After winning the Pulitzer Prize for literature and spending 2½ years on *The New York Times* best-seller list,

THE CAINE MUTINY

has become part of American folk legend. Who can forget these magnificent characters and scenes:

* **Captain Queeg,** the nervous, despotic commanding officer of the *Caine*—and the most famous captain in American fiction.

* **Willie Keith,** the careless, fun-loving Princeton boy tempered to manhood in the crucible of war.

* **Barney Greenwald,** the brilliant, enigmatic defense lawyer.

* the terrifying typhoon in which the officers of the *Caine* rebel against the captain to save the ship and themselves.

* the sensational court-martial—which became a hit Broadway play.

They all come together in a globe-spanning tale of courage and cowardice, of men and nations—truly one of the great sea dramas of all time.

D. S. HUTTON

THE CAINE MUTINY
was originally published by Doubleday & Company, Inc.

Books by Herman Wouk

Novels

Aurora Dawn
*The Caine Mutiny
The City Boy
*Don't Stop the Carnival
*Marjorie Morningstar
*The Winds of War
Youngblood Hawke

Plays

The Caine Mutiny Court-Martial
Nature's Way
The Traitor

Nonfiction

*This Is My God

*Published by POCKET BOOKS

HERMAN WOUK

THE CAINE MUTINY

A NOVEL OF WORLD WAR II

A POCKET BOOK EDITION published by
Simon & Schuster of Canada, Ltd. • Richmond Hill, Ontario, Canada
Registered User of the Trademark

THE CAINE MUTINY

Doubleday edition published 1951

POCKET BOOK edition published September, 1973
2nd printing..........July, 1973

Standard Book Number: 671-78642-3.

Printed in Canada.

This tale is for my wife,
with all my love

NOTE

This is a work of fiction in the historical setting of World War II. It contains errors of fact. Times and places of specific circumstances in actual military operations, names and missions of ships, and naval communication procedures have been distorted either to suit the story or to avoid inadvertent recounting of still-classified information. All the persons and events aboard the *Caine* are imaginary. Any resemblance to actual persons or events is coincidental. No ship named U.S.S. *Caine* exists or existed. The records of thirty years show no instance of a court-martial resulting from the relief of a captain at sea under Article 184, 185, and 186 of the Naval Regulations. The fictitious figure of the deposed captain was contrived from a study of psychoneurotic case histories to motivate the central situation and is not a portrait of a real military person or a type. This statement is made in view of an existing tendency to seek lampoons of living people in fiction. The author served under two captains of the regular Navy in three years aboard destroyer-minesweepers, both of whom were decorated for valor. One comment on style: The general obscenity and blasphemy of shipboard talk have gone almost wholly unrecorded. This good-humored billingsgate is largely monotonous and not significant, mere verbal punctuation of a sort, and its appearance in print annoys some readers. The traces that remain are necessary where occurring.

I · WILLIE KEITH

II · THE *CAINE*

VI · THE COURT-MARTIAL

VII · THE LAST CAPTAIN OF THE
CAINE

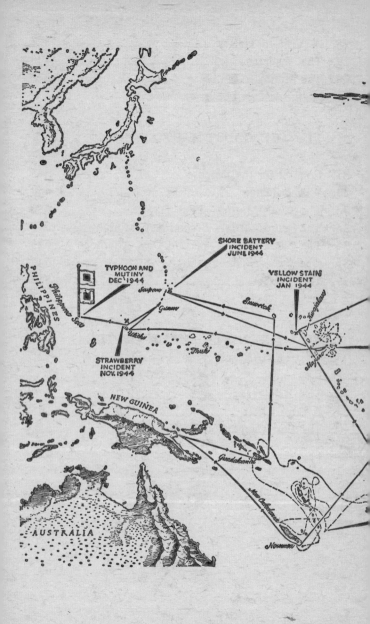

JAPAN

PHILIPPINES

Philippine Sea

SHORE BATTERY
INCIDENT
JUNE 1944

TYPHOON AND
MUTINY
DEC. 1944

YELLOW STAIN
INCIDENT
JAN. 1944

Saipan

Guam

Eniwetok

Kwajalein

Ulithi

Truk

Majuro

STRAWBERRY
INCIDENT
NOV. 1944

NEW GUINEA

Guadalcanal

New Caledonia

AUSTRALIA

Noumea

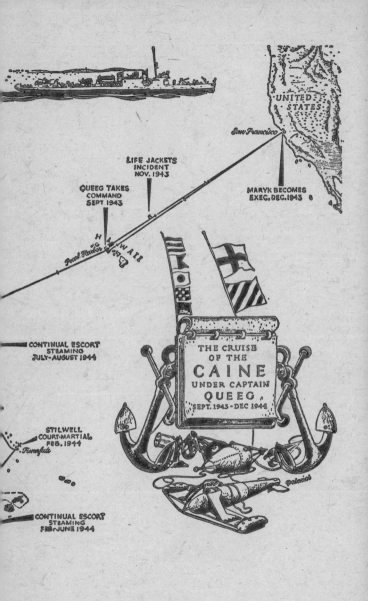

UNITED STATES

San Francisco

LIFE JACKETS
INCIDENT
NOV. 1943

QUEEG TAKES
COMMAND
SEPT 1943

MARYK BECOMES
EXEC, DEC.1943

Pearl Harbor   HAWAII

CONTINUAL ESCORT
STEAMING
JULY-AUGUST 1944

THE CRUISE
OF THE
CAINE
UNDER CAPTAIN
QUEEG
SEPT. 1943 - DEC 1944

STILWELL
COURT-MARTIAL
FEB. 1944

Funafuti

CONTINUAL ESCORT
STEAMING
FEB-JUNE 1944

From the *Navy Regulations:*

Article 184.

UNUSUAL CIRCUM-STANCES. It is conceivable that most unusual and extraordinary circumstances may arise in which the relief from duty of a commanding officer by a subordinate becomes necessary, either by placing him under arrest or on the sick list; but such action shall never be taken without the approval of the Navy Department or other appropriate higher authority, except when reference to such higher authority is undoubtedly impracticable because of the delay involved or for other clearly obvious reason. Such reference must set forth all facts in the case, and the reasons for the recommendation, with particular regard to the degree of urgency involved.

Article 185.

In order that a subordinate officer, acting upon his own initiative, may be vindicated for relieving a commanding officer from duty, the situation must be obvious and clear, and must admit of the single conclusion that the retention of command by such commanding officer will seriously and irretrievably prejudice the public interests. The subordinate officer so acting must be next in lawful succession to command; must be unable to refer the matter to a common superior for one of the reasons set down in Article 184; must be certain that the prejudicial actions of his commanding officer are not caused by secret instructions unknown to the subordinate; must have given the matter such careful consideration, and must have made such exhaustive investigation of all the circumstances, as may be practicable; and finally must be thoroughly convinced that the conclusion to relieve his commanding officer is one which a reasonable, prudent, and experienced officer would regard as a necessary consequence from the facts thus determined to exist.

Article 186.

Intelligently fearless initiative is an important trait of military character, and it is not the purpose to discourage its employment in cases of this nature. However, as the action of relieving a superior from command involves most serious possibilities, a decision so to do or so to recommend should be based upon facts established by substantial evidence, and upon the official views of others in a position to form valuable opinions, particularly of a technical character. An officer relieving his commanding officer or recommending such action, together with all others who so counsel, must bear the legitimate responsibility for, and must be prepared to justify, such action.

It was not a mutiny in the old-time sense, of course, with flashing of cutlasses, a captain in chains, and desperate sailors turning outlaws. After all, it happened in 1944 in the United States Navy. But the court of inquiry recommended trial for mutiny, and the episode became known as "the *Caine* mutiny" throughout the service.

The story begins with Willie Keith because the event turned on his personality as the massive door of a vault turns on a small jewel bearing.

I

WILLIE KEITH

1 · Through the Looking Glass

He was of medium height, somewhat chubby, and good looking, with curly red hair and an innocent, gay face, more remarkable for a humorous air about the eyes and large mouth than for any strength of chin or nobility of nose. He had graduated from Princeton in 1941 with high marks in all subjects except mathematics and sciences. His academic specialty had been comparative literature. But his real career at Princeton had consisted of playing the piano and inventing bright little songs for parties and shows.

He kissed his mother good-by on the sidewalk near the corner of Broadway and 116th Street in New York City, on a cold sunny morning in December 1942. The family Cadillac was parked beside them, its motor running, but maintaining a well-bred silence. Around them stood the dingy gray-and-red buildings of Columbia University.

"Don't you think," said Mrs. Keith, smiling bravely, "that we might stop in that drugstore first and have a sandwich?"

She had driven her son to the midshipmen school from

their home in Manhasset, despite Willie's protests. Willie had wanted to take the train. It would have seemed more like departing for the wars; he did not like being escorted to the gates of the Navy by his mother. But Mrs. Keith had prevailed as usual. She was a large, wise, firm woman, as tall as her son, and well endowed with brow and jaw. This morning she was wearing a fur-trimmed brown cloth coat instead of mink, to match the austerity of the event. Beneath her mannish brown hat her hair showed the dominant red strain that had reappeared in her only child. Otherwise there was little resemblance between mother and son.

"The Navy'll feed me, Mom. Don't worry."

He kissed her for the second time and glanced nervously about, hoping that no military men were observing the overtender scene. Mrs. Keith pressed his shoulder lovingly.

"I know you'll do wonderfully, Willie. Just as you always have."

"Aye aye, Mother." Willie strode along the brick walk past the School of Journalism, and down a few steps to the entrance of Furnald Hall, formerly a dormitory for law students. A grizzled, pudgy Navy chief with four red service stripes on his blue coat stood in the doorway. Mimeographed papers in his hand flapped in the breeze. Willie wondered whether to salute, and swiftly decided that the gesture did not go well with a brown raglan coat and green pork-pie hat. He had completely forgotten his mother.

"You V-7?" The chief's voice was like a shovelful of pebbles dropped on tin.

"Aye aye." Willie grinned self-consciously. The chief returned the grin and appraised him briefly with, it seemed, an affectionate eye. He handed Willie four sheets clipped together.

"You're starting a new line. Good luck."

"Thank you, sir." For three weeks Willie was to make the mistake of calling chiefs "sir."

The chief opened the door invitingly. Willis Seward Keith stepped out of the sunshine across the threshold. It was done as easily and noiselessly as Alice's stepping through the looking glass; and like Alice, Willie Keith passed into a new and exceedingly strange world.

At the instant that Mrs. Keith saw Willie swallowed up, she remembered that she had neglected an important transaction. She ran to the entrance of Furnald Hall. The chief stopped her as she laid a hand on the doorknob. "Sorry, madam. No admittance."

"That was my son who just went in."

"Sorry, madam."

"I only want to see him for a moment. I must speak to him. He forgot something."

"They're taking physicals in there, madam. There are men walking around with nothing on."

Mrs. Keith was not used to being argued with. Her tone sharpened. "Don't be absurd. There he is, just inside the door. I can rap and call him out."

She could see her son plainly, his back toward her, grouped with several other young men around an officer who was talking to them. The chief glanced dourly through the door. "He seems to be busy."

Mrs. Keith gave him a look appropriate to fresh doormen. She rapped on the glass of the outer door with her diamond ring and cried, "Willie! Willie!" But her son did not hear her call from the other world.

"Madam," said the chief, with a note in his rasping voice that was not unkind, "he's in the Navy now."

Mrs. Keith suddenly blushed. "I'm sorry."

"Okay, okay. You'll see him again soon—maybe Saturday."

The mother opened her purse and began to fish in it. "You see, I promised—the fact is, he forgot to take his spending money. He hasn't a cent. Would you be kind enough to give these to him?"

"Madam, he won't need money." The chief made an uneasy pretense of leafing through the papers he held. "He'll be getting paid pretty soon."

"But meantime—suppose he wants some? I promised him. Please take the money—— Pardon me, but I'd be happy to give you something for your trouble."

The chief's gray eyebrows rose. "That won't be necessary." He wagged his head like a dog shaking off flies, and accepted the bills. Up went the eyebrows again. "Madam —this here is a hundred dollars!"

He stared at her. Mrs. Keith was struck with an unfamiliar sensation—shame at being better off than most people. "Well," she said defensively, "it isn't every day he goes to fight a war."

"I'll take care of it, madam."

"Thank you," said Mrs. Keith, and then, vaguely, "I'm sorry."

"Okay."

The mother closed with a polite smile, and walked off to her Cadillac. The chief looked after her, then glanced at the two fifties fluttering in his hand. "One thing," he muttered, "we're sure as hell getting a new kind of Navy." He thrust the bills into a pocket.

Meanwhile, Willie Keith, spearhead of the new Navy, advanced to war; which, for the moment, took the form of a glittering array of inoculation needles. Willie was not angry at Hitler nor even at the Japanese, though he disapproved of them. The enemy in this operation lay not before him, but behind. Furnald Hall was sanctuary from the United States Army.

He was jabbed swiftly for several tropical ailments. The bugs thus liberated whirled down his bloodstream. His arm began to ache. He was ordered to strip naked, and his clothes were carried off in a heap by a burly sailor.

"Hey, when do I get those back?"

"Who knows? Looks like a long war," the sailor growled, and mashed the green hat under his arm. Willie followed with anxious eyes as his old identity was hauled away to camphor balls.

With forty other upright pink animals he was herded into a large examination room. His lungs, liver, heart, eyes, ears, all the apparatus he had been using since birth, were investigated by hard-eyed pharmacist's mates, who prodded and poked him like suspicious women about to buy a turkey in a market.

"Stand up straight, sir." The last pharmacist's mate of the line-up was eying him critically. Willie stiffened. It unnerved him to see, out of the corner of his eye, that the examiner looked very dissatisfied.

"Bend over and touch your toes."

Willie tried, but years of overeating barred the way. His fingers hung eight inches from his toes. He tried the ancient mode of cheating——

"*Without* bending the knees, please."

Willie straightened, took a deep breath, and tried to snap himself double. Something gave in his spine with an ugly crack. There were four inches to go.

"You wait." The pharmacist walked away, and returned with a lieutenant characterized by a black mustache, puffy eyes, and a stethoscope. "Look at that, sir."

"That" was Willie, erect as he could get.

"Can he touch?"

"Hell, no, sir. Hardly gets past his knees."

"Well, that's quite a breadbasket he's got."

Willie hauled in his stomach, too late.

"I don't care about the breadbasket," said the pharmacist's mate. "This joker has a hollow back."

The naked candidates behind Willie on line were fidgeting and murmuring.

"There is a lordosis, no doubt of it."

"Well, do we survey him out?"

"I don't know if it's that serious."

"Well, I ain't gonna pass him on my responsibility. You can, sir."

The doctor picked up Willie's record. "How about the pulse?"

"I didn't bother. What's the point if he's a lordosis?"

The doctor took Willie's wrist. His eyes emerged in surprise from the red puffs. "Ye gods, boy—are you sick?"

Willie could feel his blood galloping past the doctor's fingers. Various tropical bacteria, and above all, the shadow of the United States Army, were pushing up his pulse rate.

"No, just worried."

"I don't blame you. How on earth did you get past the receiving station? Did you know the doctor?"

"Sir, I may be chubby, but I play six hours of tennis at a stretch. I climb mountains."

"There's no mountains at sea," said the pharmacist's mate. "You're Army meat, my friend."

"Shut up, Warner," said the doctor, noticing in the record that Willie was a Princeton man. "Leave pulse and back vacant. Send him down to Captain Grimm at the Navy Yard for a recheck."

"Aye aye, sir." The doctor left. Sullenly, the pharmacist's mate took a red pencil, scrawled on a memo pad, "Lordosis—Pulse," and clipped the crimson indictment to Willie's record. "Okay. Report to the exec's office right after inspection tomorrow, Mister Keith. Best of luck."

"Same to you," said Willie. They exchanged a look of pure hate, remarkable on such short acquaintance, and Willie moved off.

The Navy now dressed him in blue jumper and trousers, black shoes, black socks, and a perky sailor hat, marked with the special blue stripe of a midshipman. Then it filled his arms with books, of all shapes, colors, sizes, and degrees of wear. As Willie left the book-issuing room, seeing his way with some difficulty over the pile of prose in his arms, a sailor at the door laid on top a stack of mimeographed sheets which brought the heap level with his eyebrows. Willie craned his neck around the corner of his burden, and siddled crabwise to the elevator—the "HOIST," said a freshly lettered sign over the push buttons.

When the elevator reached the top floor, only Willie and a skinny horse-faced sailor remained. Willie walked down the hall, scanning the names posted outside each room, and found a door labeled:

ROOM 1013
KEEFER
KEITH
KEGGS

He went in, and dropped the books on the bare springs of a cot. He heard the twang of springs again directly behind him.

"My name's Keggs," said the horse face, poking an arm toward him. Willie shook the hand, which enveloped his in a big moist grip.

"I'm Keith."

"Well," said Keggs mournfully, "looks like we're roommates."

"This is it," said Willie.

"I hope," said Keggs, "that this Keefer doesn't turn out to be too much of a drip." He looked at Willie earnestly, then his face maneuvered its length into a slow smile. He picked up *Naval Ordnance* from the pile on his cot. "Well, no time like the present." He sat on the only chair, put his legs up on the only desk, and opened the book with an unhappy sigh.

"How do you know what to study?" Willie was surprised at such industry.

"Brother, it makes no difference. It's all going to be too much for me. Might as well start anywhere."

A heap of books entered the door, walking on stout legs. "Make way, gentlemen, heah Ah come," spoke a muffled voice. The books fell and bounced all over the remaining cot, unveiling a tall, fat sailor with a cheery flushed face, small crinkling eyes and a very large loose mouth. "Well, fellas, looks like we're in for a lot of Shinola, don' it?" he said, in a high, musical Southern cadence. "Ah'm Keefer."

"I'm Keith."

"Keggs."

The fat Southerner shoved a number of his books off the cot to the floor, and stretched himself out on the springs. "Ah had me a farewell party last night," he groaned, inserting a happy giggle into the groan, "to end all farewell parties. Why do we do it to ourselves, fellas? 'Scuse me." He rolled his face to the wall.

"You're not going to *sleep!*" Keggs said. "Suppose they catch you?"

"My boy," said Keefer drowsily, "Ah am an old military man. Four years at Gaylord Academy. Don' worry about ol' Keefer. Punch me if Ah snore." Willie wanted to ask the old military man how serious lordosis might be in a war career. But as he searched for a delicate way to open the subject, Keefer's breath grew regular and heavy. Within a minute he was sleeping like a hog in the sun.

"He'll get bilged, sure," mourned Keggs, turning the pages of *Naval Ordnance*. "So will I. This book is absolute gibberish to me. What on earth is a cam? What do they mean by an interrupted screw?"

"Search me. What do you mean, 'bilged'?"

"Don't you know how they work it? We get three weeks as apprentice seamen. Then the top two thirds of the class become midshipmen. The rest get bilged. Straight to the Army."

The fugitives exchanged an understanding look. Willie's hand crept around to his back, to ascertain how hollow his hollow back really was. He began a series of frenzied efforts to touch his toes. At every bend he came nearer. He broke out in a sweat. Once he thought the tips of his fingers brushed his shoelaces, and he gurgled in triumph. With a swoop and a groan he brought his fingers squarely on his toes. Coming erect again, his spine vibrating, the room spinning, he found that Keefer, rolled over and awake, was staring at him with frightened little eyes. Keggs had backed into a corner. Willie attempted a lighthearted laugh, but he staggered at the same moment and had to clutch the desk to keep from falling over, so the effect of nonchalance was marred. "Nothing like a little setting-up exercise," he said, with drunken savoir-faire.

"Hell, no," said Keefer. "Especially three o'clock in the afternoon. Ah never miss it myself."

Three rolled-up mattresses came catapulting through the open door, one after another. "Mattresses!" yelled a retreating voice in the hall. Blankets, pillows, and sheets flew in, propelled by another disembodied voice shouting, "Blankets, pillows, and sheets!"

"Couldn't imagine what they were less'n he told us," growled Keefer, untangling himself from a sheet which had draped itself on him. He made up a bed in a few moments, flat and neat as if it had been steam-rollered. Willie summoned up boys' camp experience; his cot soon looked presentable. Keggs wrestled with the bedclothes for ten minutes while the others stowed their books and clothes, then he asked Keefer hopefully: "How's that, now?"

"Fella," said Keefer, shaking his head, "you an innocent man." He approached the cot and made a few passes of the hand over it. The bed straightened itself into military rigidity, as in an animated cartoon.

"You're a whiz," said Keggs.

"I heard what you said about me bilging," said Keefer kindly. "Don' worry. I be there on the great gittin'-up morning."

The rest of the day went by in bugles, assemblies, dismissals, reassemblies, announcements, marches, lectures, and aptitude tests. Every time the administration remembered a detail that had been omitted in the mimeographed sheets the bugle blared, and five hundred sailors swarmed out of Furnald Hall. A fair-haired, tall, baby-faced ensign named Acres would bark the new instruction, standing on the steps, jutting his chin and squinting fiercely. Then he would dismiss them, and the building would suck them in. The trouble with this systole and diastole for the men on the top floor ("tenth deck") was that there wasn't room for them all in the elevator. They had to scramble down nine flights of stairs ("ladders"), and later wait wearily for a ride up, or else climb. Willie was stumbling with fatigue when at last they were marched off to dinner. But food revived him wonderfully.

Back in their room, with leisure to talk, the three exchanged identities. The gloomy Edwin Keggs was a high school algebra teacher from Akron, Ohio. Roland Keefer was the son of a West Virginian politician. He had had a job in the state personnel bureau, but, as he cheerfully phrased it, he didn't know personnel from Shinola, and had simply been learning the ropes around the capitol when the war came. Willie's announcement that he was a night-club pianist sobered the other two, and the conversation lagged. Then he added that he was a Princeton graduate, and a chill silence blanketed the room.

When the bugle sounded retreat and Willie climbed into bed, it occurred to him that he had not had a single thought

of May Wynn or of his parents all day. It seemed weeks
since he had kissed his mother that same morning on 116th
Street. He was not far, physically, from Manhasset, no
further than he had been in his Broadway haunts. But
he felt arctically remote. He glanced around at the tiny
room, the bare yellow-painted walls bordered in black
wood, the shelves heavy with menacing books, the two
strangers in underwear climbing into their cots, sharing
an intimacy with him that Willie had never known even
in his own family. He experienced a most curiously mixed
feeling of adventurous coziness, as though he were tented
down for the night in the wilds, and sharp regret for his
lost freedom.

2 · May Wynn

Having one of the highest draft numbers in the land, Willie had passed the first war year peacefully without taking
refuge in the Navy.

There had been some talk of his returning to Princeton
after graduation for a master's degree in literature, the
first step toward a teaching career. But in September following a summer of tennis and multiple romances at his
grandparents' home in Rhode Island, Willie had found a
job in a cocktail lounge of a minor New York hotel, playing the piano and singing his original ditties. The first
earned dollar has remarkable weight in deciding a career.
Willie elected art. He was not paid much. The fee was,
in fact, the smallest permitted by the musicians' union
for a piano player. Willie didn't really care, so long as
fifty-dollar bills flowed from his mother. As the proprietor,
a swarthy, wrinkled Greek, pointed out, Willie was gain-
ing professional experience.

His songs were of the order known as cute, rather than witty or tuneful. His major piece, sung only for the larger crowds, was *If You Knew What the Gnu Knew,* a comparison of the love-making ways of animals and humans. The rest of his works leaned heavily on such devices as rhyming "plastered" and "bastard," and "twitches" and "bitches"—but instead of saying the off-color word, Willie would smile at his audience and substitute a harmless one that didn't rhyme. This usually provoked happy squeals from the kind of audiences that collected in the cocktail lounge. Willie's close-trimmed Princetonian haircut, his expensive clothes, and his childlike sweetness of face served to dress up his slender talent. He usually appeared in fawn-colored slacks, a tan-and-green tweed jacket, heavy English cordovan shoes, tan-and-green Argyle socks, and a white shirt with a tie knotted in the latest knot. Considering the entertainment merely pictorially, the Greek had a bargain in Willie.

A couple of months later the proprietor of a very dingy night club on Fifty-second Street, the Club Tahiti, saw his act and bought him away from the Greek with a raise of ten dollars a week. This transaction was concluded in an afternoon interview at the Club Tahiti, a dank cellar full of papier-mâché palms, dusty coconuts, and upended chairs on tables. The date was December 7, 1941.

Willie emerged from this meeting into the sunny street full of exultation and pride. He had risen above the minimum union wage. It seemed to him that he had overtaken Cole Porter, and was well on the way to nosing out Noel Coward. The street, with its garish, weather-beaten nightclub signs, its magnified photographs of nobodies like himself, looked beautiful to him. He stopped at a newsstand, his eye attracted by unusually big and black headlines: *JAPS BOMB PEARL HARBOR.* He did not know where Pearl Harbor was; in a passing thought he placed it on the Pacific side of the Panama Canal. He realized that this meant the United States would enter the war, but the turn of events seemed in no way comparable in importance to his engagement at the Club Tahiti. A very high draft number, in those days, helped a man to keep calm about the war.

The new rise in the entertainment world, announced to his family that same evening, was the deathblow to Mrs. Keith's faltering campaign for Willie's return to comparative literature. There was, of course, talk of Willie's enlisting. On the train ride to Manhasset he had caught some of the war fever of the excited commuters, so that his sluggish conscience stirred and gave him a prod. Willie brought up the subject at the end of dinner. "What I really ought to do," he said, as Mrs. Keith heaped his dessert dish with a second helping of Bavarian cream, "is chuck the piano *and* comparative literature, and join the Navy. I know I could get a commission."

Mrs. Keith glanced at her husband. The mild little doctor, whose round face much resembled Willie's, kept his cigar in his mouth as an excuse to remain silent.

"Don't be absurd, Willie." In a lightning estimate Mrs. Keith abandoned the distinguished phantom, Professor Willis Seward Keith, Ph.D. "Just when your career begins to look seriously promising? Obviously I've been wrong about you. If you can make such a spectacular rise so quickly, you must be very gifted. I want you to make the most of your talents. I really believe, now, you're going to be a second Noel Coward."

"Somebody's got to fight the war, Mom."

"Don't try to be wiser than the Army, my boy. When they need you, they'll call you."

Willie said, "What do you think, Dad?"

The plump doctor ran a hand through the remaining strands of his black hair. The cigar emerged from his mouth. "Well, Willie," he said, in a warm, quiet voice. "I think your mother would be very sorry to see you go."

So it was that Willie Keith sang and played for the customers of the Club Tahiti from December 1941 to April 1942 while the Japanese conquered the Philippines, and the *Prince of Wales* and the *Repulse* sank, and Singapore fell, and the cremation ovens of the Germans consumed men, women, and children at full blast, thousands every day.

In the spring two great events occurred in Willie's life; he fell in love, and he received a notice from his draft board.

He had already undergone the usual loves of a college boy with spending money. He had flirted with girls of his own class, and pressed matters further with girls of lower station. Three or four times he had considered himself plunged in passion. But the explosion into his life of May Wynn was a wholly different matter.

He arrived at the Tahiti on that slushy, drizzly day to play the piano for auditions of new acts. The Club Tahiti was dreary in all times and weathers, but most so in the afternoons. The gray light came in then through the street door and showed bare spots in the frowzy red velvet hangings of the lobby, and black blobs of chewing gum ground into the blue carpet, and blisters in the orange paint that covered the door and its frame. And the nude girls in the South Seas mural looked peculiarly mottled by reason of spatterings of drink, frescoes of tobacco smoke, and layers of plain grime. Willie loved this place exactly as it was. Looking as it did, and smelling as it did of stale tobacco, liquor, and cheap deodorant perfume, it was his domain of power and achievement.

Two girls were sitting near the piano at the far end of the chilly room. The proprietor, a pale fat man with gray stubbly jowls and a face marked with deep soured lines, leaned on the piano, chewing a half-burned cigar and leafing through a musical arrangement.

"Okay, here's Princeton. Let's go, girls."

Willie shed his dripping galoshes by the piano, stripped off his brown rabbit-lined gloves, and sat at the stool in his overcoat, inspecting the girls with the horse trader's eye of a man of twenty-two. The blonde stood and handed him her music. "Can you transpose at sight, honey? It's in G, but I'd rather take it in E-flat," she said, and from the twanging Broadway tones Willie knew at once the pretty face was an empty mask, one of hundreds that floated around Fifty-second Street.

"E-flat coming up." His glance wandered to the second

singer, a small nondescript girl in a big black hat that hid her hair. Nothing doing today, he thought.

The blonde said, "Here's hoping this cold of mine doesn't ruin me completely. Can I have the intro?" She plowed through *Night and Day* with determination, and little else. Mr. Dennis, the proprietor, thanked her and said he would telephone her. The small girl took off her hat and came forward. She placed an unusually thick arrangement on the music rack in front of Willie.

"You might want to look at this piece, it's slightly tricky." She raised her voice to address the proprietor. "Mind if I keep my coat on?"

"Suit yourself, dear. Just let me look at your figure sometime before you go."

"Might as well look at it now." The girl opened her loose brown waterproof coat and turned completely around.

"That's fine," said Mr. Dennis. "Can you sing, too?"

Willie, examining the music, missed the view, though he turned to look. The coat was closed again. The girl regarded him with a slight mischievous smile. She kept her hands in her pockets. "Does your opinion count, too, Mr. Keith?" She made a pretense of opening the coat.

Willie grinned. He pointed to the arrangement. "Unusual."

"Cost me a hundred dollars," said the girl. "Well, ready?"

The arrangement was no less ambitious a piece than Cherubino's love song from *The Marriage of Figaro,* with words in Italian. Midway it broke into a syncopated parody in clumsy English. At the end it returned to Mozart's music and Da Ponte's words. "Haven't you something else?" Willie said, noting that the singer had amazingly bright brown eyes and a handsome mass of chestnut-colored hair rolled up on her head. He wished he could see her figure, and this was a strange wish, since he was indifferent to small girls and disliked reddish hair; a fact he had explained away as a sophomore with the aid of Freud's theories as a repressive mechanism of his Oedipus complex.

"What's the matter? You can play it."

"I don't think," said Willie in a stage whisper, "that he'll like it. Too high-class."

"Well, just once, for dear old Princeton, shall we try?"

Willie began to play. The music of Mozart was one of the few things in the world that affected him deeply. He knew the aria by heart. As he called the first notes out of the battered yellowing keyboard scarred with cigarette burns, the girl leaned against the piano, resting one arm on the top so that her hand, loosely closed, hung over the edge near his eyes. It was a little hand, rather more square of palm than a girl's should be, with short, thin, strong fingers. Roughness around the knuckles told of dishwashing.

The girl seemed to be singing for the pleasure of friends, rather than for an urgently desired job. Willie's ear, trained by many years of opera-going, told him at once that this was no great voice, nor even a professional one. It was just such singing as a bright girl who had a love of music and a pleasant voice could accomplish, and it had that peculiar charm denied great performers, the caroling freshness of song for its own sake.

The melody filled the gloomy cellar with radiance. The blonde, going out at the door, turned and stopped to listen. Willie looked up at the girl, smiled, and nodded as he played. She returned the smile, and made a brief gesture of plucking the imaginary guitar accompaniment of Susanna. The motion was full of casual humor and grace. She sang the Italian words with a correct accent, and apparently knew what they meant.

"Watch for the break," she suddenly whispered at him in a pause of the singing. She reached down in a darting movement, turned the page, and pointed. Willie swung into the jazzed-up portion of the arrangement. The singer stood away from the piano, spread her hands in the conventional pose of all night-club singers, and ground out a chorus, moving her lips, wrinkling her nose, affecting a Southern accent, smiling from ear to ear, throwing her head back on every high note, and twisting her wrists. Her charm was obliterated.

The jazz part ended. As the arrangement returned to Mozart, so did the girl to her natural ease. Nothing could be pleasanter, thought Willie, than the negligent way she leaned against the piano with hands deep-thrust in her coat pockets, and trilled the fall of the song. He played the last after-echo of the melody with regret.

The proprietor said, "Darling, do you have any standard stuff with you?"

"I have *Sweet Sue, Talk of the Town*—that's all with me, but I can do more——"

"Fine. Just wait, will you? Willie, come inside a minute."

The proprietor's office was a green-painted cubicle in the rear of the cellar. The walls were plastered with photographs of actors and singers. The light was a single bulb dangling from the ceiling. Mr. Dennis wasted no money on decorations not visible to customers.

"What do you think?" he said, applying a match to a cigar stump.

"Well, the blonde is no barn-burner."

"Guess not. What about the redhead?"

"Ah—what's her name?"

"May Wynn," said the proprietor, squinting at Willie, possibly because of the burning cigar end an inch from his face.

Occasionally a name is spoken that sets up a clamor in one's heart, as though it has been shouted in a big empty hall. Often as not the feeling proves a delusion. In any case, Willie was shaken by the pronouncing of the words, "May Wynn." He said nothing.

"Why? What did you think of her?"

"What's her figure like?" replied Willie.

The proprietor choked over his cigar, and flattened its meager remains in an ashtray. "What's that got to do with the price of herring? I'm asking you about her singing."

"Well, *I* like Mozart," Willie said dubiously, "but——"

"She's cheap," said Mr. Dennis meditatively.

"Cheap?" Willie was offended.

"Salary, Princeton. Couldn't be cheaper without bringing pickets around. I don't know. Could be that Mozart thing would be a delightful novelty—distinction, class, charm. Could also be that it would clear out the place like a stink bomb—— Let's hear how she does something straight."

May Wynn's *Sweet Sue* was better than her previous jazz singing—possibly because it wasn't inserted in a framework of Mozart. There was less of hands, teeth, and hips, and a paling of the Southern accent.

"Who's your agent, dear—Bill Mansfield?" said Mr. Dennis.

"Marty Rubin," said May Wynn, a little breathlessly.

"Can you start Monday?"

"*Can* I?" gasped the girl.

"Okay. Show her around, Princeton," said Mr. Dennis, and vanished into his office. Willie Keith and May Wynn were alone among the fake palm fronds and coconuts.

"Congratulations," said Willie, extending his hand. The girl shook it briefly in a warm, firm little grasp.

"Thanks. How the devil did I get it? I murdered the Mozart——"

Willie threw himself at his galoshes. "Where would you like to eat?"

"Eat! I'm going home for dinner, thank you. Aren't you going to show me around?"

"What's there to show? Your dressing room is that one with the green curtain opposite the ladies' room. It's a hole, no window, no washbasin. We do shows at ten, twelve, and two. You're supposed to be around at eight-thirty. That's all there is to that." He stood. "Do you like pizzas?"

"Why do you want to take me to dinner? You don't have to."

"Because," said Willie, "at the moment, there is nothing else I care to do with my life."

May Wynn's eyes widened in a look of wonder, mixed with the wariness of wild game. Willie took her firmly by an elbow. "Let's go, huh?"

"I'll have to make a phone call," said the girl, allowing herself to be hauled toward the door.

Luigi's was a bright small restaurant full of little tables in rows of booths. The warmth and the spicy smell were a

pleasant change from the chill rainy twilight outside. May
Wynn sat without removing her damp coat, in a booth near
the sizzling open kitchen. Willie stared at her.

"For crying out loud, take off that coat."

"I won't. I'm cold."

"You lie. This is the hottest, stuffiest restaurant in New
York."

May Wynn rose, almost as reluctantly as if she were
being compelled to strip. "I'm beginning to think you're
very silly—— Well," she added, her face flushing, "stop
looking at me like that——"

Willie had the appearance of a startled stag—for good
enough reason. May Wynn's figure was glorious. She wore
a purple silk dress with a narrow gray belt. She sat, all in
confusion, trying not to laugh at Willie.

"You have a figure," said Willie, taking his seat in slow
motion. "I thought you probably had elephant thighs, or
no chest."

"Bitter experience," said May Wynn. "I don't like to
get jobs or make friends on the strength of my figure.
Things are expected of me that I can't deliver."

"May Wynn," said Willie thoughtfully. "I like the
name."

"That's good. It took me a long time to think of it."

"Isn't that your name?"

The girl shrugged. "Of course not. It's too good."

"What's your name?"

"If you don't mind my saying so, this is a queer conversation. Who are you to go probing at me like this?"

"Sorry——"

"I don't mind telling you, though I usually don't blab it.
My name is Marie Minotti."

"Oh." Willie looked at a waiter carrying a tray heaped
with spaghetti. "Then you're at home in here."

"Very much."

Willie's reaction to the discovery that May Wynn had an
Italian name was complicated, and quite important: a
mixture of relief, pleasure, and disappointment. It struck
away most of the girl's mystery. A night-club singer who
could carol a Mozart aria with understanding was a

wonder, for in Willie's world familiarity with opera was a mark of high breeding—unless you were an Italian. Then it became a mere racial quirk of a lower social group, and lost its cachet. Marie Minotti was someone Willie could cope with. She was pigeonholed after all as a mere night-club singer, if a very pretty one. The feeling that he was tumbling into a real relationship was an illusion. He knew perfectly well that he would never marry an Italian. They were mostly poor, untidy, vulgar, and Catholic. This did not at all imply that the fun was at an end. On the contrary, he could now more safely enjoy being with the girl, since nothing was going to come of it.

May Wynn regarded him with narrow eyes. "What are you thinking?"

"The nicest possible things about you."

"Your name, no doubt, is really Willis Seward Keith?"

"Oh, yes."

"And you come from a fine old family?"

"Oldest and finest—— My mother is a Seward, of the Mayflower Sewards. My father is something of a bar sinister, since the Keiths didn't get over here until 1795."

"Ye gods. Missed the Revolution."

"By a mile. Mere immigrants. My grandfather has made up for it slightly by being the head of surgery at the Chase Hospital, supposedly the big wheel of that branch of medicine in the East."

"Well, Princeton," said the girl with a light laugh, "obviously we can never hit it off. Talking about immigrants, my folks came over in 1920. My father runs a fruit store in the Bronx. My mother hardly speaks English."

The pizzas arrived on two large round tin platters: smoking hot flat cakes of dough covered with cheese and tomato sauce—and, in Willie's dish, sprinkled on one side with chunks of anchovy. May Wynn picked up a triangular slice, folded it expertly with a flip of her fingers, and took a bite. "My mother's pizza is better than this. As a matter of fact, I make about the best pizza in the world."

"Will you marry me?"

"No, your mother wouldn't like it."

"Great," said Willie, "we understand each other. Allow me to tell you, then, that I'm falling in love with you."

The girl's face suddenly clouded over. "Keep the blows above the belt, chum."

"No harm intended."

"How old are you?" May said.

"Twenty-two. Why?"

"You seem a lot younger."

"My baby face. I probably won't be allowed into a voting booth till I'm seventy."

"No, it's—it's you. I think I like it."

"How old are you?"

"I can't vote."

"Are you engaged, May, or do you have a sweetheart, or anything?"

"Ye gods!" exclaimed May, coughing.

"Well?"

"Let's talk about books. You're a Princeton man."

They did talk about books, between mouthfuls of wine and pizza. Willie started on current best sellers, with which May had a passable acquaintance, and worked back toward his eighteenth- and nineteenth-century favorites, whereupon the girl's answers grew lamer.

"Dickens," said Willie fervidly, riding high on a crest of comparative literature, "if I had any strength of character I'd spend my life doing research and commentary on Dickens. He and Shakespeare will be left when English is dead as Latin. Do you know his works?"

"All I've read is the *Christmas Carol*."

"Oh."

"Look, chum, I never got beyond high school. Things were tough at the fruit store when I graduated. There was a little matter of keeping myself in dresses and stockings —and the family in food, every now and then. I've worked in dime stores and orange-drink stands. I tackled Dickens a couple of times. He's hard going after a day on your feet."

"You'll love Dickens someday."

"I hope so. I think appreciating Dickens goes with ten thousand in the bank."

"I haven't a dime in the bank."

"Your mama has. Same thing."

Willie leaned back luxuriously and lit a cigarette. He was at a seminar now. "It's perfectly true that a love of fine art is a function of leisure, but that in no way vitiates the validity of the art. The ancient Greeks——"

"Shall we go? I want to work over my numbers tonight, as long as I've got a job."

It was raining hard outside. Fluorescent signs, blue, green, red, cast blurry pools of color on the wet black street. May extended her gloved hand. "Good-by. Thanks for the pizza."

"Good-by? I'll take you home in a cab."

"My boy, a cab to Honeywell Avenue in the Bronx would cost you five dollars."

"I have five dollars."

"No, thanks. Subway for the likes of me."

"Well, let's take a cab to the station."

"Cabs, cabs! Why did God give you feet? Walk me to Fiftieth."

Willie recalled some rhapsodies by George Meredith on walks in the rain, and fell in beside the singer. She took his arm. They strolled in silence, droplets hitting their faces and rolling off their clothes. The hand resting on his arm sent a soft glow through the rest of him. "There's really something rather delicious about walking in the rain," he remarked.

May glanced at him sidelong. "You wouldn't think so if you *had* to do it, Princeton."

"Oh, look," said Willie, "stop playing the poor little match girl. Is this your first singing job?"

"First in New York. I've only been singing for four months. Worked a lot of dives in New Jersey."

"How does Mozart go in a Jersey dive?"

May shuddered. "Never tried it. Out there they think *Stardust* is a heavy classic, like a Bach mass."

"Who wrote those English words of yours? You?"

"My agent, Marty Rubin."

"They're terrible."

"Write me better ones."

"I will," shouted Willie, as they crossed Broadway through a stalled jam of honking taxis and busses. "To-night."

"I was kidding. I can't pay you."

"You already have. I've never in my life enjoyed Mozart as I did this afternoon."

May slipped her hand away from his arm. "You don't have to say such things. I really dislike smooth talk. I've been fed it by the yard."

"Every now and then," Willie answered, "say, once in the course of a week, I'm honest."

May looked at his face. "I'm sorry."

They stopped at the kiosk. The shabby wrinkled news-man hawked imaginary victories in a hoarse voice, his headlines concealed under tarpaper. Crowds shouldered past them. "Thank you for dinner," said May Wynn. "See you Monday."

"Not before? I could conceivably want to. What's your phone number?"

"I haven't any phone." Willie winced. May Wynn was really out of the lower depths. "There's a candy store next door," she went on, "where I can be reached in emer-gencies, but that's all."

"Supposing an emergency arises? Give me the number of the store."

"Another time." She smiled, the wariness of her look fading for a moment into coquettishness. "Can't see you till Monday, anyway. Have to slave on my numbers. 'By."

"I'm afraid I bored you with all my book talk," said Willie, trying to fan a spark in the dying interview.

"No, I've had fun." She paused, and held out her hand. "It was an instructive afternoon."

She was swallowed up in the crowd before reaching the foot of the stairs. Willie walked away from the subway entrance with an absurd feeling of being newborn. The Roxy marquee, the black shafts of Radio City sprinkled with yellow lights, the restaurant signs, the groaning, dart-ing taxicabs swam in an aura of wonder. He decided that New York was beautiful and mysterious, like Bagdad.

At three o'clock the next morning, Willie's mother

opened her eyes in her dark bedroom, breaking out of a singularly vivid dream that she was at the opera. She listened a moment to echoes of the music that still rang in her mind, then sat up as she realized that she was hearing real music—Cherubino's love song, floating across the hallway from Willie's room. She got out of bed and put on a blue silk kimono. "Willie dear—records at this hour?"

He sat in his shirt sleeves by his portable phonograph, a pad and pencil in his hand. He looked up guiltily, and snapped off the machine. "Sorry, Mother. Didn't know it carried so."

"What are you doing?"

"Stealing a stretch of Mozart for a new number, I'm afraid."

"You're wicked." She studied her son and decided that his queer exalted look was the creative frenzy. "You usually fall into bed when you get home."

Willie stood, laying the pad upside down on the chair, and yawned. "This thing just crossed my mind. I'm tired. It'll wait till morning."

"Would you like a glass of milk? Martina made a wonderful chocolate cake."

"Had a chunk in the kitchen. Sorry I woke you, Mother. Night."

"It's a lovely piece to steal," she said, accepting a kiss on the cheek.

"None lovelier," said Willie, closing the door on her.

May Wynn's job at the Club Tahiti lasted for three weeks. Her Mozart novelty was well received. Her performance became a little better each evening, simpler, more lucidly rendered, and less loaded with gestures. Her agent and coach, Marty Rubin, came several times each week to watch her. After her performance he would spend an hour or more talking to her at a table or in her dressing room. He was a short stout moon-faced man, perhaps thirty-five, with pale hair and very thick rimless eyeglasses. The exaggerated breadth of shoulder and fullness of trouser in his suits showed they were bought on Broadway, but the colors were quiet browns or grays. Willie spoke to him casually. He was quite sure Rubin was a Jew, but thought no less of him for that. Willie liked Jews as a group, for their warmth, humor, and alertness. This was true though his home was in a real-estate development where Jews could not buy.

Except for these sessions with Rubin, May's time between shows was monopolized by Willie. Usually they sat in the dressing room, smoking and talking—Willie, the educated authority, May half respectful and half satiric as the ignoramus. After a few evenings of this, Willie persuaded her to meet him by day. He took her to the Museum of Modern Art, but that was a failure. She stared in horror at the masterpieces of Dali, Chagall, and Tchelitchew, and burst out laughing. At the Metropolitan Museum they did better. She found an immediate deep pleasure in Renoir and El Greco. She made Willie take her there again. He was a good guide. "Ye gods," she exclaimed once, as he sketched the career of Whistler for her, "do you really get all that stuff in four years of college?"

"Not quite. Mother's been taking me to museums since I was six. She's a patron here."

"Oh." The girl was a little disappointed.

Willie soon obtained the telephone number of the Bronx candy store, and they continued seeing each other after May's engagement at the club was finished. It was April. Their relationship advanced to include long walks in the blossoming new-green park, and dinners at expensive restaurants, and kisses in taxis, and sentimental presents like ivory cats and fuzzy black bears and a great many flowers. Willie wrote some bad sonnets, too, and May took them home, read them again and again, and shed warm tears over them. Nobody had ever written poetry to her before.

Late in April Willie received a postcard from his draft board, inviting him for a physical examination. Upon the sounding of this tocsin he remembered the war, and forthwith went to a Navy officer-procurement station. He was accepted for the December class of the Reserve Midshipmen School. This put him beyond the clutches of the Army, and gave him a long reprieve from service.

Mrs. Keith, however, took his enlistment as a tragedy. She was outraged at the fumblers in Washington who had permitted the war to drag on so long. She still believed that it would end before Willie put on a uniform but she had an occasional chill at heart to think that he might actually be taken away. Discreetly inquiring among influential friends, she found a peculiar stoniness everywhere to the idea of getting Willie some safe duty in the United States. So she determined to make his last free months beautiful. May Wynn was doing a pretty good job of that, but of course Mrs. Keith didn't know it. She was unaware of the girl's existence. She compelled Willie to quit his job, and carted him off, with the unresisting doctor, on a trip to Mexico. Willie, quite bored with sombreros, brilliant sunlight, and feathered serpents carved on decaying pyramids, spent his money on surreptitious long-distance calls to the candy store. May invariably scolded him for his extravagance, but the radiant tones in which she did so were quite enough consolation for Willie. When they returned in July Mrs. Keith with undimmed force dragged him to a "last wonderful summer" in Rhode Island. He managed half a dozen trips to New York on thin excuses; and lived for these excursions. In the fall May was booked by Marty Rubin for a tour of clubs in Chicago and St. Louis. She came back in November, in time for three happy weeks with Willie. He performed prodigies of invention, enough for the creation of a book of short stories, to explain his absences from home to his mother.

He and May had never talked about marriage. He sometimes wondered why she didn't mention the subject, but he was very glad that she was content to leave their relationship in the realm of wild kisses. His idea was that the sweetness would last to be enjoyed during the four months of midshipmen school; then he would go to sea, and that would be the convenient and painless end. He was quite pleased with himself for having worked the romance out for maximum fun and minimum entanglement. It indicated to him that he was a mature man of pleasure. He prided himself on not having attempted to sleep with May. The correct policy, he had decided, was to enjoy the sparkle and stimulation of the girl's company without becoming involved in a mess. It was a wise enough policy; but he deserved less credit for it than he gave himself, because it was based on a cool subconscious estimate that he probably wouldn't succeed if he tried.

3 · Midshipman Keith

Willie Keith's second day in the Navy came close to being his last in the service or on earth.

Riding on the subway that morning to the Brooklyn Navy Yard in his blue apprentice seaman raincoat, he felt conspicuously military. The fact that he was going for a check on his pulse rate and lordosis did not spoil his enjoyment of the glances of stenographers and high-school girls. Willie was collecting the homage earned by men otherwise occupied in the Solomons. In peacetime it had not been his habit to envy sailors their costume, but now suddenly these bell-bottom trousers seemed as correct and dashing as beer jackets had been on the Princeton campus.

Outside the gates of the Navy Yard Willie stopped, exposed his wrist to the raw cutting wind, and counted his pulse. It was tripping at eighty-six. He was enraged to think that his new naval aura might be stripped from him by a mere arithmetical failure of his body. He waited a few minutes, trying to relax, and took another count. Ninety-four. The marine sentinel at the gate was staring at him. Willie looked up and down the street and began walking toward a dingy drugstore at the corner, thinking, "I had a dozen physicals at college, and one at the receiving station several months ago. My pulse was always seventy-two. Now I'm worried. What the devil is an admiral's pulse rate when he sees the enemy fleet—seventy-two? I've got to take something to cancel the worry and give a normal result."

He swallowed this argument, and a double bromide; the one for his conscience, the other for his pulse. Both sedatives worked. When he hesitated for a moment outside Captain Grimm's office for a last check, his blood thumped tranquilly past his fingers at seventy-five, and he felt buoyant and relaxed. He pushed open the door.

The first object that caught his eye in the room was a blue sleeve with four gold stripes on it. The sleeve was gesticulating at a fat Navy nurse seated at a desk. Captain Grimm, gray and very tired-looking, was waving a sheaf of papers and complaining bitterly about slipshod accounting of morphine. He turned on Willie. "What is it, boy?"

Willie handed him the envelope. Captain Grimm glanced at the papers. "Oh, Lord. Miss Norris, when am I due at the operating room?"

"In twenty minutes, sir."

"All right, Keith, go into that dressing room. I'll be with you in two minutes."

"Aye aye, sir." Willie went through the white-painted door and closed it. The little room was stuffily hot, but he was afraid to tamper with the windows. He wandered around in a narrow circle, reading labels on bottles, looking out the window at the sad gray jumble of the Brooklyn waterfront, and yawning. He waited two minutes, five, ten. The bromide and the warmth took stronger hold. He stretched out on the examining table, assuring himself that a little relaxation would be good for him.

When he woke his watch read half-past five. He had slept, forgotten by the Navy, for eight hours. He washed his face in a basin, straightened his hair, and emerged from the dressing room with a look of martyrdom. The fat nurse's jaws fell open when she saw him.

"Holy Christmas! Are *you* still here?"

"Nobody ever told me to come out."

"But my God!" She jumped out of the swivel chair. "You've been here since—— Why didn't you say something? Wait!" She went into an inner office, and came out in a moment with the captain, who said, "Blazes, boy, I'm sorry. I've had operations, meetings—— Step into my office."

In the book-lined room he told Willie to strip to the waist, and inspected his back. "Touch your toes."

Willie did it—not without a loud grunt. The captain smiled doubtfully, and felt his wrist. Willie sensed hammering again. "Doctor," he exclaimed, "I'm okay."

"We have standards," said the captain. He picked up his pen. It hovered over Willie's record. "You know," he added, "Navy casualties are worse than Army in this war, so far."

"I want to be a Navy man," said Willie, and only when the words were out of his mouth did he realize that they were quite true.

The doctor looked at him, with a flicker of good will in his eye. He wrote decisively on the record: *Mild lordosis well compensated. Pulse normal—J. Grimm, Chief Med. Bklyn.* He crumpled up and threw away the red-lettered memo, and returned the other papers to Willie. "Don't suffer in silence in this outfit, boy. Speak up when something damn silly is happening to you."

"Aye aye, sir."

The captain turned his attention to a spread of papers on his desk, and Willie left. It occurred to him that his naval career had probably been saved by a doctor's shame at keeping a patient waiting eight hours, but he rejoiced at the outcome, anyway. Back at Furnald Hall he returned his medical record to the pharmacist's mate of the red pencil in the dispensary. Warner put aside a bowl of purple antiseptic to glance eagerly at the papers. His face fell, but he managed a baleful grin. "Hm, you made it. Fine."

"See you in Tokyo, Doctor," said Willie.

In his room he found Keggs and Keefer fussing with guns. A big battered rifle, with a custody card, lay on Willie's cot. "Rifles in the Navy?" he said mildly.

"Bet your behind," said Keefer. The pieces of his firing lock lay on the desk beside him. Keggs was clanking the rotating bolt back and forth with an air of futility. "We have to learn how to take one apart and assemble it in two minutes," he moaned, "by tomorrow morning. I bilge, for sure."

"Don't strain your milk," said Keefer. "Lemme get this baby together, and I'll show you. Damn this mainspring."

The Southerner gave his two roommates a patient thorough lesson in the mysteries of the Springfield rifle. Keggs got the hand of it quickly. His long bony fingers caught the critical trick, which was to force the tough mainspring back into the bolt on reassembly. He beamed at his weapon, and ran through the process several times. Willie wrestled vainly with the bolt for a while and panted, "They should have bilged me on lordosis. It would have been more dignified. I'll be out of this Navy tomorrow——— *Get* in there, lousy damn spring———" He had never touched a gun before. The potential deadliness of it meant nothing to him. It was simply a troublesome assignment: a knotty page of Beethoven, an overdue book report on *Clarissa Harlowe*.

"Jam the butt of that bolt in your stomach, see?" said Keefer. "Then press the spring down with both hands."

Willie obeyed. The spring yielded slowly. The end of it sank at last into the rim. "It works! Thanks, Rollo———" At that moment the spring, still unsecured, escaped between his fingers and leaped from the bolt. It soared across the room. The window was conveniently open. The spring sailed out into the night.

His roommates stared at him in horror. "That's bad, isn't it?" quavered Willie.

"Anything happens to your rifle, boy—that does it," said the Southerner, walking to the window.

"I'll run downstairs," Willie said.

"What, during study hour? Twelve demerits!" Keggs said.

"Come here, fella." Keefer pointed out through the window. The spring lay in a rain gutter at the edge of a steeply slanting copper-covered roof projection beneath the window. The tenth floor was set slightly back from the rest of the building.

"I can't get that," said Willie.

"You better, fella."

Keggs peered out. "You'd never make it. You'd fall off."

"That's what I think," said Willie. He was not at all a daredevil. His mountain climbing had been done in plenty of stout company, and with much gulping horror. He hated high places and poor footing.

"Look, fella, you want to stay in the Navy? Climb out there. Or d'you want me to do it?"

Willie climbed out, clinging to the window frame. The wind moaned in the darkness. Broadway twinkled far, far below. The ledge seemed to drop away beneath his trembling legs. He stretched a hand vainly toward the spring, and gasped, "Need another couple of feet——"

"If we only had a rope," said Keefer. "Look, man. One of us gets out with you, see, and hangs onto the window. And you hang onto him. That does it."

"Let's get it over with," said Keggs anxiously. "If he gets caught out there we all bilge." He sprang through the window, stood beside Willie, and gripped his hand. "Now get it." Willie let go of the window, and inched downward, clinging to Keggs's powerful grip. He teetered at the edge of the roof, the wind whipping his clothes. The spring was in easy reach. He grasped it and thrust it into a pocket.

Ensign Acres might have picked a less awkward moment to make his study-hour round of the tenth floor, but he chose this one. He walked past the room, peeped in, stopped short, and roared, "Attention on deck! What the hell is going on here?"

Keggs neighed in terror and let go of Willie's hand. Willie lunged and clutched him around the knees. The two midshipmen swayed back and forth on the ledge, not far from death. But Keggs's urge to live was slightly stronger than his fear of ensigns. He reared backward and fell into the room on his head, hauling Willie through the window on top of him. Ensign Acres glared. His chin jutted. Willie stood up and produced the spring, stammering, "I—this was out on the roof——"

"What the hell was it doing out there?" bellowed Acres.

"It flew out," said Willie.

The blood rushed into Acres' face as though he had been called a dirty name. *"Flew* out? See here, you——"

"While I was assembling my gun. It got away," Willie added in hurried, plaintive tones.

Acres looked around at the roommates. Keggs's shuddering fear, Willie's fright, Keefer's rigid attention were genuine. Two months ago he had himself been a midshipman. "You should each get fifteen demerits," he growled, by way of descending from his rage. "I have my eye on you—— Carry on." He stalked out.

"Do you suppose," Willie said in the numb pause that followed, "that some higher power doesn't want me in the Navy? I seem to be the Jonah in this room."

"Forget it, fella. You just getting the hard luck out of your system," Keefer said.

They studied fiercely as Bilging Day drew nearer. A nice balance of forces became evident in Room 1013. Keggs was strong on the paper work of navigation and engineering. His plotting charts and sketches of boilers were handsome art, and he lent his talents to the others readily. He was slow to grasp facts and theories, so he set his alarm clock two hours before reveille to give himself extra study time. His face elongated daily, and his melancholy eyes burned in deepening sockets like dim candles, but he never failed a quiz.

Keefer failed often. He calculated averages to a hair and managed to stay above the estimated expulsion level in all courses. His strong point was military wisdom. Willie never could decide whether this gift was natural or acquired, but Keefer, with the body and air of a sloven, was the most polished seaman in the school. He kept himself, his bed, and his books with the neatness of a cat. On parade his fresh-looking uniform, glittering shoes, and erect bearing quickly caught the eye of the executive officer. He was ordained a battalion commander.

Willie Keith became the oracle of the tenth floor in matters of naval ordnance. Actually he was a blockhead on the subject. Reputations are made queerly and swiftly in wartime. It happened that in the first week a terrible examination was scheduled in Ordnance, with the announced purpose of causing weaklings to go down. Everybody crammed feverishly, of course. Willie was as earnest as the rest, but one page of the book, composed in the worst Navy jargon, baffled him; a description of a thing called a Frictionless Bearing. Keefer and Keggs had given it up. Willie read the page over seventeen times, then twice more aloud, and was on the point of quitting when he noticed that whole sentences had become embedded in his memory. He worked another half hour and memorized the entire page, word for word. The chief essay question on the examination, as luck would have it, was *Explain the Frictionless Bearing.* Willie happily disgorged the words, which meant no more to him than a Hindu chant. When the results of the test were announced he stood first in the school. "Apprentice Seaman Keith," shouted Ensign Acres, squinting in the sunlight at noon assembly, "is officially commended for a brilliant Ordnance paper. He was the only man in the school to give an intelligent explanation of the Frictionless Bearing."

With a reputation to uphold, and dozens of questions to answer in every study period, Willie thereafter drove himself to a meaningless verbal mastery of all the details of naval cannons.

This lesson in Navy pedagogy was driven home shortly before Bilging Day. One night Willie came upon the following statement in his tattered green-bound manual, *Submarine Doctrine, 1935:* "Submarines, because of their small cruising range, are chiefly suitable for coastal defense." At that time the Nazis were torpedoing several American ships each week around Cape Hatteras, four thousand miles from Germany's coast. Willie pointed this out with chuckles to his roommates. The sinking of a few dozen of our own ships seemed a small price for the pleasure of catching the Navy in an absurdity. Next day in Tactics class the instructor, one Ensign Brain, called on him.

"Keith."

"Aye aye, sir."

"What is the submarine chiefly suitable for, and why?" The educator held an open copy of *Submarine Doctrine, 1935* in his hand. Ensign Brain was a prematurely baldish, prematurely wrinkled, prematurely ferocious martinet of twenty-five. He was a drillmaster. About this subject he knew nothing. But he had once learned to read.

Willie hesitated.

"Well, Keith?"

"Do you mean as of now, sir, or as of 1935?"

"I asked the question now, not in 1935."

"The Germans are sinking a lot of ships off Hatteras," said Willie tentatively.

"I am aware of that. This is not a class in current events but in tactics. Have you prepared the lesson?"

"Yes, sir."

"Answer the question."

Willie estimated the situation swiftly. This was his last chance to recite in Tactics before the bilge. "Submarines, because of their small cruising range," he declared, "are chiefly suitable for coastal defense."

"Correct," said Ensign Brain, writing down a perfect mark. "Why all the stalling?"

So Willie gave himself over to the bondage of brute memory. Doomsday came; and none of the three in Room 1013 bilged. Kalten in Room 1012 and Koster in Room 1014 were delivered into the jaws of their draft boards. Kalten, the son of a powerful Washington attorney, had flouted rules and done no studying. Willie felt much sorrier for Koster, a good-humored, effete boy brought up by maiden aunts. That evening when Willie visited Room 1014, the sight of the empty cot upset him. Years later he learned that Koster had died in the first attack wave at Salerno.

Now they were midshipmen, firmly rooted in the Navy, with blue dress uniforms, white officers' caps, and most important, freedom on Saturdays from noon to midnight. This was Friday. They had been imprisoned incommunicado for three weeks. Willie telephoned May Wynn joyously and told her to meet him outside the school at one minute past twelve next day. She was there in a taxi; and she looked so beautiful stretching her arms eagerly to him that Willie momentarily pictured a wedding and all its consequences as he hugged her. He was still kissing her when he regretfully decided against it, for all the old reasons. They went to Luigi's, and Willie was so stimulated by the beauty of his girl and the first taste of wine in three weeks that he ate a couple of pizzas. He slowed down, puffing, on the last bites, and glanced at his wrist watch.

"May," he said reluctantly, "I've got to leave you now."

"Oh? Aren't you free till midnight?"

"I ought to drop in on my family."

"Of course," said May. The glad light began to die out of her eyes.

"Just for a while—a half hour, maybe an hour. You take in a matinee. I can meet you again at"—he glanced at his watch—"half-past five."

May nodded.

"Look," he said, taking money out of his pocket and flourishing it, "a hundred and twenty dollars. We'll do the town."

"Navy pay?"

"Twenty of it, yes."

"Where'd you get the hundred?"

Willie choked a little over the word, but brought it out. "Mother."

"I doubt she'd approve of your spending it on me." May looked into his eyes. "Does she know I'm alive, Willie?"

Willie shook his head.

"You're very wise. That innocent face hides plenty of cunning." She reached across the table and touched his cheek affectionately.

"Where will we meet?" said Willie, feeling, as he rose, heavily freighted with dough, cheese, tomatoes, and wine.

"Anywhere."

"Stork Club?" he said. She gave him a wistful smile. They parted at the restaurant door. Willie slept, snoring, on the train to Manhasset. Commuter's instinct woke him up just before his station.

4 · Midshipman Keith in Trouble

The Keith home in Manhasset was a twelve-room Dutch colonial house with heavy white pillars, high-arching black wood-shingled roof, and multitudes of large windows. It stood on a knoll in the middle of two acres of lawns set with soaring old beech, maples, and oak trees and bordered by flower beds and a thick high hedge. Mrs. Keith's family had presented it to her. Her income from Rhode Island bank securities still went to keep it up. Willie believed such surroundings were normal.

He walked up the avenue of maples to the front door and entered upon a prepared triumph. His mother hugged him. Relatives and neighbors, flourishing cocktails, greeted the war hero. The best china and the best silver were set out on the dining-room table, reflecting yellow beams from flaming logs in the marble-paneled fireplace. "All right, Martina," cried Mrs. Keith, "put on the steaks! . . . We have a feast for you, Willie. Everything you love—oysters, onion soup, steak—double sirloin for you, dear—with soufflé potatoes, and Bavarian cream. You're starved, aren't you?"

"I could eat a horse, Mom," said Willie. There are heroisms in small acts. Willie sat down to his dinner, and ate.

"I thought you'd be hungrier," said his mother, watching him poke without enthusiasm at the steak.

"I'm enjoying it too much to rush it," answered Willie. He downed the steak. But when the Bavarian cream was set before him, rich, brown, and trembling, nature rebelled. Willie grew pale, turned away, and quickly lit a cigarette. "Mom, I'm through."

"Come, you don't have to be bashful, dear. We all know how sailors eat. Finish up."

Willie's father had been watching him quietly. "Maybe you had a little something before coming home, Willie."

"Just a snack, Dad, to keep me going."

Mrs. Keith permitted him to stagger off to the living room, where another fire crackled. Here the midshipman wheezily held court, describing the secrets of the Navy and analyzing the conduct of the war in all theaters. He hadn't read a newspaper in three weeks, so it was not easy to do; but he improvised, and his words were eagerly listened to.

Willie noticed for the first time when the party went into the living room that his father limped and walked with a cane. After a while Dr. Keith interrupted the question session. "Time out," he said, "while a man has a few words in private with his sailor son." He took Willie by the arm and led him into the library, a mahogany-paneled room full of leather-bound collected editions of standard authors and motley best sellers of twenty years. The windows looked out on the garden behind the house, where patches of old snow lay in shady corners of the brown empty flower beds. "How is it, really, Willie—the Navy?" Dr. Keith said, closing the door, and leaning on his cane.

"Fine, Dad. I'll get by. What's the matter with your leg?"

"Nothing much. Infected toe."

"I'm sorry. Bother you much?"

"Some."

Willie glanced at his father in surprise. It was the first time he had heard his father complain of an ailment. "Well—what can I say to a doctor? You've had it looked at?"

"Oh, yes. Nothing to be done. It will simply take time." Father and son looked into each other's eyes for a moment. "I shouldn't keep you from the company," said the doctor, limping toward the window. "But we've really never talked much, have we? I'm afraid I've let your mother do all the upbringing. And now you're off to the wars."

Willie did not know what to answer. It seemed that his father wanted to say something but could not find a way to begin.

"I never got overseas myself, Willie, in the first war. Maybe you'll be lucky, too."

"I'll take what comes," said Willie. "The Navy's spending a lot of time and work on me. Maybe I ought to go overseas if I'm good enough for it.".

Dr. Keith ran his fingers across the small black mustache. His eyes searched Willie's face. "You're changing a little. What's doing it? The Navy?"

"I'm afraid I'm the same poor lug."

"Do you get a chance to play the piano?"

"Forgetting what one looks like."

"Willie," said his father, "have you met a girl?"

Willie was too startled to lie. "Yes, sir."

"A good girl?"

"In her way, wonderful."

"Do you want to marry her?"

"No."

"Why not?"

"Well—it's not that kind of thing."

"Don't be too sure. Bring her out here to meet us."

A picture flashed across Willie's mind: the narrow dark fruit store in the Bronx which he had once visited, tended by May's mother and father. The mother was fat, wore a shapeless rusty black dress, and had a hairy face. The father was a wizened man in a dirty apron, with gaps in his brown teeth. They had both seemed warmly good-natured in the few broken sentences they had spoken to him. Another grotesque image presented itself: Mrs. Minotti and his mother shaking hands. He shook his head.

"Well, there was a nurse I once didn't marry," said his father thoughtfully. "But I have no regrets. Your mother and I have had a fine life—— Well, they'll be wondering what happened to us." Still he made no move to go.

"Dad, is there something else you want to talk about?"

The father hesitated. "Nothing that can't wait."

"Why don't you visit me down at school? It's kind of interesting."

"I'm not free much."

"Yes, I know."

"Maybe I will, though." Dr. Keith put his hand on his son's shoulder. "This isn't necessarily a bad time for you, Willie. The Navy."

"Not if I emerge in one piece. It might do me good."

"It might—— Let's go."

Willie glanced at his watch as they re-entered the living room. Five to four. He made hasty excuses to the guests, overriding his mother's loud protests. She followed him to the door. "When will I see you again, dear?" she said as he pulled the belt tight on his blue raincoat.

"Next Saturday, Mom, if I stay out of trouble."

"Oh, no. I'll come and see you before that."

It was twenty past six when he rushed into the Stork Club. Hurriedly pulling off his coat at the check room, he caught a glimpse of May. The phrases of apology faded from his mind. Marty Rubin, the agent, sat with her. "Now, what is that Jew doing here at this point?" he thought. His greeting to both of them was cool.

"Congratulations on making midshipman. May's been telling me about it," said the agent. "I envy you your uniform."

Willie glanced from his own brass-buttoned blues to Rubin's gray single-breasted suit cut too full for the taste of Manhasset and Princeton. The peering baldish fat agent seemed a living cartoon of the Civilian. "I envy you yours," he said with a quiet irony, and chose a chair opposite May, leaving Rubin between himself and the girl. "What are you drinking?"

Rubin beckoned to a waiter. "Scotch," he said. "What will you have?"

"Double scotch," said Willie.

"Good heavens," said May. She regarded Willie in an intent, not quite friendly way.

"A man's drink for a naval officer," Rubin remarked. He lifted his half-empty glass. "I'll finish mine and run along. May and I were just talking a little business till you got here."

"Don't rush off," said Willie. "Have dinner with us. Sorry I'm late, May."

"Marty is very good company. I didn't mind," answered the girl.

"Thanks," said the agent. "I know when it's time for a fill-in act to get off." He drained his drink and stood. "Have yourselves a time, kids. By the way, your dinner is paid for."

"Don't be absurd," said Willie.

"My pleasure. I've seen Frank," he said, indicating the headwaiter. "Don't let the sailor pay for anything, May. They'll be gypping him. So long."

Willie felt obliged to get up and shake Rubin's hand. "Thank you," he said. "That really wasn't necessary."

"My bit for the war effort," said Rubin, and walked off with his heavy waddling gait.

"That was sweet of Marty," said May. "I didn't know he'd done it."

"Very sweet. Also a bit vulgar," said Willie, sitting and taking a deep gulp of his drink. "I don't like favors to be pressed on me."

"Go to hell," said May. "Marty Rubin is my best friend in the world, and I include you——"

"I gather that. You're inseparable."

"I keep him around to remind me that there are decent men in the world who don't consider every girl a thing to be jumped at and pawed——"

"Sorry I'm such a beast as to find you attractive. Possibly your friend prefers tall girls."

May was conscious enough of her height to wear extra-high heels. The blow knocked out her wind for a moment, but she rallied. "How dared you talk to him like that?"

"I was very pleasant. I invited him to dinner——"

"The way you'd invite a dog to lie down by your chair."

"I wanted to be alone with you because I love you and haven't seen you for three weeks."

"Three weeks and an afternoon."

"All right."

"Plus an extra hour."

"I apologized for being late."

"It would have been better, of course, for me to sit here by myself for an hour, looking as though I wanted to be picked up."

"May, I'm glad he was with you. I'm sorry I had to leave you. We're together now. Let's start from there." He took her hand but she slipped it free.

"Possibly you don't like Jews. Or Italians, either. They have a lot in common."

"You really want to fight."

"Yes!"

"What about? Not about Marty Rubin."

"No. About us." The girl's fists were clenched in front of her on the table.

Willie's heart ached, because she was so beautiful in the gray dress, with her dark red hair falling to her shoulders. "Wouldn't you rather eat first?"

"I don't want to eat."

"Thank God. I couldn't get down an olive myself. Let's go to the Tahiti. One drink, then we fight."

"Why there? If you think I'm sentimental about that place you're wrong——"

"I said I'd meet my roommates there for a few minutes——"

"All right. I don't care."

But when they came to the Tahiti the check-room girl and Mr. Dennis and the musicians came flocking around to admire Willie's uniform and joke about his romance with May. The thread of the quarrel was broken. They sat drinking glumly while the place filled with a noisy swelling crowd, mostly Army and Navy officers with their girls. Just before the ten o'clock floor show Roland Keefer came rolling through the smoke and din. His hair was disheveled, his paper collar wilted, his eyes bloodshot. He was towing a fat blonde of about thirty-five in a pink satin dress. Her features were not clearly visible through her make-up.

"Hey, Willie! H'ya, fella! How's the old mainspring holding up tonight?"

He giggled happily and inspected May. Willie stood and

introduced him. Keefer greeted May with respectful, suddenly sober politeness. "Hey, whaddya think of old horse-face Keggs?" He dropped back into hilarity. "Went to a concert, I swear he did. They give him a free ticket at the officers' club. He wanted me to come. I said 'Shinola on that!'" He pinched the blonde's arm. "We make our own concert, hey, sweetie?"

"Don't be fresh," said the blonde. "Why don't you introduce me to your friends?"

"This here is Tootsie Weaver, folks. Tootsie, this fella comes from Princeton."

"How do you do," said Tootsie, in her best Senior Prom manner.

"See you, folks," said Keefer, dragging Tootsie off as she seemed settling herself to be sociable, "we got drinking to do."

"Don't forget," called Willie, "five demerits for every minute you're late after midnight."

"Son, you talking to the human time clock," shouted Keefer. "Bye-bye."

"Keefer has odd tastes," Willie said at he sat.

"Maybe he thinks you have," said May. "Order me another drink."

The floor show ran its usual course of comic master of ceremonies, girl singer, and knockabout comedy team in funny clothes. "With us tonight," blared the master of ceremonies after the last act, "are two great entertainers who delighted audiences here at the Tahiti for many weeks last March. May Wynn, the lovely singer who just finished a triumphant run at the Krypton Room, and Willie Keith, who is now in the service of his country." He pointed and clapped his hands. The pink spotlight swung to the couple. They rose reluctantly and the crowd applauded. When the servicemen saw May the handclapping became stronger. "Maybe we can induce this charming couple to give us a number. Don't they look nice together, folks?"

"No, no," said Willie, and May shook her head, but the applause grew.

"Mozart!" shouted the hat-check girl, and the audience,

having no idea what the cry meant, took it up all the same. "Mozart! Mozart!" There was no escape. They walked to the piano.

May sang deliciously, with sweet sadness in her tones. There was something in the performance that hushed the customers, a note of farewell and regret for passing love that cut through the fumes of tobacco and alcohol and touched all the men who were soon to leave home and fight—and even those who had intelligently arranged to remain behind were touched, too, and felt vague pangs of shame. Tootsie Weaver, squeezed in a corner of the bar, put a heavily perfumed handkerchief to her eyes.

May stumbled during the last strains of the song. At the end there was a storm of hand-clapping. She hurried back to her seat without bowing. The three-piece dance orchestra struck up, and couples jammed the floor. "First time I ever blew up like that," she muttered to Willie.

"It was wonderful, May."

"I'm ready to fight now," said the girl, draining her flat drink. "I don't want to see you any more."

"I don't believe you."

"Don't call me again at the candy store. I won't come to the telephone."

"Why? Why?"

"Let me put it another way—will you marry me?"

Willie pressed his lips together, and looked down at the glass in his hands. The trumpeter blew deafeningly into the microphone and dancers joggled their table. May said, "Don't misunderstand me, I don't expect you to. This is all my fault. You played it straight when you told me your pedigree over the pizzas. I was having a wonderful time until recently and I didn't care. But somewhere along the line I made a terrible mistake. I forgot I was Tootsie Weaver——"

"Look, May——"

"Oh, sure, skinnier, younger, and somewhat more presentable—would you take either of us home to meet your mother?"

"May, we're both kids—I'll be **out** to sea in three months——"

"I know. You're a darling, Willie. I hope you find a wonderful girl someday. I just don't want another three months as Tootsie. I don't want another evening of it. Not another minute, in fact." Her eyes filled with tears, and she stood. "Never let it be said I earned you any demerits. Let's go."

They went out and climbed into a taxi, and fell into the most racking kisses they had ever exchanged. It was not pleasure, it was torment which neither could stop. The taxi drew up under the street lamp at the entrance to Furnald Hall. Willie's wrist watch showed eleven twenty-five. "Keep going," he said chokingly to the driver.

"Where to, mister?"

"I don't care. Up and down Riverside Drive. Just so we get back here by midnight."

"Right, mister."

The driver started his motor and slid the glass panel closed between himself and his passengers. The taxi plunged downhill to the Drive. There were more kisses and broken futile words. May held Willie's head comfortingly to her bosom, and stroked his hair. "Sometimes I think you like me," she said.

"I don't know why God makes human jellyfish like Willie Keith——"

"You know what Marty Rubin says?"

"Damn Marty Rubin."

"You don't know it, Willie, but he's a friend of yours." Willie sat up. "This whole mess started with him."

"I asked him what I ought to do about you."

"And he said throw me out."

"No. He says he thinks you really love me."

"Well, hooray for Marty."

"He wondered whether I would become more acceptable to your mother if I enrolled in college."

Willie was astounded. Moaning and protesting his undying love was one thing. But this was a serious matter.

"I could do it," said May eagerly. "I could still get into the February class at Hunter. I had good marks in high school though you do consider me an ignoramus. I even have a Regents' scholarship, if it's still good. Marty says he can get me enough bookings in and around New York to keep me going. I only work nights, anyway."

Willie wanted to spar for time. His beautiful prize was drifting within reach again, but on sobering terms. May regarded him with lustrous, hopeful eyes. Her hard-boiled wariness was all gone.

"Could you stand going back to school?"

"I'm pretty tough," she said.

Willie realized that she spoke truly. She was not a companion for good times any more, but a challenger to his mother for his life. It had all changed in a few minutes; he was dizzied. "I'll tell you God's truth, May. I don't think it would make a particle of difference to my mother."

"Would it to you?"

Willie looked into her eyes, and quailed, and turned away.

"Don't trouble, darling," she said with sudden dryness. "I predicted the answer to Marty. I said I don't blame you. I don't. Tell the little man to take you back to the Navy. It's late."

But when the taxi parked again at Furnald Hall and Willie had to get out and leave May behind forever, he couldn't do it. At three minutes to twelve, he started a desperate harangue to recover lost ground. On the sidewalk outside, midshipmen were running, walking, and staggering toward the entrance. Several were kissing girls in nooks of the building. The tenor of Willie's plea was that he and May ought to live for the hour, and gather rosebuds while they might, and drink for once dead they never would return, and youth was a stuff that would not endure, and so forth. It took him the whole three minutes to round out this message. The couples outside finished their business. The stream of midshipmen disappeared. But Willie, with demerits beginning to pile up, was compelled in courtesy to wait for May's answer. He hoped it would be favorable and short.

"Listen, Willie darling," said May, "for the last time, because we're all finished. I'm a poor Bronx girl with a lot of problems. I don't want to add a hopeless romance to them. I have a mother and father with a fruit store that doesn't pay, one brother in the Army and another a plain bum that we never see except when he needs money to get out of trouble. All I want is a chance to make some money and live in peace. I was a fool to fall in love with you, and I don't know why I did, because you're a bigger fool than I am. Emotionally you're about fifteen, and when your hair stands up in back you look like a rabbit, which is frequently. I guess I'm a sucker for comparative literature. Hereafter I'll steer clear of any man with more than a public-school education and—— For God's sake," she broke off irritably, "why do you keep looking at your watch?"

"I'm getting demerits," said Willie.

"Get out—get out of my life. I'll never see you again!" stormed the girl. "You must be my punishment for not going to mass. Get out!"

"May, I love you," said Willie, opening the door.

"Drop dead," cried May. She pushed him out and slammed the door.

Willie raced into Furnald Hall. Awaiting him was a huge clock over the entrance which grinned four minutes past twelve. And under the clock, terrible in his gloating happiness, grinned Ensign Brain.

"Ah, Midshipman Keith, I believe."

"Yes, sir," panted Willie, erect and trembling.

"The check list showed you as absent over leave—the only one in Furnald, Midshipman Keith. I had hoped there was some mistake." His wreathing smiles indicated that probably he had hoped harder there was no mistake. All his wrinkles were bent upward with pleasure.

"Sorry, sir. Circumstances——"

"Circumstances, Midshipman Keith? Circumstances? The only relevant circumstance that I am aware of, Midshipman Keith, is that you now have twenty demerits, the highest figure in Furnald, Midshipman Keith. What do you think of that circumstance, Midshipman Keith?"

"I'm sorry about it, sir."

"You're sorry about it. Thank you for informing me you're sorry about it, Midshipman Keith. I was stupid enough to imagine that you were glad about it, Midshipman Keith. But probably you're used to such stupidity in your superiors. You probably think we're all stupid. You probably think all the rules of this school are stupid. Either you think that, or you think you're too good to have to obey rules made for the common herd. Which is it, Midshipman Keith?"

To help the midshipman in making this interesting choice, he thrust his corrugated face within two inches of Willie's nose. The midshipmen standing guard on the "quarterdeck" watched the dialogue out of the corners of their eyes, and wondered how Willie would get out of that particular alley. Willie stared at the sparse fuzz atop Ensign Brain's head and had the sense to keep quiet.

"Fifty demerits mean expulsion, Midshipman Keith," purred the drill-master.

"I know, sir."

"You're well on the way, Midshipman Keith."

"There won't be any more, sir."

Ensign Brain withdrew his face to a normal distance. "Wars are fought by the clock, Midshipman Keith. Attacks are made when ordered. Not four minutes late. A four-minute delay can cause ten thousand men to die. A whole fleet can be sunk in four minutes, Midshipman Keith." Ensign Brain was following the usual pattern, shading his cat-and-mouse delights into lofty morality, though the morality was sound enough. "Dismissed, Midshipman Keith."

"Thank you, sir."

Willie saluted, and walked up nine flights of steps in despair. The elevator had stopped at midnight.

5 · Orders for Midshipman Keith

The next day, Sunday, was sunny and clear, and the midshipmen were thankful. A review was scheduled for the pleasure of the commandant of the Third Naval District, a display of the whole military might at Columbia. The other sections of the midshipmen school at Johnson Hall and John Jay Hall were going to merge with the men of Furnald in an array of twenty-five hundred novice naval officers. After breakfast the midshipmen shifted into their dress blues and lined up in front of the hall, with rifles, leggings, and gun belts. They were inspected one by one as minutely as if each midshipman were about to have lunch with the admiral, rather than pass by him in a blur of heads. Demerits flew for a spot on the collar, shoes that failed to reflect the image of the inspector, hair a fraction of an inch too long. A flick of Ensign Brain's hand on the back of a midshipman's neck was an announcement of five demerits, duly recorded by the yeoman who walked close behind him. Willie was flicked. In his eminence of twenty-five demerits he floated lonely as a cloud. The closest contender had seven.

A sixty-piece band of midshipmen blasted brassy marches with more lung power than harmony, colors waved bravely on staffs, and fixed bayonets glittered in the morning sun as the ranks of midshipmen marched onto South Field. Behind the wire fences around the field were hundreds of spectators—parents, sweethearts, passers-by, college students, and satiric small boys. The band used up its repertoire, and was beginning again on *Anchors Aweigh*, when all the cohorts of Johnson, John Jay, and Furnald reached their places. They made a stirring show,

47

the immense ranks and files of white gold-trimmed hats, bristling rifles, squared shoulders in blue, and young stern faces. Individually they were scared youngsters trying to remain inconspicuous, but from their aggregate there rose a subtle promise of unexpected awkward power. A bugle call knifed across the air. "HAND SALUTE!" blatted the loudspeakers. Twenty-five hundred hands snapped at a slant to the hats. The admiral strolled onto the field, smoking, followed by a straggle of officers, walking carelessly to symbolize the privileges of rank, but straggling at distances from the admiral strictly regulated by the number of sleeve stripes on each straggler. Ensign Brain brought up the rear, also smoking. He put out his cigarette at the instant that the admiral did.

The admiral, short, stout and gray-headed, addressed the ranks briefly and politely. Then the performance began. Stepping proudly and confidently to the music after a week of rehearsal, the battalions passed in review, marching, wheeling, countermarching. The spectators clapped and cheered. The small boys marched raggedly outside the fence in imitation of the midshipmen, yelling. And the commandant watched with a smile which infected the usually grim faces of the school staff. Newsreel cameras, mounted on trucks at the edges of the field, recorded the scene for history.

Willie went through his paces in a daze of whirling thoughts about May and demerits. He was not interested in the admiral but he was mightily interested in making no more mistakes. No back was straighter, no rifle at a more correct angle in the whole parade than Willie Keith's. The martial music and the majestic passing to and fro of the ranks thrilled him, and he was proud to be in this powerful show. He swore to himself that he would yet become the most correct, most admired, most warlike midshipman at Furnald Hill.

The music paused. The marching continued to a flourish of drums signaling the last maneuvers of the parade. Then the band crashed once more into *Anchors Aweigh*. Willie's squadron wheeled toward the fence, preparing to make a flank march off the field. Willie stepped around the wheeling turn, his eye on the line, staying faultlessly in position. Then he fixed his eyes to the front once more, and found himself looking straight at May Wynn. There she stood behind the fence not twenty feet away in her black fur-trimmed coat. She waved and smiled.

"I take it all back. You win!" she cried.

"By the *left* flank—march!" bawled Roland Keefer.

At the same instant a squadron from Johnson Hall passed them and the leader shouted, "By the *right* flank—march!"

Willie, his eyes on May, his mind paralyzed, obeyed the wrong order; turned sharply, and marched away from his battalion. In a moment he was cut off from them by an oncoming file from Johnson Hall. He halted after prancing into a vacant patch of grass and realizing that he was alone. A row of newsreel cameras close by, all seemingly trained on him, photographed every move.

He glanced around wildly, and, as the last of the Johnson Hall file went past him, he saw his battalion marching away from him, far down the field beyond a stretch of empty brown grass. With each grunt of the tubas, each beat of the drums, Willie was becoming more and more alone. To get back to his place meant a solitary hundred-yard dash in full view of the admiral. To stand alone on the field another second was impossible. Spectators were already beginning to shout jokes at him. Desperately Willie dived into a single file of John Jay Hall midshipmen marching past him to the exit in the opposite direction from Furnald.

"What the hell are you doing in here? Beat it," hissed the man behind him. Willie had landed unluckily in a group of the tallest John Jay men. He formed a distinctly unmilitary gap in the line of heads. But now it was too late for anything but prayer. He marched on.

"Get out of this line, you little monkey, or I'll kick you bowlegged!"

The file jammed up at the exit and became disorderly. Willie turned and said swiftly to the big glaring midshipman, "Look, brother, I'm sunk. I got cut off from my battalion. Do you want me to get bilged?"

The midshipman said no more. The file wound into John Jay Hall. As soon as they passed the entrance the midshipmen dispersed, laughing and shouting, to the staircases. Willie remained in the lobby, staring uneasily at faded Columbia athletic trophies in glass cases. He allowed fifteen minutes to pass, wandering here and there, keeping out of sight of the office and midshipmen guarding the quarterdeck. The excitement of the review dissipated. The lobby became quiet. He screwed up his courage, and walked briskly toward the one guarded door. All the other exits were locked and bolted.

"Halt! Sound off."

Willie drew up at the summons of the officer of the day, a burly midshipman wearing a yellow armband. A few feet away an ensign sat at a desk marking examination papers.

"Midshipman Willis Seward Keith, Furnald, on official business."

"State business."

"Checking on a lost custody card of a rifle."

The OOD picked up a clipboard with a mimeographed form sheet on it. "You're not logged in, Keith."

"I came in during the foul-up after the review. Sorry."

"Show your business pass."

This was the spring of the trap. Willie cursed Navy thoroughness. He pulled out his wallet and showed the OOD a picture of May Wynn waving and smiling on a merry-go-round horse. "Take it from here, friend," he whispered. "If you want, I bilge."

The OOD's eyes widened in amazement. He looked sidelong at the ensign, then straightened and saluted. "Pass, Keith."

"Aye aye, sir." Willie saluted and emerged into the sunlight, through the one loophole that military wisdom can never quite button up—the sympathy of the downtrodden for each other.

There were three ways back to Furnald: across the field, which was too exposed; a sneak trip around through the streets, which were out of bounds; and the gravel path along the field in front of the library. Willie took the gravel path, and soon came upon a working party of

Furnald midshipmen folding up the yellow chairs which had been placed for the admiral's party on the library steps. He briefly considered mingling with them, but they wore khaki, and they gave him queer scared looks. He hurried by them. The path lay clear ahead to Furnald——

"Midshipman Keith, I believe?"

Willie spun around in unbelieving horror at the tones. Ensign Brain, concealed by a granite post at the library entrance, was seated on a yellow chair, smoking. He dropped the cigarette, ground it out daintily with his toe, and rose. "Any explanation, Midshipman Keith, for being outside your room and wandering around out of uniform during a study hour?"

All Willie's resolve and intention caved in. "No, sir."

"No, sir. An excellent answer, Midshipman Keith, making up in clarity for what it lacks in official acceptability." Ensign Brain smiled like a hungry man at the sight of a chicken leg. "Midshipman Auerbach, you will take charge of the working party."

"Aye aye, sir."

"You will come with me, Midshipman Keith."

"Aye aye, sir."

Willie got back into Furnald Hall with no trouble, under the escort of Ensign Brain. He was marched to the desk of the duty officer, Ensign Acres. The midshipmen on the quarterdeck regarded him with pale dismay. Word of his pile of demerits had spread through the school. This new disaster horrified them. Willie Keith was all their nightmares come to life.

"Holy cow," exclaimed Ensign Acres, standing, "not Keith again."

"The same," said Ensign Brain. "The same paragon of military virtue, Midshipman Keith. Out of uniform, absent without leave, and violating a study period. No explanation."

"This is the end of him," said Acres.

"No doubt. I'm sorry for him, but obviously I had to pick him up."

"Of course." Acres regarded Willie curiously, and with some pity. "Don't you like the Navy, Keith?"

"I do, sir. I've had a bad run of luck, sir."

Acres lifted his hat, scratched his head with the same hand, and looked doubtfully at Brain. "Maybe we ought to just kick his behind up nine flights of stairs."

"You're the duty officer," said Brain virtuously. "A couple of dozen midshipmen know of this already. For all I know the exec saw the whole business through his window."

Acres nodded, and squared his hat as Brain walked off. "Well, this does it, Keith. Come along."

They paused outside the exec's door. Acres said in a low voice, "Between you and me, Keith, what the hell happened?"

The uniforms of both young men seemed to fade away for the moment, in the friendliness of Acres' tone. Willie had a sudden flooding sense that this was all just a dream in Looking-glass Land, that he still had his health, that the sun still shone, and that outside Furnald Hall, just a few feet away, on Broadway, his predicament would seem a joke. There was just this one difficulty: he was inside Furnald Hall. Enmeshed in comic-opera laws, he had comically broken a few, and was going to a comic-opera doom. But this dance of nonsense impinged very strongly on the real world. It meant that in time his living body, instead of being carted across the Pacific, clad in blue, would be carted across the Atlantic, clad in brown. This fact bothered him violently.

"What's the difference?" he said. "It was nice knowing you, Acres."

Ensign Acres let the familiarity pass. He understood it. "Merton has a heart. Tell him the truth. You have a chance," he said as he knocked.

Commander Merton, a little round-headed man with bristling brown hair and a red face, sat at his desk facing the door. He was partly hidden by a bubbling Silex. "Yes, Acres?"

"Sir—Midshipman Keith again."

Commander Merton peered sternly around the coffee at Willie. "Good God. What now?"

Acres recited the indictment. Merton nodded, dismissed

him, locked the door, and flipped a key on his interoffice talkbox. "I don't want any calls or other interruptions until further notice."

"Aye aye, sir," rattled the box.

The commander filled a cup. "Coffee, Keith?"

"No, thank you, sir." Willie's knees were unsteady.

"I think you'd better have some. Cream or sugar?"

"Neither, sir."

"Sit down."

"Thank you, sir." Willie was more scared by the courtesy than he would have been by rage. There was an air about the coffee of a condemned man's last meal.

Commander Merton sipped in silence for endless minutes. He was a reserve officer, in peacetime an insurance sales manager with a fondness for boating and for the weekly reserve drills. His wife had complained often of the time he wasted on the Navy, but the war had justified him. He had gone into active service at once and his family was proud now of his three stripes.

"Keith," he said at last, "you put me into the peculiar position of wanting to apologize to you for the Navy's laws. The sum of demerits for your three new offenses, together with the twenty-five you have, puts you out of school."

"I know, sir."

"Those demerits make sense. The values were carefully weighed. Any man who can't stay within the bounds of those penalties shouldn't be in the Navy."

"I know, sir."

"Unless," said the commander, and sipped for a while, "unless extraordinary, once-in-a-million circumstances are involved. Keith, what's been happening to you?"

There was nothing to lose. Willie poured out the tale of his troubles with May Wynn, including her appearance outside the fence. The exec listened unsmilingly. When the story was done, he pressed his fingertips together and mused.

"In effect, your claim is one of temporary derangement due to a girl."

"Yes, sir. But my fault, not hers."

"Aren't you the boy," said Commander Merton, "who wrote the brilliant essay on the Frictionless Bearing?"

"Well—yes, sir."

"That was a brutal essay question, designed to knock out all but the best. The Navy can't afford, Keith, to lose a man with such a mind. You've done us a bad turn."

Willie's hopes, which had risen slightly, fell again.

"Supposing," said Commander Merton, "that I were to give you a total of forty-eight demerits and confine you to the school until graduation. Could you make the grade?"

"I'd like to try, sir!"

"Any offense would put you out—shoeshine, haircut, mussed bed. You'd live with your head on a chopping-block. Any bad luck would sink you—even the day before graduation I've bilged men who had their ensign uniforms on. You wouldn't have an evening with this girl, Miss Wynn, for three months. Are you sure you want to tackle such an ordeal?"

"Yes, sir."

"Why?"

Willie thought a moment. Why, really? Even transfer to the Army seemed a relief in comparison, after all. "I've never failed anything I've tried yet, sir," he said. "I've never tried to do much, that's true. If I'm no good I might as well find it out now."

"Very well, get on your feet."

Willie jumped to stiff attention. The movement brought him back into the Navy.

"Twenty-three demerits and confined till graduation," snapped Commander Merton, in dry, bitter tones.

"Thank you, sir!"

"Dismissed."

Willie came out of the office full of resolution. He felt in debt to Commander Merton. His roommates respected his silence when he returned to the tenth floor. He flung himself upon his books with zeal and hate.

That night he wrote a long letter to May. He promised that at the end of his imprisonment his first act would be to seek her, if she still wanted to see him. He said nothing about marriage. Next morning he got up with Keggs two hours before reveille and ground fanatically at ordnance, tactics, gunnery, navigation, and communications.

There was a visiting time each day between five and five-thirty, when midshipmen could talk with parents or sweethearts in the lobby or on the walk in front of the hall. Willie intended to study through it, but came downstairs to buy cigarettes at the vending machine. He was surprised to see his father seated in a corner of a leathercovered sofa, the cane resting across his knees, his head leaning wearily on an arm, his eyes closed.

"Hello, Dad!"

Dr. Keith opened his eyes and greeted Willie cheerfully, dispelling the picture of fatigue.

"Where's Mom?"

"She had a patrons' meeting at the museum. A few patients are pretty annoyed at me for canceling my office hours, Willie, but here I am."

"Thanks for coming, Dad. How's your toe?"

"The same—— So, this is the good ship Furnald——"

"Let's walk around. I'll show you the place."

"No. Just sit and talk. Tell me about it."

Willie explained the use of the alphabet flags hanging from the ceiling, rattled off his store of nautical language to describe the massive anchoring tackle laid out in a corner, and explained the workings of the five-inch gun decorating the middle of the lobby. Dr. Keith smiled and nodded. "You're learning fast."

"It's just a lot of talk, really, Dad. I'll be lost on a ship."

"Not as much as you think. How are things going?"

Willie hesitated. He felt glad of the chance to break the bad news to his father, rather than to his mother. He could not guess how she would receive the blow. He preferred to disclose his trouble to a man. He sketched his situation, keeping May's part in it brief. Dr. Keith lit a cigar, and watched Willie as though his son's face told him more than the words.

"Pretty bad spot."

"Bad enough."

"Do you think you'll make it?"

"If it's in me, I will. I used to think I was pretty sharp. Now I'm not sure what stuff I've got. I'm more curious than worried."

"Do you care about becoming a naval officer?"

"I guess so. I can't see myself as a new John Paul Jones, but I'd hate to be licked in this silly way."

"Did your mother tell you about Uncle Lloyd?"

"What about him?"

"His partner has gone into the Army as a colonel. Public Relations. Lloyd is almost sure they can pull you out of the Navy and get you an Army commission. Your mother has been looking into ways and means of transferring you from the Navy."

"I didn't know."

"It came up over the week end. You know your mother. She'll want to work it all out and hand it to you on a plate."

Willie glanced out through the window. Midshipmen were lounging in front of the building in the sunshine. "Could I still get an Army commission if I bilged?"

"I gather that it wouldn't make much difference. It might even expedite matters."

"Will you do me a favor, Dad?"

"Of course."

"Tell Mom, as nicely as you can, to call off Uncle Lloyd."

"Don't be hasty."

"That's what I want, Dad."

"We can always keep it in reserve, you know."

"No, thanks."

"I doubt very much you'd go overseas in that billet."

"I wish to hell I'd known about it sooner."

"Suppose you bilge next week? One smudged collar will do it, Willie."

"If I bilge," said Willie, "I'll enlist as a sailor." He had formed no such resolve. The words came to his tongue.

The gong clanged. Dr. Keith looked around and saw other visitors moving to the door. He rose awkwardly, leaning on the cane. His movements gave Willie a twinge of anxiety.

"You're not in good shape, are you?"

"I'll live," laughed the doctor. He took Willie's arm, but didn't lean on it, merely holding it as they walked to the entrance. "Well, farewell to the prisoner of Furnald. I'll break it to your mother as gently as possible."

"She can still visit me here. I hope you will, too."

"I can't help saying," Dr. Keith remarked, stopping at the door, "that your devotion to the Navy surprises me."

"I'm not devoted to it. If you want to know, what I've studied seems to me a lot of rubbish. The rules, the lingo, strike me as comical. The idea of men spending their lives in this make-believe appalls me. I used to think it was preferable to the Army, but I'm sure now that they're both the same kind of foolishness. I don't care. I picked the Navy. I'll see this stupid war through in the Navy."

"Do you need any money?"

Willie smiled ruefully. "Cigarettes are cheap here. No tax."

The doctor put out his hand. "Good-by, Willie." He held his son's grip a little longer than necessary. "Much of what you say about the Navy is probably true. But I wish I were one of your roommates."

His son grinned, surprised. "Be nice to have you here. But you're doing more for the war in Manhasset."

"I'm compelled to try to think so. Good-by."

Willie looked after the limping figure, and vaguely thought that he ought to have talked more with his father before the war.

In the weeks that followed May came often to visit him. She was contrite and cheerful. With simple tact she found out when his mother was likely to come, and stayed away on those days. Twice Willie saw her come to the entrance of Furnald, observe him talking to his mother, and depart with a discreet wave. In February her visits became less frequent; she enrolled in Hunter College, and had several late classes. But sometimes she cut these to come to him. Willie was uneasy about her return to school, but she laughed at him.

"Don't worry, dear, all that is finished. I'm not doing

this for you, but for me. You've had one good effect on me. I've decided I'd rather not be an ignorant canary all my life."

Willie stuck to his resolve to improve his shaky position with high marks, and he rose gradually to a place among the leaders in the school. In the first hours of fiery determination he had set his goal at Number One, but he soon saw that that would be denied him. A mandarin-like midshipman named Tobit, with a domed forehead, measured quiet speech, and a mind like a sponge, was ahead of the field by a spacious percentage. Bunched behind him were three other masterminds. Willie couldn't compete with their weird photographic registry of print; he soon realized this, and stopped despairing at marks which fell short of perfect. He drudged away in the niche that he found, varying between eighteenth and twenty-third in Furnald.

His struggle against odds was notorious. The midshipmen and even the ensigns were fond of telling their girls about the unhappy devil carrying forty-eight demerits. This celebrity was useful to Willie. No ensign, not even the punctilious Brain, wanted to be the one to drop the guillotine on him. Once Acres came into the room during a study period and found Willie collapsed in sleep over the desk, a plain case costing eight demerits. Willie shook all day, but the offense was never reported.

Mrs. Keith was outraged at Willie's position and violently sympathetic. She spent several visiting periods urging Willie to accept Uncle Lloyd's Army commission, but she gave up at last when she saw that Willie was evidently winning his battle and taking deep satisfaction in it.

In the last weeks, Willie faltered, partly from numb fatigue, partly from a sense that the danger was passing. When the final standings were posted, four days before graduation, he had dropped to the thirty-first place.

That same day a sensational document appeared on the bulletin board: a list of the types of duty open to graduates of Furnald. When the midshipmen returned to their rooms after morning classes they found mimeographed forms on their cots. Each midshipman was asked to list the three types of duty he most desired, and to state the reasons for his first choice.

Nobody could find out how heavily these sheets would count in deciding orders. There were rumors that everyone would get his first choice if the reasons were well put; other rumors that the sheets were just more meaningless Navy paper; still other darker rumors, the more believed for their pessimism, that the purpose was simply to trap those who wanted to avoid dangerous duty, in order to make sure they got it. Some advised asking for the riskiest duty; others were for putting down frankly the desires of the heart. Men like Willie, known for a gift of words, were pressed into service to write convincing reasons wholesale. An enterprising ex-newspaperman named McCutcheon on the eighth floor enjoyed a burst of prosperity by charging five dollars per reason.

Keefer instantly chose Staff Duty, Pacific, saying, "That's for me. Laying around on your duff in Hawaii, with all them nurses around, maybe running to get the admiral a despatch once in a while. That's my kind of war." He daringly left blank the other choices. Keggs agonized over the blank sheet for an hour and at last filled it in with a shaking hand. His first choice was Mine Disposal Training, a horrible bogey which no other man in school dared place on his sheet at all. Next he chose Submarines, Pacific—and third, in small letters, he wrote his true choice, Local Defense, Atlantic.

Willie's one aim in filling out the form was to remain near May. First he placed Staff, Atlantic, calculating that this must land him on the East Coast, possibly even in New York. Next he put Large Ships, Atlantic (large ships spent a lot of time in port). Last he wrote Submarines, Pacific, to show that he was really a daredevil at heart. This last touch was admired on the tenth floor and much imitated. Willie himself thought that his list showed an incisive knowledge of Navy mentality. For a while he was tempted to apply for communications school, a five-month course at Annapolis. Keefer had a brother, Tom, who had attended the school and enjoyed a wild time with the Baltimore girls. But it seemed to Willie that asking outright for half a year more of shore duty would show his hand. Tom Keefer had been sent to Annapolis after requesting an aircraft carrier. When Willie found that out, it decided him against listing the school.

Graduation was one day off, and during a study period the midshipmen of the tenth floor were droning over books, carrying out to the last the pretense of work though the marks were all totaled and nothing counted any more. A word crackled down the corridor like a spark. "Orders!" The midshipmen crowded to their doors. Down the hall came the mate of the deck with a bundle of envelopes. He came to 1013 and thrust two envelopes into Keefer's hand. "Good luck, mates."

"Hey," said Keefer, "there's three guys in here."

The messenger riffled through his bundle. "Sorry. Guess Keith's orders are held up. There's another batch coming."

Keefer ripped open his envelope, burst into a cheer, and danced. "Made it! Made it! Staff, Pacific, by Christ!" Willie pounded his back in congratulation. All at once Keefer sobered, and pulled himself out of the hug. "Hey, Ed—what the Shinola's eating you?"

The horse face was leaning against the wall, trembling as though he stood in a bumping trolley car. His envelope lay on the desk.

"What did you draw, Eddy?" said Willie anxiously.

"Dunno. I—I can't open it, fellows." He was staring at the envelope as though it were a live mine.

Keefer snorted. "Want me to?"

"Please."

The Southerner rasped it open and read the orders. "Jesus," he murmured. Keggs fell on his cot with his face to the wall, groaning.

"For God's sake," said Willie, "what is it?"

" 'Report to San Francisco for transportation to DMS 21—U.S.S. *Moulton*.' "

Keggs sat up. "A ship? A ship? Not Mine Disposal—a ship?"

"A ship," said Keefer. "Now what is a DMS?"

"Who cares? A *ship!*" Keggs fell back on his cot, threw

his legs and arms in the air, and neighed, wept, and giggled all at once.

Keefer drew a picture manual, *Ships of the Navy, 1942,*
from a shelf. "DMS—DMS—I swear to God there ain't
no such ship—no, wait. Here it is—DMS—page 63."

The others crowded around him as he flipped the stiff
pages to a picture of a queer narrow three-stack vessel. He
read aloud: " 'DMS—Destroyer Minesweeper. World War
I destroyer converted for high-speed sweeping.' "

"Oh, God!" breathed Keggs. "Mines. Mines." He
dropped into the chair and writhed.

"Hell, boy, that's a sight better than Mine Disposal.
Sweeping is nothing."

Willie couldn't muster up any such false cheer. The
three had often talked about minesweeping and agreed it
was the worst seagoing horror the Navy had to offer. He
pitied Keggs. All up and down the floor shouts were being
exchanged. Most of the men had received their first pref-
erences. Those who had been honest rejoiced; the others
sulked or shivered. Willie was annoyed to learn that everyone who had asked for communications school, even as
third choice, had been sent there. He had missed a chance.
But Staff, Atlantic, was fair enough.

The mate of the deck appeared in the doorway. "Here's
yours, Keith. Just came up."

Willie opened the envelope with a thrust of his forefinger and yanked out the sheaf of papers. His eye darted
to the third paragraph. The words seemed to rise up at
him with a sound of trumpets: *Report to Receiving Station, San Francisco, for transportation to*

DMS 22—U.S.S. CAINE.

II

THE *CAINE*

---

6 · Dr. Keith's Letter

When Ensign Keith followed the bellboy into his room in the Mark Hopkins Hotel in San Francisco, he was struck at once by the view of the city in the sunset. The hills were twinkling under a sky massed with clouds, pink in the west, fading to rose and violet in the east. The evening star shone clear, hanging low over the Golden Gate Bridge. Eastward the lamps were burning along the gray arches of the Oakland Bridge, a string of amber gems. The bellboy turned on lights, opened closets, and left Willie alone with the sunset and his bags. The new ensign stood by the window for a moment, stroking his gold stripe, and wondering at so much beauty and splendor so far from New York.

"Might as well unpack," he said to the evening star, and opened his pigskin valise. Most of his belongings were in a wooden crate in the hotel's check room. In the valise he carried only a few changes of clothes. On top of a layer of white shirts lay two mementos of his last hours in New York—a phonograph record and a letter.

Willie rolled the record between his fingers and wished

he had brought his portable phonograph. How perfect a setting the evening was for May's sweet voice, and the Mozart aria! She had recorded it for him in a Broadway shop one night when they were both giddy with champagne. Willie smiled as he thought of the delicious April evenings with May during his ten days' leave. He reached for the telephone, then pulled back his hand, realizing that it was near midnight in the Bronx, when all candy stores were shut and dark. Besides, he reminded himself, he was giving May up, because he couldn't marry her, and she was too good a girl to be kept dangling. His plan had been to enjoy an ecstatic farewell, then depart and never write or answer letters, allowing the relationship to die peacefully of malnutrition. May hadn't been informed of the plan. He had fulfilled the first part, now he must remember the second.

He laid aside the record and picked up his father's mysterious letter. No use holding it to the light, it was bulky and utterly opaque. He shook it, and sniffed it, and wondered for the fortieth time what could possibly be inside.

"When do you think you'll get to the *Caine?*" the father had asked, the afternoon before Willie's departure.

"I don't know, Dad—in three or four weeks."

"No more?"

"Maybe six weeks, tops. They move us out pretty fast, I hear."

Thereupon his father had limped to the desk and drawn the sealed envelope out of a leather portfolio. "When you report aboard the *Caine*—the day you get there, not before or after, open this and read it."

"What's in it?"

"Why, if I wanted you to know now I wouldn't have gotten myself a writer's cramp scrawling it, would I?"

"It isn't money? I won't need money."

"No, not money."

"Sealed orders, eh?"

"Something like that. You'll do as I say?"

"Of course, Dad."

"Fine—— Put it away and forget about it. Never mind mentioning it to your mother."

Three thousand miles from his father and the scene of the promise, Willie was tempted to peek at the contents; merely to glance at the first page, no more. He tugged at the flap. It was dry, and came loose easily without tearing. The letter was open for Willie's inspection.

But the thin strand of honor held, after all, across the continent. Willie licked the crumbled paste on the open flap, sealed the letter tight, and tucked it out of sight at the bottom of the valise. Knowing his own character, he thought it well to minimize the strain on it.

Well, he thought, he would write a letter to May after all—just one. She would expect it. Once he went to sea, silence would be understandable; now it would be cruel, and Willie didn't want to treat May cruelly. He seated himself at the desk and composed a long warm letter. May would have needed second sight to read her dismissal in it. He was writing the last tender paragraph when the phone rang.

"Willie? Doggone you, boy, how are you?" It was Keefer. "I got your wire, boy. I been phoning all day. Where you been, boy?"

"Plane got hung up in Chicago, Rollo——"

"Well, come on out, boy, time's a-wasting. We just getting a party organized——"

"Where are you—Fairmont?"

"Junior Officers' Club—Powell Street. Hurry up. There's a tall blonde on the loose here that is a dish——"

"Where's Keggs?"

"He's gone already, Willie, gone to sea. Three weeks' delay getting transportation for everybody in Frisco except old horseface——"

"How come?"

"Why, the poor boy was down in transportation office, see, he just come off the train, he was getting his orders endorsed. Wouldn't you know, the phone rings and it's the skipper of a creeping coffin that's going to Pearl, and he's got room for three more officers. Keggs gets endorsed right over to him. He never even changed his socks in

Frisco. Left Tuesday. Missed everything. This is the town, Willie. Liquor and gals till you can't stand up. Get on your bicycle———"

"Be right over, Rollo."

He felt slightly hypocritical, finishing up the letter to May. But he asserted to himself that he was entitled to any fun he could grasp before he went out to sea.

Willie considered himself a mistreated hero; he still smarted under the insult of his orders to the *Caine*. After triumphing over the handicap of forty-eight demerits and rising to the top five per cent of the school, he had been sent to sweep mines on an obsolete World War I ship! It was mortifying—twice so, because Keggs, nearest him on the alphabetical list but almost two hundred numbers below him in standing, had drawn identical duty. Obviously the Navy had disposed of the two men with no thought of what they deserved, one after another, like hogs being slaughtered. So Willie believed.

He was drawn into a round of drinking and partying that lasted twenty days. He rolled with Keefer from clubs to bars to girls' apartments. He quickly became popular because of his piano entertaining. Officers and girls alike were rapturous over *If You Knew What the Gnu Knew:* he had to sing it several times every night. He resurrected a knack developed in college days of making up rhymes on people's names as he sang:

> *Hirohito trembles when he hears of Keefer,*
> *To calm his nerves he has to light a reefer———*

Willie could go nimbly from name to name in the room, improvising such couplets to a jazzy refrain. This astounded his audiences, especially the girls, who thought his talents bordered on witchcraft. He and Keefer roared up and down the hair-raising hills in an old rented Ford, and dined mightily on Chinese food, abalones and crabs, and did very little sleeping. They were invited to fine homes and exclusive clubs. It was a great war.

Keefer became friendly with an officer in the transportation department. The result was that the roommates were assigned to a hospital ship for their voyage westward. "Nurses and fresh strawberries—that's the ticket, Willie my boy," Keefer said, proudly announcing this news. They rolled aboard the *Mercy* at dawn after a roistering farewell party, and they continued the same pace of pleasure all the while the ship was steaming toward Hawaii. Nurses clustered around Willie at the piano in the lounge every evening. There were sharp restrictions aboard the *Mercy* on place and time of meetings between the sexes, but Keefer quickly learned his way about the ship and arranged for the pursuit of happiness at all hours. They saw very little of the Pacific Ocean.

They debarked in Honolulu arm in arm with two free-thinking nurses, Lieutenants Jones and Carter; exchanged brief kisses under the huge Dole's pineapple electric sign, and agreed to meet for dinner. The two ensigns piled their luggage into the taxicab of a snub-nosed grinning Hawaiian in a rainbow-colored shirt.

"Navy Base, Pearl, please."

"Yes, gentlemans."

Keefer got off at the bachelor officers' quarters, a structure of unpainted wood. Willie went to the personnel officer in the cement office building of the Hawaiian Sea Frontier, and was told that the *Caine* was at the Navy Yard in repair berth C-4. He threw his baggage into another cab and raced out to the repair basin. Berth C-4 contained only a slosh of empty filthy water. He wandered around the yard amid deafening sounds of ship repair, asking questions of workmen, sailors, and officers. None of them had heard of the ship. Battleships, carriers, cruisers, destroyers, in drydock or alongside docks, were everywhere: gray monsters in dozens, swarming with riveters and sailors. But no *Caine*. So Willie returned to the personnel officer.

"Don't tell me," said the fat lieutenant, "they fouled up this berthing chart again——" He searched through a heap of despatches in a box on his desk. "Oh. Pardon me. Yep, she's gone. Shoved off this morning."

"Where to?"

"Sorry. Classified."

"Well, what do I do now?"

"I don't know. You should have caught her."

"My ship just got in an hour ago."

"That's not my fault."

"Look," said Willie, "all I want to know is; how do I get transportation from this point to catch up with the *Caine?*"

"Oh. You want Transportation. Well, I'm Personnel. You'll have to see Transportation." The lieutenant got up, put a nickel in a Coca-Cola machine, drew out a frosty bottle, and drank noisily. Willie waited till he had seated himself again.

"Who and where is Transportation?"

"Jesus, I don't know."

Willie walked out of the office. Blinking in the glare of the sun, he noticed a sign on the next door: *Transportation.* "He doesn't know much," muttered Willie, and entered the office. A dried-up woman of thirty-seven or so sat at the desk.

"Sorry," she said, as Willie entered, "no more scooters."

"All I want," said Willie, "is transportation to the U.S.S. *Caine.*"

"*Caine?* Where is it at?"

"I don't know."

"Then how on earth do you expect to get to it?" She pulled a Coca-Cola bottle out of a desk drawer, flipped off the cap against the edge of her desk, and drank.

"Nobody will tell me where the ship is bound for. It left this morning."

"Oh. It's not in the yard?"

"No, no. It's at sea."

"Well, then, how do you expect to get to it on a scooter?"

"I don't want a scooter," exclaimed Willie. "Did you hear me ask for a scooter?"

"You came in here, didn't you?" snapped the woman. "This is the scooter pool."

"It says 'Transportation' outside."

"Well, a scooter *is* transportation——"

THE *CAINE*   69

"Okay, okay," said Willie, "I'm new here, and very stupid. Please tell me how to get a start toward my ship."

The woman pondered, clicking the green bottle against her teeth. "Well, I guess you want Fleet Transportation. This is Yard Transportation."

"Thank you. Where is Fleet Transportation?"

"Jesus, I don't know. Why don't you ask Personnel next door?"

Willie gave up for the day. If the Navy was in no hurry to send him after the *Caine,* he was in no hurry to go. He went back to the bachelor officers' quarters, thoroughly tired of piling a crate and two bags in and out of taxis.

"Just in time, boy." Keefer was fresh and cool in newly pressed khaki shirt and trousers. Willie still wore his hot, heavy blues. "Big doings. Admiral giving a party for the nurses tonight. Jonesy and Carter got permission to bring us along."

"Which admiral?"

"Who knows? They thick as fleas on a dog's back around here. You find your ship?"

"Shoved off today. Nobody will say where."

"Fine, fine. Nice delay, probably. Shower up."

The admiral's party, at his handsome home inside the base, started as a quiet affair. Most of the guests were within earshot of an admiral for the first time and they minded their manners. The admiral, a big bald man with startling black hollows under his eyes, received everyone with genial majesty in his straw-matted, flower-filled living room. After drinks had flowed for a while the atmosphere warmed. Willie, urged on by Keefer, timidly sat at the piano and played. The admiral brightened at the first notes, and moved to a seat near the piano. He waved his glass to the rhythm of the music. "The boy has talent," he said to a captain at his elbow. "By George, these reserves bring some life into things."

"They certainly do, sir."

Keefer heard this exchange. "Hey, Willie, give us the *Gnu Knew.*"

Willie shook his head, but the admiral said, "What? What's that? Let's have it, whatever it is."

The song caused a sensation. The admiral put down his glass and applauded, whereupon everyone else did the same. He was in chuckling high spirits. "What's your name, Ensign? By George, you're a find."

"Keith, sir."

"Keith. Good name. Not a Keith from Indiana?"

"No, sir. Long Island."

"Good name anyway. Now, let's have some more music. Let's see. Do you know *Who Hit Annie in the Fanny with a Flounder?*"

"No, sir."

"Hell, I thought everyone knew that."

"If you'll sing it, sir," said Keefer eagerly, "Willie can pick it up in a second."

"By God I will," said the admiral, glancing around at the captain beside him, "if Matson here will pitch in."

"Certainly, Admiral."

Willie easily picked up the refrain of *Who Hit Annie in the Fanny with a Flounder,* and the house rocked with the chorus sung twice by all hands, male and female. The nurses giggled, cooed, and twittered. "This is the best damn party," cried the admiral, "we've ever had. Somebody give me a cigarette. Where are you stationed, boy? I want you to come again, often."

"I'm trying to catch up with the U.S.S. *Caine,* sir."

"Caine? Caine? Christ, is she still in commission?"

Captain Matson leaned over and said, "Converted DMS, sir."

"Oh, one of those. Where is she?"

"Just left today, sir." He dropped his voice. " 'Ashtray.' "

"Hm." The admiral regarded Willie keenly. "Matson, can you take care of this lad?"

"I think so, Admiral."

"Well, more music, Keith!"

When the party broke up at midnight, the captain slipped Willie his card. "Come and see me at 0900, Keith."

"Aye aye, sir."

Next morning Willie presented himself at the captain's

office in the CincPac Building. The captain rose and shook hands pleasantly.

"Sure enjoyed your music, Keith. Never saw the admiral have a better time. By God, he needs it—does him good."

"Thank you, sir."

"Well," said the captain, "if you want I can put you on a plane for Australia. Maybe you'll catch the *Caine* down there, maybe you won't. She's running convoy. Those escorts get shoved here and there by every port director who gets his hands on them——"

"Whatever you say, sir——"

"*Or,*" said the captain, "we can put you on temporary duty here in the officer pool till she gets back to Pearl. Might be a few weeks, might be a few months. Depends on whether you're in a hurry for combat duty or—— They can use you out there, sure enough. The admiral wouldn't interfere with your going out, in any way." Captain Matson grinned.

Willie glanced through the broad picture window which faced the sea and the hills. A rainbow was drifting down a palm-covered misty mountainside far away. Outside on the lawn crimson hibiscus blossoms stirred in the warm breeze, and a sprinkler twirled a sparkling spiral of water over the close-clipped grass.

"Officer pool sounds swell to me, sir."

"Fine. The admiral will be pleased. Bring your orders around to my yeoman any time today."

Willie was officially transferred to the officer pool, and took up quarters with Keefer in the BOQ. The Southerner, who had already been assigned to Third Fleet Communications, exulted as Willie unpacked his bags.

"Boy, you catching on to the military life."

"I don't know. Maybe they needed me on the *Caine*——"

"Shinola on that. You gonna get all the war you want, boy. You keep little old Keefer and the admiral happy a few weeks, that's all." He rose and swiftly knotted a black tie. "Got the duty. See you tonight."

Unpacking, Willie came upon his father's letter. He

took it up uncertainly. Months might pass now, before he reached his ship. Dr. Keith had told him to open it upon reporting for duty. He was on duty—temporary duty, to be sure, but it might last a long time. He lit a cigarette, tore open the letter, and sat down to read it. At the first words he started up. He read on, sitting on the edge of the chair, the letter trembling in his hands, the cigarette burning down between his fingers, and ashes dropping off unnoticed.

DEAR WILLIE:

By the time you read this letter, I think I will be dead. I'm sorry to startle you but I suppose there's no pleasant way to break such news. The trouble I've been having with my toe is due to a rather vicious disorder, malignant melanoma. The prognosis is one hundred per cent bad. I've known about my condition for a long time, and figured that I would probably die this summer. But the toe began to go a bit sooner. I suppose I should be in a hospital at this moment (two nights before you leave) but I hate to spoil your departure, and since there's no hope anyway, I've postponed it. I'm going to try to stall until I know you've left San Francisco. Your mother doesn't know anything yet. My guess is that I won't last more than three or four weeks, now.

I'm a little young to go, according to the insurance tables, and I must say I don't feel ready, but I daresay that's because I've accomplished so little. I look back on my life, Willie, and there's not much there. Your mother has been a fine wife, and I have no regrets on that score. But I seem to have led such a thoroughly second-rate life—not only compared to my father, but in view of my own capabilities. I had quite a feeling for research. When I fell in love with your mother I thought I couldn't marry her without undertaking general practice in a high-income community. It was my plan to make a pile in ten or fifteen years of such work, and then return to research. I really think I might have done something in cancer.

I had a theory—a notion, you might say—nothing I could have put on paper. It needed three years of systematic investigation. Nobody has touched it to this day. I've kept up with the literature. My name might have meant as much as my father's. But now there's no time even to outline the procedure. The worst of it is, I now feel your mother would have stood by me and lived modestly if I'd really insisted.

But I've had a pleasant time, I can truly say that. I've loved reading and golf, and I've had all of that I wanted. The days have gone by all too fast.

I wish I might have met this girl of yours. It seems to me that she, or the Navy, or both, are having quite a good effect on you. And believe me, Willie, that is by far the brightest thought I take with me into the hospital. I've let slide my relationship with you as I have so many other things, through plain sloth; particularly since your mother seemed anxious to take charge of you. It's too bad we had no more children. Just bad luck. Your mother had three miscarriages, which you may not know.

I'll tell you a curious thing. It seems to me that I have a higher opinion of you than your mother has. She regards you as a hopeless baby who will have to be coddled through life. But I am coming to believe that though you are pretty spoiled and soft at the surface, you are tough enough at the core. After all, I see, you have always done pretty much as you pleased with your mother, while giving her the sense of ruling you. I'm sure this was no plan on your part, but you've done it anyway.

You've never had a serious problem in your life, up to this Navy experience. I watched you in the forty-eight demerits business very closely. It had its comical side, but really it was a challenge. You rose to it in an encouraging way.

Perhaps because I know I'll never see you again I find myself sentimentalizing over you, Willie. It seems to me that you're very much like our whole country—young, naïve, spoiled and softened by abundance and good luck, but with an interior hardness that comes from your sound stock. This country of ours consists of pioneers, after all, these new Poles and Italians and Jews as well as the older stock, people who had the gumption to get up and go and make themselves better lives in a new world. You're going to run into a lot of strange young men in the Navy, most of them pretty low by your standards, I daresay, but I'll bet—though I won't live to see it—that they are going to make the greatest Navy the world has ever seen. And I think you're going to make a good naval officer—after a while. After a great while, perhaps.

This is not criticism, Willie, God knows I am pretty soft myself. Perhaps I'm wrong. You may never make a naval officer at all. Perhaps we're going to lose the war. I just don't believe it. I think we're going to win, and I think you're going to come back with more honor than you believed possible.

I know you're disappointed at having been sent to a ship like the *Caine*. Now, having seen it, you're probably disgusted. Well, remember this, you've had things your own way too long, and all your immaturity is due to that. You need some stone walls to batter yourself against. I strongly suspect you'll find plenty of them there on the *Caine*. I don't envy you the experience itself, but I do envy you the strengthening you're going to derive from it. Had I had one such experience in my younger years, I might not be dying a failure.

Those are strong words, but I won't cross them out. They don't hurt too much and, furthermore, my hand isn't the one to cross them out any more. I'm finished now, but the last word on my life rests with you. If you turn out well, I can still claim some kind of success in the afterworld, if there is one.

About your singing versus comparative literature —you may have a different outlook when the war is over. Don't waste brain power over the far future. Concentrate on doing well now. Whatever assignment they give you on the *Caine,* remember that it's worthy of your best efforts. It's your way of fighting the war.

It's surprising, how little I have to say to you in these last words. I ought to fill up a dozen more sheets, and yet I feel you are pretty good at getting your way—and in other matters any words I might write would make little sense, without your own experience to fill the words with meaning. Remember this, if you can—there is nothing, nothing more precious than time. You probably feel you have a measureless supply of it, but you haven't. Wasted hours destroy your life just as surely at the beginning as at the end—only at the end it becomes more obvious. Use your time while you have it, Willie, in making something of yourself.

Religion. I'm afraid we haven't given you much, not having had much ourselves. But I think, after all, I will mail you a Bible before I go into the hospital. There is a lot of dry stuff in the Bible about Jewish wars and rituals that may put you off—but don't make the mistake of skipping the Old Testament. It's the core of all religion, I think, and there is a lot of everyday wisdom in it. You have to be able to recognize it. That takes time. Meantime get familiar with the words. You'll never regret it. I came to the Bible as I did to everything in life, too late.

About money matters. I'm leaving all my property to your mother. Uncle Lloyd is the executor. There is a ten-thousand-dollar policy of which you're the beneficiary. If you want to get married, or go back to school, that should be enough to enable you to carry out your plans. Money is a very pleasant thing, Willie, and I think you can trade almost anything for it wisely except the work you really want to do. If you sell out your time for a comfortable life, and give up your natural work, I think you lose the exchange. There remains an inner uneasiness that spoils the comforts.

Well, Willie, it's 3 A.M. by my old leather-covered

desk clock. A waning moon is shining through the library window, and my fingers are stiff from writing. My toe is giving me the devil, too. Sleeping pills and bed for me. Thank God for barbiturate.

Take care of your mother if she lives to be very old, and be kind to her if you come back from the war with enough strength to break away from her. She has many faults, but she's good, and she has loved you and me very truly.

Willie began to sob. He read the last paragraphs through a blur of tears.

Think of me and of what I might have been, Willie, at the times in your life when you come to cross-roads. For my sake, for the sake of the father who took the wrong turns, take the right ones, and carry my blessing and my justification with you.

I stretch out my hand to you. We haven't kissed in many, many years. I liked to kiss you when you were a baby. You were a very sweet and good-natured child, with wonderful large eyes. God! Long ago.

Good-by, my son. Be a man.

DAD

The ensign rose, wiping his eyes, and hurried down-stairs to the telephone booth. He dropped a coin into the box. "I want to call the United States——"

"Sorry. Private calls only at Central Building with censor's permission. One week delay on them," said the operator with a Hawaiian accent.

Willie ran out into the naval base and went from build-ing to building until he found the telegraph office. *How is Dad?* he cabled, and paid the urgent rate, giving the office as his return address. Next morning at eight when the office opened Willie was waiting outside. He sat on the steps smoking until eleven-thirty, when the answer was brought to him. *Dad died three days ago. Sent you his love in last words. Please write. Mother.*

Willie went straight to the office of Captain Matson, who greeted him cordially.

"Have they put to work yet, Keith?"

"Sir, on reconsidering, I'd like to fly out to look for the *Caine,* if I may."

The captain's face fell. "Oh? What's the matter? They give you some rugged coding detail?"

"No, sir."

"I've already told the admiral you're set here. He was extremely pleased."

"Sir, if I may say so, it just doesn't seem like fighting the war—playing piano for the admiral."

A hard distant look came over the captain's features. "There's plenty of work to do in this establishment. You'll find that a shore billet is as honorable as any other."

"I don't doubt it, sir——"

"You were placed in the officer pool at your own request."

"Yes, sir, I know, but——"

"Your orders have been put through and sent to the Bureau. I see no reason to countermand them. Your request is denied." The captain picked up a paper before him and put on his glasses.

"Thank you, sir," said Willie, and left.

And so Willie stayed at Pearl Harbor, decoding messages which told of great actions around Rendova and Munda, of the victorious night battle at Vella Lavella, and of huge preparations for further invasions. Often he came upon the name of the *Caine* in despatches showing her in the thick of the operations. And across the world the Allies smashed into Sicily and Italy, and Mussolini fell. Meantime Willie played piano for the admiral.

7 · The *Caine*

But the soreness over his father's death lessened gradually, and Willie began to enjoy Pearl Harbor. His coding duties involved eight hours a day of drudgery in a cement vault underground, and this hardship soothed his conscience. He avoided the girls and the liquor for a couple of weeks, but then the admiral had another party, and Willie got drunk, and soon he was back at the old round. Honolulu was full of easy pleasures. The climate was soft, the sun brilliant, the moon beautiful, the air perfumed by ever-blooming flowers. Except for the curfew and the black-out and some barbed wire along the beaches the war caused little inconvenience. Willie went on many picnics with the nurses. He acquired a rosy tan and became plumper.

He continued writing tremendously affectionate letters to May. The plan for dropping her was discarded. Willie had decided that May was not too old to waste a year or two. He might marry her, he might not. But their relationship was too valuable an "experience" to be cut short. May's letters were all that could be desired: long, loving, cheery, and usually containing good news. She was enjoying college, though she felt like a grandmother, she said, among the freshmen. Her marks were high, and the language in her letters improved each month.

The roommates lay on their cots, reading newly arrived mail one sultry July afternoon. Flies buzzed at the screens, though there was no attraction inside the room but the smell of hot dry wood. Keefer lolled on his side, naked except for white shorts, his hairy stomach bulging over the

78

ike?"
urself."
on?"

d her long?"

ll long."
g."
g sometimes."
up at the head of steps leading down
Paynter honked. Three sailors lying in
easy gray boat alongside the dock rose
ed the steps. Their blue dungarees were
irttails hung outside the trousers. They
r into the boat while Paynter turned the
pool a few yards down the road. The
d into the boat and sat on cracked black
the canopy.
tball, shove off," said Paynter to the
ailor dressed in amazingly dirty rags,
new hat tilted forward almost to his

in Willie's ear and he jumped. His head
n an inch from the bell. He shifted to
The boat engineer started up the motor,
res which he commented on with filthy
in an indifferent monotone. He was
small and gaunt, with a face blackened
and half by grease, and covered with
arse black hair fell over his tiny squint-
no hat. He was addressed by the other
ble." As soon as the boat chugged away
he took off his shirt, exposing a monkey-
r.
around at the boat. The gray paint was
wood, and ragged patches showed where
been daubed over old without scraping.
portholes of the canopy had cardboard
glass.

waistband. "Christ on a bicycle!" he exclaimed, rising on one elbow. "What's the name of your ship again—*Caine,* ain't it?"

"Yes," said Willie, absorbed in a letter from May.

"Well listen, boy, I think my brother Tom is on that ship!"

Willie glanced up in surprise.

"I *think* it's the *Caine,*" said Keefer. "Never can make out my pap's doggone handwriting. Here, how do you read this?"

Willie peered at the word indicated by Keefer's thumb. "*Caine* all right."

"Sure enough. They sent him there from communications school. Whaddya know!"

"Fine. It's a lucky break. It'll be like having a relative on board. Does he like the ship?"

"Hell, no. He wrote Pap it's the foulest bucket in the Navy—— But that don't mean nothing," he added quickly, seeing Willie wince. "Hell, don't take anything that Tom says too serious. Tom's queer as a three-dollar bill. The *Caine's* probably a great ship if he don't like it."

"What kind of guy is he, Rollo?"

"Well, you try to figure how different from me a guy can get—and that's Tom. See, he's only my half brother. I've seen very little of him. His mother was dad's first wife —Catholic. They got married Protestant, and it didn't last long, and she hauled off home to Boston where she come from, with Tom."

Keefer put aside the letter, lit a cigarette, and lay back with his arms under his head.

"Tom's a high-brow, pretty much, writes short stories, plays—had some stuff in magazines. Gets real dough for them. I got to know him a little bit at William and Mary. He was a senior when I was a freshman. But he ran around with that literary crowd, you know, reading poetry by candlelight, with a few dames around for when the candles went out—that kind of Shinola. I guess he figures me for a moron, he's never bothered with me a damn. He's not a bad guy. Pretty witty and all that. You and him will probably get along good, with you reading all that Dickens and all."

It was the first of September when Willie and Keefer staggered into the BOQ at four in the morning, full of hog meat and whisky which they had consumed at a hilarious luau arranged by the nurses. They fell on their beds still giggling and singing ribald parodies of Hawaiian songs. Soon they were heavily, happily asleep.

Next thing Willie knew, he was being shaken, and a strange voice was whispering loudly, "Keith? Keith? Are you Keith?"

He opened his eyes. Day was just dawning. In the dim light he saw a short, swarthy ensign in shapeless frayed khakis standing over him.

"Yes, I'm Keith."

"Better come along. I'm Paynter, from the *Caine*."

"The *Caine?*" Willie sat up. "She's here?"

"Yep. We're shoving off at 0800 to do some target towing. Get your gear together."

Willie sleepily reached out for his trousers. "Look, I'll be glad to report aboard, Paynter, but I'm still attached to the officer pool here."

"No, you're not. That's all fixed. We've got a visual despatch detaching you. We've been waiting for you a long time, Keith."

He said it pleasantly, but Willie felt obliged to defend himself. "I did what I could. Missed you by a few hours back in May when you shoved off. They stuck me into the officer pool——"

"Hell, I wouldn't blame you if you never showed up," said Paynter. "I hate to be the guy who does this to you. Can I help you with your gear?"

All this talking was in low tones. Keefer snored obliviously. As Willie emptied drawers of the bureau into his wooden foot locker, he said, "Do you have an officer aboard named Keefer? Tom Keefer?"

"My department head," said Paynter.

"That's his brother." Willie pointed to the sleeper. Payn-

---

ter looked a
noticed that t

"How screw
"Why? Is y
"I didn't say
waiting on us."
"Are we leav
"Why?"
"If we are I
"No. We're
ing to orders."
"Fine." Willi
He shouldered
the door. Paynt
don't be surpri
civilization for a
Outside the B
small gray Nav
Paynter, "but tha
Pile in."
They rattled d
Willie's luggage j
though trying to
wondering at the
"Moored to a b
"Are you regula
"No."
"Are there any r
"Three."
"Are you V-7?"
"Yes."
"Deck?"
"No, engineering.
"What are your d
"Communications
Willie was startle
an engineer?"
"Not on the *Caine*
"I take it you don'
"I didn't say that."

"What's the ship
"You'll see for yo
"Seen a lot of acti
"Yes and no."
"You been aboar
"Depends."
"On what?"
"On what you ca
"I call a year lon
"I call a week lo
The truck pulled
to the fleet landing
a half-canopied gr
wearily and mount
ragged, and the sh
loaded Willie's gea
truck in to a car
two officers steppe
leather seats inside
"All right, Me
coxswain, a fat
with a pure-whit
nose.
A bell clanged
was no more tha
another cushion.
after several fail
epithets delivere
perhaps nineteen,
half by stubble
pimples. Long, c
ing eyes. He wo
sailors as "Horri
from the landing
like growth of ha
Willie looked
blistering off the
new paint had
Two of the thre
in them instead o

"Mr. Paynter," shouted the engineer over the racket of the motor, "can we stop off and pick up a movie?"

"No."

"Christ, we ain't seen no movie forever," whined Horrible.

"No stopping."

Horrible thereupon blasphemed and cursed for a couple of minutes. Willie, appalled at his freedom of language in the officer's presence, expected Paynter to bring him up short. But the stream of gutter talk appeared to trouble Paynter no more than the lapping of the water. He sat immobile, his fingers folded in his lap, his eyes closed, chewing a rubber band that protruded from his lips.

"Say, Paynter," Willie shouted, "what duties do you suppose I'll get aboard ship?"

Paynter opened his eyes. "Mine," he said, with a brief happy smile, and closed them again.

The gig rounded a point of Ford Island and headed into the western channel. "Hey, Mister Paynter," called Meatball, standing tiptoe on the stern thwart, leaning on the tiller, "the ship's gone."

"You're crazy, Meatball," said Paynter. "Look again. She's in R-6, forward of the *Belleau Wood*."

"I'm telling you, sir, the buoys are empty. For Christ's sake, take a look."

He clanged the bell with a pull cord. The boat slowed, and wallowed in the waves. Paynter climbed out on the gunwale. "I'll be damned. She *is* gone. Now what the hell?"

"Maybe she sank," said the sailor crouched on the bow, a small baby-faced youngster with a highly obscene tattoo on his chest.

"No such luck," said Meatball.

"Could be," said Horrible. "Chief Budge had 'em scraping bilges in number-two engine room. I *told* him there wasn't nothin' keepin' the water out but that rust."

"What do we do now, Mister Paynter?" said Meatball.

"Well, let's see. They wouldn't put out to sea without the gig," said Paynter slowly. "Probably they've just shifted berths. Look around."

Horrible killed the motor. The boat drifted gently in dead quiet past a bobbing red channel buoy. From the water rose an effluvium of fuel oil and rotten vegetables. "There she is," said Meatball, and clanged the bell.

"Where?" said Paynter.

"Repair basin. Right there starboard of the *St. Louis*——" The coxswain thrust the tiller over. The boat swung about.

"Yeah." Paynter nodded. "Guess we get our alongside period after all." He dropped back under the canopy.

Willie, staring in the direction Meatball had been looking, could see nothing that resembled the *Caine*. The repair basin was crammed with ships of every shape except the DMS silhouette which Willie had memorized from pictures. "Pardon me," he shouted to Meatball, "can you point the ship out to me?"

"Sure. There." The coxswain jerked his head meaninglessly.

"Do you see her?" Willie said to Horrible.

"Sure. She's in that nest of cans in C-4."

Willie wondered whether his vision had gone bad.

Paynter said, "You can't see nothing but the trucklight from here. You'll see her soon enough."

It humiliated Willie not to be able to recognize his ship by the trucklight. He punished himself by standing up and taking spray in his face for the rest of the ride.

The gig came alongside a limp chain ladder hanging over the side of a new destroyer, the outer ship of four in the repair berth. "Let's go," said Paynter, "the *Caine's* the one inboard of this. The men will bring your gear."

Willie went up the jingling ladder, saluted the smart OOD of the destroyer, and crossed the deck. A tarry plank laid between the ships over four feet of open water led to the *Caine*. Willie got no distinct impression of his ship at first glance. He was too concerned about the plank. He hung back. Paynter mounted the board, saying, "This way." As he crossed, the *Caine* rolled and the plank wobbled violently. Paynter jumped off it to the *Caine* deck.

It occurred to Willie that if Paynter had fallen from the plank he would have been crushed between the two ships.

With this picture bright in his mind Willie set foot on the plank and pranced across like a circus acrobat. Halfway, hanging over the open water, he felt the plank heave upward. He leaped for life, and landed on the *Caine* in the arms of the OOD, staggering him.

"Ho! Don't be so eager," said the OOD. "You don't know what you're jumping into."

"Rabbitt, this is the long-lost Ensign Keith," said Paynter.

"So I gathered." Lieutenant (jg) Rabbitt shook Willie's hand. He was of middle size, with a narrow face and an air of rustic good humor. "Welcome aboard, Keith. Say, Paynter, this Ensign Harding showed up too, half an hour ago."

"All kinds of new blood," said Paynter.

The focus of Willie's mind widened beyond the plank now and took in the quarterdeck of the *Caine*. It was a place of noise, dirt, bad smells, and thuglike strangers. Half a dozen sailors were clanking at the rusty deck with metal scrapers. Other sailors were walking past, cursing under crates of cabbages on their backs. One man in a welding mask was burning a bulkhead with a crackling sour-smelling blue flame. All around were patches of new gray paint, patches of old gray paint, patches of green prime coat, and patches of rust. A tangle of snaky hoses, red, black, green, yellow, brown lay all over the deck. The deck was covered with orange peel, fragments of magazines and old rags. Most of the sailors were half naked and wore fantastic beards and haircuts. Oaths, blasphemies, and one recurring four-letter word filled the air like fog.

"God knows where you go," said Rabbitt. "There are no more bunks in the wardroom."

"The exec will think of something," said Paynter.

"Okay, Keith, you're logged aboard," said Rabbitt. "Paynt, will you take him down to the exec?"

"Sure. Follow me, Keith."

Paynter led Willie down a ladder and through a dark stifling passageway. "This is the half deck." He opened a door. "This is the wardroom."

They passed through an untidy rectangular room as wide as the ship, mostly filled by a long table set with a stained cloth, silver, boxes of breakfast cereal, and pitchers of milk. Magazines and books were scattered on the lounging chairs and black leather couch. Willie noted with horror several secret publications among comic-strip books, leg-art magazines, and frayed *Esquires*. Leading forward from the middle of the wardroom was a passageway of staterooms. Paynter entered the first room on the right. "Here's Keith, sir," he said, pushing aside the curtain in the doorway. "Keith, this is the executive officer, Lieutenant Gorton."

An enormously fat, husky young man, nude except for tiny drawers, sat up on a raised bunk, scratching his ribs and yawning. The green bulkheads of the room were decorated with colored cutout pictures of girls in flimsy underwear. "Greetings, Keith. Where the hell you been?" said Lieutenant Gorton in a high voice, and swung mammoth thighs out of the bed. He shook Willie's hand.

Paynter said, "Where do we put him?"

"Jesus, I don't know. I'm hungry. Are they bringing some fresh eggs off the beach? Those eggs we got in New Zealand will dissolve your fillings by now."

"Oh, here's the captain, maybe he has an idea," said Paynter, looking off into the passageway. "Sir, Ensign Keith has reported aboard."

"Collared him, did you? Nice work," said a voice full of irony and authority, and the captain of the *Caine* came to the doorway. Willie was even more startled by him. The captain was absolutely naked. In one hand he carried a cake of Lifebuoy soap, in the other a lighted cigarette. He had a creased old-young face, blond hair, and a flabby white body. "Welcome aboard, Keith!"

"Thank you, sir." Willie felt an urge to salute, to bow, in some way to express reverence for supreme authority. But he remembered a regulation about not saluting a superior when he was uncovered. And he had never seen a more uncovered superior than his commanding officer.

Captain de Vriess grinned at Willie's discomfiture, and

scratched his behind with the soap cake. "I hope you know something about communications, Keith."

"Yes, sir. That's what I've been doing for CincPac while—while waiting for the ship, sir."

"Good. Paynter, you're an assistant engineering officer again as of now."

"Thanks, sir." Paynter's gloomy face was suffused with fleeting happiness. He sighed like a horse having a saddle taken off. "Got any idea, Captain, where we stash the new communicator?"

"Did Maryk put a bunk in the clipping shack?"

"Yes, sir. That's where we've stuck this other new one, Harding."

"Well, tell Maryk to hang another bunk in there."

"Pretty damn crowded in that clip shack even for one, Captain," said the exec.

"War is a terrible thing. I've got to shower, before I curdle." Captain de Vriess puffed his cigarette, ground it out in an ashtray on the desk made of a three-inch shell, and walked off. The fat lieutenant shrugged, and drew on a pair of tentlike trousers.

"That's it," he said. "Take him to the clip shack, Paynt."

"Sir," said Willie, "I'm ready to get to work any time."

Gorton yawned, and regarded Willie with amused eyes. "Don't burn out any bearings. Just mosey around the ship for a couple of days. Get used to it. It's going to be your home for a long, long time."

"Suits me, sir," said Willie. "I'm due for some sea duty." He had resigned himself to a stay of six months to a year. It was his year in the wilderness, the ordeal of which his father had written, and he was ready to face it.

"Glad you feel that way," said the exec. "Who knows, maybe you'll beat my record. I got sixty-seven months on this bucket, myself."

Willie divided by twelve and quailed. Lieutenant Gorton had been on the *Caine* for five years.

"There's something about the DMS outfit," went on Gorton cheerfully, "that makes the Bureau reluctant to shift personnel. Maybe the file is lost back in Washington. We got two chiefs aboard with more than a hundred months. Captain de Vriess has seventy-one. So you'll get your sea duty—— Well—glad to have you aboard. Take it easy."

Willie stumbled after Paynter to the clipping shack, a metal box on the main deck about seven feet high, six long, and three wide. A doorway was the only opening. A shelf ran along one side, waist-high, piled with empty clipping belts for machine-gun bullets and cases of ammunition. Ensign Harding was sleeping on a bunk which had been recently welded into the wall close to the deck; the weld was still bright and angry-looking. Sweat was pouring off Harding's face, and his shirt was dark with wet streaks. The temperature in the shack was about 105 degrees.

"Home sweet home," said Willie.

"This Harding has *Caine* blood in him," Paynter said. "He's starting off right—— Well, there'll be some transfers any day. You guys'll be down in the wardroom right soon." He started to go.

"Where can I find Mr. Keefer?" said Willie.

"In his sack," said Paynter.

"I mean later in the day."

"So do I," said Paynter, and departed.

Willie wandered around the *Caine* for a couple of hours, poking his nose down ladders and hatchways and into doorways. He was ignored by the sailors as though he were invisible, except when he faced one in a passageway. Then the sailor would flatten automatically against the bulkhead, as though to allow a big animal to pass. Willie's sight-seeing tour confirmed his first impression. The *Caine* was a pile of junk in the last hours of decay, manned by hoodlums.

He drifted down to the wardroom. Overhead the metal scrapers pounded loudly. The long table was covered with green baize now and the magazines and books had been shelved. The room was empty except for a very tall skinny colored boy in sweaty white undershirt and trousers, who was listlessly dabbing at the deck with a mop. "I'm the new officer, Ensign Keith," said Willie. "Might I have a cup of coffee?"

"Yassuh." The steward's mate put down the mop, and sauntered to a Silex on a metal bureau in the corner.

"What's your name?" said Willie.

"Whittaker, suh, steward's mate second. Cream and sugar, suh?"

"Please." Willie glanced around. A tarnished brass plaque on the bulkhead informed him that the ship had been named for one Arthur Wingate Caine, commander of a destroyer in World War I who had died of wounds received in a gun battle with a German submarine. Above the plaque on a shelf among a lot of naval books was a leather-bound loose-leaf volume, *Ship's Organization, U.S.S. Caine, DMS 22*. Willie took it down. The steward's mate set the coffee before him.

"How long have you been on the *Caine*, Whittaker?"

"Fo' months, suh."

"How do you like it?"

The Negro backed away, his eyes bulging as though Willie had whipped out a knife. "Bes' ship in de whole Navy, suh." He grabbed the mop and ran out the door.

The coffee was lukewarm and muddy but Willie drank it. He needed stimulation badly. One hour of sleep had allowed him little recovery from the luau. He read the statistics of the *Caine* blearily. It had been built in 1918 in Rhode Island ("Before I was born," he muttered). It was 317 feet long and 31 feet wide and could make a flank speed of 30 knots. Upon conversion for minesweeping one of its four stacks and a boiler had been removed to make for more fuel tanks, thus increasing the cruising radius.

Overhead the clanking became louder; another work party was starting to chip paint. The air in the wardroom was growing hot and foul as the sun rose higher. *The mission of the high-speed minesweeper,* Willie read, *is primarily to sweep in enemy waters ahead of invasion or bombardment forces.* He dropped the book on the table, laid his head on it, and groaned.

"Hullo," said a voice, "are you Keith or Harding?" The speaker stumbled sleepily past him toward the Silex, dressed in nothing but an athletic supporter. It occurred to

Willie that the conventions of modesty aboard the *Caine* were simpler than those among the Iroquois Indians.

"Keith," he answered.

"Fine. You work for me."

"You're Mr. Keefer?"

"Yes."

The communications officer leaned his back against the bureau and gulped coffee. There was little resemblance to his brother in the long lean face. Tom Keefer was over six feet tall, small-boned and stringy. Deep-set blue eyes with much white showing gave him an intense, wild look. His mouth like Roland's was wide, but the lips, far from being fleshy, were narrow and pale.

Willie said, "Sir, I know your brother Roland. We were roommates in midshipmen's school. He's here in Pearl now at the BOQ."

"Really? We'll have to get him down here." Keefer coolly put down the coffee cup. "Come into my room and tell me about yourself."

Keefer lived in an iron cubicle crisscrossed with pipes at the head of the passageway. There were two bunks installed against the curving hull, and a desk piled three feet high with books, pamphlets, wire baskets full of papers, and registered publications in a scrambled heap, on top of which was a stack of freshly laundered khakis, socks, and underwear. There was a prone naked figure in the upper bunk.

While the communications officer shaved and dressed, Willie described his days at Furnald Hall with Roland. His eye rambled around the stuffy room. In shelves welded over the desk and along Keefer's bunk were crammed volumes of poetry, fiction, and philosophy. The collection was impressive; it was like a college list of the Hundred Best Books, somewhat heavy on the modern side with the works of Joyce, T. S. Eliot, Proust, Kafka, Dos Passos, and Freud, with several books on psychoanalysis and a few that bore Catholic publishing house imprints. "You've really got the books," said Willie.

"This life is slow suicide, unless you read."

"Roland told me you're a writer."

"I was trying to be one before the war," said Keefer, wiping lather off his face with a wet ragged towel.

"Get to do any writing now?"

"Some. Now, about your duties—we'll make you custodian of registered pubs, and of course there'll be coding——"

The steward's mate Whittaker inserted his face through the dusty green curtain. "Chadan," he said, and withdrew. The mysterious word resurrected the figure in the upper bunk; it rose, thrashed feebly, jumped to the deck, and commenced dressing itself.

"Chadan?" said Willie.

"Chow down, in steward patois—lunch," said Keefer. "The name of this vegetable with a face is Carmody. Carmody, this is the elusive Mr. Keith."

"Hello," said Willie.

"Um," said the figure, groping for shoes in the bottom of a black closet.

"Come along," said Keefer, "and break bread with the officers of the *Caine*. There is no escape, Keith. And the bread itself isn't too terrible."

8 · Captain de Vriess

Willie planned to sleep after lunch. He was longing for sleep with every cell of his body. But it was not to be. He and Harding were collared after coffee by the "vegetable with a face," Ensign Carmody.

"Captain de Vriess says for me to take you two on a tour of the ship. Come along."

He dragged them for three hours up and down ladders, and across teetering catwalks, and through narrow scuttles. They went from broiling engine spaces to icy clammy bilges. They splashed in water and slipped on grease and scratched themselves on metal projections. Willie saw everything through a reddish haze of fatigue. He retained only a confused memory of innumerable dark holes cluttered with junk or machines or beds, each hole with a novel odor imposed on the pervading smells of mildew, oil, paint, and hot metal. Carmody's thoroughness was explained when he mentioned that he was an Annapolis man, class of '43, the only regular officer aboard beside the captain and exec. He had narrow shoulders, pinched cheeks, small foxy eyes, and a tiny mustache. His conversation was spectacularly skimpy. "This is number-one fireroom," he would say. "Any questions?" Harding seemed as tired as Willie. Neither of them offered to prolong the tour with a single question. They stumbled after Carmody, exchanging haggard looks.

At last, when Willie was honestly expecting to faint and even looking forward to it, Carmody said, "Well, I guess that does it." He led them forward to the well deck. "Just one more thing now. You climb that mast."

It was a wooden pole topped by a radar, and it looked about five hundred feet high. "What the hell for?" whined Willie. "A mast is a mast. I see it, that's enough."

"You're supposed to explore the ship," said Carmody, "from the bilges to the crow's-nest. *There's* the crow's-nest." He pointed to a tiny square iron grille at the very top of the mast.

"Can't we do that tomorrow? I'm a tired old man," said Harding, with a wistful smile. His face was youthful and kindly; his hair receded deeply at the crown, leaving only a narrow blond peak in the middle. He was slight and had pallid blue eyes.

Carmody said, "I'm supposed to report compliance prior to dinner. If you don't climb that mast I can't report compliance."

"I have three kids," said Harding, shrugging and setting his foot on the lowest of the metal brackets that studded the mast to the top. "Hope I see 'em again."

Slowly, painfully, he began to go up. Willie followed, clutching each bracket convulsively. He kept his eyes on the seat of Harding's trousers, ignoring the dizzying view around him. The wind flapped his sweat-soaked shirt. They reached the crow's-nest in a couple of minutes. As Harding scrambled up on the platform Willie heard the ugly thump of a skull striking metal.

"Ouch! Christ, Keith, watch out for this radar," moaned Harding.

Willie crawled onto the crow's-nest on his stomach. There was barely room on the rickety grille for the two men side by side. They sat with feet dangling into empty blue space.

"Well done!" came Carmody's voice thinly from below. "Good-by now. I'm going to report compliance."

He disappeared into a passageway. Willie stared down at the faraway deck, then quickly pulled his eyes away and took in the surrounding view. It was a fine one. The harbor sparkled beneath them, plain as a map in all its contours. But Willie took no pleasure in it. The height made him shudder. He felt he could never climb down again.

"I regret to tell you," said Harding in a small voice, his hand to his forehead, "that I am going to have to vomit."

"Oh, Christ, no," said Willie.

"Sorry. Height bothers me. I'll try to keep from getting any on you. Jesus, though, all those guys down below. It's awful."

"Can't you hold off?" begged Willie.

"Not a chance," said Harding, his face a poisonous green. "Tell you what, though. I can do it in my hat." He pulled off his officer's cap, adding, "Though I hate to. It's my only hat——"

"Here," said Willie swiftly, "I have two others." He offered Harding his new officer's cap, upside down.

"This is damned cordial of you," gasped Harding.

"You're perfectly welcome," said Willie. "Help your-self."

Harding threw up neatly into the extended hat. Willie felt a terrible urge to do likewise, but he fought it down. Harding's color improved somewhat. "God, thanks, Keith. Now what do we do with it?"

"Good question," said Willie, staring at the mournful object in his hands. "A hatful of—that—is an unhandy thing."

"Scale it out over the side."

Willie shook his head. "It might turn over. Wind might catch it."

"It's a cinch," said Harding, "you can't put it back on."

Willie unfastened the chin strap and looped the hat carefully to a corner of the crow's nest, bucket-fashion. "Let it hang here forever," said Willie, "as your salute to the *Caine*."

"I can never get down from here," Harding said feebly. "You go ahead. I'll die and rot here. Nobody will miss me except my family."

"Nonsense. Do you really have three kids?"

"Sure. My wife's on the way to a fourth."

"What the hell are you doing in the Navy?"

"I'm one of those silly jerks who thought he had to fight the war."

"Feeling better?"

"A little, thanks."

"Come on," said Willie. "I'll go first. You won't fall. If we stay up here much longer we'll get so sick we'll both fall off."

The descent was an endless slippery horror. Willie's sweating hands slid on the shallow brackets, and at one ghastly point his foot slipped. But they both reached the deck. Harding tottered, his face beaded with drops. "I'm going to lie down and kiss the deck," he muttered.

"There are sailors around," whispered Willie. "It's all in the day's work. Come on, let's hit the clip shack."

There were two bunks in the little tomb now. Harding dived into the bottom one, and Willie fell on the top bunk. For a while they lay silently, panting. "Well," spoke Harding wearily at last. "I've heard of friendships sealed in blood, but never in puke. All the same, Keith, I'm obliged to you. You did a noble deed with your hat."

"I'm just lucky," said Willie, "that you didn't have to do the same for me. No doubt you'll have plenty of chance on this happy cruise."

"Any time," said Harding, his voice trailing off. "Any time, Keith. Thanks again." He rolled over and fell asleep.

It seemed to Willie that he had barely dozed off when a hand reached into his bunk and shook him. "Chadan, suh," said the voice of Whittaker, and his steps receded on the deck outside.

"Harding," groaned Willie, "do you want dinner?"

"Huh? Dinner already? No. Sleep is what I want———"

"We better go. It'll look bad if we don't."

There were three officers at the wardroom table including the captain. The rest were off on shore leave. Willie and Harding took chairs at the lower end of the long white cloth and began eating in silence. The others ignored them and made incomprehensible jokes among themselves about things that had happened at Guadalcanal and New Zealand and Australia. Lieutenant Maryk was the first to glance their way. He was burly, round-faced, and pugnacious-looking, about twenty-five, with a prison haircut. "You guys look kind of red-eyed," he said.

Willie said, "We were caulking off for a few minutes in the clip shack."

"Nothing like caulking off to start your career right," the captain said to a pork chop, out of which he took a large bite.

"Kind of hot in there, isn't it?" said Adams, the gunnery officer. Lieutenant Adams wore fresh prim khakis. He had the long aristocratic face and negligent superior look which Willie had seen often at Princeton. It meant good family and money.

"Kind of," Harding said meekly.

Maryk turned to the captain. "Sir, that doggone clip shack is over the engine room. These guys'll fry in there———"

"Ensigns are expendable," the captain said.

"What I mean, sir, I think I could hang a couple of bunks just as easy in Adams' and Gorton's room, or even in here over the couch———"

"The hell with that," Adams said.

"Isn't that a hull modification, Steve?" the captain said,

chewing pork. "You'd have to get permission from Bu-
Ships."

"I can look it up, sir, but I don't think it is."

"Well, when you get around to it. The shipfitters are
way behind as it is." Captain de Vriess glanced at the
ensigns. "Do you gentlemen think you can survive a week
or two in the clip shack?"

Willie was tired, and the sarcasm irritated him. "Nobody's complaining," he said.

De Vriess raised his eyebrows and grinned. "That's the
spirit, Mr. Keith." He turned to Adams. "Have these
gentlemen started on their officers' qualification courses
yet?"

"No, sir—Carmody had them all afternoon, sir——"

"Well, Mr. Senior Watch Officer, time's a-wasting. Get
them started after dinner."

"Aye aye, Captain."

The officers' qualification courses were bulky mimeographed sheafs of coarse paper turning brown around the
edges. They were dated 1935. Adams brought them out
of his room while the ensigns were still drinking coffee,
and handed a course to each of them. "There are twelve
assignments," he said. "Complete the first by 0900 tomorrow and leave it on my desk. Thereafter complete one
a day while in port and one every three days while at sea."

Willie glanced at the first assignment: *Make two
sketches of the Caine, port and starboard, showing every
compartment and stating the use of each.*

"Where do we get this information, sir?"

"Didn't Carmody take you around the ship?"

"Yes, sir."

"Well, just write down what he told you, in diagram
form."

"Thank you, sir," said Willie.

Adams left the two ensigns to themselves. Harding
murmured wearily, "What say? Want to start on it?"

"Do you remember anything Carmody said?"

"Just one thing. 'Climb that mast.'"

"Well, it's due first thing in the morning," Willie said.
"Let's have a go at it."

They collaborated over a sketch, blinking and yawning, with frequent arguments about details. At the end of an hour their work looked like this:

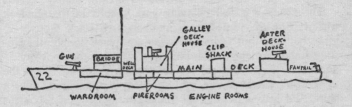

Willie sat back and examined it critically. "I think that does it——"

"Are you crazy, Keith? There are about forty compartments we have to stick in a label——"

"*I* don't remember any of those bloody compartments——"

"Neither do I. Guess we'll just have to go around the ship again——"

"What, for another three hours? Man, I'll get a heart attack. I'm failing fast. Look, my hands are shaking——"

"Anyway, Keith, the whole thing's out of proportion. It looks like some misbegotten tugboat——"

"It is."

"Look, I have an idea. There must be blueprints of this ship somewhere. Why don't we just get hold of them and—— It's not cricket maybe but——"

"Say no more! You're a genius, Harding! That's it. We'll do *exactly* that. First thing in the morning. Me for the Black Hole."

"Right with you."

Outside the clip shack, under a brilliant yellow floodlight, some civilian yard workers were burning with blowtorches and sawing and banging at the deck, installing a new life-raft rack. Harding said, "How the devil can we sleep with that going on?"

"I could sleep," said Willie, "if they were doing all that

to me instead of to the deck. Let's go." He stepped into
the shack and backed out, coughing like a consumptive.
"Ye gods!"

"What's the matter?"

"Go in there and take a breath—a shallow one."

The shack was full of stack gas. A shift in the wind
was wafting the fumes from number-three stack directly
into the little hut, where, having no place to go, they
stayed and fermented. Harding took a sniff at the doorway
and said, "Keith, it's suicide to sleep in there——"

"I don't care," Willie said desperately, pulling off his
shirt, "I'd just as lief die, all things considered."

He crept into his bunk, holding his nose, and Harding
followed. For a couple of hours he tossed and thrashed in
an eerie doze full of nightmares, wakened every few minutes by a burst of clattering from the workmen. Harding
passed into a dead stupor. At midnight the workmen quit,
but the sudden quiet and gloom brought no relief; it
merely made Willie more conscious of the heat, and of
the stinking miasma of the stack gas. He staggered out on
deck in his drawers, stumbled down to the wardroom, and
passed out on the couch. His body was covered with soot.

And again—and this was to be his most characteristic
experience aboard the *Caine,* and his longest memory of
it—he was being shaken out of his sleep. Lieutenant
Adams was standing over him, dressed for a watch with
gun belt and pistol, sipping coffee. Willie sat up. Through
the porthole he saw black night.

"Bear a hand, Keith. We've got the four-to-eight."

Willie went back to the clipping shack, got into his
clothes, and dragged himself to the quarterdeck. Adams
gave him a gun belt, showed him the leather-bound logs
and battered *Watch Officers' Guide* which were kept in a
rickety tin desk by the gangway, and introduced him to
the quartermaster and messenger of the watch, two sleepy
sailors in dungarees. The clock on the desk under the
shaded yellow electric bulb read five past four. All the
ships in the nest were dark and still. "The four-to-eight is
a pretty routine watch," said Adams.

"That's good." Willie yawned.

"I don't know," said the gunnery officer, "but what I'll lay below till reveille. Think you can handle it?"

"Uh-huh."

"Fine. There's nothing to it, really, except making damn sure none of your watch-standers sit down or fall asleep standing up. There are guards on the fo'c'sle and the fantail. Okay?"

"I got it," said Willie, saluting. Adams returned the salute and left.

The messenger, a small seaman first class named Mackenzie, promptly sat down on a crate of cabbages, with a happy sigh. Willie was stupefied by this defiance. "Get up, Mackenzie," he said uncertainly.

"Aw, why? I'm here if you need me for a messenger. Hell, sir," said Mackenzie, with an ingratiating smile, leaning back comfortably, "you don't have to pay no attention to Lieutenant Adams. He's the only officer that makes us stand up. Captain de Vriess don't care."

Willie suspected that this was a lie. He glanced at the gangway petty officer, Engstrand, a tall broad-shouldered first-class signalman, who was leaning against the desk, enjoying the byplay with a toothy grin.

"If you're not on your feet in two seconds," said Willie, "you're on report."

Mackenzie got up at once, muttering, "Christ, another of these lousy fireballs."

Willie was too embarrassed to object further. "I'm going to inspect the guards," he said.

"Aye aye, sir," said Engstrand.

On the forecastle, where a pleasant breeze blew and the night was blazing with stars, Willie found the guard curled up against the anchor windlass, his gun across his knees, fast asleep. This really shocked him. He had learned at Furnald Hall that the penalty for sleeping on watch in wartime was the firing squad. "Hey you," he yelled, "wake up." The guard was oblivious. Willie poked him with a toe, then shook him fiercely. The guard yawned and stood, shouldering his rifle. "Do you know," barked Willie, "what the penalty is for sleeping on watch?"

"Who was sleeping?" said the guard, with sincere outrage. "I was sending Morse code mentally."

Willie wanted to put this felon on report, but he hated to be responsible for his court-martial. "Well, whatever you were doing, stay on your feet and don't do it again."

"I was on my feet," said the guard angrily. "Just crouching to keep warm."

Willie left in disgust to inspect the guard at the stern. He passed the quarterdeck and found Mackenzie supine on a pile of life jackets. "Hell's fire," he shouted. "Get up, Mackenzie! Engstrand, can't you keep this man standing up?"

"Sir, I'm sick," moaned Mackenzie, sitting up. "I had a rough liberty."

"He is in bad shape, sir," said Engstrand, with a slight smile.

"Well, get someone else to stand the watch, then."

"Hell, sir, the whole crew is in terrible shape," replied Engstrand.

"*Get up, Mackenzie!*" roared Willie. Mackenzie pulled himself up on his feet, with ghastly moans.

"Okay, stay that way." Willie strode aft. The guard on the fantail was asleep on the deck, curled in a ball like a dog. "Jesus, what a ship," Willie muttered, and gave the guard a tremendous kick in the ribs. The guard jumped up, seized his rifle, and came to attention. Then he peered at Willie incredulously.

"Holy cats," he muttered, "I thought sure you was Mr. Maryk."

"I'm Mr. Keith," said Willie, "and what's your name?"
"Fuller."

"Well, Fuller, if I ever find you off your feet again on watch you get a general court-martial, do you hear?"

"Sure," said Fuller affably. "Say, are you from the Academy like Mr. Carmody?"

"No." Willie returned to the quarterdeck. Mackenzie was asleep on the life jackets again, and Engstrand was sitting on a hatch, smoking a cigar. He rose hastily when he saw Willie.

"Sorry, sir. Just taking a blow."

"Oh, God," exclaimed Willie. He was exhausted, enraged, and sick at the stomach. "And you a first-class petty officer. Three cheers for the good ship *Caine*. Look, Engstrand, you can sit, lie, or drop dead, for all I care, but keep this horizontal bastard *on his feet* for the rest of the watch, or I swear I'll put you on report."

"Get up, Mackenzie," said Engstrand, in a dry crisp tone. The sailor sprang off the life jackets, walked to the rail, and leaned against it, staring sullenly. Willie went to the desk and opened the *Watch Officers' Guide* with trembling hands, waiting for Mackenzie's next move. But the sailor stood in the same place for ten minutes, and seemed to find no difficulty at all in standing. At last he spoke up.

"All right with you, Mr. Keith," he said, with no rancor, "if I smoke?" Willie nodded. The sailor offered him a pack of Luckies. "Use 'em yourself?"

"Thanks."

Mackenzie lit Willie's cigarette, and then, to seal the good-fellowship thus established, he began to tell the new ensign about his sex career in New Zealand. Willie had heard some pretty frank talk late at night in college bedrooms, but Mackenzie's explicitness was something new. Willie was first amused, then disgusted, then fiercely bored, but there seemed no way to turn off the sailor's cloacal drone. The sky paled, and a dull streak of red appeared on the horizon. Willie was profoundly grateful when Lieutenant Adams came out of the wardroom hatchway, rubbing his eyes. "How's it going, Keith? Any strain?"

"No, sir."

"Let's inspect the lines."

He walked around the ship with Willie, kicking the manila ropes that tied the *Caine* to the next destroyers. "This number-three line needs chafing gear, the chock is rubbing. Tell Engstrand."

"Yes, sir—— Mr. Adams, frankly I had a hell of a time keeping the guards and the messenger from flaking out."

Adams grinned wryly, then his face became long and stern. "That's damned serious."

"They didn't seem to think so."

Adams pursed his lips, and stopped to light a cigarette, leaning against the life lines. "Tell you what, Keith. You've got something to contend with. This ship has been in the forward area since March 42. It's been through a lot of action. The men are all Asiatic. They probably think a fantail watch in Pearl Harbor is foolishness. The trouble is, the skipper thinks so, too. It's the port director's orders, so we post the guards. You've just got to bear down."

"What actions were you in, sir?"

"Hell, about everything. Marshalls raid, Coral Sea— first Savo, second Savo—Rendova, Munda——"

"What were you doing—minesweeping?"

"Who ever heard of a minesweeper minesweeping? Mostly we ran av-gas for the marine fliers at Henderson Field. Ran torpedoes up from New Zealand. That was a happy deal, live torpedoes lashed all over the deck and getting strafed. Ran dogfaces up to relieve the marines on Guadal. Ran convoys all over the ocean. Supply scow, troop transport, screen, mail carrier, or what dirty job have you? That's the *Caine*. So if she's a little run down, you know why."

"A little run down is putting it politely," said Willie.

Adams straightened up, glared at him, threw his cigarette into the water, and walked aft. Over the loudspeaker came the chirp of the boatswain's pipe, then the words, "Reveille for all hands. Reveille." Adams snapped over his shoulder, "Check reveille in the after crew's quarter, Keith. Make sure they're all out of their sacks."

"Aye aye, sir."

Willie decided that he had better guard his mouth. Adams and the other officers had been aboard the *Caine* so long, they must be blind to the fact that it was a filthy wreck. They might even be proud of the ship. He swore to himself that he would be different. He would keep perspective, and he would never rest until, one way or another, he had gotten himself off the *Caine*. He set six months as his limit. After all, there was an admiral who was fond of him.

A narrow round hatchway and a steep ladder led to the after crew's quarters. Willie put his face to the opening and peered down. It was dark as a cave inside, and the smell was like a very hot and dirty gymnasium. Willie lowered himself through the hatchway and shouted, trying to use a fierce tone, "All right! What the hell about reveille, here?"

A light snapped on in a far corner, revealing tiers of shadowy bunks full of sleepers. "Aye aye, sir," spoke a lone voice, "I'm the master-at-arms. I'll get 'em up. We didn't hear reveille called away, sir. Come on, you guys —up! There's an officer here."

A few naked sailors rolled out of the bunks, but the response was sluggish and small. The master-at-arms turned on a brilliant central light, and went from one tier of bunks to another, shaking, poking, pleading. The sailors were stacked like corpses in a mausoleum. Willie was ashamed of intruding on their wretchedness. The deck was as nasty as a chicken yard with butts, papers, clothing, and moldering scraps of food. The fetid air sickened him.

"Hurry it," he said. He fled up the ladder.

"How's it going back there?" said Adams when he returned to the quarterdeck. The sun was shining, and boatswain's pipes and loudspeaker's calls were filling the air in the repair basin. Barefoot sailors were hosing down the deck.

"They're getting up," said Willie.

Adams nodded satirically. "Excellent. You may secure now. Lay below and get yourself some eggs and coffee."

"Aye aye, sir." Willie took off the gun belt, and his haunches felt pleasantly light.

In the wardroom the officers were already at breakfast. Willie fell into his chair and ate what was placed before him, not knowing or caring what it was. He wanted to fill his gnawing stomach and return to the clip shack and stay there for the day, stack gas or no stack gas.

"Say, Keith," said the communications officer, buttering a roll, "I saw Roland last night. Says he's coming out here later today to pay us a visit."

"Swell," said Willie.

"We've gotten kind of stacked up on messages, by the

way," added Keefer. "How's about decoding for a couple of hours after breakfast?"

"Love it," said Willie, a little desperately.

Captain de Vriess looked up at him from under thick blond eyebrows. "What's the trouble, Keith? Saddle bothering you?"

"No, sir!" exclaimed Willie. "I'm glad to have something to do."

"Fine. Ambition becomes an ensign."

An hour later, as Willie toiled over a decoding device spread out on the wardroom table, the letters suddenly became a blur. The wardroom jerked back and forth, and began to rotate gently. His head fell on his hands. The fact that Lieutenant Maryk was reading official mail at the table beside him made no difference. He was done in.

He heard the opening of a door, and then the captain's voice: "Well, well. Siesta time for Ensign Keith."

He did not dare raise his head.

"Sir," he heard Maryk say, "that clip shack is no place to sleep. The kid is shot."

"Kind of ripe in port, but it'll be fine under way. Hell, Maryk, this boy's had four months' temporary in Pearl. Like to know how the hell he arranged it. He ought to have soaked up enough sleep to go without for a month."

The captain's voice was mocking and cruel. It filled Willie with rage. What right had De Vriess to be so damned red hot? De Vriess was the man who permitted all the filth and sloth of the *Caine,* for which he deserved a court-martial. He seemed to reserve all his energies for baiting ensigns. Willie's accumulated resentment, weariness, and disgust coagulated at that moment into hatred of Captain de Vriess. The ship was the measure of the commanding officer. He had fallen into the hands of a bullying stupid sloven. He gritted his teeth, and as soon as De Vriess was gone he pulled himself erect and resumed decoding with new energy released by hate.

There was an enormous pile-up of coding traffic. He had to keep working until lunch time, and then for an hour after that. At last it was done. He dropped the decodes on Keefer's cluttered desk, went aft to the clipping shack, and fell asleep instantaneously.

It was Adams again who shook him awake. "Keith, you have visitors in the wardroom——"

"Huh—visitors?"

"Keefer's brother, and two of the prettiest nurses I've ever seen. Lucky boy——"

Willie sat up, suddenly refreshed. "Thank you, sir. Sir, what's the procedure for getting off the ship?"

"You check out with the senior watch officer—me."

"Thank you, sir. I'd like to check out." Willie reached for his clothes.

"Sure. Just let me have the assignment."

Willie had to search his memory. Through the cloud of recent happenings came a dim recollection of the officers' qualification course. "I haven't had time to touch it, sir."

"Sorry, Keith. Better clear with the skipper, then. Orders are that assignments must be up to date prior to any shore leave."

Willie dressed and went down to the wardroom. He found the captain, in smart tropical khakis festooned with campaign ribbons, chatting with the nurses and the Keefer brothers. He disliked begging permission like a schoolboy in the presence of the girls, but there was no help for it.

"Pardon me, Captain."

"Yes, Keith?"

"I request permission to go ashore."

"Of course. I wouldn't think of depriving you of such charming company," said the captain with elephantine gallantry. The nurses giggled. Miss Jones said, "Hi, Keither."

"Thank you, sir."

"I presume you've checked out with Adams?"

"Well, that's it, sir. That's why I'm checking with you." The captain gave him a quizzical look. "See, there's an assignment in my qualification course I haven't completed. It was handed to me yesterday and I've been on the go every second since and——"

"Every second? Seems to me I've seen you at rest once or twice. What were you doing just now?"

"I—I plead guilty to about three hours of sleep in the past forty-eight, sir——"

"Well, why don't you sit down and bat that assignment out now? It won't take long. The girls will wait. I'll do my best to amuse them."

"The sadist," said Willie to himself. Aloud, "Thank you, Captain, but——"

"I'll give you a ti-ip," said De Vriess, in a teasing sing-song. "The sketches you need are right up there in the ship's organization book. All you have to do is trace them. That's all I did in my day." He resumed his chitchat with the girls, who seemed fascinated by him.

Willie took down the book and found the sketches. He calculated that it would require three quarters of an hour to trace the diagrams and copy the names of the spaces.

"Pardon me, Captain."

"Yes?" said De Vriess pleasantly.

"This being a purely mechanical chore, as you say, would it be acceptable to you if I promise to turn it in prior to 0800 tomorrow? I can do it tonight."

"No telling what shape you'll be in tonight, Keith. Better do it now."

The nurses laughed, and Miss Jones said, "Poor Keither."

"Use my room, Keith," said the communicator. "There's a ruler and tracing paper in my upper right-hand drawer."

Blushing, seething, Willie bolted from the wardroom. "War is hell," he heard the captain say, and the girls gurgled. Willie made the sketches in twenty minutes, grinding his teeth each time he heard feminine laughter from the wardroom. With the papers in his hand he climbed up on deck through a scuttle to avoid the captain and the girls, and went looking for Adams. But the senior watch officer had left the ship. There was no help for it; Willie had to go below and, his cheeks flaming, hand the sketches to the captain. De Vriess inspected them carefully while the girls cooed and whispered. "Very nice," he said after a long, humiliating pause. "A little hasty, but under the circumstances, very nice."

Brief giggle by Nurse Carter.

"May I go now, sir?"

"Why not?" said the captain magnanimously. He rose. "May I give you people a lift? I have a station wagon."

"No, thank you, sir," Willie growled.

The captain raised his eyebrows. "No? Too bad. Goodby, Miss Carter—Miss Jones: Very pleasant having you aboard." He walked out, putting on his hat with a self-satisfied tilt.

The party that followed was a dampened one. Willie covered his fury with a dull silence. The girls found little to say. In Honolulu they picked up a third nurse earmarked for Tom Keefer, an extravagantly stupid, beautiful blonde. She displayed a marked and instant liking for Roland. Tom retreated into long drunken quotations from *Paradise Lost* and the poems of T. S. Eliot and Gerard Manley Hopkins while Roland and the blonde carried on a boisterous flirtation. This was during dinner at a Chinese restaurant. Willie drank more than he ever had in his life. They went on to a Danny Kaye movie at CincPac, which he saw blurrily, as through a rainy window. He fell sound asleep in the middle of it; and never really woke, though he walked obediently wherever he was led, until he found himself riding in a taxi with Tom Keefer.

"Where are we? What time is it? Where are the others?" he grumbled. His mouth tasted sickeningly of rum and Chinese food.

"We're on the way home, Willie. Home to the *Caine*. Party's over."

"The *Caine*. The *Caine* and De Vriess——"

"Afraid so."

"Mr. Keefer, am I wrong, or is De Vriess a complete lout and moron?"

"Your estimate is a little generous, otherwise correct."

"How does such a man get command of a ship?"

"He isn't commanding a ship. He's commanding the *Caine*."

"He's made the *Caine* what it is."

"Very likely."

"Say, where's Roland?"

"Out getting married to the blonde. I hope so, anyway.

He ought to make an honest woman of her after what they were doing at that movie."

"He sure cut in on you."

"Roland isn't responsible," said Keefer, "for the deeds that his thyroid puts him up to. It's a classic instance of what Kant calls *arbitrium brutum*. You recall the passage, no doubt."

"Of course," said Willie, and fell asleep again.

Keefer led him aboard the *Caine* and dumped him into the clipping shack. Willie was only half aware of what was happening. An hour later he was being shaken out of his sleep. He opened his eyes and looked into the face of Paynter. "Whassamatter now?" he mumbled.

"Message to be broken, Keith."

"What time is it?"

"Quarter past three."

"Jesus, can't it wait till morning?"

"Nope. *Caine* is information addressee. Any message where we're an addressee is busted at once. Captain de Vriess's orders."

"De Vriess," snarled Willie. "De Vriess. Why doesn't the Navy send him back to high school to mature?"

"Come on, Keith."

"Pal, let someone else break it. I'm too tired to see."

"Assistant communicator always handles these night breaks," said Paynter, "as I know only too goddam well. Come on, Keith, I've got to get back to the gangway."

Willie slid out of the bunk and descended to the wardroom, leaning heavily on bulkheads and railing. He propped his spinning head on one arm and set about decoding. The message was addressed to the aircraft carrier *Brandywine Creek* for action. Halfway through the message Willie jumped up and uttered a cry of joy. He poured himself a cup of sludgy coffee, drained it, and raced through the rest of the decoding. With the penciled message he ran up to the quarterdeck, threw his arms around Paynter, and kissed him. The dour engineer pushed him away in distaste. "What the hell?"

"Look, friend, look. Tidings of comfort and joy."

Paynter took the slip of paper to the light over the

desk. Shielding it from the side glances of the watch, he read: *Lieutenant Commander Philip F. Queeg USN detached. Proceed to Anti-submarine Warfare School San Francisco for training. Upon completion proceed to relieve Commanding Officer Caine DMS 22.*

Paynter looked mildly pleased.

"Well," said Willie in a low tone, standing beside him, "aren't you going to kiss me back?"

"I'll wait," said Paynter, "until I see this Queeg."

"When you're at the bottom, there's no place to go but up," said Willie. "Can you imagine anyone *worse* than De Vriess?"

"Well, it's conceivable. I'll take this in to the skipper——"

"No, no, allow me that luxury."

Willie ran down the ladder to the wardroom and rapped at the captain's door.

"Come in——"

"Good news, Captain," cried Willie, as he opened the door. The captain snapped on his bed light and squinted at the message, leaning on an elbow, his face streaked with red marks from the creases of his pillow.

"Well, well," he said, with a small wry smile. "Call that good news, do you, Keith?"

"I guess it is for you, sir, after six years. You'll probably get a new destroyer. Maybe shore duty."

"You're all for shore duty, eh, Keith? That's a thoroughly salty viewpoint. You've picked it up real quickly."

"Why, I sort of think you rate it, sir, that's all."

"Well, I hope the Bureau agrees with you. Thanks, Keith. Good night."

Willie left with a feeling that his sarcasm had somehow bounced off the captain's hide. But he didn't care. He could suffer through the next weeks on the *Caine* gladly now. Deliverance was on the way, in the person of Lieutenant Commander Philip F. Queeg.

9 · First Day at Sea

After four days of repairs, the *Caine* was ordered to sea for minesweeping exercises in waters near Oahu. "Well, well," said Captain de Vriess, when Willie brought him the decoded message, "minesweeping, eh? Looks like our friend Queeg will be relieving me just in time."

"Does that mean we're going to minesweep for real in —in the near future, sir?".

"Could be."

"Has the *Caine* ever done any sweeping, sir?"

"Sure, dummy mines by the hundreds. Never in any operation, thank God." De Vriess climbed out of his bunk and reached for his trousers. "I'll like minesweeping, Keith, when they figure out one simple problem."

"What's that, sir?"

"Who sweeps ahead of the minesweepers— Well, tell Steve Maryk to come in here, will you? And tell Whittaker I'd like some coffee."

"Yes, sir."

"Not the black tar that's been cooking down since this morning. Fresh."

"Yes, sir."

Roland Keefer came aboard that evening for dinner, bringing a batch of mail for Willie from the BOQ. As usual, Willie ripped open May's letter first. She had returned to college for the autumn session. It was a sacrifice, for during the summer Marty Rubin had obtained a midday radio booking for her, and she might have continued on it. The pay was a hundred dollars a week.

But I don't care, dear. The more I read and study, the less ambitious I become. Last year I was sure I wanted nothing in life but a top salary as a top singer. I despised the girls I met at Hunter at first because they couldn't earn a nickel. But I'm beginning to wonder whether it's sensible to give up all my days and nights for a salary. I love to sing, I guess I always will. As long as I have to earn money I'm glad I can do it at a fair rate in work I enjoy rather than as a typist in some stale office. But I know I'll never be a first-rate singer—haven't the voice, haven't the style, haven't the looks (no, I haven't, dear). What I want now, I think, is to trap some kindhearted sugar daddy who will help me have a couple of babies and otherwise let me read in peace.

Score one for you, my love. Dickens is *terrif.* Sat up all night reading *Dombey and Son*—for a book report, mind you, that isn't due till next week—and now have huge black bags under my eyes. Glad you can't see me.

What a lie that last sentence is. Are you ever coming home? When is this war going to end? I thought after Italy surrendered that I'd be seeing you any day. But it seems to be bogging down for another long stretch. The European news is usually good but I'm afraid I care mostly about the Pacific. And it may be unpatriotic, but I'm awfully glad you haven't caught the *Caine* yet.

I love you.

MAY

"Well," said Roland as they sat down to dinner, "looks like I'll be saying good-by to you all for a while. Staff's piling aboard the *Yorktown* tomorrow. Guess the admiral wants some sea pay."

Tom Keefer's face darkened. He threw down his knife and fork. "Wouldn't you know. A new flattop."

"That hurts, doesn't it, Tom?" said De Vriess, grinning.

"What's the matter, Tom?" said Maryk. "Don't you like minesweeping?" All the officers laughed at the standard joke about the communicator.

"Hell, I just want to see some war, as long as my sands are running out uselessly——"

"You came aboard too late," said Adams. "We saw plenty of war before——"

"You saw some errand-boy duty," said Keefer. "I'm interested in essences, not accidents. The nub of this Pacific war is the duel of flying machines. Everything else is as routine as the work of milkmen and filing clerks. All uncertainty and all decision rides with the carriers."

"I've got some friends on the *Saratoga*," said the captain. "Pretty routine life aboard her, too, Tom."

"War is ninety-nine per cent routine—routine that trained monkeys could perform," said Keefer. "But the one per cent of chance and creative action on which the history of the world is hanging right now you'll find on carriers. That's what I want to be part of. So my dear bother, who would like nothing better than to rest his duff in Hawaii for the rest of the war——"

"Tom, you are but so right," threw in Roland cheerfully.

"—gets carted aboard a carrier on a silver charger, and I ride the *Caine*."

"Have some more liver, Tom," said Maryk. The first lieutenant, who resembled a prize fighter or drill sergeant with his bullet head, short wide nose, and close-clipped hair, had a surprisingly innocent, affectionate smile which changed his whole appearance.

"Why don't you send in another transfer request, Tom?" said the captain. "I'll approve it again."

"I've given up. This ship is an outcast, manned by outcasts, and named for the great outcast of mankind. My destiny is the *Caine*. It's the purgatory for my sins."

"Any interesting sins, Tom? Tell us about 'em," said Gorton, leering over a heavy forkful of liver.

"Sins that would make even the naked whores in your picture collection blush, Burt," said Keefer, raising a hoot of laughter at the exec.

The captain regarded Keefer admiringly. "That's the literary mind for you. I never thought of *Caine* being a symbolic name——"

"The extra *e* threw you off, Captain. God always likes to veil His symbols a bit, being, among His other attributes, the perfect literary artist."

"Well, I'm glad I stayed aboard for dinner," said Maryk. "You haven't opened up for a long while, Tom. Been off your form."

"He just got tired of casting his pearls before swine," said the captain. "Let's have the ice cream, Whittaker."

Willie had noticed a curious mixture of respect and satire in the captain's attitude toward Tom Keefer. He was beginning to realize that the wardroom was a tangle of subtle, complex evaluations by the officers of each other, knotting centrally, as it were, in the person and attitudes of the captain. It seemed to him that De Vriess must have an insoluble difficulty in facing a subordinate so much more cultured and gifted than himself. Yet somehow De Vriess struck a note with Keefer that enabled him to use an amiable condescension, where he had no right to condescend.

Harding broke his accustomed silence to remark, "Friend of mine was sent to a destroyer called the *Abel*. Wonder what you'd say if you were aboard her, Mr. Keefer?"

"I'd probably say that I was sacrificing my first fruits aboard her, as God knows I am here, and had some hope they'd be acceptable," rejoined Keefer.

"What first fruits, Tom?" said Gorton.

"My young years, my early vigor, the time in which Sheridan produced *The Rivals,* and Dickens, *Pickwick,* and Meredith, *Richard Feverel*. What am I producing? A lot of decodes and registered pub inventories. My freshness is spending its wavering shower in the dust. At least if I were on a carrier——"

"You stole that line," said Willie proudly, "from Francis Thompson."

"Christ," exploded the captain, "this ship is becoming a damned literary society. I'm glad I'm getting off."

"Well, it seems to me, Mr. Keefer," said Harding, "that you can twist any ship's name into a symbolical meaning. Caine, Abel——"

"The world is an endless treasury of symbols," said Keefer. "That's grade-school theology."

"I think Harding means that you're an endless treasury of plays on words," said Willie.

"Salvo for the junior ensign," cried Gorton, signaling with a fat forefinger for a third helping of ice cream.

"All intelligent conversation is playing on words," said Keefer. "The rest is definitions and instructions."

"What I mean," persisted Harding, "you can go on spinning those symbols forever, and one's as good as another——"

"Not quite," said Keefer, with a brief nod of appreciation at the point, "because the test of the validity of any symbol is the extent to which it's rooted in reality. What I said about the *Abel* was a specious verbalism to answer you. But you see I am aboard the *Caine.*"

"Then we're all outcasts for our sins," said Willie.

"Hell, what sins? Keith looks as though butter wouldn't melt in his mouth," said Maryk. "Look at that sweet face."

"Who knows? Maybe he robbed his mother's purse once," said Keefer. "Sin is relative to character."

"Wonder what I ever did," said Gorton.

"It's hard to know what would be sin in a born degenerate," said Keefer. "You probably worship Satan in that private stateroom."

"I," said the captain, rising, "am going to see that Hopalong Cassidy movie on the *Johnson.* Tom gives me mental indigestion."

The *Caine* left Pearl Harbor at dawn in a rain squall.

The light was still dim on the bridge when Maryk bawled into a greenish brass speaking tube, "Ready in all respects to get under way, Captain!" Willie, stationed on the bridge as junior OOD, was utterly bewildered by the rapid reports and orders which went before this word. He stood out in the warm rain in his khakis, shielding his binoculars under his arm, denying himself the protection of the pilothouse in the vague intention of demonstrating that he was a real seaman.

Captain de Vriess came up the ladder. He paced the

bridge slowly, leaning over the bulwarks to look at the lines, estimating the wind, peering astern at the channel, issuing brief orders in a dry pleasant tone. His bearing was very impressive, Willie admitted to himself, because it was natural, perhaps unconscious. It was not a matter of a stiff spine, squared shoulders, and a sucked-in stomach. Knowledge was in his eye, authority in his manner, decision in the sharp lines of his mouth.

"Well, hell," Willie thought, "if a destroyer captain can't get a ship away from alongside, what *is* he good for?" He had already adopted the *Caine* mode of shading the truth toward the glamorous side by regarding the ship as an honest-to-goodness destroyer.

His meditations were interrupted by a shocking blast on the ship's steam whistle. The stern of the destroyer next to the *Caine* swung away sluggishly, pulled by a small tug, leaving a narrow triangle of open water bubbling under the rain.

"Take in all lines to port," said the captain.

A goateed sailor named Grubnecker, who wore headphones, reported in a moment, "All lines taken in fore and aft, sir."

"Port back one third," said the captain.

The fat ship's yeoman at the engine telegraph, Jellybelly, repeated the order and rang it up. The engine-room pointer answered. The ship began to vibrate, and slowly to move backward. Willie had an intuitive flash that this was a historic moment, his first time under way aboard the *Caine*. But he pushed it from his mind. This ship was not going to be important in his life—he was determined to see to that.

"Stand clear of the bulkhead, Mr. Keith," said De Vriess sharply, leaning over the side.

"Beg pardon, sir," said Willie, leaping aside. He mopped the streaming rain from his face.

"All engines stop," ordered De Vriess. He walked past Willie, remarking, "Don't you know enough to get in out of the rain? Go in the pilothouse."

"Thank you, sir." He took shelter gladly. A stiff wind

was slanting the rain across the channel. Drops drummed on the windows of the wheelhouse.

"Fantail reports channel buoy a hundred yards dead astern," called Grubnecker.

"I see it," said the captain.

Maryk, in a dripping mackintosh, peered down the channel through binoculars. "Submarine coming down the channel, Captain. Making ten knots. Distance one thousand."

"Very well."

"Fantail reports battle wagon and two tin cans coming up-channel past the gate, sir," said the telephone talker.

"Forty-second Street and Broadway out here today," said De Vriess.

Willie looked out at the choppy channel, thinking that the *Caine* was in difficulties already. The wind was moving her swiftly down on the channel buoy. There was little space to maneuver between the bobbing buoy and the ships in the docks. The battleship and the submarine were rapidly closing from both sides.

De Vriess, unperturbed, issued a swift series of engine and rudder orders, the purpose of which escaped Willie. But the effect was to swing the minesweeper around in a backing arc, heading down-channel, well clear of the buoy, falling in line behind the departing submarine. Meanwhile the battleship and its escorts passed down the port side with plenty of room. Willie observed that none of the sailors commented or seemed impressed, so he assumed that what had appeared knotty to him was a matter of course to an experienced seaman.

Maryk stepped into the pilothouse and swabbed his face with a towel hung on the captain's chair. "Damn! Puget Sound weather." He noticed Willie standing around, looking uncommonly useless. "What the devil are you doing in here? You're supposed to stand lookout on the starboard side——"

"Captain told me to get in out of the rain."

"Hell, you probably were under his feet. Come on out. You won't melt."

"Gladly, sir." Willie followed him out into the weather, irritated at being in the wrong whatever he did.

"Learn anything," asked Maryk, peering down-channel, "from that backing maneuver?"

"Seemed pretty routine," said Willie.

Maryk dipped his binoculars and looked at Willie, showing all his teeth in a mystified grin. "You ever been on a bridge before, Keith?"

"No, sir."

Maryk nodded, and resumed his search of the channel through the glasses.

"Why," said Willie, wiping rain from his eyes, "was there anything remarkable about it?"

"Christ, no, no," said Maryk. "Any ensign could have handled the ship the way the old man did. I thought maybe you were impressed for no good reason." He grinned again and walked to the other side of the bridge.

The squall passed and the sun came out brilliantly as the *Caine* cleared the channel entrance. When Willie came off watch he went to the forecastle to enjoy the view of Diamond Head and Oahu's green hills. The ship knifed through calm blue water at twenty knots. He was agreeably surprised at the old minesweeper's brisk speed. There were traces of destroyer grandeur yet in the rusty ruin. The deck rolled steeply, and sparkling spray flew up from the bow wave, and Willie was proud of not being in the least seasick. For the first time since his arrival on the *Caine* he felt moderately happy.

But he made the mistake of going below for a cup of coffee. Keefer captured him and set him to work correcting publications. This was the dreariest of all communication chores. Willie hated the red ink, the scissors and smelly paste, and the interminable niggling corrections: "Page 9 para. 0862 line 3: change *All prescribed gunnery exercises* to read *All gunnery exercises prescribed by USNF 7A.*" He had visions of thousands of ensigns all over the globe straining their eyes and crooking their backs over these preposterous trifles.

The motion of the ship, heaving the green table up and down as he bent over it, began to trouble him. He noticed with annoyance that some of the corrections which Keefer had dumped on him in a heap were very old. Several of them he had himself entered in CincPac's books, months ago. At one point he threw down the pen with an exclamation of disgust. He had spent an hour minutely entering a set of ink corrections which were obsolete; further down in the pile there were new printed pages to replace them. "Damn," he said to Carmody, who was decoding messages beside him, "doesn't Keefer ever enter corrections? These things are piled up since the last war."

"Lieutenant Keefer's too busy with his novel," burst out Carmody bitterly, stroking his faint mustache.

"What novel?"

"He's writing some kind of novel. Half the time at night when I'm trying to sleep he's pacing around talking to himself. Then in the daytime he flakes out. Why, he can work these damn decoding gismos ten times faster than anybody in the wardroom. He spent six months on the beach studying them. He could clear up the whole traffic in a couple of hours a day. But we're always behind, and you, Rabbitt and I are clearing about ninety per cent of it. I think he's a foul ball."

"Have you read any of the novel?"

"Hell, I have no time to read novels by good authors. Why should I bother with his tripe?" Carmody twisted his blue-and-gold Annapolis ring nervously with his thumb. He rose and poured himself coffee. "Want some Joe?"

"Thanks—— Well, look," said Willie, accepting the cup, "this kind of thing must be horribly dull to a man of his talents."

"What talents?" Carmody dropped into a chair.

"He's a professional author, Carmody. Didn't you know that? He's had stories in magazines. The Theatre Guild had an option on one of his plays——"

"So what? He's on the *Caine* now, just like you and me."

"If he brings a great novel off the *Caine,*" said Willie, "it'll be a far greater contribution to America than a lot of decodes."

"His assignment is communications, not contributions to America——"

Keefer entered the wardroom in underwear and went to the coffee corner. "How are you doing, lads?"

"All right, sir," said Carmody with sudden subservience, pushing away his coffee cup and taking up a coded message.

"Except we think you ought to do some decoding for a change," said Willie. He had no fear of Keefer's higher military rank. He was sure the communicator laughed at such gradings. His respect for Keefer, already high, had risen sharply on learning that he was composing a novel.

Keefer smiled and came to the table. "What's the matter, class of '43," he said, slouching in a chair, "want to go talk to the chaplain?"

Carmody kept his eyes down. "The coding watch is part of an ensign's work on a small ship," he said. "I don't mind. Every line officer should learn the essentials of communications, and——"

"Here," said Keefer, draining his coffee, "give me that gismo. I've been doping off. Go study *Navy Regulations*." He pried the device out of Carmody's hands.

"No, I can do it, sir. Happy to——"

"Run along."

"Why, thank you, sir." Carmody rose, bestowed a brief arid smile on Keith, and went out.

"There goes a happy man," said Keefer. He began whipping the coding machine through its motions. It was as Carmody had said. He was incredibly fast.

"He tells me you're working on a novel."

Keefer nodded.

"Got much of it done?"

"About forty thousand words out of four hundred thousand."

"Gosh. Long."

"Longer than *Ulysses*. Shorter than *War and Peace*."

"Is it a war novel?"

Keefer smiled ironically. "It takes place on a carrier."

"Got a title?"

"Well, a working title."

"What is it?" said Willie very curiously.

"Doesn't mean much, by itself."

"Well, I'd like to hear it."

Keefer hesitated, and spoke the words slowly. *"Multitudes, Multitudes."*

"I like it."

"Recognize it?"

"Bible, I imagine."

"Book of Joel. 'Multitudes, multitudes in the valley of decision.' "

"Well, I put in right now for the millionth copy, autographed."

Keefer gave him the whole-souled smile of a flattered author. "I'm a little way from that, yet."

"You'll make it. May I read some of it?"

"Perhaps. When it's in better shape." Keefer had never stopped decoding. He finished his third message and began a fourth.

"You really whiz through those," marveled Willie.

"Perhaps that's why I let 'em pile up. It's like telling a child Red Riding Hood for the thousandth time. The thing is infantile and dull to start with, and becomes maddening with repetition."

"Most of the Navy is repetition."

"I don't mind it, when there's only fifty per cent waste motion. Communication is ninety-eight per cent waste motion. We carry a hundred and twelve registered publications. We use about six. But all the rest have to be corrected, one set of corrections superseding another every month. Take decoding. Actually about four messages a month concern this ship in any way. Commander Queeg's orders, for instance. The minesweeping-exercise despatch. All the rest of this garbage we rake over because the captain, bless his intellectual curiosity, wants to snoop on the fleet's activities. For only one reason. So that at the officers' club he can say to some classmate of his, very casually, don't you know, 'Well, I hope you like screening that southern attack group in the next push.' Makes him sound like a friend of the admirals. I've seen him do it a dozen times."

He kept racing through the decoding steps as he talked. Willie was fascinated by his negligent speed. Already he had done more work than Willie could perform in an hour; and Willie was the speediest of the ensigns.

"I can't get over the way you polish those off."

"Willie, aren't you wise to the Navy yet? It's all child's play. The work has been fragmentized by a few excellent brains at the top, on the assumption that near-morons will be responsible for each fragment. The assumption is sound enough for peacetime. There's a handful of brilliant boys who come into the Navy with the long purpose of becoming the nation's admirals, and they succeed invariably because there's no competition. For the rest the Navy is a third-rate career for third-rate people, offering a sort of skimpy security in return for twenty or thirty years of a polite penal servitude. What self-respecting American of even average gifts, let alone superior ones, will enter such a life? Well, now, comes a war, and the gifted civilians swarm into the service. Is it any wonder that they master in a matter of weeks what the near-morons painfully acquire in years? Take code devices. Navy plodders grind out maybe five, six messages an hour with them. Any half-baked reserve communicator can learn to whip out twenty an hour. No wonder the poor peons resent us——"

"Heresy, heresy," Willie said, rather startled and embarrassed.

"Not at all. Plain fact. Whether it's the fragment of coding, the fragment of engineering, the fragment of gunnery—you'll find them all predigested and regulated to a point where you'd have to search the insane asylums to find people who could muff the jobs. Remember that one point. It explains, and reconciles you to, all the Navy Regulations, and all the required reports, and all the emphasis on memory and obedience, and all the standardized ways of doing things. The Navy is a master plan designed by geniuses for execution by idiots. If you're not an idiot, but find yourself in the Navy, you can only operate well by pretending to be one. All the shortcuts and economies and common-sense changes that your native intelligence suggests to you are mistakes. Learn to quash them. Constantly ask yourself, 'How would I do this if I were a fool?' Throttle down your mind to a crawl. Then you'll never go wrong—— Well, that cleans up brother Carmody's traffic," he added, pushing aside the heap of despatches. "Want me to do yours?"

"No, thank you, sir—— You're pretty bitter about the Navy——"

"No, no, Willie," said Keefer earnestly. "I approve of the whole design. We need a navy, and there's no other way to run one in a free society. It simply takes a little time to see the true picture, and I'm passing on to you the fruits of my analysis. You have wit and background. You'd come to the same conclusion in a few months. Remember Socrates' slave who worked out the *pons asinorum* with a stick in the sand? A fact of nature emerges by itself after a while. It would come pretty quickly to you."

"So that's your *pons asinorum* of shipboard life? 'The Navy is a master plan designed by geniuses for executoin by idiots.' "

"An excellent demonstration," Keefer smiled, nodding, "of obedient memory, Willie. You'll be a naval officer yet."

A few hours later Willie was on the bridge again with Maryk for the noon-to-four watch. Captain de Vriess dozed in his narrow chair on the starboard side of the pilothouse. The remains of his lunch in a tin tray rested on the deck under the chair: a broken corn muffin, fragments of Swiss steak, and an empty coffee mug. The weather was clear and hot, the sea choppy with whitecaps. The *Caine* rolled and creaked, cutting across the troughs of the waves at fifteen knots. A telephone buzzed. Willie answered it.

"Forward fireroom requests permission to blow tubes," croaked the phone. Willie repeated the request to Maryk.

"Granted," said the OOD, after a glance at the fluttering flag on the mast. There was a rumble from the stacks and inky smoke billowed out and floated away perpendicularly to leeward. "Good time to blow tubes," said Maryk. "Wind on the beam. Carries the soot well clear.

Sometimes you have to change course to get the wind right. Then you ask the skipper's permission."

The ship took a long steep roll. The rubber mats on the wheelhouse deck slid in a heap to one side. Willie clung to a window handle as the quartermaster rescued the mats. "Sure rolls with the wind on the beam," he observed.

"These buckets roll in drydock," said Maryk. "Lot of freeboard forward and too much weight aft. All that sweep gear. Pretty poor stability. Wind on the beam really pushes her over." He strolled out on the starboard wing, and Willie followed him, glad of the chance to let some fresh air blow in his face. The rolling bothered him in the narrow stuffy pilothouse. He decided he would do most of his watch-standing on these open wings. It would give him a nice sunburn.

The first lieutenant peered constantly seaward, sometimes making a slow sweep of the horizon with his binoculars. Willie imitated him, but the sea was empty, and he soon became bored.

"Mr. Maryk," he said, "what do you think of Mr. Keefer?"

The first lieutenant gave him a brief surprised side glance. "Damn keen mind."

"Do you think he's a good officer?" Willie knew he was trampling on etiquette, but curiosity was too strong. The first lieutenant put his binoculars to his eyes.

"Gets by," he said, "like the rest of us."

"He doesn't seem to think much of the Navy."

Maryk grunted. "Tom don't think much of a lot of things. Get him started on the West Coast sometime."

"Are you from the West Coast?"

Maryk nodded. "Tom says it's the last primitive area left for the anthropologists to study. He says we're a lot of white tennis-playing Bushmen."

"What did you do before the war, sir?"

Maryk glanced uneasily at the dozing captain. "Fisherman."

"Commercial fishing?"

"Look, Keith, we're not supposed to shoot the breeze

on watch. If you have questions about the ship or the watch that's a different matter, of course."

"Sorry."

"Skipper's easygoing about it. But it's a good idea to keep your mind on the watch."

"Certainly, sir. There just wasn't much happening, so——"

"When anything happens it generally happens fast."

"Aye aye, sir."

After a while Maryk said, "There they are."

"Where, sir?"

"One point to starboard."

Willie trained his glasses in that direction. Behind the iridescent edges of the empty waves there was nothing— except—he thought there might be two, no, three, faint black points like bristles on an unshaven chin.

Maryk woke the captain. "Three cans hull down, sir, about three miles west of rendezvous."

The captain mumbled, "Okay, go to twenty knots and close 'em."

The three hairlines became masts, then the hulls appeared, and soon the ships were plain to see. Willie knew the silhouettes well: three stacks with an untidy gap between the second and third; feeble little three-inch guns; slanting flush deck; two cranes crooked queerly over the stern. They were sister bastards to the *Caine*, destroyer-minesweepers. The captain stretched, and came out to the wing. "Well, which ones are they?"

The signalman Engstrand seized a long telescope and squinted at the bow numbers. "*Frobisher*——" he said. "*Jones—Moulton.*"

"*Moulton!*" exclaimed the captain. "Look again. She's in SoPac."

"DMS 21, sir," said Engstrand.

"What do you know. Duke Sammis with us again, hey? Send 'em 'Greetings to the Iron Duke from De Vriess.' "

The signalman began blinking the shutter of a large searchlight mounted on the flagbag. Willie picked up the telescope and trained it on the *Moulton*. The three DMS's were coming closer every minute. Willie thought he saw the long sad face of Keggs hanging over the rail on the bridge. "I know someone on the *Moulton!*" he said.

"Fine," said De Vriess. "Makes the operation more cozy—— Keep the conn, Steve, and fall in a thousand yards aft of the *Moulton,* column open order."

"Aye aye, sir."

Willie had been one of Furnald Hall's champions of the blinker light. He was proud of his ability to send Morse at eight words a minute. Nothing seemed more natural than for him to take the shutter handle, when Engstrand relinquished it, and start blinking at the *Moulton.* He wanted to greet Keggs, and he also thought that his prowess at Morse might cause the captain to think a little more highly of him. The signalmen—Engstrand and two assistants—stared at him, appalled. "Don't worry, my lads," he said. "I can send." How like sailors it was, he thought, to hug their little accomplishments, and resent an officer who could match them. The *Moulton* returned his call. He began spelling out "H-E-L-L-O K-E-G-G-S— W-H-A-T A——"

"Mister Keith," said the captain's voice at his ear, "what are you doing?"

Willie stopped blinking, resting his hand on the shutter lever. "Just saying hello to my friend, sir," he replied blandly.

"I see. Get your hand off that light, please."

"Yes, sir." He complied with a yank. The captain took a long breath, expelled it slowly, then spoke in patient tones. "I should make something clear to you, Mister Keith. The communication facilities of a ship have nothing in common with a public pay telephone. Only one person aboard this ship has the authority to originate messages, and that is myself, so hereafter——"

"This was in no sense an official message, sir. Just hello——"

"Confound it, Keith, you wait till I'm through talking! Whenever this ship breaks radio or visual silence for any reason whatever, with any manner of signal whatever, that is an official communication for which I and I alone am held responsible! Is that clear, now?"

"I'm sorry, sir. I just didn't know, but——"

De Vriess turned and snarled at the signalman, "Damn it to hell, Engstrand, are you asleep on watch? This light is your responsibility."

"I know, sir." Engstrand hung his head.

"The fact that some officer happens to be uninformed on communication procedure is no excuse for you. Even if the *exec* puts a hand on that light you're supposed to kick him the hell across the bridge away from it. That happens again, you're out ten liberties. Get on the ball!"

He stalked off into the wheelhouse. Engstrand glanced reproachfully at Willie and walked to the other side of the bridge. Willie stared out to sea, his face burning. "The boor, the big stupid egotistic boor," he thought. "Looking for any excuse to throw his weight around. Picking on the signalman to humiliate me more. The sadist, the Prussian, the moron."

10 · The Lost Message

At four o'clock the minesweepers formed a slanting line, a thousand yards apart, and began to launch their sweep gear. Willie went to the fantail to watch.

He could make no sense of the activity. The equipment was a foul tangle of greasy cables, shackles, floats, lines, and chains. Half a dozen deck hands stripped to the waist swarmed about under the eye of Maryk, uttering hoarse cries and warnings larded with horrible obscenities as they wrestled the junk here and there on the heaving fantail. Waves broke over their ankles when the ship rolled, and water sloshed around the gear. To Willie's eye it was a scene of confusion and panic. He surmised that the *Caine* crew were unfitted for their jobs, and were fulfilling the ancient adage:

> *When in danger or in doubt,*
> *Run in circles, scream and shout.*

After twenty minutes of this bawling and brawling, the boatswain's mate in charge of the war dance, a chunky, frog-voiced, frantic chief named Bellison, shouted, "All set to starboard, Mr. Maryk!"

Willie, perched clear of the water on an immense steam windlass, expressed to himself a strong doubt that anything was really "set" in that heap of scrap metal.

"Keith," yelled Maryk, "get clear of that windlass."

Willie jumped into an arriving wave, soaking his trousers halfway to the knees; waded to the after-deckhouse ladder, and climbed up to see what would happen. The sailors cranked an egg-shaped paravane up on a crane. At a word from Maryk, they dumped all the gear over the side. Came clanks, rattles, splashes, yells, puffing of steam, creaking turns of the windlass, and a frenzy of running around, and a great cadenza of obscenity. Then sudden quiet ensued. The paravane was streaming neatly outward to starboard in a fanning arc, sinking slowly beneath the surface with a red float above it to mark the place. The serried cutting cable payed out from the windlass evenly. All was correct and orderly as a diagram in the mine-sweeping manual.

The wild scramble began again with the gear of the port paravane. Willie was no longer sure whether the faultless first launching had been a matter of luck or skill. When the turmoil and blasphemy reached their height as before he was inclined to attribute it to luck. But splash, grind, yowls, curses, silence—and the second paravane was streaming as neatly as the first. "I'll be damned," he said aloud.

"Why?"

Willie jumped a little at the voice. Captain de Vriess was leaning over the bulwark beside him, watching the operation.

"Well, sir, it looked pretty sharp to me, that's all."

"That was the lousiest launching I've ever seen," said De Vriess. "Hey, Steve, what in the Christ took you forty-five minutes?"

Maryk smiled up at him. "Hello, Captain. Why, I didn't think the boys did too bad, for a four-month layoff. Look, sir, none of the other ships have even started to launch."

"Who cares about those snafu buckets? We streamed at Noumea in thirty-eight."

"Sir, that was after four days' practice——"

"Well, I want it done in thirty tomorrow."

"Yes, sir."

The dirty, sweating, ragged sailors stood around, hands resting on their belts, looking singularly self-satisfied under the captain's criticism.

"Sir, it was my fault," spoke up the boatswain's mate. He began an alibi which sounded to Willie like this: "The port bandersnatch got fouled in the starboard rath when we tried to galumph the cutting cable so as not to trip the snozzle again. I had to unshackle the doppelganger and bend on two snarks instead so we could launch in a hurry."

"Well," said De Vriess, "couldn't you have vorpaled the sillabub or taken a turn on the chortlewort? That way the jaxo would be clear of the varse and you could forget about the dudelsak. It would have done the same thing."

"Yes, sir," said Bellison. "That might work okay. I'll try it tomorrow."

Willie's heart sank. He was certain that if he sailed a hundred years on the Caine he would understand such abracadabra no better than he did at that moment. "Sir," he said to the captain, "is there a standard time for launching the gear?"

"Book calls for one hour," said De Vriess. "The standard on this ship is thirty minutes. I've never been able to make these stumblebums do it. Maybe your friend Queeg will have better luck."

"That's a curious use of the word 'standard,' sir," ventured Willie.

De Vriess gave him a satiric look. "Well, that's Navy

jargon for you—— All right," he called down, "you of the minesweep detail. All things considered it wasn't too terrible a job."

"Thank you, sir," said the sailors, grinning at each other.

The other minesweepers got their gear launched and an afternoon of practice maneuvers began. Willie was dizzied by the turns and twists and changing formations. He tried hard to follow what was happening. Once he went to the bridge and asked Carmody, the junior officer of the deck, to explain the proceedings. Carmody answered with extended gibberish about Baker Runs, George Runs, and Zebra Runs. Willie gathered at last by using his eyes that the ships were pretending to be in a mine field and simulating various emergencies and disasters. A lugubrious business, he thought. The sun was low and the clouds were reddening when word came over the p.a., "Cease present exercises. Recover sweep gear." Willie at once returned to the after deckhouse, partly to learn what he could about hauling in paravanes, but mainly to enjoy the cursing of the sailors. He had never heard anything like it. There was a fine dithyrambic sweep to *Caine* obscenity in hot moments.

He wasn't disappointed. The minesweep detail worked in a fever, racing against time to get the two paravanes aboard. They kept a constant watch on the two black balls hanging on the yardarms of the other ships; the drop of a ball would mean that a paravane had been recovered. In fifteen minutes the *Caine* dropped its ball on the port yardarm; and they had the starboard paravane in sight before the *Moulton* hauled down a ball. Lieutenant Maryk worked with the sailors, stripped to the waist, pouring sweat. "Come on," he shouted, "twenty-eight minutes so far! Best yet! Let's get that damned egg aboard." But at the last moment there was a calamity. The sailor Fuller, who was pulling the little red float out of the water, juggled it and dropped it. The float bobbed away in the ship's wake, free.

The other sailors gathered around Fuller and discharged such a flood of inspired cursing that Willie wanted to applaud. Maryk sent word to the bridge. The *Caine* stopped and then backed slowly. Maryk tore off all his clothes and wrapped a line around his waist. "No sense fooling around with the gig. I'll swim for the goddamn thing. Tell the captain to stop the screws," he said to the chief, and dived over the side.

The sun had set. The float was a red dot on the purple waves, about two hundred yards off the port quarter. The sailors lined the rail, watching the first lieutenant's head slowly approach the float, and Willie heard them muttering about sharks. "I saw a goddamn hammerhead five minutes ago," Bellison said. "I'm damned if I'd swim for it. Save five minutes for the old man and get my behind snatched off———"

Somebody was tapping Willie on the shoulder. He turned impatiently. "Yes, yes, what is it?"

A radioman stood behind him with a flapping despatch in his hand. "This just came over Fox, sir. We're the action addressee. Mr. Keefer says you got the coding duty———"

Willie took the message and glanced at it. "Okay, okay. I'll break it in a few minutes." He thrust the sheet in his pocket and looked to sea. Maryk's head was barely visible now on the dark water. He had reached the float. He thrashed around in it for a minute or so, kicking up white foam, then leaped half out of the water and waved his arms. His shout came feebly on the wind, "Okay, haul in!" The sailors began to pull the wet line back aboard frantically. The float came cutting through the water with Maryk clinging to it.

Willie, tingling with excitement, scampered down the ladder to the fantail. He lost his footing on the slippery deck and fell. A wave of warm salty water broke over him, drenching him. He got himself up, spitting water, and grabbed a life line. The dripping float clanked on the deck. "Haul down the ball to starboard!" Bellison yelled. A dozen arms reached for Maryk as his head bobbed up near the propeller guard. He clambered aboard.

"Christ, sir, you didn't have to do that," said Bellison. Maryk gasped. "What was the time of recovery?"

The telephone talker said, "Forty-one, sir, when the float got aboard."

"Beat 'em all, sir," said a sailor, pointing seaward. Black balls still hung at the yardarms of the other ships.

"That's fine," grinned Maryk. "Never have heard the end of it if one of those buckets beat us." His eye fell on the bedraggled figure of Willie. "What the hell happened to you, Keith? Did you dive in, too?" The sailors noticed Willie now and snickered.

"Got too interested watching you," said Willie. "That was great work."

Maryk swept water from his broad brown chest and shoulders with his palms. "Hell, I've been looking for an excuse to take a dip."

"Weren't you worried about sharks?"

"Sharks don't bother you if you keep moving. Hell," said the first lieutenant, "I'd take a shark any day rather than the old man if Iron Duke Sammis beat him recovering sweep gear—— Come on, Keith, you and me need new clothes."

Willie dumped his sodden khakis in a heap in a corner of the clipping shack. He had completely forgotten the despatch in his pocket. There it lay, dissolving to a pulp inside the crumpled khakis, while the ship steamed through maneuvers for the next two days.

The weather was good, and with the novelty of the different minesweeping gadgets, electric, moored, and acoustic, for entertainment, Willie found himself enjoying the trip as an amused spectator. In his watches on the bridge he got on a little better with Captain de Vriess by making a mighty effort to please. Taking as his rule Tom Keefer's dictum, "How would I do this if I were a fool?" he play-acted a struggling overconscientious ensign. He stood erect for the whole four hours, peering to sea. He never spoke, except when spoken to, or to report an object he sighted through binoculars. Even if it seemed absurd to mention it—a floating log, a tin can, a spread of garbage dumped from a ship—he gravely announced it; and the captain invariably thanked him in pleased tones. The more he slipped into character as a plodding dolt, the better De Vriess seemed to like him.

On the third day the formation moved in to shallow waters near a beach and swept some dummy mines. Not till Willie saw the yellow-painted horned iron balls bobbing on the foamy blue waves did he truly realize that the fantastic rig of cables and paravanes was good for anything but races against time between the captains of minesweepers. He took a strong interest in this part of the show. Once the *Caine* narrowly missed a mine cut by the *Moulton.* Willie pictured what might have happened had the mine been a live one, and began to wonder whether he ought to wait six months before applying to the admiral for rescue.

The last sweep was completed two hours before sunset. There remained a chance that the ships could get back into Pearl Harbor before the submarine nets were closed for the night, by running for home at twenty knots. Unluckily the *Moulton,* which had the squadron commander aboard, lost a paravane in the last moments of recovery, and fished for it for an hour while the other vessels waited and the crews fretted. When the *Moulton* grappled its paravane at last the sun was setting. The four old sweepers had to steam all night outside the channel entrance in futile circles.

When they went in next morning, the *Caine* and *Moulton* were paired in one buoy berth. As soon as the gangplank was laid between the ships Willie got Gorton's permission to cross over and visit Keggs.

He was startled by the difference between the two ships the moment he set foot on the other quarterdeck. In structure they were identical. It was hardly conceivable that they could look so unlike. There was no rust here, no splashes of green prime coats. The bulwarks and decks were a clean uniform gray. The cording on ladder railings was new-white. The leather wrappings of the life line, tightly sewed, were a natural rich brown, where those of the *Caine* were frayed, hung loose, and were covered with cracked gray paint. The dungarees of the sailors were clean, and the shirts tucked inside the trousers, whereas a flapping shirttail would have been a proper heraldic device for the *Caine*. Willie saw that it was not necessary for a DMS to look like his ship; it was only necessary for the outcast *Caine* to look like what it was.

"Keggs? Sure, he's in the wardroom," said the OOD, neat as an admiral's aide.

Willie found Keggs at the green-covered table, drinking coffee with one hand and working a coding device with the other. "Hello, Keggsy boy! Knock off for a minute, for Pete's sake——"

"Willie!" The cup clattered to the saucer. Keggs jumped up and grabbed Willie's outstretched hand with both his own. Willie thought the other's hands were trembling. He was disturbed by his friend's appearance. Thin as he had been, he had lost more weight. The bones protruded from his cheeks and the pallid skin seemed to stretch with difficulty the long distance to his jaw. There were a few strands of gray in his hair which Willie had never noticed before. His eyes were ringed in blue shadow.

"Well, Ed, stuck you in communications, too, did they?"

"I relieved the communication officer last week, Willie. I've been his assistant for five months——"

"Department head already, eh? Nice going."

"Don't make jokes," said Keggs haggardly.

Willie accepted coffee and sat. After they chatted awhile he said, "Have you got the duty tonight?"

Keggs pondered foggily. "No—not tonight——"

"Great. Maybe Roland hasn't shoved off yet. We'll hit the beach and hunt him up——"

"Sorry, Willie. I'd love to, but I can't."

"Why not?"

Keggs looked over his shoulder. There were no other officers in the immaculate wardroom. He dropped his voice. "The paravane."

"The one you lost? What about it? You recovered it."

"The whole ship is restricted for a week."

"The whole ship? Officers, too?"

Keggs nodded. "Everybody."

"Why, in God's name? Who was responsible for losing it?"

"Everybody is responsible for everything on this ship, Willie—it's the way——" Keggs suddenly stiffened, sprang to his feet, and swept the coding device off the table. "Oh, God," he said. Willie saw or heard no reason for the act except a muffled door slam overhead.

"Excuse me, Willie——" Keggs frantically stowed the code machine in a safe, locked it, and seized a clipboard of decoded despatches hanging on a hook in the bulkhead. He stared at the wardroom door, gulping. Willie rose and stared, too, an uneasy fear possessing him despite himself.

The door opened and a straight thin man with scanty light hair, knitted brows, and a mouth like a puckered scar, stepped in.

"Captain Sammis, this—this—is an acquaintance of mine, sir, from the *Caine*, sir, Ensign Keith."

"Keith," said Sammis tonelessly, extending his hand. "My name is Sammis."

Willie touched the cold hand, and it withdrew. Captain Sammis sat in the chair Keggs had been using.

"Coffee, sir?" quavered Keggs.

"Thank you, Keggs."

"This morning's traffic is ready, sir, if you wish to look at it."

The captain nodded. Keggs scrambled to pour the coffee, then he drew despatches from the board and presented them for the Iron Duke's view one by one, bowing slightly each time, and murmuring a comment. Sammis inspected each despatch and handed it back to Keggs without speaking. It was a picture of flunky and master such as Willie had never seen outside of costume movies.

"I don't see number 367," remarked Sammis.

"Sir, I was breaking that down when my friend came. It's three quarters finished. I can complete it in two minutes, sir—right now if you desire——"

"What precedence is it?"

"Deferred, sir."

Sammis cast a bleak look at Willie, showing awareness of

his presence for the first and last time after the handshake. "You may wait," he said, "until your visitor has gone."

"Thank you very much, sir."

Iron Duke Sammis sipped the rest of his coffee at leisure, looking neither left nor right, while Keggs stood at his elbow in respectful silence, clutching the despatch board. Willie leaned against the bulkhead, marveling. The captain patted his mouth with a handkerchief, lit a cigarette with a flick of a gold-plated lighter, rose, and walked out.

"Banzai," murmured Willie, as the door closed.

"Sh!" Keggs shot him an imploring look and fell into a chair. After a few moments he said hollowly, "He can hear through bulkheads."

Willie put his arm compassionately around Keggs's bowed shoulders. "Ye gods, man, how did you ever let him get you so buffaloed?"

Keggs looked at him in mournful surprise. "Isn't your skipper like that?"

"Hell, no. I mean, he's a low brute in his own way, but—good God, this one is comical——"

"Take it easy, Willie," Keggs begged, glancing over his shoulder again. "Why, I imagined all captains were pretty much the same——"

"You're crazy, boy. Haven't you been on any other ship?"

Keggs shook his head. "I picked up the *Moulton* at Guadalcanal and we've been operating ever since. I haven't even been ashore in Pearl yet."

"The captain doesn't live," said Willie through his teeth, "who can make me do monkey tricks like that."

"He's a pretty good skipper, Willie. You just have to understand him——"

"You just have to understand Hitler, for that matter," said Willie.

"I'll come over to your ship, Willie, as soon as I can. Maybe later today." Keggs took the coding device out of the safe with unconcealed anxiety to get to work. Willie left him.

On the rusty littered quarterdeck of the *Caine,* by the

OOD's desk, stood a strange figure: a marine corporal in faultless dress uniform, straight as a tin soldier, his buttons glittering in the sun. "Here's Ensign Keith now," said the OOD, Carmody, to the marine. The stiff figure strode up to Willie and saluted. "With the compliments of Rear Admiral Reynolds, sir," he said, presenting Willie with a sealed envelope.

Willie opened it and read a typewritten note:

Ensign Willis Keith is cordially invited to a reception for Rear Admiral Clough at the home of Rear Admiral Reynolds tonight at 2000. Transportation will be furnished by ComCarDiv Twenty barge which will arrive at the *Caine* at 1915.

Captain H. Matson,
by direction.

"Thank you," said Willie. The marine saluted rigidly again, went through all the forms of leaving the quarter-deck with the jerkiness of an animated doll, and climbed down the chain ladder outboard to a sleek admiral's barge with a white-fringed canopy. Carmody dismissed the boatswain, and the barge purred away.

"My God," said the little Annapolis man, pulling at his mustache and regarding Willie with awe, "what kind of drag do you have?"

"Keep it quiet," said Willie jauntily. "I am Franklin D. Roosevelt, Jr., traveling incognito." He strolled off to the forecastle, the mystified stare of Carmody warming him like champagne.

Willie walked to the stem, where a cool breeze fluttered the blue starry jack. He sat on the deck, leaning against the jackstaff, and gave himself up to thorny analysis of recent scenes. What he had observed aboard the *Moulton* confused all his ideas about his own ship. In the first place, he had considered De Vriess a tyrant; but compared to Iron Duke Sammis his captain was lazily benevolent. Then, the *Moulton* was a model of naval order and efficiency, the *Caine* a wretched Chinese junk by comparison. Yet the smart ship had dropped a paravane; the

rusty tramp had led all the ships in minesweeping performance. How did these facts fit together? Was the loss
of the paravane a meaningless accident? Was the *Caine's*
working skill another accident, owing to the presence of
the fisherman Maryk? In the hybrid world of destroyer-
minesweepers all rules seemed to be confounded. The
words of Tom Keefer came back to him: "The Navy
is a master plan designed by geniuses for execution by
idiots," and "Ask yourself, 'How would I do this if I
were a fool?'" He respected the communicator's mind; he
had heard Maryk acknowledge its keenness. These maxims
must guide him, he decided, until he could piece together
his own views and make——

*"Ensign Keith, report to the captain's cabin on the
double!"* The announcement rasped through the loudspeaker, bringing him to his feet. As he ran to the wardroom he rapidly reviewed possible reasons for the summons, and guessed that perhaps Carmody had told the
captain about the admiral's barge. He knocked gaily at
the captain's door.

"Come in, Keith."

De Vriess, in trousers and undershirt, sat at his desk,
glowering at a long list of despatch headings, one of
which was circled in heavy red crayon. Beside him stood
Tom Keefer and the radioman who had brought Willie the
forgotten message three days ago. The radioman twisted
his white cap in his hands and gave the ensign a frightened
look. Keefer shook his head at Willie.

The sight told Willie all. He experienced a longing to
vanish or die.

"Willie," said the captain in a level, not unkind tone,
"three days ago this ship received a despatch addressed
to us for action. I learned this interesting fact for the
first time five minutes ago while making a routine check
of the headings of all despatches received while we were
at sea. I always do that when we come into port. These
dull habits sometimes pay off. Now, the radio shack has
orders to shoot action despatches to the coding officer the
instant they come in. Snuffy Smith here claims he gave the
message to you three days ago. Is he lying?"

The radioman blurted, "Sir, I gave it to you on the after deckhouse while they were recovering paravanes. You remember!"

"You did, Smith," said Willie. "I'm sorry, Captain. It's my fault."

"I see. Have you decoded the message?"

"No, sir. I'm sorry, but it——"

"Very well. Smith, lay up to the radio shack and bring Lieutenant Keefer the Fox sked on the double."

"Aye aye, sir." The sailor darted out of the cabin.

The "Fox skeds" were the log sheets on which all despatches sent to Navy ships at sea were copied by the radio operators. These were preserved for several months, then destroyed. Despatches concerning the ship were re-copied on separate forms. It was such a retyped form that lay moldering in Willie's khakis in the clip shack.

"The next thing, Tom," said the captain calmly, "is to break that message faster than you've ever done anything in your life."

"I will, sir. I really think there's no great cause for concern. It's routine precedence. Maybe a BuShips modification or——"

"Well, let's see, shall we?"

"Yes, sir." As the communicator walked out he said in low tones of reproach, "Good God, Willie."

Captain de Vriess paced the narrow cabin, taking no notice of Willie. Except that he puffed his cigarette faster than usual, he gave no sign of being disturbed. In a few moments the coding machine began clicking in the wardroom. The captain went out, leaving the door open, and peered over Keefer's shoulder as he whirled through the message, working from the long white Fox schedule. De Vriess took the completed decode from Keefer's hands and scanned it.

"Thank you, Tom." He came into his cabin, closing the door. "Too bad you didn't break it when it came, Mister Keith. It might have interested you. Read it."

He handed the breakdown to Willie. *Lieutenant Commander William H. de Vriess USN detached when relieved. Report to BuPers by air transportation for further assign-*

ment. Class two priority authorized. Training duty of Lieutenant Commander Philip F. Queeg has been canceled and he is proceeding to relieve at once.

Willie returned the despatch to the captain. "I'm sorry, sir. It's incredible stupidity and carelessness on my part," he said, choking over the words. "I don't know what else to say, sir, except——"

"What happened to the despatch Smith gave you?"

"It's still in the pocket of some dirty khakis. Smith handed me the despatch while Mr. Maryk was swimming for the float. I stuck it in my pocket and—I guess I became interested in the float recovery and forgot all about it. . . ." The words sounded so lame to his own ears that he blushed.

De Vriess leaned his head on his hand for a moment. "Have you any idea, Keith, how serious the mislaying of an action despatch can be?"

"Yes, sir."

"I'm not sure you have." The captain ran his hands through his hanging blond hair. "Conceivably this ship might have failed to carry out a combat assignment—with all that that entails. I hope you realize that for such failure I would have borne sole responsibility at the court-martial."

"I know, sir."

"Well, how does that fact register on you?"

"With a determination never to let it happen again."

"I wonder." The captain picked up a stack of long yellow forms on his desk. "By a coincidence which is perhaps unlucky, I've been filling out the work sheet of your fitness report this morning, together with those of the other officers. I have to submit them to the Bureau when I'm detached."

A tremor and tingle of alarm passed through the ensign.

"How do you suppose this incident ought to affect your fitness report?"

"It's not for me to say, sir. Anybody can make one mistake——"

"There are mistakes and mistakes. The margin for error is narrow in the Navy, Willie. There's too much life and property and danger involved in every act. You're in the Navy now."

"I realize that, sir."

"Frankly, I don't think you do. What just happened calls for me to give you an unsatisfactory fitness report. It's an unpleasant, dirty thing to do. These sheets lie in the Bureau forever. Everything written on them becomes part of your name. I don't like to wreck a man's naval career, even when he regards it lightly."

"I don't regard it lightly, sir. I've made a bad mistake and I'm desperately sorry. I've made that as clear as words can make it."

"Maybe now is the time to clean up your report," said the captain. He pulled out one of the forms from the batch, picked up a pencil, and started to write.

"May I say one thing more, sir?" Willie put in quickly.

"Certainly." The captain looked up, pencil poised.

"You're writing that report with this incident pretty fresh in your mind. It's bad enough, I know. But I wonder whether twenty-four hours from now your phrasing might not be a little fairer——"

De Vriess smiled in the familiar sarcastic way. "A good point. But I'll look over all the sheets tomorrow anyway before giving them to the yeoman. Perhaps I'll be feeling more charitable then, in which case I'll make the necessary changes."

"I'm not asking for charity, sir."

"Very well." De Vreiss wrote several lines in his unexpectedly neat small hand. He gave the report to Willie. Underneath *General Remarks* he had written this:

Ensign Keith seems a bright and apt young man. He has been aboard less than two weeks. He shows promise of becoming a competent officer. But he must first overcome a somewhat light and careless approach to his duties.

Above this there was a space in which was printed, *I consider this officer: Outstanding—Excellent—Above Av-*

erage—Average—Unsatisfactory. De Vriess had erased a check beside *Excellent* and moved it to *Above Average.*

This was, in Navy usage, a blackball. The fitness report was so dread an instrument that few commanding officers had the bowels to be coldly honest. As a result the average officer was judged "Excellent" on these forms. To call a man "Above Average" was to inform the Bureau that he was a nonentity. Willie knew all this. He had typed dozens of the reports at CincPac. He read the report with rising anger and disturbance. This was damning with faint praise, skillful and malicious, beyond hope of repair. He returned the sheet to the captain, trying to keep his face blank of emotion. "Is that all, sir?"

"Do you consider that summary unfair?"

"I'd rather not comment, sir. The fitness report is your province——"

"My duty to the Bureau requires as honest an opinion as I can give. That report is by no means unsatisfactory, you know. You can erase it with one good one."

"Thank you very much, sir." Willie was trembling with suppressed irritation. He wanted nothing but to leave the cabin at once. He felt De Vriess was detaining him merely to gloat over him. "May I go, sir?"

De Vriess looked at him, his expression mingling wry sadness with his habitual mockery. "It's my duty to inform you that if you feel the report is unjust you have the right to attach a letter challenging it."

"I've nothing to add to it, sir."

"All right, Willie. Don't mislay any more action despatches."

"Aye aye, sir." Willie turned and put his hand on the doorknob.

"One moment, please."

"Yes, sir?"

The captain tossed the fitness report on his desk and swiveled his chair back and forth slowly. "I think there's a matter of disciplinary action to be considered."

Willie threw a bitter look from the captain to the yellow form.

"The report, at least to my limited mind, doesn't come

under that heading," observed De Vriess. "The punitive use of the fitness report negates the value of the system and is strictly forbidden by a SecNav directive."

"That's good to know, sir." Willie considered that a bold ironic thrust, but it made no dent on De Vriess.

"I'm putting you in hack for three days, Willie—the same length of time you held up that message. Perhaps that will drive the feathers out of your head."

"I'm sorry to be ignorant, sir. Exactly what does that involve for me?"

"Confinement to your room except for meals and calls of nature—— On second thought," added the captain, "confinement to the clip shack would be cruel and unusual punishment, no doubt of that. Let's say you're confined to the limits of the ship for three days."

"Aye aye, sir."

"Well, I guess that's all."

As Willie turned to go, a thought penetrated his red haze of anger. He pulled the admiral's invitation from his pocket and silently handed it to De Vriess. The captain pursed his lips. "Well, well. Admiral Reynolds, hey? Pretty good company. How do you know the admiral?"

"I happened to meet him socially, sir."

"Why does he want *you* at this particular shindig?"

"I'm sure I don't know, sir." But this sounded too surly, so he added, "I play the piano a bit. The admiral seems to enjoy it."

"You do? I didn't know that. I play a sax myself, a little bit, when I'm home. You must be pretty good to get requisitioned by the admiral. Like to hear you play sometime."

"Delighted to oblige, sir, any time at your convenience."

De Vriess regarded the invitation, smiling. "Tonight, hey? Well, far be it from me to dampen the admiral's party. Let's say your confinement begins at 0800 tomorrow. How's that?"

"Whatever you say, sir. I don't want any special treatment."

"Well, we'll leave it at that. Have a good time tonight. Don't drown your sorrows too heavily."

"Thank you, Captain. Is that all?"

"That's all, Willie." He returned the invitation to the ensign, who turned and walked out, closing the door rather hard.

Willie dashed up the ladder and ran to the clipping shack. His course was clear to him now. His position on the *Caine* was hopeless. The new captain would read the fitness report and mark him once for all as an unreliable fool—not a fool in Keefer's sense, but in the Navy sense. There was only one thing to do: get off this cursed ship and make a fresh start. The penalty for his mistake was paid in the damning fitness report. "I can, and I will, erase that description from my record, so help me God," he swore to himself. "But not on the *Caine*. Not on the *Caine!*" He was sure that the admiral would get him transferred. Several times the great man had embraced him after a chorus of *Who Hit Annie in the Fanny with a Flounder,* and had declared that he would do almost anything to get Willie on his staff permanently. "Just say the word, Willie!" He had been joking; but it was a joke with a core of truth, Willie knew.

He dragged the qualification course from a grimy drawer in the clipping shack. He calculated the number of lessons due by this date. He spent the rest of the morning and the whole afternoon grimly filling out those assignments. After dinner he presented himself in Lieutenant Adams' room, shaved, glossy, and dressed in his last precious set of shore-laundered khakis. "Request permission to leave the ship, sir."

Adams glanced at him sympathetically. His eye moved to the four assignments in Willie's hand, and he smiled. "Granted. Give my love to the admiral." He took the assignments and laid them in his workbasket.

As Willie mounted the ladder to the main deck he met Paynter coming down with both fists full of wrinkled, moldy letters. He said, "Anything for me?"

"I dropped yours in the clip shack. This is all old stuff that chased us around SoPac for a couple of months. Just caught up with us."

Willie went aft. Sailors were milling around the mail

orderly on the quarterdeck in the twilight as he shouted names and passed out letters and packages. Four dirty weather-stained canvas sacks of mail were heaped on the deck at his feet.

Harding was lying on his bunk in the gloomy clipping shack. "Nothing for me," he said sleepily. "I wasn't on the *Caine* mailing list way back then. You sure were."

"Yes, my folks thought I was going straight to the *Caine*——" Willie snapped on the dim light. There were several old crumpled letters from May and his mother, and a few others; also a battered oblong package that looked like a book. His nerves were shocked when he saw his father's handwriting on the package. He tore it open, and found a black-bound Bible with a wrinkled note protruding from it.

Here's the Bible I promised you, Willie. Luckily I found one right here in the hospital bookstore, otherwise I'd have had to send out for it. I guess Bibles go well in hospitals. If my handwriting seems a little cramped it's because I'm sitting up in bed to write this. Everything's proceeding on schedule, I'm afraid. They're operating tomorrow. The surgeon is old Dr. Nostrand, who should know better than to try to kid me. But I appreciate his optimism only too eagerly, all the same.

Well, my son, take a look at Ecclesiastes 9:10, will you? I'll let that stand as my last word to you. Nothing more now, but good-by, and God bless you.
DAD

Willie turned to the Bible passage with shaking hands.
Whatsoever thy hand findeth to do, do it with thy might; for there is no work, nor device, nor knowledge, nor wisdom, in the grave, whither thou goest.

The words were underlined with wavering ink lines. Beside them Dr. Keith had written in the broad margin: "He's talking about your job on the *Caine,* Willie. Good luck."

Willie turned out the light, threw himself on his bunk,

and buried his face in the sooty pillow. He lay so, motion-less, for a long while, heedless of the creasing of his last shore-laundered khakis.

Someone reached in and touched his arm. "Ensign Keith?" He looked up. The admiral's marine orderly stood just outside the shack. "Pardon me, sir. The barge is at the gangway for you."

"Thank you," said Willie. He raised up on an elbow, covering his eyes with his hand. "Look, will you please tell the admiral I'm terribly sorry, but I can't come tonight? It seems I have the duty."

"Yes, sir," said the marine in a wondering tone, and departed. Willie dropped his face into the pillow again.

The next morning, Lieutenant Commander Philip Francis Queeg reported aboard the *Caine*.

They exchanged pleasant smiles, and De Vriess led his successor forward. When they were out of earshot Winston said to the officer of the deck, "Looks like a good Joe."

"For Christ's sake," said Harding, tightening his gun belt two notches, "let's see what we can do about this quarterdeck."

The two commanding officers sat in De Vriess's cabin, drinking coffee. Queeg leaned back comfortably in the low black leather armchair. De Vriess was in the swivel chair at his desk.

"Kind of sudden, this whole deal," said De Vriess.

"Well, I didn't much like being yanked out of anti-submarine school," said Queeg. "I'd moved my wife and family down to San Diego and we were all set for six good weeks, anyway. First shore billet I'd had in four years."

"I'm sorry for your wife."

"Well, she's a pretty good sport."

"They have to be." After a moment of silent sipping De Vriess said, "You're class of '34?"

"Thirty-six," said Queeg.

De Vriess knew this. He also knew Queeg's precedence number, his class standing, and several other facts about him. But it was a nice point of etiquette to simulate ignorance. It was a courtesy, too, to place Queeg by mistake in an earlier class; it implied that Queeg was obtaining a command for which he was rather young. "They're moving you fellows up now pretty fast."

"I guess they want you somewhere in pretty much of a hurry, too. New construction, I suppose?"

"I don't know. I hope they give me a supply depot in the middle of Utah. Some place with no water."

"Not much chance of that."

"Guess not." De Vriess gave a false sigh of despair. Both men were stepping gingerly around the point uppermost in both their minds: namely, that De Vriess was getting off, and Queeg getting on, an obsolete ship. De Vriess said, "Had much to do with minesweeping?"

"Not a hell of a lot. Seems to me they might have sent

me to Mine Warfare School. But I guess somebody in the Bureau had his pants on fire for some reason."

"Well, hell, you know as much as I did when I came aboard. Not a whole lot to it—— More coffee?"

"No, thanks."

De Vriess took Queeg's cup and set it on the desk. Queeg reached into his pocket. De Vriess, expecting him to pull out cigarettes, picked up a packet of matches. But Queeg brought out a couple of bright steel ball bearings the size of marbles, and began rolling them absently between the thumb and fingers of his left hand. "I imagine," said Queeg casually, "that it's mainly a matter of towing rigs of one sort and another."

"That's about all there is to it," said De Vriess, even more casually. His question about minesweeping had not been random. In the back of his mind was the conjecture that Queeg was being groomed to command the squadron. But that possibility he now ruled out. He indicated a large battered blue book in the rack above his desk. "All the dope is in BuShips 270, the *Minesweeping Manual*. You might take a look at it one of these days."

"I've read it. Seems simple enough."

"Oh, it is. Pure routine. The boys back aft are pretty fair hands at it. And your first lieutenant, Maryk, is a crackerjack. You won't have any trouble. We just ran off a very satisfactory exercise last week. Sorry you weren't aboard."

"Maryk," said Queeg. "Regular?"

"No. There are only two regulars beside yourself. The way they're hauling those boys off to radar schools and what not, you'll probably have a solid reserve wardroom by January."

"That's one against how many—twelve?"

"Ten—theoretically. The complement is eleven. We've been down to seven and up again. There'll be eleven now, counting yourself."

Queeg stopped rolling the steel balls, and began rattling them slowly in his fist. "Good bunch?"

"Not bad. Some good, some so-so."

"Made out their fitness reports?"

"Yes."

"Might I have a look-see?"

De Vriess hesitated. He would have preferred simply to talk about the officers, touching briefly on their defects and high-lighting their good points. He cast about for a diplomatic way to refuse the request, but none occurred to him. He pulled open his desk drawer. "If you want to," he said, and passed the bundle of long yellow sheets to his successor.

Queeg glanced at the first three in silence, rolling the balls ceaselessly between his fingers. "Pretty nice. This about Maryk, especially. For a reserve."

"He's one in a hundred. Used to be a fisherman. He knows more about seamanship than some chief boatswain's mates."

"Fine." Queeg read on. He flipped quickly through the sheets, ignoring the elaborate mathematical scores, glancing at De Vriess's general summary of each officer's character. De Vriess felt more and more strongly that he was abetting a kind of peeking. He was relieved when Queeg handed the reports back to him, saying, "Seems like a good wardroom, all in all."

"As good as you'll find, I think."

"What's the matter with this Keith?"

"Nothing. He's going to be a good officer. Needed a kick in the pants, and I gave it to him. I don't know but what I'll rewrite that before I shoot it in. He's willing and has a good head."

"Why did he need a kick in the pants?"

"Well, he mislaid a despatch. Not an important one, but on general principles—when he's just getting started, you know—I thought he ought to be brought up short."

Queeg pursed his lips, then smiled agreeably. "I suppose no despatch is unimportant, really."

"Well, you're right, there."

"Did your communications officer catch the mistake—this Keefer?"

"Keefer does very well. Of course no system is foolproof. He's a strange duck, by the way. Brilliant mind. A writer. Read about all the books in the world. Son of a gun's been working on a novel in off hours——"

"Did you discipline Keith?"

"Put him in hack for three days."

"How about Keefer?"

"I ought to make one thing as clear as I can," said De Vriess in a firm, pleasant tone. "I regard both those men as excellent officer material: Keith may turn into an outstanding officer after some seasoning. As for Keefer, he has brains enough to do anything superlatively, but he's older, and his interests are somewhat divided. You engage his loyalty and he'll deliver the goods. Stands a fine OOD watch under way."

"Nice to know. How are we on watch-standers?"

The far-off thumping of metal scrapers was augmented by a new sound directly overhead, a terrific clatter and clanking of another party of paint chippers. Queeg winced. De Vriess leaped up, pressed a buzzer, and roared into a brass speaking tube at the head of his bed, "Engstrand! Tell the damn deck force to stop trying to split my skull!" The two men looked at each other in wry amusement for a few deafening seconds, and the noise suddenly subsided.

"Lot of that going on," observed Queeg.

"Every time we're in port the deck boys turn to. Only way to stay ahead of the rust."

"I wonder why? Scrape her down to flat bright metal and give her a good double coat, and that ought to be the end of it for a long while."

"There isn't any flat bright metal," said De Vriess. "These decks have taken too much salt water. They're pitted. The rust starts up from a pit and just spreads under the new paint like a skin disease. It's not a bad thing. Chipping paint is good exercise. We've killed a hell of a lot of dead time for the crew chipping paint."

"How does the ship handle?"

"Like any destroyer. All the power you need. She won't turn on a dime like these new destroyer-escorts. But you can maneuver her."

"Wind take her much, coming alongside?"

"Well, you have to watch the wind."

"Good line-handling parties?"

"No kick there. Maryk has them trained up pretty fair."

"I like fast line handling."

"So do I. You've handled destroyers?"

"Well," said Queeg, "I guess I've had a few million hours as OOD under way."

"How about coming alongside and so forth?"

"Well, I've seen it done often enough. Given the orders and so forth."

De Vriess regarded his successor narrowly. "Were you exec on this *Bristol*-class destroyer?"

"Well, just a month or so. Had almost every other department—it was the *Falk*—guns, hull, black gang, communications—I was just breaking in as exec when they yanked me over to a carrier——"

"Skipper give you the conn much?"

"Well, there wasn't much chance. A few times."

De Vriess offered Queeg a cigarette and lit one himself. "If you like," he said carelessly, waving out the match, "we can take her out for a couple of runs before you take over. I can stand by while you shoot a few approaches, and getting away from alongside, and maybe some power turns and so forth——"

"Thanks, that won't be necessary."

De Vriess puffed twice on his cigarette in silence. "Well," he said, "I'm at your service. How do you want to go about this?"

"Well, I'll have to sight the registered publications and execute a transfer report," said Queeg. "Guess maybe we can do that pretty soon, like today. And I'd appreciate having a look around——"

"Let's do that this morning."

"I suppose all the reports are up to date? Let's see— logs, war diary, hull, burn reports, personnel roster, and so forth?"

"If they aren't they will be when you're ready to relieve."

"How about the Title B inventory?"

De Vriess compressed his lips.

"Well, I'm sorry to say that's pretty fouled up. I'd be kidding you if I told you anything else."

"What's the trouble?"

"The trouble is simply that this ship has steamed about a hundred thousand miles since the war started," said De Vriess, "and we've been through so many strip-ships and night actions and storms and what not that half our Title B gear is gone and we don't know where the hell it's gone to. When you lose a snatch block over the side in the middle of towing some silly bastard off a reef under air attack you just don't make the entry on the Title B card. You ought to, but you don't."

"Well, running off a fresh inventory and sending in a survey report on the lost gear would take care of that."

"Sure it would. A Title B inventory takes two weeks. If you want to wait around till we push one through, I'll be happy to get it rolling——"

"Hell, no, I can attend to it as well as you," said Queeg. "I thought maybe I'd relieve tomorrow—if I could see the registered pubs and the reports today."

De Vriess was pleased and startled. He had relieved his own commanding officer on the *Caine* in forty-eight hours; but, as executive officer, he had been fully as familiar with the ship as the captain. Queeg was stepping into a vessel of a new type, about which he knew almost nothing. He would have been justified in requesting several days at sea, in order to observe all the ship's equipment in action. De Vriess had figured that the transfer of command might take a week. But it was absolutely outside naval manners to make any comment. He rose. "Good enough," he said. "Pretty nice to think of seeing my wife in three days. How about a quick Cook's tour of the ship?"

"Okay." Queeg dropped the steel balls into his pocket.

"If I'd known you were coming," said De Vriess, "I'd have run off a captain's inspection and shined her up for you a bit. The boys can do a good job, though you may not think so to look at her now."

"Pretty cool for Hawaii, this time of year," said Queeg.

*   *   *

Willie Keith lay on his bunk in the clipping shack that afternoon, trying without success to read Kant's *Critique of Pure Reason,* which he had borrowed from Keefer. Curiosity gnawed at him; he could hardly resist leaving his self-imposed jail to have a look at the man who had come to free him from the tyranny of De Vriess. He read the same page over four times, while his mind kept wandering to the task of constructing Queeg from Harding's description, as scientists construct cave men from a piece of a jawbone.

"Mistuh Keith, suh?"

Willie looked up into the sad loose-lipped face of Whittaker, a couple of inches from his own. "Yes, Whittaker?"

"Cap'n want you in de wardroom."

Willie jumped to the deck and put on his cleanest khakis, stabbing the ball of his thumb in his hurry to change the collar pins. When he walked into the wardroom, therefore, he was sucking his thumb; a perhaps unfortunate touch of immaturity. The two commanding officers were drinking coffee at the green-covered table. "Ensign Keith," said De Vriess with sardonic formality, "Lieutenant Commander Queeg."

The new captain rose and greeted Willie with a firm handshake and a friendly smile. In one anxious glance Willie took in these details: a small man, slightly shorter than himself; natty blues with two campaign ribbons and one battle star; an oval, somewhat plump fair face with small narrowed eyes; and some strands of sandy hair across an almost bald head, with thicker fringes at the sides. "Hello, Mr. Keith," said Queeg with cordial good humor, and a gay lift in the tones.

Willie liked him at once. "How do you do, sir."

"Willie," said De Vriess, "are you all set to run off a registered pubs inventory and a transfer report? Commander Queeg wants 'em this afternoon."

"Certainly, sir."

"Not missing anything, are we?"

"No, *sir.*" Willie allowed himself a slight contemptuous emphasis. With the new captain present, power seemed to be draining out of De Vriess.

"Good." The captain turned to his successor. "He's all yours. If I can be of any further assistance, let me know."

De Vriess stepped into his cabin and closed the door. Willie turned to his new commanding officer. He could not repress a mischievous grin. "Nice to have you aboard, sir."

"Why, thank you, Willie," said Queeg, with a lift of the eyebrows, and a warm smile. "Let's get started, shall we?"

Next morning at eleven the crew lined up at quarters on the forecastle, and the ceremony of transferring command was enacted in a perfunctory way. The officers had tried very hard to make the crew look respectable for the occasion; but despite the shoeshines and new dungarees and shaved faces the general effect was that of a group of tramps freshly deloused by the Salvation Army.

After the ceremony the two commanding officers went below together. The captain's cabin was heaped with tumbled luggage of both officers. De Vriess picked his way to the desk. He opened the small safe, took out several tagged keys and some sealed envelopes, and handed them to Queeg. "Envelopes are various safe combinations you'll want to have. . . . Well, I think that's it." He glanced around the room. "I left you a stack of mysteries. I don't know if you like 'em, but that's all I can read. Distract me from whatever's bothering me. Never remember what I'm reading from one page to the next, anyway."

"Thanks. I guess I'll have all I can do to keep up with official reading for a while."

"Sure enough. Well—I'm off." De Vriess cocked his head and looked his successor in the eye. Queeg met the glance for a moment, then offered his hand to De Vriess.

"Best of luck with your new construction."

"If I get it. You've got a good ship here, Queeg, and a good crew."

"I hope I'm up to handling it."

De Vriess grinned, and said hesitantly, "I'm wondering if you don't think it's a pretty sloppy lash-up."

"Oh, I quite understand," said Queeg. "You've been in a forward area a hell of a long time———"

"It isn't that. You can do things with some ships that

you can't do with others," said De Vriess. "Between you and me, these damn buckets ought to be melted down to razor blades. They roll and pitch too damn much, the power plant is shot, all the machinery is obsolete, and the men are crowded like animals. These are the only fire-rooms left in the Navy where the black gang has to work under air pressure. If anything goes wrong a blowback can kill them all. The men know the kind of deal they've got. The strange thing is, most of the crazy bastards like it. Damn few of them put in for transfers. But they have to do things their own way. It's the hooligan navy, to look at them. But give them a chance, and they deliver. They've backed me up in some bad spots——"

"Well, thanks for the dope," said Queeg. "Is the gig standing by for you?"

"I think so." De Vriess ground out his cigar, and opened the door. "Whittaker! How about bearing a hand with my gear?"

Willie was at the gangway, buckling on his gun belt, when two steward's mates came up with the bags, followed by De Vriess.

"Where's the gig, Willie?"

"Oh. I didn't think you were shoving off till four, sir. I just sent it over to the *Frobisher* to trade movies. It'll be back in ten minutes. Sorry, sir."

"No harm done. Drop the bags here, men."

"Yassuh," said the steward's mates. "Good-by, Captain."

"Don't bring the new skipper any of that cold coffee up to the bridge."

"Nosuh." The colored boys grinned.

De Vriess put his foot up on a life line and stared out over the harbor. He looked strangely impressive in dress blues. Sailors chipping paint on the quarterdeck threw curious glances at him and exchanged low remarks. Willie, oppressed by a heavy gap of embarrassment between himself and his ex-captain, felt obliged to make conversation. "How does it feel, sir?"

"How does what feel?" said De Vriess, not looking at him.

"Well, leaving the ship after—how long—over five years, isn't it?"

De Vriess bent his head sidewise and inspected Willie coldly. "Happiest damn moment of my life," he growled.

"I hope you get a good ship, sir."

"It's about time I had one." De Vriess walked away. He paced aft to the fantail, looking down at his shoes. A knot of chiefs and petty officers appeared in the port passageway by the galley. They watched the ex-captain as he came forward again. The oldest chief, a fat, ham-faced water tender named Budge, whose belly bulged over his underslung belt, stepped up to him. "Pardon me, Captain."

"What now?"

Budge took off his greasy khaki cap, revealing a bald head, fumbled with the cap and put it on again. "Well, nothing, sir. Except a few of the guys chipped in and got this." He hauled a long flat box out of his pocket, and opened it, displaying a silver wrist watch. De Vriess stared at the watch, and then looked around at the fidgeting sailors.

"Whose idea was this?"

"Well, everybody's, sir."

"Well, everybody's a damn fool. I can't accept it. It's against Navy Regulations."

Budge glanced helplessly at the others. "I told them that, sir. But we thought——"

A tall, tousle-headed shipfitter, De Lauche, spoke up, "You don't always go by regs, sir——"

"That's my goddamn trouble," said De Vriess, "I've been in the hooligan navy too long."

Budge scanned the captain's unfriendly face, awkwardly juggled the open box, and set it on the dirty screen cover of a ventilator. "We meant it for the best, sir——"

The dinging of a bell and the asthmatic cough of a motor announced that the gig was coming alongside. "You guys take an even strain with the new skipper," said De Vriess. "You chiefs and first-class P.O.'s run the ship, as you know damn well. Keep the men in line and give things a chance to break in——" He turned to Willie. "I am leaving the ship, sir."

"Aye aye, Captain." They exchanged salutes.

De Vriess put his hand on the ladder. His eye fell on the watch, glittering in the sun. "Whaddya know," he said. "Some silly bastard left a watch lying around." He picked it out of the box and strapped it on. "Might as well steal myself a souvenir of this old bucket. Not a bad watch, at that," he said, glancing at it critically. "What time is it, Mister Keith?"

"Four o'clock, sir," said Willie.

"Three-thirty," grunted De Vriess, adjusting the hands. "I'll always keep it half an hour slow," he said to the sailors, "to remind me of the fouled-up crew of the *Caine*. Somebody toss down my gear."

He began to descend the ladder, and went out of sight. Then his head and arms reappeared. He looked up at the sailors and threw them a salute. "Thanks," he said, and dropped down into the gig. The bags were lowered; the boat pulled away. Willie watched it go, expecting to see De Vriess take a long lingering farewell look at his ship. But he did no such thing. The last Willie saw of the ex-captain, he was slouched on the cushions under the canopy, reading a paper-bound mystery.

"Attention on deck!" called the gangway petty officer.

Willie turned, stiffening. Captain Queeg, dressed in khaki shirt and trousers, was coming out of the starboard passageway. He looked different without the double-breasted blues. He had surprisingly narrow, sloping shoulders, and was hollow-chested and potbellied. His forehead was furrowed, and there were three deep vertical wrinkles in the center; his eyes squinted as though he were trying to see a long distance. Willie saluted. Queeg, peering around at the quarterdeck, ignored the gesture. "Gig gone?"

"Yes, sir."

"Willie, you're out of hack as of now. Amnesty, you might say."

"Thank you, Captain," Willie said warmly.

Queeg stopped at the gangway desk and cast his eye here and there, rolling the steel balls absently in his left hand. The sailors worked busily and without talking, heads bent. Queeg glanced down at the quartermaster's log. "Captain de Vriess hasn't been logged out."

"I was about to do that, sir," spoke up Engstrand, the gangway petty officer.

"Very well. Note the exact time of departure."

"Aye aye, sir."

Queeg watched Engstrand write the notation. The back of the signalman's blue dungaree shirt was stenciled in red, *Killer Engstrand. Hands off.* The captain said, "Mr. Keith."

"Yes, sir."

"Pass the word to your relief that while we're in Pearl the gangway watch will be stood in undress whites."

This was the uniform of the watch on the *Moulton,* and on most of the destroyers Willie had seen. The order pleased him. The *Caine* was being restored to the Navy, with no time lost. "Aye aye, sir," he snapped.

Queeg resumed his scrutiny of the ship, ceaselessly rolling the balls, his shoulders lowered, his head moving to and fro. "Okay," he said. "Pass the word. Meeting of all officers in the wardroom at 1630."

"Aye aye, sir. Shall I get a chief to stand by for me? I'll still have the watch then——"

"Have chiefs been standing OOD watches in port?"

"Well, yes, sir——"

"Never mind getting a chief. You're excused from the meeting." The new commanding officer of the *Caine* walked off toward the port passageway. "Get a couple of your prisoners-at-large with some turpentine," he said over his shoulder to Willie, "and have this mess cleaned up." He pointed to the remains of the morning's oil stain.

"We have no prisoners-at-large, sir."

"Oh? . . . Well, then, the deck force. Get it cleaned up." Captain Queeg went forward.

12 · The New Order

At four-thirty the officers of the *Caine* were all seated around the wardroom table, except for Keith, Gorton, and the captain. Keefer and Maryk were drinking coffee. The others smoked or drummed their fingers on the green baize. Nobody spoke. The room was unnaturally tidy for that time of day. The magazines and paper-bound novels were racked, and the coding devices usually scattered on the table were absent.

"This is known in literature," Keefer remarked in a low tone, stirring his coffee, "as a pregnant pause."

"Go easy on the smart talk for a while, Tom," murmured Adams.

"I'm simply observing," said Keefer, "that our new captain has a sense of drama. I thoroughly approve."

"Knock it off," whispered Maryk, as the knob of the captain's door turned. Gorton came out and looked around the table. "All present, Captain," he called through the open door. Queeg entered the wardroom. With a scrape of chair legs the officers stood. The *Caine* officers had not performed this courtesy in a year; several of them had never done it; but they all rose instinctively.

"Sit down, sit down, gentlemen," said Queeg in a light, joking tone. He sat in his chair, laid a fresh pack of cigarettes and a packet of matches in front of him, and looked around with a smile as his officers took their seats. He tore open the pack deliberately, lit a cigarette, and took the two steel balls out of his pocket. Rubbing them softly back and forth in his fingers, he began to speak. Occasionally he glanced up at their faces; otherwise he kept his eyes on the cigarette or the steel balls.

"Well, gentlemen, I just thought we ought to get acquainted. We're going to be shipmates for a long time. You're probably wondering about me, and I confess I'm a little curious about you, though I've formed some pretty good first impressions. I think this is a fine ship with a splendid wardroom of officers. I think we're going to have a good cruise, and, I hope, as Captain de Vriess put it, some good hunting. I intend to give you every co-operation, and I expect the same in return. There is such a thing as loyalty upward, and such a thing as loyalty downward. I desire and expect to get absolute loyalty upward. If I do, you'll get loyalty downward. If I don't—well, I'll find out why, and I'll see to it that I do." He laughed, indicating that this was a joke, and the officers nearest him smiled.

"Now, there are four ways of doing a thing aboard ship—the right way, the wrong way, the Navy way, and my way. I want things on this ship done my way. Don't worry about the other ways. Do things my way, and we'll get along—— Okay. Now, are there any questions?"

He looked around. There were no questions. He nodded with smiling satisfaction. "Now, I'm a book man, as anyone who knows me will tell you. I believe the book is there for a purpose, *and* everything in it has been put in it for a purpose. When in doubt, remember we do things on this ship by the book. You go by the book and you'll get no argument from me. You deviate from the book and you better have a half dozen damn good reasons—*and* you'll still get a hell of an argument from me. *And* I don't lose arguments on board this ship. That's one of the nice things about being captain." He laughed again, and received the same smiles. Keefer was slowly shredding a cigarette as he listened.

"I want you to remember one thing," Queeg went on. "Aboard my ship, excellent performance is standard. Standard performance is sub-standard. Sub-standard performance is not permitted to exist. Now, Rome wasn't built in a day, and this ship has been sailing a hell of a long time without me, and as I say, I regard you as a splendid wardroom of officers. If there's anything that I want changed in anybody's department you'll find out about it fast enough. Meantime you will go on with your duties as before, remembering, as I say, that on my ship excellent performance is standard."

Keefer dropped the shred of the cigarette slowly into his coffee cup.

"Well, now that I've shot my face off," said Queeg, "I'll give anyone else who wants to the chance to do the same. . . . Nobody? Okay. Then let's have taut watches beginning as of now, if you feel that in any way you haven't been standing taut watches. And let's have a taut ship. *And,* as I say, remember about loyalty upward and loyalty downward, and about excellent performance being standard. And, as I say, I regard you as a fine set of officers, and it's a privilege to be in a wardroom with you, and—and let's keep it that way. And that's all I have to say. And I thank you, and"—he laughed once more, an informal laugh that dismissed any tinge of martial austerity in what he had said—"all ashore that's going ashore."

He rose, picking up his cigarettes. The officers stood. "Don't get up, don't get up," he said. "Thank you all." He went into his cabin.

The officers looked around at each other. After a moment's stillness Gorton inquired, "Anybody got anything on his mind?"

"When is the gig shoving off for the beach?" said Keefer.

"At 1800," said Gorton. "I'm glad you asked, because you'll have the gangway then."

"In a pig's eye," said Keefer genially. "I'll be in the gig. I've got me a date with a college graduate from the OWI office. She knows words of two syllables. It promises to be a highly intellectual evening, after life on the *Caine.*"

"Well, in words of one syllable, you're a dead duck," said Gorton. "New watch-standing orders. Four officers aboard at all times in port. Me or the captain, and all three—repeat, all three—officers of the duty section. I believe your section has the duty?"

Keefer looked around and said, "Okay. Who's standing by for good old Tommy?"

"I'll take it, Tom," said Maryk.

"Thanks, Steve. I'll do the same——"

"Sorry, boys," put in Gorton. "No stand-bys."

Keefer gnawed at his lips, scowling. Barrow rose, polishing his fingernails on his gabardine lapel. "I can take a dictionary along in the gig, Tommy," he said daintily, "and bone up on two-syllable words. Does she know how to say 'Gladly'?" There was a bark of male laughter from all the officers.

"Oh, look, Burt," pleaded Keefer. "It's absolutely pointless. We're standing a cold-iron watch. There's nothing to do but log vegetables aboard. Hell's bells, in Tulagi we didn't keep four aboard, with the Tokyo Express running every night."

"Tom, I have never heard anything more persuasive," said Gorton. "Your arguments move me to tears. Now will you go in and straighten out the captain?"

Carmody yawned and put his head on his hands. He said sleepily, "I see where the great American novel gets another chapter written tonight."

Keefer rose, uttered a short, blistering obscenity, and went to his room. He picked up the volume of Aurelius from his cluttered desk, and flung himself on his bunk. For ten minutes he read the soothing stoicisms of the Roman emperor. Then Gorton poked his head into the room.

"Skipper wants to see you. Put on your saddle and report to the sawdust ring."

"With pleasure," growled Keefer, leaping out of his bed.

Captain Queeg was standing at the washbasin in his room, shaving. "Hello, hello, Tom," he said. "Be with you in a minute." He did not invite Keefer to sit. De Vriess had also ignored that formality with his department heads. They had been in the habit of dropping into the armchair without being asked. Keefer was not sure of his ground with Queeg. He leaned against the captain's bunk, and lit a cigarette to show that he was not overawed. Queeg scraped away at his lathered face, humming. He wore only short drawers, and Keefer inspected with secret amusement the unprepossessing figure: flat hairless white chest, bulging little round stomach, and pallid skinny legs.

"Lousy light," remarked Queeg, squinting at his image in the mirror. "A wonder De Vriess didn't cut his throat."

"We can get you a brighter bulb, sir."

"Well, I don't think that will be necessary—— Tell me, Tom, what do you think of your assistant, Keith?"

"Willie? He's a good kid."

"I mean, as an officer?"

"Well, he has a lot to learn, like any ensign. He'll be fine."

"I'm not interested in what he'll be. As of now, I agree with you that he's a nice kid—and also extremely immature. Particularly for a custodian of registered publications."

Keefer said hastily, "Sir, I'm certain Keith can handle that assignment to perfection——"

"What training has he had for it?"

"Training?"

"I understand you had five months in communication school."

"Yes, sir. But you don't need that to——"

"Has he studied the registered publications manual?"

"I assume that in V-7 school they gave them the basic——"

"You can't assume a *damn thing* in the Navy, Tom," said Queeg sharply, shifting his eyes to Keefer's face and away again. "Could he pass a test on that manual this afternoon?"

"Well, without warning——"

"Could *you?*"

"I certainly could," snapped Keefer, offended.

Rinsing his razor, Queeg said pleasantly, "I'm sure of it. That's why I think you should resume the duties of custodian."

"But, sir——"

"The boy obviously knows nothing about classified stowage, Tom. Why, secret pubs are jammed and flopped around in that safe like garbage. And he has pubs in the radio shack, pubs on the bridge—not a single custody receipt to show for them, either. Is that *your* idea of registered stowage, hey?"

It was exactly Keefer's idea, as a matter of fact. Willie had inherited an appalling mess, but the novelist had airily laughed, saying, "This isn't a battleship, Willie. Forget about that custody-receipt malarkey. We're all pals together on the *Caine*." The ensign had innocently believed him.

Keefer said, "Well of course, sir, things could be a bit more ship-shape—I'll get on his tail——"

"Nothing doing. You *relieve* him."

"Sir, pardon me, there isn't a ship in this squadron with a full lieutenant as custodian—it's an ensign's collateral duty—always is——"

"Well, I don't want to be unreasonable about it," said Queeg. "How long do you think it would take you to train up Keith as a custodian?"

"A few days, a week at most, and Willie can know that manual by heart."

"Fine. We'll let it go at that."

"Aye aye, sir. Thank you."

"Don't get me wrong," said Queeg. "Meantime I want you to relieve him. This evening."

"What! And go through an inventory and a transfer report? And then, again, in reverse, three days from now?"

"We have lots of time and transfer forms."

"Sir, a department head who's a top watch-stander doesn't have an infinite amount of time. If you expect efficient performance of my main duties——"

"I expect efficient performance of all your duties. This business may cut into your novel-writing a little. But of course, none of us is aboard to write novels." In the poisoned silence that followed, Queeg opened his drawers. They slid to the deck, and he kicked them into a corner. "Well," he said cheerfully, picking up a towel, "I hope the shower has hot water."

Keefer said in a slow, strangled tone, "Sir, do you object to my working on a novel?"

"Not at all, Tom," said Queeg, taking a faded blue bathrobe out of his narrow closet. "An outside interest of an intellectual kind is recommended for all officers, as a stimulant to clear thinking and alertness."

"Fine," said Keefer.

"So long as your department is in every respect up to the mark, of course," said Queeg. "I mean all reports up to date, all changes entered, all correspondence cleared, all enlisted training at the maximum, your own training accomplished, and, in general, everything so perfectly in hand that nothing remains to be done in your spare hours. Until such time, I think the Navy has first call on you."

"I don't suppose there are many officers in the Navy who can say their departments are in such shape——"

"Not one in a hundred, maybe. The average officer nowadays is lucky if he can keep abreast of his work and get six hours' sleep a night. I guess that's why we don't have many novelists in the Navy," said Queeg with a giggle. "But Captain de Vriess described you as a man of exceptional ability and I have every reason to hope that his judgment was sound."

Keefer put his hand on the doorknob. "Don't rush off," said the captain, unwrapping a soap cake. "Like to talk a bit more."

"I thought you were going to take a shower, sir."

"Well, we can still talk. Come along.

"Now, Tom, what kind of radio guard are we standing at the moment?" he shouted over the drumming of the water on the metal deck of the shower room.

A conference during a shower was new to Keefer. He pretended not to hear Queeg. After a moment the captain turned around, glowering from under his eyebrows as he soaped his groin. "Well?"

"I can't hear you very well over that water, Captain."

"I said what kind of *radio guard* are we standing?"

Two hours earlier, Keefer's chief radioman had reported to the communications officer that Queeg had been in the shack, minutely cross-examining him about the radio guard. The new captain had been violently displeased to learn that they were merely copying local harbor broadcasts. So Keefer phrased his answer carefully. "Well, sir, we're following standard Pearl Harbor procedure. We copy the harbor circuit."

"What!" Captain Queeg looked amazed. "How about the Fox schedule? Aren't we guarding that?" He lifted his leg and soaped underneath it.

"We pick up the skeds from the *Betelgeuse*. They guard for all destroyers in port. It's standard procedure," shouted Keefer.

"You needn't scream. I hear you. Standard procedure for whom? For destroyers in the same nest as the *Betelgeuse*? We're an hour away by motor whaleboat. What happens if an urgent despatch comes through for us?"

"They're supposed to give it to us at once over the harbor circuit."

"Supposed to. And suppose they don't?"

"Look, Captain, suppose the *Betelgeuse* blows up? Suppose *we* do? You have to assume certain normal conditions——"

"You can't assume a *goddamned* thing in this Navy," said Queeg. "Get that idea out of your head. Nothing will be assumed on this ship from now on, not a *goddamned thing.*" He rinsed the soap from his body and shut off the water. "Hand me that towel, please." Keefer complied.

"Now listen, Tom," said the captain, in pleasanter tones, rubbing himself with the towel, "in this Navy a commanding officer gets a chance to make one mistake—just one mistake, that's all. They're just waiting for me to make that one mistake. I'm not going to make that mistake, and nobody on this ship is going to make it for me. I can keep my own radio gang from doping off, if it takes six months' restriction apiece, and breaking them all to seaman second class, to wake them up. But I can't do anything about some silly ape who dopes off on the *Betelgeuse*. Therefore I won't have the *Betelgeuse* standing guard for me. We'll stand our own guard, and we'll stand it around the clock, and we'll stand it beginning as of now. Is that clear?"

"That's clear, sir."

Queeg looked at him amiably. "Say, how about coming to the club with me and having a few?"

"Sorry, sir. Under the new watch orders I have to stay aboard."

"Oh, damn," said the captain regretfully, as though he and Keefer were both victims of a silly rule. "Well, another time. Say, I'd like to read your novel one of these days. Has it got plenty of sex in it?" He giggled hopefully.

Keefer said, "Will that be all now, sir?"

"That's all, Tom," said Queeg, shuffling down the passageway.

The communications officer went into his room. He lay back on his bunk and picked up Aurelius. He lit a cigarette and took quick, deep puffs. Soon he lay in a cloud of gray curling smoke, reading.

Willie Keith came to the quarterdeck at eleven o'clock that night, looking for Keefer. The gangway petty officer, spruce and surly in white uniform, told him that the OOD was inspecting the forward lines. Willie walked out on the breezy forecastle and found Keefer sitting on a folded blanket, his back against the anchor, his feet dangling over the side, his gun belt lying on the deck. He was smoking, and staring up at the black starry night. "Hi," said Willie.

"Hi."

"Busy?"

"Not very. Composing a sonnet."

"Sorry to disturb you."

"Not at all. It's a stinking sonnet. What can I do for you?"

"I've been hitting that registered pubs manual for three hours. I think I've got the first part memorized."

"Well done."

"Mind if I go over and visit my friend on the *Moulton?*"

"Go ahead."

"I looked in on Mr. Gorton to ask him. But he was asleep."

"Hell, you don't need the exec's permission to visit in the nest. Shove off."

"Thanks. Lots of luck with the sonnet."

In the immaculate wardroom of the Moulton several officers were sitting around in dejected attitudes, reading magazines or drinking coffee, but Keggs was not among them. Willie went up the passageway to Keggs's room, and pulled aside the green curtain. His friend was slumped at the desk, snoring, his long face resting on a pile of unfolded blueprints. The desk lamp was shining directly upon his closed eyes. His hands dangled awkwardly, the knuckles brushing the deck. Willie hesitated, then touched Keggs's shoulder. The ensign started up wildly, with a gasp. He glared at Willie in horror for a moment, then recognition dawned and he greeted his friend with a sweet, sad smile. "Hello, Willie."

"What the hell are you studying blueprints for?" said Willie.

"I'm taking an engineering course."

"Engineering? You're a deck man."

"Skipper's got all the engineering men studying deck and all the deck men studying engineering. Makes us rounded officers, he says."

"That's great," said Willie, "providing you don't have to run a department and stand watches and fight a war—— I thought we could play a game of chess, maybe."

"Jesus, I'd love it, Willie," said Keggs cautiously. He peeked out into the passageway. "Looks like the coast is clear. I'm game. Come on." They went into the wardroom. Keggs took down a board and a box of red and black plastic chessmen, saying to a pudgy lieutenant, "When will he be back?"

"Not before midnight, I guess," mumbled the lieutenant, who was slouched almost horizontal in an armchair, gazing dully at a ragged *Life.*

"This is great, Willie. Glad you came over. Say, the hell with it. Let's have a couple of cokes."

"Sure."

Keggs disappeared into the pantry and emerged in a moment with two frosty bottles. "Anybody else?" he queried, looking around. Most of the officers ignored him. Two of them turned lackluster eyes on him and shook their heads. "If I drink another coke," said the sloucher in the armchair, "I'll go into shock."

Willie said, "You fellows still restricted?"

"Till Sunday," said Keggs.

"When we'll probably get a despatch," said the sloucher, "to proceed to Truk and sweep mines."

As Willie set up the chessmen, Keggs took a long pull at the coke bottle. "Ah, this is a great coke. I feel good. You guys mind if I turn on the radio?" Nobody answered. He switched on a blast of jazz. "Hot dog. For a change, no Hawaiian music. Get those men ready, Willie. I'm going to take your pants. Breep-de-broop, breep-de-broop——"

He danced as he sang, a queer angular jig, his elbows stuck out, his arms dangling. The lieutenant in the armchair regarded him with a mixture of disgust and pity. "It's amazing," he said, "what a cat nap will do for that poor fagged-out son of a bitch."

Keggs dropped into the chair opposite Willie and moved the red king's pawn. "Look, Willie, just remember this. When you hear a buzzer ring twice, that's it. Game's over. That's the signal from the gangway that he's come back on board. Just disappear, like the rest of us. Use the starboard passageway and you probably won't run into him——"

"Suppose I do run into him?"

"Be nonchalant," spoke up the lieutenant in the armchair. "Kiss his behind and stroll off whistling *Anchors Aweigh.*"

"How's your new skipper?" said Keggs.

"A human being, for a change."

A couple of the officers yawned, stretched, and went to their rooms. "This is wonderful," said Keggs, draining his coke. "We should do this more often, Willie."

The wardroom door opened, and Iron Duke Sammis entered, followed by Queeg. Keggs was unperturbed. He moved a bishop and looked up, grinning. Then he saw the other officers getting to their feet, their faces dead blank. He uttered a strangled, sorrowful neigh and leaped up, overturning the chessboard. The chessmen bounced and clattered all over the deck.

"Gentlemen," said Iron Duke Sammis, "this is Commander Queeg, the new commanding officer of the *Caine*. Good evening, Mr. Keith."

"Good evening, sir. Good evening, Captain," said Willie.

"Well, I'm glad to see I own a chess player," said Queeg. "I've always wanted to pick up the game."

"Wonderful relaxation," said the Iron Duke. "Too bad it eats up so much time. I haven't shot a game since the war started. But since my communicator seems to have the leisure, I may go in for it again——"

"Sir, all tonight's decodes are on your desk," said Keggs tremulously, "and I did two and a half engineering assignments this evening——"

"Could you interrupt your game long enough to let Captain Queeg and myself have a little fresh coffee?"

"Yes, sir. Certainly, sir."

The two captains went into Sammis' cabin. Keggs ran to the pantry and came out with Silexes full of clear water.

"What the hell," said Willie, "are you a steward's mate, too? Where's your burnt cork?"

"Easy, Willie. I'm wardroom mess treasurer. It's quicker to make it myself than to go roust out a mess boy, that's all." He began to pick up the chess pieces.

"Game's over, I take it."

"Oh, hell, yes."

"Well, I'll stick around for some of that coffee—if I'm allowed to drink from the same bowl as the gods."

Keggs looked over his shoulder at the captain's cabin. "Sure, stick around. But please, Willie, don't say those things—he hears."

When Willie left Keefer on the forecastle to go to the *Moulton*, the communications officer stared skyward for a while, then took a pad, pencil, and flashlight from his pocket and began to scribble verses. In a few minutes the dim figure of Maryk came up the forecastle. Greeting Keefer morosely, the first lieutenant pulled open a narrow hatch forward of the anchor engine, reached his hand inside, and turned a switch. A shaft of yellow light rose from the hatch. Keefer said, "What goes on in the paint locker, this time of night?"

"Title B inventory."

"Are you still at that? Sit down for a second, you beast of burden."

Maryk scratched his round, close-cropped head, yawned, and accepted a cigarette. The light streaming up from the paint locker accentuated the lines of fatigue in his face and the puffy creases under his eyes. "Well, it's going to be a close call," he said, "but I think I'll make it by 0900 Friday. What are you doing—working on your book?"

"Well, doing a little writing."

"Maybe you better secure on that stuff for a while, Tom —at least while you're on watch—until this new skipper gets squared away."

"What the hell is an eight-to-midnight gangway watch in Pearl, Steve? We ought to have one petty officer and a messenger, and that's all."

"I know. But this bird is fresh off a carrier."

"What do you think of him?"

Maryk puffed at his cigarette, and a worried, thoughtful expression came over his face. He had ugly, yet not unpleasant features: a wide mouth, a small nose, protruding brown eyes, and round, heavy jaws. His massive body gave him an air of power and determination, weakened by the gentle, good-natured puzzlement visible now in his face. "I'm not sure."

"Better or worse than De Vriess?"

Maryk paused and said, "Captain de Vriess wasn't a bad officer."

"For crying out loud, Steve. He ran this ship like a garbage scow. Stand her up against the *Moulton*——"

"Pretty good ship handler, though."

"Sure. Is that all being a captain means? I think Queeg's what the doctor ordered for the *Caine*. I wouldn't be surprised if someone in ServPac alerted the Bureau to send us a red-hot book man, to clean things up."

"Well, I don't know if you can change the nature of a ship overnight. I've been aboard a lot longer than you, Tom. Everything gets done that *has* to get done—not the

Navy way, maybe, but it gets done somehow. She gets under way, she goes where she has to go, the gun crews shoot pretty good, the engine plant holds together—Christ knows how, mostly with baling wire and chewing gum—but the *Caine* has spent less time getting repaired than any other four-piper I know of, since the war started. What's Queeg going to do, except try to get things done by the book, instead of the *Caine* way? Is that an improvement? All De Vriess cared about was results."

"The book way is the right way, Steve. Let's face it. I don't like it any more than you, but it's true. The wastage, and lost motion, and plain dumb luck by which things get done on the *Caine* are simply staggering."

"I know." Maryk's face became more perplexed. They smoked in silence for a while. "Sure, the book way is the right way," spoke up the first lieutenant, "for the right ship. By the book, though, the *Caine* should be in the boneyard. Maybe this ship has to be run screwy because it's screwy for her to be afloat at all——"

"Look, Steve. Your trouble is the same as mine, except that I see through it. We're civilians, free citizens, and it burns us to be treated as dumb slaves by these Queegs, who are the most colossal ignoramuses in the world except for their book. Don't forget one thing. Right now, the book is all that matters, because of the war. Look. Suppose all of a sudden the whole survival of America hung on shining shoes. Never mind how. Suppose it did. What would happen? All of us would become shoeshiners, and the professional bootblacks would take over the country. Well, how do you think the bootblacks would feel toward us? Humble? Hell, no. They'd figure that at last they'd come into their own—that for the first time in their lives the world was showing a proper respect for shoeshining. And by God, they'd lord it over us, and find fault, and nag, and crab, and bully us to shine shoes their way. And they'd be *right*. That's the story, Steve. We're in the hands of shoeshine boys. It's irritating when they act as though we're fools and they know all wisdom—it hurts to take orders and guff from them—but it's their day. Pretty soon all the shoes will be shined, the war will be over, they'll be nickel-and-dime bootblacks again, and we'll look back and laugh at the whole absurd interlude. The point is, if you understand it now, you can be philosophic, and take anything that comes——"

The gangway petty officer came trampling up the forecastle. "Mr. Keefer, the captain has returned aboard, and Mr. Gorton wants to see you in his room. On the double."

"Gorton? I thought he was asleep."

"He just phoned up from the wardroom, sir."

Keefer rose, hitching his gun belt and yawning. "Flash red, no doubt."

"Skipper missed you at the gangway," said Maryk. "Good luck, Tom. Remember your philosophy."

"Sometimes I get so bored," said Keefer. Maryk jumped down into the paint locker.

In the wardroom Keefer found the executive officer in his underwear in an armchair, drinking coffee and looking sleepy, mussed, and cross. "Jesus, Tom," Gorton said. "How much trouble can one guy cause in one day? Why the hell weren't you at the gangway when the skipper came aboard?"

"Why, you young fat fraud," said Keefer. "You, who broke me in to watch standing, and slept through every in-port night watch you had until you became exec——"

Gorton slammed down the cup and saucer on the arm of the chair. Coffee splashed to the deck. "*Mister* Keefer, we are not discussing anything but tonight's watch," he said, "and be careful of your tone in addressing me."

"Hold on, Burt. Take an even strain. No offense meant. Did the old man eat you out?"

"You're damned right he did. Do you secure your brains when you're not writing your goddamn novel? The first night a new skipper is aboard, can't you be a little careful?"

"Sorry. I did think of it, but I got to talking to Steve and forgot to watch the clock——"

"Well, that's only half of it. What the hell is Keith doing over on the *Moulton?*"

Keefer's face crinkled in disgust. "Oh, Burt. That's too

much. Since when is the duty section not allowed to cross the gangplank to the ship alongside?"

"Since always. Read the standing orders again. Why didn't he check out with me?"

"He looked in on you. You were asleep."

"Well, he should have waked me up."

"Burt, anybody waking you up with such a fool request before tonight would have gotten a copy of *Snappy Stories* in his puss."

"Well, tonight's another night. We're back on standing orders, and no kiddling——"

"Okay, okay, that's simple enough. Just so we know about it——"

"Meantime," said Gorton, looking down into his empty cup, "you're restricted to the ship for twenty-four hours."

"What!" flared Keefer. "Says who?"

"Says me, God damn it," snapped the executive officer. "Good enough?"

"Not by a long shot. If you think you can suddenly pull regs on me that have been dead-filed for two years, and start slapping me with penalties——"

"Shut up!" said Gorton.

"I have a date tomorrow night. It's the one I broke tonight, and I'm not breaking it again. If you don't like it tell the skipper I defied you, and recommend a general court-martial——"

"You stupid bastard, do you think I'm the one who's restricting you? Get this through your thick Reserve head, *the heat is on.* I'll be the guy everybody will hate. That's okay. I'm the exec of this ship, and I'll carry out my orders, do you hear?"

A radioman poked his pale face into the wardroom. "Pardon me, Mr. Keefer, do you know where I can find Mr. Keith? He doesn't seem to be anywhere——"

"What's up?"

"Priority, action *Caine.*"

Keefer took the despatch sheet. "Okay, Snuffy." The radioman withdrew. Gorton said, "Who's the originator?"

"ServPac."

The exec's sullen face lit up. "ServPac? Priority? Could be a stateside convoy run. Break it, for crying out loud."

Keefer started decoding; he had deciphered about fifteen words when he stopped, muttered a curse, and resumed the work with all eagerness gone.

"Well, what's the dope?" said the exec.

"Convoy run, all right," said Keefer listlessly. "But you're a little matter of 180 degrees off in direction."

"Oh, no," groaned Gorton. "No."

"Yes, indeed," said Keefer. "The *Caine* is going to Pago Pago."

13 · The Best Goddamned Target-towing Ship

Next day Willie went to his post on the bridge as junior officer of the deck shortly after sunrise. It was a lovely morning, bright and fragrant. The harbor was blue, and the surrounding hills of Oahu a soft yellow-green, flecked here and there by the fat shadows of puffy clouds which drifted over the north mountains, evaporating on the fairweather side of the island without shedding rain. Willie was full of fresh eggs and coffee. The lively zest that comes over a ship's company upon getting under way— no matter where bound—infected him. Pago Pago was far behind the combat zone, almost as safe as Hawaii, but at least it lay southwestward, and it was Somerset Maugham country. Romantic adventure seemed to be opening before him at last. Perhaps there would be encounters with submarines, he thought, and he could begin to redeem himself for his months of piano playing in Pearl Harbor.

Captain Queeg came up to the bridge, brisk and smiling,

with a pleasant greeting for each sailor and officer. Willie recognized the narrow blue book under his arm: *On a Destroyer's Bridge,* a manual of ship handling. "Good morning, Captain. All lines singled up, sir," Willie said, saluting smartly.

"Ah, good morning. Thank you, thank you, Willie." Queeg leaned over the bulwark, taking a quick look at the mooring lines. The *Caine* was tied to the *Moulton,* which was secured fore and aft to buoys. The two ships lay in the far corner of West Loch, a narrow inlet of the harbor. Ahead, astern, and to starboard there were muddy shallows. The *Caine* had a few hundred yards of dredged channel in which to maneuver its way out of the corner.

"Tight squeeze, hey?" Queeg said jovially to Maryk and Gorton, who stood together on the port wing, awaiting with interest the new captain's first demonstration of ship handling. The two officers nodded respectfully. Queeg called, "Take in all lines!"

The manila ropes came snaking aboard the *Caine.* "All lines taken in, sir!" said the telephone talker.

"Kay." Queeg glanced around the wheelhouse, wetted his lips, dropped the book on the chair, and said, "Well, let's go. All engines back one third!"

The ship vibrated, and things began to happen so fast that Willie couldn't tell exactly what went wrong or why. As the *Caine* moved backward the sharp fluke of the decked anchor came ripping down along the forecastle of the other ship, bending several stanchions and ripping two out by the roots. It then gashed a jagged hole in the *Moulton's* bridge with a ghastly metallic screech. At the same time a gun on the galley deckhouse went battering along the *Moulton's* side, carrying way two ammunition boxes and an antenna, which squealed and crunched and then fell into the water. Captain Queeg shouted a tangle of wheel and engine orders; the stacks vomited billows of black smoke which poured down on the bridge; there ensued a few moments of wild yelling and running around in the smoky gloom. Then it was all over. The *Caine* was stuck fast by the stern in the mud on the other side of the loch, canted over about ten degrees.

In the shocked quiet that followed, Captain Queeg seemed the least disturbed person on the bridge. "Well, well, beginner's luck, hey?" he said smiling, as he peered astern. "Mr. Gorton, lay aft and find out if there's been any damage." He sent a blinker message to Captain Sammis apologizing for the mishap. The executive officer returned in a few minutes, staggering on the slanted deck, and reported that there was no visible damage to the hull, and the propellers were buried in mud to their hubs.

"Kay, a little mud bath never hurt a propeller," Queeg said. "Shine 'em up a little, maybe." He was looking out toward the harbor.

"Guess we'll have to send a grounding report despatch to ServPac, Captain," Gorton said. "Shall I——"

"Maybe we will and then again maybe we won't," Queeg said. "See that tug? Over there by the point? Give him a call on your blinker light."

The tug obligingly turned out of the main channel and came chugging into West Loch. A towline was soon rigged, and the *Caine* was easily pulled off the mud. Queeg shouted his thanks through a megaphone to the tug captain, a grizzled chief boatswain, who waved cordially and steamed off. "So much for that," Queeg said affably to Gorton. "And so much for your grounding report, Burt. No sense getting old ServPac in an uproar over nothing, hey? All engines ahead one third."

He conned the ship confidently across the harbor to the fueling dock where they were to spend the day taking on oil, food, and ammunition. He stood on the starboard wing, steadily rolling the two steel balls in the fingers of his right hand, his elbows hanging on the bulkhead. Coming alongside the fueling dock, he gave everybody on the bridge a bad scare. He tore in toward the dock at a sharp angle at fifteen knots. Gorton, Maryk, and Willie huddled together on the wing behind him, exchanging pallid looks. A crash with the stern of a tanker in the berth ahead of theirs seemed inevitable. But in the very last seconds Queeg backed down emergency full, and the *Caine* slowed, shuddering fearfully, and dropped into its berthing space as neatly as a New York taxicab parking. "Kay," said

Queeg as the mooring lines flew over to the dock. "Double up all lines. Out smoking lamp and commence fueling." He dropped the balls into his pocket and sauntered off the bridge.

"Jesus," Willie heard Maryk mutter to the exec, "a wild man from way back."

"Shifty as hell, though," Gorton murmured. "How about the way he dodged that grounding report? De Vriess would never have dared——"

"Why the hell didn't he get his stern out before we left the *Moulton?* Wind on the beam outboard——"

"Christ, Steve, first time out—give him a chance——"

That afternoon Willie interrupted his coding to write off a letter to May, the last before the start of the voyage. He filled it with warm affectionate descriptions of how badly he missed her, and he praised her doughty persistence in going to Hunter College. He felt impelled to write something about Queeg, though up till now he had remained purposely vague about life on the *Caine.*

> Our new captain is a rather strange man, like most of these regular officers, but I think he's just what the ship needs. He's a strict perfectionist and a hard taskmaster, and pure Navy through and through. Yet at the same time he has a remarkably pleasant disposition. He seems to be a very daring seaman, maybe a little inexperienced, but full of zip. All in all I think the *Caine* has had a wonderful change in luck, and I expect my spirits are going to improve accordingly. I've really been pretty low . . .

A radioman knocked at his open doorway. "Pardon me, Mr. Keith. Action from ComServPac. Just come over the harbor circuit."

"Sure, give it here." Willie went to the coding machine and broke the despatch. *A written report is desired explaining grounding of Caine this morning in West Loch. Include explanation of failure to report grounding via despatch to this command.*

Willie had very little desire to face Captain Queeg with

this unpleasant message, but there was no way to avoid it. He brought the decode to the captain's room. Queeg was sitting in his underwear at the desk, working over a pile of official mail. When he read the message he sat upright with a loud squeak of the swivel chair. He stared at the sheet for a long time while Willie tried to think of a good excuse to sneak out of the room.

"Fussy so-and-so, this ComServPac, hey, Willie?" Queeg looked at him sidewise.

"Wonder how he got the dope, sir——"

"Hell, nothing hard about that. Damn mustang on that tug just skipped on home and reported the whole thing. First useful duty he's performed in a month, no doubt. I might have thought of that——" Queeg picked up the balls from his desk and rolled them rapidly, eying the despatch. "Well, hell, he wants a grounding report. We'll give him a grounding report. Spruce up, Willie, and stand by to deliver it by hand. Seems to have his pants on fire for some reason."

"Aye aye, sir."

Riding to the ComServPac building on the yard bus an hour later, Willie's curiosity about the grounding report became too strong for him. The manila envelope was closed only by a flexible metal clasp. He glanced from side to side in an automatic guilty gesture; none of the passengers were watching him. He slid the report out of its envelope on his lap and read it.

Grounding of USS CAINE (DMS 22) in West Loch, 25 September 1943—Report on.

1. Subject vessel ran slightly aground on mudbank in subject area on subject date at 0932. It was floated off by YT 137 at 1005. There were no casualties or damage.
2. The reason for the grounding was failure of the engine room to respond in time to engine orders telegraphed from the bridge.
3. This command has recently been relieved. The state of training aboard is believed to warrant a dras-

tic drilling program to bring performance of crew up to proper standards. Such a program has been instituted.

4. It was intended to submit a grounding report in full tomorrow morning by messenger. Report was not made by despatch to ComServPac at the time because help was at hand, damage was nil, and the matter appeared to be disposable without troubling higher authority unnecessarily. Regret is expressed if this estimate was erroneous.

5. It is believed that the intensive drilling already instituted in this command will rapidly bring about competent performance, and such incidents will not recur.

PHILIP FRANCIS QUEEG

That night at the officers' club in the Navy Yard the *Caine* wardroom had a drinking party to celebrate their departure from Pearl. Captain Queeg joined his officers for an hour or so before moving on to another party of lieutenant commanders in the patio. He was full of jocular good humor, drank faster than anybody else without becoming fuzzy, and entertained them with long anecdotes about the invasion of North Africa. Good feeling ran high. Willie was more convinced than ever that BuPers had sent the *Caine* a prince of a skipper to replace the sour sloven, De Vriess. He snuggled down in the clip shack at three in the morning, feeling that his term aboard the minesweeper was going to be pretty good, after all, while it lasted.

He was shaken out of his sleep by Rabbitt when day was just dawning. "Sorry to bother a man with a hangover, Keith," the OOD said, "but we just got an action from ComServPac."

"Right, Rab." Willie pulled himself wearily out of the clip shack and went to the wardroom. While he was clacking away at the coding machine Gorton came out of his room naked and watched over his shoulder, yawning. The words formed one by one: *Caine departure Pago Pago canceled. Moulton replace Caine convoy duty. Caine remain Pearl target-towing duty. Obtain towing gear target repair base.*

"Now what the hell?" said Gorton. "What kind of quick switch is that?"

"Ours not to reason why, sir——"

"Hope that goddamn grounding didn't—— Well." Gorton scratched his bulging belly. "Okay, put on your asbestos suit and take it in to the skipper."

"Think I ought to wake him, sir? Reveille's only——"

"Hell, yes. Right away."

Willie disappeared into the captain's cabin, and the executive officer paced the wardroom, chewing his lips. In a couple of minutes the ensign came out, grinning. "Well, it didn't seem to faze the skipper any, sir."

"No? What did he say?"

"Why, he just said, 'That's fine, fine. Nobody can get me mad by switching me to Pearl Harbor duty. The more the merrier.' "

Gorton shrugged. "I guess I'm crazy. If he's not worried, no reason why I should be."

Through the loudspeaker came the shrill boatswain's piping of reveille. Gorton said, "Well, time to retire. Call me if anything else comes in."

"Aye aye, sir." Willie left.

The exec went into his room, wallowed into his bunk like a big pink bear, and dozed off. The captain's buzzer brought him sharply awake an hour later. He threw on a bathrobe and went to Queeg's cabin. He found the captain sitting cross-legged on his bunk in his underwear, unshaven and frowning. "Burt, take a look at the despatch on my desk."

"I saw it, sir, while Keith was breaking it——"

"Oh, you did, hey? Well, that's something we can start knocking off right now. Nobody, repeat *nobody,* will have access to action despatches except the coding officer and myself until such time as I release them. Is that clear?"

"Yes, sir. Sorry, sir——"

"Kay, kay, just so's you know," Queeg grumbled. "Well, if you've seen it, what do you make of it?"

"Well, sir, it seems to me we tow targets instead of going to Pago Pago——"

"Do you take me for an idiot? I can read English, too. What I want to know is, what does it mean? Why the changed orders?"

Gorton said, "Sir, it bothered me, too. But according to Keith, you were perfectly satisfied——"

"Hell, I'd rather stay here in Pearl any day than go moseying out west—if there's no more in it than meets the eye. That's what I'm beginning to wonder about. I want you to get dressed and haul yourself over to Com-ServPac. Find out what this is all about."

"From whom, sir—the operations officer?"

"I don't care from whom. You can go to the admiral for all I care. But don't come back without *the* dope, understand?"

"Aye aye, sir."

The office building of Commander, Service Squadron Pacific, was a U-shaped white wooden structure atop a hill behind some warehouses in the Navy Yard. Lieutenant Gorton appeared there at eighty-thirty, dressed in his cleanest, newest khakis, with gleaming fresh collar pins. He went to the operations office and, not without misgivings, presented himself to Captain Grace, a fierce-looking old officer with a square red face and heavy white eyebrows.

"What can I do for you, Lieutenant?" Grace growled. He was sipping coffee from a paper cup. He looked as though he had been at his desk since dawn.

"Sir, I'm here with regard to your despatch 260040 to the *Caine*."

The operations officer picked up a loose-leaf file of despatches on green tissue paper and flipped through them. "What about it?"

"Well, sir—I—I wonder if you can tell me why our orders were changed."

Captain Grace wrinkled his nose at Gorton. "You're the commanding officer?"

"No, sir. Exec."

"What!" The operations officer banged the despatch file to his desk. "What in blazes does your skipper mean, sending you over to question orders? You go back and tell your captain—what's-his-name——"

"Queeg, sir—Lieutenant Commander Queeg——"

"You go tell Queeg that if he has any inquiries about operations he's to come here in person, and not send subordinates. Is that clear?"

"Yes, sir."

"That's all." Captain Grace picked up a letter and made a show of contracting his heavy white eyebrows over it. Gorton, bearing in mind Queeg's injunction not to come back without *"the* dope," nerved himself for one more try.

"Sir—pardon me—did the change have anything to do with our grounding in West Loch yesterday?"

Captain Grace looked as startled at the sound of Gorton's voice, speaking after being dismissed, as though he had heard an ass bray in his office. He turned and stared at Gorton's face for perhaps thirty very long seconds. Then his eyes shifted to Gorton's Annapolis ring, and he stared at that for a good long while. Then he stared at Gorton's face again, shook his head incredulously, and turned to the letter. Gorton slunk out.

At the gangplank of the *Caine* the OOD, Carmody, saluted the exec and said, "The captain wants to see you in his cabin the minute you return aboard, sir."

Gorton went below and knocked at the captain's door. There was no answer. He knocked louder, then cautiously turned the knob and peeked into a black room. "Captain? Captain?"

"Oh. Come in, Burt." Queeg switched on his bed light and sat up, scratching his stubbly face. He reached to the shelf over the bunk and took down the two steel balls. "Well? What's the dope?"

"I don't know, sir. The operations officer wouldn't tell me."

"What!"

Gorton, perspiring, described the interview with Captain Grace. Queeg glowered at the rolling balls.

"And you let it go at that, hey?"

"I didn't see what more I could do, sir. I was practically thrown out——"

"Did you think of snooping around among some of the ensigns on the staff?"

"No, sir."

Queeg turned his head to glare briefly, then resumed looking at the balls. "Well, why didn't you?"

"I——" Gorton was baffled by the question. "Well— I——"

"I'm not delighted," said the captain after a silence. "When I send an officer out for *the* dope, I expect him to return with *the* dope, and to use whatever ingenuity is called for to get it—— That's all."

He lay back on his pillow. Gorton said diffidently, "Will you be going down there, sir? I'll arrange transportation——"

"Maybe I will and then again maybe I won't," said Queeg. "I don't appreciate being placed in the position where I might get read off like a midshipman for the stupidity of the *Caine's* engine-room personnel——" There was a knock at the door. "Come in!"

Signalman Third Class Urban entered, carrying a despatch board in one hand and his frayed hat in the other. His dungarees were faded and streaky, and his shirt hung outside his trousers. He was an undersize roly-poly sailor with a round, red, perpetually puzzled face. "Visual from ComSerPac, Cap'n."

Captain Queeg took the board and read: *Caine under way 29 September 0600. Pick up target and operation order at target repair base.*

"Kay," said the captain, initialing the despatch and returning the board to the sailor.

"Thank you, sir." Urban scuttled out.

"Now," said Queeg, rattling the balls in his fist, "that's another thing I want knocked off right away, Mr. Gorton."

"What, sir?"

"You know damn well what. Since when do uniform regulations permit the crew to wear their shirts outside their trousers? They're sailors, not Filipino bus boys."

"Aye aye, sir," said Gorton resignedly.

"Aye aye, sir, hell!" snapped Queeg. "I'm serious about this, Burt. You will make the following announcement in the plan of the day tomorrow. 'Hereafter all shirts will be tucked inside trousers. Failure to comply will result in heavy disciplinary action.' "

"Yes, sir," said Gorton. "They've been doing it for years on this ship. I don't know if we can change them overnight——"

"Those are *orders*," said Queeg, "and sailors don't have to be changed overnight to obey orders. If there's any trouble we'll hand out a few captain's masts, and if necessary we'll hand out deck courts, and if necessary we'll hand out general court-martials for defiance of orders—but there will be no more flapping shirttails on my ship! Is that clear?"

"Yes, sir."

"And I want a meeting of all officers in the wardroom at 1300."

"Aye aye, sir." The exec went out, closing the door softly. Captain Queeg lay back on his bed and stared at the green overhead. Rub, rub, rub, rub, went the little steel balls.

The officers of the *Caine* sat around the green table, chatting in low tones, a ring of perplexed, sullen faces. "Two wardroom meetings in a week," said Keefer aside to Maryk. "De Vriess didn't have two all the time he was captain."

"Take it easy, Tom," muttered Maryk.

"I'm just beginning to wonder, that's all," said Keefer, very low.

Gorton came out of Queeg's room. "The captain, gentlemen."

All the officers rose. Keefer slouched, his hands in his pockets. Captain Queeg entered at a businesslike pace, head down, rolling the balls as usual. "Kay," he said. "Kay, gentlemen." He sat, and the officers did, too. He pulled out a fresh package of cigarettes, opened it, took out a cigarette, lit it, and laid the cigarettes and matches carefully on the table.

"Gentlemen," he said at last, looking out from under his eyebrows at the empty air over the table, "I regret to say that I am displeased."

His eyes shifted momentarily from side to side, taking in the faces around him, and he resumed his stare at nothing. "I am displeased, gentlemen, because I have told you that on my ship I expect excellent performance to be standard—and—well, it isn't standard. No, it isn't standard. You all know what I'm talking about, so I won't embarrass the department heads by going into particulars. Perhaps some of you feel that in your departments excellent performance *is* standard. Well, in that case, I'm not addressing you. But those whom the shoe fits—well, they'd better get on the ball, that's all.

"Now, as you know, this ship was supposed to go to Pago Pago. Well, this ship isn't going to Pago Pago. This ship is going to stay at Pearl Harbor and tow targets. Nice, soft, pleasant duty. The only question is, why have we been favored so generously by ComServPac?

"Well, your guess is as good as mine. A naval officer isn't supposed to speculate about his orders. He's supposed to execute them. That's exactly what I intend to do, and don't kid yourselves about that!" He looked around at blank faces. "Kay, any questions? No? Then I assume you all know exactly what I'm driving at, is that correct? Kay. Now I would like to point out that there are only two possible reasons why we got our orders changed. Either ComServPac decided that this ship is so outstanding that it deserves some extra-nice duty—*or* ComServPac decided that this ship is so lousy that it might not be competent to carry out an assignment in the forward area. Can anybody here suggest any other possible reason?

"Kay. Now, I'm not saying which I think it is. But if this ship is not outstanding now it had damn well better become so P.D.Q., meaning pretty damn quick. Now, it happens I had occasion to report to ComServPac recently that the engineering performance of this ship was below par, and it's entirely possible that that's why our orders were changed. But as I say, a naval officer is supposed to execute his orders, not speculate about them, and that's how it's going to be on this ship!"

Keefer was seized with a fit of coughing. He bent double over the table, his shoulders shaking. The captain glanced at him in annoyance.

"Sorry, sir," gasped Keefer, "some smoke went down the wrong way."

"Kay," said Queeg. "Now I want you gentlemen to remember that anything that's worth doing at all is worth doing well—and furthermore on this ship what's difficult we do at once, and the impossible takes a little longer, and—— Now, our duty for the next few weeks seems to be target towing. Well, we're just going to be the best goddamn target-towing ship this Navy has ever seen, and—— And as I say, we're supposed to execute our orders, not speculate about them, so let's not worry about anything that's happened. As far as the grounding of the ship is concerned I feel that I'm not responsible for the state of training in which I found the ship, and I'm certain that ComServPac will see eye to eye with me on that and so—that's that. But I am damn well responsible for anything that happens on this ship from here on in. I don't intend to make a single mistake *and*—I won't tolerate anybody making any mistakes for me, and I kid you not. And, well, I think you get the idea without my drawing you a picture, and—oh, yes, I knew there was something else." He looked about and said, "Who's the morale officer?"

Glances of puzzlement traveled around the table. Gorton cleared his throat. "Ha—hem. Captain, an ensign named Ferguson had that as collateral duty last I knew. It seems to me it was never reassigned when he got detached——"

Queeg shook his head slowly, and rasped the balls in silence for several moments. "Kay," he said. "Mr. Keith, as of now, you're the morale officer, in addition to your other duties."

"Aye aye, sir."

"Your first task is to see to it that every man on this ship begins to tuck his shirttail inside his pants."

Willie looked startled.

"I don't want to see a flapping shirttail again while I'm captain of this ship, I don't care what steps you take. You can be as tough as you please. I'll back you to the limit. If we want these men to start acting like sailors we've got to make them start looking like sailors. Woe betide the officer during whose watch I see a sailor with a flapping shirttail—and woe betide that sailor's department head—and woe betide the morale officer. I kid you not.

"Well, gentlemen, that concludes my business, and, as I say, let's get excellent performance established as the standard around here, and—and has anybody got any comment to make? No? You, Gorton? You, Maryk? You, Adams? . . ." In this way he went around the table, darting a forefinger at each officer. They shook their heads, one after another. "Fine. In that case I can assume that you all fully understand and enthusiastically support what I've said today, is that correct? And—well, that's all I have to say, and—and remember that we are now running the best goddamn target-towing ship in the Navy, and—and let's get on with the ship's business."

All the officers rose for the ceremony of the captain's withdrawal. "Kay, kay, thank you," he said, and hurried off into his room.

During the next two weeks, the "best goddamn target-towing ship in the Navy" carried out several towing assignments without mishap.

Queeg's ship handling underwent a striking change after the brush with ComServPac. His dashing first manner disappeared, replaced by painful inching toward a dock or away from it. The exaggerated caution fretted the nerves of the crew, who were used to De Vriess's spirited ease and accuracy. But there were no crashings or groundings.

Willie Keith posted a long notice in the crew's quarters, headed: *Morale—Smart Seamanlike Appearance as an Improver of*. In five paragraphs of rolling prose he asked the crew to tuck in their shirttails. Much to his amazement, he was obeyed; the flapping tails vanished. He read his notice over and over, in a proud agony of authorship, and decided that he had a literary gift which could move men's souls. This was optimistic. The crew, wise as wolves, knew perfectly well where the order came from. They were walking softly with their new captain. For the *Caine* had fallen on fat days; a stretch of Pearl Harbor duty was the dream of all the destroyer sailors in the Pacific. It meant fresh fruit in the pantry, and milk, and cream, and steaks, and revelry by night in the bars and byways of Honolulu. Nobody wanted to be restricted to the ship for the small luxury of a hanging shirttail.

The trouble started one morning when there was a fog. Captain Queeg came on the bridge at dawn and saw nothing but a blue blur, dimly relieved by yellow blotches of lamps on the dock. The air was muggy and smelled of mildew. "The hell with this," the captain snorted. "Secure special sea details. We'll get under way when this mess is gone. The sun'll dry it up."

But the blue turned light gray, then a drizzly white, and the channel echoed with the mournful, irritated hoots of foghorns, and the clock stood at 0815. From the bridge, the cranes on the fantail could barely be seen; beyond that was blank whiteness. Captain Queeg had been pacing the bridge for an hour, muttering. "Stand by to get under way," he snapped at last.

Sounding fog signals, with the engines at dead slow, the *Caine* backed out into the channel. The dock was swallowed in drifting mist. The blind ship floated in a steamy void, rocking, and around it the foghorns suddenly seemed louder. They bawled and screeched from every direction, as hard to place as crickets in a dark cellar. Queeg ran from wing to wing, straining his eyes at the dripping blank windows and at the tumbling mists astern. His jaw was slack; his lips trembled. "Get out of my way, God damn it," he yelled at Willie on the port wing, and the ensign leaped backward.

All at once a blast shattered the air, a tremendous fog-horn apparently right on top of the *Caine*. Willie bit his tongue in sudden fright. Queeg came racing past him, bawling, "All engines stop! Who sees it! Where is it? Doesn't anybody *see* anything?" He ran past Willie again and again, circling the bridge in frenzy four times, stopping each time for an instant in the wheelhouse to yank the foghorn cord. Again the big horn blasted, and a monstrous shadowy shape, a tanker, loomed through the fog, slipped past the *Caine's* stern, and disappeared.

"Whew!" said Queeg, arresting his orbit beside Willie. He went to the charthouse door. "Navigator, how about giving me a course here? What the hell is the holdup?"

Gorton looked up from his chart in surprise. The course from this point was 220 degrees straight to the target base. Captain Queeg knew it as well as he. "Aye aye, sir, I——"

"What do you mean, aye aye, sir? *What's the course?*" squeaked the captain, pounding his fist against the iron bulkhead.

Gorton stared at him. "Sir, I didn't think you wanted a course until we turned around——"

"Turned around?" exclaimed Queeg. He glared at Gorton for a moment, then rushed into the pilothouse and issued the engine and rudder orders to turn the ship around. In a moment the minesweeper began to shudder as its screws pounded in opposite directions. The circle of gleaming green numbers on the black face of the gyroscope compass ticked steadily counterclockwise and the heading increased: 95 degrees, 100, 105, 120, 150. Queeg watched the compass intently for a few moments. Then he said to the helmsman, "Call out every twenty degrees of course change," and ran out on the wing. Maryk, with both hands gripping the bulwark, was squinting out into the mist. The water was visible now around the ship for a couple of hundred yards, and overhead the whiteness had become dazzling.

"I think she's breaking up, sir," said the first lieutenant.

"About time," growled Queeg, panting a little.

"Heading 180," called the helmsman, a gunner's mate second class named Stilwell. He was tall, and had thick straight black hair and sensitive boyish features. He gripped the wheel and stood with his legs apart, eyes fixed on the gyrocompass.

"I guess maybe we'll get out of here today yet," said Queeg. He called to the navigator's shack, "What's the course to the gate, Tom, 220?"

"Yes, sir."

"Heading 200," called the helmsman.

The foghorn blasts were diminishing in number, and stretches of black water could now be seen around the ship. "Bet she's clear up at the channel entrance already," said Maryk.

The helmsman called, "Steadying up on 220, sir."

"WHAT?" yelled Queeg. He dived into the pilothouse. "Who gave you the order to steady up?"

"Sir, I thought——"

"You thought! You *thought!* You're not being paid to think!" the captain screeched. "You just do as you're goddamn told and don't go thinking—*please!*"

The helmsman's legs were trembling. His face was white and his eyes seemed to be popping from his head. "Aye aye, sir," he gasped. "Shall I come left again——"

"Don't do ANYTHING!" Queeg screamed. "What course are you on?"

"Tu—tu—two-two-five, sir, coming right——"

"I thought you steadied on 220——"

"I stopped steadying, sir, when you said——"

"For Christ's sake will you stop telling me what I said? Now, you come *left* and steady on 220!! *Is that clear?*"

"Aye aye, sir, l-left and steady on 220."

"Mr. Maryk!" shouted the captain. The first lieutenant came running into the wheelhouse. "What's this man's name and rating?"

"Stilwell, sir, gunner's mate second——"

"If he doesn't watch himself he'll be *seaman* second. I want him relieved and I want an experienced man at this wheel hereafter when we're in the channel, not a green stupid idiot——"

"He's our best helmsman, sir——"

"*I want him relieved, do you hear——*"

Willie Keith put his head in. "Something looks like a battleship, dead ahead, Captain, three hundred yards!"

Queeg looked up in horror. A vast dark bulk was bearing down on the *Caine*. Queeg opened and closed his mouth three times without uttering a sound, then he choked out, "All engines back full—bah—bah—belay that——— All stop."

The order had barely been countermanded when the battleship slipped down the starboard side of the *Caine*, hooting angrily with perhaps ten feet of open water between the hulls. It was like a steel cliff going by.

"Red channel buoy, one point port bow," called down a lookout from the flying bridge.

"No wonder," said Maryk to the captain. "We're on the wrong side of the channel, sir."

"We're not on the wrong side of *anything*," snapped the captain. "If you'll tend to your business and get another helmsman, I'll tend to my business and conn my ship, Mr. Maryk!"

The *Caine* suddenly drifted through a gray curtain into sparkling sunshine and green water. The way was clear to the target repair base, in plain view about half a mile down-channel. The fog lay on the channel astern like a pile of cotton.

"Kay," said Queeg. "All engines ahead one third." He reached a shaking hand into his trousers and brought out the two steel balls.

The atmosphere on the bridge remained unpleasant long after the shore sank from sight and the *Caine* was steaming peacefully over calm blue water. It was the first time the new captain had burst out against a sailor; and it was the first time in the memory of anyone aboard the *Caine* that a helmsman had been summarily relieved. It wasn't even clear to the crew what Stilwell had done wrong.

Willie, relieved of the watch when the ship left the channel, went to the clipping shack and told Harding the story. "I may be crazy. I hope I am," he said. "It seemed to me that the captain just lost his head in the fog, and got scared, and took out his scare on the handiest sailor."

"Well, I don't know," said Harding from directly beneath him, lying back and smoking. "A helmsman isn't supposed to steady up without an order."

"But he knew the captain wanted course 220. He heard

him say so to the navigator. Isn't a sailor ever supposed to use his head?"

"Willie, it takes time to get used to a new captain's ways, that's all."

The delicate question arose, when Stilwell's turn came to relieve the wheel that afternoon, whether he had been banished perpetually from the bridge, or merely dismissed from his post for that one time. He asked his chief petty officer; the chief asked Lieutenant Adams; Adams asked Gorton; and Gorton reluctantly decided that he would have to ask Queeg.

The *Caine* at that time was steaming placidly on a straight course, the target trailing in its wake a mile behind, and on the horizon to starboard a division of destroyers was deploying into position for the last firing run of the afternoon. Gorton approached the captain and asked him about Stilwell. Queeg laughed pleasantly and said, "Hell, of course let him stand his watch. I've got nothing against the boy, he seems like a clean-cut sailor. Anybody can make a mistake. Just tell him not to go doing things to the helm without orders."

Stilwell came up to the bridge at a quarter to four dressed in brand-new dungarees and a newly bleached white hat. He was freshly shaved and his shoes were shined. He saluted the captain smartly. "Ah, good afternoon, good afternoon, Stilwell," said Queeg with a smile. The gunner's mate took the wheel, and studied the compass with painful concentration, trying to keep the ship from drifting even half a degree off course.

Over the TBS, the short-wave speaker in the wheelhouse, the squadron leader of the destroyers spoke up: "Gwendolyn, Gwendolyn, this is Tarzan. Ready to commence final run. Out."

"Two-block Baker!" called the captain.

The signalman ran the red flag to the yardarm. Yellow flashes appeared all along the leading destroyer. Splashes shot up near the target as the boom of the five-inch guns came rolling over four miles of water. Again and again came the salvos, and then the second ship in line began firing.

Willie Keith was lolling on the fantail with his shirt off, enjoying the show and acquiring a sunburn. His lazy thoughts were of May Wynn, of walks through snow and rain along Broadway, of long languorous kisses in taxi-cabs——

"Ensign Keith, report to the bridge on the double!"

When a note of emotion managed to filter through the public-address system, as it did in this strident announcement, the effect was frightening. Willie jumped to his feet, put on his shirt, and scuttled up the main deck. A horrid sight confronted him on the bridge. The little moon-faced signalman, Urban, stood at cataleptic attention, his face frozen in lines of fear. His shirttail hung outside his pants. On one side of him stood the captain, glowering out to sea and rolling the balls. On the other side was Keefer, nervously twisting the lenses of his OOD binoculars.

"Ah, the morale officer," said Queeg, turning sharply as Willie approached. "Mr. Keith, have you any explanation for the appearance of this sailor?"

"Sir—I—I didn't know——" Willie turned on the signalman. "Didn't you read my notice?" he said as fiercely as he could.

"Ye-yes, sir. I just forgot, sir. I'm sorry, sir——"

"Well, damn it," said Willie, "the least you can do is tuck in your damned shirttail now!"

"Sir, the captain won't let me," bleated Urban.

Willie glanced at the captain. "Of course not," said Queeg irritably. "First I wanted you to see what a lousy job you were doing, Ensign Keith, and——"

"Gwendolyn, Gwendolyn, this is Tarzan," came from the wheelhouse. Queeg ran inside and seized the receiver.

"This is Gwendolyn. Go ahead."

"Gwendolyn, cease present exercise and return to base. Well done. Out."

"Roger, thank you, out," said Queeg. He turned to the helmsman. "Right standard rudder."

"Right standard rudder, sir," said Stilwell, with a glance

at the captain that showed all the white of his eyes. He spun the wheel hard.

The captain went out to the starboard wing. "Kay. Now, first of all, Keith, do you or don't you have an explanation for this?"

"Sir, I was on the fantail, and——"

"I didn't ask for an alibi! I'm talking about your failure to carry out my orders, and impress this ship's crew with my desires regarding uniforms!"

The *Caine,* responding to the helm, swung around in a wide arc to the right. The target and towline, lagging behind on the turn, drifted up the starboard side.

"Kay," said Queeg, "you will submit a written report, Mr. Keith, explaining this failure."

"Aye aye, sir."

"Now then, Mr. Keefer," said the captain, wheeling on the officer of the deck, who was watching the target. "Have you any explanation for the fact that the first man to violate my uniform orders is in your department?"

"Sir, there are limits to what a department head can do while he has the deck——"

"Well, there are no limits," shrilled Queeg, "to the duties of the officer of the deck! He is responsible for every goddamned thing that happens aboard ship during his watch, every goddamned thing!"

The ship was swinging in a circular path. The target and towline were well forward of the beam. The helmsman was staring at the target, his mouth gaping. The turning diameter of the *Caine* was a thousand yards, and the towline was twice that long; it was therefore obvious to Stilwell that at the present rate the ship was going to cut far inside the target, and pass over its own towline. Ordinarily he would have called this fact to the captain's attention; but today he would have bitten his tongue out before speaking. He held the helm at right standard rudder.

"Kay, Mr. Keefer," Queeg was saying, "you will submit a written report explaining (a) why this man's shirt was out when he is in your department and (b) why this man's shirttail was out when you had the deck. Is that clear?" (The target was now drifting across the bow.)

"Aye aye, sir."

Chiefs Budge and Bellison were sitting on a ventilator on the forecastle, enjoying a smoke in the salt breeze. Bellison suddenly dug a bony elbow into the water tender's fat ribs. "Budge, am I seeing straight? Are we cutting back across the towline?"

Chief Budge stared out at the target, then looked wildly at the bridge, then catapulted his heavy body to the life lines, and peered over the side of the water. "Christ, yes. What's the matter with the old man?"

Bellison said, "Should I yell?"

"It's too late. We can't stop any more——"

"Jesus, the screws, Budge—suppose that tow cable wraps around the screws——"

The chiefs held their breath and clung to the lifelines, fearfully watching the bobbing target, far on the port beam. The *Caine* majestically steamed over its own tow cable. There was a slight jar, no more, and the old ship continued on its way. Nothing, apparently, happened to the target.

The two chiefs turned to each other. Bellison uncorked a flood of horrible profanity, which, translated, meant, "This is extremely unusual." They stared at the sea and the ship's curving wake for a long while, half stunned. "Budge," said Bellison at last in a low, shaken tone, "I'm an unholy son of a bitch. This ship has gone around a full circle, and *is starting around again!*"

Budge, his stomach resting heavily on the life line, nodded in wonder. On the sea the ship's wake was a complete circle of smooth green water flecked with bubbles, a mile across. The *Caine* was plowing into the same track again, still heeled over by the rudder. "What the Christ are we steaming in circles for?" said Bellison.

"Maybe the old man's slipped his trolley——"

"Maybe the rudder's jammed. Maybe the cable's cut. Let's see what the hell goes on——" They ran off the forecastle.

Meanwhile, on the bridge, Captain Queeg was winding up the shirttail emergency, after a long general harangue on the subject. "Kay, Signalman Third Class Urban. You may now adjust your uniform." The little signalman frantically stuffed his shirt into his trousers and snapped to rigid quivering attention again. "There," said Queeg. "Don't you think you look better? More like a sailor in the United States Navy?"

"Yes, sir," choked Urban.

The *Caine* had now steamed partly around the circle for the second time, and once more the target lay ahead. Queeg walked away from the palpitating sailor, with a curt "Dismissed." He saw the target, started with surprise, and threw a savage glance at Keefer and Keith. "What the hell is that target doing up there?" he exclaimed. "Where the hell are we? What the hell's going on?" He scurried into the wheelhouse and took a look at the rapidly rotating compass. "What the hell are you doing?" he screamed at Stilwell.

"Sir, you told me right standard rudder. I'm holding at right standard rudder," said the helmsman desperately.

"'Kay, that's right, I did tell you right standard rudder," said Queeg, turning his head from side to side, looking first at the target, then at the departing destroyers. "Why the hell isn't that target coming around after us? That's what I want to know—— All engines stop! Steady as you go!"

The *Caine* wallowed to a stop. The target drifted on the port beam, about five hundred yards away. The telephone talker poked his head into the wheelhouse. "Pardon me, Captain——" he said, in a scared voice. "It's Chief Bellison, sir, from the fantail. He says we ain't got the target no more. The towline's broken."

"How the hell does he know it's broken?" Queeg snapped. "Tell him not to be so goddamn positive when he's just making a goddamn surmise."

Grubnecker moved his lips, as though rehearsing the message, then spoke into the phone strapped on his neck. "Chief, the captain says not to be so goddamn positive with your goddamn sammizes."

"All engines ahead standard! Rudder amidships! We'll see whether we've got a target or not."

The *Caine* steamed two miles. The target dwindled to a

bobbing dot on the waves, not moving at all. Utter silence hung in the wheelhouse. "Kay," said the captain. "Now we know what we want to know. We haven't got the target." He looked at Keefer and shrugged humorously. "Well, Tom, if ComServPac gives us cables that part when we come right a few degrees that's his lookout, hey? . . . Willie, give me a despatch blank."

He wrote, *Defective towline parted southwest corner gunnery area Charlie. Target adrift, menace to navigation. Am returning to base. Suggest tug recover or destroy target at dawn tomorrow.*

"Send it out on the harbor frequency," he said.

As Willie took the despatch Maryk came running into the wheelhouse, his khaki shirt black with sweat. "Sir, the motor whaleboat is swung out and the target detail is standing by. It'll take us about an hour to recover. If we close to about fifty yards——"

"Recover what?"

"The *target* sir." The first lieutenant seemed amazed at the question.

"Show Mr. Maryk the despatch, Willie," said Queeg, grinning. The first lieutenant ran his eye over the scribbled sheet. Queeg went on, "As I see it, Mr. Maryk—maybe your insight is more profound than mine—my responsibility doesn't include emergencies arising from defective gear. If ServPac gives me a towline that parts my duty is to let him know and then get back home and await the next operation, instead of fooling away the Navy's time out here to no purpose—— Mr. Keefer, kindly ask the navigator for a course back to Pearl."

Maryk followed Keefer out to the port wing and tugged at his shirt sleeve. "Tom," he whispered, "doesn't he know that we went around in circles and cut the target loose?"

"Steve," murmured the communications officer, shaking his head, "don't ask me what goes on in his mind. We're in trouble with this joker, Steve. I'm not fooling."

The two officers went into the charthouse, where Gorton was calculating a sun line. Keefer said, "Skipper wants a course to Pearl, Burt."

Gorton's mouth fell open. "What! How about the target?"

Maryk told him Queeg's reasoning on the subject and added, "Burt, if you want to keep him out of trouble, try to talk him into recovering it——"

"Listen, Steve, I ain't talking the old man into anything he——"

Queeg's scowling face poked into the charthouse. "Well, well? What's the staff conference all about? I'm still waiting for a course to Pearl——"

"Captain, I'm sorry if I seem pigheaded, sir," Maryk blurted, "but I still think we ought to try to recover that damn target. It's worth thousands of dollars, sir. We can do it if——"

"How do you *know* we can do it? Has this ship ever recovered one?"

"No, sir, but——"

"Well, I haven't got such a high opinion of *Caine* seamanship as to think they can do such a specialist job. Fool around here all afternoon, maybe get some of these enlisted dumbheads drowned on us, miss the closing of the gate—how do I know the next op-order isn't waiting for us right now? We're supposed to be back prior to sunset——"

"Sir, I can recover it in an hour——"

"So you say—— Mr. Gorton, what's your opinion?"

The exec looked unhappily from Maryk to the captain. "Well, sir—I think Steve can be relied on—if he says——"

"Oh hell," said Queeg, "get Chief Bellison up here."

The boatswain's mate came into the charthouse in a few minutes, dragging his feet. "Yes, Captain?" he croaked.

"Bellison, if you had to recover that target how would you go about it?"

Bellison screwed up his face into a thousand wrinkles. After a pause he rattled off a confusing answer involving heaving lines, U-bolts, swivels, pelican hooks, slip hooks, pad eyes, spring lines, and chains.

"Hm, hm," Queeg said. "How long would it take?"

"Depends, sir. Sea ain't bad—maybe forty minutes, an hour——"

"And nobody would get killed, hey?"

Bellison peered at the captain like a suspicious monkey. "Nuthin' to get killed about, Cap'n——"

Queeg paced the bridge, muttering, for a few minutes, and then sent another despatch to ComServPac: *If you prefer can attempt recover target. Request instructions.*

The minesweeper steamed in a long lazy circle around the target for an hour. The answer came from ComServPac: *Act at discretion.* Willie delivered the despatch to the captain on the port wing, where he stood with Gorton and Maryk, watching the target.

"Helpful, aren't they?" Queeg said crankily, passing the despatch to the exec. He glanced up at the sun, which was about an hour and a half above the horizon. "That's the Navy for you. Pass the buck and get a receipt. Act at discretion, hey? Well, that's exactly what I'm going to do, and I kid you not. They're not hanging the responsibility on *me* for missing tomorrow's exercise and maybe breaking some thick sailor's neck. Let's head for the barn."

But no exercise was scheduled for the next day, and the *Caine* lay alongside the dock, doing nothing. At eleven o'clock in the morning Gorton sat at the wardroom table, sipping coffee as he worked through a basketful of correspondence. The door was opened by a smart sailor in dress blues, who whipped off a snowy hat and said to the exec, "Pardon me, sir, where is the captain's cabin?"

"I'm the executive officer. What can I do for you?"

"Sir, I have a mailgram to be delivered to the captain personally."

"Mailgram from whom?"

"ComServPac, sir."

Gorton pointed at the captain's cabin. The sailor knocked. When the door opened Gorton caught a glimpse of Queeg in underwear, his face heavily lathered. In a moment the sailor emerged, said to Gorton, "Thank you, sir," and went out, his steps echoing up the half-deck ladder. Gorton sat still, waiting. He waited perhaps forty-five seconds, then he heard the buzzer in his cabin ring frantically. Draining off the coffee at a gulp, he pushed himself out of his chair and trudged in to the captain's cabin.

Queeg sat at his desk, lather still on his face, the ripped-open envelope on the floor, a sheet of flimsy paper in his right hand. His head was sunk down between his shoulders, and his left hand, resting on his knee, trembled. He glanced up sidewise at the exec for a moment, then silently held out the mailgram to him, looking away.

At 1300 22 October commanding officer Caine will submit in person repeat in person written report on latest fiasco to operations officer ComServPac.

The captain rose, and fished the steel balls out of khaki trousers hanging on a hook. "Will you tell me, Burt," he said thickly, "what you think that means?"

Gorton shrugged unhappily.

"Fiasco! In an official mailgram!—— I'd sure as hell like to know why he calls it a fiasco. Why should *I* have to submit a written report? Didn't they tell me to act at discretion? Tell me frankly, Burt, was there anything I could possibly have done that I didn't do? Any mistake *you* think I made?" Gorton was silent. "I'd appreciate your telling me if there was anything. I regard you as my friend."

"Well, sir——" Gorton hesitated. He thought ComServPac might have heard about the cutting of the towline; such stories traveled fast in the Navy. But he was afraid to mention it, because Queeg had yet to acknowledge that it had happened.

"Speak up, Burt, you needn't fear offending me."

"The only thing is, sir," said the exec, "you—I think maybe you overestimated the difficulty of recovering. I've seen it done. We were once out on a shooting exercise with the *Moulton,* back in '40. The towline parted. They recovered it, no strain, in about half an hour."

"I see." Queeg compressed his mouth, staring at the balls, and was silent for a while. "Mr. Gorton, can you explain why this vital piece of information was not given to me at the time, when it would have decisively influenced my command decision?"

Gorton gaped at the captain.

"Maybe you think I'm pulling a fast one on you, Mr. Gorton. Maybe you think I was supposed to read your mind for any relevant information. Maybe you don't think that the primary duty of a second-in-command is to give his superior informed advice when asked."

"Sir—sir, if you recall, I recommended that you allow Mr. Maryk to recover——"

"Did you tell me *why* you recommended that, hey?"

"No, sir——"

"Well, why didn't you?"

"Sir, I assumed that when you said——"

"You assumed. You assumed! Burt, you can't assume a *goddamn thing* in the Navy. Not a goddamn thing. That's why I have to submit a written report to Com-ServPac, because you *assumed.*" Queeg struck the desk with his fist, and glowered silently at the wall for perhaps a minute.

"I readily grant you," he said, "that it called for a little intelligence on your part to understand your duty in this matter and give me all the dope. But it was definitely your responsibility. Hereafter, of course, if you want to be treated as if you don't have the professional background which I respect in you, why, that can easily be arranged."

Queeg sat, nodding to himself, for a long while. Gorton stood dumfounded, his heart pounding.

"Kay," said the captain at last. "It's probably not the first butch you've ever pulled, Burt, and it may not be your last, but I damn well hope it's the last you pull as my executive officer. I like you personally, but I write fitness reports on the basis of professional performance only. That's all, Burt."

14 · Queeg on the Carpet

Willie Keith came into Keefer's room shortly after the captain left for his interview with ComServPac. The ensign's hair was rumpled, his boyish face full of strain. "Say, Tom, excuse me," he said. "How about this written report on Urban's shirttail? What the devil are you going to say?"

Keefer yawned and smiled. "What the hell are you worrying about? Write anything. What does it matter? Whose eyes are going to see it? Take a look at what I wrote. It's on the desk there under those sneakers."

Willie pulled out the typewritten sheet and read:

Subject: Urban, Signalman 3/C—Violation of Uniform Regulations by.

1. On 21 October 1943 subject man was out of uniform due to inadequate supervision.
2. Undersigned officer, as OOD, and also as department head of subject man, was responsible for adequate supervision of subject man. Due to insufficient attention to duty this was not done.
3. The failure to adequately supervise subject man is regretted.
4. Steps have been taken to ensure that such incidents do not recur.

THOMAS KEEFER

Willie shook his head in rueful admiration. "Jesus, that's perfect. How long did it take you to do it? I've been sweating over mine since reveille."

"Are you kidding?" said the communications officer. "I wrote that as fast as I could type it. Probably a minute and a half. You just have to develop an ear for Navy prose, Willie. For instance, note that split infinitive in paragraph three. If you want a letter to sound official, split an infinitive. Use the word 'subject' very often. Repeat phrases as much as possible. See my beautiful reiteration of the phrase 'subject man.' Why, it's got the hypnotic insistence of a bass note in a Bach fugue."

"I wish I could copy yours verbatim. But I guess he'd catch on———"

"Hell, I'll bat one out for you."

"Would you?" Willie brightened. "I don't know, I thought I could write, but composing an official report on Urban's shirttail has me licked."

"Which is exactly the idea," said Keefer. "By making you write a report about a silly thing, he makes you sweat ——and that's all he's after, to make you sweat. A written report by its nature should be about something important. It's a terrific effort to write an official document about a shirttail without sounding impudent or idiotic———"

"That's just it," broke in Willie eagerly. "All my drafts sound as though I'm kidding the skipper, or insulting him———"

"Of course our little circle-steaming friend ran afoul of me, because I'm a gifted writer. I actually enjoy writing Navy letters. It's like a concert pianist improvising on *Chopsticks*. Don't let it get you, Willie. Queeg is a refreshing change from De Vriess, whose bullying technique was sarcasm, about as subtle as a rhinoceros charge. Queeg hasn't got the personal force of De Vriess, who could look anybody in the eye. So he adopts technique 4-X. This consists of retreating into his official identity, like a priest inside a mumbo-jumbo idol, and making you address him through that scary image. Standard Navy. That's the whole idea of these reports. So get used to them, because there'll be plenty of them, and———"

"Pardon me, when will you write that second improvisation on *Chopsticks*? He'll be back soon."

Keefer grinned. "Right away. Bring me Gorton's portable."

Captain Grace, chewing on the stem of an enormous black pipe which emitted a column of blue smoke and occasional sparks from the bowl, accepted the envelope offered by the captain of the *Caine* and motioned him to a yellow wooden chair beside his desk. Queeg, natty as his bulbous figure permitted in gabardine khakis, sat with his fingers laced tightly together in his lap.

Grace rasped the envelope open with a wicked-looking Japanese paper cutter, and spread the report before him on the desk. He put on heavy black-rimmed glasses, and read the document. Then he deliberately removed his glasses, and shoved the report aside with the hairy back of his hand. He inhaled on his pipe, and puffed up a volcanic cloud from the hissing bowl. "Unsatisfactory," he said, looking straight at Queeg.

The commander's lower lip trembled. "May I ask why, sir?"

"Because it says nothing I didn't know before, and explains nothing I wanted explained."

Queeg unconsciously began to roll imaginary balls between the fingers of both hands.

"I gather," Grace went on, "that you divide the blame among your exec, your first lieutenant, your chief boatswain's mate, and your predecessor, Captain de Vriess."

"Sir, I accept full responsibility for everything," Queeg said hastily. "I'm well aware that the mistakes of subordinates are no excuse for an officer but simply reflect on his ability to lead. And as for my predecessor, why, sir, I am cognizant that the ship spent a very long time in the forward area and I have no complaints about the ship, but facts are facts, and the state of training is definitely not up to snuff, but I have taken steps which will quickly remedy the situation, and so——"

"Why didn't you recover the target, Commander?"

"Sir, as I state in my report the chief boatswain's mate seemed to have no clear idea how to go about it and my officers were equally vague and uncertain, and failed to give me precise information, and a captain has to lean on his subordinates to some extent, it's inevitable. And I judged that it was more important for the *Caine* to report back to base for such further duty as might be assigned instead of wasting God knows how much time in futile complicated maneuvering. If this decision was erroneous it is regretted, but that was my decision."

"Hell, man, there's nothing complicated about recovering a target," Grace said irritably. "You can do it in half an hour. DMS's out here have done it a dozen times. Those damn things cost money. God knows where that target is now. The tug we sent out can't find it."

"I'm not commanding that tug, sir," Queeg said with a sly little smile at his hands.

Grace screwed up his eyes and peered at Queeg as though he were in a very poor light. He rapped the ash out of his pipe against a horny palm into a heavy glass ashtray. "See here, Commander," he said in a pleasanter tone than he had hitherto used, "I understand how you feel about your first command. You're anxious to make no mistakes—it's only natural. I was that way myself. But I made mistakes, and paid for them, and gradually grew into a fairly competent officer. Let's be frank with each other, Commander Queeg, for the sake of your ship and, if I may say so, your future career. Forget that this is an official interview. From here on in everything is off the record."

Queeg's head was sinking down between his shoulders, and he regarded Grace warily from under his eyebrows.

"Between you and me," Grace said, "you didn't try to recover that target because you just didn't know what to do in the situation. Isn't that the truth?"

Queeg took a long, leisurely puff at his cigarette.

"If that's the case, man," said Grace in a fatherly way, "for Christ's sake say so and let's both put this incident behind us. On that basis I can understand it and forget it. It was a mistake, a mistake due to anxiety and inexperience. But there's no man in the Navy who's never made a mistake——"

Queeg shook his head decisively, reached forward, and

crushed out his cigarette. "No, Captain, I assure you I appreciate what you say, but I am not so stupid as to lie to a superior officer, and I assure you my first version of what happened is correct and I do not believe I have made any mistake as yet in commanding the *Caine* nor do I intend to, and, as I say, finding the caliber of my officers and crew to be what it is, I am simply going to get seven times as tough as usual and bear down seven times as hard until the ship is up to snuff which I promise you will be soon."

"Very well, Commander Queeg." Grace rose, and when Queeg started to get up he said, "Stay where you are, stay where you are." He went to a shelf on the wall, took down a round purple tin of expensive English tobacco, and refilled his pipe. When he was lighting the pipe with a thick wooden match he inquisitively regarded the *Caine* captain, who was rolling nonexistent balls again.

"Commander Queeg," he said suddenly, "about the— puff puff—defective towline—puff puff—that broke. How much of a turn were you making?"

Queeg's head tilted sidewise; he darted a look full of suspicion at the captain. "I was using standard rudder, of course, sir. I have never exceeded standard rudder with the target, as my logs will show——"

"That's not what I mean." Grace returned to his seat, and leaned forward, waving the smoking pipe at Queeg. "How far did you turn? Twenty degrees? Sixty degrees? Were you reversing course 180 degrees—or what?"

The *Caine* skipper gripped the arms of the chair with bony knuckles, saying, "I'd have to check in my logs, sir, but I don't see what bearing it has on the matter *how* much of a turn it was, so long as——"

"Did you come around in a complete circle, Commander Queeg, and cut your own towline?"

Queeg's jaw dropped. He closed and opened his mouth a couple of times and at last said in a low, furious tone, stammering a little, "Captain Grace, with all submission, sir, I must tell you that I resent that question, and regard it as a personal insult."

Grace's stern expression wavered. He looked away from

Queeg. "No insult intended, Commander. Some questions are more unpleasant to ask than to answer—— Did that happen or didn't it?"

"If it did, sir, I think I ought to have recommended my own general court-martial."

Grace stared hard at Queeg. "I must tell you, Commander, that you have troublemakers aboard your ship. We received such a rumor here this morning. I seldom take cognizance of such scuttlebutt. However, the admiral heard it, and in view of several other actions of yours which have seriously troubled him, why, he ordered me to put the question to you. However, I suppose I can take your word as a naval officer that it didn't happen——"

"May I know, sir," Queeg said in a faltering tone, "in what respect the admiral finds fault with me?"

"Well, hang it man, first time under way you run up on the mud—of course, that can happen to anybody—but then you try to duck a grounding report and when you *do* send one in upon request, why, it's just a phony gundeck job. And then what do you call that despatch to us yesterday? 'Dear me, I've lost a target, please, ComServPac, what shall I do?' Admiral blew up like a land mine. *Not* because you lost the target—because you couldn't make a decision that was so obvious a seaman second class could have made it! If the function of command isn't to make decisions and take responsibility, what is it?"

Queeg's upper lip raised, showing his teeth in a mechanical half-smile. "By your leave, sir, I made my estimate of the situation and my decision. Then, considering the expense of the target which you have just mentioned and all, I made another decision, which was that the matter ought to be referred to higher authority. As for the grounding report I did not try to duck it, sir, I did not wish to trouble higher authority with a despatch about a trivial matter. It seems to me that I am being reproved here in one case for bothering higher authority, and in the other case for not bothering higher authority. I respectfully submit, sir, that the admiral ought to make up his mind as to which policy he prefers." There was a glimmer of triumph in the down-hung face.

The operations officer ran his fingers through his gray hair. "Commander," he said, after an extremely long pause, "do you really see no difference between those two situations?"

"Obviously they were different. But in *principle* they were the same. It was a question of consulting higher authority. But as I say, sir, I accept full responsibility for whatever happened, even if it means a general court-martial——"

"Nobody's talking about a general court-martial." Grace shook his head with a pained, exasperated expression. He stood, with a motion to Queeg to keep his seat, and paced the little office several times, whirling spirals in the layers of smoke that hung in the air. He came back to the desk and rested one haunch on the corner. "See here, Commander Queeg. I'm going to ask you a couple of straight off-the-record questions. I promise you your answers will go no farther than this room unless you wish. In return, I would greatly value a couple of forthright answers." He looked into Queeg's eyes in a friendly yet searching way.

The *Caine* skipper smiled, but his eyes remained opaque and expressionless. "Sir, I've tried to be as forthright as possible in this interview, and I certainly will not stop being forthright at this point——"

"Okay. Number one. Do you think your ship, in its present state of training, and with the caliber of subordinates you have, is capable of carrying out combat assignments?"

"Well, sir, as to a definite yes-and-no commitment on that nobody can predict the future and I can only say that with the limited resources at my command I will to the utmost of my ability strive to carry out any orders I may receive, combat or otherwise, and—as I say——"

"You'd be happier if the Bureau had given you another assignment, wouldn't you?"

Queeg grinned with one side of his mouth. "Sir, I respectfully submit that that's a question nobody would care to answer, not even the admiral."

"True enough." Grace paced in silence for a long time.

Then he said, "Commander Queeg, I believe it's possible to transfer you to a state-side assignment—with no reflection whatever," he added hastily, "on your performance of duties aboard the *Caine*. The transfer would be a single correction of an unjust and erroneous assignment. Among other things, as you know, you're rather senior for this post. I understand the squadron is filling up with CO's who are reserve lieutenant commanders and even lieutenants——"

Queeg, frowning at the air in front of him, his face gone pale, said with difficulty, "And I wonder how that would look in my record, sir—relieved of my first command after one month!"

"I believe I could guarantee you a fitness report that would remove any possible doubt on that score——"

Queeg suddenly plunged his left hand into his pocket and brought out the steel balls. "Don't misunderstand me, sir. I don't say that CO of the *Caine* is the best assignment any officer has ever had, or even that it's the assignment I deserved. But it happens to be the assignment I've got. I don't pretend to be the cleverest or smoothest officer in the Navy, Captain, by a long shot—I wasn't first in my class by any manner of means, and I never got very good grease marks—but I'll tell you this, sir, I'm one of the stubbornest. I've sweated through tougher assignments than this. I haven't won any popularity contests, but I have bitched and crabbed and hollered and bullied until I've gotten things done the way I wanted them done, and the only way I've ever wanted things done is by the book. I'm a book man. The *Caine* is far from what I want it to be, but that doesn't mean I'm going to give up and sneak off to some shore billet. No, thank you, Captain Grace." He looked for a moment at the operations officer, and resumed his glowering address to the invisible audience in front of and a little above him. "I am captain of the *Caine*, and I intend to remain captain, and while I'm captain the *Caine* will carry out all its assignments or go to the bottom trying. I'll promise you one thing, sir—if stubbornness, and toughness, and unremitting vigilance and supervision by the commanding officer are of any avail, the *Caine* will come through any combat duty assigned. And I'll stand by the fitness report I'll get when my tour of duty is over, sir. That's all I have to say."

Grace leaned backward, hooking his arm over the back of his chair. He regarded Queeg with a slight smile, and nodded his head slowly several times. "Professional pride and a sense of duty, both of which you obviously have, can carry an officer a long way in this outfit." He stood, and put out his hand to Queeg. "I think we've each spoken our piece. I'm going to accept your report. As to these mistakes of yours, or unfortunate incidents, as you prefer to call them, well, they say a bad beginning makes a good ending—— You know, Commander," he went on, rapping his pipe on the glass ashtray, "we got a lot of indoctrination at the Academy about the degree of perfection that's expected in a naval officer, and the fact there's no margin for error, and so forth. Well, I sometimes wonder whether all that wasn't laid on a bit too thick."

Queeg glanced questioningly at the operations officer, who laughed.

"Sounds like heresy, hey? Well, all I've got to say is, I've seen so much motion wasted and ink spilled and hot air issued in this outfit, trying to make a plain dumb mistake fit into this pattern of perfection, *after* the fact—— Well, maybe I'm getting too old to keep the game up, or something." He shrugged. "If I were you, Commander, I'd worry a little less about making mistakes, and a little more about doing the most sensible and useful thing that occurs to you in any given circumstances."

"Thank you, sir," said Queeg. "I have always endeavored to make only sensible and useful decisions, and in view of your kind advice I shall redouble my efforts in that direction."

The captain of the *Caine* returned by bus to the dock where his ship was moored. Descending among a group of yard workmen, he was unnoticed by anyone on the *Caine* until he came walking up the gangway. Unluckily, the gangway petty officer, Stilwell, was leaning on the

OOD's desk, leafing through a comic book which he had idly picked off the deck; and Queeg saw this, though the gangway messenger bellowed "Attention on deck!" and Stilwell spun around and froze in a stiff salute.

The captain returned the salute, apparently unperturbed. "Where's the officer of the deck?"

"Ensign Harding is on the forecastle, sir," Stilwell rapped out, "getting new chafing gear put on number-one line, sir."

"Kay. Messenger, call Ensign Harding to the quarter-deck." They waited in silence, the gunner's mate at rigid attention, the captain smoking, and glancing curiously around the deck. Sailors who issued whistling or humming from the passageways stopped their song, and either shrank back into the gloom or continued on with rapid steps, squaring their hats and averting their eyes. Harding came out of the starboard passageway and exchanged salutes with the captain.

"Mr. Harding," said Queeg, "are you aware that your gangway petty officer was reading on watch?"

The ensign, shocked, turned to the gunner's mate. "Is that true, Stilwell?"

Queeg snapped angrily, "Of course it's true! Do you take me for a liar, sir?"

The OOD shook his head dizzily. "I didn't mean to imply——"

"Mr. Harding, did you know he was reading on watch?"

"No, sir."

"Well, why didn't you?"

"Sir, number-one line was beginning to fray, and I was——"

"I didn't ask you for an alibi, Mr. Harding. An officer of the deck has no alibis. He is responsible for every goddamned thing that happens during his watch, *every goddamned thing,* do you hear?" Queeg was shouting, and the crew men working on the galley deckhouse and the afterdeck turned to hear. "You will call your relief, Mr. Harding, and you will notify the senior watch officer that you have been removed from the watch bill until such time as you seem to have acquired some dim notion of an officer of the deck's duties and responsibilities! Is that clear?"

"Aye aye, sir," Harding said hoarsely.

"As for this man," said Queeg, pointing at Stilwell with his thumb, "you will place him on report, and we'll see whether six months' restriction to the ship will teach him not to read on watch, and whether that lesson suffices for the rest of the crew, or anyone else needs the same dose—— Carry on."

Queeg walked off the quarterdeck and went below to his cabin. On his desk lay the two written reports about Urban's shirttail. He tossed his cap on his bed, took off his jacket, loosened his tie, dropped into the swivel chair, and read the reports through hastily, rattling the balls in his fist. Then he rang a buzzer and picked up the telephone on a bracket by the desk. "Tell the gangway messenger to find Lieutenant Keefer and have him report to my cabin." In a few minutes there was a knock at the door. Queeg, who had been sitting with his head in his hands, picked up Keefer's report, turned to the second page, and called over his shoulder, "Come in!"

The communications officer entered, and closed the door. After a moment Keefer said, addressing the captain's back: "You sent for me, sir?"

Queeg grunted, and rustled the papers. With a patronizing grin, Keefer propped his long, thin frame against the captain's bunk, resting on his elbows, and waited. The captain dropped the report to the desk, and pushed it aside with the back of his hand. "Unsatisfactory!"

"Oh?" said the communications officer. "May I ask why, sir?"

But he allowed a little too much aristocratic amusement to creep into his tone. Queeg looked up at him swiftly. "Stand at attention, Mr. Keefer, when you're in conference with your commanding officer!"

Keefer straightened in a leisurely way, an irritating ghost of a grin remaining on his face. "I beg your pardon, sir."

"Take that back," said Queeg, contemptuously indicating the report with his thumb. "Rewrite and resubmit prior to 1600 today."

"Aye aye, sir. May I respectfully inquire in what way it is inadequate?"

"It tells me nothing I didn't know before, and explains nothing I wanted explained."

"Sorry, sir. I'm afraid I don't understand that."

"I see." Queeg picked up the other report, which Keefer had rattled off for Willie Keith's signature, and flourished it. "Well, Mr. Keefer, I suggest you consult your assistant, Ensign Keith, in that case. He can teach you a great deal about composing a written report, strange as it may seem. This letter which he submitted on the same subject is absolutely excellent."

"Thank you, sir," said Keefer. "I'm happy to know I have such talent in my department."

Queeg smiled, evidently judging that he had pricked Keefer's core of vanity. He nodded several times and said, "Yes, as a matter of fact, Tom, you take this report of Keith's, and study it. Try to see why Willie has written a perfect report whereas yours is a phony gun-deck job."

In his own room, Keefer performed a series of grotesque monkeylike capers, during which he several times rubbed both reports forcibly against his behind. Then he dived into his bunk and buried his face in his pillow, shaking with choked laughter.

Captain Grace stood beside the admiral's heavy mahogany desk in a wood-paneled, green-carpeted room.

"I wish you'd have let *me* see the report before accepting it," the admiral was grumbling. He was a lean, wintry little man with piercing blue eyes.

"I'm sorry, Admiral."

"It's all right. What's your impression of this Queeg? That's the main thing."

Grace drummed on the desk softly with his fingers for a moment. "An old lady, I'm afraid, sir. I think he's earnest enough and probably pretty tough, but he's one of those that are never wrong, no matter how wrong they are —always some damn argument to defend himself, you know—and I don't think he's very bright. One of the low men in his class. I've been checking around."

"How about that towline? What's the story? Did he cut it or didn't he?"

Grace shook his head dubiously. "Well, it's one of those things. He got terribly offended when I asked about it —seemed sincere enough. I more or less had to take his word that it didn't happen. You'd have to run a court of inquiry to get at the definite facts, sir, and I don't know——"

"Hell, we can't go tracking down scuttlebutt with courts of inquiry. But I don't like the cut of the man's jib, Grace. Too many questionable occurrences too fast. Do you think I ought to recommend to the Bureau that he be relieved?"

"No, sir," said Grace promptly. "In all fairness to the man, he's done nothing that we know of definitely to warrant that. Overtension in his first command could account for everything that's happened so far."

"Well, then—look here, CincPac wants me to send two destroyer-minesweepers back to the States for overhaul and new radar installations, to go on the Flintlock push," said the admiral. "What's wrong with sending the *Caine?*"

"Nothing, sir. It's been in the forward area twenty-two months——"

"Okay. Get up the despatch recommending the *Caine.* Let this Queeg pull his next butch somewhere else."

A yard overhaul in the States was the most precious, prayed-for assignment of the war. In a year of combat steaming De Vriess had been unable to earn it for the old disintegrating *Caine*. Queeg had achieved it in his first four weeks, commanding the Navy's best goddamn target-towing ship.

15 · Joys of the Homeward Voyage

When the despatch came, it was New Year's Eve, Fourth of July, and every man's birthday and wedding day aboard the *Caine*. Willie Keith, too, felt his blood bubbling, though by *Caine* standard he was a Johnny-come-lately who had scarcely wiped off the lipstick of his last state-side farewell. He wrote to May and to his mother, hinting strongly to May that her presence on the pier when the *Caine* pulled into San Francisco would be an overwhelmingly fine surprise (he omitted any such hint to his mother). He composed the letter to May in the clipping shack, crawling into his hole like an animal to enjoy his delight in dark solitude; and he took long pauses in the writing, with the ink caking on the nib of his fountain pen, while he stared at the paper and his mind rioted through Mohammedan fantasies.

A shadow fell across the page. Looking up, he saw Stilwell standing in the doorway. The sailor wore the immaculate dungarees and highly polished shoes in which he had appeared for trial at captain's mast that morning, shortly before the arrival of the despatch.

"Yes, Stilwell?" said Willie sympathetically.

As officer of the deck Willie had recorded Stilwell's sentence in the log: six months' restriction to the ship. He had observed the mast ceremony on the quarterdeck with some wonderment—the solemn array of scared offenders in stiff new blue dungarees, the accusing officers lined up at attention opposite the culprits, and Queeg, calm and pleasant, receiving the prisoners' red service folders one by one from Jellybelly. It was a curious sort of justice. So far as Willie knew, all the offenders had been placed on report by order of Captain Queeg. Ensign Harding, for instance, appeared to accuse Stilwell, but he had not seen the sailor reading on watch. Since Captain Queeg never placed anyone on report himself, but always turned to the nearest officer and said, "I want this man placed on report," the triangle of justice was maintained in form, accuser, accused, and judge. And Queeg was ceremoniously interested and surprised by the accuser's narration of the offense which he himself had ordered reported. Willie had watched this strange business for a while and had indignantly concluded that it was an outrage against civil liberties, and constitutional rights, and habeas corpus, and eminent domain, and bills of attainder, and every other half-remembered phrase which meant that an American was entitled to a fair shake.

"Sir," said Stilwell, "you're the morale officer, aren't you?"

"That's right," said Willie. He swung his legs to the deck, put aside his stationery box, and screwed his fountain pen shut, converting himself with these motions from a girl-hungry youngster to a naval functionary.

He liked Stilwell. There are young men, slim, well built, and clean-faced, with bright eyes and thick hair, and an open, cheery look, who invite good feeling, and make things pleasant wherever they are, almost in the way pretty girls do, by the pure morning light that is on them; the gunner's mate was one of these.

"Well, sir," said Stilwell, "I got a problem."

"Let's hear it."

Stilwell plunged into a rambling tale, the meat of which was that he had a wife and child in Idaho, and that he had reasons to doubt his wife's faithfulness. "What I want to know is, sir, does this restriction mean I don't get to go home on leave? I haven't been home in two years, sir."

"I don't think it does, Stilwell, I can't imagine that it would. Any man who's been in the combat area as long as you have is entitled to go home unless he's committed murder or something."

"Is that the regulations, sir, or is it just how you figure it?"

"It's how I figure it, Stilwell, but, unless I tell you otherwise, and I'll find out pretty damn soon, well, you can count on it."

"What I want to know, sir—can I write home that I'm coming, like all the other guys are doing?"

The answer to this, as Willie well knew, was that Stilwell had better wait until the captain's views were explored. But the hungry appeal in the sailor's face, and Willie's own slight defensiveness about his lack of information, led him to say, "I'm sure you can, Stilwell."

The gunner's mate brightened so marvelously that Willie was glad he had ventured to be positive. "Thank you, Mr. Keith, thanks a whole lot," stammered Stilwell, his mouth trembling a little, his eyes glistening. "You don't know what that means to me, sir." He put on his hat, straightened, and saluted Willie as though he were an admiral. The ensign returned the salute, nodding pleasantly.

"Okay, Stilwell," he said. "Glad to be chaplain for you any time." Willie resumed writing the letter to May Wynn; and in the spangled excitement of the images that went shimmering through his brain he forgot the conversation.

The talk in the wardroom at lunch next day was warm and jolly for the first time since the change of command. Old jokes were revived about romantic escapades in Australia and New Zealand. Maryk took the worst drubbing, for a liaison with a middle-aged waitress in an Auckland teashop. The number of moles on the lady's face was thoroughly discussed, Gorton putting the number at seven and Maryk at two, with votes for figures in between from the others.

"Well, I think Steve is right, after all," said Keefer. "I guess two were moles. The rest were warts."

Whittaker, the steward's mate, who with his usual mournful expression was passing around a platter of fried ham, suddenly broke into a scream of laughter and dropped the platter, narrowly missing the captain's head. The red greasy meat slices tumbled all over the deck. In holiday mood, Captain Queeg said, "Whittaker, if you have to throw food at me don't throw meat, throw vegetables, they're cheaper." By wardroom tradition any witticism of a captain is automatically hilarious. There was great laughter.

Maryk said to the fat exec, "Well, okay, if she did have seven moles, at least she was real. I'm not satisfied, like some guys, with a lot of French magazines and postcards."

"Steve, I have a wife to be faithful to," said Gorton cheerily. "She can't divorce me for looking at pictures. But if I were a free agent like you, and couldn't do better than that New Zealand wart hog, I think I'd go in for postcards."

"Damn clever idea I came across once," said Queeg, obviously in a rare good humor, for he usually took no part in wardroom chatter. The officers fell silent and listened respectfully for the captain's table talk. "Speaking of postcards, that is. I don't know how I got on this mailing list but I did and—well, all you had to do was send this company a dollar a month, see, and they sent you these pictures, real big and glossy prints, about six by four, I guess." He indicated a rectangle with his two thumbs and forefingers. "Well, what was so clever—you know, you can't send pictures of naked ladies through the mail, well—these gals weren't naked, no sir, they had on the prettiest little pink pants and bras you ever saw, all nice and legal. The only thing was, their undies were washable. All you had to do was pass a wet cloth over the picture and—well, there you were—— Damn clever." He looked around with a happy snigger. Most of the officers managed to produce smiles. Keefer lit a cigarette, covering his face with his cupped palms, and Willie stuffed a whole slice of ham into his mouth.

"By the way," the captain went on, "none of you fellows have used up your liquor ration at the club, have you? Or if anyone has, say so." None of the officers spoke up. "That's fine. Anybody have any objection to selling his ration to me?"

The ration was five quarts of bottled liquor per month, which could be bought at the officers' wine mess in the Navy Yard for a fraction of the price in the United States. Queeg caught his officers off guard; they hadn't been thinking ahead to the cost of liquor back home. With varying shades of grumpiness they all consented except Harding.

"Captain," he said plaintively, "I plan for my wife and me to drink up my year's pay, and anything I can save will be a big help."

Queeg laughed appreciatively, and excused him. That same evening, therefore, the *Caine's* officers, shepherded by the captain, lined up at the liquor counter of the club and bought some thirty quarts of scotch and rye whisky. Captain Queeg directed them one by one, with many thanks, as they came away from the counter carrying armloads of bottles, to a jeep that stood outside in the gloom of the driveway. When the jeep had taken on a full cargo the captain drove off, leaving the knot of *Caine* officers looking at each other.

Carpenter's Mate Second Class Langhorne was summoned to the captain's cabin next morning at seven-thirty. He found the captain, in wrinkled stained gabardines, leaning over his bunk chewing a dead cigar stub, and counting an array of bottles spread across the blanket. "Hello, Langhorne. What kind of crate can you fix me up for thirty-one bottles?" The carpenter, a dour Missourian with a long bony face, protruding lower jaw, and lank black hair, goggled at the contraband. Captain Queeg said with a chuckle and a wink, "Medical supplies, Langhorne, medical supplies. Outside your province, and if asked, you've never seen these bottles and know nothing about them."

"Yes, sir," said the carpenter. "Fix up a crate, say, three by two, something like that—pack it with excelsior——"

"Excelsior, hell, this stuff is precious. I want partitions between the bottles *and* excelsior packed between the partitions——"

"Sir, we ain't got no thin stuff for partitions, no plywood nor nothin'——"

"Well, hell, get some sheet tin from the metalsmith's shop."

"Yes, sir, I'll fix it up nice, sir."

Late that afternoon Langhorne came staggering into the wardroom, his face pouring sweat, bearing on his back a box made of fresh-sawed white boards. He stumbled into Queeg's cabin and let the crate down to the deck with fearsome grunts and grimaces, as though it were a piano. Mopping his streaming face with a red bandanna, he said, "Jesus, sir, them sheet-lead partitions are heavy——"

"Sheet *lead?*"

"Metalsmiths were fresh out of sheet tin, sir——"

"But Christ, *lead*. Good stiff cardboard would have done just as well——"

"I can rip them lead sheets out, sir, and make it over——"

"No, leave it as it is," grumbled Queeg. "It just means some seamen are going to be getting some healthy exercise in a few days, which is just as well—— Probably I can use a supply of sheet lead back home, at that," he muttered.

"Pardon me, sir?"

"Never mind. Get some excelsior and pack away those bottles." He pointed to the treasure, ranged on the deck under the washbowl.

"Aye aye, sir."

"Now hear this. General drills will commence at 1400."

The *Caine* was steaming in her position at the right end of the semi-circular screen of escorts, which plowed in the van of the convoy of four fleet oilers, two transports, and three merchant ships. They were far out of sight of land, rocking over calm blue water. The ships were disposed in a neat pattern on the sunlit sea.

Ensign Keith, junior officer of the deck, was greatly enjoying this voyage. No submarines had been reported east of Hawaii for a year, but still, there was no doubt at all that Willie Keith was JOOD on a ship which was sniffing for Jap submersibles. If the OOD should drop dead or fall over the side it was conceivable that he, Ensign Keith, might take the conn, sink a submarine, and win great glory. If was not likely—but it was possible, whereas it was not possible, for example, that his mother might do it. The OOD, Keefer, added to his exaltation by putting him in charge of the zigzag plan, allowing him to give the orders to the helm. Willie tried to snap the orders out at the instant when the second hand of the bridge chronometer was cleaving the dot over twelve o'clock. The war had at last begun for him.

Captain Queeg came on the bridge at two minutes before two, squinting around in an irritated way, followed by Gorton, who had a whipped-dog look. The exec had, in fact, just received a raking for his failure to conduct general drills more often, and was mentally composing the opening paragraphs of a written report explaining why he hadn't held them. Queeg had come across a CincPac letter in his correspondence that morning, desiring written reports from all ships on the number of drills conducted each month. "Kay," said the captain to Engstrand. "Hoist 'I am conducting general drills.'"

The signalman ran up a halyard display of colored flags. Willie, at a nod from the captain, walked to the red-painted general alarm handle in the wheelhouse, and yanked it. Then, while the whang-whang-whang shook the air, he inspected with satisfaction his image in one of the bridge windowpanes. Confronting him was the shadowy figure of a World War II sea warrior, complete with bulbous helmet, bulky gray kapok life jacket and attached flashlight, and gray flash-burn paint on his face and hands. Everybody on the bridge was similarly dressed.

Elsewhere on the ship things were different. The *Caine* crew, after more than a year of general quarters under Japanese air attacks, followed by a couple of months of Pearl Harbor indolence, were not inclined to take pains with a mock general alarm in the peaceful waters between Honolulu and San Francisco. Half of them appeared at their battle stations minus either helmet or life jacket, or both. Queeg peered here and there, frowning horribly.

"Mr. Keefer!"

"Yes, sir?"

"I want you to make the following announcement over the loudspeaker: 'Every man who is not wearing a helmet or a life jacket is docked one day's leave in the United States. Every man who is wearing neither is deprived of three days' leave. The names are to be reported at once via the telephone talkers to the bridge.' "

Keefer looked stunned. He stammered, "Sir, that's kind of tough——"

"*Mister* Keefer," said the captain, "I did not ask you to pass an opinion on such disciplinary measures as I deem necessary for the instruction and safety of my crew. If these men are going to commit suicide by coming to GQ unprotected, well, nobody is going to say it's because I didn't impress on them the importance of wearing battle gear. Make the announcement."

The men at the gun stations, hearing the words from the loudspeakers, could be seen turning their heads toward the bridge, their faces showing incredulity and rage. Then a boiling activity began among them, and helmets and life jackets began to appear magically, mushrooming all over the ship and passing from hand to hand.

"Now I want that knocked off!" roared Queeg. "I want those names, and I don't want any man putting on any jacket or helmet until every single name is turned in to the bridge! Mr. Keefer, you announce that!"

"*What* shall I announce, sir?"

"Don't be so goddamn stupid, sir! Announce that they're to stop putting on that goddamn gear and report those names to the bridge!"

Sailors were throwing helmets and life jackets from concealed places up to the deckhouses; a rain of the gear was flying through the air. Queeg screamed, "Send for the master-at-arms! I want whoever's throwing those helmets and jackets put on report!"

"Chief Bellison, master-at-arms," droned Keefer into the microphone, "please report to the bridge on the double."

"Not to the bridge, you ass," screeched Queeg, "tell him to go behind the galley deckhouse and arrest those men!"

"Belay that last word," said Keefer, turning his face away from the captain to grin, "Chief Bellison, lay aft of the galley deckhouse and arrest whoever's throwing helmets and life jackets."

The words had scarcely died in the speakers when the deluge of gear stopped. It had served its purpose, however. There was gear on the deckhouses to spare for all hands, and they were rapidly dressing themselves. Queeg ran frantically here and there on the bridge, watching the men disobeying his orders wholesale, and yelled, "Stop putting on that gear! You, down there! . . . Come here, Mr. Gorton! What's the name of that man on number-three gun? Put him on report!"

"Which one, sir?"

"Hell, the redheaded one. He just put on a helmet. I saw him!"

"Sir, if he's got a helmet on I can't see his hair."

"Christ on a crutch, how many redheaded men are there on that gun?"

"Well, sir, I believe there's three. Wingate, Parsons, Dulles—no, Dulles is more of a blond—but I think maybe he's on gun four now, ever since——"

"Oh, Christ, *forget* it," snapped Queeg. "Of all the lousy fouled-up failures to execute orders I've ever seen, Burt, this is the worst! The *worst*."

By this time every man aboard the *Caine* was wearing a helmet and a life jacket. Queeg peered around the ship, with an angry balked glare. "Kay," he said. "Kay. I see these birds think they have me licked."

He walked into the wheelhouse, and picked up the microphone. "This is the captain speaking," he said, and the angry tone filtered through all the distortion of the speakers. "Now, I am displeased to note that some misguided sailors on this ship believe they can pull a fast one on their captain. They are very much mistaken. I have asked for the names of the men who came to GQ out of uniform. The names don't seem to be forthcoming. Kay. Since I have no other way of dealing out justice to the numerous cowards who are disobeying my orders to turn in their names, I am hereby depriving every man on this ship of three days' leave in the States. The innocent must suffer with the guilty, and you'll simply have to punish the guilty ones among yourselves for bringing this penalty on the whole crew—— Kay. Now proceed with general drills."

The convoy ran into stormy seas halfway to San Francisco, and Willie Keith began to get a clearer idea of the limitations of World War I destroyers. Towing targets on the smiling seas around Hawaii, the *Caine* had done plenty of rolling, and Willie had been proud of his sea legs and his quiet stomach; now he realized that he had been a little premature in congratulating himself.

He was awakened one night to go on the midwatch after an hour and a half of dozing on the wardroom couch, and found that he could hardly stand. He fell down while groping around to make himself some coffee. He struggled into a blue woolen windbreaker, because the air streaming in from the ventilation duct felt cold and damp, and he went zigzagging across a deck that was wobbling like a room in an amusement park Crazy House. When he came topside, clutching the stanchion that held up the hatchway, the first thing he saw was a wall of greenish-black water on the port side, towering high over his head. As he opened his mouth to yell the wall fell away, replaced by a sky of torn moonlit clouds, and an equally horrendous wall rose on the other side of the ship. He inched up the bridge ladder, holding his hat in the expectation of a blast of wind, but there was very little wind. He found the bridge watch all clinging to handholds in the dark wheelhouse, their bodies swaying back and forth with each roll. Even here, high on the bridge, when the ship heeled over Willie found himself looking upward at tossing water.

"Good Christ," he said to Carmody, who had one arm braced through the back of the captain's chair, "how long has this been going on?"

"How long has what been going on?"

"This rolling!"

"This isn't rolling." The rubber mats on the deck all slid sideward and heaped up against his legs.

Willie relieved Carmody, and as the watch wore on his terror abated. The *Caine* was apparently not going to founder. But it seemed an entirely reasonable possibility to him that it might come apart. At the extreme limit of a roll, the whole ship groaned from end to end like a sick man, and Willie could see the bulkheads bending and swaying. It struck him forcibly that nothing now stood between him and the black cold waters except the guess of an engineer (now probably dead) made thirty years ago as to how much stress such a ship should be built to stand.

Evidently he had guessed well, for the *Caine* kept up this careening into the next day, and held together.

Willie went up to the forecastle after a lunch of roast pork, feeling oddly aware of the fact that he had a stomach. He was not seasick, of that he was certain. But he could feel the stomach hanging there in his midriff, palpitating, full, and hard at work at its usual tasks. This second sight into his body induced in Willie a desire for a lot of fresh air blowing in his face. He pulled open the watertight door to the forecastle, and saw Stilwell in a pea jacket and wool cap crouched by number-one gun, tying down the blue canvas cover, which had worked loose and was flapping loudly.

"Afternoon, Mr. Keith."

"Afternoon, Stilwell." Willie dogged the door shut and leaned against the life lines, gripping the stanchion. The wind and cold spray in his face were delightful. When the ship rolled to port he could see the convoy plunging along through the gray choppy swells.

"How do you like the rolling, sir?" called Stilwell, over the rushing and bubbling of the bow waves.

"What rolling?" said Willie, with a brave grin.

The sailor laughed. He slid across the deck to the life line and made his way cautiously to the ensign. "Sir, did you ever talk to the captain about—you know, about my leave?"

A little ashamed, Willie said, "Haven't had a chance, Stilwell. But I'm sure it will be okay."

The sailor's face went gloomy. "Well, thanks, sir."

"I'll talk to him this afternoon. Come to the clipping shack at three and see me."

"Thanks a million, Mr. Keith." The gunner's mate

smiled, undogged the door, and slipped through to the well deck.

Willie took several deep breaths of the medicinal wind, and went below to the captain's cabin.

Queeg was lying on his bunk in his underwear, fiddling with a wooden Chinese puzzle, a ball of interlocking pieces. The captain had confiscated it one day, upon poking his head into the radar shack and finding the watchstander playing with it. He had been working at it ever since, and though he told Gorton he had solved it nobody had ever seen the pieces apart. "Yes, Willie, what can I do for you?" he said, jiggling the puzzle under his reading lamp.

Willie stated his errand, while the captain worked away at his puzzle. ". . . So, sir, I just thought I'd check and be sure. Did you mean Stilwell's restriction to apply during the overhaul?"

"What do you think I meant?"

"Well, I didn't think so, sir——"

"Why not? When a man's in jail for a year they don't let him out for two weeks at Christmas, do they? Restriction to the ship means restriction to the ship."

The close air in the room, and the swaying deck, and the jiggling of the puzzle before his eyes began to trouble Willie. "But—but sir, isn't this a little different? He's not a criminal—and he's been fighting a war for two years overseas——"

"Willie, if you start getting sentimental about naval discipline you're licked. Every man in a brig or a guardhouse in the forward area has been fighting a war. When a war is on you've got to get tougher with enlisted men, not easier." (Jiggle, jiggle, jiggle.) "They're under a strain, and there's a lot of damned unpleasant duty to do, and if you let up the pressure even once your whole goddamn organization's apt to blow up in your face." (Jiggle, jiggle.) "The sooner you learn that elementary fact, Willie, the better morale officer you'll be."

Willie's stomach put in an appearance again, throbbing and heavy. He pulled his hypnotized glance away from the puzzle, and his eyes fell on the wooden crate under the captain's washbasin. "Sir, there are offenses and offenses," he said, his voice a little weaker. "Stilwell is a good sailor. Before you came aboard, nobody bore down on these men for peeking at a magazine during a watch. I know it was wrong but——"

"All the more reason for bearing down now, Willie. You tell me a better way to get my wishes obeyed on this ship and I'll take it under consideration. Do you think all reading on watch would stop if I gave Stilwell a letter of commendation, hey?"

Willie's dizziness got the better of his discretion and he blurted out, "Sir, I'm not sure that reading on watch is any greater violation than transporting whisky aboard ship."

The captain laughed amiably. "You've got a point there. But rank hath its privileges, Willie. An admiral can wear a baseball cap on the bridge. That doesn't mean the helmsman can. No, Willie, our job is to make damn sure that the enlisted men do as we say, not as we do." (Jiggle, jiggle, jiggle.) "And, as I say, the one way to make them do as we say is to get goddamn tough with them and make it stick."

Willie felt himself breaking out in a sweat.

The captain droned on, "Now, if it was Stilwell's tough luck to get caught first so that I had to make him the horrible example, well, as I say, reading on watch has got to be knocked off on this ship, and" (jiggle, jiggle) "it's just too bad that he's worried about his wife, but I've got the whole U.S.S. *Caine* to worry about, and" (jiggle) "sometimes one man has to suffer for——"

But he left the sentence unfinished, because at that point Willie Keith made a queer stifled noise and threw up violently. The ensign managed to turn his green face away from Queeg just in time. Gasping apologies, he seized a towel and began dabbing at the deck. Queeg was surprisingly genial about it. "Never mind, Willie. Send a steward's mate in here and go topside for some fresh air. Lay off the pork till you get your sea legs."

So ended Willie's plea for Stilwell. He could hardly face

the sailor, but Stilwell took the news with a stiff blank face. "Thanks for trying anyway, sir," he said dryly.

Another day and another passed of rough seas and lowering skies; of rolling and pitching, cold winds, and cold damp eating into bones softened by tropic warmth; of a treadmill of watches in a wheelhouse dank and gloomy by day and danker and gloomier by night; of sullen silent sailors and pale dog-tired officers, of meals in the wardroom eaten in silence, with the captain at the head of the table ceaselessly rolling the balls in his fingers and saying nothing except an infrequent grumpy sentence about the progress of the work requests. Willie lost track of time. He stumbled from the bridge to his coding, from coding to correcting publications, from corrections back up to the bridge, from the bridge to the table for an unappetizing bolted meal, from the table to the clipping shack for sleep which never went uninterrupted for more than a couple of hours. The world became narrowed to a wobbling iron shell on a waste of foamy gray, and the business of the world was staring out at empty water or making red-ink insertions in the devil's own endless library of mildewed unintelligible volumes.

One morning Willie stirred in his bunk, opened his eyes, and felt a strange and delicious sensation: the bunk was neither rolling nor pitching, but remaining level. He bounded out of the clipping shack in his underwear. The ship was gliding between the green banks of a channel about a mile wide. The sky was blue, the air cool and mild. The *Caine* moved as steadily as a ferryboat. Willie craned his neck out over the life lines and peered forward. Above the green round bulge of a hill he saw the piers of the Golden Gate Bridge, misty red, far inland. His eyes filled with tears; he dived back into the clipping shack.

He was on the bridge when the *Caine* steamed under the vaulting crimson span. But his poetic thoughts were jangled by a colloquy between the captain and Gorton, standing behind him.

"Kay, when we pass Alcatraz we'll head over to Oakland. Give me a course, Burt."

"Sir, Pier 91 isn't in Oakland——"

"I know. We're going to lie off Oakland for a while before we tie up at the pier."

"But sir——"

"What the hell is all this arguing for, Burt? I want a course to Oakland!"

"Sir, I just wanted to say there's a rugged tide current at Pier 91, five knots or better. It's slack water now, we can make our landing easy. If we delay for an hour it'll be a damn tough approach——"

"Let me worry about landing this ship. You give me a course to Oakland."

"Aye aye, sir."

"*Mister* Keith. Are you doing anything besides sight-seeing?"

Willie shriveled away from the bulkhead and faced the captain. Queeg, strangely dapper in a blue-and-gold bridge coat, white hat, and white silk scarf, was scanning the widening bay through binoculars. "No, sir——"

"Kay. That crate in my cabin—get yourself a working party and load it into the gig. You'll be boat officer."

At the expense of sundry mashed fingers, splinters under fingernails, crushed toes, and a spectacular fireworks of obscenity, the working party lodged the captain's stone-heavy crate in the boat. Willie's contribution was to stand well clear of the murderous box as it teetered in the air, and to make occasional mild suggestions which were totally ignored.

The *Caine* lay to near the Oakland shore, and the gig went puttering toward a concrete landing at the foot of a deserted street. Queeg sat in the stern sheets, his feet on the crate, rolling the balls and squinting around at the bay. Willie marveled at the crew of the gig. Horrible, Meatball, and Mackenzie were unrecognizable; washed, combed, shaved, powdered, dressed in starched whites, they seemed to be of a different race of man than the dismal savages who had first brought Willie to the *Caine*. He knew the reason for the Cinderella change, of course; the sailors wanted their leave, and were afraid of Queeg.

Once the motor died. The captain snapped irritably,

after the sailors had fussed with the engine for a couple of minutes, "If this gig isn't under way in thirty seconds someone's going to be goddamn sorry." Agonized thrashing of arms, and banging of wrenches, and sulphurous cursing ensued; and mercifully the motor started up again at the twenty-eighth second, and the gig reached the shore. "Kay," said Queeg, leaping off the gunwale to the landing, "bear a hand with that crate. I'm late as hell."

Two of the working party jumped to the dock, and the third sailor with Horrible and Meatball got one end of the crate up over the gunwale with much heaving and grunting. The men on the dock seized the crate and pulled; those in the gig pushed from below. The box hardly moved.

"Well, well, what's taking so long?"

"Sir, she won't slide," panted Horrible, his black hair falling over his eyes. "Too heavy."

"Well, stand up on the gunwale and lift her then. Haven't you any brains?" The captain looked around and saw Mackenzie standing on the dock with the bowline in his hand, staring vacantly at the struggle. "Well, what are *you* doing, standing there with your thumb in your bum and your mind in neutral? Bear a hand."

Mackenzie at once dropped the line and jumped to help the men on the dock. This was a mistake on the part of captain and sailor alike. Mackenzie had been performing the necessary function of holding the gig close to the dock. With the bowline free, the gig fell away, imperceptibly at first and then faster. A crack of open water widened under the crate. "Oh Christ!" gasped Horrible, tottering on the gunwale, his fingers under one edge of the crate. "The bowline! Someone grab the bowline!" Mackenzie let go of the crate and rushed back to the rope. The men on the dock staggered. There was an instant of chaotic yelling, cursing, and crunching, over which rose the soprano scream of Queeg, "Watch out for that goddamn crate!"

Horrible and the crate fell into the water with a tremendous splash, soaking Queeg. Horrible floated, a blob of white on the muddy water. The crate went down like an anvil, with a bubbly groan. There was a moment of gruesome silence. Queeg, dripping, leaned over the edge of the landing and peered down into the brown water. "Kay," he said. "Get out your grappling irons."

Half an hour of grappling efforts followed. Queeg smoked up half a pack of cigarettes, taking only a few puffs each time and dashing the cigarettes into the water. Horrible crouched on the dock, his teeth chattering loudly.

"Sir," said Meatball at last in a weak, small voice.

"Yes?"

"Sir, pardon me, I think she's sunk in ooze. Even if we find her I don't think we can bring her up. This line won't take the strain, and anyway I think the grappling iron would just come splintering out of the wood. Pardon me, sir, but that's what I think."

Queeg stared at the water where the crate had vanished. "Kay. I think you're right, at that. It's just too goddamn bad."

The gig was halfway back to the *Caine* before he spoke again. "Willie, who was in charge of that working party?"

"I—I guess I was, sir."

"I guess you were, too. Well, then, how do you explain that fiasco?"

"Sir, I beg your pardon, you didn't tell me to take charge of the unloading——"

"I don't tell you to wipe your nose, either, Mr. Keith, when it needs it. There are certain things that an officer is assumed to understand for himself." The captain stared out from under his eyebrows at nothing for several seconds and said, "I don't appreciate a foul-up by a working party for which you're responsible, Willie, especially when the foul-up costs me about a hundred and ten dollars."

"Sir, that crate is in pretty close to shore, after all. I'm sure the harbor police can grapple for it and recover it, if you——"

"Are you out of your mind?" said the captain. "And have them ask me about the contents, hey? Sometimes you're not so bright, Willie—— Damn. Friend of mine up in Oakland would have taken that crate and shipped it back home for me—— Well." After a pause he added, "No, you'd just better think it over, Willie, and—well, just try to see where you bitched things up, and what you'd better do about it."

"Do you want me to submit a written report, sir?"

"Just think it over," said Queeg irritably.

Seventy or eighty people, most of them women, were crowded on Pier 91 when the old minesweeper drew near. They fluttered handkerchiefs and uttered thin sweet cries, and in their brightly colored coats they made as decorative a welcoming display as rows of flags.

"Kay," said Captain Queeg, posted on the port wing, squinting unhappily at the tide current swirling past the dock. "All engines slow to one third. Line-handling parties stand by the port side."

Willie went to the starboard wing out of the captain's sight, and began scanning the women on the wharf through binoculars. All over the ship sailors crowded the rails and life lines, trying to find familiar faces, shouting and waving.

The *Caine*, with its screws beating at five knots, drifted impotently sidewise, making no headway toward the dock against the current.

"Kay," said the captain, rolling the steel balls swiftly, "I can see this approach is going to be fun—— Tell the line handlers to stand by their line-throwing guns. All ahead two thirds! Right full rudder!"

The *Caine* churned forward against the brown tumbling tide, and swung in toward the pier. Gray gulls wheeled and darted between the ship and the dock, making raucous, jeering noises. In a few seconds the ship drew parallel to the dock—but yards and yards of open water lay between. "Kay, we'll breast her in! All stop! Shoot those heaving lines over!"

The line-throwing guns cracked fore and aft, and the crowd cheered as two arcs of white cord came sailing across the water. The forward line reached the dock, but the after line splashed short. The *Caine* drifted away from the pier. "Christ, what's the matter with that after line-handling party?" stormed Queeg. "Tell 'em to shoot over another line on the double!"

Gorton, standing at the captain's elbow, said, "It's not going to reach, sir. We're drifting too fast——"

"*Why* are we drifting too fast? Because these goddamn line handlers are all goddamn zombies! Kay. Recover all lines! I'm going to make another approach."

The *Caine* backed out into the main channel. Willie Keith's heart gave a mighty throb, for he suddenly saw May Wynn at the far end of the pier, almost hidden by women in front of her. She wore a perky gray hat with a veil, a gray traveling suit, and a white fur shoulder piece. She looked as she had in Willie's waking dreams, not a touch less beautiful or desirable. She was peering anxiously at the ship. Willie wanted to dance and scream, but he refrained, and merely took off the hat which made him a nameless naval officer. In a moment May's eyes turned to him, and her face became brilliant with joy. She raised one white-gloved hand and waved. Willie returned the wave with a careless, masculine dip of the binoculars, but he became weak in the knees all the same, and prickles of pleasure ran along his skin.

"All right, we'll try again," he heard the captain shout, "and if there's any more doping-off by the line-handling parties it'll be too goddamn bad for a lot of people!"

Queeg tore in toward the dock at fifteen knots, swung the ship hard right, and backed the engines, in an apparent attempt to duplicate his historic red-hot landing alongside the fuel dock in Hawaii. But luck or skill did not favor him with the same hair-raising success this time. He backed down too late. The *Caine* came crashing into the wharf at an angle of about twenty degrees, still going fast. A hideous splintering din arose, mingled with the shrieks of the lady spectators scurrying to the other side of the wharf.

"Back down emergency full! Emergency full!" squeaked the captain, as the destroyer, its bow imbedded in the dock, quivered like an arrow shot into a tree trunk. The *Caine* pulled clear in a moment, with more tearing and banging, leaving a monstrous shaving several feet thick and twenty yards long gouged out of the pier.

"God damn this current, why don't they have a god-damn tug standing by when a ship has to go alongside?"

Willie shrank out of the captain's sight, and flattened against the charthouse bulkhead, as he had often seen the signalmen do. With his girl almost within his grasp, and an infuriated captain loose, it was time to be invisible.

"Kay, we'll try once more," announced Queeg, as the old ship backed into open water, "and this time we'd better make it, for the sake of all hands, that's all I've got to say!—— All ahead two thirds!"

The *Caine* shuddered and started forward again.

"Right full rudder! All engines stop!"

Willie cautiously came up to the bulwark and saw that the *Caine* was slipping fairly into position alongside the dock, except that the bow was closer than the stern.

"Kay, let's get that stern in now! Port back one third."

"Port, sir?" said Jellybelly at the engine telegraph, in a suprised tone.

Queeg screamed, "Yes, port, and ring it up, God damn it! . . . Kay! Get those lines over!"

Ensign Keith caught another good look at his sweetheart's face. He was dizzy with love and longing.

"What the hell is the matter with that after line-handling party?" screeched Queeg, and on the instant came the pop of the line-throwing gun. But the current, and Queeg's unfortunate mistake of backing the wrong screw, had swiveled the stern too far out, and the line fell into the water again. Meantime the men of the forecastle, with desperate speed, had gotten one manila line over to the dock, where the waiting sailors had secured it to a bollard. By this one tether the *Caine* now hung precariously, swinging out so that it was perpendicular to the wharf.

As the ship swung so, the starboard wing came in view of the dock again, and to Ensign Keith's ears came a cry of a very familiar voice: "Will—EE! Will—EE darling!" His mother stood near the manila line, waving a handkerchief!

Queeg came bolting through the wheelhouse and almost knocked Willie down as he dashed for the rail. "Mr. Keith, get out from underfoot! Signalman, signalman, raise that tug!"

With the help of the passing tug, the ship's stern was

pushed in toward the dock. The ladies on the dock sent up a derisive cheer, not unmixed with hoots, and catcalls, and inquiries as to whether the ship belonged to the Chinese Navy, when the *Caine* was finally secured. Queeg came into the pilothouse, his face white, his forehead crawling with wrinkles, his eyes glaring out at nothing. "Officer of the deck!"

Lieutenant Maryk followed him through the door. "Officer of the deck, aye aye."

"Kay," said Queeg, with his back to Maryk, rubbing the steel balls in his fingers so that they made a loud rasp. "You will pass the following word: 'Due to the lousy seamanship of the after line-handling party, the entire crew is deprived of two days' leave.' "

Maryk stared at the captain, his blunt face showing disbelief and disgust. He did not move. After a few seconds the captain whirled. "Well? What are you waiting for, Mr. Maryk? *Pass the word.*"

"Pardon me, Captain, if I'm talking out of turn, but that's kind of rugged, sir. After all, there wasn't much the guys could——"

"*Mister* Maryk, let me remind you that I am captain of this ship! If I get another word of back talk from you I will triple the penalty and include all the officers as well. *You pass that word.*"

Maryk wet his lips. He went to the squawk box, pressed the lever, and said, "Now hear this. Due to the lousy seamanship of the after line-handling party, the entire crew is deprived of two days' leave." The snap of the lever, as he released it, echoed in the wheelhouse.

"Thank you, Mr. Maryk. And let me tell you that I don't appreciate your grandstand play in the presence of the bridge watch in a matter of discipline. I consider it conduct unbecoming an officer, amounting to insubordination, and it will be reflected in your fitness report."

Head down, the captain hurried from the wheelhouse and trampled down the bridge ladder. All over the ship, and on the dock, where the announcement had been clearly heard, faces were drawn with shock and dismay—young faces of sailors, weary faces of chiefs, pretty faces of sweethearts, and old faces, such as the face of Willie Keith's mother. Mrs. Keith did not yet have the consolation of realizing that Ensign Keith was an officer and therefore exempt from the penalty.

When the gangplank was put over, Willie was one of the first to disembark. He saw no escape from his situation; it would simply have to be faced. Mrs. Keith was standing at the foot of the gangway; and May, her expression a touching mixture of confusion, gladness, and fear, had placed herself directly at the mother's elbow. Mrs. Keith embraced Willie wildly as he set foot on United States soil once more—if a wharf, that is, can qualify as soil. "Darling, darling, darling!" she exclaimed. "Oh, it's so wonderful to have you close again!"

Willie disengaged himself gently, smiling at May. "Mother," he said, taking her hand and May's hand, "I'd like you to meet—ah—Marie Minotti."

SHORE LEAVE

16 · Shore Leave

Willie and May were huddled together in the moonlight beside a tall pine on the floor of the Yosemite Valley, in front of the Ahwanee Hotel. Their cheeks touched; their breath mingled in a cloud of white vapor. They heard a deep masculine voice call, in long-drawn tones echoing between the sheer valley walls, "Let the fire fall!" From the peak of a cliff a red cascade of embers came tumbling straight down through the darkness, a glowing, floating fiery column a mile high. Somewhere in the gloom cowboy musicians began a melancholy little love song. Willie and May turned to each other and kissed.

After a while they walked arm in arm into the hotel. Through the bright lobby decorated with multicolored Indian hangings, and skins, and horns, they strolled to the red-lacquered elevator. They rode up three floors and got out together. It was all of a long winter night before Willie returned to his own room, and sank into an armchair in an excess of stupefied pleasure, still thinking with joy of his last glimpse of May, enchanting in her simple white nightdress, with her red hair tumbled on her bare shoulders, smiling up at him as he closed her door. It was a perfectly satisfying picture, and he had no way of knowing that in her room below May was crouched in a chair, shivering and crying.

It was the familiar story: the young man back from the war, eager for his love, impatient of the cautious rules of peacetime; his girl no less eager for him, and ready to do anything to make him happy; and so, good-by rules! Willie had never tried to force May to yield to him. He had feared the entanglement more than he wanted this last intimacy, and their relationship had been full of sweetness without it. Nor did he force her this night. It happened; and it happened the more easily because they had both read lots of books which dismissed the rules as pretty primitive taboos and asserted that all morals were relative to time and place. Willie, floating in a daze of well-being, was certain at this moment that the books contained true wisdom. May, for some reason, wasn't so sure. Anyway, the deed was done.

A couple of hours later, after May had telephoned him and both had confessed that they were wide awake, they sat at a table in the dining room, eating breakfast in a flood of white sunshine. Through the tall cathedral-like window they could see the nearby towering cliff, and pine forests dark green against the snow, and, far away, the everlasting white peaks of the Sierras; an especially agreeable contrast for a table set with a fine cloth, and fresh flowers, and fragrant bacon and eggs and hot coffee. They were both very gay. Willie leaned back and said with a luxurious sigh, "Well, it cost me a hundred and ten dollars, but it was worth it."

"A hundred and ten dollars? For what? Two days in this place?"

"No, no. That was the ransom I paid to get off the *Caine*."

He told May about the lost liquor crate, and described how, when he had requested a seventy-two-hour pass, Captain Queeg had hemmed and hawed, and finally said, "Well, now, Willie, it seems to me you've still got that fiasco with the crate on your record." Whereupon the ensign had quickly answered, "Sir, I accept complete responsibility for my stupidity, and will try never to repeat such a bad performance. The least I can do, sir, is reimburse you for a loss which was my fault, and I hope you'll permit me to do so." At this Queeg had turned very pleasant; and, after a few gracious remarks to the effect that an ensign wouldn't be an ensign if he didn't make mistakes, he had agreed to let Willie go.

May was flabbergasted. She began to question Willie about his life on the *Caine*, and became more and more appalled as he talked, the Stilwell narrative shaking her most of all. "Ye gods, this Queeg, he's a—he's a monster, a maniac!"

"Well, more or less."

"Is the whole Navy like that?"

"Oh, no. The skipper before Queeg was a grand guy, and damned capable, too." The words were out of his mouth before it occurred to him to smile at his change of heart about De Vriess.

"Can't you *do* anything about him?"

"But what, May?"

"I don't know. Report him to an admiral. Write a letter to Walter Winchell. *Something!*"

Willie grinned, and put his hand over hers. They were silent for a while. Then May patted her lips with a napkin, opened her purse, and began repainting her mouth skillfully and quickly with a small brush which she dipped into a little black pot of rouge. Willie hadn't seen such a cosmetic technique before, and he found it a bit glaring and over-professional, but he pushed the distaste from his mind with the thought that a night-club singer must carry with her a trace or two of her trade. The hope flitted across his mind that May wouldn't bring out the brush if ever they dined with his mother. Lovers are supposed to come near the telepathic state; perhaps for this reason May gave him a keen look as she put away the brush and said, "Nice of your mother to let you run off like this."

"Well, I pretty well do as I please, darling——"

"I know—but after she came across the country, and all—you just leave her flat-footed——"

"I didn't ask her to come. She surprised me. Anyway, she's going to stay on, and you have to go back. It's only natural. She knows the score."

"I wonder," said May, with a little rueful smile. Willie pressed her hand, and they both colored a little.

"What does she think of me?" asked May, as forty billion poor girls have asked in their time.

"She thinks you're swell."

"I'll bet she does—— Really, what did she say? I mean the very first time she had a chance, when I walked off the pier and went back to the hotel? What were her exact words?"

Willie reviewed the awkward triangle scene on the wharf in his mind, the lame exchanges, the forced smiles, May's deft withdrawal in a few minutes, and his mother's remark, "Well, well. My Willie is keeping secrets from his old mother, eh? She's remarkably pretty. Model, or show-girl?"

"Her exact words, as I recall them," said Willie, "were, 'There goes a very beautiful little girl.' "

May snorted delicately and said, "Your memory isn't so hot, or you're a liar. Little of both, I guess—— Ow!"

A large blond young man in skiing clothes, walking past the table and chatting lovingly with a girl in a bright red ski suit, had cracked May's head with his elbow. There were apologies, and the young couple went off, fingers interlaced, swinging their arms and laughing into each other's eyes. "Goddamn honeymooners," muttered May, rubbing her head.

"What do you say, would you like to try skiing?" Willie said.

"No, thanks. I like my spine the way it is." But May's eyes brightened.

"Look, they have slopes that your grandmother wouldn't get hurt on——"

"I have no clothes, no skis—neither have you——"

"We'll buy 'em or rent 'em. Come on!" He sprang up and tugged at her hand.

drank coffee. "What would you like to do today?" said Willie.

"Anything you want."

"Did you sleep?"

"So-so."

"I'm sorry about last night," said Willie suddenly, though he had not had any intention of apologizing.

May smiled at him wanly and answered, "There's nothing to be sorry about, Willie."

Willie was seized with a feeling of vertigo, an actual dizziness, as though he were teetering at the edge of a deck, looking into a turbulent sea, and experiencing an impulse to jump overboard. His mouth became dry. He swallowed hard, and jumped. "What would you think of spending the rest of your life with a monster like me?" he said with difficulty.

May looked at him, a little amused, a little saddened. "What's this, now, dear?"

"I don't know, it seems to me maybe we ought to start talking about getting married," Willie said doggedly.

May put her hand on his, and said with a quiet smile, "Do you want to make an honest woman of me, Willie?"

"I don't know what else we're going to do with our lives," Willie said. "If you think I'm crazy, say so."

"I don't think you're crazy," said May. "Only I wish you didn't look as though you were taking a dose of medicine like a man."

Willie laughed. He looked into her face for a long moment. "Well, what do you say?"

May looked away, and glanced around the sunny dining room. Most of the tables were empty. In a corner near a window the honeymooners in the bright ski suits were leaning toward each other, the bride feeding a bit of coffee cake into her husband's mouth. "What do I say about what, Willie?"

"About our getting married."

"I haven't heard you propose."

"I propose to you that we get married," said Willie with extreme distinctness.

"I'll think about it," said the girl. She took her lip brush and rouge from her purse, then glanced up at Willie demurely. He wore a look of such pained surprise that she burst out laughing. "Oh, look, darling," she said, putting her cosmetics on the table, and touching his arm, "this is terribly sweet of you. I'm sure it's the best you can manage. But everything's all wrong this morning. I can't jump at your words and hold you to them just because you're feeling sheepish, and sorry for me. If we're going to get married, why, I guess maybe we will sometime. I don't know. Talk about other things."

Willie, in a fog of bewilderment, watched her skillfully paint her mouth. Every word that they had both spoken seemed printed on his mind, and as he scanned the interview it seemed to him an unbelievable exchange. He had often pictured proposing to May, but nothing he had ever imagined resembled this devious, inconclusive reality. The possibility had never occurred to him that, several minutes after allowing himself to speak the fateful words, he might still be free.

May, for all her apparent calm, for all the steadiness with which she traced the carmine outline of her lips, was as confused and dizzied as Willie. All her reactions and words had come to her unbidden. She had not expected Willie to propose, and even less had anticipated that she could fail to accept. Yet now the scene was done, and nothing had been solved. "I think I'd like to ride a horse," she said, still looking in the mirror. "A nice gentle one. Would you like that?"

"Sure," said Willie. "Hurry with the paint job."

They rode sad old horses through the snow on bulky Western saddles, May clutching the saddle horn and laughing breathlessly whenever her nag gamboled forward in a brief trot. Willie was an experienced rider, and the diversion was tame for him, but he enjoyed the crystal air, and the awesome scenery, and above all the beauty and good humor of his girl. They were hungry at lunch time, and ate huge steaks. In the afternoon they went for a sleigh ride, nestling under horsy-smelling blankets and exchanging mild caresses while the garrulous old driver droned geological facts about the valley. Back at the hotel, they started drinking long before dinner, and wafted through an evening of dancing and chatter in a pleasant haze of affection and good feeling. Willie left May at her door that night, after a short but wholehearted kiss, and went upstairs, glowing with manly virtue and alcoholic exaltation.

The bus ride back to San Francisco next day was long. It was pleasant enough to look out of the window at the snowy thick-forested peaks and gorges of the Sierras, holding hands and saying nothing. But when the bus rolled out into the San Joaquin Valley and sped quietly along U.S. 99 between endless plum groves and truck gardens, all wintry brown and bare, Willie became more and more aware that the time was at hand for serious talk. Not only San Francisco and the *Caine* lay at the end of this long straight macadam trail. There was also his mother. "Darling," he said.

May turned and gave him an affectionate look.

"Have you thought about us?" Willie said.

"Sure, lots." May sat up in her seat and disengaged her hand to light a cigarette.

"Well—what do you say?"

Between the moment that the match flared and the time she dropped it in the ashtray, May's mind raced through a long series of thoughts. The gist of them was a sense of insecurity and dissatisfaction, and a suspicion that she was in a bad corner. "What do you want me to say, Willie?"

"That you'll marry me."

May shrugged. This tepid, matter-of-fact courtship was no part of love and marriage as she had vaguely imagined it. But common sense was her strong point, and she thought she had better take what was offered. She wanted Willie. "You know me, Willie—hard to get," she said, with an abashed, confused smile and a blush. "When? Where? What do you want to do?"

Willie, with a heavy sigh, clasped her hand tightly and said, "Those are the things we have to think about next."

May sat up straight and shot a glance at him full of her old wariness. "Look dear, let's get one thing straight. If you're starting a little home for fallen women, I'm not interested. I don't want you to marry me because you're sorry for me, or because you want to do the manly thing by me, or anything like that."

"I love you, May."

"You'd better think about the whole thing some more."

"I don't want to think about it any more," said Willie, but his tone lacked conviction. He was confused about his motives, and suspected that misguided chivalry might be at the bottom of his proposal. Willie Keith was steeped in suburban morality, and he was inexperienced, and more-over, he was not the brightest young man on the planet. The night he had spent with May had sunk the girl in his esteem though it had heightened her as an object of desire. He did not really know what he ought to do, and on the whole was as miserable as a young man might be with a beautiful girl like May at his side and within his grasp.

"Are you going to talk to your mother about it?"

"Well, I guess she'd better know, the sooner the better."

"That's a conversation I'd like to hear."

"I'll repeat it for you tonight, after I talk to her," said Willie. "Word for word."

After a long silence Willie said, "There's the matter of religion. How strongly do you feel about—about yours?" It was a great effort to bring the words out. He was embarrassed by a feeling that he was being stupidly and falsely solemn about something that was totally unreal.

May said, "I'm afraid I'm not a good Catholic by any means, Willie. That won't be a problem."

"Well, fine." The bus turned in to a roadside restaurant and stopped. Willie jumped up with great relief. "Come on, let's get some coffee or I'll die."

An old lady who was unpacking a lunch basket on her lap in one of the forward seats glanced up with sentimental pleasure at the pretty red-haired girl in the camel's-hair coat, and the young pink-cheeked ensign in his long, gold-buttoned bridge coat, white silk scarf, and white officer's cap. "Now there," she said to the old gentleman by her side, whose eyes were on the lunch basket, "*There* goes a darling couple."

17 · Two Bottles of Champagne

Maryk was awakened from an uneasy sleep by the sound of a metal drill directly over his face, a few inches from his skull. He threw aside the piled blankets on his bunk and leaped down, shuddering as his naked feet touched the clammy deck. He put on grease-stained khakis by the light of an electric lantern.

He had that most miserable of Navy watches, the twenty-four-hour stretch as duty officer on a cold ship in drydock. The *Caine* was a corpse of iron. Heat, light, power were gone. Boilers and main engines lay disemboweled. The fuel oil was all pumped out, and the purr of the ventilators, the vessel's breathing noise, was stilled. A thousand rattles, bangs, screeches, scrapes, and grinding shocks replaced it. Yard workmen were executing yet another rejuvenation by plastic surgery on the scarred old ship. The foggy San Francisco air drifted stagnantly through the passageways, rancid with the smell of mildew, and the staterooms and crew's quarters were a chaos of scattered books and magazines and dirty linen.

The officers and crew were billeted in nearby barracks. Only the duty officer and a gangway watch remained to connect the defunct shell with its former identity. Captain Queeg had shot off to his home in Arizona a couple of hours after the ship had entered the dock, leaving Gorton in charge. Adams, Carmody, Rabbitt, and Paynter had gone on leave, and the crew seethed unhappily in the barracks, waiting for the fifth day in the States, when their leaves could commence. Their spirits were at such ebb, the atmosphere in their barracks so funereal, that even

Maryk, friendly though he was with the sailors, could hardly bear to visit them for a muster.

He went topside, emerging into a gray cloudy morning, and picked his way carefully over and around the litter of pipes, hoses, parts of machines, lumber, tarpaulins, and crates. At the gangway he found the duty petty officer, Meatball, in dirty wrinkled whites, asleep on a coil of manila rope. He roused him without bitterness, and sent the yawning coxswain across the long gray gangplank that spanned the gulf of the drydock, to buy coffee and doughnuts.

At eight o'clock Ensign Harding staggered aboard, his face bluish-gray. He relieved the first lieutenant, wobbled to the wardroom, and fell asleep on the couch on a prickly pile of knives and forks.

Maryk went to the BOQ and tried to rouse Keefer, but the novelist groaned, "See you St. Francis lunch one o'clock," and fell obstinately asleep in an instant. The first lieutenant changed into dress blues still rank of camphor despite a cleaning, and caught a bus to the city.

San Francisco was his boyhood home, and he had been full of nostalgia for it from the moment the *Caine* had steamed under the Golden Gate Bridge. But finding himself on Market Street again, he didn't know what to do with himself. He killed time in aimless dull wandering until one o'clock.

Keefer was waiting for him in the lobby of the St. Francis, slouched in an armchair, looking pallid and weedy. They went to the ornate dining room and ate an elaborate costly lunch. The novelist insisted on ordering a bottle of champagne to celebrate their temporary freedom from Queeg. He drank most of it himself. Maryk thought it tasted like sweet beer. "What's the matter, Steve?" said Keefer. "You're way down in the dumps."

"I know."

"Why?"

"Couldn't tell you. Ever have one of those days, Tom, when you feel something bad is in the air—something bad's going to happen to you before the day's out?"

"Sure. That your trouble?"

"Maybe so. Ever since I got up, I don't know, everything's seemed so gray and lousy." He glanced around. "I feel damn funny in this place. Steve Maryk eating in the St. Francis. When I was a kid I thought only millionaires ate here."

"How does Frisco look to you after—how many years?"

"Ten, I guess—we moved to Pedro in '33. Lousy. I feel like a goddamn ghost."

"That's your trouble, then. Seeing your childhood home will do it to you—the sense of the passing of time. It's the cold breath of death, Steve, on the back of your neck."

Maryk grinned wryly. "Cold breath of death. Stick it in your novel."

Rain began to splatter against the window by which they sat. Maryk said, "There goes the plan to walk across the Golden Gate Bridge, if you were still figuring on it."

"Hell, that was romantic nonsense. I get carried away sometimes. We're going out to Berkeley. I've got something on the fire there."

"What?"

"I know an English prof there. Phoned him this morning. He invited us out to a literary tea. Main thing is, the literary club is ninety per cent girls."

"I'll try anything."

"You'll have to listen to me talk on 'The Novel in World War II,' God help you."

"That's okay." Maryk lit a cigar.

Both officers felt the queerness of being away from the ship, in a luxurious hotel, in dress blues. They looked like strangers to each other. And, like strangers thrown together, they began to talk of very personal things. They exchanged full accounts of their family backgrounds. In a half hour Maryk found out more about Keefer's family and love affairs than he had learned in a year of sailing with him on the *Caine*. He told the novelist about his fishing experiences, and was flattered by Keefer's eager probing questions.

"Sounds like a marvelous life, Steve."

"Well, it isn't. It boils down to making a dollar the

hardest way there is. Break your back, and the market is never right—when you catch shad, nobody wants shad—when you catch mackerel, there's so much goddamn mackerel you can't sell it for manure—and that's how it goes. And the jobbers on the beach scrounging every quarter they can. It's a business for dumb foreigners, like my father. I'm dumb, too, but I'm not a foreigner. I'll find something else to do."

"Meaning the Navy?"

"Okay, I'm stupid. I like the Navy."

"I don't understand it, Steve. There's something so honest and useful about fishing. Not a motion wasted, not a drop of fuel oil burned without a purpose. You break your back, yes, but at the end of a run you've got *fish*. You of all people, to want the Navy! Paper, paper, paper —nothing but phony kowtowing and gun-decking and idiotic drills, all to no purpose whatever—utter waste— Christ, and the *peacetime* Navy—Sunday school every day of the week for grown men——"

"Don't you think the country needs a navy?"

"Sure."

"Who's going to man it?"

"The Queegs, of course. Not useful citizens."

"Sure. Leave it to the Queegs. Then along comes the war, and you get a Queeg over you, and you scream bloody murder."

"Screaming helps pass the time."

"The Navy isn't all Queegs by a long shot."

"Of course not. He's a waste product of the system. Buckled into a monster because his feeble little personality can't stand the pressure of Navy standards—— This is fine champagne, by the bye, pity you don't appreciate it—— But Steve, the real Navy is a tight little father-and-son group. It's a tradition, like the British governing class. You don't shine in. You'd just be one of the lowly time-servers——"

"You think fishing is useful. Well, I think manning Navy ships is useful. They're coming in goddamn handy at this point——"

"So help me, you're a patriot, Steve."

"In a pig's eye. I know seamanship, and I'd a damn sight rather put in twenty years for the Navy and get a pension than get arthritis and a sprung back hauling fish out of the water. At least that's how I figure it with my thick head."

"Well, bless you, my boy. Here's to Fleet Admiral Maryk, CincPac of 1973." He sloshed champagne into Maryk's glass and made him drink it. "How's your premonition doing, boy?"

"Well, it goes away when I don't think about it."

"The little Berkeley girls will fix everything. Let's shove off."

Professor Curran, a pudgy man with a pink face and a little soft mouth like a child's, led the two officers into a reception room alive with twittering coeds. Here and there were gawky boys of bad complexion. The arrival of two battle veterans in blue and gold electrified the air. The girls lost their real nonchalance and assumed false nonchalant attitudes; and there was a violent activity in powder puffs and lipsticks.

The professor's introduction of Keefer was long and fulsome. This was one of the rising literary stars of America, he told the shining-eyed girls. He mentioned that several of Keefer's short stories and verses had appeared in the *Yale Quarterly* and such fine periodicals. He dwelt on his play, *The Amaranthine Weed,* which the Theatre Guild had held under option for a year. "But," he added archly, "lest you get the idea that Thomas Keefer is just another writer for the high-brow coterie, let me inform you that he has also sold stories to *Esquire* and the *Ladies' Home Journal*—yes indeed, the very best of the 'slicks,' as they are known." The girls giggled and exchanged knowing looks. It was all news to Maryk, sunk in the corner of a decrepit green couch in the back of the room. Keefer had never talked about his writing. It was unnerving to realize that his shipmate was a real young author of consequence. He was ashamed to think that he had joined in the coarse wardroom jokes about Keefer's novel.

"And so we are going to have the unexpected pleasure of hearing about the Novel in World War II—not from me—but from a young man who may well write the novel of World War II—Lieutenant Thomas Keefer, of the U.S.S. *Caine*."

Keefer acknowledged the loud applause with a charming smile, and began to talk easily. The girls seemed to soak up the speech, but Maryk derived nothing from it but the sad reassurance that his flunking grades in English had been well deserved. In the tangle of names—Kafka, Proust, Hemingway, Stein, Huxley, Crane, Zweig, Mann, Joyce, Wolfe—he recognized only one, Hemingway. He dimly recalled having started to read a twenty-five-cent reprint of a Hemingway novel, attracted by the cover picture of a naked girl sitting up in bed talking to a fully dressed soldier; but the tale had seemed too well written to be a sex story, and he had abandoned it.

Keefer talked for half an hour, leaving Maryk completely baffled and humiliated. Then the girls swirled and frothed around the speaker in a circle four or five deep, while Maryk leaned against the wall and conducted a dry stumbling conversation with a couple of the least good-looking ones, whose interest in him was confined to such information as he could give them about Keefer. Maryk wondered whether this was the fulfillment of his foreboding: an afternoon in which his nose had been rubbed painfully in his own ignorance and stupidity. He wasn't sure he could ever talk naturally with Keefer again.

After a while the novelist captured two of the prettiest girls, and they went to dinner in a candlelit French restaurant overlooking the bay. Maryk telephoned the ship's office, a routine check at eight o'clock. He came back to the table gnawing his lips; his eyes were prominent. "They want us back aboard, Tom."

"What! When?"

"Right now."

"What's the dope?"

"I spoke to Jellybelly. He wouldn't say. Gorton wants us back."

The girls uttered tiny chirps of dismay. They drove away unhappily in their red Buick convertible, and the officers hailed a cab. Keefer cursed the bad luck and offered wild conjectures about the summons. The first lieutenant sat silent, rubbing his wet palms on his coat sleeves.

In the glare of a yellow floodlight at the foot of the gangplank, Gorton and Harding stood beside a knot of hooded welders crouched over their blue flames on the deck. "What's the dope?" yelled Keefer, trampling behind Maryk down the gangplank.

"You'd better get on the ball, Mr. Maryk," said Gorton with a crafty grin. "The exec is supposed to keep the duty officer informed of his whereabouts. I've been calling every hotel bar in town for you——"

The first lieutenant screwed up his blunt features. "What are you talking about?"

"You heard me. You've got it, Steve," said Gorton. "Adams and I received our orders this afternoon. You're the new exec of the *Caine*." He took the astounded officer's hand and shook it heartily.

"*Me?*" stammered Maryk. "*Me?*"

"It's happening in the whole squadron, Steve. Over on the *Simon* a bird who made lieutenant in October has got exec. And their new skipper is a reserve lieutenant. The whole deal is busting wide open. We've got a night's work ahead of us——"

"Did I get orders?" Keefer interrupted eagerly.

"No, and you ain't ever going to, Tom. This does it. They peeled off Carmody, too. You and Steve will ride her into the boneyard. You'll be exec in a year."

Keefer took off his white hat and dashed it to the deck. It bounced, rolled to the side, and disappeared. Gorton leaned over the life lines. "Dear me," he said, "smack into a puddle of bilge. Looks like the new senior watch officer needs a new hat."

"God damn the *Caine*," said Keefer, "and strike everyone aboard it, including me, with a curse."

Maryk peered gloomily around at the old ship, as though he were reporting aboard for the first time. "This is it," he thought—but he could not have said what he meant by "it."

It was not hard for Mrs. Keith to see that her Willie was not the same lad who had left for Yosemite three days earlier. They were having dinner at the Mark Hopkins Hotel in her suite overlooking the bay. The view was fine, the dinner was excellent, the champagne a rare French vintage; but Willie ignored the view, picked at his dinner, and left the wine sloshing in the bucket of melting ice, except when his mother reminded him to pour.

Mrs. Keith was aware that the *Caine* had changed Willie. His face was narrower. The innocent curves which she affectionately thought of as baby fat were disappearing, and her own marked cheekbones and square jaw were taking shape in her son's countenance. His eyes and mouth gave less the impression of his old easy good humor than of fatigue and a certain petulant doggedness. His hair seemed thinner, too. These things Mrs. Keith had noted in the first moments on the pier. But there was a deeper change now, an uneasiness and gloomy abstraction, and the mother had a good idea of what the trouble was. "May Wynn is a remarkably pretty young woman," she said, breaking a long silence, pouring tea for Willie.

"She sure is."

"How do things stand between you and her?"

"I think I may marry her, Mother."

"Oh? Pretty sudden, isn't it?"

"No. I've known her for a long time."

"How long?" Mrs. Keith smiled. "You've been very cagey about it all, I must say, Willie."

He told his mother briefly about the romance, and explained that he hadn't talked to her of it because until recently he hadn't regarded it seriously.

"But now you do, eh?"

"Obviously, Mother."

"Well, you underestimated her from the first, Willie. She's extraordinarily attractive. What's her background? Do you know her parents?"

Willie admitted everything. He added some sentiments

about the equality of all Americans and the need to
judge people on their merits rather than their background.
He put in a good word for May, in conclusion, by disclosing that she was working her way through college so
as to be more worthy of him. Mrs. Keith took the whole
revelation calmly, allowing Willie to talk himself out. She
lit a cigarette, left the table, and stood at the window,
looking out at the bay. Willie had the curious sensation
that he had been through such scenes before. He realized
that he had felt the same way in childhood, discussing a
bad report card with his mother.

"Have you proposed to her?"

"Yes."

"You proposed out at Yosemite, didn't you?"

"Yes."

"I rather thought so."

"She hasn't exactly accepted me," said Willie, stating
the fact as though it added to May's stature. "She said
I'd better think about it some more, and tell you."

Mrs. Keith smiled pityingly over her shoulder at her
son and said, "I think she'll accept you, Willie."

"I hope she will."

"Willie—what's your exact relationship with this girl?"

"That's a hell of a question, Mother."

"I think you've answered me, Willie."

"Don't get any wrong ideas. She isn't a tramp, and I
haven't been living with her——"

"I'm sure she's not a tramp——"

"She's a sweet, good girl, and you'll just have to take
my word for that."

"Willie, you're through with your dinner, aren't you?
Come here and sit with me on the sofa. I want to tell you
a story."

She sat close beside him, and took his hand in hers.
Willie disliked the touch; it was too intimate, too parental,
made him too much the confused child needing guidance,
but he lacked the heart to pull his hand away. "Before
your father married me," said Mrs. Keith, "while he was
a medical student and an intern, he lived for three years
with a nurse. I don't suppose you know that."

Willie did remember his father's short, bleak reference to the nurse, in their one conversation about May, but he said nothing.

"Well, I never met her, but I saw her picture and found out a lot about her. Her name was Katherine Quinlan, and she was a tall, beautiful brunette, with lovely large eyes—a little cowlike, if you'll forgive my saying it, but lovely—and a gorgeous figure. I knew about her before we married. Your dad told me the whole story. It almost broke up our engagement. I was furiously jealous." She gave a soft reminiscent sigh. "Well, I took his word that it was all over, and it was. But he too, Willie, at one time, had wanted to marry this girl. It was natural. His father persuaded him not to, simply making your dad face facts about himself. Your dad liked to mingle with the best people, and to live easily and luxuriously, Willie. He used to talk a lot about a Spartan life of research, but it was just a dream with which he amused himself. Had your father married the nurse he would have had his Spartan life, and he would have been sorry for it. That was why he waited to get married until he met me—— Give me a cigarette, please."

She continued, "Any man has a feeling of debt toward a decent girl with whom he has had an affair. Furthermore, he acquires a taste for her. All that is inevitable. The point is, any girl with half a brain knows these things. And if she really wants a man, and feels that her chances are good, she'll risk it. It's the last throw of the dice."

Willie's cheeks became red, and he started to speak. His mother rode over him. "Willie dear, this is all a process, natural and inevitable. It's happened a million times. Anybody can get caught up in it. Only remember, a marriage shouldn't be based on a bad conscience, or a taste for a girl's looks, but on similar background and values. If you get married out of a guilty feeling, very well, the guilty feeling passes—to a certain extent—but what else have you got? Now, honestly—do you think you love this girl—or do you feel obligated to her?"

"Both."

"That means you feel obligated to her. Naturally you're trying to tell yourself you love her, to make the marriage as palatable as possible. Willie, do you want this night-club singer to bear your children? Do you want the Italian fruit peddlers in the Bronx—I have no doubt they're decent, good people—but do you want them for your in-laws, coming into your home whenever they choose, being the grandparents of your sons and daughters? Can you picture it?"

"How do I know I'll ever do better? At least I want this girl. She's the only one I've ever wanted."

"Willie, you're twenty-three. Your dad married at thirty. You'll meet a thousand girls in the next six years."

"You keep saying I want to marry her because I feel guilty. How do you know what I feel? I love her. She's beautiful, she's good-natured, she's not stupid, I'm sure she'll make a good wife, and if her background is crude, what of it? I think I'll be sorry the rest of my life if I let her go——"

"Darling, I broke two engagements before I married your father. Each time, I thought the world had come to an end."

"What do I need background in a wife for? If I ever come back from this blasted war, what will I be? A piano player——"

"There you're wrong, and you know you are. Willie, you're growing up fast. Does show business still appeal to you, really? Aren't you beginning to realize that there's more to you than fooling with a piano?"

It was a good blow. In the long watches on the *Caine* Willie had come nearer and nearer to the decision that at the piano he was an untalented dilettante. What he wanted after the war was a university career, at a quiet, noble school like Princeton, teaching literature, perhaps eventually (this his innermost dream, hardly confided even to himself) writing works of scholarship, or even a novel or two. "I don't know what I'm going to do. It's all so far in the future——"

"*I* know what you're going to do. You're going to be a distinguished scholar. And when I'm gone you'll be wealthy, and independent, and you'll move in the circle of educators and philosophers—Conant, Hutchins, people like that are your kind—and in the name of truth, Willie, does May fit into that picture? Could she be happy as a faculty wife? Do you see her pouring tea for Dean Wicks or chatting with Dr. Conant?"

He rose, went to the table, and fished the bottle out of the bucket. There was only half a glass of flat wine left. He poured it and drank it off.

"Willie dear, I'm telling you what your dad would have told you. God knows he would have been less crude and tactless. I'm sorry, but I've done my best. If I'm all wrong, just ignore me."

She walked quickly to her purse on a bureau, and touched a handkerchief to her eyes. Willie immediately came and put his arm around her shoulders. "Mother, I'm not angry. I know you're doing what you think is right. This is one of those tight corners. Somebody's got to be hurt——"

"So long as it isn't you, Willie, I don't care."

Willie left her side and walked into the bedroom, where he paced between the twin beds and the dresser, noting even as his mind gyrated the spare neatness with which his mother had laid out her slippers and flowered silk night robe, and the silver toilet set he had given her for her fiftieth birthday.

His position was crumbling. It was true that he had proposed to May out of a guilt feeling; true that he suspected her of gambling for marriage by yielding to him; true that he was ashamed of her background; true that he couldn't picture her as his partner in an academic life. He was not sure that he loved her. The night in Yosemite had clouded his feelings, and spread a murk of doubt and ill will over his whole tie to May. Was he a trapped fool, or an eager lover? There was no doubt whatever that he felt much more like a trapped fool. His self-respect gave way, and he was wretchedly pale. "You pitiful jackass," he murmured at the mirror, and went back to the sitting room. His mother stood where he had left her. "Look Mother, let's not talk about it any more." He dropped into an armchair and put a hand over his eyes. "Nothing's going to be done tomorrow. Give me a chance to think."

"Weren't you planning to get married during this trip to the States, dear?"

"I don't know, I don't know. We hadn't made definite plans. I told you she hadn't even accepted me."

"She's very wise. Oh, Willie, wait at least until you come back again. It's not fair to any girl to tie her up when you're going back out into the war. Promise me you won't get married this time. That's all I ask, and believe me I ask it for your sake."

"I believe you, Mother. I probably won't. But I can't tell you I'll give her up, because I probably won't do that, either."

"I'm satisfied, darling." She put her hand comfortingly on his shoulder, and walked into the bedroom. Her son remained wilted in the armchair. After a few moments she called to him, while she powdered her nose at the dressing table, "You know what I'd like to do, dear?"

"What?"

"I'd like to have a couple of stiff brandies, and then go see a very funny and silly movie. Do you know whether there's one playing in town?"

"Sorry, Mother. I'm meeting May a little later."

"Oh. Well," she said cheerily, "have you time for a drink with me first?"

"Sure."

"Where is May staying?"

"At a small hotel near the St. Francis."

"Oh. Well, maybe you can drop me off at a movie on the way down."

"Certainly, Mother." Willie walked to the window, and leaned his forehead on the cool pane, without seeing anything. He had never felt more empty and sick. His mouth rested against the wooden frame of the window. Unthinking, he bit into the wood, made a deep print of teeth in it, and got a mouthful of cracked varnish and dust. He wiped his mouth with his handkerchief, and stared ruefully at the two rows of tooth marks in the wood.

"Well," he thought, "some people carve hearts on trees."

Next day he saw May off at the airport. Their parting kiss was passionate. Nothing was settled. He had lied to May about the talk with his mother. They were vaguely and informally engaged, but there was to be no ring, and no definite planning, until after the war. May seemed satisfied; at any rate she didn't argue.

18 · Stilwell's Leave

Suspend all work on Caine not thirty per cent or more complete. Cut overhaul period to three weeks. Caine under way for Pearl not later than 29 December.

Willie brought the despatch to Maryk in the temporary ship's office in a warehouse near the drydock: one desk, actually, in a corner of a big, busy shipping room, where the new executive officer and Jellybelly spent most of the day transacting ship's business on an extremely senile typewriter, surrounded by toppling heaps of records, forms, files, reference books, and miscellaneous papers of all sizes and colors.

"Stabbed, by God," said Maryk.

"What does it mean?" said Willie. "No leave for the second section?"

Jellybelly paused in his pecking at the typewriter and, though he did not look up, his face seemed to grow appreciably longer.

"I hope not. Jellybelly, get the captain on the phone."

The yeoman put through the call to Phoenix, while the officers fidgeted. "Sir," he said, putting his hand over the mouthpiece, "it's Mrs. Queeg. She says the captain was out late last night and is still asleep. She wants to know whether it's urgent."

Glancing at the wall clock, which showed a quarter past twelve, the exec said, "Tell her it's urgent."

The yeoman obeyed and hastily handed Maryk the receiver. After perhaps two minutes, Maryk heard Queeg's voice, hoarse and cranky, "Hello? What's the trouble now?"

The exec read the despatch slowly over the telephone. There was a pause during which he heard the captain breathing heavily. "Kay. Those are our orders. Carry them out," said Queeg. "Notify the yard repair officer, and so forth. You know what to do—— Or do you?"

"Yes, sir."

"I see no necessity for me to come up there, but I will if you think you can't handle it."

"I think I can, sir. I wanted to ask you about the leave situation."

"Hm. Well, what about it? I can't spare you, Steve. I'm sorry, it's just one of those tough breaks——"

"Sir, I was thinking mainly about the men. The way things are now the second section won't get any leave at all."

"Well, that's not my fault. It's just one of those things——"

"I only thought, sir, if we could get the first section back early, we might still give the others a week—at least most of them."

"How the hell can you do that? They're scattered all over the country."

"Well, I have all their forwarding addresses. I'll wire them."

"Ha! You don't know sailors. They'll say they never got the wires."

"Well, I'll order them to acknowledge by return wire. The ones that don't answer, I'll telephone. The ones I don't get by telephone, I'll send special-delivery registered letters to."

"Who's going to pay for all these wires and phones and special deliveries?" said the captain peevishly. "We have no appropriation for——"

"We have a surplus in the ship's welfare fund, sir."

There was a silence. Then the captain said, "Well, if you want to go to all that trouble I have no objection. I want to see the men get their leave as much as you do, bearing in mind, however, that there are other important things to be done at this point, too. Go ahead with your wires and phone calls. For every man that comes back you can send one on leave."

"Thank you, sir. How about the officers?"

"No, I'm afraid the officers are just out of luck. We'll recommend extended leave for them whenever they get orders. How's everything coming?"

"Well, this despatch will foul us up pretty badly, sir. But I guess it'll just be a question of buttoning up again as fast as we can."

"Those new officers reported aboard yet?"

"Two of them have, sir—Jorgensen and Ducely."

"Well, get them started at once on their qualification courses. They're to turn in an assignment a day, or no shore leave."

"Aye aye, sir."

"All right. Don't hesitate to call me if there's any doubt in your mind about anything. Will we get those new radars installed?"

"Yes, sir. That work is more than half finished."

"Well, good, that was the main idea, anyway. Kay. Good-by."

"Good-by, sir."

The yeoman ran out clumsily, clutching a list of the sailors in the first section and a scribbled copy of the telegram dictated by Maryk to recall them. He brushed past Stilwell, who approached the desk, twisting his hat.

"Sorry to bother you, Mr. Maryk," the gunner's mate said in a shaky voice. "Hello, Mr. Keith." He took a wrinkled telegram from his trouser pocket and gave it to the exec. Maryk frowned over it and showed it to Willie.

MOTHER VERY SICK. DOCTOR SAYS MAY NOT LIVE. COME HOME. PAUL.

"Paul's my kid brother," the sailor said. "Do you think I could get emergency leave, Mr. Maryk?"

"Your case is a little complicated, Stilwell—— Willie, what's the procedure on emergency leave?"

"Don't know. Hasn't come up since I've been morale officer——"

"Jellybelly knows, Mr. Maryk," Stilwell put in. "De Lauche, he got emergency leave when we were down at Guadal. His father died——"

"Willie, call the yard chaplain. Ask him about procedure."

The chaplain was not in his office; but his yeoman told Willie that it was customary to check with the sailor's minister in his home town or with the local Red Cross, to verify the seriousness of the illness.

"How can we get in touch with your minister, Stilwell? Do you know his address?" said Maryk.

"Don't belong to no church, sir."

"Well, then, it's the Red Cross, I guess. Willie, send a wire——"

"Sir, I live in a small town," broke in the sailor. "I don't remember no Red Cross office——"

Willie, watching the sailor carefully, said, "The Red Cross will track down the case, Stilwell, don't worry——"

"By that time my mother may be dead. Sir, you've got my brother's wire, what more do you want?"

Willie said, "Stilwell, step away from this desk a moment. I want to speak to the exec."

"Yes, sir." The sailor withdrew to the other side of the room, and slouched against the wall, his thumbs hooked in his trousers, his hat tilted back on his head, his face sullen and despairing.

"Stilwell got his brother to send that wire," Willie told the exec. "There's nothing wrong with his mother. He's worried about his wife—apparently she's the kind you have to worry about. I'm surprised he didn't go over the hill a week ago."

Maryk rubbed his palm slowly against the back of his head. "I know about Stilwell's wife. What am I supposed to do?"

"Let him shove off, sir. He lives in Idaho. He can fly home in a few hours. Give him a seventy-two-hour pass. The captain may never even know about it. If he does, there's the telegram to excuse it."

"If the captain finds out, the telegram isn't going to help me, Willie."

"Sir, Stilwell is human. He didn't do anything to deserve being chained up like a beast."

"I'm supposed to carry out the captain's orders and intentions. I know damn well what his intention would be in this case. Hell, if his mother really *was* dying Captain Queeg might not let him go——"

"You're not Queeg, sir."

Maryk gnawed his lips. "This is just the beginning. To let Stilwell go is wrong, Willie. Gorton wouldn't have done it. If I start wrong I'm going to finish wrong."

Willie shrugged. "I beg your pardon for arguing with you so much, sir."

"Hell, I don't blame you. I'd be arguing, too, if someone else was the exec. Call Stilwell over."

The sailor responded to Willie's wave by strolling listlessly back to the desk. "Stilwell," said the exec, touching the phone, "I'm going to call the captain about you."

"Don't waste your time, sir," said Stilwell, in a tone edged with hate.

"Do you expect me to conduct the ship's business in a manner contrary to what the captain wants?" The sailor did not answer. Maryk looked at him for a long while, with a pained grimace. "How long would it take you to get home from here?"

Stilwell gasped, and stammered, "Five hours, sir, tops, by plane and bus——"

"Would a seventy-two do you any good?"

"Christ, sir, I'll kiss your feet——"

"Never mind that damn foolishness. Will you give me your word to come back at the end of seventy-two hours?"

"I swear, sir, I swear I will——"

Maryk turned to the ensign. "There's a file of forms in that yellow folder on top of the mail log. Instead of waiting for Jellybelly, how's for you to type out a seventy-two now? I'll sign it and he can shove off. The sooner the better."

Willie flew into a frenzy of motion and clatter; and in three minutes he passed the papers to Maryk. Stilwell stood by in a daze. The exec signed the papers. "Do you have an idea, Stilwell," he said, "what it means to me to have you back on time?"

"Yes, sir. I hope to die if I'm not back, sir."

"Shove off."

"God bless you, sir."

The officers looked after the sailor as he scampered out. Maryk gloomily shook his head, and picked up his work progress chart. Willie said, "An exec sure has the power to do a hell of a lot of good. I guess it's the best part of the job."

"The duty of an exec," Maryk said, coloring a line of squares on the chart with a red pencil, "is to do exactly what the captain would want him to do. It's the only way to run a ship. Don't bring any more requests like that to me, Willie. I'm not going to go soft in the head any more."

Unfortunately, Stilwell didn't return to the *Caine* at the end of seventy-two hours, and Captain Queeg did.

Willie learned these two unpleasant facts by telephone at six-thirty in the morning, in his mother's hotel suite, where he had spent the night. Jellybelly telephoned him, apologizing for disturbing him and explaining that the captain had arrived and wanted a muster at eight o'clock.

"Okay, I'll be there," Willie said sleepily, and added, "Hey, is Stilwell back yet?"

"No, sir."

"Jesus."

When he arrived at the Navy Yard the shrunken crew of the *Caine* had already gathered in ragged lines at the edge of the drydock. He fell in place with the officers, yawning, wishing he had had time to eat breakfast. A few drops of rain spattered down from massed gray clouds as

Maryk and the captain came up the gangplank. The men assumed a dreary semblance of attention. Queeg, freshly shaved and wearing a new blue raincoat, looked spruce, but his eyes were bloodshot and his face puffy and pallid.

"Well, I won't keep you men long," he said, peering around at the crew and pitching his voice high above the riveting and the snorts of the cranes. "Our California sunshine is a little damp this morning. I just want you to know I'm making every effort to see to it that you all get some kind of leave despite the curtailing of the overhaul. It's just one of those things. As you know, there's a war on, and we can't all have things just the way we want them. I want to caution you all as strongly as I can against taking it on yourselves to go over the hill. Just remember, leave is not a right, but a special privilege, and if the Navy wants to work you 365 days out of 365 and one extra in leap year, why, there just isn't a damn thing you can do about it, so nobody owes you any apologies. As I say, I'll see what I can do, but don't go taking French leave, any of you. The Navy will find you even if you're down in a coal mine, and they'll send you back to the *Caine* even if the ship is in the Indian Ocean. And so I hope you're all having a pleasant stay in San Francisco and—well, Mr. Maryk, let's dismiss the men before we all get soaked."

Willie watched Queeg's face for a sign of wonder or displeasure at the absence of Stilwell; but the captain maintained a look of jolly good humor. The crew trotted off to their barracks, and the officers straggled after the captain and exec for a conference at the BOQ. Willie saw Stilwell come out of a side street, out of the captain's view, and go bounding down the gangplank to report to the duty officer. The ensign was immensely relieved. He wanted to whisper the good news to Maryk, but the exec was talking to Queeg.

The officers grouped around a couch in a corner of the BOQ lobby, drinking Coca-Colas. Queeg handed out the new departmental assignments. Keefer became gunnery officer. Willie was exalted to communications officer.

Willie had his first good look at the two newcomers to the wardroom. Ensign Jorgensen was a tall, heavyish fellow with curly blond hair, thick glasses over narrow peering eyes, and a fixed apologetic smile. He was remarkably sway-backed; his rump projected like a small bustle. Ensign Ducely was thin and cream-faced, and had girlish features and long slender hands. Willie suspected that physical standards had been lowered since his Furnald Hall days. Ensign Jorgensen's lordosis was cavernous compared to Willie's; yet here he was with a glistening gold stripe.

"By the bye," said Queeg suddenly to Maryk, "did I see our friend Stilwell at muster or didn't I? Seems to me I didn't."

"Why, sir——" Maryk began, but Willie quickly struck in: "Stilwell is here, sir."

"Are you sure?" said the captain dryly. "How do you know he hasn't gone over the hill?"

Willie said, addressing Maryk more than the captain, "Well, sir, I *saw him* at the gangway just a few seconds after muster."

"I see." The captain appeared convinced. He grumbled, rising from the couch, "Well, no reason for him to be late for muster, is there, Mr. Maryk? Put him on report."

Willie thought he had saved the situation. He was appalled when Maryk said, "Sir, I gave Stilwell a seventy-two."

Queeg sank back on the couch, astounded. "You did? And just why did you do that, sir?"

"He had a telegram that his mother was dying."

"Did you think of calling me and asking my permission?"

"Yes, sir."

"Well, why didn't you? Did you verify the telegram through the Red Cross?"

"No, sir."

"Why didn't you?"

Maryk looked at the captain, his face dull and blank.

"Well, let's get on with ship's business, Mr. Maryk. Where's the work progress chart?"

"In my room, sir."

Willie trembled for Maryk and himself.

In the exec's room, Queeg burst out, "God damn it, Steve, what kind of stupid trick was that with Stilwell?"

"Well, sir, an emergency——"

"Emergency, my behind! I want you to write the Red Cross and find out whether his mother died or whether she was sick at all, or what the exact truth was. I owe all the trouble I had with ComServPac to that little sneak. Remember when we cut the towline? That started it——"

(Maryk was startled. It was the first time the captain had ever admitted that the line had been cut.)

"——and it was Stilwell's fault. Imagine a helmsman not warning the commanding officer that the ship was in such danger! I know why he kept his mouth shut, of course. I'd bawled him out in the morning for being too goddamn fresh and making his own decisions at the helm, and he was just playing it real smart, see, letting me get myself in trouble. Kay. I know his kind. These vindictive little troublemakers that bear grudges are just my meat. I'm gunning for that little squirt and I'm going to get him, believe you me. You write the Red Cross this morning, do you hear?"

"Aye aye, sir."

"Let's see your chart."

They discussed the progress of repairs for a quarter of an hour. Queeg was not very interested; he checked off the items and asked a desultory question or two about each. He stood, putting on his raincoat. "Steve, there's one thing we'd better get straight," he said casually, fastening his belt. "I don't appreciate your evasiveness and generally sloppy handling in this Stilwell deal one bit. And I want to know frankly whether you're going to straighten up and fly right." He glanced sidewise. The exec's face was set in a miserable frown. "It's obvious to me that Stilwell has your sympathy. That's all every well. But let me remind you that you're my executive officer. I know damn well that the whole ship is against me. I can handle that. If you're against me, too, why I can handle that, too. There are fitness reports to be made out in due time. You'd just better make up your mind whose side you're on."

"Sir, I know I was wrong not to call you about Stilwell," the exec said haltingly, rubbing his moist palms together and looking down at them. "I'm not against you, sir. I've made one bad mistake. I won't repeat it in the future, Captain."

"Is that a man-to-man promise, Steve, or are you just applying the grease?"

"I don't know how to apply grease, sir. As far as my fitness report goes you'd be justified in giving me an Unsat in loyalty, on the Stilwell deal. But that's the first and last time."

Queeg held out his hand to the exec, who rose from his bunk and grasped it. "I accept what you say, and I'm willing to forget this incident," Queeg said. "I regard you as a damn good officer, Steve, far and away the best on the ship, and I consider myself lucky to have you. The rest are willing enough, and bright, but there isn't a sailor among them, and the two new ones don't look like prize packages, either——"

"I think we have a pretty good wardroom, sir——"

"Why, I said so. For a lot of wartime recruits, they're fine. But you and I have to run this ship. Now, I'm well aware that I'm not the easiest man in the world to get along with, and not the smartest either. I probably have done a lot of things that strike you as damned queer, and I'll probably go right on doing them. I can only see one way to run this ship, Steve, and come hell or high water that's how it's going to be run. And you're my exec, and so you're in the middle. I know all about that. I was exec for the unholiest son of a bitch in the Navy for three months, and during that time I did my duty, and was the second unholiest son of a bitch. That's how it goes."

"Yes, sir."

With a friendly smile, Queeg said, "Well, I'm off."

"I'll walk you down, sir."

"Why, thank you, Steve. That'll be very pleasant."

In the days that followed the *Caine* was hastily put back together by the yard workmen, none of its parts much the better for the disassembly; and the general hope, as in the case of a clock taken apart by a child, was not that it would perform in an improved manner, but rather that it might begin ticking again as well as before. Some of the worst decay in the engineering plant was patched and the ship had new radars. Otherwise it was the same mangy old *Caine*. Nobody knew why the overhaul time had been cut in half, but Keefer was vocal on the point, as usual. "Someone finally figured out that the bucket won't hold together for more than one invasion, anyway," he theorized. "So they just souped her up enough for one last gasp."

On the thirtieth of December, the *Caine* steamed out through the Golden Gate at sunset, minus some twenty-five of her crew, who had elected court-martial for missing ship rather than another cruise with Queeg. Willie Keith was on the bridge, and his spirits were low as the last hills slipped past the bow, and the ship issued forth on the purple sea. He knew this meant a long, long parting from May. There would be hundreds of thousands of miles of steaming, and probably many battles, before the ship would come into these waters again with its bow pointed the other way. The sun, dead ahead, sinking beneath ragged banks of dark clouds, shot out great spokes of red light which fanned across the western sky. It was an uncomfortable similitude of the flag of Japan.

But he had a good steak dinner in the wardroom, and he wasn't posted for a night watch. And what cheered him most of all was that he went to sleep in a room, not the clipping shack. He had inherited Carmody's bunk, and Paynter was his new roommate.

With a sense of great luxury and well-being, Willie crawled to the narrow upper bunk and slid between the fresh, rough Navy sheets. He lay only a few inches beneath the plates of the main deck. He had not much more room than he would have had under the lid of a coffin. A knotty valve of the fire main projected downward into his stomach. The stateroom was not as large as the dressing closet in his Manhasset home. But what did all that matter? From the clipping shack to this bunk was a great rise in the world. Willie closed his eyes, listened with pleasure to the hum of the ventilators, and felt in his bones the vibration of the main engines, transmitted through the springs of his bunk. The ship was alive again. He felt warm, and safe, and at home. Drowsiness came over him almost at once, and he slept deliciously.

V

THE MUTINY

19 · The Circle of Compliance

Any recent book of military history is likely to contain the
remark that by the beginning of 1944 World War II was
really won. Quite rightly, too. The great turning points,
Guadalcanal, El Alamein, Midway, and Stalingrad, were
in the past. Italy had surrendered. The murdering Germans were at last recoiling. The Japanese, their meager
power spread thin over a swollen empire, had begun to
crack. The industrial power of the Allies was coming to
flood; that of their enemies was waning. It was a bright
picture.

But Ensign Keith had a worm's-eye view of the war
remarkably different from that of the post-war historians.
Standing in the black cold wheelhouse of the *Caine* at midnight on New Year's Eve, as the ship plowed its old snout
through the murky sea toward the west, he took a very
gloomy view of the world situation.

In the first place, he decided, he had been an idiot to go
into the Navy instead of the Army. Russia was doing the
real dirty work in Europe. The smart man's place in this
war—unlike the last—was in the infantry, wallowing in

idleness in England while the asses who had taken refuge in the Navy tossed on sickening seas, on the way to assault the terrible barrier of the Japanese mid-Pacific islands. His destiny now was coral and blasted palms and spitting shore batteries and roaring Zeros—and mines, hundreds of them, no doubt—and the bottom of the sea, perhaps, in the end. Meantime his opposite numbers in the Army would be visiting Canterbury Cathedral or the birthplace of Shakespeare arm in arm with pretty English girls, whose good will toward Americans was already a global legend.

It seemed to Willie that the war against Japan would be the largest and deadliest in human history, and that it would probably end only in 1955 or 1960, upon the intervention of Russia, a decade after the collapse of Germany. How could the Japanese ever be dislodged from their famed "unsinkable carriers," the chain of islands, swarming with planes which could massacre any approaching fleet? There would be, perhaps, one costly Tarawa a year. He was sure he was headed for the forthcoming one. And the war would drag on at that rate until he was bald and middle-aged.

Willie didn't have a historian's respect for the victories at Guadalcanal, Stalingrad, and Midway. The stream of news as it burbled by his mind left only a confused impression that our side was a bit ahead in the game, but making painful slow work of it. He had often wondered in his boyhood what it must have been like to live in the stirring days of Gettysburg and Waterloo; now he knew, but he didn't know that he knew. This war seemed to him different from all the others: diffuse, slogging, and empty of drama.

He was on his way to fight in battles as great as any in the histories. But these would appear to him mere welters of nasty, complicated, tiresome activity. Only in after years, reading books describing the scenes in which he had been engaged, would he begin to think of his battles as Battles. Only then, when the heat of youth was gone, would he come to warm himself with the fanned-up glow of the memory that he, too, Willie Keith, had fought on Saint Crispin's Day.

For two days the *Caine* wallowed through gray cold rainy weather. There was the usual eating of damp sandwiches while clinging to stanchions, and sleeping in fits between pitches and rolls. Contrasted to the golden days of shore leave, this spell of misery seemed worse to the officers and crew than any they had ever undergone. There was a general feeling that they were all damned forever to a floating wet hell.

On the third day they broke into the sunny blue of the South Seas. Dank pea jackets, sweaters, and windbreakers vanished. Officers in creased khakis and crew in dungarees began to look familiar to each other. Furniture was unroped. Hot meals were resumed at breakfast time. The pervading gloom and taciturnity gave way to a freshet of laughing reminiscence and boasts about the leave period. In a way, the shorthandedness of the crew helped the recovery process. Those who had preferred court-martial to further adventures with Captain Queeg were the crafty, the discontented, the easily discouraged. The sailors who had returned to man the *Caine* were jolly boys, ready to take the bad with the good, and fond of the old ship, however heartily and horribly they cursed it.

On this day Willie took a mighty leap upward in life. He stood the noon-to-four watch as officer of the deck. Keefer was present to correct any disastrous mistake, and Captain Queeg himself perched in his chair throughout the watch, alternately dozing or blinking placidly in the sunshine. Willie conducted a faultless watch. It was a simple matter of staying on station in the screen while the convoy zigzagged. Whatever his inner shakiness, he kept a bold front, and maneuvered the ship firmly. When the watch was over he penciled in the log:

12 to 4—Steaming as before.

Willis Seward Keith
Ensign, USNR

He had signed many logs for port watches, but this was different. He put an extra flourish to his signature, and thrilled as though he were entering his name in a historic document.

In a state of quiet exaltation, he went down the ladders to the wardroom, and ripped merrily into a stack of decoded messages. He kept at it until the new steward's mate, Rasselas, a sweet-faced, pudgy colored boy with huge brown eyes, touched his arm and begged permission to lay the table for dinner. Willie folded away his codes, poured a cup of coffee from the Silex, and lay on the wardroom couch with his legs up, sipping. The radio was purring a Haydn quartet: the boys in the radio shack had not yet noticed and strangled it. Rasselas spread a fresh white cloth, and clinked the silver into place. From the pantry, where Whittaker in his new khaki uniform of a chief steward lorded it over the mess boys, there floated an aroma of roast beef. Willie sighed with contentment, and snuggled in the corner of the gently rocking couch. He looked around at the wardroom, freshly sprayed with a light green paint, its brown leather fitting renewed, the brass polished, the chairs gleaming. After all, he said to himself, there were worse places in the world than the wardroom of the *Caine*.

The other officers came straggling in, shaved, dressed in clean clothes, good-humored, and hungry. All the old jokes were brought out. They seemed funny and gay to Willie: Harding's procreative fertility, Keefer's novel, the foulness of the ship's fresh water ("Paynter's Poison"), Maryk's New Zealand girl of the seven warts, and, latest of all, Willie Keith's stature as a Don Juan. The officers and sailors of the ship had caught glimpses of May Wynn during the overhaul, and her voluptuousness had become a matter of fable. Linked with the remembrance of the pretty nurses who had visited Willie in Pearl Harbor, the appearance of May had established for the ensign a reputation for mystic power over women.

It was a fine new topic for wardroom banter. Sex was the subject, therefore anybody could be a comedian. A properly timed grunt was a great witticism. Willie for his part was delighted. He protested, and denied, and pretended to be vexed, and kept on prolonging the joke long after the others were ready to drop it; and sat down to dinner in very high spirits indeed. He felt a warm bond with the other officers, made stronger by the presence of the two bashful newcomers, Jorgensen and Ducely. He realized now how green, how intrusive, he and Harding must have seemed five months ago to the vanished Gorton, Adams, and Carmody. He put a spoonful of pea soup to his lips, and at that instant the ship passed over a high swell and pitched violently. He noticed the practiced motion of his arm with which he neutralized the pitching and kept the spoon from spilling even a drop; and he uttered a low happy laugh, and drank it off.

After dinner he said to Ducely, as the fragile-looking ensign was about to leave the wardroom, "Let's have a walk on the forecastle, shall we? Have to start talking about communications sometime."

"Yes, sir," said his new assistant meekly.

They stepped through the door of the forecastle into a cool purple twilight. The only brightness was a patch of fading gold in the west. "Well, Ducely." Willie rested one leg on the starboard bitts, and leaned on the life lines with both hands, enjoying the flow of the salt wind. "Getting used to the *Caine?*"

"As much as I ever will, I guess. Horrible fate, isn't it?"

Willie turned an annoyed glance at the ensign. "I suppose so. Every ship has good points and bad——"

"Oh, of course. I guess there isn't much to do on one of these old rattletraps, which is something. And then I suppose we'll spend most of our time in Navy yards getting patched up, which suits me, too. If it only weren't so cramped and filthy! The wardroom is like a chicken coop."

"Well, you get more or less used to it, Ducely. I guess you don't like the clip shack too much, eh?"

"It's revolting. I almost died in there the first night. Why, that stack gas!"

"Awful, isn't it?" said Willie, with huge enjoyment.

"Abominable."

"Well, after a while you won't mind it so much."

"No fear. I don't sleep there any more."

The grin faded from Willie's face. "Oh? Where do you sleep?"

"In the ship's office, on the half deck. Nobody uses it at night. I have a folding cot. It's swell in there. Real airy."

This information irritated Willie extremely. "I don't think the captain will approve of that. He's very particular about——"

"I asked him, sir. He said I could sleep anywhere that I could find six vacant feet."

Willie said to himself that he would be damned. *He* had suffered five months without thinking of this simple escape. "Hm. Well, now, you're supposed to assist me in communications, and——"

"I'll be glad to try, sir, but I don't know beans about communications——"

"What *do* you know about?"

"Practically nothing, sir. You see, my—that is, I got a direct commission into the Navy. My mother owns most of a shipyard in Boston, and so—the whole thing is just a mess. Just one letter of the alphabet fouled me up—one letter. When they were making out my commission they asked me whether I wanted to be an S or a G. I didn't know. They said S meant Specialist and G meant General. So I asked which was better and they said that a G was regarded as much superior. So naturally, I asked for G. That was my mistake. My God, it was all arranged. I was supposed to go into Public Relations. I did, too. But I got ordered to some hole down in Virginia. And suddenly one day this directive came through saying that all ensigns designated G were to be sent out to sea. It all happened so fast there just wasn't a thing my mother could do about it. So, here I am."

"Tough."

"Oh, I don't mind. Public Relations is worse than the *Caine,* I think. The *paper* work! If there's one thing I'm no good for, it's paper work."

"Too bad. Communications is *all* paper work, Ducely. You'll just have to get good at it——"

"Well, don't say I didn't warn you, sir," said Ducely with a resigned sigh. "Naturally, I'll do my best. But I'm just not going to be worth a damn to you——"

"Can you type?"

"No. And what's worse, I'm absent-minded. I can't remember where I've put a paper two seconds after I've laid it down."

"Beginning tomorrow you'll get yourself a typing course from Jellybelly and learn to type——"

"I'll try, but I don't think I'll ever learn. I'm all thumbs——"

"And I think you'd better get started on decoding right away. Do you have a watch tomorrow morning?"

"No, sir."

"Fine. Meet me in the wardroom after breakfast and I'll show you the codes——"

"I'm afraid that'll have to wait, sir. Tomorrow morning I have to finish my officers' qualification assignment for Mr. Keefer."

It had grown dark now, and the sky was crowded with stars. Willie peered at the dim face of his assistant and wondered whether he himself had ever seemed such a mixture of effrontery and stupidity. "Well, stay up a little late tonight and finish your assignment."

"I will if you insist, Mr. Keith, but I'm really horribly fagged out."

"The hell with it. Get a good night's sleep by all means," said Willie. He started to walk away. "We'll start decoding in the afternoon. Unless, of course, you have something more important to do."

"No, sir," said Ducely, with bland sincerity, tagging after him, "I don't believe I have."

"Great," said Willie. He twisted the dogs on the forecastle door viciously, motioned his assistant through, and slammed the door with a clang that was heard in the after crew's quarters.

This force will assault and capture Kwajalein Atoll and other objectives in the Marshall Islands, with the purpose

*of establishing bases for further attacks to the west-
ward*——

Willie stared at the blotchy mimeographed words. He
tossed aside the thick operation order and snatched a war
atlas from the bookshelf. Turning to a map of the Central
Pacific, he saw that Kwajalein was the largest of the atolls,
in the very heart of the Marshalls, surrounded by Jap
strongholds. He whistled.

Official mail was heaped two feet high on his bunk. He
had dumped the tumbled mass of envelopes stamped with
crimson secrecy warnings out of three gray mail sacks
which lay crumpled on the deck. The stuff had accumulated in Pearl Harbor for a month. It was all his now, to
log, file, and be responsible for; his first batch of secret
mail since inheriting Keefer's job.

Willie threw a blanket over the rest of the mail and
brought the operation order up to the captain. Queeg was
in the cabin on the main deck which had formerly housed
two officers. It had been altered at the Navy Yard under
his careful direction so that it contained one bed, a wide
desk, an armchair, a lounge seat, a large safe, and numerous speaking tubes and squawk boxes. The captain paused
in his shaving to riffle through the sheets, dripping soap
on them. "Kwajalein, hey?" he said casually. "Kay. Leave
this stuff here. You'll discuss this with nobody, of course,
not even Maryk."

"Aye aye, sir."

When Willie began to log and file the mail he made
unpleasant discoveries. Keefer had turned over to him a
set of dog-eared ledgers and the keys to the filing cabinet,
and had offhandedly added several handfuls of secret mail
which lay on the deck of his closet under shoes and dirty
laundry. He assured Willie that the correspondence was
"meaningless garbage."

"I've been figuring on logging it in when the next batch
came. You may as well do it," he said, yawning. He
climbed back on his bunk and resumed reading *Finnegan's
Wake.*

Willie found the file cabinet in a hopeless jumble. Letters in it would have been easier to locate had they been

stuffed in a gunnysack. The ledgers contained an idiotically complicated system for entering the arrival of mail, using four different notations for each letter. Willie calculated that it would take him five or six solid working days to log the mail. He went to the ship's office and watched Jellybelly logging tremendous sackfuls of non-secret correspondence. The yeoman typed entries on green form sheets, and in less than an hour disposed of as much mail as Willie had in his room. "Where'd you get that system?" he asked the sailor.

Jellybelly turned a bored, bleary glance at him. "Didn't get it nowhere, sir. Navy system."

"How about these?" Willie thrust the ledgers at Jellybelly. "Ever see them?"

The yeoman shrank away from the books, as though they were leprous. "Sir, that's your job, not mine——"

"I know, I know——"

"Mr. Keefer, he tried half a dozen times to get me to log in that secret stuff. It's against regulations for an enlisted man to——"

"All I want to know is, are these ledgers official, or what?"

The sailor wrinkled his nose. "Official? Christ, that system would give any yeoman third class a hemorrhage. Mr. Funk, he invented it back in '40. He give it to Mr. Anderson, *he* give it to Mr. Ferguson, *he* give it to Mr. Keefer."

"Why didn't they use the Navy system? It seems so much simpler——"

"Sir," said the yeoman dryly, "don't ask me why officers do anything. You wouldn't like my answer."

In the next weeks Willie overhauled his entire department. He installed standard Navy systems of filing and logging. He burned some sixty obsolete registered publications, and he sorted the rest into order, so that he could find any book in an instant. In this process he caught himself wondering often about Keefer. It became obvious that the novelist had wasted a fearful amount of time in communications. Willie remembered searches for letters or publications that had consumed whole afternoons, searches punctuated with a fire of Keefer's sour wit about the Navy's foul-ups. He remembered the communicator bending over the ledgers for hours, cursing. Willie knew that above all things the novelist prized time in which to write and read. He knew, too, that Keefer had the cleverest mind on the *Caine*. How, then, could this man have failed to see that he was defeating himself and blaming the Navy for his own mistakes? Willie began to look at Keefer with different eyes. The novelist's wisdom seemed to tarnish a bit.

During the remaining time before the Kwajalein sortie Captain Queeg fell into a furious lassitude. He could be found at almost any hour of the day in his bunk, or at his desk in his underwear, playing with a jigsaw puzzle. He emerged only at night, when they were in port, to watch the movie on the forecastle. At sea, during rehearsal maneuvers, whole days passed when he was not seen on the bridge. He gave orders to the OOD's through the speaking tube. The rasp of the captain's buzzer became as common a sound on the bridge as the ping of the sound-search gear. He stopped coming to the wardroom for meals, and ate almost nothing but enormous quantities of ice cream with maple syrup, brought to his cabin on a tray.

The other officers imagined that Queeg was busy memorizing the documents of the operation, but Willie knew better. When he brought decodes to the captain's cabin he never found Queeg studying any battle plans or books of tactics. His occupation was either sleeping, or eating ice cream, or reading a magazine, or simply lying on his back, staring with round eyes at the overhead. He acted, thought Willie, like a man trying to forget a terrible sorrow. The ensign guessed that perhaps Queeg had had a quarrel with his wife during the overhaul, or else had received bad news of some other kind in the flood of mail. It never crossed the ensign's mind that the bad news might have been the operation order.

Willie's attitude toward the coming battle was a mixture of excitement, faint alarm, and a very immediate pleasure at knowing the secret. There was something reassuring in the great **bulk** of the operation order, in the lengthy cat-

alogue of ships that were to take part, in the very excess
of dry detail which made the blurry gray sheets so hard to
read. He felt, deep down, that he was pretty safe, ventur-
ing out against the Japs under the Navy's wing.

On a bright warm January day, a horizon-spanning
horde of ships swarmed out of the harbors of Hawaii,
formed itself into a vast circular pattern, and set a course
for Kwajalein.

The armada moved peacefully over the wastes of the
sea, through quiet days and nights. There was no sign of
the enemy, nothing but rolling waters, blue by day and
black by night, an empty sky, and ships of war in every
direction as far as the eye could see, steaming in a great
majestic diagram under the stars and the sun. Radar, the
ghostly measuring rod, spanning empty space accurately to
within a few yards, made the preservation of the diagram
a simple matter. This vast formation, so precise and rigid,
yet so quick and fluid to change course or rearrange itself,
a seagoing miracle surely beyond the dreams of Nelson
himself, was maintained with careless ease by hundreds of
officers of the deck, not one in ten of whom was a professional seaman: college boys, salesmen, schoolteachers,
lawyers, clerks, writers, druggists, engineers, farmers, piano
players—these were the young men who outperformed
the veteran officers of the fleets of Nelson.

Willie Keith was a full-fledged officer of the deck now,
and he took for granted all the mechanical aids that eased
his task. He did not consider the work easy. He was
enormously and continually impressed with his quick-won
mastery of the sea, and with his military authority. He
prowled the wheelhouse, lips compressed, chin high, forehead puckered in a squinting scowl, shoulders hunched
forward, hands clenching the binoculars through which he
frequently frowned at the horizon. Histrionics apart, he
was a competent OOD. He quickly developed the impal-
pable nervous feelers, reaching from stem to stern of the
ship, which are the main equipment of a conning officer.
In five months on the bridge he had picked up the tricks
of station keeping, the jargon of communications and

reports, and the ceremonial pattern of the ship's life. He knew when to order the boatswain's mate to pipe sweepers, when to darken ship, when to call away cooks and bakers in the early morning, when to rouse the captain and when to allow him to sleep. He could gain or lose a few hundreds yards by slight changes of rudder or engines, and could calculate course and speed to a new screening station in ten seconds by drawing a single pencil line on a maneuvering diagram. The dense blackness of a rain squall at midnight did not scare him; not while the radar scope picked out the task force for him in a neat pattern of green dots.

The *Caine* was placed on the right flank of the formation, in the inner anti-submarine screen. Two belts of destroyers surrounded the troop transports, carriers, cruisers, battleships, and landing craft. Each destroyer constantly searched a narrow cone of water for echoes, and the cones overlapped. No submarine could approach the formation without causing telltale pings aboard one of the destroyers. A single screen would have been enough; the double screen was an instance of the American taste for generous safety factors. The *Caine* was in a position abaft the beam of the guide, where an approach of a submarine was almost impossible, because the attacker would have been committed to a stern chase under water. The minesweeper was therefore a safety factor added to a safety factor. For an American man of war her combat role lacked something of the dash of the *Bonhomme Richard* attacking the *Serapis*. Nevertheless she was sailing into the waters of the foe, pinging. Had John Paul Jones been OOD instead of Willie Keith, he could have done no more.

As the attack force steamed slowly through the wheeling days and nights, life aboard the old minesweeper fell into a cycle that repeated with the circlings of the clock. It became more and more clear that a new pattern of living was hardening on the *Caine,* after the churning flux caused by the change of command.

One morning in Pearl Harbor, just before the sortie, Captain Queeg had seen some cigarette butts mashed on the deck. After excoriating the OOD he had gone to the ship's office and dictated this document:

Ship's Standing Order #6–44.
1. The main deck of this vessel will always be spotlessly clean.
2. Failure to comply will result in heavy disciplinary action for the entire crew.

P. F. QUEEG

The order was prominently posted. Next morning he found a cigarette butt in a scupper of the forecastle, and canceled all liberty for the crew. During the next couple of days the deck force kept the main deck constantly swept. As soon as the *Caine* sailed for Kwajalein the order was shelved, and the deck was as dirty as before, except at sweeping times; but one of the deck hands was detailed to keep cleaning the small patch of the deck between the captain's cabin, the bridge ladder, and the hatchway leading to the wardroom.

This was typical of the new order. The crew with its vast cunning had already charted most of the habits and pathways of the captain. He was moving now in a curious little circle of compliance that followed him like a spotlight, extending to the range of his eyes and ears; beyond that, the *Caine* remained the old *Caine*. Now and then the captain would make an unexpected sally out of the circle. A discordant hubbub would ensue, and Queeg's disapproval would be crystallized on the spot into a new ship's law. This fresh edict, whatever it might be, was carefully observed—within the circle of compliance; in the rest of the ship it was ignored. It was not a conscious conspiracy. Individual sailors of the *Caine* would have been surprised at such a description of life aboard their ship. Probably they would have denied its accuracy. The attitude of the crew toward Queeg varied from mild dislike, as a general thing, to poisonous hate in a few men who had run foul of him. He was not without partisans. Outside the circle of compliance life was easier, filthier, and more lawless than ever; anarchy, indeed, tempered only by the rough community rules of the sailors themselves and a certain respect for two or three officers, especially Maryk. There were sailors, those who enjoyed dirt or gambling or late sleeping, who pronounced Queeg the best skipper they had ever known, "just so's you keep out of his sight."

It was well known among the crew that Stilwell was the particular object of Queeg's dislike. The gunner's mate was suspended in an agony of worry about the letter that Maryk had sent to the Red Cross regarding his mother's illness. No answer had come yet. The sailor was growing gaunt as the weeks slipped by and he waited for the ax to fall. Every watch he stood at the helm within range of Queeg was torture for him. The sailors who were against Queeg went out of their way to be friendly with the gunner's mate, and tried to cheer him up; and so the opposition came to center around him. The rest of the crew avoided Stilwell. They feared that the captain's hatred might spread out to include his cronies.

In the wardroom there were three distinct parties. One was Queeg himself, daily more frosty and secluded. One was Maryk, retreated into a stolid, humorless silence, maintaining whatever contact existed between the captain and his ship. The executive officer saw what the crew was doing. He was aware that it was his responsibility to enforce the captain's rules; he was also aware that most of the rules were either impossible of enforcement on the overworked, overcrowded, rough-minded crew, or enforceable only at an unacceptable cost to the ship's narrow margin of seaworthiness. He winked at the circle of compliance, and set himself the task of keeping the ship functioning adequately outside that circle.

The third party included all the other officers, with Keefer as ringleader. A strong open detestation of Queeg began to serve as a bond of affection among them, and they passed hours in sarcastic joking about him. The new officers, Jorgensen and Ducely, quickly absorbed the air of the wardroom and were soon in full cry after Queeg with the rest. Willie Keith was regarded as the captain's pet, and was the target of much joking for it; and, in point of fact, Queeg was warmer and pleasanter in manner to

Willie than to any of the others. But he joined vigorously in satirizing the captain. Maryk alone took no part in the ribaldry. He either kept silence or tried to defend Queeg, and if the jokes became too prolonged he would leave the wardroom.

This was the condition of the U.S.S. *Caine* when it crossed the mythical line on the broad sea, five days out of Pearl Harbor, and steamed into Japanese waters.

20 · The Yellow Stain

The evening before the fleet was due to arrive at Kwajalein, Willie had the eight-to-midnight watch. He observed an increased tension among the sailors on the bridge. Silence, even in the captain's absence, hung heavily in the wheelhouse. The perpetual discussion of sex in the black radar shack, among ghostly faces lit by the dim green glow of the scopes, had not ceased; but it was sluggish, and dwelt mainly on venereal disease. The signal gang crouched on the flagbags over cups of rancid coffee, muttering.

There had been no official word passed that the ship would be at Kwajalein in the morning, but the crew had its intelligence agent in the quartermaster who solved the star sights each night with Maryk. They knew the distance from the objective as well as the captain.

Willie did not share the general gloom. His mood was buoyant and devilish. Within twelve hours he would be in battle; within twenty-four hours he would be a man who had risked his life for his country. He felt invulnerable. He was rolling toward an edge of danger, he knew, but it seemed an entertaining kind of danger, like a jump over a high hurdle on horseback. He was proud of his lack of fear, and this buoyed him yet more.

He alone, beside the captain, knew that the *Caine* was going to perform a hazardous mission at dawn. One of the top-secret guard-mail letters had contained new orders. The minesweeper was to shepherd a wave of attack from their transport to a line of departure only a thousand yards from the beach, fairly into the muzzles of the shore batteries; the reason being that correct navigation would be hard for the low-lying boats by themselves. Willie plumed himself on being in better spirits than the men though they were combat veterans and he wasn't; though he knew of a great impending risk and they didn't.

His optimism was really founded on a cunning estimate of his position (but a completely unconscious one) made by his viscera and nerves. He was not going to land on any beach; there was no risk of face-to-face encounter with stocky little yellow men brandishing bayonets. What confronted him was an increased likelihood of some crippling misfortune befalling the *Caine*, in the shape of a shell, a torpedo, or a mine. The odds in favor of his living through the next twenty-four hours had dropped from, say, a normal ten thousand to one to a smaller but still comfortable figure: seventy or eighty to one, maybe. So reasoned Willie's nervous tissue; whereupon it sent up to his brain some stimulating fluid that produced the ensign's glow of bravery.

The nerves of the crew made less cheerful calculations for a simple reason. The crew had seen the results of misfortunes of battle; ships burning red and yellow, ships sinking, men scrambling over dripping slanted hulls, men soaked in oil, men ripped bloody, and floating dead men. They were inclined to think less of the odds than of the disagreeable possibilities.

"Officer of the deck!" It was the voice of Queeg, resonating in the speaking tube from the charthouse. Surprised, Willie glanced at the dim phosphorescent clockface. Ten-thirty, time for the captain to be in his cabin. He stooped to the conical brass mouthpiece of the tube.

"Keith, aye aye."

"Come in here, Willie."

The captain, fully clothed, with his life jacket on, had crawled into the canvas bunk that hung over the navigator's table. This picture flashed on Willie when he closed the door of the charthouse, automatically lighting the room with one red shaded bulb on the bulkhead. The air was foul with cigarette smoke. "How are things going, Willie?"

"Everything normal, sir."

The captain rolled over on his side and peered at the ensign. His face was drawn and bristly in the red light. "You read my night orders?"

"Yes, sir."

"Call me if there's anything the least bit unusual, do you understand? Don't worry about interrupting my beauty sleep. *Call* me."

"Aye aye, sir."

But the watch passed in the routine of pinging, zigzagging, and maintaining station. Harding stumbled up to him in the breezy gloom of the starboard wing at a quarter to twelve. "Ready to relieve you," he said sadly, exhaling a faint fragrance of coffee.

"Well, forty miles to go, and still nothing."

Willie hesitated before going below, and considered curling up in a corner of the main deck. Coming down the bridge ladder, he saw that half the crew had had the same idea. There were no corners left on the deck, and no very wide pathways for walking. The sight made Willie disdainful and bold. He went below, took off his clothes, and slipped between the sheets. Despite the hour, it felt queer to be in his bunk, somewhat as though he had fallen ill and taken to bed in the daytime. He was still congratulating himself on his hardihood when he fell asleep.

GHANG, ghang, ghang, ghang, ghang . . .

The general alarm had not yet stopped ringing when he came bolting out on deck in his underwear, clutching shoes, socks, shirt, and trousers. He saw a calm sea, a starry black sky, and ships crisscrossing here and there in the melting formation. Sailors went thundering through the murky passageways and up and down ladders; no need to penalize any of them this time for not wearing helmet and life jacket! As Willie stepped into his pants the hatchway to the wardroom clanged shut behind him, and sailors of the forward repair party dogged it down hard. The ensign slipped his shoes on his naked feet and scrambled up the bridge ladder. The clock in the wheelhouse showed three-thirty. The little space was crowded with shadowy figures. Willie could hear the rasping of steel balls rubbed together. He took his life jacket and helmet from a hook and approached the stoop-shouldered form of Harding. "Ready to relieve you. What's up?"

"Nothing. We're there." Harding pointed off the port bow and handed Willie the glasses. Willie saw, at the horizon, on the line between sea and sky, a thin irregular smudge, perhaps a fingernail wide. "Roi-Namur," said Harding.

Tiny yellow flashes appeared along the smudge. Willie said, "What's that?"

"The battle wagons peeled off and went ahead a couple of hours ago. I guess maybe that's them. Or maybe it's planes. Somebody's giving that beach hell."

"Well, this is it," said Willie, a little annoyed at the thumping of his heart. "If there's no change, I relieve you."

"No change."

Harding shuffled off the bridge. Now the sound of the shore bombardment came rolling across the sea to Willie's ears, but at this distance it was a mere trivial thumping, as though sailors were beating out mattresses on the ship's forecastle. Willie told himself that these vague noises and little colored flashes represented hellish destruction that was being rained on the Japs, and tried for a moment to imagine himself as a slant-eyed soldier crouching and shivering in a flaming jungle, but the picture had the unsatisfying false effect of a magazine story about the war. In plain fact, Willie's first glimpse of combat was a disappointment. It appeared to be an unimportant night gunnery exercise on a very small scale.

The night paled to blue-gray, the stars disappeared; and day was brightening over the sea when the fleet came to a halt, three miles off-shore. Attack boats began to drop from the davits of the transports, clustering and swarming on the water like beetles.

And now Willie Keith found himself in an honest-to-goodness war; one-sided, because there was still no firing from the beach, but the real deadly business, none the less. The green islands trimmed with white sand were already aflame and smoking in many spots. Tubby old battleships, targets of so many journalists' sneers in peacetime, were briskly justifying thirty years of expensive existence by volleying tons of shells into the tropic shrubbery every few seconds, with thundering concussions. Cruisers and destroyers ranged beside them, peppering at the atoll. Now and then the naval fire stopped, and squadrons of planes filed overhead and dived one by one at the islands, raising clouds of white smoke and round bursts of flame, and sometimes a skyscraping mushroom of black, as an oil dump or ammunition pile went up with a blast which jarred the decks of the *Caine*. All the while the transports kept disgorging attack boats, which were fanning out along the gray choppy water in neat ranks. The sun rose, white and steamy.

The appearance of the atoll was not yet marred by the attack. The orange billows of flame here and there were decorative touches to the pleasant verdant islands, and so were the freshly blossoming clouds of black and white smoke. The smell of powder drifted in the air, and, for Willie, somehow completed the festive and gay effect of the morning. He could not have said why. Actually, it was because the odor, with the incessant banging, reminded him of fireworks on the Fourth of July.

Keefer paused beside him for a moment on the port wing. Wisps of black hair hung out from under the gray dome of the novelist's helmet. His eyes glittered in their deep shadowed sockets, showing all the whites. "Like the show, Willie? Seems to be all ours."

Willie swept an arm around at the swarms of ships closed in on the frail-looking islands in the pearly sunrise. "Multitudes, multitudes. What do you think of the Navy at this point, Tom?"

Keefer grinned, twisting one side of his mouth. "Christ," he said, "the taxpayers ought to be getting something for their hundred billion dollars." He bounded up the ladder to the flying bridge.

Queeg appeared, hunched almost to a crouch, his head moving ceaselessly to and fro over the bulky collar of his kapok life jacket. His eyes were squinted nearly shut, and he seemed to be smiling gaily. "Kay, Mr. OOD. Where's this bunch of LVT's we're supposed to take in to the beach?"

"Well, I guess it's that bunch there, sir, by APA 17." Willie pointed to a huge gray transport some four thousand yards off the port bow.

"APA 17, hey? You're sure that's the ship they're supposed to come from?"

"That's what the orders said, sir. Jacob Group Four from APA 17."

"Kay. Let's get over to APA 17. Standard speed. You keep the conn."

The captain vanished behind the bridgehouse. Willie stalked into the wheelhouse, swelling with self-importance, and began barking orders. The *Caine* dropped out of the screen and headed toward the transports. The roaring and blasting of the battleship salvos grew louder with each hundred yards that the *Caine* moved inward. The ensign was feeling a little dizzy and exalted, as though he had drunk a highball too quickly. He went from wing to wing, taking bearings on the APA, calling for radar ranges, shouting rudder changes with inebriated confidence.

A long line of attack boats emerged from the clusters around the APA and headed for the old minesweeper. Willie went looking for the captain and found him perched on a flagbag, out of sight of the transports and the beach, smoking, and chatting casually with Engstrand. "Sir, Jacob Group Four seems to be heading our way."

"Kay." Queeg glanced vaguely out to sea, and puffed at his cigarette.

Willie said, "What shall I do, sir?"

"Whatever you please," said the captain, and giggled. The ensign stared at his commanding officer. Queeg resumed telling an anecdote about the invasion of Attu to the signalman. Engstrand rolled his eyes momentarily at the officer of the deck, and shrugged.

Willie returned to the pilothouse. The attack boats were bumping toward the *Caine* in showers of spray. Peering through binoculars, Willie could see an officer standing in the stern of the leading boat with a large green megaphone under his arm. Spray flew all over his life jacket and khakis, and drenched the backs of the crouching marines in front of him. The glasses gave a prismatic blurriness to the boat and its occupants. Willie could see the men shouting at each other but could hear no sound; it was like a glimpse of a worn-out silent movie. He didn't know what to do next. He thought the ship ought to be stopped but he was afraid to make such a command decision.

Maryk came into the wheelhouse. "Say, where's the captain? We're going to run those birds down!"

The ensign pointed out of the starboard doorway with his thumb. Maryk strode across and glanced back at the flagbag. "Well," he said quickly. "All engines stop." He took a battered red cardboard megaphone from a bracket under the port window, and walked out on the wing. The *Caine* slowed and rocked. "Boat—a—hoy," Maryk called.

The officer in the attack boat called back, in a voice that came faintly over the water, young, strained, and unmistakably Southern, "Jacob Group Four. Ready to proceed to point of departure."

Queeg poked his face in at the doorway of the pilothouse, exclaiming irritably, "What's going on here? Who said anything about stopping? Who's yelling to whom here?"

The executive officer shouted to the captain from the other wing, "Sorry, sir, it looked like we were overshooting these boys, so I stopped. It's Jacob Four. They're ready to proceed."

"Well, all right," called the captain. "Let's get it over with, then. What's course and distance to the point of departure?"

"Course 175, distance 4000, sir."

"Kay, Steve. You take the conn and get us there."

Queeg disappeared. Maryk turned toward the attack boat, and the boat officer put his megaphone to his ear to catch the message. "We—will—proceed," the executive officer boomed. "Follow—us. Good—luck."

The boat officer waved the megaphone once, and crouched low in the boat as it began to churn forward again. His little landing craft was only fifty yards from the side of the *Caine* now. It was an LVT, one of the numerous land-and-water monsters evolved in World War II; a small metal boat incongruously fitted with caterpillar tracks. It could waddle on land or wallow through the sea for short distances, and though it could perform neither feat well, it existed because it could do both at all. Willie pitied the drenched men in the little craft, which pitched and rolled on the open sea like a toy.

Maryk steered for the atoll. There was nothing between the *Caine* and the Japanese island of Enneubing (which the Navy had nicknamed "Jacob"), but a few thousand yards of choppy water with whitecaps. Willie could see details on the beach now: a hut, an abandoned rowboat, oil drums, shattered palm trees. He thought he had never seen a green so deep and rich as the green of Jacob Island, nor a white so white as its sands. There were two pretty orange fires on it, showing above the treetops; and not a movement of life anywhere. He looked around at the string of LVT's bobbing behind, and noticed a sailor in the lead boat frantically waving semaphore flags. The ensign signaled with his arms. "Go ahead." The flags rapidly spelled out, *C-H-R-I-S-T S-L-O-W D-O-W-N.* Several times the sailor fell off his signaling perch as the LVT dived into foaming troughs. Curtains of spray were dousing the attack boats every few seconds.

Queeg came around the bridgehouse and scurried up to Willie. "Well, well, what is it?" he said impatiently, and "What the hell do they want?" and "Well, can you read it or can't you?"

"They want us to slow down, Captain."

"That's too goddamn bad. We're supposed to be on the line of departure at H-hour. If they can't keep up with us we'll throw over a dye marker when we reach the spot, and that'll have to do." Queeg squinted at the island, and ran into the pilothouse. "Jesus Steve, do you want to run up on the beach?"

"No, sir. About fifteen hundred yards to go to the line of departure."

"*Fifteen hundred?* You're crazy! The *beach* isn't fifteen hundred yards away——"

"Captain, the cutoff tangent on Roi Island is 045. Tangent now is 065."

Urban, at the port alidade, called out, "Left tangent Roi, 064."

The captain darted out on the port wing and pushed the little signalman aside. "You must be blind. He put his eye to the alidade. "I thought so! Zero *five* four and that's allowing nothing for set and drift along the line of bearing. We're inside the departure point now. Right full rudder! Right full rudder!" he shouted. "All engines ahead full! Throw over a dye marker!"

The stacks puffed billows of black smoke. The *Caine* heeled sharply to starboard and scored a tight white semicircle on the sea as it sped around on the reverse course. Within a minute the LVT's of Jacob Group Four were a line of bobbing specks far astern. Near them on the sea was a spreading stain of bright yellow.

Later in the day, however, the *Caine* steamed bravely through the channel between Jacob and Ivan, together with a hundred other ships of the attack force. The American flag was flying on both islands. The *Caine* dropped anchor in the lagoon. Queeg ordered the posting of armed guards all along the sides of the ship to shoot any stray Japanese swimmers, and dismissed the crew from battle stations. There was nothing else to do. Hemmed in by transports, cargo ships, and destroyers, the *Caine* couldn't have fired at the beach even if ordered to. The grateful sailors left their gun posts, where they had been lolling for fourteen hours, and most of them went below at once to sleep. Sensitive as cats to the likelihood of danger, they knew that none threatened any more at

Kwajalein. Willie's eyes stung with sleepiness, too, but he went up to the flying bridge to watch the show.

It was a queer battle, the fight for Kwajalein, to be a young man's initiation into warfare. Possibly it was the queerest that has ever been fought. It had been won thousands of miles away, months before a shot was fired. The admirals had guessed correctly that the Mikado's "unsinkable carriers" were short of an important commodity: planes. Too many Japanese aircraft had been clawed out of the sky in the broils around the Solomons. As for warships, the remaining ones had become precious to the empire; and frugally guarded weapons are no weapons at all. With the mere arrival of the American array of ships and men, the battle was theoretically over. There was nothing at Kwajalein but a few thousand Japanese soldiers to face the monstrous fleet rising out of the sea; they were blasted into utter impotence in a few hours by an avalanche of bombs and shells. A white flag should have flown from each island at sunrise, by all the logic of war. Since the Japs appeared illogically unwilling to surrender, the naval bombarders set about annihilating them with an oddly good-humored, ribald ferocity.

Willie enjoyed and applauded the spectacle with no thought of its fatality. Under a garish pink-and-blue sunset, the bombardment was taking on the air of Mardi Gras. The green islands were blazing in wide red splotches now. Pretty crimson dotted lines of tracer bullets laced across the purple waters; the gouts of flame at the big guns' muzzles grew brighter and yellower in the twilight, and concussions regularly shook the atmosphere, while the smell of powder hung everywhere, strangely mingled, in the puffs of the breeze, with the spicy sweetness of crushed and burning tropic foliage. Willie leaned on the bulwark of the flying bridge, his life jacket dumped at his feet, his helmet pushed back from his damp forehead; and he smoked, and whistled Cole Porter tunes, and occasionally yawned, a tired but thoroughly entertained spectator.

This cold-bloodedness, worthy of a horseman of Genghis Khan, was quite strange in a pleasant little fellow like Ensign Keith. Militarily, of course, it was an asset beyond price. Like most of the naval executioners at Kwajalein, he seemed to regard the enemy as a species of animal pest. From the grim and desperate taciturnity with which the Japanese died, they seemed on their side to believe they were contending with an invasion of large armed ants. This obliviousness on both sides to the fact that the opponents were human beings may perhaps be cited as the key to the many massacres of the Pacific war. The Kwajalein invasion, the first of these, was a grand classic of sea warfare, a lesson for the generations. There has never been a more wisely conceived and surgically executed operation. As a young man's first taste of war, however, it was too rich, too easy, too fancy, too perfect.

Whittaker poked his head over the top of the ladder to the flying bridge, and said, "Chadan, Mistuh Keith." Stars were already winking in the sky. Willie went below, and fell to with the other officers on an excellent steak dinner. When the table was cleared, Willie, Keefer, Maryk, and Harding remained around the green baize, drinking coffee.

"Well," said Keefer to Maryk, lighting a cigarette, "what did you think of the performance of Old Yellowstain today?"

"Knock it off, Tom."

"That was something, wasn't it, turning tail before we ever got to the line of departure and leaving those poor slobs in the LVT's to navigate for themselves?"

"Tom, you weren't even on the bridge," said the executive officer shortly. "You don't know what you're talking about."

"I was on the flying bridge, Steve, old boy, seeing and hearing everything."

"We dropped a marker. They knew just where they were——"

"We dropped when the cutoff bearing was out almost twenty degrees——"

"Ten degrees. The captain read fifty-four, not sixty-four——"

"Oh, you believed that?"

"—and our advance while turning carried us another six or seven hundred yards. The dye marker was probably right on."

Keefer turned on Willie suddenly. "What do *you* say? Did we funk off like a scared rabbit or didn't we?"

Willie hesitated for several seconds. "Well, I wasn't on the alidade. Urban could easily have read the bearing wrong."

"Willie, you had the deck all day. Did you ever see Captain Queeg on the side of the bridge that was exposed to the beach?"

The question startled Willie, and in a shocking flash he realized that he never had. The shuttlings and disappearances of the commanding officer during the day had puzzled him extremely, especially since it had been Queeg's custom in previous maneuvers to stay fixed in the wheelhouse, where he could hear the TBS and watch the helmsman. But the novelist's suggestion was monstrous. Willie stared at Keefer and could not speak.

"Well, what's the matter, Willie? Did you or didn't you?"

Maryk said angrily, "Tom, that's the goddamnedest remark I've ever heard."

"Let Willie answer, Steve."

"Tom, I—I was pretty busy trying to keep myself straightened out. I wasn't worrying about the captain. I don't know——"

"You do and you're lying, like an honorable little Princeton boy," said the novelist. "Okay. Take a bow for trying to protect the honor of the *Caine* and the Navy." He got up and carried his cup and saucer to the Silex. "That's all very well, but we're responsible for the safety of this ship, not to mention our own necks, and it's not wise to be anything but realistic." He poured fresh coffee, light brown and steaming, into his cup. "There is a new fact that all of us have got to live with, and let's face it, lads. Queeg is a poltroon."

The door opened, and Queeg came in. He was freshly shaved, still wore his helmet, and carried his life jacket under his arm. "I'll have a cup of the same, Tom, if you don't mind."

"Certainly, Captain."

Queeg sat in the chair at the head of the table, dropped his life jacket on the deck, and began rubbing the steel balls in his left hand. He crossed his legs and danced the upper one, so that his whole slumping body bobbed rhythmically. He stared straight ahead, with a peevish, pouting look. There were heavy green shadows under his eyes, and deep lines around his mouth. Keefer put three spoons of sugar in a cup of coffee and set it before the captain.

"Thanks. Hm. Fresh, for once." These were the last words spoken in the wardroom for ten minutes. Queeg glanced swiftly at the officers from time to time and returned his eyes of his coffee cup. At last, draining the last mouthful, he cleared his throat and said, "Well, Willie, as long as you don't seem to be doing much of anything, how about letting me see some decodes, here? There are about twenty-seven numbers I'm still waiting for."

"I'll get on it right away, sir." The ensign opened the safe and languidly brought out the code devices.

"Tom," said the captain, staring into his empty cup, "my records show that Ducely's twelfth officers' qualification assignment is due today. Where is it?"

"Sir, we've been at battle stations since three o'clock this morning——"

"We're not at GQ now and haven't been for two hours."

"Ducely's entitled to eat, and clean himself, and rest, sir——"

"Rest is something you do when your duties are fulfilled. I want that assignment on my desk tonight before Ducely turns in, and you're not to turn in, either, until you receive it from him and correct it. Is that clear?"

"Aye aye, sir."

"And watch those smart-alecky tones a little bit, Mr. Keefer," the captain added, rising, his eyes on the wall. "Fitness reports include such things as willingness and subordination." He went out of the wardroom.

"Think he heard?" Willie whispered.

"No, don't worry," Keefer said in a normal tone. "That was sullen face number two. Ordinary fatigue plus maybe an ulcer twinge or two."

"You better watch your goddamn tongue," Maryk said.

The novelist laughed. "You can't say he isn't on the ball. Invasion or no invasion, Ducely does his assignment. You never saw a more fearless wielder of a check list than Old Yellowstain——"

Maryk rose and walked to the door, setting a frayed overseas cap on his head. "All right," he said, in a dry voice. "Mr. Keefer, the name of the commanding officer of this ship is Captain Queeg. I'm his executive officer. I don't want any more of this name-calling in my presence, do you hear? None of this Old Yellowstain or anything but plain Captain Queeg."

"Turn me in, *Mister* Maryk," said Keefer, opening his eyes wide so that the whites glittered. "Tell Queeg what I think of him. Let him court-martial me for insubordination."

Maryk uttered a brief obscenity and went out.

"Well, I guess I'll hunt up poor Ducely," Keefer said, "and screw that assignment out of him."

Harding said, "My audit of the ship's service accounts is due." He tossed aside a magazine and yawned. "Guess I'd better do it before I turn in. Last month he sent for me at one o'clock in the morning and asked for it."

"Brilliant administrator, our captain," Keefer said as he went out.

Harding and Keith looked at each other with identical expressions of wry, worried amusement. Harding scratched his head. "Willie," he said softly, "did the captain keep dodging to the covered side of the bridge?" His tone appealed to the brotherhood of three months in the clip shack, of two green ensigns sick together at the top of a mast.

"Hardy, I'm not sure," answered Willie, in a tone involuntarily hushed. "It seems to me I saw a lot less of him than usual. But—hell, you know how Keefer hates the captain." He dropped his eyes to the code machine.

Harding stood. "That's great—great."

"Maybe he's all wrong."

"What happens if this ship gets in a jam?" Harding's lips were tight in vexation and fear. "The purpose of a captain is to get us out of jams, Willie, not to check off due dates on reports and assignments. Christ, this ship's service audit is ludicrous! I'm a graduate CPA. I've done audits for Onondaga Carbide. Christ knows what my boss would say if he saw me in that canteen, counting Oh Henry bars and tubes of toothpaste! . . . Well, all that doesn't matter, see? I volunteered for the Navy, and I'm on the *Caine,* and if it helps the *Caine* for a professional CPA to audit the nickel-and-dime ship's service, why, I'll audit it. But in return the Navy's supposed to give me a ship that goes, and a captain that fights—— That's what all this muck is for, isn't it?"

"Look, it's an old story by now. We're stuck with a lemon. Misfortune of war. We could be in a Jap prison camp. We've got to see it through, that's all——"

"Willie, you're a good guy," Harding said, getting up, "but you're not a married man. We're different animals. I'm scared for five people, me, my wife, and three kids. One kid in particular. A six-year-old boy with a very nice smile. Remind me to show you his picture sometime."

Harding hurried up the passageway and disappeared behind the green curtains of his stateroom.

21 · Death and Ice Cream

At dawn next day another entertainment was staged for Ensign Keith by the Northern Attack Force.

The whining bangs of the general alarm brought him, half dressed, scampering up to the bridge, in a misty blue twilight torn by zigzags and parabolas and bursts of red-and-orange fire. The crash of big guns made his ears ring. He hastily chewed up two of the sheets of toilet paper he kept tucked in his life jacket for this purpose, and thrust the wet wads in his ears. At once the explosions dimmed to comfortable thuds. This was his own invention, devised when cotton had once run short during a gunnery exercise.

The *Caine's* three-inch pop guns had no part to play in the barrage. Queeg kept the crew at battle stations until the sun rose, and then dismissed them. Willie remained on the bridge to enjoy the thumping, blazing show. At half-past eight a long arc of assault boats crept across the quiet waters toward Roi-Namur, main northern fortress of the atoll. The islands were no longer green at all, but sandy gray, spotted here and there with black. Little fires flickered on them, pale in the white sunlight. The foliage had all burned or withered away, leaving splintered, criss-crossed tangles of tree trunks, through which could be seen ruins of squat buildings, and some empty broken walls. Willie watched through binoculars the arrival of the assault boats on the beaches, the swarming forward of the tanks and the marines, the unexpected puffs of white and orange from the inner gray wastes of the islands. He saw some marines fall. The sight was thrilling and a little saddening, like seeing a fighter knocked out.

He turned on the special short-wave radio, the JBD 640, and eavesdropped eagerly on the talk of the embattled men in the tanks ashore. He was surprised to notice that they had dropped the phrases of Navy communications. They spoke to each other, and to the ships trying to protect them with gunfire, in short, angry, vicious sentences. They used fearful obscenity. There was a half-comic contrast between the formal, apologetic tones of the men on the ships and the bitter heat of the men on shore. It was such an interesting novelty that Willie listened for almost two hours. He had the thrill of hearing one man die in the middle of an incredibly foul stream of cursing. At least he surmised the death, because the man was pleading for naval shelling to eliminate a block-house that was spraying him with machine-gun fire; and suddenly his words were cut off. Willie had a vague shame-ful sense that he was storing up anecdotes for future parlor chats while other men were perishing, and that such behavior showed a want of feeling. But he didn't turn off the radio.

However, he was troubled at lunch, at one particular instant. He was pouring thick chocolate sauce over his ice cream when a shocking explosion, more violent than any he had heard so far, made the silverware and glasses rattle; it felt palpable in the air against his face. He jumped up, with Keefer and Jorgensen, and ran to the starboard scuttle. Jorgensen yanked the tin wind scoop out of the opening, and the officers peered through. A colossal black cloud was climbing skyward over Namur. Long, ugly vermilion flames licked out of its boiling base. "Main ammunition dump, no doubt," observed Keefer.

"I hope it blew a few thousand Japs to kingdom come," said Ensign Jorgensen, adjusting his glasses.

"I doubt that it did," Keefer returned to his seat. "They're all in nice deep holes, what's left of 'em. Some of our guys went up with it, though, that's for sure."

Willie stared at the holocaust for a minute or so, while a warm fragrant breeze fanned his face, and Ensign Jorgensen breathed on his neck, audibly chewing meat. Then Willie sat at his place again, and dug his spoon into the mound of white cream attractively laced with brown. It occurred to him that there was an unsettling contrast between himself, eating ice cream, and marines on Namur a few thousand yards away, being blown up. He was not sufficiently unsettled to stop eating the ice cream, but the thought worked around like grit in his mind. At last he spoke it aloud.

The other officers gave him vexed looks. None of them stopped eating their desserts. But Ducely, who was in the habit of dousing his plate with chocolate sauce in quanti-ties that sickened the others, paused in the act of reaching for the sauce; then he poured only a thin spiral of brown on his ice cream, and put the pitcher down furtively.

Keefer, pushing back his clean-scraped plate, said, "Willie, don't be an ass. War is a business in which a lot of people watch a few people get killed and are damn glad it wasn't them." He lit a cigarette. "Tomorrow they may have us sweeping mines in the lagoon. The islands will probably be secured. A lot of marines sitting around on their duffs on the beach, eating lunch, may see us all blown sky-high. None of them will skip a bite."

"At least they'll be eating K-rations, not ice cream with sauce," said Willie. "It's so—so luxurious, some-how."

"Look, nobody will court-martial you if you don't eat your ice cream," said Keefer.

"We ferried a bunch of marines along the coast one night at Guadal," said Maryk, spooning up his dessert. "Calm night, but they all got sick as dogs. This marine captain was laying over on that couch. He says, 'I sure as hell don't like Guadalcanal, but I'd rather stay on it a year than on this bucket a week.' He said he'd jump ship if he heard we were going to sweep mines. He says, 'Of all the lousy deals I know of in this war, sweeping mines is the worst. I don't know how you guys can sleep nights just knowing you're on a minesweeper.' "

"Can this ship really sweep mines?" said Ducely. "It seems so unbelievable, really——"

"You just handed in an assignment," said Keefer, "explaining in seven pages exactly how we do it."

"Oh, that. You know I copied it straight out of the *Minesweeping Manual*. I don't even know what the words mean. What is that paravane thing they keep talking about?"

"Mr. Keith," said Maryk, with a small groan, "take your assistant by the hand, right after lunch, and show him a goddamn paravane."

"Aye aye, sir," said Willie, and he squinted over his cigarette like an old sea dog.

The table was still being cleared when a radioman brought Willie an action message. He broke it in a hurry. The *Caine* was ordered to proceed to Funafuti Atoll next day, escorting an LST group. Funafuti was far south, well clear of the battle zone. Willie was regretful at the thought of leaving the attack force.

He stopped at the rail outside the captain's cabin to see the sights, but the show had tamed down. Sporadic fire-support shelling was still going on, but the mass barrages were over. The fleet in the lagoon was losing its warlike air. Naked sailors were diving off some of the anchored ships, splashing merrily in water which was no longer blue, but yellow-brown and full of garbage. Other ships were airing bedding in ragged white patches along the life lines.

"Funafuti, hey?" The captain, at his desk, was eating ice cream out of a soup plate with one hand, and fitting pieces into a jigsaw puzzle with the other. "Kay. Tell Maryk to come up here. And tell Whittaker to send me up another big plate of ice cream, and some coffee——"

A knock sounded at the door, the tentative rap of an enlisted man. It was the radioman, Smith, grinning in apologetic fright. "Beg pardon, Captain. They told me Mr. Keith was here—— Big day, Mr. Keith. Another action message——"

Queeg said, "Give it here." The radioman placed the despatch on the captain's desk and backed out hastily. Queeg glanced at the heading, half started out of his chair, then leaned back, and said very calmly, "What do you know! Bureau of Personnel. Orders for somebody, no doubt——"

Willie's hand shot forward. "I'll break it, sir, right now."

"Good, Willie, do that. Might even be me. I'm somewhat senior for the good old *Caine*." The captain gave him the paper offhandedly, and as Willie went out the door he added, "And just remember, orders are classified military information."

"Aye aye, sir."

Willie had hardly set up the coding machine in the wardroom when Queeg came strolling in. The captain poured himself a cup of coffee. "How're you coming, Willie?"

"Here she goes, sir."

Queeg stood over him as he ticked off the message.

The orders were for Lieutenant (jg) Rabbitt, assigning him to the destroyer-minesweeper *Oaks,* under construction in San Francisco.

"Rabbitt, hey? New construction, hey? Mighty nice. I'll take that message, Willie." Queeg pulled the decode out of the machine, reaching over Willie's shoulder. "Get one thing straight, Willie. I and I alone will decide when Mr. Rabbitt is to know about his orders, understand me?"

"But, Captain, aren't the orders addressed to him?"

"God damn it, Willie, you're turning into the worst sea lawyer I've ever seen! For your information this message is addressed to the *Caine,* of which I am the captain, and I can detach Mr. Rabbitt at my pleasure, now that I know the desires of the Bureau. I haven't the least confidence in Harding as a relief for Rabbitt, not yet, and until such time as Harding seems to measure up, why, Rabbitt can just ride along on the *Caine,* like the rest of us. Is that clear?"

Willie swallowed, and said, "Quite clear, sir."

Suppressing the knowledge of Rabbitt's orders was torture for Willie. He sat opposite the first lieutenant at dinner, stealing glances at the pale, patient, worried face, with its perpetual cowlick of straight brown hair falling over the left eye. He felt like a party to a crime.

The ensign realized now that he had grown fond of Rabbitt. It was into the arms of this man that he had jumped when he first boarded the *Caine,* and he still remembered the drawled welcome, "Ho, don't be so eager! You don't know what you're jumping into." At first Willie had considered him a dull rustic. But, in time, other qualities of Rabbitt had emerged. He was never late in relieving the deck. He couldn't refuse to do a favor, and he executed favors as though they were orders of the captain. The sailors snapped to obey his commands, though he issued them in easy, joking tones. He wrote up his logs on time, and often volunteered to help Willie with decoding when traffic piled up. And Willie had never heard him say a derogatory word about anybody, except in the general wardroom banter about Queeg.

But Willie feared the captain too much to whisper the

great news to Rabbitt. The first lieutenant stood the midwatch that night and stumbled to his bunk in the misty
dawn, unaware that his visa out of misery lay on the
captain's desk; or that it lay on the conscience of the
communicator, too, so that Keith could hardly sleep.

Willie was drearily deciphering the day's traffic in the
wardroom after breakfast when Queeg came in, followed
by a commander—evidently a newly appointed one, for
the leaves on the visor of his cap were bright untarnished
yellow. The ensign jumped to his feet.

"Commander Frazer, this is my communicator, Ensign
Keith."

Willie shook hands with a tall tanned man of about
thirty, with a long jaw, clear blue eyes, and blond hair cut
down to bristles. The commander's khaki shirt was beautifully ironed. Queeg looked shabby beside him, in grays
faded by the *Caine's* vitriolic laundry.

"Go right ahead with your work, Willie," said Queeg.

"Aye aye, sir." He moved his coding material to the
far end of the table.

Whittaker came in with a steaming jug, and poured
coffee for Queeg and his guest. It developed that Frazer,
the captain of a destroyer, had just been ordered back to
the States to assume command of a new destroyer-minesweeper, new in the sense that a modern destroyer, not a
World War I relic, was being converted for sweeping. He
had come aboard, he said, for a look-see, because he knew
nothing about minesweeping. "They're converting a whole
squadron of them," said Frazer. "The boss man of my
squadron, Captain Voor, thinks I'm being yanked back
to get a div or squad command. I don't know. I'd sure as
hell better bone up on sweeping, that's for sure." He began
to light a curved brown pipe.

Queeg said, "I'll be happy to show you around, sir,
and tell you whatever little we know, here. What ship did
they give you, sir?"

"*Oaks,*" said Frazer.

Willie's heart bounded. He saw Queeg glance toward
him; he bent low over his work to avoid the look. "*Oaks,*

hey? Sixteen-fifty-tonner. I had a year on one of those
as a jg. Nice ships."

"Bureau was nice enough to send me a tentative roster
of my new wardroom," said Frazer. He pulled a flimsy
sheet out of a breast pocket. "Seems as how I'm kidnaping
a man from you. What's the name? Oh—here. Rabbitt."

Queeg drank coffee.

"His orders haven't come through yet to you?" Frazer
asked.

Queeg took another swallow of coffee, and said, "Oh,
yes, we have the orders."

Frazer smiled. "Well, fine. I rather thought you had. I
saw the BuPers despatch to you on the Fox sked and had
my boys break it—— Well. He's your first lieutenant,
isn't he? Guess he's pretty well up on sweeping."

"Competent officer."

"Well, maybe I'm in luck then. I can get some pretty
high NATS priorities. Maybe Rabbitt can fly back with me
and give me a long fill-in on the way."

"Well, but we're getting under way this afternoon, going
south."

"No strain. Send him over to my ship for berthing. I
think I can get us out of here in a couple of days. My
relief is aboard and ready to take over."

"Well, there's still the question of Rabbitt's relief," said
Queeg, with a chuckle. It was a strange solitary sound in
the wardroom.

"What do you mean, Captain? Doesn't Rabbitt have a
qualified relief aboard?"

"Depends on what you mean by qualified—— More
coffee, Commander?"

"No, thank you—— Are you *that* shorthanded, Commander Queeg? How long has Rabbitt's assistant been
aboard?"

"Harding? Oh, I'd say five-six months."

"Is he a weak sister?"

"Well, that's pretty harsh."

"Hell, Captain, there isn't an officer on my ship, outside
of the exec, that I couldn't detach in twenty-four hours.

I figure it's part of the job to maintain that level of training."

"Why, it's all a question of standards, sir," said Queeg. "I daresay on a good many ships Ensign Harding would be considered qualified in every respect. It's just that, well, on my ship, excellence is the standard, and I'm not sure Harding has quite achieved excellence."

"I believe I will have some more coffee, please," said Frazer.

Queeg said, "Willie, would you be good enough——" The ensign leaped up and poured for the senior officers.

"Well, Commander Queeg," said Frazer, "I see your viewpoint and I appreciate your high standards. On the other hand, the *Oaks* needs a first lieutenant to start putting her in commission right away, and I particularly need someone around me who knows a little minesweeping. After all, we're in a war. People have to learn fast, and do their best——"

"Well, I don't know," said Queeg, with a wise smile, "it sort of seems to me that in war standards of officer training should be higher, not lower. There are lives at stake, you know."

Frazer stirred canned milk into his coffee slowly, and studied Queeg's face with narrowed eyes. The captain of the *Caine* slouched in his chair, and stared at the wall, still smiling; in one hand hung over the back of the chair, the steel balls rolled with a little crackling noise.

"Captain Queeg," said the blond commander, "your point is well taken. Only thing is, it wouldn't make sense for me to hold up commissioning the *Oaks* while we waited for this relief of Rabbitt's to come up to your standards, would it? I have to stop over in Washington to report to the Bureau. Suppose I tell them frankly that you've had difficulty in training up a replacement for Rabbitt to suit your standards, and just request that another officer be assigned——"

"I've had no difficulty of any kind, and I'll match the state of officer training on this ship with any ship in the fleet, sir," said Queeg quickly. When he put his coffee cup down it rattled. "As I say, by anybody's standards but my own Harding is perfectly qualified, and in fact by my own standards his state of training is damned good, and, as I say, if Rabbitt left this afternoon the *Caine* would still be qualified to carry out all assignments, but all I was getting at——"

"I'm glad to hear that, Captain, and I'm sure it's true," said Frazer, grinning. "And that being the case, how about letting me have Rabbitt this afternoon?"

"Well, sir——" Queeg's head wagged heavily from side to side, and sank down between his shoulders. He peered out from under his eyebrows. "Well, as I say, since apparently it would work such a hardship to the *Oaks* if Rabbitt stayed aboard here another few days, which is all I ever intended, and gave Harding some concentrated indoctrination, why—— I fully realize that the *Caine* is an obsolescent vessel and the battle mission of the *Oaks* is far more important, sir, but for that very reason I regard training as one of the primary missions of this ship, and if I seem overzealous for excellence, well, I don't know as you can blame me or the Bureau could, either."

"On the contrary, you deserve commendation for your high standards." Frazer stood, and picked up his cap. "Suppose I send my gig over for Rabbitt, say, 1600, Captain. Save your boat a trip. Will that suit you?"

"That'll be fine. If you have any friends in the Bureau, you might tell them that Queeg, Philip, class of '36, is fairly due for some orders, too. . . . I'll escort you to the gangway, sir," Queeg said, as Frazer moved toward the door.

"Thank you. Nice meeting you, Keith."

"It was an honor and a pleasure, sir, I'm sure," said Willie. He failed in his effort to keep the gladness out of his voice. Queeg shot a baleful side glance at Willie as he left.

Ordinarily when a detached officer quitted the *Caine* nobody took notice except the gangway watch, who had to log the exact time of his leaving. But Willie, who had the watch that afternoon, began to see around three-thirty that something extraordinary was going on. Sailors were

congregating near the sea ladder, talking in low tones.
The officers began to drift to the quarterdeck, too, one
by one. Officers and men alike watched the movements of
troops and machines on the battered gray islands, or made
jokes about the physiques of swimmers splashing around
a destroyer anchored close by, or gawked at the deck
hands painting number-three stack slate blue. The sweet
oily smell of paint was strong in the warm air.

"Here she comes," someone said. A trim gig appeared
around the bow of a transport and clove through the
muddy water toward the *Caine*. A rustling sigh passed
through the watchers, as through an audience at a transition moment of a play. Whittaker and a steward's mate
came through the port passageway, carrying a weather-
beaten wooden foot locker with two blue canvas handbags
piled on it. Rabbitt emerged on the quarterdeck behind
them. He blinked in amazement at the crowd. The officers
shook hands with him one by one. The sailors stood with
their thumbs hooked in their belts, or their hands in their
pockets. A few of them called out, "So long, Mr. Rabbitt."

The gig clanged to a stop beside the sea ladder. Rabbitt
went up to Willie and saluted. His lips were sharply
pressed together, and his eyes were winking nervously.
"Request permission to leave the ship, sir."

"Permission granted, sir," said Willie, and added im-
pulsively, "You don't know what you're getting out of."

Rabbitt grinned, pressed Willie's hand, and went down
the ladder. The gig pulled away. Willie, at the gangway
desk, looked at the array of backs lined along the rail.
They reminded him of shabby spectators roped off at the
entrance to a wedding. He went to the rail himself, and
gazed after Rabbitt. The gig disappeared around the transport. There was only the fading foamy curve of the wake.

Within the hour Captain Queeg threw a fearful tantrum.
Paynter brought him a fuel and water report which showed
that the crew's consumption of water had risen ten per cent
during the Kwajalein operation. "They're forgetting the
value of water, hey? Kay, Mr. Paynter," the captain
shrieked. "No water for officers' and crews' personal use

for forty-eight hours! Maybe that'll show 'em I mean business, here!"

The *Caine* weighed anchor half an hour later, and headed out of Kwajalein Lagoon, bound for Funafuti.

22 · The Water Famine

In the days of sail, a following wind was a blessing; not so in the days of steam.

En route to Funafuti, two hundred miles out of Kwajalein, the *Caine* was wallowing along at ten knots under masses of clouds like vast dirty pillows. It was enveloped in its own miasma, from which it could not escape. The breeze blew from astern at about ten knots. Relative to the ship there was no movement of air at all. The minesweeper seemed to be traveling in a nightmare calm. The stack gas swirled and rolled on the main deck, sluggish, oily, almost visible. It stank; it coated tongues and throats with an itchy, foul-tasting film; it stung the eyes. The air was hot and damp. The smell of the crated cabbages on the after deckhouse made a singularly sickening marriage with the stack fumes. The sailors and officers of the *Caine*, sweating, dirty, unable to obtain the relief of a shower, looked at each other with lolling tongues and dulled sad eyes, and worked with their hands to their noses.

The *Caine* and a destroyer-escort were screening six LST's, lumbering fat shells more than three hundred feet long, shaped like wooden shoes, and withal strangely frail-looking; a determined assault with a can opener, one felt, on one of these paunchy hulls might bring about the abandon-ship alarm. The LST's wobbled over the waves at eight knots, and the zigzagging escorts went slightly faster.

Queeg's water ban was about twenty-four hours old when Maryk presented himself in the captain's cabin. The *Caine's* commanding officer lay flat on his back in his bunk, naked. Two fans, buzzing at full speed, blew streams of air down on him; nevertheless sweat stood in beads on his white chest. "What is it, Steve?" he said, not moving.

"Captain, in view of the extraordinary wind conditions, how about securing the water regulations after one day instead of two? Paynter tells me we've got plenty to last us until Funafuti——"

"That's not the point," exclaimed Queeg. "Why is everybody so goddamned stupid on this ship? Don't you think I know how much water we have? The point is, the men on this ship have been wasting water, and for their own good they've got to be taught a lesson, that's all."

"Captain, they've learned their lesson. One day of this is like a week without water."

The captain pursed his lips. "No, Steve, I said forty-eight hours and I meant forty-eight hours. If these men get the idea that I'm one of these shilly-shallyers who doesn't mean what he says there'll be no controlling them. Hell, I'd like a shower myself, Steve. I know how you feel. But we've got to put up with these inconveniences for the sake of the men's own good——"

"I wasn't asking for myself, sir. But the men——"

"Now don't give me any of that!" Queeg raised up on one elbow, and glared at the executive officer. "I'm as interested in the men's welfare as you are, and don't you go playing the hero. Did they or didn't they waste water? They did. Well, what do you want me to do about it— give them all letters of commendation?"

"Sir, consumption went up ten per cent. It was an invasion day. It wasn't really what I'd call wasting——"

"All right, all right, Mr. Maryk." Queeg lay back on the bed. "I see you simply want an argument for argument's sake. Sorry I can't accommodate you, but it's too hot and smelly at the moment. That's all."

Maryk heaved his broad chest in a painful sigh. "Sir,

how about one fifteen-minute shower period after the sweep-down?"

"God damn it, no! They'll get enough water in their soup and coffee to keep from getting dehydrated. That's all that matters. Next time they'll remember not to waste water on my ship! You can go, Steve."

The following wind did not desert the *Caine* that night nor the next day. Below decks, the air that came through the ventilators was intolerable; most of it was stack gas. The sailors swarmed out of the compartments and slept in clusters on the after deckhouse or on the main deck, as far from the stacks as they could get. Some of them brought mattresses, but mostly they curled themselves on the rusted deck plates, with life jackets for pillows. On the bridge everyone breathed in gasps through the night. During certain legs of the zigzag the breeze blew at a slight angle, instead of from dead astern, and then it was possible, by stretching one's neck far out over the bulwark, to catch a gulp or two of warm, fresh, unbelievably sweet air.

A hot sun rose out of the sea next morning and glared redly on a ship which appeared stricken by a plague. Dirty half-naked bodies sprawled all over the decks, apparently lifeless. The boatswain, piping reveille, wrought only a halfhearted resurrection. The bodies stirred, and rose, and began to move through chores with leaden limbs, like the crew of dead men in the *Rime of the Ancient Mariner*. The *Caine* was now fifty miles from the equator, sailing almost due south. With each hour that the sun rose in the sky the air grew hotter and more humid. And still the ship wallowed over the glittering sea, trapped in its own stench of stack gas and cabbages.

Around noon, human nature revolted. The black gang began to bootleg water in the after engine room, where the evaporators were, so that no pressure would be found by Queeg in any pipes. The word passed through the ship like a telegram. The two narrow steel ladders descending to the broiling, clanking engine space became choked with sailors. Paynter quickly discovered what was happening, and reported it to Maryk in the charthouse. The executive officer shrugged. "Can't hear a word you're saying," he said. "Stack gas has got my ears ringing."

This blessed relief was available only to the crew. Word of it soon reached all the officers; but, unanimously disloyal though they were to Queeg, a vague yet pervasive sense of the symbolism of an officer's cap kept them from descending the engine-room ladders.

Ducely, indeed, dropped his head on his arms beside the coding machine at three o'clock, and bleated to Willie that he could stand it no more; he was going aft to get a drink in the engine room. Willie glared at him. Ensign Keith bore small resemblance at this moment to the chubby, cheery-faced piano player who had walked into Furnald Hall fourteen months earlier. He had marked lines around mouth and nose; cheekbones and chin stood out from the round face. His eyes were sunk in smudged sockets. His face was grimy, and brown hairs bristled all over it. Trickles of sweat ran down his face into the neck of his open collar, staining the shirt dark brown. "You go back aft, you sad little bastard," he said (Ducely was three inches the taller of the two), "and you had better start living in your life jacket. I swear to God I'll throw you over the side."

Ducely moaned, lifted his head, and resumed picking feebly at the coding machine.

In one respect Captain Queeg's isolation from his officers was not as complete as he might have wished; having no private toilet, he was compelled to come below to use the officers' head in the wardroom passageway. These periodic appearances of the captain at odd hours sometimes led to trouble. It had become instinctive with all the officers to listen for the clang of the captain's door, and to spring into attitudes of virtue as soon as they heard it. One would leap out of his bunk and pick up a fistful of official mail, another would dart at a coding machine, a third would seize a pen and a mess statement, and a fourth would flip open a logbook.

Since Willie and Ducely were honorably employed, the bang of the captain's door at this moment did not trouble them. Queeg appeared a few seconds later and flapped through the wardroom in his run-down slippers, pouting morosely at vacancy as usual. The two officers did not look up from their coding. There was quiet while one might count ten, then a sudden frightful yammering in the passageway. Willie jumped up, thinking, or rather half hoping, that the captain had touched some defective light socket and electrocuted himself. He ran up the passageway, followed by Ducely. But there was nothing wrong with the captain, except that he was screeching unintelligibly into the officers' shower room. Ensign Jorgensen, naked as a cow, his large pink behind jutting like a shelf from his sway back, stood under the shower, his shoulders unmistakably wet, the iron deck under his feet covered with droplets. One hand gripped the shower valve, and with the other he was mechanically fumbling at his ear to adjust glasses that weren't there. His face wore an idiotically pleasant smile. Out of the captain's jumbled sounds emerged the words, "—dare to violate my orders, my express orders? How dare you?"

"The water left in the pipes, sir—in the pipes, that's all," babbled Jorgensen. "I was just using the water in the pipes, I swear."

"The water in the pipes, hey? Very good. That's what the officers on this ship can all use for a while. The crew's water restriction goes off at five o'clock. The officers' restriction will continue for another forty-eight hours. You inform Mr. Maryk of that fact, Mr. Jorgensen, and then submit a written report to me explaining why I should not make out an unsatisfactory fitness report for you" (he spat out the word "fitness" as though it were an oath) "at once!"

"The water in the pipes, sir," groaned Jorgensen, but Queeg had flounced into the head, and slammed the door. Keith and Ducely stared at Jorgensen, with stern, hating faces.

"Fellows, I've got to have my shower or I don't feel human," said Jorgensen, with injured self-righteousness. "I was only using the water in the pipes, really."

"Jorgensen," said Willie, "the water supply for nine

men dying of thirst has coursed away into that huge cleft between your buttocks. That's the right place for it, since your whole personality is concentrated in there. I hope you enjoyed it."

The officers of the *Caine* went without water for two more days. They all took turns at cursing Jorgensen, and then forgave him. The breeze changed, and the horror of the stack gas and cabbage fumes abated, but the weather continually grew hotter and stickier. There was nothing to do but suffer, and slander the captain. The officers did plenty of both.

Funafuti Atoll was a necklace of low islands richly green, flung on the empty sea. The *Caine* entered it shortly after sunrise, steaming slowly through a gap of blue water in the long white line of breakers on the reef. Half an hour later the minesweeper was secured to the port side of the destroyer tender *Pluto,* outboard of two other ships. Lines for steam, water, and electric power were hurriedly run across; the fires were allowed to die on the *Caine;* and the ship commenced to nurse itself at the generous dugs of the *Pluto.* The tender with its litter swung to a heavy anchor chain, fifteen hundred yards from the beach of Funafuti Island.

Willie was one of the first over the gangplank. A visit to a destroyer tender's communication office saved him whole days of decoding. It was part of the tender's service to decode and mimeograph fleet messages. These AlPacs, AlComs, AlFleets, GenPacs, PacFleets, AlNavs, NavGens, SoPacGens, and CentPacGens were what broke the backs of overburdened destroyer communicators.

There was a choppy swell in the lagoon. Willie airily crossed the unsteady planks over the sucking, churning, murderous little spaces between the ships. From the destroyer next to the *Pluto* a broad, stout gangplank on rollers slanted upward. Willie mounted it and found himself in a roaring machine shop. He groped around the cavernous tender, through zigzagging passageways and up and down ladders, passing in and out of a blacksmith shop, a barbershop, a carpenter shop, a laundry, a stain-

less-steel kitchen where hundreds of chickens were frying, a bakery, and twenty other such civilized enterprises.
Throngs of sailors moved sedately through these clean,
fresh-painted spaces, most of them eating ice cream out of
paper cups. They looked different from his own crew;
generally older, fatter, and more peaceful; a species of
herbivorous sailor, one might say, as contrasted to the
coyotes of the *Caine*.

He stumbled at last upon the immense wardroom.
Brown leather couches stretched along the bulkheads, and
officers in khaki stretched upon the couches. There were
perhaps fifteen of these prostrate figures. Willie walked up
to a bulky body and touched the shoulder. The officer
grunted, rolled over, and sat up, blinking. He stared at
Willie a moment, and said, "I'll be goddamned—the
demerit king, Midshipman Keith."

The jowly face had familiar, half-obliterated features.
Willie studied the officer with some embarrassment and
put out his hand. "That's right," he said, and added, with
a sudden jolt of recognition, "Aren't you Ensign Acres?"

"Good for you. Only it's Lieutenant jg." Acres uttered
a wheezy laugh. "They don't always recognize me. Coffee?"

"Yes," he said, a few minutes later, stirring his cup,
"I've put on at least forty pounds, I know. You do, on
these damn tenders. There's so much of everything——
You look pretty good. Skinnier. Sort of older, somehow.
You got a good deal?"

"It's all right," Willie said. He was trying to keep himself from staring in wonder at Acres. The once stern,
handsome drill officer was a fat wreck.

"Can't beat this deal," said Acres. "Oh, you see these
guys?" He swept a scornful thumb around at the sleepers.
"Ask them, and half of them will cry that they hate this
dull noncombatant life, being stuck forever in a godforsaken atoll. All they want is action, action, they say.
They want to be part of this great battle, they say. When,
oh when, will orders ever come, taking them to a fighting
ship? . . . Horse feathers. I handle the ship's correspondence. I know who puts in transfer requests and who

doesn't. I know who kicks and screams when the possibility arises of giving 'em some temporary staff duty with a commodore on a tin can. They all love this deal. I do, and I admit it. Want a cheese sandwich? We have some terrific roquefort."

"Sure."

The roquefort was exquisite, and so was the fresh white bread.

"The thing is, Keith, that all of us supine bastards are actually doing a damn good and damn necessary job. Have you tried the facilities of this ship? Destroyers beg a few days alongside the *Pluto*. We are the can-do ship. We've got it so well organized, and there's so little waste motion, no steaming here and there and buttoning up for sea and going to GQ and all that combat crap that eats up honest worktime——" He took another slice of bread and lavishly smeared roquefort cheese on it. "You married, Keith?"

"No."

"I am. Got married I guess during the next class after the one you were in. You were the December '42 bunch, weren't you? It's all getting hazy. Well, anyway, I met this girl, blonde, she was a secretary in the English Department at Columbia. Got married in three weeks." Acres grinned, and sighed, and noisily sucked up his cup of coffee and poured more. "Well, you know, we instructors had a pretty good deal, Keith. What we put in for, we got. I always had figured that when my year of teaching was up I'd put in for subs. Had read up all the submarine doctrine—well. That was before I married. I studied all the ships in the fleet roster, Keith, and put in for destroyer tender. Smart. The mail comes here mighty regularly, and I live for it, Keith. Got a baby two months old I've never seen. Girl. . . . I'm the communicator on this bucket. I should have asked you before, is there something I can do for you?"

Acres took Willie to the communication office, a spacious room on the main deck furnished with new chairs and desks of green-enameled metal, bubbling coffee makers, and several sleek scrubbed yeoman in fresh blue dungarees. At a word from Acres the yeomen sprang up, and out of clean cabinets and flawlessly regular files they produced in a few minutes all the decodes Willie wanted, and a series of new fleet letters. Weeks of piled-up work melted away for the *Caine's* communicator. He looked around at the shelves of books in alphabetical order, at the wire baskets almost clear of correspondence, at the handsome plexiglass file boards of Fox skeds and decodes, and wondered at this weird antiseptic efficiency. His gaze rested on Acres, whose belly bulged in two khaki rolls above and below his belt. The *Pluto's* communicator, flipping through a sheaf of AlNavs, glanced up at Willie's collar pin. "Is that gold or silver?"

"Gold."

"Should be silver, Keith. You make jg on the new AlNav. Class of February. Congratulations."

"Thanks," said Willie, shaking hands, "but my skipper still has to approve."

"Oh, hell, that's automatic. Buy yourself some collar pins while you're here. Come on, I'll show you where. Got everything?"

When Willie left Acres at the gangway, the communicator said, "Come on over and eat with me any time. Lunch. Dinner. We'll shoot the breeze some more. We have strawberries and cream all the time."

"Sure," Willie said. "Thanks a million."

He crossed the nest to the *Caine*. As he came over the gangplank and set foot on the rusty, littered quarterdeck, he straightened like a German and threw Harding a salute which brought a smile of mournful amusement to the first lieutenant's face. "I report my return aboard, sir!"

"Got the jerks, Willie? A salute like that can break your arm."

Willie walked forward. He smiled at the dirty, ragged Apaches of the crew, passing here and there on the deck in their accustomed tasks. Mackenzie, Jellybelly, Langhorne of the long bony jaw, Horrible with his pimples, Urban, Stilwell, Chief Budge, one after the other they went by and Willie realized that he had never had relatives or friends whom he knew as well and could estimate as clearly as any second-class seaman of the *Caine*. "Jelly-belly," he called, "six fat sacks of mail for us on the tender—four official, two personal——"

"Aye aye, sir. Get 'em right away."

On the well deck a group of deck hands were dividing and devouring an immense round yellow cheese, plunder from the *Pluto*, with the shrill chattering of blue jays. Crumbs of the cheese were scattered on the deck. Willie accepted a broken, fingerprinted yellow morsel from the redheaded Jew, Kapilian, and crammed it in his mouth.

In his room Willie stuck the lieutenant junior grade bars into the collar of a new khaki shirt he had bought on the *Pluto*. He drew the green curtain, put on the shirt, and examined himself in the mirror by the dim yellow overhead light. He noted his flat stomach, his lean face, his tired, black-rimmed, dogged eyes. His lips were dragged downward and compressed.

He shook his head. With that gesture, he gave up a plan which he had been secretly harboring for a week. There was a chaplain on the *Pluto;* he had passed his office; but Willie knew now that he was not going to hunt up the chaplain and tell him the story of the water famine. "You may not be much," he said aloud to his mirror image, "but you don't have to go weeping to anybody on the *Pluto*. You're Lieutenant Keith of the *Caine*."

23 · Court-martial of Stilwell

"Mistuh Keith, exec want to see you, suh."

"Okay, Rasselas." Willie reluctantly dropped on his desk the nine mildewed letters from May that had just come in the mailbags from the *Pluto,* and went to the exec's room.

"Things are closing in, Willie." Maryk handed him a long typed letter on Red Cross stationery. Willie read it, squatting on the coaming of the doorway. He felt sick, as though he himself were trapped. "Captain seen it?"

Maryk nodded. "Summary court-martial for Stilwell day after tomorrow. You're going to be the recorder."

"The what?"

"Recorder."

"What's that?"

The exec shook his head and grinned. "Don't you know any Navy regulations? Get out *Courts and Boards* and get hot on summary court-martials."

"What do you think will happen to Stilwell?"

"Well, that's up to Keefer, Harding, and Paynter. They're the court."

"Well, then, he'll be okay."

"Maybe," Maryk said dryly.

A couple of hours later Rasselas went searching the ship for the communicator and found him flat on his face on the flying bridge, asleep in the sun. Jellybelly's ragged copy of *Courts and Boards* lay open on the deck beside him, the pages flapping in the breeze. "Suh, Mistuh Keith, suh. Cap'n wants you, suh."

"Oh, God. Thanks, Rasselas."

Queeg looked up from his jigsaw puzzle with a remarkably pleasant, youthful smile when Willie came into his cabin. It brought back forcibly to Willie how much he had liked Queeg at their first handshake so long, long ago.

"Well, Mr. Keith, here's something for you." Queeg took several clipped sheets from an overflowing wire basket and gave them to the communicator. They were Willie's appointment to lieutenant junior grade. Queeg stood, and offered his hand. "Congratulations, Lieutenant."

Willie had been comforting himself for months with a dark fantasy. He had resolved that if ever a moment came when Queeg offered to shake hands with him, he would refuse. With that one gesture he would tell the captain once for all what the world of gentlemen, in the person of

Willie Keith, thought of people like Queeg. Now it had
suddenly come, the chance to make the daydream real—
but the sad fact is, Willie meekly took the captain's hand
and said, "Thank you, sir."

"Not at all, Willie. We have our little differences,
naturally, but as an officer you measure up very well—
very well, on the whole. Now then. All set to be recorder
at the court-martial?"

"Well, sir, I've been boning up on this *Courts and
Boards*—seems I'm a combination prosecutor and legal
adviser——"

"Yes, well, don't let all that legal gobbledegook throw
you. I've been a recorder five, six times and the last thing
I know anything about—or want to know anything about
—is law. The important thing is to have a yeoman who's
on the ball and gets the whole thing typed up right, according to the form in the book. Porteous knows his stuff,
so you'll be okáy. Just bear down on him and make sure
he dots the *i*'s and crosses the *t*'s. Stilwell's going to get
a bad-conduct discharge and I want to be damn sure it
sticks."

Willie blurted in plain puzzlement, "How do you know
what he's going to get, sir?"

"Hell, he's guilty, isn't he? A fraud like that calls for
the stiffest sentence a summary court can give, which is a
BCD."

"Sir, it's just that—well, it sure *looks* as though Stilwell is guilty—but—to prove it legally may be a little
tougher than——"

"Prove it, hell! Here's his confession." Queeg snatched
a typewritten sheet from the wire basket and tossed it on
the desk in front of Willie. "There's a way of doing these
things. The court-martial is a formality, that's all. How
the hell could four ignoramuses like you and Keefer and
those two others try a not-guilty plea? You'd make a
million mistakes. You take that confession now."

"Aye aye, sir." Willie folded the paper away carefully.

"Now if there are any questions, any points that you
and Porteous can't figure out between you, why, remember to bring the record up here to me. I don't want the

big boys to throw it out on some goddamn technical point. I want this thing to stick, do you understand?"

Willie took the confession to his room and read it. At first he was sure that Stilwell was lost. Then he opened *Courts and Boards* to the section on confessions, and studied it carefully, underlining several sentences. He sent for Stilwell. In a few minutes the sailor appeared in the doorway. He wore painfully clean dungarees, and wrung a new white hat in his hands. "You want me, Mr. Keith?"

"Come in. Draw the curtain. . . . Sit down on that bunk." The sailor closed the curtain, and stood with his back to it. "Pretty sad business, Stilwell."

"I know, sir. I'll take what's coming to me. Whatever it is, it was worth it. If that's all——"

"Why did you confess?"

"Hell, the captain had me cold, sir, with that Red Cross letter."

"Oh, he showed that to you?"

"He says, 'Take your choice. A clean breast of it, and a summary court on the ship, or try to bluff through, and get yourself a general court back in the States, and probably ten years.' What would *you* do, sir?"

"Stilwell, what has the captain got against you?"

"Holy Christ! You tell *me,* sir."

Lieutenant Keith pulled forward the open copy of *Courts and Boards* on the desk. He read the section on confessions aloud to the sailor. At first Stilwell's face lit with desperate hope, but the liveliness quickly went out of his face. "What's the use, sir? It's too late now. I didn't know about that book."

Lighting a cigarette, Willie leaned back in his chair and stared at the overhead, smoking in silence for a minute. "Stilwell, if you quote me to the captain as saying this, I'll call you a liar. But if you'll call on me to bear you out from the book, I will. Do you see the difference? I want to tell you two things to think about overnight."

"Yes, sir?"

"First, if you repudiate that confession it can't possibly be used against you in court. That, I swear. Second— and don't ever tell the captain I said this—if you plead not guilty I think it's almost impossible for a summary court-martial on this ship to convict you."

"Sir, that Red Cross letter——"

"It doesn't *prove* anything. Your brother sent that wire. It's up to the court to prove that you instigated him. Without your testimony—and they can't make you testify against yourself—how can they possibly prove it? Where's your brother? Where's any record of a conversation between you?"

Stilwell looked at him suspiciously. "Why would you rather have me plead not guilty?"

"Look, I don't give a damn what you plead! My duty as recorder is to point out to you in my dumb way what the best legal course for you seems to me to be. Don't take my word. Go ask a chaplain, or the legal officer on the *Pluto.* Ask them about *Courts and Boards* yourself. Section 174."

The sailor repeated mechanically, *"Courts and Boards* 174—174—174. Okay, sir. Thanks, sir." He went out. Willie fought down his irritation. It was only natural, he reasoned, that in the nostrils of the crew all the officers were acquiring the odor of Queeg.

Stilwell was back next morning with a stiff new copy of *Courts and Boards* under his arm. "Mr. Keith, you're right. I'm gonna plead not guilty."

"Oh? Who convinced you?"

The sailor said eagerly, "Well, see, Engstrand, he's got a cousin on the *Bolger,* second can outboard. This cousin, he's big buddies with the first-class yeoman on the ship. Well, this yeoman, he's a fat Irish guy, bald, maybe forty years old. In civilian life he's a politician, they say. Only reason he ain't an officer, he never went to college. Well, he sold me this book. He says it ain't nothing secret, anybody can buy it off the government for a couple of bucks. Is that right?"

Willie hesitated, and turned to the title page of his copy. At the bottom, in small print, was a legend he had not noticed before: *For sale by the Superintendent of Documents, U.S. Government Printing Office, Washington 25, D.C.* "That's right, Stilwell." His tone contained a touch of his own surprise. He had assumed, for no good reason, that the book was restricted.

"Well, Jesus, I don't know why every sailor in this goddamn outfit don't own one!" said the gunner's mate. "I been up all night reading it. I never knew I had all them rights. Well, anyway, sir, this Callaghan, this yeoman, he said I sure as hell ought to plead not guilty. He says I'm a cinch to get acquitted."

"He's not an officer, so you can probably believe him."

"That's how I figure it, sir," the sailor said with perfect seriousness.

"Okay, Stilwell—— Well. This brings up a lot of problems. You have to have counsel, and I have to prepare exhibits, and dig up witnesses, and in general the whole thing turns into a trial, just like in the movies——"

"You think I'm doing the right thing, don't you, sir?"

"I'd rather not see you get convicted, naturally, if there's a way out. I think I'd better talk to the captain right away. You wait here."

Stilwell clutched the brown book tightly in both hands, and ran his tongue over his lips. "Ah—aye aye, sir."

Willie hesitated outside Queeg's door for a couple of minutes, rehearsing answers to hypothetical shrieks and snarls of the captain. He knocked. "Come in!"

It was dark in the cabin. The black-out curtain hung over the porthole. Dimly, Willie could see the bulge of the captain's form in the bunk. "Who is it and what do you want?" said a voice muffled by a pillow.

"Sir, it's Keith. It's about the court-martial. Stilwell wants to plead not guilty."

The captain reached a curved talon out from under the pillow and snapped on the bed lamp. He sat up, squinting, and scratching his naked chest. "What's all this? Not guilty, hey? Just a born troublemaker, that man! Well, we'll fix him. What time is it?"

"Eleven, sir."

Queeg rolled out of the bunk, and began splashing water on his face at the basin. "How about his confession? How in hell can he plead not guilty after confessing, hey? Did you ask him that?"

"He's going to repudiate his confession, sir."

"Oh, he is, hey? That's what he thinks—— Pass me that tube of toothpaste, Willie."

The young lieutenant waited until the captain's mouth was full of foam. Then he said cautiously, "He seems to have been getting some legal advice from a very savvy yeoman on another ship in the nest, sir. He's got himself a copy of *Courts and Boards*——"

"I'll Courts and Boards him," mumbled the captain around his toothbrush.

"He says there's no evidence that he sent any fraudulent wire, and the confession, he says, he dictated under duress, and it doesn't mean anything."

The captain blew out a mouthful of water explosively. "Duress! What duress?"

"He claims you said something about a general court-martial——"

"For plain, wrongheaded, inside-out stupidity you can't beat an enlisted man who suddenly gets hold of a goddamn book of regulations! Duress! I was offering him a way out of a general court-martial. I could probably get a reprimand for such undercover clemency. And that little sneak calls it duress! . . . Give me a towel."

Queeg mopped his face and hands. "Kay," he said, tossing the towel aside and picking a shirt off the back of his chair, "where is our poor little mistreated innocent?"

"In my room, sir. He just told me——"

"Send him up here."

Stilwell was in the captain's cabin for an hour. Willie lurked on the well deck, perspiring in the vertical bluish glare of the noon sun, watching the captain's door. At last the gunner's mate came out. In one hand he carried his *Courts and Board,* in the other a sheet of white paper. His face was lead-colored, and trickling with sweat. Willie ran up to him. "What's the dope, Stilwell?"

"Look, Mr. Keith," the sailor said hoarsely, "maybe you mean well, but I don't know, every time I have anything to do with you I wind up in worse trouble than before. Lay off me, will you? The captain told me to give you this. Here it is."

Willie read a handwritten scrawl: *I hereby state that the confession made by me on 13 February 1944 was made voluntarily, under no duress. I was glad to be given a chance to make a clean breast of it, and I have been given no inducement or promises of better treatment for confession. I will repeat these true facts under oath if necessary.* It was signed by Stilwell in a schoolboyish hand; the bright blue ink and the broad pen nib identified the instrument as Captain Queeg's fountain pen.

Willie said, "Stilwell, this isn't the end. He got this under duress, too. If there's anything you want me——"

"Please, Mr. Keith!" A sudden desperate glare came into the sailor's eyes. "That's it, see? That's the way I want it, that's the truth, that's how it's gonna be. There wasn't no duress, see? Duress!" Stilwell flung *Courts and Boards* over the side. "I never heard of duress! Keep your goddamn nose out of my business!"

He ran off down the port passageway. Willie mechanically looked over the side. *Courts and Boards* lay under water, caught between the two hulls, amid floating splinters and garbage. The ships rolled slowly together; the book was squashed to a shapeless wad.

The beer was icy, golden, keenly gratifying and delicious, gurgling out of the triangular holes in the misted cans. Keefer, Maryk, Harding, and Willie lay under palm trees in sweet breezy shade and rapidly drank off a couple of cans each, to quench thirst. Then, more slowly, they began their social drinking. The spot they had chosen was a secluded curve of the recreation beach. They were alone with sand and palms. Far out on the green-blue lagoon the *Pluto* drifted slowly back and forth at the end of her anchor chain, carrying the six nursing destroyers with her.

Willie had resolved to say nothing to the other officers about the Stilwell matter. It seemed unethical for the prosecutor and court members to gossip over the case on the day before the trial. But a few beers dissolved his resolution. He told them about the abortive not-guilty plea, and the documents Queeg had extorted from the sailor.

None of the others spoke for a while. Harding rose and

began plunging holes in three more cans of beer. Keefer
sat with his back to the bole of a palm, smoking a pipe.
Maryk lay face down on the sand, his head on his arms.
He had rolled into this position halfway through the story,
and remained so.

The novelist accepted a beer can from Harding and
drank deeply. "Steve," he said in a quiet tone. Maryk
turned his head sideways. "Steve, has the thought ever occurred to you," said Keefer, gravely and calmly, "that
Captain Queeg may be insane?"

The executive officer sat up with a grunt, and squatted
cross-legged, red-brown and thick, white sand clinging to
the folds of his skin. "Don't bust up a good afternoon,
Tom," he said.

"I'm not making jokes, Steve."

"There's no point in that kind of talk," said the exec,
shaking his head impatiently like an animal.

"Look, Steve, I'm no psychiatrist, but I've read a lot. I
can give you a diagnosis of Queeg. It's the clearest picture
I've ever seen of a psychopathic personality. He's a
paranoid, with an obsessive-compulsive syndrome. I'll bet
a clinical examination would back me up a hundred per
cent. I'll show you the description of the type in the
books——"

"I'm not interested," said the exec. "He's no crazier than
you are."

"You're in a big jam, Steve."

"I'm in no jam."

"I've seen this coming for a long time." The novelist got
up, tossed his beer can aside, and punched holes in another. Foam boiled over his hands. "See, Steve, about a
week after Queeg came aboard I realized he was a psychopath. The shirttail obsession, the little rolling balls, the
inability to look you in the eye, the talking in secondhand
phrases and slogans, the ice-cream mania, the seclusion—
why, the man's a Freudian delight. He crawls with clues.
But that doesn't matter. Some of my best friends are psy-
chopaths. It could be argued that that I'm one. The thing
is, Queeg is an extreme case, bordering on the twilight
zone between eccentricity and real psychosis. And because

he's a coward, I think that being in a combat zone is beginning to drive him over the red line. I don't know whether there'll be a sudden crack, or——"

"Tom, it's a known fact that you read a hell of a lot more than I do and talk better, and all that. The only thing is, common sense is worth more than all the talk and all the books in the world." Maryk lit a cigarette in a swift scratch of flame and spurt of smoke. "You're all wound up in big words, paranoid, psychopath, and all that. Captain Queeg is nothing but a strict guy who likes to have his own way, and there are a thousand skippers more or less like him. Okay, he rolls little balls. You sit in your room before reveille filling your desk drawers with a lot of scribbling. Everybody is a screwball in their own way. It doesn't make them crazy."

Keith and Harding looked from one speaker to the other with the intensity of children at a family quarrel.

"You're whistling in the dark," said Keefer. "Ever hear of a captain in his right mind trying to rig a court-martial as crudely as he's doing it?"

"It happens every day. What the hell is a summary court-martial but a farce? Nobody on a ship ever knows any law. Hell, how about De Vriess with Bellison—and Crowe?"

"That was different. De Vriess fixed the court to let them off. He was going through the forms because the Auckland police were so sore about the riot. But rigging a trial to convict a man—moral considerations aside, he's violating all his Navy principles. That's what makes me think he's going off his head. You know damn well that the enlisted man is God in this Navy. For two reasons, first, because he *is* the Navy, and second, because his relatives back home pay the Navy's appropriations. Sure, hounding the officers is standard emotional ping-pong for skippers. But the *enlisted* man? The regulations bristle with his rights. Queeg's juggling dynamite and giggling happily."

"When it comes right down to it, Stilwell is guilty," said Maryk.

"Of what? Christ, Steve! Wanting to see his wife, when

poison-pen letters from home were accusing her of adultery?"

"Look, try the trial tomorrow," said Maryk. "Give us a beer, Harding. Drop it, Tom, or I'm going to semaphore for the gig."

The rest of the afternoon went by in increasingly sullen beer drinking.

The plan of the day read: *1400. Summary Court-Martial of Stilwell, John, GM 2/C, in the wardroom.*

Shortly after lunch Queeg sent for Harding. Then he sent for Paynter. In another quarter hour, Paynter brought the same message for Keefer. The novelist rose. "Nothing like polling the jury for the verdict before the trial starts," he said. "Eliminates all that unpleasant suspense."

Willie was in the ship's office, his mind whirling in a fog of legal rituals and phrases. The yeoman, obese as a pudding in shrunken dress whites, was helping him arrange the papers for the trial. When Chief Bellison, the master-at-arms, came to the door, smooth-shaven and immaculate, his shoes gleaming black, and announced, "Fourteen hundred, Lieutenant Keith. Ready in all respects for the court-martial," Willie had a panicky moment. It seemed to him that he was utterly unprepared for his task. He blindly followed the yeoman and the chief into the wardroom, where the three officers were ranged around the green table, looking strangely dressed up in their black ties, and grave and embarrassed. Stilwell came shambling in, picking at his cap, a meaningless half-smile on his face. The trial began.

Willie sat with *Courts and Boards* open before him, carefully acting out the ritual step by step. Jellybelly prompted him, and he prompted the accused and the court. As Willie pushed the limping trial along he was reminded continuously of his high-school fraternity initiation, which had been enacted shamefacedly from a printed script by perplexed boys, half amused, half solemn, in a dim room around a steaming skull.

It was the simplest possible situation, a guilty plea with a typewritten confession in the record, and yet time wasted and wasted in entrances and exits, clearing of the court, wrangles over the meanings of words in *Courts and Boards,* and searchings through *Navy Regulations* and the court-martial manual. At the end of an hour and a half of this weariness, Keefer declared the trial finished, whereupon Stilwell roused himself from a horselike apathy and announced that he wanted to make a statement. This occasioned further flurries of debate. At last he was allowed to proceed.

"The captain give me six months' restriction for reading on watch, and that's why I had to get that phone wire sent. I had to see my wife or my marriage would of busted up," Stilwell said, in halting, self-conscious tones. "I didn't think reading a comic book at the gangway was enough reason to ruin my life. But I'm guilty. Only I think the court ought to remember why I done it."

Willie swiftly copied down as much of this as he could, and read it back to Stilwell. "Is that the substance of your statement?"

"That's fine, Mr. Keith. Thanks."

"All right," Keefer said. "Clear the court."

Willie led out the yeoman, the accused, and the orderly. He waited in the ship's office for forty minutes, and then Bellison called him and the yeoman back to the wardroom.

"Court finds specification proved by plea," Keefer said. "Sentence is loss of six liberties."

Willie stared around at the three officers. Paynter sat like a mahogany idol; Harding was trying to look solemn, but a grin was bursting through; Keefer appeared half irritated and half amused. "Well, that's it," the communications officer said. "That's our verdict. Record it."

"Aye aye, sir." Willie was appalled. This was a direct insult to Queeg. Stilwell was already confined for half a year; the punishment was meaningless. It amounted to an acquittal. He glanced at Jellybelly, whose face was as blank as a fish's. "Got that, Porteous?"

"Yes, sir."

The officers were finishing their evening meal when Jellybelly, still in whites, perspiring and cross, came into the wardroom for signature and authentication of the

typed record. "Okay, Jellybelly," said Keefer, the last to
sign. "Bring it up to him."

"Aye aye, sir," said the yeoman, getting an extraordinary amount of church-bell timbre into the three words,
and he left.

"We have time for one more cup of coffee, I think,"
said Keefer.

"Before what?" said Maryk suspiciously.

"You'll see," said Willie. "Hold onto your hat." Silence
settled over the wardroom made more palpable by the
clinks of spoons in coffee cups.

The rasp of the telephone buzzer came almost immediately. Maryk leaned back in his chair and with a
weary gesture yanked the phone out of its bracket. "Maryk
speaking. . . . Yes, sir. . . . Aye aye, Captain. What time?
. . . Yes, sir. How about the officer at the gangway? . . .
Aye aye, sir." He put the phone back, and said to the expectant officers with a sigh, "Meeting of all officers in the
wardroom in five minutes. Somebody's done something."

Queeg came in head down, shoulders hunched, his face
gray with rage. He announced that he was now convinced
there was no loyalty whatever to him in the wardroom.
Therefore all gentle treatment of officers was at an end.
He laid down several new edicts. There would be five
points off a fitness rating for any mistake in a log; another
five points off for every hour that a report or statement
was overdue; and an automatic unsatisfactory fitness rating if any officer was caught sleeping any time after eight
o'clock in the morning or before eight at night.

"Sir," said Keefer pleasantly, "how about officers who
have come off the midwatch? They have no sleep at all
before morning———"

"Mister Keefer, the midwatch is a duty like any other,
and nobody deserves a letter of commendation for standing
a midwatch. As I say, if you gentlemen had played ball
with me I might have played ball with you, but you gentlemen have made your bed and now you're going to get the
book thrown at you. *And* as for the goddamn childish
vindictive stupidity that was perpetrated this afternoon,
and especially that so-called statement of Stilwell which

was phrased specifically and lyingly to embarrass me I don't know who's responsible, but I have a pretty good idea—and, well, as I say, there's a new policy here in this wardroom now, and it had better pay dividends!"

The door crashed shut.

Keefer was sitting on his bed in his shorts, reading the poems of T. S. Eliot.

"Say, Tom!" It was the voice of Maryk from across the passageway. "How about coming in here for a second if you're not busy?"

"Sure."

Maryk, also in shorts, sat at his desk, fingering a pile of Navy letters. "Pull the curtain, Tom. . . . Now, just for the hell of it, tell me this. Can you figure what it is the captain has against Stilwell?"

"Sure, Steve, I know, but you'll just brush me off——"

"Let me hear."

"Okay. He hates Stilwell for being handsome, healthy, young, competent, and naturally popular and attractive—all the things that Queeg is not. Ever read *Billy Budd,* by Melville? Read it. That's the whole story. Stilwell is a symbol of all the captain's frustrations, all the things he would like to smash because he can't have them, like a child wanting to break another child's toys. Infantilism is very strong in our captain. I'm leaving out a conjectural element which I also think is important, maybe even decisive—the sexual——" Maryk made a disgusted grimace. "—I know, we start wading in slime at this point. But repressed desire can turn to hate, and all of the captain's maladies could fall into a pattern on the theory of an unconscious, violently repressed inversion which fits in beautifully with——"

"Okay, Tom. I've heard enough. Thanks." The exec got up and hoisted himself onto his bunk. He sat at the edge, his thick bare legs dangling. "Now, would you really like to know why the captain has it in for Stilwell?"

"Sure," said Keefer. "No doubt you have a much more profound theory, and I——"

"I don't know any theories. I'm just a dumb comic-book reader who made a straight C-minus at college. But I know a fact or two that you don't. The captain is out to get Stilwell because he blames him for the time we cut our own towline. He thinks Stilwell deliberately didn't warn him, just to get him in trouble."

Keefer was startled. "How do you know? We don't even know that he realizes we *did* cut the towline——"

"He realizes. He told me in San Francisco what I just told you."

"I'm damned!"

"And the captain feels that all his trouble with Com-ServPac, and for that matter with the *Caine* officers and crew, stems from that incident. He knows what an idiot that made him out to be. Don't underrate the captain, Tom——"

The novelist shook his head in wonder. "You know, that's the first backstage glimpse I've been allowed into the strange mind. Imagine, blaming Stilwell! When he himself——"

"How about all those theories of yours now, Tom? Frustration, Billy Buck, infantilism, inversion, and all that——?"

Keefer said, with an embarrassed grin, "You think you've caught me, don't you? Not necessarily. What he told you may still be just a surface symptom of my diagnosis——"

"Okay, Tom. How about this? Will you come up with me tomorrow morning to the medical officer of the *Pluto,* and tell him what you think of the captain?"

Keefer took a long pause before answering. "Not me," he said. "You can go. It's your place, not mine."

"I can't explain all that psychological stuff. That's your line."

"Did you ever hear of a thing called conspiracy to undermine authority?" said the novelist.

"But if he's crazy——"

"I never said he was crazy. I said he was teetering on the edge. That kind is almost impossible to nail. Once you accuse them, they shrink back into the most convincing goddamn normal attitudes you ever saw. They're as cun-

ning as acrobats at treading that thin line between being a
bastard and being a lunatic. It would take a state-side civilian clinic to see into Queeg. Here we'd just hang ourselves."

"All right, Tom." The executive officer jumped off his
bunk, and faced the gangling novelist, looking up into his
eyes. "That was a request to put up or shut up. You won't
put up. Then *shut up* this talk about the captain being
crazy. It's like running around in a powder magazine with
a goddamn blowtorch. You understand? I swear to Christ
I'll report to the captain any further statements you make
along that line. Friendship, on this point, no longer means
anything to me. That's the straight dope."

Keefer listened with a grave, tense face; only there was
a tinge of mockery in the wrinkling of his eyes. "Aye aye,
Steve," he said quietly, and went out through the drawn
curtain.

Maryk crawled up on his bunk. Propping himself on an
elbow, he drew from under his pillow a red-bound volume,
with the black and gold label, *Mental Disorders*. Across
the top of the pages was an oval blue rubber-stamp mark,
Property of Medical Officer, U.S.S. Pluto. He flipped open
the book to a place marked with a burned match.

24 · Maryk's Secret Log

It became known among the officers, shortly after the ship
left Funafuti in a convoy to Noumea, that Steve Maryk
had taken to writing late at night. He would draw his curtain, and through the gaps when it swayed he could be
seen in the desk lamp's blob of light, knitting his forehead
over a yellow pad, and chewing the end of a pen. When
anyone entered he would hastily turn the pad upside down.

the everlasting buzz of the wardroom phone and the message, "Captain wants to see you in his cabin." And all the time Maryk doggedly kept adding to his secret log.

Early in June they were rescued from the treadmill delirium of Seventh Fleet duty. The operation order for the invasion of Saipan arrived aboard, and the *Caine* was assigned to the screen of the main body of attack transports. There was genuine joy among the officers and crew when the old ship set out on a high-speed run by itself through dangerous waters to join up with the attack force at Eniwetok. As between gunfire and a prolongation of the tedium, they would probably have voted twenty to one for the gunfire. It was pleasanter to be shot at than to rot.

On the first day of the invasion Maryk made one of the briefest and most important entries in his medical log: an incident involving Willie Keith.

An hour before dawn of the invasion day, with the night fading to blue and Saipan beginning to show on the horizon, a humped black shape, Willie was surprised to find himself badly scared. It humiliated him to be afraid, approaching his second combat experience, when he had been so valorously carefree the first time. His innocence was gone. The flame and noise and ruin and falling figures of Kwajalein had penetrated to his bones and viscera even while he had hummed *Begin the Beguine*.

But when the sun came up, Willie momentarily forgot his fear in enchantment at the beauty of Saipan. Terraced and gardened, it was like Japanese scenes on lacquered screens and porcelain jars; a broad island of rolling green cultivated hills dotted with rustic homes, rising out of the gray waste of the sea. A flower-scented breeze blew from it across the water. Glancing down at the dirty forecastle, where the number-one gun crew stood in a blue phalanx of ragged dungarees, life jackets, and helmets, peering at the shore, Willie felt a tiny flash of sympathy for the Japanese. He sensed what it might be like to be short and yellow-skinned and devoted to a picture-book emperor, and to face extermination by hordes of big white men swarming from everywhere in flaming machines. Although the sea and air bombardment had enlivened the island's bucolic prettiness with patches of flame and mushrooms of dust and smoke, there was no such obliteration of the greenery here as there had been on Kwajalein. The rows of attack boats seemed to be crawling toward a recreation park instead of a murderous island fortress.

The *Caine* was sent to an anti-submarine patrol sector as soon as the invasion got under way, and there it steamed endlessly in a figure-eight path several thousand yards long. Twelve other ships moved in unison with it, back and forth at ten knots, in a protective fanning curtain around the transports anchored close to the beach. It seemed like a safe place, and Willie's spirits improved as the hours passed. His morale stiffened when he observed that Queeg was really shuttling from one side of the bridge to the other so as to remain sheltered from the beach. There was no mistaking it this time, because the ship kept reversing course every few minutes; and regular as clockwork, each time it presented a new side to Saipan, Queeg would come strolling around to the seaward wing. This gave Willie a dearly cherished chance to display his contempt for the captain by doing exactly the opposite. He sensed that the sailors were noticing Queeg's conduct; there was a lot of sly grinning and muttering. Willie ostentatiously moved to the exposed side with each turn of the ship. Queeg took no apparent notice.

Things were so quiet in the patrol sector that the captain secured the crew from battle stations at noon, and went below to his cabin. Willie was relieved of the deck. He was desperately tired, having been awake for more than thirty hours, but the captain's edict against daytime sleeping made retirement to his bunk too risky. He knew Queeg was heavily asleep in his cabin; but there was always the chance that a call of nature would bring the captain down to the wardroom. Willie went up to the flying bridge, nestled down on the hot iron deck, and slept in the blazing sun like a cat for four hours. He went back to the wheelhouse for the afternoon watch much refreshed.

Shortly after he took over the binoculars from Keefer, a

Navy Corsair came flying across the northern hills of the island toward the *Caine*. All at once it burst into a rosette of flame, and arced into the water with a great splash half-way between the minesweeper and another patrol vessel, the new destroyer *Stanfield*. Willie telephoned the captain.

"Kay, head over there at twenty knots," was the sleepy reply. Queeg arrived on the bridge wearing khaki shorts and bedroom slippers, yawning, as the *Caine* and the *Stanfield* were closing to within a thousand yards of each other at the place of the crash. There was no remnant of the plane on the water; only a rainbow-colored film of gasoline.

"Bye-bye Corsair," said Queeg.

"Went down like a stone," murmured Willie. He glanced at the paunchy little captain, and felt a stir of shame. What had happened to his sense of proportion, he wondered, that a comic-opera monster like Queeg could annoy or upset him? A man had just died before his eyes. The buzzing TBS transmissions spoke of thousands more dying on the shore. He had not yet seen blood spilled on the *Caine* except in careless handling of tools. Thought Willie, "I'm in danger of becoming a self-pitying whiner after all, the scum of military life——"

Towers of white water suddenly grew out of the sea on both sides of the *Stanfield*. For half a second Willie was puzzled, and thought they might be a queer tropical weather trick. Then the words burst from his throat: "Captain! The *Stanfield's* being straddled!"

Queeg looked at the subsiding splashes and shouted into the pilothouse, "All engines ahead full! hard right rudder!"

"*There*, Captain!" Willie pointed to an orange flash following by a puff of black smoke, high on a cliff to the north. "That's the battery, sir!" He ran out on the wing, and shouted up to the flying bridge, "Gun watch!"

Jorgensen poked his head over the bulwark. "Yes, Mr. Keith?"

"Shore battery bears 045 relative, distance 4000, top of the cliff! *There*, see that flash? Train the main battery on it!"

"Aye aye, sir! . . . All guns, shore battery, 045 relative, elevation 10, distance 4000!"

The *Stanfield* was whirling in a tight circle through a rain of splashes, and, even as it turned, it blasted an ear-splitting salvo from its five-inch guns. Willie saw the *Caine's* gun crews jump to their places. The line of three-inch guns swung parallel, pointing more and more astern each second as the ship turned.

"Rudder amidships! Steady as you go!" Willie heard Queeg say. The minesweeper was now headed directly away from the shore battery, leaping through the water at twenty knots. Willie ran into the pilothouse.

"Captain, main battery manned and on target!" Queeg seemed not to hear. He stood at an open window, with a squinting smile on his face. "Captain, request permission to come broadside and fire at the shore battery! We're on the target, sir!" The guns of the *Stanfield* roared two more salvos astern. Queeg paid no attention. He did not turn his head or his eyes. "Sir," said Wilie desperately, "I request permission to open fire with number-four gun! A clear shot over the stern, sir!"

Queeg said nothing. The officer of the deck ran out on the wing and saw the destroyer, a dwindling shape, fire its guns again. A thick ball of dust enveloped the place on the cliff where the battery had been. Flames darted out of the dust as the salvo struck. Again the *Stanfield* was straddled. It fired four rapid salvos. There were no answering shots; at least there seemed to be no more splashes rising near the destroyer. Already the *Caine* was too far away for Willie to be certain.

He whispered the story to Maryk after dinner. The exec grunted, and made no comment. But late that night he wrote in his log:

19 June. Saipan. I did not see this at first hand. It was reported to me by an OOD. He states that this vessel was investigating the scene of an air crash with a destroyer. The destroyer, 1000 yards on our beam, was taken under fire by a shore battery. Captain re-

versed course and left scene without firing a shot,
though battery was well within our range and our
guns were manned and ready.

The Saipan campaign was not yet over when the *Caine*
was detached from the attack force and ordered to escort
a damaged battleship to Majuro. That was the end of the
minesweeper's part in the Marianas battle. It missed the
Turkey Shoot and the invasion of Guam; while these brilliant events were going forward the *Caine* sank back into
escort duty. From Majuro it accompanied a carrier to
Kwajalein, a dull, domesticated Kwajalein all knobby with
Quonset huts. Blighted yellowish greenery was appearing
again around the edges of the sandy air strips, and there
was a continuous crawling on the beach of bulldozers and
jeeps. Willie thought it curious that, with the coming of the
Americans, the once-charming tropic islands had taken on
the look of vacant lots in Los Angeles.

The old minesweeper went on with the carrier to Eniwetok, and was sent back to Kwajalein with some LST's,
and then to Eniwetok again with a tanker. The year
rounded into August and the *Caine* still plied among the
atolls of the Central Pacific, trapped once more in tedious
shuttling, this time in the grip of Com Fifth Fleet.

The ship's life remained a static vexatious weariness.
There were no grand incidents for a while, and Maryk's
log writing dwindled. Everything was known. All per-
sonalities had been explored, and even Queeg, it seemed,
had at last run through his surprises. What happened today had happened yesterday, and would happen tomorrow:
heat, zigzagging, little nervous spats, paper work, watches,
mechanical breakdowns, and steady scratchy nagging by
the captain.

The taste of this wretched time was preserved for Willie
in the score of *Oklahoma!* Jorgensen had picked up the
album at Majuro. He played it day and night in the wardroom; and when he was not playing it the boys in the radio
shack borrowed it and piped it through the loudspeakers.
For the rest of his life, Willie would be unable to hear

Don't—throw
Bo—kays at me,

without being overwhelmed by a flashing impression of heat, boredom, and near-to-screaming nervous fatigue.

Willie had an extra burden to carry. Once the captain's favorite, he had suddenly become the wardroom goat. The turn seemed to come immediately after the *Stanfield* episode. Until then Keefer had been Queeg's main target; but thereafter everyone noticed a marked shift of the captain's hounding to Lieutenant Keith. One evening at dinner the novelist ceremoniously presented to Willie a large cardboard head of a goat cut from a beer advertisement. The transfer of this *Caine* heirloom was accompanied with great laughter, in which Willie wryly joined. The summons, *"Mr. Keith, report to the captain's cabin,"* boomed over the p.a. system a couple of times each day; and seldom did Willie lie down for a few hours of sleep between watches, without being shaken awake by a mess boy and told, "Cap'n wants to talk to you, suh."

Queeg's complaints in these interviews were about the slowness of decoding, or the routing of mail, or the correction of publications, or a smell of coffee coming from the radio shack, or an error of a signalman in copying a message—it did not much matter what. Willie began to develop a deep, dull hate for Queeg. It was nothing like the boyish pique he had felt against Captain de Vriess. It was like the hate of a husband for a sick wife, a mature, solid hate, caused by an unbreakable tie to a loathsome person, and existing not as a self-justification, but for the rotten gleam of pleasure it gave off in the continuing gloom.

Out of this hate, Willie achieved an unbelievable thoroughness and accuracy in his work. It was his one joy to frustrate the captain by anticipating his complaints and stopping his mouth. But there was a permanent hole in his defenses: Ducely. When the captain, droning nastily in triumph, faced Willie with a mistake or an omission in his department, it nearly always traced back to the assistant communicator. Willie had tried rage, contempt, invective, pleading, and even a bitter interview in the presence of Maryk. At first Ducely, blushing and boyish, had made promises to reform. But he had remained exactly as vague and slovenly as before. In the end he had retreated into petulant assertions that he was no good, and knew it, and never would be any good, and there was nothing for Willie to do but report him to Queeg for court-martial or dismissal. Willie took a belligerent pride in never blaming his assistant to the captain, by word or hint. It gave him perverse pleasure to know that Ducely had received an excellent fitness report.

August dragged, and dragged, and expired into September, with the *Caine* en route from Kwajalein to Eniwetok in the company of ten green crawling LCI's.

During the first two weeks of September an increasingly tense, restless expectation spread among the officers. It was now twelve months since Queeg had been ordered to the *Caine,* and they knew that few captains held their posts longer than a year. Willie took to going to the radio shack and scanning the Fox skeds as they came out of the radiomen's typewriters, seeking the prayed-for BuPers despatch. Queeg himself showed stirrings of the same eagerness. Several times Willie found him in the shack, glancing through the skeds.

They say the watched pot never boils. It is equally true that the watched Fox sked never contains the captain's orders. The vigil simply increased the nervous irritation in the ship, spreading down from the officers to the men. Eccentricities, those fungi of loneliness and boredom, began to flourish rankly on the *Caine.* The men grew queerly shaped beards, and had their hair cut in the shapes of hearts, crosses, and stars. Paynter caught a fiddler crab on the beach at Kwajalein, a thing the size of a pie, with one huge multicolored claw. He brought it aboard, and kept it in his room, walking it every evening on the forecastle at the end of a string like a dog. He called the hideous creature Heifetz. Paynter and Keefer had a falling-out when the crab escaped, walked in on the novelist while he sat naked at his desk, composing, and nipped one of his toes with the big claw. Keefer danced shrieking into the wardroom. He attempted to exterminate Heifetz with the ship's cutlass, and Paynter threw himself between the crab and the maddened nude Keefer. Bad blood existed between the two officers thereafter.

Ensign Ducely went queer, too, falling ragingly in love with a corset advertisement in the *New Yorker*. To Willie's eye the nameless maiden in the advertisement was like a thousand other clothing models he had seen in magazines —arched brows, big eyes, angular cheeks, pouting mouth, a fetching figure, and a haughty, revolted look, as though someone had just offered her a jellyfish to hold. But Ducely swore that this was the woman he had searched for all his life. He wrote off letters to the magazine and the clothing firm asking for her name and address, and he also wrote to friends in three New York advertising agencies, begging them to track her down. If his efficiency had been around twenty-five per cent of normal before, it now dropped to zero. He languished on his bunk, sighing over the corset ad, by day and by night.

Willie took uneasy note of these peculiarities. They reminded him of incidents in novels about men on long sea voyages, and there was a not quite pleasant amusement in seeing the classic symptoms popping out in his shipmates. And then he himself was stricken. One day the thought occurred to him, as he was drinking coffee on the bridge during a watch, that it would be rather elegant to have his own monogrammed coffee mug. In itself the notion was not odd, but his response to it was. In a few minutes, a monogrammed coffee mug came to seem to him the most wonderful imaginable possession on earth. He could not pay attention to the watch for thinking of the mug. He could see it floating in the air before his eyes. When he was relieved he rushed to the shipfitter's shack, borrowed a small file, and spent several hours gouging "WK" into a crockery cup with a jeweler's precision and delicacy, while the dinner hour passed and night fell. He filled the excavated letters with a rich blue paint, and laid the mug tenderly in his desk drawer to dry, cushioned with socks and underwear. When he was wakened at 4 A.M. to go on watch his first thought was of the mug. He took it out of the drawer and sat gloating over it like a girl over a love letter, so he was ten minutes late in relieving, and drew a snarl from the weary Keefer. The following afternoon he brought the cup up to the bridge and casually handed it to the signalman Urban, asking him to fill it from the radar-shack Silex. The envious, admiring glances of the sailors filled Willie with pleasure.

Next morning, coming on the bridge again with his wonderful cup, Willie was enraged to see Urban drinking out of a mug monogrammed "LU," just like his own. He took this as a personal insult. He soon saw that a rash of monogrammed mugs had broken out throughout the ship. The boatswain's mate Winston carried one etched with an insignia in fine Old English lettering, with heraldic flourishes. Willie's monogram was a kindergarten work compared to this, and to a dozen other sailors' cups. He angrily threw his mug into the sea that night.

In this long nightmare time, Willie spent hundreds, perhaps thousands, of hours daydreaming about May Wynn, staring at her pictures, or reading and re-reading her letters. She was his one link with what had once been his life. His civilian existence now seemed a perfumed glamorous unreality, like a Hollywood movie about high society. Reality was the rolling minesweeper, and the sea, and shabby khakis, and binoculars, and the captain's buzzer. He wrote wildly passionate letters to the girl, and with the greatest difficulty edited out any references to marriage. It made him uneasy and guilty to send off these letters, because as time passed he suspected more and more that he was not going to marry May. If he ever came back alive he wanted peace and luxury, not a struggling inept marriage with a coarse singer. So his reason informed him; but reason had little to do with the hours of romantic fantasy with which he doped himself to beguile the tedium and deaden the pain of Queeg's nagging. He knew his letters were queerly evasive and contradictory; but such as they were, he sent them off. In return, in the rare times when the minesweeper encountered a fleet post office, he would get batches of warm happy letters from May, which at once intoxicated and worried him. She gave herself completely to him in these letters, and followed his silent treatment of the subject of marriage. In this strange love affair on paper Willie found himself becoming more and more attached to May and at the same time increasingly aware that he was being unjust to her. But the dreamworld was too precious an anodyne to be broken up; and so he persisted in his fervid pointless love letters.

25 · A Medal for Roland Keefer

On October 1, with Captain Queeg still in command, the old minesweeper steamed into Ulithi Atoll, an atoll like any other atoll, a ragged ring of islands, reefs, and green water, halfway between Guam and the newly captured Palaus. As the captain was maneuvering the nose of the ship into the center of the anchoring berth, Willie, yawning on the starboard wing, felt a tap on his shoulder. He turned. Keefer, pointing off to the right, said, "Willie dear, look yonder and tell me it's a hallucination."

A thousand yards away an LST, painted with brown-and-green tropic camouflage, was anchored. Tied to the open ramp at the bow were three sixty-ton target sleds. Willie said sadly, "Oh, Christ, no."

"What do you see?" said Keefer.

"Targets. *That's* why we were sent down to this hole, no doubt." The despatch ordering the *Caine* to proceed from Eniwetok to Ulithi alone at high speed had been the subject of extended guessing in the wardroom.

"I am going below to fall on my sword," said the novelist.

The weary old *Caine* went back to work, hauling targets around the open sea near Ulithi for the fleet's gunnery practice. Day after day, dawn found the ship steaming out of the channel with the sled, and dusk was usually purple over the atoll before it dropped anchor again. The effect of this on Captain Queeg was marked. In the first couple of days of target-towing he was more irascible and cantankerous than ever. The pilothouse echoed with his screeches and curses. Then he fell into a comatose condition. He turned over the conning of the ship entirely to Maryk, even to weighing anchor in the morning and steaming into the channel at night. Occasionally in fog or rain he would come to the bridge and take the conn. Otherwise be lay in his bunk, day and night, reading, or playing with a jigsaw puzzle, or staring.

Personal to Lieutenants Keefer and Keith. Greetings, sweepers. How about coming over tonight? I have the duty. Roland.

The *Caine,* returning to Ulithi in the sunset, received this blinker message from a carrier far up in the lagoon, one of a large number which had come in during the day and now were crowded at the north end of the anchorage, a mass of oblong shapes, black against the red sky. Willie, who had the deck, sent the boatswain's mate to fetch Keefer. The novelist came to the bridge when the *Caine's* anchor was splashing into the water. "What is that lucky clown doing on the *Montauk?*" Keefer said, peering through binoculars at the carriers. "Last I heard he was on the *Belleau Wood.*"

"When was that?" Willie said.

"I don't know—five, six months ago. He never writes."

"He just commutes from carrier to carrier, I guess."

Keefer's face twisted in a wry grin. The evening breeze stirred his lank black hair. "I could almost believe," he said, "that BuPers is deliberately and systematically insulting me. I have put in about seventeen requests for transfer to a carrier—— Well. Think we can risk a reply without bothering Queeg? The answer is no, of course, don't bother saying it. Guess I'll have to pay a visit to Grendel's cave. Christ, it's been a year since we saw Rollo last in Pearl, isn't it?"

"I guess so. Seems longer."

"Rather. This cruise under Queeg seems to me to be lasting about as long as the Renaissance. Well. Here's hoping he's not in a blood-drinking mood."

Queeg, lying on his bunk, yawning over a wrinkled old *Esquire,* said, "Well now, Tom, let's see. Seems to me you had a registered publications inventory due on 1 October. Have you turned it in?"

"No, sir. As you know we've been at sea every day and——"

"We haven't been at sea at night. I daresay you've managed to write quite a bit of your novel lately. I've seen you at it almost every night——"

"Sir, I promise to do the inventory tonight when I get back, even if it means staying up all night——"

The captain shook his head. "I've got my methods, Tom, and they're the result of a hell of a lot of observation of human nature. What's more I'm a damn softhearted guy, strange as that may sound to you, and if I make one exception I'll start making more and my whole system will fly to pieces, and whatever you may think of the way I run this ship at least it's been run properly and I've made no mistakes yet. So I'm sorry and it's nothing personal but permission is denied until such time as you turn in that inventory."

Keefer and Willie took inventory that night, to the accompaniment of some picturesque cursing by the gunnery officer. It had been galling him for a year that Queeg had never permitted him to transfer custody of the secret publications. In Pearl Harbor, Queeg had compelled him to take the books back from Willie, saying it would only be for a week or two, until Willie mastered the manual; but thereafter the captain had balked at allowing the transfer, month after month.

"I finally stopped trying to persuade that criminal lunatic to let me off the hook," Keefer said between grunts, hauling armfuls of books out of the safe, "because I realized that he would never give up the luxury of those revolting interviews where he had me begging him for something. He would hold me on as custodian of the *Caine* if I rose to admiral, so long as he was an admiral one number higher than me. The man's a classic psychotic. A full-dress analysis of him would supersede all the studies of the Jukes and the Kallikaks." He went on in this vein for several hours. Willie threw in some sympathetic remarks, to hide the fact that he was meanly amused.

Next morning Keefer brought the inventory to the captain's cabin, and handed it to Queeg with a shamefaced smile. "Permission to use the gig to visit the *Montauk*, Captain?"

"Permission granted. Thank you, Tom," said the captain, flipping the pages of the report. "Enjoy yourself."

"Willie Keith would like to come along, sir."

Queeg frowned. "Why doesn't he ask permission himself? . . . Well, I'm just as glad not to have to look at his stupid face. He can pick up some of these AlPacks and AlComs that he's always behind on, while he's at it."

When Keefer came out on the well deck Willie was waiting for him, looking drooped despite fresh khakis and a gleaming shoeshine. "Tom, the carriers are under way——"

"Oh, Christ, no——"

"A couple of them are in the channel already. *Montauk's* chain is straight up and down."

"Let's see." The novelist ran up the bridge ladder. He stood by the bulwark, staring grimly northward. Four carriers were steaming toward the *Caine.*

Willie said, "Maybe they're just going to the south anchorage." Keefer did not answer.

Towering high over their heads, the leading carrier drew abreast of the *Caine,* a moving mountain of gray-painted iron, no more than a hundred yards away. The minesweeper rocked in the wash. "Let's go up on the flying bridge," Keefer said.

It was only eight o'clock, but the sun was already hot on the unprotected flying bridge. Keefer squinted at the carriers, seven of them now, moving slowly over the glittering water. The *Montauk* was sixth in line. Down-channel, the leading carrier swung ponderously to port and headed out toward the open sea. "Wrong way for the south anchorage," Keefer said bitterly.

"They didn't stay long," Willie said. He felt apologetic, as though in some way Keefer's disappointment was his fault. The two officers watched the vast procession for a while in silence.

"This must be the Philippines," Keefer said, gnawing at his lower lip. "Preliminary strike. Or maybe they're rendezvousing with the transports. That is it, Willie. The push."

"Well, Tom, I'm just as glad to stay here and tow targets. I'm like Roosevelt. I hate war."

Two more carriers went slowly past. The *Caine* rolled and pitched, straining at its anchor chain. "All I've ever wanted since this war began," murmured the novelist, looking up at the airplanes clustered on the stern of the *Arnold Bay,* "is to serve on a carrier." Another carrier slipped by, and another.

"I think I see him," said Willie. "Look there, in that gun tub, the twin-forty on the hangar deck, just aft of the hawse. There, that's him. He's waving a megaphone."

Keefer nodded. He pulled a green megaphone from a bracket in the bulwark, and flourished it over his head. As the *Montauk* approached, Willie had a clear look at Roland Keefer through binoculars. His old roommate, wearing a purple baseball cap, had the same good-humored grin, but his face was much leaner. He resembled his brother more. It might almost have been the novelist in the gun tub.

Roland bawled something through his megaphone, but it was muffled by the sucking, washing noises of the water between the ships. "Repeat—repeat," yelled Keefer. He put the megaphone to his ear. Roland was now directly opposite, about twenty feet above them, recognizable without binoculars. As he slipped past he shouted again. A few words came across, ". . . luck . . . next time for sure . . . Shinola . . . 'By, Tom . . ."

The novelist roared, "Good luck, Roland. You'll tell me all about the war next time."

They could see Roland laugh and nod. He was far ahead of them in a moment. He called back once more, but nothing was distinguishable except the word ". . . brother . . ."

Willie and Keefer stood watching the purple dot of the baseball cap as the *Montauk* swung into Mugai Channel, increased speed, and headed out to sea.

The people in the United States knew more about the great Battle of Leyte Gulf when it happened than the sailors who fought it, and much more, of course, than the men of the *Caine* becalmed in Ulithi. On the old mine-sweeper the development of the battle trickled through slowly in terse coded despatches, mostly damage reports, fogged with unfamiliar names—Surigao, San Bernardino, Samar. Willie was decoding one of these on the morning of October 26, when he struck the name *Montauk*. He worked on for a while, his face grave, and then brought the unfinished message to Keefer's room. The novelist sat at his cluttered desk, striking out a paragraph on a yellow manuscript sheet with thick red crayon lines. "Hi, Willie. How's our side doing?'

Willie handed him the message. Keefer said quickly, *"Montauk?"*

"Fourth paragraph."

The gunnery officer shook his head over the message, and glanced up at Willie with sickly embarrassment. He handed back the despatch, shrugged, and laughed a little. "My brother, being the lucky clown he is, came through okay, don't worry, Willie. Probably earned himself a Congressional Medal of Honor. He's indestructible."

"I hope he's all right——"

"Did he ever tell you about the auto accident he was in, in prep school, when four kids got killed and he came out with a sprained ankle? People run to patterns. He has a lucky life."

"Well, Tom, we ought to know for sure in a couple of days. They'll be in here——"

"A suicide plane, Christ, they really bought it——"

Willie said, "How's your novel coming?"

The gunnery officer laid his hand protectingly on the manuscript. "So-so. Old Yellowstain has really slowed the progress of American literature. I've done less in a year than in two months under De Vriess."

"When do I get to read some of it?"

"Pretty soon," said Keefer vaguely, as he had said a dozen times before.

Two days later, toward evening, Keefer was drinking coffee in the wardroom, when the phone buzzed. "This is Willie, Tom. I'm on the bridge. *Montauk* is standing in."

"Coming right up. How does she look?"

"Banged up."

Keefer came to the bridge with a despatch blank initialed by Queeg. "Get one of your boys to send this, Willie. It's okay."

Engstrand flashed the *Montauk* as it turned into the anchorage. The signal light on the carrier's buckled, blackened bridge gleamed in reply: *Boat will come to Caine when we anchor.* Keefer spelled the Morse aloud. He turned to Willie and said irritably, "What the hell kind of answer is that?"

"Tom, they're all fouled up over there. Don't worry——"

"I'm not worried. It's just a damn lamebrained answer."

When they saw a motor whaleboat put out from the carrier and head toward their berth the officers went down to the main deck and stood by the sea ladder. "There he is, in the stern sheets," said Keefer, looking at the boat through glasses. "Lost his admiral's cap, that's all." He handed Willie the binoculars. "That's him, isn't it?"

Willie answered, "Sure looks like him, Tom." The officer in the boat did not resemble Roland at all. He was slight and slope-shouldered, and Willie thought he had a mustache.

In a minute or so Keefer said, "That isn't Roland." Harding, the OOD, joined them. The three officers stood in silence as the *Montauk's* boat drew alongside. A young, scared-looking ensign with a blond mustache and thin childish lips came up the ladder. His left hand was wrapped in a heavy bandage stained yellow. He introduced himself as Ensign Whitely. "What's the story on my brother?" said the novelist.

"Oh. You're Lieutenant Keefer?" said the ensign. "Well, sir." He looked at the others, and back at Keefer. "Sir,

I'm sorry to be the one who tells you. Your brother died of burns yesterday. We buried him at sea."

Keefer nodded, his face calm and apparently half smiling. "Come on below, Mr. Whitely, and tell us about it. Keith here is an old friend of Rollo's."

In the wardroom he insisted on pouring the coffee for all three of them, though Willie tried to take the pot from him.

"Well, I'll tell you this, Mr. Keefer, your brother saved the *Montauk*," Whitely began, after a nervous gulp of half the cup of coffee. "He'll get the Navy Cross. His name's already gone in. I realize that doesn't mean much—I mean, to you and your family, compared to—but anyway, it's a sure thing, and he deserved it——"

"It'll mean a very great deal to my dad," said Keefer in a tired tone. "What happened?"

Ensign Whitely began to tell of the surprise encounter of Admiral Sprague's escort-carrier force with the main battle line of the Japanese Navy off Samar, in a chaos of rain squalls and smoke screens. His picture of the action was fragmentary and confused. He became more coherent in describing the damage to the *Montauk*.

"The shells started the fires aft. It was bad because secondary conn was knocked out and the exec got it, and ordinarily he took charge at the scene of a fire—at drills, you know. Damn good guy. Commander Greeves. Well, anyway, Roland was damage-control officer and he took over. A lot of av-gas went up on the hangar deck so it made things bad, but Roland got the torpedoes and ammo jettisoned. He kept his head real good and had the fire-fighting parties going strong, see. And it looked as though we were okay. He had the fire pretty well cornered on the port side amidships, mostly on the hangar deck. And then this goddamn suicide just came flying through the smoke screen and the rain and smashed into the bridge. Must have been carrying a torpedo because this time all hell really broke loose. Terrific explosion, fire everywhere you looked, big roaring red flame all over the flight deck, and the ship took a list to starboard. Nobody could raise the bridge on the phones and it was a cinch the old man had got it, and it was nothing but confusion and guys running every which way like ants and some of them jumping overboard. I had a damage-control party on the port side, that's why I'm alive. Mostly the starboard side got it. Well, the loudspeaker system had failed, too, power connections all torn out around the bridge. The ship was steaming around in a crazy circle, making flank, and destroyers dodging out of our way—and all this goddamn fire and smoke, and the gas attack alarm started screaming, too, for no bloody reason, and nobody could shut it off—Christ——

"Well, Roland really took over. There was a gasoline generator for stand-by communications power on the hangar deck port side. First thing, he cut that in and started directing the fire fighting over the loudspeakers. He got 'em to flood the magazines and turn on all the sprinklers and carbon-tet systems and all that, then the steering engine room got through to him on sound power phones and told him they weren't getting any steering orders, so Roland started conning the ship, too, over the loudspeaker, running out on the catwalk to see what was doing up ahead.

"Well, some big goddamn flaming wreckage came tumbling down from the flight deck all over him out on the catwalk—I don't know what it was, nobody does. He was pinned under it. They dragged him free and dumped the junk off the catwalk, and he was in bad shape. But he kept on with the fire fighting and conning. A couple of sailors holding him up and greasing him and bandaging him and giving him morphine——

"Well, about that time the air officer, Lieutenant Commander Volk, he came crawling out of the mess on the bridge, and he was pretty stunned but still in better shape than Roland, and he was senior surviving officer, so he took over the conn, and Roland passed out and they took him down to sick bay. But by that time he had all the guys back to doing everything they always did at drills, and of course that's what counts. So as I say, Commander Volk wrote him up for a Navy Cross, and of course he'll get it——"

"Did you see him after that?" Keefer said. His eyes were reddened.

"Sure. I was down in sick bay for hours with him. See, I was taking over his department, and he was telling me what to do, talking through a hole in the bandage all over his face. He was weak but still on the ball. Made me read the damage-report despatch to him and told me how to correct it. Doctor said he had a fifty-fifty chance of pulling through. About half his body was third-degree burns. But then he got pneumonia on top of it, and that did it. . . . He told me to come to see you in case——" Whitely paused, picked up his cap, and fumbled with it. "He was asleep when he died. He went off easy, as far as that goes, with the dope, and all——"

"Well, thanks, I appreciate your coming." The novelist stood.

"I—I've got his gear in the boat—there isn't a hell of a lot——" Whitely rose, too. "If you want to look it over——"

"I think," Keefer said, "you'd better send it all on intact to his mother. She's listed as next of kin, isn't she?"

Whitely nodded. The novelist put out his hand, and the young officer from the *Montauk* shook it. He ran a forefinger over his mustache. "I'm sorry, Mr. Keefer, he was a damn good guy——"

"Thank you, Mr. Whitely. Let me see you to the gangway."

Willie sat, elbows on the green baize, staring at the bulkhead, reliving the fire on the *Montauk*. Keefer returned to the wardroom in a few minutes. "Tom," said Willie, getting up when the door opened, "I know how tough this must be——"

The novelist grinned with one side of his mouth, and said, "Rollo did pretty well, didn't he, though?"

"Damn well——"

"Give me a cigarette. Makes you wonder. Maybe a military-school upbringing has its points, Willie. Could you have done what he did, do you think?"

"No. I'd have been one of the first guys over the side

when the plane hit. Roland was wonderful at midshipmen school, too—just took to it——"

Keefer dragged noisily at the cigarette. "I don't know what I'd have done. It's decided below the threshold of intelligence, that's for sure. It's instinct. Rollo had good instincts. You never really know till you're tested—— Well." He turned and started to walk to his room. "Kind of wish I'd gotten to see him last week——"

Willie reached out a hand and touched his arm. "I'm sorry, Tom. For Roland, and for you, too."

The novelist paused. He put a palm over both his eyes and rubbed hard, saying, "We were never really very close, you know. We lived in different cities. But I liked him. We had a chance to get better acquainted at college—I'm afraid I thought he was too dumb. My dad's always preferred Rollo to me. Maybe he knows something." Keefer went into his room, drawing the curtain.

Willie walked up to the forecastle and paced back and forth for an hour, glancing often across the water at the twisted, sooty hull of the *Montauk*. A tremendous red sunset flared and died, and a cool breeze flickered over the rippling lagoon. All the while he kept trying to fit the sly, profane, lazy, fat Roland Keefer into the heroic role he had played at Leyte. He could not do it. He noticed the evening star gleaming in the sky over the palm trees of Ulithi, and beside it the merest silver knife edge of a moon. The thought came on him that Roland Keefer wouldn't see such sights any more, and he crouched down beside the ready ammunition box and cried a little.

Willie came off watch that night at twelve o'clock and tumbled heavily into bed. He was dozing amid brightening visions of May Wynn when a hand poked his ribs. He groaned, burying his face in the pillow, and said, "You want Ducely. Other bunk. I've just been on watch."

"I want you," said the voice of Queeg. "Wake up."

Willie jumped out of bed naked, his nerves prickling. "Yes, Captain——"

Queeg, shadowy against the dim red light of the passageway, held a Fox sked in his hand. "There's a BuPers

despatch for us on this sked. It came in two minutes ago."
Mechanically Willie reached for his drawers. "Never mind
putting anything on, it isn't cold in the wardroom, let's
get this thing *broken*."

The leather of the wardroom chair felt clammy on
Willie's naked thighs. Queeg stood over him, watching
each letter as it emerged from the code machine. The
despatch was short: *Ensign Alfred Peter Ducely detached.
Proceed best available air transportation to BuPers Washington for reassignment. Class four priority.*

"That's all of it?" said the captain in a choked tone.

"That's it, sir."

"How long has Ducely been aboard, anyway?"

"Since January, sir—nine, ten months."

"Hell, that cuts us down to seven officers—the Bureau
is crazy———"

"We have those two new ones on the way, sir. Farrington and Voles. If they ever catch up with us."

"Mr. Ducely can damn well wait to be detached until
they do. Guess I overdid his fitness report, or something."

As the captain shuffled to the door, slouching in his
ragged bathrobe, Willie said with sleepy malice, "His
mother owns a shipyard, sir."

"Shipyard, hey?" said Queeg, and slammed the door.

Nobody except the pharmacist's mate saw the captain
for a week after the arrival of the Ducely despatch; he was
plagued with migraine headache, he informed Maryk by
phone. The executive officer took over the ship completely.

26 · A Gallon of Strawberries

I got the Yellowstain Blues,
Old Yellowstain Blues.
When someone fires a shot,
It's always there that I'm not,
I got the Old Yellowstain Blues——

Willie Keith, at the battered little piano of the officers' bar on Mogmog Island, was reviving his rusty gift for improvising. He was quite drunk, and so were Keefer, Harding, and Paynter, who clustered around him, highballs in hand, half giggling and half singing. The gunnery officer exclaimed, *"I'll* do the next stanza!

I got the Yellowstain Blues,
Old Yellowstain Blues.
You should see strong men quail,
When he spies a shirttail—
Oh, Yellowstain, Yellowstain Blues.

Willie laughed so hard that he fell off the piano stool. When Paynter bent to pick him up, he spilled his highball all over Willie's shirt in a ragged brown stain, and the guffaws of the *Caine* officers attracted stares from less hilarious groups in the bar.

Jorgensen came staggering toward them with his arm around the neck of a tall, pudgy ensign, with protruding teeth, freckles, and the brash expression of a schoolboy. "Fellows, do any of you like strawberries with your ice cream?" Jorgensen said, leering. He was answered with drunken affirmative roars. "Well, that's nice," he said, "because this here is my old roommate from Abbot Hall, Bobby Pinckney, and what ship do you think he's assistant first lieutenant on but the dear old U.S.S. *Bridge,* where all the chow is——"

The *Caine* officers overwhelmed Ensign Pinkney with handshakes. He grinned toothily and said, "Well, it happens the wardroom mess just brought half a dozen gallons of frozen strawberries up out of the hold, and I know how tight things are for you guys on those old four-pipers. And I'm the wardroom mess treasurer so—any time Jorgy or any one of you wants to stop by in the next day or two——"

Keefer glanced at his watch and said, "Willie, flag the gig. We're going to get some strawberries."

"Aye aye, sir." Willie played the closing bars of *Anchors Aweigh* fortissimo, banged the piano shut, and ran out.

Back in the wardroom, the officers bolted dinner greedily, impatient for dessert. The steward's mates served the ice cream at last with smiling pomp. Each dish was heaped over with rosy strawberries. The first round was gobbled up, and there were cries for more. Queeg suddenly came into the wardroom, in his bathrobe. The talk and laughter stopped, and in silence the officers stood one by one. "Don't get up, don't get us," the captain said amiably. "Who am I to thank for the strawberries? Whittaker just brought me a dish."

Maryk said, "Jorgensen got them from the *Bridge,* sir."

"Well done, Jorgensen, very well done. How much have we got?"

"A gallon, sir."

"A whole gallon? Fine. I'd like to see some more of this enterprise around here. Tell Whittaker I want another dish, with plenty of strawberries."

The captain sent down again and again for helpings, the last time at eleven o'clock, when all the officers were sitting around in rare good-fellowship, exchanging sex reminiscences as they smoked and drank coffee. Willie went to bed that night happier than he had been for a long time.

Shake, shake, shake . . . "What now?" he murmured,

opening his eyes in the darkness. Jorgensen stood over him. "I've got no watch——"

"Meeting of all the officers in the wardroom, right away." Jorgensen reached up and poked at the other bunk. "Come on, Duce, wake up:"

Willie said, peering at his watch, "Jesus Christ, it's three o'clock in the morning. What's the meeting about?"

"Strawberries," said Jorgensen. "Get Duce up, will you? I've got to rouse the others."

In the wardroom the officers sat around the table in various stages of undress, hair mussed, faces creased with sleepiness. Queeg was at the head of the table, slouched in his purple robe, glowering straight ahead at nothing, his whole body nodding rhythmically as he rolled the steel balls in one hand. He made no sign of recognition when Willie tiptoed in, buttoning his shirt, and dropped into a chair. In the long silent pause that followed Ducely entered, then Jorgensen, followed by Harding, who wore the OOD's gunbelt.

"All present now, sir," said Jorgensen, in the quiet unctuous tone of an undertaker. Queeg made no response. Roll, roll, went the balls. Minutes of dead silence passed. The door opened, and Whittaker, the chief officer's steward, came in, carrying a tin can. When he set it on the table Willie saw that it brimmed with sand. The Negro's eyes were rounded in fright; perspiration rolled down his long, narrow cheeks, and his tongue flickered across his lips.

"You're sure that's a gallon can, now," spoke Queeg.

"Yes, suh. Lard can, suh. Got it often Ochiltree, suh, in de galley——"

"Very well. Pencil and paper, please," said the captain to nobody. Jorgensen sprang up and offered Queeg his pen and pocket notebook. "Mr. Maryk, how many helpings of ice cream did you have this evening?"

"Two, sir."

"Mr. Keefer?"

"Three, Captain."

Queeg polled all the officers, noting down their answers. "Now, Whittaker, did your men have any straw-berries?"

"Yes, suh. One helpin' each, suh. Mr. Jorgensen, he said okay, suh."

"I did, sir," said Jorgensen.

"Just one helping each. You're sure, now," said Queeg, squinting at the Negro. "This is an official investigation. Whittaker. The penalty for lying is a dishonorable dis-charge, and maybe years in the brig."

"Hope to die, suh. I served 'em myself, Cap'n, and lock away de rest. One helpin', suh, I swear——"

"Very well. That's three more. And I had four." The captain murmured to himself, adding the total. "Whittaker, bring a soup tureen, here, and the spoon with which you ladled out the strawberries."

"Aye aye, suh." The Negro went into the pantry and returned in a moment with the implements.

"Now—dole into that tureen an amount of sand equal to the amount of strawberries you put on one dish of ice cream."

Whittaker stared at the can of sand, and spoon, and tureen, as though they were elements of a bomb which, brought together, might blow him up. "Suh, I dunno ex-actly——"

"Be as generous as you please."

Reluctantly the Negro dumped a high-heaped spoonful of sand from the can into the tureen. "Pass the tureen around the table. Inspect it, gentlemen. . . . Now then. Do you gentlemen agree that that is approximately the amount of strawberries you had on each dish of ice cream? Very well. Whittaker, do that again, twenty-four times." Sand diminished in the can and piled in the tureen. Willie tried to rub the blinking sleepiness out of his eyes. "Kay. Now, for good measure, do it three more times. . . . Kay. Mr. Maryk, take that gallon can and tell me how much sand is left."

Maryk looked into the can and said, "Maybe a quart, or a little less, sir."

"Kay." The captain deliberately lit a cigarette. "Gentle-men, ten minutes before I called this meeting, I sent down for some ice cream and strawberries. Whittaker brought me the ice cream and said 'They ain't no mo' strawberries.' Has any of you gentlemen an explanation of the missing quart of strawberries?" The officers glanced covertly at each other; none spoke. "Kay." The captain rose. "I have a pretty good idea of what happened to them. However, you gentlemen are supposed to keep order on this ship and prevent such crimes as robbing of wardroom stores. You are all appointed a board of investigation as of now, with Maryk as chairman, to find out what happened to the strawberries."

"You mean in the morning, sir?" said Maryk.

"I said now, Mr. Maryk. Now, according to my watch, is not the morning, but forty-seven minutes past three. If you get no results by eight o'clock this morning I shall solve the mystery myself—noting duly for future fitness reports the failure of the board to carry out its assignment."

When the captain was gone Maryk began a weary cross-examination of Whittaker. After a while he sent for the other steward's mates. The three Negro boys stood side by side, respectfully answering questions shot at them by different officers. The story, painfully extracted from them, was that the container, when locked away for the night at eleven-thirty—they didn't remember who had placed it in the icebox—had contained some strawberries—they didn't know how many. Whittaker had been called by the OOD at three in the morning to bring the captain another sundae, and had found the container empty except for a scraping of red juice at the bottom. The officers badgered the Negroes until dawn without upsetting this account. Maryk wearily dismissed the stewards at last.

"It's a dead end," said the exec. "Maybe they ate the stuff up. We'll never know."

"I wouldn't blame them if they did. There wasn't enough for another meal," said Harding.

"Thou shalt not muzzle thy mess boy," yawned Willie, "when he treadeth out the strawberries."

"Steve and I have no worries about fitness reports," said Keefer, laying his head on his arms. "Just you small fry.

Either one of us could be Queeg's relief. We're outstanding officers, no matter what. I could call him a dirty name to his face—I practically have. I still drew a 4.0 on the last report."

Ducely, his head slumped on his chest, emitted a blubbering snore. With a disgusted glance at him Maryk said, "Tom, suppose you bat out a report before you turn in, and I'll adjourn the meeting now."

"It will be on your desk," murmured the novelist, "in about a hundred twenty seconds." He staggered to his room, and the typewriter began clacking.

The wardroom telephone buzzer rang promptly at eight o'clock; it was Queeg, summoning the executive officer to his room. Maryk unhappily put down a forkful of griddle-cake, drank off his coffee, and left the breakfast table. He was cheered on his way by these remarks:

"Operation Strawberries, phase two."

"Stand by to make smoke."

"How are your saddle sores, Steve?"

"If things get tough, throw over a dye marker."

"Who's your next of kin?"

Queeg was at his desk, dressed in fresh clothes, his puffy face shaved and powdered. This struck Maryk as ominous. He handed the captain the investigation report, headed: *Strawberries, disappearance of—Report of board of investigation.* Queeg, rolling the balls, read the two typewritten sheets carefully. He shoved them away with the back of his hand. "Unsatisfactory."

"Sorry, Captain. The boys may be lying, but it's a dead end. The story hangs together——"

"Did your board investigate the possibility that they might be telling the truth?"

Maryk scratched his head, and shuffled his feet, and said, "Sir, that would mean someone broke into the wardroom icebox. For one thing, Whittaker made no claim that the padlock had been tampered with——"

"Did it occur to you that someone on the ship might have a duplicate key to the icebox?"

"No, sir."

"Well, why didn't it?"

Maryk stammered, "Why—well, the thing is, sir, I bought that lock myself. There were only two keys. I have one, Whittaker has the other——"

"How about the possibility that someone once stole Whittaker's key, when he was asleep, and made himself a duplicate—did you look into that?"

"Sir, I—Whittaker would have to be an exceptionally heavy sleeper for that, and I don't think——"

"You don't *think*, hey? Do you *know* that he's not an exceptionally heavy sleeper? Did you ask him?"

"No, sir——"

"Well, why didn't you?"

The executive officer looked out of the small porthole. He could see in a nearby anchor berth the bow of the light cruiser *Kalamazoo,* which had been hit by a suicide plane at Leyte. The bow was buckled and twisted to one side so that Maryk was looking at jagged blackened deck plates, from which a torn ventilator dangled crazily. "Sir, I guess there are an infinite number of remote possibilities, but there wasn't time to go into all of them last night——"

"There wasn't, hey? Did you sit in continuous session until just now?"

"I believe the report states that I adjourned the meeting at ten minutes past five, sir."

"Well, you might have found out a hell of a lot in the three hours you spent in your sacks. And since nobody appears to have dreamed of any adequate solution, I shall take over the investigation, as I said I would. If I solve the mystery, and I'm pretty sure I will, the board will have to suffer the penalty for making the commanding officer do its work for them. . . . Send Whittaker up to me."

The steward's mates followed each other into the captain's cabin all morning, at intervals of about an hour. Willie, who had the deck, kept the mournful procession moving. At ten o'clock he was distracted from the strawberry crisis by the arrival of the two new ensigns, Farrington and Voles, in a landing craft from the beach. The OOD inspected the uneasy recruits as they stood on the quarterdeck, waiting for the sailors to pass up their gear from the boat, and decided he liked Farrington and didn't like Voles. The latter was round-shouldered, and had a greenish complexion and a high voice. He seemed several years older than Farrington, who looked like an ensign in a cigarette advertisement, ruddy, handsome, and blue-eyed. The muss and fatigue of travel, and a certain mischievous humor with which he looked around at the dirty old ship, relieved his good looks. Willie liked him for his soiled gray shirt and his impish smile. Voles's shirt was stiffly starched. "Wait here, gentlemen," he said. He went forward and knocked at the captain's door.

"What is it?" called Queeg irritably. The captain sat in his swivel chair, the balls rolling swiftly in one hand hung over the back. The Negro Rasselas stood against the bulkhead, his hands behind him, showing all his gums in a smile, sweat dripping off his nose.

"Pardon me, Captain," said Willie. "Voles and Farrington are here."

"Who?"

"The new officers, sir——"

"Well. About time, too. Kay. I have no time to see them now. Send 'em to Maryk. Tell him to quarter them and so forth."

"Aye aye, sir." As Willie turned to go his eyes met Rasselas'. The Negro gave him the beseeching dumb look of a calf being led down the road on a rope. Willie shrugged and went out.

At noon the captain sent for Maryk. "Kay, Steve," he said—he was reclining on his bunk—"everything's going exactly as I figured, so far. The steward's mates are telling the truth. I know how to handle those black apes, I've done plenty of it in my mess-treasurer days. You can rule them out as suspects."

"That's fine, sir."

"Scared the living hell out of them, I'm afraid, but that's good for their souls every now and then." The captain chuckled. Scaring the steward's mates had put him in a pleasant humor. "So far as anyone taking Whittaker's key goes we can rule that out, too. He slept in his clothes, and it was chained to his belt. And he's a light sleeper.

I found that out." Queeg glanced at the exec with sly triumph. "Now then. That narrows the case to where we can begin working on it, hey?"

Maryk kept his eyes respectfully on the captain's face, and stood at attention—resolved not to utter a word unless forced to.

"Tell you a little story, Steve. Dates back quite a ways to peacetime. Had a little mystery like this aboard a destroyer, the *Barzun,* back in '37, when I was a lowly ensign, in charge of general mess. Matter of a discrepancy of five pounds of cheese in the cook's accounts. Cheese wasn't in the refrigerator, and it hadn't been cooked, or served in sandwiches, or anything. I proved that. Just vanished in thin air, like these strawberries. Well, the exec pooh-poohed it, and said, 'Forget it, Queeg,' but as you know, I'm kind of a stubborn cuss. Through devious inquiry and bribes and one thing and another I found out that a big sloppy chowhound named Wagner, a snipe, had made himself a wax impression of the cook's key one night while he slept, and got himself a duplicate key, and was showing up in the wee hours of the morning every chance he got. Made him confess, and he pulled a BCD at a summary court—— I got myself a nice little letter of commendation in my promotion jacket, too, but that's neither here nor there, though for an ensign in those years that meant plenty in the way of promotion credit—— Well. Get my point?"

Maryk smiled vaguely.

"All we have to do now," said Queeg, "is find out which bright boy on the *Caine* has made himself a duplicate key to the wardroom icebox. That shouldn't be hard."

Maryk said, after a long pause, "You assume, sir, that that's what happened?"

"I am not *assuming* a goddamned thing," snapped the captain in sudden irritation. "You can't assume anything in the Navy! I *know* someone's made a duplicate key. All other possibilities have been eliminated, haven't they? What do *you* say—that the strawberries just melted into thin air?"

"Well, I'm not sure what to think, sir——"

"Damn it all, Steve, a naval officer is supposed to be capable of following simple logic. I have just taken great pains to prove to you that there is no other possible solution." Thereupon the captain repeated the entire chain of reasoning which he had developed in the interview. "Now then, did you follow me that time?"

"I followed you, sir."

"Well, thank heaven for small favors. Kay. . . . Now, here's the next step. Call the crew to quarters. Tell them every man is to write out a statement describing all his movements and whereabouts between the hours of 11 P.M. last night and 3 A.M. this morning, name two men who can substantiate his statement, and swear to the truth of it when he hands it in to you. All statements to be in by 1700 today, and on my desk."

Urban knocked and came in, carrying a penciled despatch. "Visual from the beach, sir," he said, nervously feeling at his tucked-in shirt. The captain read the despatch and passed it to Maryk. It was orders for the *Caine* to leave Ulithi that afternoon to escort the *Montauk*, the *Kalamazoo*, and two damaged destroyers to Guam.

"Kay," said Queeg. "All departments prepare to get under way. We ought to have some fun on this trip for a change, what with our little detective work to do."

"Aye aye, sir," Maryk said.

"At this point, Tom, we can use a little of your silver tongue," said the captain. He was at his desk, the crew's statements spread out in disorderly heaps before him. Keefer was leaning with his back to the door. It was nine o'clock of the following morning, and the *Caine* was steaming smoothly through an oily doldrums calm in the screen of the damaged ships. "Sit down, Tom, sit down. Park yourself on my bunk. Yes, it's breaking wide open, just as I figured," the captain went on. "I'm practically certain I've got my bird. It all adds up. Just the man who'd pull such a stunt, too. Motive, opportunity, method—everything clicks."

"Who is it, sir?" Keefer perched himself gingerly on the edge of the bunk.

"Ah hah. That's my little secret, for a while. I want you to make a little announcement. Get on the p.a. system, will you, Tom, and say—putting this in your own words, you know, which is a hell of a lot better than I can do—tell 'em the captain knows who's got a duplicate key to the wardroom icebox. The guilty party gave himself away by his own statement, which is the only one in the whole ship that doesn't check and—well, then say he's got till 1200 to turn himself in to the captain. If he does it'll be a lot easier for him than if I have to make the arrest. . . . Think you can get all that across?"

Keefer said dubiously, "I think so, sir. Here's about what I'll say." He repeated the substance of the captain's threatening offer. "Is that it, sir?"

"That's fine. Use exactly those words, if you can. Hurry up." The captain was in a glow of smiling excitement.

Willie Keith, with the OOD's binoculars around his neck, was prowling the starboard wing, squinting up at the sky. The smell of stack gas was strong on the bridge. The novelist approached him and said, "Request permission to make an announcement, by order of the captain——"

"Sure," said Willie. "Come here a minute, though." He led Keefer to the aneroid barometer affixed to the rear of the pilothouse. The needle on the gray dial inclined far to the left at 29.55. "How about that," said Willie, "on a nice quiet sunny blue day?"

Keefer pushed out his lips judiciously. "Any typhoon warnings?"

"Steve's got 'em all plotted in the charthouse. Come take a look."

The two officers unfolded and scanned a large blue-and-yellow chart of the Central Pacific. There were three storm tracks dotted in red on the chart, none of them within hundreds of miles of their position. "Well, I don't know," said Keefer, "maybe a new one cooking up around here. They're in season. Did you tell the captain?" Willie nodded. "What did he say?"

"He didn't say. He went 'ugh' at me, the way he does nowadays."

Keefer went into the pilothouse, pressed the talk lever of the p.a. box, and paused a moment. He said, "Now hear this. The following announcement is made by order of the captain." Slowly and distinctly he repeated Queeg's message. The sailors in the pilothouse exchanged narrowed glances, and resumed their vacant stares.

Queeg waited in his cabin all morning. Nobody came. At a quarter past twelve the captain began sending for various members of the crew, sometimes singly, sometimes by twos and threes. A new summons boomed over the loudspeakers every fifteen or twenty minutes. The procession of cross-examinations went on until four o'clock; then Queeg called for Maryk and Keefer. When the officers came into the cabin they found Jellybelly undergoing questioning. The yeoman's fat white face was expressionless. "I'd tell you if I knew, sir," he was saying. "I just don't know. I slept all through it——"

"My observation," said Queeg, hunched in the back-tilted swivel chair, rolling balls in both hands, "is that the ship's yeoman generally can find out everything there is to know on a ship. Now I'm not saying you know anything. I'm not telling you to squeal on anybody. I'm just saying that I'd like very much to approve your application for chief yeoman's school at San Francisco. Once this mystery is cleared up, the culprit punished, and the summary court typed up and all that, why, I think I'll be able to spare you, Porteous. That's all."

A flicker of interest enlivened the yeoman's dull eyes. "Aye aye, sir," he said, and left.

"Kay, boys," the captain said zestfully to the officers. "Now we close in."

"Going to make the arrest, sir?" said Keefer.

"I certainly am," said Queeg, "as soon as we check for one more bit of evidence. That's where you two come in. It's going to take a bit of organizing."

"The crew expected an arrest at noon," said the exec.

"Always good to keep 'em guessing. The next thing we've got to do—the last thing, actually—is find that duplicate key. And how do you gentlemen suggest we do that?" Queeg grinned from one officer to another. "Pretty tough, you think, hey? Well, here's what we're going to do. It's three simple steps. Step one. We're going to collect every single key aboard ship, tagged with the name of the owner. Step two. We're going to make an intensive search of the ship and a personal search of everybody to be *sure* we've got all the keys. Step three. We test all the keys on the wardroom padlock. The one that opens it, well, the tag on it gives you the name of the guilty party."

Keefer and Maryk were dumfounded. The captain glanced at their faces and said, "Well, any questions? Or do you agree that that's the way to go about it?"

"Captain," said Keefer cautiously, "I thought you told me this morning you knew who stole the strawberries."

"Of course I do. I spoke to the man this afternoon. He lied in his teeth, of course, but I've got him nailed."

"Then why not arrest him?"

"There's a little matter of evidence if you want a conviction," Queeg said sarcastically.

"You said his statement gave him away——"

"Of course it does. Logically. Now all we need is the key itself."

"Sir, do you realize there may be a couple of thousand keys on the ship?" said Maryk.

"What if there are five thousand? Sort 'em out, it'll take maybe an hour, and you'll only have a few hundred that could possibly fit the padlock. You can check one a second, sixty a minute, that's one thousand eight hundred keys in half an hour. Anything else bothering you?"

The exec rubbed his hand over his head, took a deep breath, and said, "Sir, I'm sorry, but I don't think the plan has any chance of working. I think you'll upset and antagonize the crew for nothing——"

"And why won't it work?" Queeg looked down at the rolling balls.

"Tom, do *you* think it'll work?" Maryk turned to the gunnery officer.

Keefer glanced sidewise at Queeg, then threw a wink at

the exec and shook his head. "I don't know how it can hurt to try it, Steve."

"I'd like to know your objections, Mr. Maryk," said Queeg through his nose.

"Captain, I don't know where to begin. I don't think you've thought it through. Why—first of all, we don't know there *is* such a key——"

"Let me interrupt you right there. *I* say there is, therefore for your purposes there is——"

"All right, sir. Assume there is. Assume this search starts. There are a hundred million holes and ducts and cracks and boxes and crannies on this ship where a key could be hidden. It could be tossed over the side. The chances of our *finding* it are nil. And as for a man handing it in to you with his name tagged on it, do you think anyone would be that crazy?"

"The world is full of crazy people," said Queeg. "Frankly, since you're talking to me as though I were a goddamned idiot, I *don't* think he'll hand it in. But I think he'll hide it and we'll find it, which'll prove my case. As for dropping it over the side, don't worry, he's not going to do that after all the trouble he had getting it——"

"Sir, you could hide a key in the forward fireroom and I could search for a month and not find it, just in that one space——"

"All you're saying is you're not competent to organize a thorough search, and I guess maybe you're right. Therefore *I* shall organize the search——"

"Captain, you said a personal search of all hands, too. That means stripping the men——"

"We're in a warm climate, nobody'll catch cold," said Queeg, with a giggle.

"Sir, let me ask you, with due respect, is it worth doing all this to the crew for a quart of strawberries?"

"Mr. Maryk, we have a pilferer aboard ship. Do you propose that I let him go on pilfering, or maybe give him a letter of commendation?"

"Captain, who is it?" Keefer struck in.

Queeg assumed an air of sly secrecy, and hesitated.

Then he said, "This stays among the three of us, of course—— Well, it's Urban."

Both officers exclaimed involuntarily, in the same amazed tones, "Urban?"

"Yes. Innocent little Urban. Surprised me, too, a little, until I went into the psychology of Urban. He's a thief type, all right."

"That's amazing, Captain," said Keefer. "Why, he's the last one I would have suspected." His tone was kind and soothing.

Maryk looked at Keefer sharply.

The captain said, with great self-satisfaction, "Well, it took quite a bit of figuring, I'll tell you that, Tom, but he's the one—— Well. Let's get to work. Steve, start the key collecting at once. Announce the search for ten o'clock tomorrow morning, and tell 'em anyone who has a key of any kind on him or in his belongings at that time gets a summary. I shall personally direct the search tomorrow."

The two officers went out, and in silence descended the ladder to the wardroom. Keefer followed Maryk into his room, and pulled the curtain. "Well, Steve—is he, or is he not, a raving lunatic?" he said in a low voice.

Maryk dropped into his chair and rubbed his face hard with both palms. "Lay off, Tom——"

"I *have* laid off, haven't I, Steve? I haven't talked about it since the Stilwell thing. This is something new. This is over the red line."

Maryk lit a cigar and puffed blue clouds. "All right. Why?"

"It's a genuine systematized fantasy. I can tell you exactly what's happened. Ducely's orders did it. They were a terrible shock to the captain. You saw what a spin he went into. This is the next step. He's trying to restore his shattered ego. He's re-enacting the biggest triumph of his naval career—the cheese investigation on the *Barzun*. The strawberries don't mean anything. But the circumstances were a perfect take-off for a detective drama by which he could prove to himself he's still the red-hot Queeg of 1937. He's invented this duplicate key to our icebox because there's *got* to be one, for his sake—not because it's logical. It isn't logical. It's crazy——"

"Well, what do *you* say happened to the strawberries, then?"

"Oh, Christ, the mess boys ate them, of course. You know that. What else?"

"He cross-examined them all yesterday morning. Scared them white. And he's satisfied they didn't——"

"I'd like to have heard those interviews. He forced them to keep up their lies. He *wanted* them to be innocent. Otherwise he couldn't act out the great drama of the key, don't you understand——"

"You've got nothing, Tom. Just another one of your fancy theories."

"I've got a captain with paranoia, or there's no such thing as paranoia," retorted Keefer. Maryk impatiently picked up a log sheet on his desk and began reading it. The novelist said quietly, "Steve. Are you familiar with Articles 184, 185, and 186 of the *Navy Regulations?*"

The exec jumped up. "For Christ's sake, Tom," he muttered. He put his head through the curtain for a moment to peer up the wardroom passageway. Then he said, "Watch your voice."

"Are you, though?"

"I know what you're talking about." The exec took a deep breath, and puffed out his cheeks. "You're the one that's crazy. Not the captain."

"Okay," said Keefer. He looked the exec squarely in the eye, turned, and went out.

That night the executive officer wrote a long entry in his medical log. When he was through he put away the folder, locked his safe, and took down the fat blue-bound *Navy Regulations* volume. He opened the book, looked over his shoulder at the curtained doorway, then rose and slid shut the metal door, which was almost never used in the tropics. He turned to Article 184 and read aloud slowly, in a monotonous mutter: *"It is conceivable that most unusual and extraordinary circumstances may arise in which the relief from duty of a commanding officer by a subordinate becomes necessary, either by placing him under arrest or on the sick list; but such action shall never be taken without the approval of the Navy Department or other appropriate higher authority, except when reference to such higher authority is undoubtedly impracticable because of the delay involved or for other clearly obvious reason. . . ."*

27 · The Search

Flat gray clouds closed in overhead. A strong wind from the west whipped the bridge clean of stack gas, and heeled the *Caine* over steeply each time it rolled to starboard. Lines of white spray began to appear on the blackish rough surface of the sea. Sailors staggered here and there, collecting keys, distributing tags, borrowing pens and pencils, and maintaining a murmur of rebellious cursing.

By seven o'clock Willie Keith had interviewed all the men in his department. On his bunk was a large cardboard carton which contained a tangle of some four hundred tagged keys. He hefted the box, wobbled through the wardroom with it, backed up the rolling ladder to the main deck, and inched along the rainy, slippery passageway to the captain's cabin. He kicked at the door; it rang hollowly. "Open, please, sir. Both arms full."

The door opened, automatically blacking out the interior of the cabin. Willie stepped over the coaming into the darkness. The door clanged behind him, and the lights flashed up brightly.

There where four people in the room: the captain, Ensign Voles, Jellybelly, and Chief Bellison. The captain's bunk was a sea of keys—there seemed to be a hundred thousand of them, brass keys, steel keys, iron keys, of all shapes, tangled and knotted in each other and in the cords of the white tags. The deck was piled with cardboard cartons. Jellybelly and Bellison were clinking the keys into two separate heaps. Ensign Voles was passing the keys from the smaller heap one by one to the captain. Queeg, sitting at his desk, white-faced and red-eyed, but full of enthusiasm, plunged the keys one by one into the padlock, tried to turn them, and discarded them into a box between his feet. He glanced up at Willie, snapped, "Don't stand there gawking, dump 'em and run along," and resumed the regular smothered clank of key into lock, key into lock, key into lock. The air was fetid and smoky. Willie dumped his keys on the captain's bed, hastened from the room, and went out on the forecastle.

Slant waving lines of rain were blowing across the bow. The wind whipped his trouser legs and water spattered his face. Willie wedged himself in the lee of the bridgehouse. The bow plunged into a trough, and cut a wave into two foaming black streams as it rose again. Spray blew past Willie and drenched the deck and the bridge, dripping down on him.

He loved these lonely moments on the forecastle, in all weathers. There was balm in the wide sea and the fresh wind for all the itchy afflictions of life on the *Caine*. In the late stormy twilight he could see the dim forms of the *Montauk,* the *Kalamazoo,* and the nearest destroyers of the screen, small tossing shapes of an intenser black on the gray-black of the ocean. Inside those shapes were light, and warmth, and noise, and all the thousand rituals of Navy life, and—for all he knew—crises as wild and unlikely as the strawberry affair on the *Caine*. Which of the watchers on the other bridges, seeing the narrow old minesweeper plunging through the steep waves, could guess that its crew was full of mutinous mutterings, and that its captain was immured in his room, testing innumerable keys in a padlock, his eyes gleaming?

The sea was the one thing in Willie's life that remained larger than Queeg. The captain had swelled in his consciousness to an all-pervading presence, a giant of malice and evil; but when Willie filled his mind with the sight of the sea and the sky, he could, at least for a while,

reduce Queeg to a sickly well-meaning man struggling
with a job beyond his powers. The hot little fevers of the
Caine, the deadlines, the investigations, the queer ordi-
nances, the dreaded tantrums, all these could dwindle and
cool to comic pictures, contrasted with the sea—momentarily. It was impossible for Willie to carry the vision back
below decks. One rake on his nerves, a wardroom buzzer,
a penciled note, and he was sucked into the fever world
again. But the relief, while it lasted, was delicious and
strengthening. Willie lingered on the gloomy splashing forecastle for half an hour, gulping great breaths of the
damp wind, and then went below.

It was still raining next morning when the *Caine* entered
Apra Harbor in Guam, and the craggy hills of the island
were misty gray. The ship tied up at a mooring buoy,
alongside a new 2200-ton destroyer, the *Harte.* As soon
as the lines were secured, Queeg ordered armed guards
posted every twenty feet along the port side, to prevent
anybody from passing the key across to some friend on
the destroyer. He also sent Jorgensen over to the *Harte,*
requesting the chief censor to notify the *Caine's* captain
if any keys appeared in the mail on the *Harte.* The censor,
a skinny lieutenant with black-rimmed hollow eyes, looked
at Jorgensen as though he suspected him of being insane,
and made him repeat the request twice. Then he reluctantly nodded.

Meanwhile, Willie was helping the jubilant Ducely pack
his belongings. Queeg had at last detached the ensign, who
had arranged to go to the beach with the boat of the *Harte*
at ten o'clock. "Why don't you stick around and watch the
search?" said Willie.

Ducely giggled, snapping the brass fasteners on his
beautiful pigskin suitcase. He was dressed in blues redolent
of camphor, the left breast decorated with a new yellow
ribbon and two battle stars. "Willie, I'm getting off this hell
ship while the getting is good. I have hated every single
second of it, and there have been far too many seconds,
already. As far as the search goes, you're not going to find
any key. There isn't any."

"I don't think so, either, but the spectacle will be something——"

"I'm not saying what I *think,* Willie. I know there isn't any key." The ensign stooped to look in the mirror and combed his long blond hair.

"What do you know, exactly?"

"Nothing that I'll tell you. I'm not going to get involved again with that potbellied little maniac, when I'm about to go free." Ducely shook pink hair oil on his brush, and stroked his locks carefully. Willie grabbed his shoulder and spun him around.

"Duce, damn your whipped-cream soul, do you know anything that can clear up this crazy mess? Tell me, or I'll tell Queeg you're holding something out, so help me——"

The ensign laughed. "Now, Willie, you won't tell Old Yellowstain anything. I know you. I've been abusing that weakness of yours for ten months. I'm sorry I threw you, Willie. I told you the first time we talked that I was no good. That's me. I have a certain slight charm in New York, where I can——"

"What do you know about those goddamn strawberries, Duce?"

The willowy ensign hesitated, and bit his nails. "It's a shame not to tell you, really, but I insist on a deal. You say nothing about it until twenty minutes after I've left——".

"All right, all right. What do you know?"

"It was the mess boys. I saw them scraping out the container. It was one o'clock in the morning. I came down off the midwatch to use the head. They were having such a good time, I guess they didn't see me pass the pantry——"

"Why the hell didn't you speak up at that meeting?"

"Willie, have you no heart? Did you see Whittaker's face that night? Red-hot wires under my nails wouldn't have dragged it out of me." He swung his bag off the bed. "God, to think that I'm going free, *free* of this madhouse——"

"Lucky boy," snarled Willie. "Did you take your corset ad?"

Ducely looked embarrassed, and laughed, and turned red. "I guess you can blackmail me about that after the war. Willie, for ten days she seemed absolutely divine to me. I don't know. If I stayed on this ship much longer I think I'd begin insisting I was Lord Nelson." He held out his hand. "Willie, I'm no good, but I can respect a hero. Shake."

"Go to hell," muttered Willie, taking his hand.

Whittaker came to the doorway. "Meetin' fo' all officers, Mistuh Keith, suh——"

The wardroom was crowded with officers, chiefs, and first-class petty officers ranged around the table, most of them standing. Queeg, at the head, was rolling the balls, smoking, and silently studying several red-crayon diagrams spread before him on the table. Ducely threaded through the crowd unnoticed, and went out. Queeg began to outline his search plan. He had worked up a scheme for herding the men topside, stripping and searching them by groups, and returning them below to spaces that had meantime been searched. The point of the arrangement was that at no time could the missing key be moved from an unsearched to a searched space; and in this respect, Willie perceived, the plan was ingenious and effective. He felt a little sorry for Queeg. The captain was transformed with pleasant excitement; he seemed genuinely happy for the first time in many months; and it was pathetic to consider that the whole explosive burst of energy was for nothing. When the meeting adjourned Willie tapped Maryk's shoulder. "Got to talk to you, Steve." They went into the exec's room, and Willie told him Ducely's story.

"Good Christ," said Maryk, resting his head wearily against his fist. "So that's it, after all—the mess boys——"

"Going to tell the old man?"

"Well, of course, right away. Why turn the whole ship upside down now? I'm sorry for the boys, but they'll have to take the consequences. They had no right to eat the damn strawberries——"

Maryk went up to the captain's cabin. Keys were still

heaped in thousands in boxes on the deck. The captain was in his swivel chair, idly playing with the padlock. He was dressed in new clothes, and shaved, and his shoes were brightly shined. "Hello, Steve. Ready to let her roll? I want you to run it, of course, but I'll be supervising pretty closely. Any time you say——"

"Captain, something has come up." Maryk repeated Ducely's information. As Queeg gathered the import his head began to sink between his shoulders, and the old angry glare at nothing appeared in his eyes.

"Let's get this straight. Ducely told Keith, and Keith told you. Ducely's supposed to be the one who saw it, and he's gone. Right?"

"Yes, sir."

"And how do we know either Ducely or Keith is telling the truth?"

"Captain, they're both naval officers——"

"Oh, don't give me that poppycock." Queeg took a pair of steel balls from the bowl on his desk. "Ducely's capable of a parting prank, he's perfectly irresponsible, and anyway, we don't even know he said it. Keith picked a mighty convenient time to tell us about it—*after* Ducely left——"

"Sir, Ducely made him promise——"

"I know, you said that. Well, I could take good care of Ducely if I didn't have other fish to fry. He thinks he's escaped, does he? Well, I could summon him back from the beach as a material witness—his plane isn't gone yet —and keep him here till hell froze over. But as I say, Keith may have made up the whole thing, so——"

"Sir, why on earth would Willie do that——"

"How do I know who he's trying to protect?" said Queeg. "His loyalty upward is zero, that's for sure. Maybe it extends downward in some peculiar direction. Anyway, I'm not going to sit here psychoanalyzing Mr. Keith, when we've got important business to do."

Maryk said after a small silence, "Sir, you want to go ahead with the search?"

"Why not? Neither Mr. Ducely nor Mr. Keith produced the key, which is all that interests me——"

"Captain . . . Captain, *there is no key,* if the messboys

ate the strawberries. Are you going to assume that two of your officers have lied to you?"

"I'm not assuming a goddamned thing," Queeg exclaimed through his nose, "and that's exactly why we're going to look for that key. Nobody's going to kid me into assuming it *doesn't* exist. Now let's get going!"

Heavy swells were rolling into the harbor from the storm on the open sea. The *Caine* and the *Harte,* plunging and rubbing and rolling against each other, were mashing their fenders to splinters. Willie, relaxing in the captain's chair in the empty wheelhouse, was watching Bellison and three sailors slipping and cursing on the forecastle in the thick rain as they put across extra lines and doubled the canvas chafing gear in the chocks. Maryk came into the pilothouse, his black raincoat streaming, and switched on the p.a. system. Willie heard both the normal voice and the denatured boom of the loudspeakers: "Now hear this. Commence search. Commence search. All hands go topside. Clear all spaces. Personal searches will be conducted forward on the well deck under the tarpaulin and aft in the crew's shower."

Willie jumped out of his chair. "Steve! Didn't you tell him what Duce said?"

"He says we search anyway——"

"But that's pointless—why, it's—it's crazy——"

"Bear a hand, Willie. What's your assignment?"

"Personal searches aft. Christ, in this weather, too—well——"

"Farrington and Voles aren't assigned. Pick one of them up to help you if you want——"

Willie made his way aft. The rocking, pitching main deck was all confusion. Sailors in dripping rain gear or soaked dungarees milled on the well deck around Harding and Paynter. Two men stood naked, strangely pink and white in the drab crowd, their faces expressing embarrassment, defiance, and amused scorn. The officers fumbled through their clothes. The guards spaced along the starboard side slouched, leaning on their rifles, and joked with the other sailors. Ensign Farrington stood in the entrance of the wardroom hatchway, one hand hanging on the top

of the hatch, observing the search with the half-enter-
tained, half-horrified look of a boy at a freak show.

"Farrington," Willie called, crossing the well deck, "you
come along with me. You'll assist me."

"Aye aye, sir," the ensign said, and fell into step behind
Willie. Walking down the port passageway, the lieutenant
observed over his shoulder, "This strikes you as a queer
business, no doubt."

"Well, Mr. Keith, I was feeling outside of things, and
pretty useless. I'm glad of a chance to help."

Willie couldn't see his face, but the tone of sober
deference was unmistakable. It was the tone in which
Willie had addressed Lieutenant Maryk and Lieutenant
Gorton fifteen months ago, when they had seemed to him
infinitely senior, battle-wise men of the sea. For an instant
he was flattered; and he reflected that the *Caine* itself was
perhaps so bewildering and odd to Farrington that the
search scarcely surprised him, after all. It was becoming
hard for Willie to picture the effect of the *Caine* on newcomers, and to reconstruct the emotions of fresh ensigns.

They emerged from the passageway into another crowd
of wet, sullen sailors, drifting here and there in the rain.
Willie herded the men into places of shelter, and organized
an alphabetical sequence for the stripping. The men came
in pairs into the shower room to take off their clothes.
Farrington went to work systematically and unsmilingly,
helping Willie rummage through the dank garments. Willie had the grateful feeling that another officer had at last
come aboard the *Caine*.

One of the first men to be stripped was Meatball. Naked,
hairy, and squat, he stood grinning, while Willie felt
through the dungarees and in the shoes, wrinkling his nose
at the powerful animal smell. He handed them back
hastily. "Okay, Meatball, get dressed."

"Why, Mr. Keith," said the coxswain innocently, "ain't
you gonna look up my behind?"

The note was good-humored, and Willie swiftly decided
not to take offense. "No, thanks. I don't want any medals
for extraordinary heroism."

"Old man is really Asiatic, sir, ain't he?" said Meatball, stepping into his trousers.

"Never mind about the captain," said Willie sharply. "Keep a respectful tongue in your head."

"Christ, sir, I'm only sayin' what Mr. Keefer said to a whole bunch of us———"

"I'm not interested. No wise talk about the captain to me, understand?"

"Aye aye, sir," whined the coxswain, looking so abashed that Willie instantly felt guilty and apologetic. The process of stripping the sailors rasped his nerves; it seemed to him an almost German rape of their personal rights; and the fact that they were submitting so tamely was an indication of the way the Queeg regime had weakened the crew's spirit. Their only remonstrance was obscene and impudent joking. It gave Willie a twinge to see how easily the coxswain was cowed out of even that small comfort.

The head of Queeg poked around the doorway into the shower room. "Well, well, well. Everything getting under way nicely?"

"Yes, sir," said Willie.

"Fine, fine. Put Farrington to work, hey? Fine, fine." The head grinned, and nodded, and disappeared.

"Who's got a cigarette?" said Willie, a little shakily.

"Right here, sir." Meatball extended a pack, and swiftly struck a match, shielding it with a cupped fat palm. He said genially, as Willie puffed, "Gives a guy the heebie-jeebies, don't it, sir?"

Captain Queeg walked forward with rapid steps, ignoring the malevolent looks of the sailors clustered in doorways and under tarpaulins. Raindrops bounced from his yellow poncho. He encountered Maryk climbing out of the narrow hatchway of the forward engine room. "Well, well, Steve. How's it going down there?"

"Okay, sir." The exec was flushed and sweating. "Just started, of course—it'll take about four hours—but they're really going at it———"

"Fine, fine. Budge is a man you can rely on. Yes, sir. Fact, Steve, I think all our chiefs and first-class are doing themselves proud, and the officers, too, for that matter. Why, even Keith———"

"Pardon me, sir." The yeoman, Jellybelly, was at the captain's elbow. He saluted, panting, with a glance at Maryk.

"Yes, Porteous?"

"You—wanted a report, sir, from me. I've got it for you———"

"Oh, yes, yes. Excuse me, Steve. Keep an eye on things. Keep 'em moving. Come along, Porteous."

Queeg closed his cabin door and said, "Well?"

"Sir, you meant that about yeoman's school in Frisco?" Jellybelly's look was cunning and timorous.

"Of course I did, Porteous, I don't kid about such things. If you have any information which can be proved———"

"It was the mess boys, sir," whispered the fat yeoman.

"Oh, hell, it was not. Damn it, why do you waste my time———"

"Sir, Chief Bellison saw them. It was around one o'clock that night. He was coming back from breaking up a crap game in the forward crew's compartment. He passed the pantry. He told a couple of chiefs, and———"

"Are you trying to tell me that my chief master-at-arms would see pilfering, and not make an arrest, and not even report to me?" Queeg pulled steel balls out of his pocket and began to roll them. The happy look was fading from his face, the sick wrinkles reappearing.

"Well, sir, he didn't think nothing of it, see, because the mess boys, well, they're always chowing up on wardroom leftovers, it ain't nothing new. And then when this big fuss was kicked up, he felt sorry for them, he thought they'd all pull BCD's, so he kept quiet. But it's all over the ship, sir, this morning—you can prove it easy———"

Queeg dropped into his swivel chair, and looked around dully at the myriad keys stacked on the deck. His mouth hung slightly open; his lower lip was pulled in. "Porteous, this conversation of ours is to remain confidential."

The yeoman, his face twisted in a rueful leer, said, "It certainly will, sir, I hope."

"Type out your application for that school, with an approving endorsement, and I'll sign it."

"Thank you, sir."

"That's all, Porteous."

After a half hour, Maryk began to wonder what had become of the captain. The plan called for Queeg to supervise topside and forward while the exec concentrated on the labyrinthine engineering spaces, but the busy, smiling figure of the commanding officer had vanished from the search scene. Maryk went to Queeg's cabin and knocked. "*Come* in," called a harsh voice. The captain was lying on his bunk in his underwear, staring at the ceiling, rolling balls in both hands. "What is it, Mr. Maryk?"

"Pardon me, sir—I thought you were supervising topside——"

"I have a headache. You take over."

The exec said uncertainly, after a pause, "Aye aye, sir. I don't know if I can give the thorough coverage you want——"

"Delegate someone to assist you, then."

"Aye aye, sir. I wanted to ask you—do you think we have to pull out that lead ballast in the bilges and look under all the blocks? That's a terrific job, sir——"

"I don't care what you do. Leave me alone. I'm sick of the whole stupid business. Nothing gets done on this ship unless I wet-nurse it along. Do it any old way you please. Of course you'll find nothing, and I don't give a damn if you don't. I'm used to the idea that nothing I want done on this ship is ever done adequately, and of course a sloppy search is no search at all, but go ahead, do it your way. Leave me out of it."

"Sir," said the exec, baffled, "do you want the search to continue?"

"OF COURSE I want it to continue! Why shouldn't I?" yelled the captain, rising on one elbow, and glaring at Maryk with red eyes. "I still want this ship searched from stem to stern, every damn inch of it! Now please get out, I have a headache!"

Though Maryk glumly persisted in the search, the crew

very quickly sensed that something had changed. The captain's disappearance and the perfunctory manner of the exec were soon reflected in an increasing slackness of the search party, officers and petty officers alike, and in bolder jokes and effrontery from the sailors. By noon the search had dwindled to a shabby farce, embarrassing for the officers, and amusing to the men. The searchers were merely going through lazy motions, like customs inspectors who had been bribed. At one o'clock Maryk called a halt, accepting tongue-in-cheek reports from all his subordinates that their parts in the search had been carried out. The rain had stopped, and the air was steamy and close. The exec went to the captain's cabin, and found the shades drawn, and Queeg naked in his bunk, wide awake. "Well, did you find it?" said Queeg.

"No, sir."

"Exactly as I predicted. Well, at least I gauged the caliber and loyalty of my subordinates correctly." The captain rolled over, his face to the bulkhead. "Kay. Get these keys out of here and return them."

"Yes, sir."

"And you can pass the word around that if anybody thinks I'm licked they've got another think coming. I'll make my arrest in due time."

"Aye aye, sir."

The exec ordered some sailors to haul the cartons of keys out on the well deck. He summoned Willie Keith, Voles, and Farrington to redistribute them. The crew jammed the little space between the bridge and the galley deckhouse, laughing, yelling, and wrestling with each other, as the officers began the tedious job of unscrambling thousands of keys, calling off the names on the tags, and passing them out to the owners. A carnival of foolishness broke loose. Prim sailors on the *Harte* lined the rail, staring in astonishment at the mopping and mowing, and walking on hands, and obscene singing, and wild jigging of the *Caine* crew. Engstrand brought out his guitar to accompany such ditties as *Roll Me Over in the Clover, Hiho Gafoozalum, The Bastard King of England,* and *The Man Who Shagged O'Reilly's Daughter.* Meatball appeared, dressed in nothing but a pair of gigantic pink panties, from the waist of which there protruded a huge black key. The officers were too enmeshed in the tangled masses of keys to interfere with the boiling merriment. All this was taking place within a few feet of the captain's cabin. The hilarious sounds may have penetrated the dark, hot room; but there was no word of protest from Queeg.

Maryk, meanwhile, had gone below to his room. He took off all his clothes, lit a long cigar, and brought the "medical log" out of his desk safe. Settling himself on his bunk, the folder propped on his knees, he began reading at the first page. The cigar was half smoked when he turned over the last sheet and put the log aside. He smoked away, staring at the green bulkhead, until the butt felt hot to his lips when he drew on it. He crushed it out, and pressed a buzzer beside his bed. Whittaker appeared at the doorway in a moment. "Suh?"

Maryk smiled wryly at the Negro's scared look. "Relax, Whittaker. I just want you to hunt up Mr. Keefer and ask him to come to my room if he's free."

"Yes, *suh*." Whittaker grinned and ran off.

"Close the door, Tom," said Maryk when the novelist arrived. "Not the curtain. The door."

"Aye aye, Steve." Keefer slid the squeaking metal door shut.

"Okay. Now, I've got something for you to read." Maryk handed over the folder. "Get comfortable, it's pretty long."

Keefer sat in the chair. He glanced quizzically at the exec when he saw the first paragraphs. He read a couple of pages. "Jesus, even *I'd* forgotten some of this," he murmured.

"Don't say anything till you've finished——"

"So this is the mysterious novel you've been writing all these months, hey, Steve?"

"You're the novelist, not me. Go ahead and read it."

The gunnery officer read through the entire log. Maryk sat on his bunk, slowly rubbing his naked chest with his palms, watching the other's face. "Well, what do you think?" he said when Keefer put the folder down on the desk.

"You've got him cold, Steve."

"You think so?"

"I congratulate you. It's a clinical picture of a para-noiac, a full case history, not a doubt in the world of it. You've *got* him, Steve. It's an amazing job you've done——"

"Okay, Tom." Maryk swung his legs over the edge of the bunk, and leaned forward. "I'm ready to go up to Com Fifth Fleet here on the beach and turn in the skipper, under Article 184. Will you come with me?"

Keefer drummed his fingers on the desk. He pulled a cigarette out of a pack in his breast pocket. "Sure you want me along?"

"Yes."

"Why?"

"Tom, I told you why long ago when we were alongside the *Pluto*. You're the one who knows psychiatry. If I start talking about it I'll make a goddamn idiot of myself and flub the whole thing——"

"You don't have to talk. Your log does all the talking."

"I'm going to be walking in on admirals, and they'll be calling in doctors, and I just can't present the thing my-self. Anyway, I'm no writer. You think the log is enough. A hell of a lot is in the way a thing is written up, for an outsider. You *know* all these things happened, but when someone reads about them cold—I've got to have you along, Tom."

There was a long silence. "The son of a bitch kept me from seeing my brother," Keefer said unsteadily. His eyes glared.

"That's beside the point, Tom. If the old man's sick in the head there's nothing to be sore about."

"True enough—— I'll—I'm with you, Steve."

"Okay, Tom." The exec jumped to the deck and of-fered his hand, looking up into Keefer's eyes. The squat barrel-chested fisherman and the slender writer clasped hands. "Better put on a fresh uniform if you've got one," Maryk said.

Keefer looked down at his grease-smeared clothes, and smiled. "That's what happens when you go wriggling through magazines looking for a nonexistent key."

Maryk was lathering his face when a radioman brought him a message. "TBS, sir. I knocked at the captain's door and looked in but he seemed to be fast asleep——"

"I'll take it." The despatch read: *All ships Apra Harbor prepare to get under way not later than 1700. Task units will steam southward and maneuver to avoid typhoon Charlie approaching Guam.* Wiping his face wearily with a damp towel, the exec took his phone from the wall bracket and buzzed the captain several times. Queeg answered at last, and sleepily told him to get the ship ready for sea.

Keefer was in his underwear, shining his shoes when the exec came into his room and showed him the message. The novelist laughed and tossed aside the shoebrush. "Reprieve."

"Not for long. We do it first thing when we come back——"

"Sure, Steve, sure. I'm with you. But I'm not looking forward to it——"

"Neither am I."

28 · A Visit to Halsey

For two days the *Caine* steamed through rain, gusty winds, and ugly cross-swelling seas, in a motley company of ships which had bustled out of Apra Harbor. The typhoon blew by, a hundred fifty miles to the north. On the third morning the sea subsided, and a temperate wind blew a gray drizzle over the water. The ships separated into two groups, one returning to Guam, the other proceeding to Ulithi; the *Caine* went in the screen of the Ulithi group.

Merely from the backwash of the storm, the old mine-sweeper and its crew had taken a miserable beating. The rolling and plunging had smashed dishes, chairs, bottles, and small instruments, had tumbled stores helter-skelter out of shelves in dirty heaps on the deck, had shipped water which sloshed about in the passageways, filthy brown, and had sprung leaks in many places of the rusty hull. Antennas were down, and a boat davit and both depth-charge racks were buckled. There had been no hot food for two days. The unwashed, hairy crew had slept for only minutes at a time in their gyrating bunks. Ulithi, sunny and green, its lagoon an azure mirror, looked like Paradise to the men of the *Caine*—on this particular arrival. They were accustomed to refer to it as a hole, with varying foul modifiers.

"Halsey's here on the *New Jersey*," said Maryk in a low voice to Keefer, on the port wing, as the *Caine* steamed into Mugai Channel. "It's flying Sopus and a four-star flag."

Keefer peered through binoculars at the new gray battleship riding to a slack anchor chain near the channel entrance. "We're under Com Fifth, aren't we?" he whispered. "We missed our chance at Guam. If we go back, well——"

Queeg, on the other wing, was shouting to the helm, "Steady as you go! I said steady, damn it! Don't run down that channel buoy!"

The exec said, "Halsey's good enough for me. It's an emergency. We'll go over there as soon as we drop the hook——"

"*Mister* Maryk," called Queeg, "if you'll be kind enough to give me my anchor bearings——"

The two officers sat in the stern sheets of the gig, staring at the myriad gray jellyfish which pullulated under the shining surface of the lagoon. Keefer smoked. Maryk beat a tattoo on the brown leather portfolio containing the medical log. The gig chugged placidly down-channel toward the imposing *New Jersey*, two miles away. "Sun's too damn hot. Let's get under the canopy," said the novelist, flipping his cigarette into the water. "Just our luck," he went on in a low voice, when they were settled on the cracked leather cushions, screened from the gig crew by the noise of the motor, "that he's been so goddamned normal the past week."

"Well, it's been that way right along," said the exec. "Some crazy thing, then a spell when he's okay, then something even crazier."

"I know. Steve, d'you suppose there's a chance we'll get sent up to Halsey himself?"

"I think maybe so. I don't think Article 184 comes up every day——"

"I don't know how I'll like looking Halsey in the eye and telling him I've got a crazy captain."

"I don't like the idea of it much myself."

"Fact is, Steve, Old Yellowstain handled the ship fairly well in the storm, you must admit that. Far be it from me to defend him, but what's true is true——"

"Listen, for a sick man he did fine," said the exec. "Only thing is, I never sleep good, waiting for him to go off his rocker again."

"It's amazing," Keefer said, lighting another cigarette, "how cleverly these paranoids walk the narrow dividing line between outright lunacy and acts which can be logically explained. It's their distinguishing characteristic. In fact, once grant their basic premise, which may only be out of phase with reality by thirty degrees or so—not necessarily a hundred eighty degrees—and everything they do becomes justifiable. Take Old Yellowstain. What is his basic premise? That everyone on the *Caine* is a liar, a traitor, and a funk-off, so that the ship can only function if he constantly nags and spies and threatens and screeches and hands out draconic punishments. Now, how do you go about proving that his premise is wrong?"

"You couldn't ever prove it to him," said Maryk. "That's his sickness, isn't it? But any outsider *knows* that there's no ship with such a thoroughly no-good complement."

"Well, let's hope an outsider named Halsey figures it that way."

After a while Keefer said, "Take that log of yours. Individually, every one of those items could be justified by Queeg. Stopping the movies for six months? Why not? Contempt of the CO is one of the worst offenses in the Navy book. Raising hell about shirttails? Commendable strictness regarding uniforms, unusual in a minesweeper captain. The water famine? Wise prudence, perhaps a bit too conservative, but right within doctrine, to avoid a shortage. How do you prove he was really taking revenge on the crew for Rabbitt's escape? Luckily, when you add everything up, it becomes crystal-clear, but still——"

Clang, clang! The gig slowed, and Meatball shouted, "Coming alongside *New Jersey* gangway, Mr. Maryk!"

The two officers scrambled out on the gunwale. The vast flat steel wall of the battleship's side confronted them. It towered like a skyscraper and stretched away, seemingly for blocks, on either side, hiding the atoll. Maryk leaped to the landing platform, a small square wooden grille bleached by salt water at the bottom of the steep gangway ladder. Keefer followed. "Lie off and wait for us," the exec shouted to Meatball. They mounted the ladder, jingling the guy chains. The OOD was a short, round-faced lieutenant commander, gray at the temples, wearing very clean, very starched khakis. Maryk asked for the location of the flag office. The OOD briskly gave him directions. The *Caine* officers left the quarterdeck and walked slowly aft, looking around at the majestic main deck of the *New Jersey.*

It was another world; and yet, somehow, the same world as the *Caine,* transfigured. They were on a forecastle, with anchor chains, wildcat, pelican hooks, and bitts, with ventilators and life lines. But the *New Jersey's* pelican hook was as big as the *Caine's* main guns; one link of the battleship's anchor chain would have stretched across the minesweeper's entire bow; and the main battery, the long, long cannons with their turrets, seemed bigger than the whole *Caine.* There were sailors and officers everywhere, the same crowd of blue and sprinkling of khaki, but the sailors were clean as Sunday-school boys, and the officers looked like their teachers, grown up and fussily neat. The great central citadel of bridge and stacks jutted out of the deck skyward, a pyramid of metal, nervous with anti-aircraft batteries and radars; the deck dwindled aft beyond it for hundreds of feet. The *New Jersey* was awesome. "I guess we go in here," said Maryk. "Third door, starboard side, under the twin five-inch——"

"Okay," said Keefer, with a glance upward at the towering bridge in the brilliant sunlight.

They threaded through cool dim immaculate passage-ways. "Here we are," said Maryk. The black plastic plate on the green door read *Flag Lieutenant*. He put his hand on the knob.

Keefer said, "Steve, maybe this isn't the right place to start——"

"Well, they'll give us a steer, here, anyhow." He opened the door. There was nobody in the long, narrow, desk-filled room but a lone sailor in whites, reading a rainbow-colored comic magazine under the fluorescent lamp of a desk at the far end. "Where's the flag lieutenant, sailor?" Maryk called.

"Chow," said the sailor, not looking up.

"When will he be back?"

"Dunno."

"What's his room number?"

The yeoman glanced up with languid curiosity. He was white-faced, like most yeomen, and he could yawn as widely as a tiger, like most yeomen. He demonstrated this accomplishment for the benefit of the *Caine* officers, and then said grumpily, "What's it about?"

"Official business."

"Well, whatever it is, you can leave it with me. I'll take care of it."

"No thanks. What's his room number?"

"Three eighty-four," said the yeoman, with another huge red yawn, and turned back to the comic magazine, adding, "But he don't like nobody bothering him in **his** room. You won't get no favors that way."

"Thanks for the tip," said Maryk, closing the door.

He looked up and down the passageway and began to walk aft. "Which way do you suppose is 384?"

"Steve."

"Yes?"

"I think we ought to talk a little bit."

Maryk stopped, and looked back at Keefer. The novelist was not following him. He was leaning with his back against the flag lieutenant's door.

"What about?"

"Let's go out on deck."

"We don't have a lot of time——"

"Come on. I see daylight down at the other end there." Keefer hurried along the passageway and Maryk trudged after him. Rounding a corner into a shaft of sunlight, the novelist almost ran into a marine in full-dress uniform guarding a green-curtained doorway. The marine executed a salute with his rifle, and stared ahead glassily. Over the doorway the nameplate, decorated with four silver stars, read, *Admiral William F. Halsey, USN.*

Maryk grabbed Keefer's elbow. "Flag quarters! How about barging in and taking our chances? The hell with the chain of command. If he's here he'll listen to us——"

Keefer pulled his arm free. "Come on outside a minute." He led the exec to the rail. They stood in the shadow of the citadel, looking out over the blue crowded lagoon. The breeze, blowing aft from the sun-baked forecastle, was hot and damp. "Steve," said the novelist, "I'm getting cold on this deal."

Maryk stared at him.

"You would be, too, if you had any imagination. Can't you feel the difference between the *New Jersey* and the *Caine?* This is the Navy, here, the real Navy. Our ship is a floating booby hatch. Everybody's Asiatic on the *Caine,* and you and I must be the worst of all, to think we could get away with pulling Article 184 on Queeg. Steve, they'll ruin us. We haven't got a chance. Let's get out of here——"

"What the hell, Tom! I don't understand you. What's the *New Jersey* got to do with it? Is the captain nuts or isn't he?"

"He's nuts, of course he is, but——"

"Then what the hell is there to be afraid of? We've *got* to tell the highest available authority——"

"It won't stick, Steve. We haven't got enough on him. When this damn war is over I'm going to be a scribbler again, same as before. But you want to stay in the Navy, don't you? You'll smash yourself, Steve, against a stone wall. You'll be finished in the Navy forever. And Queeg will go right on commanding the *Caine*——"

"Tom, you said yourself my log on Queeg nailed him down——"

"Sure, I thought so—on the *Caine*. It does, too. It would, for a competent psychiatrist. But we've got to tell it to the Navy, not a psychiatrist. That's what I'm waking up to. Don't you know the state of mind of these benighted bastards by now? Sure, they can conn ships, and fight, but their minds are back in the feudal system! What the hell does Halsey know or care about paranoia? He'll think we're a couple of goddamn mutinous reserves. Have you read those articles carefully? 'Action under this article involves the most serious possibilities . . .' *Mutiny,* that's what it involves——"

Maryk, squinting and scratching his head, said, "Well, I'm willing to take the chance. I can't go on steaming around with a skipper who I think is crazy——"

"That's by your standards. By Navy standards, for all you know, he's still a commendable disciplinarian——"

"Oh, Jesus, Tom. Turning the ship upside down for a key that never existed—cutting off the water for days at the equator—running away from shore batteries——"

"All those things can be taken two ways. Steve, for Christ's sake listen to me and wait. Maybe in a week or two he'll go absolutely ga-ga. If he starts galloping around the decks naked or seeing ghosts or something we've really got him—and it can happen any time——"

"I think we've got him now——"

"I don't. I've changed my mind, Steve. If you think I'm crawfishing, I'm sorry. I'm really doing you the greatest favor of your life."

"Tom, let's go and try to see Halsey——"

"I won't go with you, Steve. You'll have to do it alone."

Maryk wet his lips, and grimaced at Keefer for a long moment. The novelist faced him, his jaw muscles trembling slightly. "Tom," said Maryk, "you're scared, aren't you?"

"Yes," answered Keefer, "I'm scared."

The exec shrugged, and puffed out his cheeks. "You should have said so sooner. I can understand getting scared—— Well, let's call away the gig." He started to walk forward.

"I would like you to admit," said the novelist, hurrying to his side, "that at this point the wise and logical reaction is to get intelligently scared. Sometimes getting scared and beating it the hell away is the correct solution of a——"

"Okay, Tom. Let it go at that."

"We started out to do a rash and disastrous thing. We backed off in time. There's nothing wrong with that. We should be glad of it——"

"Don't say 'we.' I'm still ready to go through with it——"

"Well, Christ," Keefer said angrily, "go ahead and hang yourself, then."

"I can't do the thing alone."

"That's a stall. You've been pulling it right along. I'm frank enough to admit I'm scared, that's the difference between us——"

Maryk stopped walking. He said mildly, "Listen, Tom. All this was your idea from the start. I never knew the word 'paranoia' until you pulled it on me. I'm still not sure what the hell it means. But I think now you're probably right about the skipper going sick in the head. I think it's wrong for us to keep quiet about it. Your trouble is, you want to back down when the going looks tough, and you also want me to congratulate you for doing it. You can't have it both ways, Tom. That's like Queeg."

Keefer bit his lower lip and said with a twisted smile, "Them's harsh words——"

"I see the gig," said Maryk, going to the rail and semaphoring with both arms. "Let's get back to the Caine."

29 · The Typhoon

Giant after giant after giant, the new battleships and carriers were ranked in Ulithi Lagoon, an orderly multitude of floating iron skyscrapers, incongruously bordered by a delicate ring of palm trees. The Navy had gathered its main striking power in the atoll for the assault on Luzon; and it was the most formidable sea force that the planet has ever borne. Willie Keith sat for hours on the forecastle of the runty, rusty *Caine,* printing the marvel of this task force on his memory. The array thrilled him, dulled as he was by now to the sights of the war. All the brute energy of human history seemed to him to be concentrated and made visible in Ulithi. He remembered walking along Riverside Drive in peacetime when the fleet was in, and philosophizing—it was during his sophomore year—to the effect that warships were merely big toys, and that national minds were children's minds, so that nations judged each other by the number and size of each other's toys. Since then he had seen the toys in action, settling the issues of life and death, and freedom and slavery, for his time; and he had swung so far away from his undergraduate wisdom that he now regarded the Navy's big ships with reverent awe.

And in so regarding them, he was still only an older sort of sophomore; because what was Ulithi, after all? A tiny enclosure of coral in the empty, empty ocean. A ship sailing within ten miles of it wouldn't even have seen it; and all the great Third Fleet, sinking at once, would not have raised the level of the sea by a thousandth of the breadth of a hair. The world's arena remains, to this hour, somewhat too big for the most ambitious human contrivances. The fact is, a typhoon, just one little racing whirlpool of air in one insignificant corner of the ocean, can be too big.

Maryk was in the charthouse, plotting typhoon warnings on the large Pacific chart from a file of despatches giving latitudes and longitudes of storm centers. Willie wandered in and stood looking over his shoulder. "Steve, d'you suppose I could sort of assistant-navigate one of these days?"

"Hell, yes." Maryk at once handed over the dividers and parallel rulers. "You can start right now plotting these storm positions."

"Thanks." Willie began pricking in the locations neatly, marking them with little red squares.

"When we go out this morning you shoot the sun lines," said the exec. "Engstrand will punch the stop watch. If we don't make it back by nightfall you can work out star sights and check your posit against mine."

"Okay. I've shot a few sun lines, last couple of weeks, just for the fun of it."

"Willie, you're asking for trouble." The exec grinned. "Don't you have enough collateral duties?"

"Oh, sure. But the old man will just keep me decoding till I rot. Laundry and morale and ship's service are all very well, but—ocean's crawling with typhoons."

"Well, this time of year——"

Maryk lit a cigar and went out on the wing. He leaned his elbows on the bulwark, enjoying the contentment of unexpected relief from a trivial chore. He knew Willie Keith would plot the warnings reliably. The pressure from below of a junior officer soberly reaching for more responsibility gave the executive officer a pleasant sense of the fruitfulness of time. He remembered Willie as he had been in his first days on the *Caine,* a baby-faced, flip ensign, callow and careless, pouting at Captain de Vriess like a spanked child. "De Vriess had Willie's number, though," Maryk thought. "He told me right off he would be okay after his behind had been kicked bloody."

Willie appeared beside him. "All plotted."

"Very well." Maryk puffed at his cigar.

The communications officer leaned on the bulwark, looking out at the anchorage. "Quite a sight, isn't it?" he said. "I never get tired of looking at it. That's *power*."

Next morning the big ships steamed out to sea. The *Caine* tagged along, dragging its target, and for a merry day and night the Third Fleet, division by division, took turns at gunfire practice while advancing westward. Then the minesweeper turned back with its tattered burden, and the task force went on to strike at the airfields of the Philippines. Ulithi looked deserted and shabby when the *Caine* returned; a reviewing stand after the parade, a ball-room after the ball. Only the service ships were left— oilers, minesweepers, and some concrete supply barges, and the ever-present ugly landing craft. Jellyfish were bat-tening on the drifting garbage of the great ships that were gone.

Down splashed the anchor, and dull days went by, while Willie followed the exploits of Halsey's force in the Fox schedule despatches. His only other diversion was keeping up the typhoon chart.

Willie had been in some of the dirty weather which swirls around the edges of typhoons, but he had never steamed through one. His picture of these whirlwinds was therefore a mingling of half-remembered pages of Conrad and some recently studied sections of the *American Practical Navigator*. On the one hand he retained the immortal image of the squeaking Chinese passengers rolling from one end of a black hold to another in a single fluid lump, accompanied by loose bouncing, clinking silver dollars. On the other hand he knew that typhoons started as a result of a collision of warm air and cold air: the warm air rose like a bubble in a tub, the cold air rushed into the resulting void, a twist was imparted to the path of the cold air by the earth's rotation, and so you had a rotating windstorm. He wasn't exactly sure why they rotated in opposite directions north and south of the equator; nor why they mostly happened in the fall; nor why they moved northwest in a parabolic path. But he had noticed that the account in the *American Practical Navigator* closed with an apologetic muttering to the effect that certain aspects of typhoons had never been satisfactorily explained. This gave him an excuse not to bother his head about the scientific account too much. He memorized the methods for locating the direction and distance of the center, and the rules of seamanship for the left and right semicircles; and these he puzzled through until he saw the logic of them. Thereafter he considered himself an informed mariner on the subject.

He knew, in fact, almost as much as one can know about typhoons without having been through one. It was as much as an innocent divinity student, feeling obliged to learn something about sin in order to fight it, might find out by reading *Ulysses* and the poems of Baudelaire.

The monotony was broken by an action despatch flashed to the *Caine* one afternoon from the beach: not a target-towing order, but a screening assignment with tankers which were to rendezvous with the Third Fleet for refueling at sea. The prospect of quasi-combat service stirred up some gaiety in the languid crew. The officers, too, perked up. They indulged in hideous part-singing that night after dinner, concluding with the sailors' hymn, *Eternal Father, Strong to Save;* wherein especially cacophonous harmonies were bawled on the last lines,

> *O hear us when we cry to Thee*
> *For those in peril on the sea.*

The ocean was calm, the sky clear, and the sun bright when the tanker group stood out from Mugai Channel. The *Caine's* station was at the extreme right of the screen, five thousand yards from the guide. The zigzag plan was an old familiar one. The squat fat tankers plowed placidly along, and the destroyers rolled in the van, probing under the sea with long fingers of sound. The patterns and precautions of war were as customary to the seafarers of this task group as fireside habits. It was a voyage of sleepy dullness.

Willie Keith's typhoon chart was empty of red squares in all the blue space between Ulithi and the Philippines.

He assumed, therefore, that there were in fact no typhoons in those waters, and went about his chores in quietness of spirit. However, as Captain Queeg had often pointed out, you can't assume a goddamn thing in the Navy. Not, at least, where typhoons are concerned.

On the night of December 16 the *Caine* began to roll pretty hard. There was nothing unusual in that. Willie had often clung swaying to a stanchion while the inclinometer on the bridge dipped to forty-five degrees, and green whitecapped seas filled the view through the side windows. He was reading *The Old Curiosity Shop* in his room. After a while he felt the slight headache that preceded nausea when he read in too-rough weather. He wedged the book into a shelf and went to bed, bracing his body with knees and soles so that the motion hardly disturbed him.

He was shaken out of sleep by the boatswain's mate. As always, his eyes sought his watch. "What the hell—it's only two-thirty——"

"Captain wants to see you on the bridge, sir."

This was slightly strange. Not the summons; Queeg called Willie out of his sleep two or three nights each week to discuss some point of accounting or decoding; but as a rule he was in his cabin. Hanging onto the upper bunk with one hand as he pulled on trousers, Willie sleepily reviewed in his mind the accounts he had recently audited. He decided that the laundry statement was probably at issue this time. He staggered topside, wondering whether the rolling was really as steep as it seemed. The wind, wet and warm, was on the starboard quarter, stiff enough to be whining through the life lines and guy wires. Black ragged seas climbed toward the sky with each roll. There were no stars.

Harding said, "He's in the charthouse."

"Condition Bligh?"

"Not really. Convulsion second class."

"Well, good—— Rolling a bit."

"A bit."

The red light flashing up in the charthouse as Willie shut the door showed Queeg and Maryk bent over the desk, both in their underwear. The captain glanced sideways, closing one eye, and said, "Willie, you've been keeping this typhoon chart, hey?"

"Yes, sir."

"Well, since Mr. Maryk has been unable to explain satisfactorily why such a serious responsibility was delegated without my permission or approval, I suppose you have no explanation, either?"

"Sir, I figured that anything I did to improve my professional competence would be very welcome."

"Well, you're quite right there, it certainly can stand improving—but—well, then, why are you making such a botch of it, hey?"

"Sir?"

"Sir, my foot! Where's any typhoon warnings between the Philippines and Ulithi? You mean to tell me there aren't any, this time of year?"

"No, sir. It's unusual, I know, but the area's all clear——"

"*Unless* your radio gang has fouled up some call sign or doped off copying some storm warning or it got lost in your efficient files instead of being decoded and plotted on his chart——"

"I don't think that's happened, sir——"

Queeg made the chart rattle, tapping it with his forefinger. "Well, the barometer's dropped fourteen points tonight and the wind's shifting every couple of hours to the right and it's force seven right now. I want you to doublecheck the skeds for the last forty-eight hours, and I want all storm warnings broken instantly and brought to me, and hereafter Mr. Maryk will keep the typhoon chart."

"Aye aye, sir." A sudden sharp roll threw Willie off balance and he fell against Queeg. The feel of the captain's dank naked skin was horrid to him. He jumped away. "Sorry, sir."

"'Kay. Get going."

Willie went to the radio shack, checked through the Fox schedules, and found nothing. He drank coffee with the bleary, white-faced operators and left, glad to escape from the nightmarish beep-beeps. He had hardly dozed off in his bunk when the same radioman who had brought the coffee shook him awake. "Storm warning, sir. All ships from CincPoa. Just came in."

Willie decoded the message and brought it up to the charthouse. Queeg was lying in the bunk, smoking. Maryk perched on the stool, his head resting on his arms on the desk.

"Ah, found something, did you? I thought so." The captain took the message and read it.

"Sir, I didn't find it in any back skeds. It came in ten minutes ago——"

"I see. Just another one of those funny coincidences that dot your career, Willie, hey? Well, I'm glad I got you to check, anyway, although of course it just came in. Plot it, Steve."

"Aye aye, sir." The exec studied the penciled slip and picked up his dividers. "That might be it, sir. East and south of us—three hundred miles—— Let's see. Three hundred seventeen, exactly—— They call it a mild circular disturbance, though——"

"Well, fine. The milder the better."

"Sir," said Willie, "if you think I'm lying about that despatch you can check in the radio shack——"

"Why, Willie, who's accusing anybody of lying?" The captain smiled slyly, his face lined with black wrinkles in the red light, and puffed on his cigarette. The glowing end was queerly whitish.

"Sir, when you say a funny coincidence——"

"Ah, ah, Willie, don't go reading meeen-ings," sang the captain. "That's the sure sign of a guilty conscience. You can go now."

Willie felt the all-familiar knotted sickness in the stomach and pounding of the heart. "Aye aye, sir." He went out on the wing and stood where the fresh air could blow in his face. When the ship rolled to port his chest pressed on the bulwark until he seemed to be lying on a metal projection looking down into the sea. The next moment he had to cling to the bulwark to keep from toppling backward. He felt his hands trembling on the dark, slippery edge of the bulwark. He stayed on the bridge, snuffing the

wind and staring out over the heaving, choppy sea until
Paynter came up to relieve the deck. Then he went below
with Harding, and the two officers drank coffee standing
up in the dark wardroom, each with an elbow hooked
around a stanchion. A small red glow came from the heat-
ing grill of the Silex.

"Rolling's worse," Harding said.

"Not as bad as outside Frisco last year."

"No. . . . Any typhoons around?"

"No. Mild disturbance to the southeast. We're probably catching the swell from it."

"My wife is worried as hell about typhoons. She wrote
me she keeps dreaming we get caught in one."

"Well, hell, what if we do? We put the wind on our
quarter or bow, depending where we are, and get the hell
out. I hope that's our worst trouble on this cruise."

They wedged their cups and saucers into the indented
board on the side table, and went to their rooms. Willie
decided against taking phenobarbital. He switched on his
bed lamp, read Dickens for about a minute, and fell asleep
with the light shining in his face.

"How the hell are they going to fuel in this sea?"

Willie and Maryk stood on the careening port wing. It
was ten o'clock in the morning. In the dismal yellow-gray
daylight the sea was heaving and bubbling like black mud.
White streaks of foam lay along the tops of the deep
troughs. The wind pulled at Willie's eyelids. All around
there was nothing to be seen but ridges and valleys of
water, except at moments when the old minesweeper
labored to the top of a swell. Then they caught glimpses
of ships everywhere, the great battleships and carriers, the
tankers, the destroyers, all plunging through waves which
broke solidly on their forecastles and smashed into creamy
streams. The Caine's forecastle was inches deep in water
all the time. The anchors disappeared every few minutes
under black waves, and foam boiled down along the deck,
piled against the bridgehouse, and sloshed over the side. It
was not raining, but the air was like the air of a bathhouse.
Dark gray clouds in masses tumbled overhead. The ship

was rolling less than during the night, and pitching much more. The rising and dropping deck felt like the floor of an elevator.

"I don't know," said the exec, "but the damned tankers are all flying Baker. They're going to try."

"Mister officer of the deck," called the captain from the wheelhouse. "Barometer reading, please?"

Willie shook his head wearily, went aft to glance at the instrument, and reported at the door of the pilothouse, "*Still* steady at 29.42, sir."

"Well, why do I have to keep asking for readings, here? You give me a report every ten minutes, now."

"Christ," muttered Willie to the exec, "it's been steady for seven hours."

Maryk trained his binoculars forward. The *Caine* shuddered for several seconds on the crest of a long swell, and dropped with a jarring splash into a trough. "Some can fueling from the *New Jersey* up there—broad on the bow —I think the fueling line parted——"

Willie waited for the *Caine* to rise again, peering through his glasses. He saw the destroyer yawing violently near the battleship, trailing a snaky black hose. The fueling gear dangled crazily free from the battleship's main deck. "They're not going to get much fueling done here."

"Well, maybe not, at that."

Willie reported the accident to Queeg. The captain snuggled down in his chair, scratched his bristly chin, and said, "Well, that's their tough luck, not ours. I'd like some coffee."

The task force kept up the attempt until early in the afternoon, at the cost of a lot of fueling hoses and steadying lines and dumped oil, while junior officers like Willie, on all the ships, made witty comments on the mental limitations of the fleet commander. They did not know, of course, that the admiral was committed to an air strike in support of a landing by General MacArthur on Mindoro, and had to fuel his ships, or else deprive the Army of air cover. At half-past one the task force discontinued fueling and began to run southwest to get out of the storm.

Willie had the deck from eight to midnight. He came to

the slow realization, during the watch, that this was extremely bad weather; weather to worry about; during a
couple of steep rolls he had flickers of panic. He drew
reassurance from the stolidity of the helmsman and the
quartermasters, who hung onto their holds on wheel or
engine-room telegraph, and droned obscene insults at each
other in fatigued but calm tones, while the black wheelhouse rolled and fell and rose and trembled, and rain
drummed on the windows, dripping inside in trickles on
the deck. The other ships were invisible. Willie maintained station by radar ranges and bearings on the nearest
tanker.

At half-past eleven a drenched radioman staggered up
to Willie with a storm warning. He read it and woke
Maryk, who was dozing in the captain's chair, gripping the
arms in his sleep to keep from pitching out. They went
into the charthouse. Queeg, heavily asleep in the bunk
over the desk, his mouth open, did not stir. "Hundred fifty
miles away now, almost due east," Maryk murmured,
pricking the chart with dividers.

"Well, then, we're over in the navigable semicircle," said
Willie. "By morning we'll be pretty well out of it."

"Could be."

"I'll be glad to see the sun again."

"So will I."

When Willie returned to his room after being relieved,
he derived a curious warm confidence from the familiar
surroundings. Nothing had come adrift. The room was
tidy, the desk lamp glowed brightly, and his favorite books
stood firm and friendly on the shelf. The green curtain and a
dirty pair of khaki trousers on a hook swayed back and
forth with each groaning roll of the ship, sticking out at
queer angles as though blown by a strong wind. Willie
wanted very much to sleep deeply and wake to a smiling
day, with all bad weather behind. He swallowed a phenobarbital capsule, and was soon unconscious.

He was awakened by loud crashing, smashing sounds
from the wardroom. He started up and jumped to the
deck, and noticed that it was slanting steeply to starboard;
very steeply; so steeply that he could not stand on it. With

horror he realized, through the fog of sleep, that this was
not merely a roll. The deck was *remaining* slanted.

Naked, he ran frantically to the dim red-lit wardroom,
holding himself off the starboard side of the passageway
with both hands. The deck began slowly to come level
again. All the wardroom chairs were piled up on the starboard bulkhead in a shadowy tangle of legs and backs and
seats. As Willie came into the wardroom they started sliding to the deck again, repeating the wild clatter. The
pantry door hung open. The china cupboard had broken
loose and pitched its contents to the deck. The wardroom
crockery was a tinkling, sliding heap of pieces.

The ship came upright, and dipped to port. The chairs
stopped sliding. Willie checked the impulse to flee naked
topside. He ran back to his room and began pulling on
trousers.

Once more the deck heaved up and fell to starboard,
and before Willie knew what was happening he had
tumbled through the air into his bunk, and lay on the
clammy hull itself, his sheeted mattress like a white wall
beside him, leaning over him more and more. He believed
for an instant that he was going to die in a capsized ship.
But slowly, slowly, the old minesweeper labored back to
port again. This was like no rolling Willie had ever experienced. It was not rolling. It was death, working up
momentum. He grabbed shoes and a shirt and scampered
to the half deck and up the ladder.

He cracked his head against the closed hatch; he felt a
hot dizzying pain and saw zigzag lights. He had thought
that the blackness at the top of the ladder was open night.
Now he glanced at his watch. It was seven o'clock in the
morning.

For a few moments he scrabbled wildly at the hatch
with his nails. Then he came to himself and remembered
that there was a small round scuttle in the hatch cover. He
twisted the lock wheel with shaking hands. The scuttle
opened, and Willie threw his shoes and shirt through and
wriggled out to the main deck. The gray light made him
blink. Needles of flying water stung his skin. He caught a
glimpse of sailors packed in the passageways of the galley

deckhouse, staring at him with white round eyes. Forgetting his clothes, he darted up the bridge ladder in bare feet, but halfway up he had to stop and hang on for his life as the *Caine* rolled over to starboard again. He would have fallen straight downward into a gray-green bubbling sea had he not clutched the handrail and hugged it with arms and legs.

Even as he hung there he heard the voice of Queeg, shrill and anguished on the loudspeaker, "You down in the forward engine room, I want power, POWER, on this goddamn starboard engine, do you hear, emergency flank POWER if you don't want this goddamn ship to go down!"

Willie dragged himself up to the bridge, hand over hand, while the ship rose and fell on huge swells, still leaning steeply. The bridge was clustered with men and officers, all clutching flagbag rails or bulwarks or cleats on the bridgehouse, all with the staring white-rimmed eyes Willie had seen in the men on deck. He grabbed Keefer's arm. The novelist's long face was gray.

"What the hell goes on?"

"Where have you been? Better put on your life jacket——"

Willie heard the helmsman yell in the wheelhouse, "She's beginning to answer, sir. Heading 087!"

"Very well. Hold her at hard left." Queeg's voice was almost falsetto.

"Zero eight six, sir, sir! Zero eight five! She's coming around now."

"Thank Christ," said Keefer, chewing his lips.

The ship veered back to port, and as it did so a violent wind from the port side tore at Willie's face and hair. "Tom, what's happening? What is it?"

"Goddamn admiral is trying to fuel in the center of a typhoon, that's what's happening——"

"Fuel! In *this?*"

There was nothing in sight all around the ship but gray waves streaked with white. But they were like no waves Willie had ever seen. They were as tall as apartment houses, marching by majestic and rhythmical; the *Caine* was a little taxicab among them. It was no longer pitching and tossing like a ship plowing through waves, it was rising and falling on the jagged surface of the sea like a piece of garbage. Flying water filled the air. It was impossible to see whether it was spray or rain, but Willie knew without thinking that it was spray because he tasted salt on his lips.

"A couple of cans are down to ten per cent," Keefer said. "They've got to fuel or they won't live through it——"

"Christ. How are we on fuel?"

"Forty per cent," spoke up Paynter. The little engineering officer, his back to the bridgehouse, was hanging onto the rack of a fire extinguisher.

"Coming around fast now, Captain!" called the helmsman. "Heading 062—— Heading 061——"

"Ease your rudder to standard! Starboard ahead standard! Port ahead one third!"

The ship rolled to starboard and back again, a terrifying sharp roll, but in a familiar rhythm. The tightness in Willie's chest eased. He now noticed the sound that was almost drowning out the voices in the wheelhouse. It was a deep, sorrowful whine coming from nowhere and everywhere, a noise above the crashing of the waves and the creaking of the ship and the roar of the black-smoking stacks, "Ooooooooo EEEEEEEEEEE eeeeeeeeeeeeee," a universal noise as though the sea and the air were in pain, "Ooo EEEEEEE, ooooo EEEEEE——"

Willie staggered to the barometer. He gasped. The needle trembled at 29.28. He went back to Keefer. "Tom, the barometer—when did all this break loose?"

"It began dropping while I was on the mid. I've stayed here ever since. The captain and Steve have been on deck since one o'clock. This terrific wind just came up—I don't know, fifteen or twenty minutes ago—must be a hundred knots——"

"*Heading 010, sir!*"

"*Meet her! Steady on 000! All engines ahead two thirds!*"

"Why the Christ," said Willie, "are we heading *north?*"

"Fleet course into the wind to fuel——"

"They'll *never* fuel——"

"They'll go down trying——"

"What the hell happened on those big rolls? Did we have a power failure?"

"We got broadside to the wind and she wouldn't come around. Our engines are okay—so far——"

The whine of the storm rose in intensity, "OOOOH—EEEE!" Captain Queeg came stumbling out of the wheelhouse. His face, gray as his life jacket, bristled with a black growth; his bloodshot eyes were almost closed by puffs around them. "Mr. Paynter! I want to know why the hell those engines didn't answer when I called for power——"

"Sir, they were answering——"

"God damn you, are you calling me a liar? I'm telling you I got no power on that starboard engine for a minute and a half until I started yelling over the loudspeaker——"

"Sir, the wind——"

("Oooo—eeee—OOEEEE!")

"Don't give me any back talk, sir! I want you to get below to your engine spaces and stay there and see to it that my engine orders are obeyed and fast——"

"I have to relieve the deck, sir, in a few minutes——"

"You do *not*, Mr. Paynter! You are *off* the watch list! Get below to those engines and stay there until I tell you to come up, if it takes seventy-two hours! And if I have another power delay you can start preparing your defense for a general court-martial!" Paynter nodded, his face placid, and went carefully down the ladder.

With its head to the wind the *Caine* rode better. The fear that had enveloped the officers and crew started to thin. Jugs of fresh coffee were brought up to the bridge from the galley, and soon spirits rose to the degree that profane jokes were heard again among the sailors. The up-and-down pitching of the ship was still swift and steep enough to cause a queerness in the stomach, but the *Caine* had done a great deal of pitching in its time, and the motion was not scary like long rolls which hung the bridge over open water. The unusual crowd on the bridge diminished; the remaining sailors began to reminisce about the scare in relieved tones.

This burst of optimism discounted the wind, which sang its eery lament as loud as ever, and the flying scud, which was still thick, and the barometer, which had fallen to 29.19. The men on the old minesweeper were used to the idea, now, that they were in a typhoon. They wanted to believe that they would come through safely; and because there was no immediate crisis, and because they wanted so much to believe, they believed. They did not tire of repeating remarks like "This is a lucky ship," and "You can't sink this old rusty son of a bitch."

Willie's feelings were very much those of the crowd. With the coffee warm in his stomach he began to sense the exhilaration of being in a tight spot, and unafraid. He recovered enough presence of mind to apply some of his lore from the *American Practical Navigator* to the storm, and calculated that the center was about a hundred miles due east, approaching at twenty miles an hour. He even looked forward with some pleasure to the possibility that the calm eye of the storm might pass over the *Caine;* he wondered whether a ring of blue sky would be visible in the black heavens.

"I hear you're going to relieve me instead of Paynt." Harding had come up to him unobserved as he faced the wind and made calculations.

"Sure. Shall I take over now?"

"Like that?"

Willie looked down at himself, naked except for sopping trousers, and grinned. "Slightly out of uniform, hey?"

"I don't know that the situation calls for dress blues with sword," said Harding, "but you might be more comfortable with clothes on."

"Be right back." Willie went down and slipped through the hatchway scuttle, noticing that the sailors were gone from the main deck passageways. He found Whittaker and the steward's mates in the wardroom, all in life jackets, laying a white tablecloth, straightening out the chairs, and picking tumbled magazines off the deck. Whittaker said to him mournfully, "Suh, I dunno how we gonna have breakfast less'n I get some tin trays offen general mess. We ain't got enough crockery left but for maybe two officers, suh——"

"Hell, Whittaker, I think you can forget about breakfast down here. Check with Mr. Maryk. I think sandwiches and coffee topside is all anybody expects."

"Thank you, suh!" The faces of the colored boys brightened. Whittaker said, "You, Rasselas, belay settin' dat table. You go ask the man like Mr. Keith says——"

It amused Willie to consider, as he struggled to dress in his galloping room, that the issue of the morning had dwindled so quickly from life-or-death to a question of the wardroom's breakfast. He was cheered by the steward's mates' solemn persistence in routine, and by the quiet yellow-lit sameness of his room. Down here he was Willie Keith, the old immortal, indestructible Willie, who wrote letters to May Wynn and decoded messages and audited laundry statements. The typhoon topside was a sort of movie adventure, exciting and mock-dangerous, and full of interest and instruction, if only he could remember to keep his head. He thought someday he might write a short story about a typhoon, and use the touch of the steward's mates worrying about breakfast. He went back to the bridge, dry and buoyant, and relieved the deck. He stood in the pilothouse, safe from the flying spray, his elbow hooked around the captain's chair, and grinned into the teeth of the typhoon, which wailed louder than ever, "OOOO! EEEEE!"

The barometer stood at 29.05.

30 · The Mutiny

A steamship, not being a slave to the wind like a sailing vessel, is superior to ordinary difficulties of storms. A warship is a special kind of steamship, built not for capaciousness and economy, but for power. Even the minesweeper *Caine* could oppose to the gale a force of some thirty thousand horsepower; energy enough to move a weight of half a million tons one foot in one minute. The ship itself weighed little more than a thousand tons. It was a gray old bantam bursting with strength for emergencies.

But surprising things happen when nature puts on a freak show like a typhoon, with wind gusts up to a hundred and fifty miles per hour or more. The rudder, for instance, can become useless. It works by dragging against the water through which it is passing; but if the wind is behind the ship, and blows hard enough, the water may start piling along as fast as the rudder so that there is no drag at all. Then the ship will yaw or even broach to. Or the sea may push one way on the hull, and the wind another, and the rudder a third, so that the resultant of the forces is very erratic response of the ship to the helm, varying from minute to minute, or from second to second.

It is also theoretically possible that while the captain may want to turn his ship in one direction, the wind will be pushing so hard in the other direction that the full force of the engines will not suffice to bring the ship's head around. In that case the vessel will wallow, broadside to, in very bad shape indeed. But it is unlikely. A modern warship, functioning properly and handled with wisdom, can probably ride out any typhoon.

The storm's best recourse in the contest for the ship's life is old-fashioned bogeyman terror. It makes ghastly noises and horrible faces and shakes up the captain to distract him from doing the sensible thing in tight moments. If the wind can toss the ship sideways long enough it can probably damage the engines or kill them—and then it wins. Because above all the ship must be kept steaming under control. It suffers under one disadvantage as a drifting hulk, compared to the old wooden sailing ship: iron doesn't float. A destroyer deprived of its engines in a typhoon is almost certain to capsize, or else fill up and sink.

When things get really bad, the books say, the best idea is to turn the ship's head into the wind and sea and ride out the blow that way. But even on this the authorities are not all agreed. None of the authorities have experienced the worst of enough typhoons to make airtight generalizations. None of the authorities, moreover, are anxious to acquire the experience.

The TBS message was so muffled by static and the noise of wind and waves that Willie had to put his ear to the loudspeaker: *Chain Gang from Sunshine. Discontinue fueling. Execute to follow. New fleet course 180. Small Boys reorientate screen.*

"What? What was it?" said Queeg at Willie's elbow.

"Discontinuing fueling, sir, and turning south. Execute to follow."

"Getting the hell out, hey? About time."

Maryk, squat and enormous in his life jacket, said, "I don't know how she'll ride, sir, with her stern to the wind. Quartering seas always murder us——"

"Any course that takes us out of here is the right course," said Queeg. He peered out at the ragged waves, rearing and tossing everywhere as high as the ship's mast. The flying spray was like a cloudburst. A few hundred yards beyond the ship the gray mountains of water faded into a white misty wall. The spray was beginning to rattle against the windows, sounding more like hail than water. "Kay, Willie. Call Paynter and tell him to stand by his

engines for some fast action. Steve, I'm going to conn
from the radar shack. You stay here."

The TBS scratched and whined. The voice came through
gurgling, as though the loudspeaker were under water:
*"Small Boys from Sunshine. Execute reorientation. Make
best speed."*

"Kay. All engines ahead full. Right standard rudder.
Steady on 180," said Queeg, and ran out of the wheelhouse. The *Caine* went plunging downhill into a foaming
trough. Stillwell spun the helm, saying, "Christ, this wheel
feels loose."

"Rudder's probably clear out of the water," Maryk said.
The nose of the ship cut into the sea and came up slowly,
shedding thick solid streams. The wheelhouse trembled.

"Rudder is right standard, sir," said Stillwell. "Jesus,
she's getting shoved around fast. Heading 010, sir—
020——" Like a kite taking the wind, the minesweeper
heeled, and swept sharply to the right. Fear tingled in
Willie's arms and legs as he was swung against the wet
windows. "Heading 035, sir—040——"

Hanging increasingly to starboard, the *Caine* was rising
and falling on the waves, blown sidewise, riding more like
flotsam again than a ship under control. Spray blew across
the forecastle in clouds. Instinctively Willie looked to
Maryk, and was deeply relieved to see the exec hanging
with both arms to an overhead beam, his back planted
against the bulkhead, calmly watching the swift veer of the
forecastle across the water.

"Say, Willie!" The captain's voice was angry and shrill
through the speaking tube. "Get your goddamn radio
technician up here, will you? I can't see anything on this
goddamn radar."

Willie roared, "Aye aye, sir," into the speaking tube
and passed a call for the technician over the p.a. He was
beginning to feel nauseous from the dizzy sidewise slipping
of the *Caine* and the queer rise and fall of the slanted
deck.

"Mr. Maryk," the helmsman said in a changed tone,
"she's stopped coming around——"

"What's your head?"

"Zero nine three."

"We're broadside to. Wind's got her. She'll come slow."

"Still 093, sir," said Stilwell, after a minute of bad wallowing—heavy slow rolls upright and swift sickening drops to starboard. It was hard to tell whether the *Caine* was moving through the water at all, or simply being flung sidewise and forward. The sense of motion came entirely from the sea and the wind; yet the engines were making twenty knots.

"Bring your rudder hard right," said Maryk.

"Hard right, sir—— Christ, sir, this goddamn wheel *feels like the wheel ropes are broken!* Just sloppy——" The hair of Willie's head prickled to see the looks of fright on the sailors. He felt the same expression forming on his own face.

"Shut your yap, Stilwell, the wheel ropes are okay," said Maryk. "Don't be such a baby. Haven't you ever had the wheel in a sea before——"

"Now God damn it, Steve," came the squeak of Queeg, "what the hell's going on out there? Why aren't we coming around?"

Maryk yelled into the speaking tube, "Wind and sea taking charge, sir. I've got the rudder at hard right——"

"Well, use the engines. *Get* her around. Christ on a crutch, do I have to do everything here? *Where's* that technician? There's nothing but grass on this radar——"

Maryk began to manipulate the engines. A combination of standard speed on the port screw and slow backing on the starboard started swinging the ship's head slowly to the south. "Steady on 180, sir," Stilwell said at last, turning his face to Maryk, his eyes glinting with relief.

The ship was tossing and heeling from side to side. But there was no alarm in the steepest rolls any more, so long as they were even dips both ways. Willie was getting used to the sight of the three rusty stacks lying apparently parallel to the sea, so that between them he saw nothing but foaming water. The whipping of the stacks back and forth like gigantic windshield wipers was no longer a frightening but a pleasant thing. It was the slow, slow dangling rolls to one side that he dreaded.

Queeg came in, mopping at his eyes with a handkerchief. "Damn spray stings. Well, you finally got her
around, hey? Guess we're okay now."

"Are we on station, sir?"

"Well, pretty near, I guess. *I* can't tell. Technician says
the spray is giving us this sea return that's fogging up the
scope. I guess if we're too far out of line Sunshine will give
us a growl——"

"Sir, I think maybe we ought to ballast," said the exec.
"We're pretty light, sir. Thirty-five per cent on fuel. One
reason we don't come around good is that we're riding so
high——"

"Well, don't worry, we're not capsizing yet."

"It'll just give us that much more maneuverability,
sir——"

"Yes, and contaminate our tanks with a lot of salt
water, so we lose suction every fifteen minutes once we
refuel. Sunshine has our fuel report. If he thought there
was any danger he'd issue ballasting orders."

"I also think we ought to set the depth charges on safe,
sir."

"What's the matter, Steve, are you panicky on account
of a little bad weather?"

"I'm not panicky, sir——"

"We're still supposed to be an anti-submarine vessel, you
know. What the hell good are depth charges set on safe if
we pick up a sub in the next five minutes?"

Maryk glanced out of the blurred window at the colossal
boiling waves. "Sir, we won't be making any sub runs in
this——"

"How do we know?"

"Sir, the *Dietch* in our squadron got caught in a storm
in the Aleutians, and got sunk by its own depth charges
tearing loose. Blew off the stern. Skipper got a general
court——"

"Hell's bells, if your heart is so set on putting the depth
charges on safe go ahead. I don't care. Just be damn sure
there's somebody standing by to arm them if we pick up a
sub——"

"Mr. Maryk," spoke up Stilwell, "the depth charges are on safe, sir."

"They are!" exclaimed Queeg. "Who says so?"

"I—I set 'em myself, sir." The sailor's voice was shaky. He stood with legs spread, clutching the wheel, his eyes on the gyrocompass.

"And who told you to do that?"

"I got standing orders, sir, from Mr. Keefer. When the ship is in danger I set 'em on safe——"

"And who said the ship was in danger, hey?" Queeg swung back and forth, clinging to a window handle, glaring at the helmsman's back.

"Well, sir, on that big roll around seven o'clock, I—I set 'em. The whole fantail was awash. Had to rig a life line——"

"God damn it, Mr. Maryk, why am I never informed of these things? Here I am, steaming around with a lot of dead depth charges——"

Stilwell said, "Sir, I told Mr. Keefer——"

"You speak when you're spoken to, you goddamned imbecile, and not otherwise!" shrieked Queeg. "Mr. Keith, place this man on report for insolence and neglect of duty! He told Mr. *Keefer!* I'll attend to Mr. Keefer! Now, Steve, I want you to get another helmsman and keep this stupid idiot's ugly face out of my sight from now on——"

"Captain, pardon me," said the exec hurriedly, "the other helmsmen are still shot from last night. Stilwell's our best man and we need him——"

"Will you stop this back talk?" screamed the captain. "Great bloody Christ, is there one officer on this ship who takes orders from me? I said I want——"

Engstrand stumbled into the wallowing wheelhouse and grabbed at Willie to keep from falling. His dungarees ran with water. "Sorry, Mr. Keith. Captain, the barometer——"

"What about the barometer?"

"Twenty-eight ninety-four, sir—twenty-*eight*——"

"Who the hell's been watching the barometer? Why haven't I had a report for a half hour?" Queeg ran out on the wing, steadying himself from hand to hand on the windows, the engine-room telegraph, the doorway.

"Mr. Maryk," the helmsman said hoarsely, "I can't hold her on 180. She's falling off to port——"

"Give her more rudder——"

"I got her at emergency right, sir—heading 172, sir—falling off fast——"

"*Why* is the rudder emergency right?" Queeg bellowed, lurching in through the doorway. "Who's giving rudder orders here? Is everybody on this bridge going crazy?"

"Captain, she's yawing to port," said Maryk. "Steersman can't hold her at 180——"

"One *six* zero, sir, now," said Stilwell, with a scared look at Maryk. It was the dreaded weather-vane effect, taking charge of the *Caine*. The rudder was not holding, and the ship was skidding sideways at the pleasure of wind and waves. The head was dropping off from south to east.

Queeg grabbed at the helmsman and steadied himself to stare at the compass. He jumped to the telegraph and signaled "Flank Speed" with one handle and "Stop" with the other. The engine-room pointers answered instantly. The deck began to vibrate with the one-sided strain on the engines. "That'll bring her around," said the captain. "What's your head now?"

"Still falling off, sir, 152—148——"

Queeg muttered, "Needs a few seconds to take hold——"

Once again the *Caine* took a sickening cant to starboard and hung there. Waves coming from the port side broke over the ship as though it were a floating log. It wallowed feebly under the tons of water, but did not right itself. It came halfway back to level and sagged further to starboard again. Willie's face was pushed against the window and he saw water no more than inches from his eyes. He could have counted little bubbles of foam. Stilwell, hanging to the wheel, with his feet sliding out from under him, stammered, "Still falling off, sir—heading 125——"

"Captain, we're broaching to," said Maryk, his voice lacking firmness for the first time. "Try backing the starboard engine, sir." The captain seemed not to hear. "Sir, sir, *back the starboard engine."*

Queeg, clinging to the telegraph with his knees and arms, threw him a frightened glance, his skin greenish, and obediently slid the handle backward. The laboring ship shuddered fearfully; it continued to drift sidewise before the wind, rising and falling on each swell a distance equal to the height of a tall building. "What's your head?" The captain's voice was a muffled croak.

"Steady on 117, sir——"

"Think she'll grab, Steve?" murmured Willie.

"I hope so."

"Oh holy Mother of Christ, make this ship come around!" spoke a queer wailing voice. The tone made Willie shiver. Urban, the little signalman, had dropped to his knees and was hugging the binnacle, his eyes closed, his head thrown back.

"Shut up, Urban," Maryk said sharply. "Get on your feet——"

Stilwell exclaimed, "Sir, heading *120!* Coming right, sir!"

"Good," said Maryk. "Ease your rudder to standard."

Without so much as a glance at the captain, Stilwell obeyed. Willie noticed the omission, for all that he was terror-stricken; and he noticed, too, that Queeg, frozen to the telegraph stand, seemed oblivious.

"Rudder is eased to standard, sir—heading 124, sir——" The *Caine* stood erect slowly and wabbled a little to port before heeling deep to starboard again.

"We're okay," said Maryk. Urban got off his knees and looked around sheepishly.

"Heading 128—129—130——"

"Willie," said the exec, "take a look in the radar shack. See if you can tell where the hell we are in the formaton."

"Aye aye, sir." Willie staggered out past the captain to the open wing. The wind immediately smashed him against the bridgehouse, and spray pelted him like small wet stones. He was astounded and peculiarly exhilarated to realize that in the last fifteen minutes the wind had actually become much stronger than before, and would blow him over the side if he exposed himself in a clear space. He laughed aloud, his voice thin against the guttural "Whooeeee!" of the storm. He inched himself to the door of the radar shack, freed the dogs, and tried to pull the door open, but the wind held it tightly shut. He pounded on the wet steel with his knuckles, and kicked at it, and screamed, "Open up! Open up! It's the OOD!" A crack appeared and widened. He darted through, knocking down one of the radarmen who was pushing against the door. It snapped shut as though on a spring.

"What the hell!" exclaimed Willie.

There were perhaps twenty sailors jammed in the tiny space, all in life jackets with waterproof searchlights pinned to them, all with whistles dangling around their necks, all with the same round-eyed bristly white face of fear. "How are we doing, Mr. Keith?" spoke the voice of Meatball from the rear of the crush.

"We're doing fine———"

"We gonna have to abandon ship, sir?" said a filthy-faced fireman.

Willie suddenly realized what was so very strange about the shack beside the crowd. It was brightly lit. Nobody was paying any attention to the dim green slopes of the radars. He let loose a stream of obscenity that surprised him as it came out of his mouth. The sailors shrank a little from him. "Who turned on the lights in here? Who's got the watch?"

"Sir, there's nothing on the scopes but sea return," whined a radarman.

Willie cursed some more, and then said, "Douse the lights. Get your faces against these scopes and keep them there."

"Okay, Mr. Keith," said the radarman, in a friendly, respectful tone, "but it won't do no good." In the gloom Willie quickly saw that the sailor was right. There was no trace of the pips of the other ships, nothing but a blurry peppering and streaking of green all over the scopes. "You see, sir," said the voice of the technician, patiently, "our masthead ain't no higher than the water most of the time, and, anyway, all this spray, why, it's like a solid object, sir. These scopes are jammed out——"

"All the same," said Willie, "the watch will be maintained on these radars, and you'll keep trying till you do get something! And all the guys who don't belong in here —well—well, stay here, and keep your faces closed so the watch-standers can do their duty——"

"Sir, are we really okay?"

"Will we have to abandon ship?"

"I was ready to jump on that last roll——"

"Will the ship come through it, Mr. Keith?"

"We're okay," shouted Willie. "We're okay. Don't lose your heads. We'll be back chipping paint in a few hours——"

"I'll chip this rusty old bitch till doomsday if she just rides out this blow," said a voice, and there was a ripple of small laughs.

"I'm staying up here if I get a court-martial for it——"

"Me, too——"

"Hell, there are forty guys over on the lee of the bridge——"

"Mister Keith"—the gutter twang of Meatball again— "honest, does the old man know what the Christ he's doing? That's all we want to know."

"The old man's doing great. You bastards shut up and take it easy. Couple of you help me get this door open."

Wind and spray blasted in through the open crack. Willie pulled himself out and the door clanged. The wind blew him forward into the pilothouse. In the second that elapsed he was drenched as by buckets of water. "Radars are jammed, Steve. Nothing to see until this spray moderates——"

"Very well."

Despite the whining and crashing of the storm, Willie got the impression of silence in the wheelhouse. Queeg hung to the telegraph as before. Stilwell swayed at the wheel. Urban, wedged between the binnacle and the front window, clutched the quartermaster's log as though it were a Bible. Usually there were other sailors in the wheelhouse—telephone talkers, signalmen—but they were avoiding it now as though it were the sickroom of a cancer victim. Maryk stood with both hands clamped to the captain's chair. Willie staggered to the starboard side and glanced out at the wing. A crowd of sailors and officers pressed against the bridgehouse, hanging to each other, their clothes whipping in the wind. Willie saw Keefer, Jorgensen, and nearest him, Harding.

"Willie, are we going to be okay?" Harding said.

The OOD nodded, and fell back into the wheelhouse. He was vexed at not having a flashlight and whistle, like everyone else. "Just my luck to be on watch," he thought. He did not really believe yet that the ship was going to founder, but he resented being at a disadvantage. His own man-overboard gear was in his desk below. He thought of sending the boatswain's mate for it; and was ashamed to issue the order.

The *Caine* yawed shakily back and forth on heading 180 for a couple of minutes. Then suddenly it was flung almost on its beam-ends to port by a swell, a wave and a gust of wind hitting together. Willie reeled, brought up against Stilwell, and grabbed at the wheel spokes.

"Captain," Maryk said, "I still think we ought to ballast —at least the stern tanks, if we're going to steam before the wind."

Willie glanced at Queeg. The captain's face was screwed up as though he were looking at a bright light. He gave no sign of having heard. "I request permission to ballast stern tanks, sir," said the exec.

Queeg's lips moved. "Negative," he said calmly and faintly.

Stilwell twisted the wheel sharply, pulling the spokes out of Willie's hands. The OOD grasped an overhead beam. "Falling off to *starboard* now. Heading 189—190—191——"

Maryk said, "Captain—hard left rudder?"

"Okay," murmured Queeg.

"Hard left rudder, sir," said Stilwell. "Heading 200——"

The exec stared at the captain for several seconds while

the minesweeper careened heavily to port and began its nauseating sideslipping over the swells, the wind flipping it around now in the other direction. "Captain, we'll have to use engines again, she's not answering to the rudder. . . . Sir, how about heading up into the wind? She's going to keep broaching to with this stern wind——"

Queeg pushed the handles of the telegraph. "Fleet course is 180," he said.

"Sir, we have to maneuver for the safety of the ship——"

"Sunshine knows the weather conditions. We've received no orders to maneuver at discretion——" Queeg looked straight ahead, constantly clutching the telegraph amid the gyrations of the wheelhouse.

"Heading 225—falling away fast, sir——"

An unbelievably big gray wave loomed on the port side, high over the bridge. It came smashing down. Water spouted into the wheelhouse from the open wing, flooding to Willie's knees. The water felt surprisingly warm and sticky, like blood. "Sir, we're shipping water on the god-damn *bridge!*" said Maryk shrilly. "We've *got* to come around into the wind!"

"Heading 245, sir." Stilwell's voice was sobbing. "She ain't answering to the engines at all, sir!"

The *Caine* rolled almost completely over on its port side. Everybody in the wheelhouse except Stilwell went sliding across the streaming deck and piled up against the windows. The sea was under their noses, dashing up against the glass. "Mr. Maryk, the light on this gyro just went out!" screamed Stilwell, clinging desperately to the wheel. The wind howled and shrieked in Willie's ears. He lay on his face on the deck, tumbling around in salt water, flailing for a grip at something solid.

"Oh Christ, Christ, Christ, Jesus Christ, save us!" squealed the voice of Urban.

"Reverse your rudder, Stilwell! Hard right! Hard right!" cried the exec harshly.

"Hard right, sir!"

Maryk crawled across the deck, threw himself on the engine-room telegraph, wrested the handles from Queeg's

spasmodic grip, and reversed the settings. "Excuse me,
Captain——" A horrible coughing rumble came from the
stacks. "What's your head?" barked Maryk.

"Two seven five, sir!"

"Hold her at hard right!"

"Aye aye, sir!"

The old minesweeper rolled up a little from the surface
of the water.

Willie Keith did not have any idea of what the executive
officer was doing, though the maneuver was simple enough.
The wind was turning the ship from south to west. Queeg
had been trying to fight back to south. Maryk was doing
just the opposite, now; seizing on the momentum of the
twist to the right and assisting it with all the force of engines and rudder, to try to swing the ship's head completely northward, into the wind and sea. In a calmer moment Willie would easily have understood the logic of the
act, but now he had lost his bearings. He sat on the deck,
hanging stupidly to a telephone jack-box, with water sloshing around his crotch, and looked to the exec as to a
wizard, or an angel of God, to save him with magic
passes. He had lost faith in the ship. He was overwhelmingly aware that he sat on a piece of iron in an angry
dangerous sea. He could think of nothing but his yearning
to be saved. Typhoon, *Caine,* Queeg, sea, Navy, duty,
lieutenant's bars, all were forgotten. He was like a wet cat
mewing on wreckage.

"Still coming around? What's your head? *Keep calling
your head!*" yelled Maryk.

"Coming around hard, sir!" the helmsman screamed as
though prodded with a knife. "Heading 310, heading 315,
heading 320——"

"Ease your rudder to standard!"

"Ease the rudder, sir?"

"Yes, ease her, ease her!"

"Ru-rudder is eased, sir——"

"Very well."

Ease, ease ease—the word penetrated Willie's numb
fogged mind. He pulled himself to his feet, and looked
around. The *Caine* was riding upright. It rolled to one side,

to the other, and back again. Outside the windows there was nothing but solid white spray. The sea was invisible. The forecastle was invisible. "You okay, Willie? I thought you were knocked cold." Maryk, braced on the captain's chair, gave him a brief side glance.

"I'm okay. Wha-what's happening, Steve?"

"Well, this is it. We ride it out for a half hour, we're okay—— What's your head?" he called to Stilwell.

"Three two five, sir—coming around slower, now——"

"Well, sure, fighting the wind—she'll come around—we'll steady on 000——"

"Aye aye, sir——"

"We will not," said Queeg.

Willie had lost all awareness of the captain's presence. Maryk had filled his mind as father, leader, and savior. He looked now at the little pale man who stood with arms and legs entwined around the telegraph stand, and had the feeling that Queeg was a stranger. The captain, blinking and shaking his head as though he had just awakened, said, "Come left to 180."

"Sir, we can't ride stern to wind and save this ship," said the exec.

"Left to 180, helmsman."

"Hold it, Stilwell," said Maryk.

"Mr. Maryk, fleet course is 180." The captain's voice was faint, almost whispering. He was looking glassily ahead.

"Captain, we've lost contact with the formation—the radars are blacked out——"

"Well, then, we'll find them—— I'm not disobeying orders on account of some bad weather——"

The helmsman said, "Steady on 000——"

Maryk said, "Sir, how do we know what the orders are now? The guide's antennas may be down—ours may be—call up Sunshine and tell him we're in trouble——"

Butting and plunging, the *Caine* was a riding ship again. Willie felt the normal vibration of the engines, the rhythm of seaworthiness in the pitching, coming up from the deck into the bones of his feet. Outside the pilothouse there was only the whitish darkness of the spray and the dismal

whine of the wind, going up and down in shivery glis-
sandos.

"We're not in trouble," said Queeg. "Come left to 180."

"Steady as you go!" Maryk said at the same instant.
The helmsman looked around from one officer to the other,
his eyes popping in panic. "Do as I say!" shouted the
executive officer. He turned on the OOD. "Willie, note the
time." He strode to the captain's side and saluted. "Captain, I'm sorry, sir, you're a sick man. I am temporarily
relieving you of this ship, under Article 184 of *Navy
Regulations*."

"I don't know what you're talking about," said Queeg.
"Left to 180, helmsman."

"Mr. Keith, *you're* the OOD here, what the hell should
I do?" cried Stilwell.

Willie was looking at the clock. It was fifteen minutes
to ten. He was dumfounded to think he had had the deck
less than two hours. The import of what was taking place
between Maryk and Queeg penetrated his mind slowly. He
could not believe it was happening. It was as incredible as
his own death.

"Never you mind about Mr. Keith," said Queeg to Stilwell, a slight crankiness entering his voice, fantastically
incongruous under the circumstances. It was a tone he
might have used to complain of a chewing-gum wrapper on
the deck. "I told you to come left. That's an order. Now
you come left, and fast——"

"Commander Queeg, you aren't issuing orders on this
bridge any more," said Maryk. "I have relieved you, sir.
You're on the sick list. I'm taking the responsibility. I
know I'll be court-martialed. I've got the conn——"

"You're under arrest, Maryk. Get below to your room,"
said Queeg. "Left to 180, I say!"

"Christ, Mr. Keith!" exclaimed the helmsman, looking
at Willie. Urban had backed into the farthest corner of
the wheelhouse. He stared from the exec to Willie, his
mouth open. Willie glanced at Queeg, glued to the telegraph, and at Maryk. He felt a surge of immense drunken
gladness.

"Steady on 000, Stilwell," he said. "Mr. Maryk has the responsibility. Captain Queeg is sick."

"Call your relief, Mr. Keith," the captain said at the same instant, with something like real anger. "You're under arrest, too."

"You have no power to arrest me, Mr. Queeg," said Willie.

The shocking change of name caused a look of happy surprise to appear on Stilwell's face. He grinned at Queeg with contempt. "Steady on 000, Mr. Maryk," he said, and turned his back to the officers.

Queeg suddenly quit his grasp on the telegraph stand, and stumbled across the heaving wheelhouse to the starboard side. "Mr. Keefer! Mr. Harding! Aren't there *any* officers out there?" he called to the wing.

"Willie, phone Paynter and tell him to ballast all empty tanks on the double," Maryk said.

"Aye aye, sir." Willie seized the telephone and buzzed the fireroom. "Hello, Paynt? Listen, we're going to ballast. Flood all your empty tanks on the double—— You're goddamn right it's about time——"

"Mr. Keith, I did *not* issue any orders to ballast," said Queeg. "You call that fireroom right back——"

Maryk stepped to the public-address system. "Now, all officers, report to the bridge. All officers, report to the bridge." He said aside to Willie, "Call Paynter and tell him that word doesn't apply to him."

"Aye aye, sir." Willie pulled the phone from the bracket.

"I said once and I say again," Queeg exclaimed querulously, "both of you are under arrest! Leave the bridge, right now. Your conduct is disgraceful!"

Queeg's protests gave Willie a growing sense of gladness and power. In this shadowy careening wet wheelhouse, in this twilit darkness of midmorning, with a murderous wind shrieking at the windows, he seemed to be living the happiest moment of his life. All fear had left him.

Maryk said, "Willie, think you can grab a look at the barometer without being blown over the side?"

"Sure, Steve." He went out on the port wing, clinging

carefully to the bridge structure. As he crept up to the charthouse door it came open, and Harding, Keefer, and Jorgensen emerged, clasping each other's hands. "What's the dope, Willie? What goes on?" yelled Keefer.

"Steve relieved the captain!"

"What?"

"Steve relieved the captain! He's got the conn! He's put the captain on the sick list!" The officers looked at each other and lunged for the wheelhouse. Willie edged to the rear bulkhead and peered around at the blurry barometer. He dropped to his hands and knees and crawled back to the pilothouse. "Steve, it's up," he cried, jumping to his feet as he came to the doorway. "It's up! Twenty-eight ninety-nine, almost 29.00!"

"Good, maybe we'll be through the worst of it in a while." Maryk stood beside the wheel, facing aft. All the officers except Paynter were grouped, dripping, against the bulkhead. Queeg was hanging to the telegraph again, glaring at the exec. "Well, that's the story, gentlemen," Maryk said, his voice pitched high over the roar of the wind and the rattle of spray on the windows. "The responsibility is entirely mine. Captain Queeg will continue to be treated with the utmost courtesy, but I will give all command orders——"

"Don't kid yourself that the responsibility is all yours," Queeg interposed sulkily. "Young Mr. Keith here supported you in your mutinous conduct from the start and he'll pay just as you will. And you officers"—he turned, shaking his finger at them—"if you know what's good for you, will advise Maryk and Keith to put themselves under arrest and restore command to me while the restoring is good. I may be induced to overlook what's happened in view of the circumstances, but——"

"It's out of the question, Captain," said Maryk. "You're sick, sir——"

"I'm no sicker than you are," exclaimed Queeg with all his old irritation. "You'll all hang for collusion in mutiny, I kid you not about that——"

"Nobody will hang but me," said Maryk to the officers. "This is my act, taken without anybody's advice,

under Article 184, and if I've misapplied Article 184, I'll
get hung for it. Meantime all of you take my orders.
There's nothing else you can do. I've taken command, I've
ballasted on my own responsibility, the ship is on the
course I ordered——"

"Mr. Maryk!" Stilwell shouted. "Something up ahead, a
ship or something, close aboard, sir!"

Maryk whirled, squinted out through the windows, and
grabbed at the telegraph handles, hurling Queeg roughly
aside. The captain staggered and grasped a window handle.
"Hard right rudder!" the exec shouted, ringing up full
astern on both engines.

Visibility had improved so that the sea was in sight
through the driving spray some fifty yards beyond the
bows. A vast dim red shape bobbed on the black swells,
slightly to port.

The *Caine* veered quickly, shoved sideways by the wind
as soon as it turned a little. The thing drifted closer. It was
immense, long and narrow, longer than the *Caine* itself,
bright red. Waves were breaking over it in showers of
foam.

"Holy Mother of God," said Keefer. "It's the bottom of
a ship."

Everybody stared in awe at the horror. It slipped slowly
down the port side, endlessly long and red, rolling gently
under the breaking waves. "Destroyer," Harding said in a
choked voice.

The *Caine* was moving well clear of it. Part of the wreck
was already gone in the gloom. "We'll circle," said Maryk.
"All engines ahead full, Willie."

"Aye aye, sir." The OOD rang up the order. There was
a hideous sickness at the pit of his stomach.

Maryk went to the p.a. box and pressed the lever. "Now
all hands topside keep a sharp lookout for survivors. We
will circle the capsized ship twice. Report anything you
see to the bridge. Don't get excited. Don't anybody get
blown overboard, we have enough trouble as it is."

Queeg, braced in a forward corner against the windows,
said, "If you're so worried about the safety of this ship,
how can you go monkeying around looking for survivors?"

"Sir, we can't just steam by and forget it——" said the exec.

"Oh, don't misunderstand me. I think we should look for survivors. In fact I order you to do so. I'm simply pointing out your inconsistency for the record——"

"Left standard rudder," said Maryk.

"I should also like to point out," said Queeg, "that twenty minutes before you illegally relieved me I ordered you to get rid of that helmsman and you disobeyed me. He's the worst troublemaker on the ship. When he obeyed you instead of me he became a party to this mutiny, and he'll hang if it's——"

A roaring wave broke over the *Caine's* bridge and buffeted the ship far over to port, and Queeg tumbled to his hands and knees. The other officers slid and tottered about, clutching at each other. Once again the minesweeper labored in difficulties as the wind caught it and swept it sideways. Maryk went to the telegraph stand and manipulated the engines, altering the settings frequently, and shouting swift-changing rudder orders. He coaxed the ship around to the south, and steamed ahead until the hulk came vaguely in view again. Then he commenced a careful circling maneuver, keeping the *Caine* well clear of the foundering wreck. It was entirely awash now; only when a deep trough rode under it did the round red bottom break to the surface. The officers muttered among themselves. Queeg, his arm around the compass stand, stared out of the window.

It took forty minutes for the *Caine* to maneuver through a full circle around the lost ship against wind and waves, and all the time it wallowed and thrashed as badly as it had been doing since morning, and took several terrible rolls to leeward. Willie was scared each time. But he now knew the difference between honest fright and animal terror. One was bearable, human, not incapacitating; the other was moral castration. He was no longer terrorized, and felt he no longer could be, even if the ship went down, provided Maryk were in the water near him.

The exec was out on the wing, shielding his eyes from the hurtling spray with both hands, peering around at the heaving spires of black water, as the *Caine* steadied on north again. He came into the wheelhouse, trailing streams from his clothes. "We'll come around once more and then quit," he said. "I think it's gone under. I can't see it—— Left standard rudder."

Willie groped to the barometer once more and saw that it had risen to 29.10. He crawled to Maryk's side and reported the reading, yelling into the exec's ear. Maryk nodded. Willie rubbed his hands over his face, fevered with the sting of the flailing spray. "Why the hell doesn't it let up, Steve, if the barometer's rising?"

"Oh, Jesus, Willie, we're thirty miles from a typhoon center. Anything can happen in here." The exec grinned into the wind, baring his teeth. "We may still catch all kinds of hell—— Rudder amidships!" he shouted through the doorway.

"Rudder amidships, sir!"

"Getting tired, Stilwell?"

"No, sir. Wrestle with this son of a bitch all day if you want me to, sir!"

"Very good."

The door of the radar shack pushed open, and the telephone talker, Grubnecker, poked out his whiskered face. "Something that looks like a raft on the starboard quarter, sir, Bellison reports."

Maryk, followed by Willie, went trampling through the wheelhouse to the other side of the bridge, shouting at Stilwell as he passed, "Hard right rudder!"

At first they saw nothing but peaks and troughs of water veiled by spray; then, broad on the beam, as the *Caine* rose to the top of a swell, they both spied a black dot sliding down the slant of a wave.

"I think there's three guys on it!" shrieked Willie. He danced aft to the flagbag rails for a better look. A stiff gust of wind sent him sprawling on his stomach on the canvas cover of the flagbag. As he gasped and clutched wildly at the halyards to keep from rolling over the side, swallowing salt water from the puddle on the canvas, the wind stripped his trousers clean off his legs, and they went flapping away over the bulwark into the sea. He pulled himself to his feet, paying no attention at all to the loss.

Queeg stood in the doorway, face to face with the executive officer. "Well, Mr. Maryk, what are you waiting for? How about rigging your cargo net to starboard and having your deck forces stand by with life buoys?"

"Thank you, sir. I was about to give those orders, if you'll let me pass."

Queeg stepped aside. The exec went into the pilothouse, and passed the instructions over the loudspeaker. He began to maneuver the lurching ship toward the object, which soon showed clear, a gray balsam raft, with three men on it and two more heads bobbing beside it in the water.

"You'll be interested to know, gentlemen," Queeg said to the officers while Maryk manipulated engines and rudder, "that I was about to issue orders to ballast and head into the wind when Mr. Maryk committed his panic-stricken criminal act. I had previously determined in my own mind that if the fleet guide had given no orders by 1000 I would act at my own discretion——"

Maryk said, "All right, Stilwell, head over to the right some more. Hard right——"

Queeg went on, "And I saw no reason for confiding my command decisions to Mr. Maryk, who seemed to be treating me like a feebleminded idiot, and I'll say as much over the green table, and there'll be plenty of witnesses to——"

"Don't run 'em down, Stilwell! Rudder amidships!" Maryk stopped the engines and went to the loudspeaker. "Now throw over your buoys!"

The survivors were pulled aboard. A white-faced, wild-eyed sailor, naked except for white drawers, streaked with broad smears of oil, with a bleeding gash in his cheek, was brought to the bridge by Bellison. The chief said, "It was the *George Black*, sir. This here is Morton, quartermaster third. The others are down in sick bay."

Morton stammered a brief, horrid tale. The *George Black* had been thrown broadside to the wind and all combinations of engines and rudder had failed to bring it around. Ventilators, ammunition boxes, and davits were ripped off the decks by the seas; water began flooding the engine rooms; power failed; the lights went out. The helpless ship drifted for ten minutes, rolling further and further to starboard, with all hands screaming or praying, and finally took a tremendous roll to starboard and never stopped rolling. His next recollection was being under water in complete blackness, and after that he was at the surface, being dashed against the red bottom of his ship.

"We'll keep circling," said Maryk. He peered out at the streaked sea, visible now for several hundred yards. "I think it's letting up some. Take him below, Bellison."

"I am resuming the conn, Mr. Maryk," said Queeg, "and we will drop the matter entirely until the storm has abated——"

Maryk turned wearily to the captain. "No, sir. I've got it. I respectfully ask you to lay below to your cabin. Contradictory orders will endanger the ship——"

"Are you putting me off my bridge, sir?"

"Yes, Captain."

Queeg looked to the officers. Their faces were scared and somber. "Do all you gentlemen concur in this act? ... Do you, Mr. Keefer?"

The novelist gnawed at his lips, and turned his glance to Maryk. "Nobody is concurring. Nobody has to concur," the exec said quickly. "Please leave the bridge, Captain, or at least refrain from giving orders——"

"I shall remain on the bridge," said Queeg. "The ship is still my responsibility. Mutiny doesn't relieve me of it. I shall not speak unless your acts appear to me to be endangering my ship. In that case I shall speak even at pistol point——"

"Nobody's pulling pistols on you, sir. What you say suits me." The exec nodded to the officers. "Okay, no need for you to hang around. We'll have a meeting as soon as weather permits."

The officers began straggling out of the wheelhouse. Keefer went up to Willie, saluted, and said with a pallid grin, "I am ready to relieve you, sir."

Willie looked at the clock in astonishment. Time had stopped running in his mind. It was a quarter to twelve. "Okay," he said. The formulas of the relieving ceremony came mechanically to his lips. "Steaming on various courses and speeds to look for survivors of the *George Black*. Steaming on boilers one, two, and three. Depth charges set on safe. Condition Able set throughout the ship. Last time I saw the barometer it had risen to 29.10. Fleet course is 180, but we've lost contact with formation due to jammed radars, and I don't know where we are. About one hundred and fifty miles east of Ulithi, I'd say. You can check our 0800 dead reckoning position. We're in the same place, more or less. The captain has been relieved under Article 184, and is still on the bridge. The executive officer has command and is at the conn. I guess that's all."

"Just a routine watch," said Keefer. Willie smiled ruefully.

Keefer saluted. "Okay, I've got it." He grasped Willie's hand, pressed it warmly, and whispered, "Good work."

"God help us all," murmured Willie.

VI

THE COURT-MARTIAL

31 · Counsel for the Defense

Watery sunlight of a misty San Francisco morning, falling
on the desk of Captain Theodore Breakstone, USNR,
district legal officer of Com Twelve, illuminated a fat
manila folder on top of an untidy clutter of papers, labeled
in crude red-crayon letters, "CAINE." Breakstone, a thick-
faced man with bristly hair and a large knobby nose, sat
in his swivel chair with his back to his desk, staring out
at the harbor, regarding with mingled yearning and irritation an attack transport far below which swung slowly
in the tide current to its anchor chain. Captain Breakstone
longed to go to sea, and his dream was to command a
transport—he was an amateur boat enthusiast, and he had
navigated a destroyer briefly in World War I—but he was
trapped by his excellent civilian record as a lawyer. The
Bureau ignored his applications. He assuaged his disappointment by being salty in language and demeanor, and
growling "hell" and "damn" as often as possible.

In his lap was a sheaf of long white sheets of paper
ruled on either side with a blue line: the report of the
board of investigation into the unauthorized relief of

Lieutenant Commander P. F. Queeg, commanding officer of the U.S.S. *Caine*. Captain Breakstone had held thousands of such sheafs in his hairy hands during the past three years. The phrases, the attitudes, the glints of emotion through the stilted rubbish of words, were as commonplace to him as the nicks and grooves of an old familiar staircase to an old scrubwoman. He could not recall a case that had unsettled and depressed him more. The inquiry had been a botch. The recommendations were stupid. The facts of the case, so far as they had been uncovered, were a hideous tangled mess. He had turned away from the desk, halfway through a re-examination of the report, to fight down a nauseous headache such as he got from reading on a bumpy train.

He heard a tapping on the glass partition between his cubicle and the clattering office full of desks, files, and blue-shirted Waves. He swiveled around, throwing the papers on his desk. "Hello, Challee. Come in."

A lieutenant commander walked in through the open doorway. "I've thought of a guy, sir——"

"Good. Who?"

"You don't know him, sir. Barney Greenwald——"

"Regular?"

"Reserve, sir. But a pretty red-hot officer. Fighter pilot. Lieutenant——"

"What the hell does a fly boy know about law?"

"He's a lawyer in civilian life, sir——"

"A lawyer and a *fighter pilot?*"

"He's quite a guy, sir——"

"Greenwald, you say his name is? Dutch, or what?"

"He's a Jew, sir——" Captain Breakstone wrinkled his big nose. Challee pulled himself a little more erect. He stood with one hand in his jacket pocket, the other holding a black portfolio, his attitude nicely mixing familiarity and deference. He had wavy, sandy hair, and his round face wore a look of good-humored alertness. "—but as I say, sir, quite an exceptional guy——"

"Hell, I've got nothing against Jews, you know that. This is a damn touchy case, that's all——"

"I'm sure he's the guy for us, sir——"

"What makes you so sure?"

"I know him pretty well, sir. He was at Georgetown Law when I was going through—class ahead of me, but we got friendly——"

"Well, sit down, sit down. What's he doing around Com Twelve?"

Challee seated himself in the chair beside the desk, holding his back straight. "He's just come off the sick list. He was hospitalized for third-degree burns. They've got him on temporary limited duty, officer personnel placement for air. He's waiting for a medical okay to go back to his squadron——"

"How did he get burned? Shot up?"

"No, sir. Crashed a barrier. His plane burned up but they pulled him out——"

"Not so heroic——"

"Well, so far as flying goes, I don't know that Barney's any great shakes. I think he's got two Japs——"

"What makes you think he'd be good for the *Caine* case?"

"Well, sir, Maryk is a dead pigeon, the way I see it, and Barney goes for that kind of case." Challee paused. "I guess you'd call him odd in a way. Very odd. I'm used to him. He's from Albuquerque. Barney is interested as hell in the Indians. You might say he's nuts on the subject. He specialized in Indian cases after getting out of law school—won a lot of them, too. He was working up a pretty good general practice in Washington, before he joined up——"

"What was he, ROTC?"

"No. V-7, then switched to air."

Breakstone pulled at his nose with thumb and forefinger for several seconds. "Sounds like he might be pinko."

"I don't think so, sir."

"Have you talked to him?"

"Not yet, sir. Thought I'd ask you first."

Captain Breakstone laced his fingers together and cracked his knuckles. He swiveled from side to side. "Christ, can't we get a regular? If there's one kind of smell we don't want to have hung on this case, it's regulars versus reserves—it's bad enough the way it is——"

"I talked to eight guys, sir, on the list you gave me. It's a hot potato. They're afraid of it. And two guys have been detached and gone to sea——"

"Did you talk to Hogan?"

"Yes, sir. He begged off practically with tears in his eyes. He says it's a lost case and all the defense counsel can do is get himself permanently fouled up with the Navy——"

"That isn't so——"

"I'm just quoting him——"

"Well, maybe it is so, at that, a little bit." Breakstone pulled at his nose. "Hell, somebody's got to defend the case. When can you get this Greenwald up here?"

"I guess this afternoon, sir——"

"Get him up here. Don't tell him what it's about. I want to talk to him first."

Lieutenant Greenwald came to Captain Breakstone's office late that day. After a brief, grumpy questioning the legal officer gave him the *Caine* folder. Next morning when the captain came to his cubicle he found the skinny pilot waiting outside, slumped on a chair.

"Well, come on in, Greenwald. Think you can handle the case?" He took off his raincoat and draped it on a hanger, noticing that the folder lay on his desk.

"I'd rather not, sir."

Breakstone glanced around in annoyed surprise. The pilot stood awkwardly in the doorway, looking at his shoes. He had a loose, adolescent mouth and a pale face, curly brown hair, and long dangling hands. "Looks more like Harold Teen than red-hot Jewish lawyer," thought Breakstone, as he had thought the previous day, too. He said, "Why not?"

"Well, several reasons, sir." Greenwald kept his eyes bashfully down. "If there's any other case you need help on—I mean I don't want to seem unco-operative——"

"What's the matter? Case too tough for you?"

"Well, I don't want to waste your time with my opinions on it, sir—seeing that——"

"I'm *asking* you to waste my time. Sit down." Break-stone's eyes were drawn to the terrible fire scars on the pilot's hands, hanging between his knees; the dead blue-white grafted skin, and the raw red edges, and the wrinkled stringy scar tissue. He looked away with an effort. "Challee told me you were a great one for defending the under-dog——"

"These men are no underdogs, sir. They deserve to get slugged."

"Oh, you think so? Well, frankly, so do I, but they're still entitled to a good defense, and they can't find themselves counsel, so——"

"I think they'll be acquitted. That is, sir, if there's a halfway intelligent defense——"

Breakstone arched his brows. "Oh, you do?"

"Keith and Stilwell certainly will be. So will Maryk, if the case is handled with any brains. I guess I could get them off."

The legal officer was baffled by this arrogance, expressed in hesitant, diffident tones by the slouching lieutenant. "Please tell me how."

"Well, the charge is absurd, for one thing. Making a mutiny. There's no question of force or violence or dis-respect. Maryk was damned careful to stay on legal ground. He misapplied Article 184 to commit a mutinous act, but the article's there in the books. The toughest charge that could possibly stick would be conduct to the prejudice of good order or discipline—as I say, though, it's none of my affair——"

The captain's opinion of Lieutenant Greenwald took a sharp turn upward, because Greenwald's criticism of the charge was a point he had noted himself. "Don't forget you're reading the board of investigation's recommenda-tions, Greenwald, not the formal charge. *I'm* drawing up the formal charge, and as a matter of fact it *is* conduct to prejudice. It was a one-man board, a captain from the mine force here, and I don't think he ever saw *Courts and Boards* before they sent him over to the *Caine*. That's the trouble around here, we're shorthanded, and nobody who's available knows any law. When a guy like yourself comes along, and you're on the loose, pretty much, why, I think it's your duty to make yourself available——"

Breakstone pressed a buzzer, and lit a cigar with gestures of short temper. Lieutenant Commander Challee came to the doorway.

"Yes, sir? Hello, Barney——"

"Challee, your friend here seems to think the case is too easy or something. He can lick you with one hand tied behind him, only he doesn't want to, or words to that effect——"

"Captain Breakstone, I'm sorry I ever got involved," said Greenwald. "Jack asked me if I minded helping out on a court—he didn't tell me any details—and I said I'd be glad to. Making out air priorities is pretty dull work. I just don't want to defend these *Caine* people. Captain Queeg obviously is not crazy. The psychiatrist's report proves it. These fools find a paragraph in Navy Regs that gives them ideas, and they gang up on a skipper who's mean and stupid—as a lot of skippers are—and make jackasses of themselves, and put a ship out of action. I'm a damn good lawyer and a very expensive one, and I don't see contributing my services to get them acquitted. If you've——"

"You're pretty goddamn cocksure about getting an acquittal," said Breakstone, chewing his cigar.

"They can be gotten off."

"I'd like to know how," said Challee. "If ever I saw a plain case——"

"Lieutenant Greenwald, nobody can compel you to defend these birds," said the legal officer. "But you seem to be pretty red hot on principles, to hear you talk. I think you've talked yourself into defending Maryk. Eight officers, including four legal specialists, have ducked the case. I haven't heard anybody except you give him a chance of getting off. The first requirement for a good counsel is confidence in his case. I trust you believe in the principle that the worst criminal is entitled to the best defense?"

Greenwald looked down at his fingernails, his boyish mouth loosely open, his eyes sad. "I'd be here forever on this case. Suppose I get my medical okay——"

"There'll be plenty of war left for polishing your medals," said the legal officer.

"Are you going to try all three?"

"Maryk first. We'll hold off on the Keith and Stilwell cases till we see what happens. That's what I'm recommending to the admiral, anyway. He generally does what I say."

"When will the court-martial start?"

Breakstone looked to his assistant, who said, "I think we can get it on in two weeks, sir, if Captain Blakely's available to preside. He said he'd let me know this afternoon."

"Where's the *Caine* now?" said Greenwald.

"Drydocks, Hunters Point," said Challee.

"May I go out and talk to Maryk before I commit myself?"

Breakstone nodded. "Challee, provide transportation for Lieutenant Greenwald."

"Aye aye, sir."

Greenwald rose. "I'll go now, I guess."

"Jeep will be at the main entrance in ten minutes, Barney," said Challee.

"Okay." The pilot put on his white peaked cap. The braid was crusty and green. He had the look of a poverty-stricken college boy, one who waited on tables and spent his money for phonograph records instead of food. He went out, his big scarred hands swinging.

Challee said, "He'll take the case, sir."

"Queer buzzard," said the legal officer. "Looks so futile and apologetic, but he has a damn high opinion of himself."

"He's a good lawyer," said the assistant. "But he won't get Maryk off."

Lieutenant Greenwald was used to aircraft carriers. The *Caine*, resting on keelblocks in a drydock, rusty and cluttered, looked to him like a little river boat. He went down the long steep wooden gangway stretching across the gulf of the dock to the minesweeper. Amid the rubble on the main deck he noticed a jagged hole, perhaps four feet across, roped off near the after davit of the motor whale-boat. Twisted rusty cables and pipes like entrails projected around the hole. "Like to see Lieutenant Maryk," he said to the moon-faced short sailor in whites at the gangway desk.

"He ain't here, sir."

"Where is he?"

"I guess the *Chrysanthemum,* sir. Excursion boat they got rigged up for a BOQ at Pier 6."

"Where's your captain?"

"Captain White won't be back till six o'clock, sir."

"Captain who? White?"

"Yes, sir."

"What's your name?"

"Urban, sir."

"Oh, yes. Urban." Greenwald inspected the sailor who was going to be a star witness for Challee. "Where's Captain Queeg, Urban?"

"Captain White has the ship now, sir." A wary, sullen look clouded the signalman's face.

"Don't you know where Queeg is?"

"I don't know nothing about Captain Queeg, sir."

"What's that hole in the deck?"

"We took a suicide in Lingayen."

"Anybody hurt?"

"Nobody hurt. It bounced and fell over the side."

"Who was commanding the ship then? Captain White?"

"No, sir." Urban scowled very suspiciously, and turned to the gangway desk.

"Well, who, then? Was Mr. Maryk still in charge?"

Urban grunted, opened the quartermaster's log, and made a show of scribbling in it. Greenwald turned, went up the gangway, and made his way to the *Chrysanthemum.*

His first sight of Maryk astonished the lawyer. On the basis of the board of investigation's report he had formed a clear picture of the exec: slight, thin, nervous, dark, and with the self-satisfied expression of a petty intellectual. In fact he had pictured Bill Pelham, a loud-mouthed Marxist of his college days, in a naval uniform. The husky, bullet-headed, blunt-faced officer who sat blinking amid tumbled bedclothes on the edge of his cot, rubbing his palms on his broad naked chest, dislocated Greenwald's entire conception of the *Caine* affair.

"Well, anyone they want to appoint is okay with me," Maryk said dully. "I don't know anybody. It doesn't matter a whole hell of a lot, I guess. You'll be buying yourself a lot of trouble——"

"What are you going to plead?"

"I don't know."

"Why did you relieve him?"

"I thought he was nuts."

"Don't you still think so?"

"I don't know what I think any more."

"Where did you get all that dope on paranoia you put out to the investigation officer?"

"Read it in a book," Maryk growled.

"Well, pardon me, Maryk, you don't seem to know much about it."

"I never claimed to. Christ, instead of asking me about the ship or the typhoon or the captain he cross-examined me for an hour about paranoia. I'm a stoop about those things and I know it. I made a jackass of myself, and I knew I would. And I will again, at the court-martial." He glanced at Greenwald, his brows contracted in a baffled, hurt way over hollow eyes. "I'll tell you this, the same things seem goddamn different in the middle of a typhoon when they're happening, and six thousand miles away in the Federal Office Building when you're talking about them——"

The door opened and Keefer came in, spick-and-span in freshly pressed blues, his breast-pocket ribbons crowded with battle stars. The lower gold stripes on his sleeves were faded, the upper ones bright yellow. He carried a small leather satchel. "Steve, I'm shoving off. Got time for some lunch?"

"I don't think so, Tom—— Lieutenant Greenwald, Lieutenant Keefer, our gunnery officer—— Get your plane priority okay?"

"Yes, by dint of a great deal of charm lavished on a

dried-up old pig in Transportation. I thought I might have to marry her first."

Maryk smiled sourly. "Well, have yourself a time."

The gunnery officer patted the satchel. "Recognize this?"

"The novel?"

"First half. I'm going to try to peddle it back East."

"Hope you make a million dollars, boy."

Keefer glanced at Greenwald, hesitated, looked back at Maryk, and said with a grin, "Well, I'm off, in a blaze of sheep dung." The door closed.

"Look," said Greenwald, slouched, studying the toes of his shoes. "I'm a pretty good lawyer, as it happens."

"You have to be goddamned good to get me out of this."

"Why do you say that?"

"Because as far as the thing will ever get in the Federal Office Building, I'm guilty. For all I know I'm guilty any way you look at it. Give a lamebrain enough time and he'll foul himself up——"

"I'm hungry," said the lawyer. "Where can we get some chow and talk about it?"

"There's a cafeteria over at Pier 8——"

"Come along."

Maryk looked at the lawyer and shrugged. "Okay," he said, reaching for blue trousers crumpled at the foot of the bed.

"If you're going to plead guilty," said Greenwald—his voice was pitched high over the clatter of cutlery and tin trays, and the gabble of hundreds of Navy Yard workers feeding themselves amid steamy odors of tomato soup, cabbage, and human being—"then the whole thing becomes a formality. Even in that case the idea is not just to stand up and say 'Guilty' in open court. You bargain with Challee. It's a queer case, and a messy one, and for the sake of a sure score Challee might go easy——"

The exec listlessly forked scrambled eggs into his mouth and took a swallow of coffee. "I'm no good at that bargaining——"

"Well, of course, your counsel does that for you——"

"Look, Greenwald, I may be guilty by the book but I

don't feel like pleading guilty. Christ, I wasn't trying to take over the ship, I was trying to save it. If I was wrong about Queeg being nuts, well, that's one thing, but I was trying to do what I thought was right——"

Greenwald nodded, lolling his tongue on his lower lip. "No criminal intent."

"That's it. No criminal intent."

"Well, *don't* plead guilty then. Make them work to hang it on you—— What did your friend Keefer think of Captain Queeg?"

The exec's eyes shifted in a narrow surly side glance. "Look, it's all my responsibility—that's the way it's got to be——"

"Did Keefer think Queeg was a paranoiac, too?"

"I don't know what he thought. Leave him out of it."

Greenwald played with his nails. "He looks like a guy I once knew in school. Fellow name of Pelham."

The exec's face was sullen and bitter, his gaze far away. He drank off his coffee. "Pretty lousy joe they serve here."

"See here, Maryk, I'm willing to be your defense counsel, if you want me."

Maryk nodded, and looked into the lawyer's eyes, his frown fading into timid gratitude. "Well, okay, thanks. I need somebody——"

"Don't you want to know my qualifications?"

"I guess they're okay or the legal office wouldn't have sent you around——"

"Well, listen anyway. I am a red-hot lawyer in civilian life. I was making twenty thousand a year when I was only out of school four years." Greenwald's boyish face took on a peculiar inner smile, a mere glow around the eyes; he held his head bashfully sidewise, looking at a spoon with which he traced rings in a slop of coffee on the table. "Not only that, my third year out of school I pried a hundred thousand dollars out of the government for some Cherokees who'd been cheated out of their land forty years ago."

"Jesus. Maybe you *can* get me off," said the exec, staring at Greenwald skeptically.

"I better tell you one more thing. I'd rather be prosecuting you than defending you. I don't know yet just how guilty you are. But you're either a mutineer or one of the dumbest goofs in the whole Navy. There's no third possibility." Maryk blinked in astonishment. "If you're going to give me all the dope, say so, and we'll work out your defense. If you're going to stay clammed up because you're so proud and noble and hurt, say so, and I'll go on back to town."

"What do you want to know?" the exec said after a pause filled with cafeteria noise.

"All about you, and Keefer, and Keith, and everything else that explains how you pulled your dumb stunt——"

"Sure, you call it dumb," exclaimed Maryk. "Everyone does, now that we're all alive to talk about it. If Queeg and me and the whole ship were at the bottom of the sea —I guess the only way I could have been proved right was if I *hadn't* relieved Queeg and the ship had capsized, as it damn near did. Three cans went down in that typhoon, you know——"

"Sure. About forty of them stayed afloat, though, without the exec relieving the skipper."

Maryk looked extremely surprised. He took out a cigar, and regarded it thoughtfully as he stripped off the crinkling cellophane.

He really was surprised. Greenwald had jarred him into uncovering his secret self-justifying thought, a comfort he had proudly, silently applied to his feelings throughout the official ordeal he was undergoing. The lawyer's sarcastic twist of viewpoint had never occurred to the exec, preoccupied as he was with his own misunderstood heroism and the treachery of Keefer, and the evil fate closing in on him. "Where are you from?" he said.

Greenwald showed no surprise at the irrelevancy. "Albuquerque."

"Oh. I thought maybe you were from New York— though you don't talk much like a New Yorker, at that——"

"Well, I'm a Jew, if that's what you mean," the pilot said, with a little grin at his shoes.

Maryk laughed, and said, "I'll tell you anything you want to know. Let's go over to the *Chrysanthemum*."

They sat on a leather couch in the lounge of the excursion boat, and for an hour Maryk told the story of how he had become convinced that Queeg was crazy. He ran out of words at last and sat silent, staring out of the window at the clanking yard, bristling with cranes, funnels, and masts. The lawyer lit a cigar which the exec had given him, and puffed at it awkwardly, blinking. After a while he said, "Did you ever read your friend Keefer's novel?"

Maryk looked at him with the empty puzzlement of a man wakened from sleep. "He never shows it to anybody. It must be long as hell. He's always kept it in that black satchel."

"Probably a masterpiece."

"Well, Tom's smart, no getting away from that——"

"I'd like to read it. I'm sure that it exposes this war in all its grim futility and waste, and shows up the military men for the stupid, Fascist-minded sadists they are. Bitching up all the campaigns and throwing away the lives of fatalistic, humorous, lovable citizen-soldiers. Lots of sex scenes where the prose becomes rhythmic and beautiful while the girl gets her pants pulled down." Greenwald saw Maryk's mystified suspicious smile, and shrugged. "Well, I can tell, because war novels are coming out already and the war is still on. I read 'em all. I like novels where the author proves how terrible military guys are, and how superior sensitive civilians are. I know they're true to life because I'm a sensitive civilian myself." He puffed at the cigar, made a mouth of distaste, and threw it into a brass jar half full of sand. "How can you smoke those things? . . . Well, I'll tell you, Maryk. Your sensitive novelist friend is the villain of this foul-up, all right, but it doesn't do us any good——"

"I want him left out of it," said Maryk doggedly.

"He's got to be. If I can help it he'll never be put on the stand. What you did, you did. Actually it's better that you did it out of your own mistaken but noble judgment than that you took the psychiatric opinions of a sensitive novelist as straight dope. The fact that he's running for cover now—well, he warned you on the *New Jersey,* didn't he? He had all the insight of a sensitive novelist. Sounding off about Old Yellowstain—wonderful name, by the way—behind his back was one thing, but he knew damn well when it came to a showdown what the outcome would be."

"After everything I told you," said Maryk, with childish appeal, "you don't think Queeg was nuts?"

"No."

"Then I get hung," said Maryk shakily.

"Not necessarily. Tell me one more thing. How did it happen that they let you take the ship on to Lingayen Gulf?"

Maryk wet his lips and looked away. "Is that important?"

"I don't know until you tell me."

"Well, it was goddamn strange." The exec took another cigar from his breast pocket. "See, after the typhoon when we got back to Ulithi we were in pretty good shape. Boat stove in and a couple of paravanes gone and some topside stuff buckled and smashed. But we were operational. We could still sweep." Greenwald held out a flaming match, and the exec puffed the cigar aglow. "Thanks—— When we came in I reported right away to the beach there, to the commodore, I think he was ComServRon Five, and told him what had happened. Well, he got all excited and got Queeg on the beach that morning, and had the head doctor go over him. Well, the upshot of the doctor's examination—he was an old fat four-striper with a real rummy nose—the doctor said he didn't think Queeg was crazy at all. Said he seemed to be an intelligent normal officer, maybe a little fatigued. But he wouldn't give Queeg clearance to go back on duty. Said he was no psychiatrist and Queeg had been four years at sea and the best thing was to fly him back to the States for a psychiatric checkup. Commodore was sore as hell at me. He had me in the office when the doctor made his report. He said the admiral had been building a fire under him for more sweepers for Lingayen because so many had been knocked out in the typhoon, and he'd be goddamned if he was going to pull the *Caine* out of the line-up. So after a lot of talk back and forth he got Queeg into the office, too, and he gave Queeg a big pitch about how bad the admiral needed sweepers. And he asked Queeg whether he thought I could take the *Caine* to Lingayen. He asked him to think of the good of the Navy and not his personal feelings, and he said he was sure I'd get everything that was coming to me after Lingayen. Well, Queeg really surprised me. He was calm and quiet. He said I'd been his exec for eleven months and after that much training he thought he had trained me up for ship handling even though I had a disloyal and mutinous character. He recommended that I take the ship to Lingayen. That's how it happened."

Greenwald was twirling a paper clip which he had twisted into the shape of a question mark. He sent it spinning out through the window. "Where's Queeg now?"

"Down at his home in Phoenix. The doctors here discharged him and said he was fit for duty. He's on temporary duty attached to Com Twelve, just sitting around waiting for the court-martial."

"He made a mistake, recommending you for Lingayen —from the viewpoint of hanging you."

"That's what I think. Why do you suppose he did it?"

The pilot stood and stretched, baring his streaked, mutilated hands and wrists. The slick scar tissue ran up into his sleeves. "Well, maybe, like the commodore told him, he was thinking of the good of the Navy—— I'll go back to Com Twelve and start beating Jack Challee over the head——"

"What are we going to plead?" The exec looked up at his lanky counsel anxiously.

"Not guilty, of course. You're really a great naval hero. I'll be seeing you."

32 · Willie's Leave

Willie Keith was on his way to New York in a plane. Captain Breakstone had advised the new commanding officer of the *Caine* to let him go. "He can have ten days, anyway, before the court starts," the legal officer had told Lieutenant White over the phone. "Send the poor beggar off while the sending is good. God knows when he'll ever be in the clear again." Willie had asked for the leave for only one reason. He was going home to break with May.

In the last turbulent months he had advanced in his thinking about her to the point of realizing that his conduct toward her, even in their correspondence, was abominable. He still yearned for her. If the word "love" meant anything, and if the descriptions in novels and poetry of the emotion were accurate, he supposed he loved her. But he had a deep-seated, unshakable intuition that he would never depart from his upbringing enough to marry her. It was a familiar old conflict in literature; and it was dreary and sad to find himself trapped in it in real life. But he understood now that the real victim of the situation was May, and he was determined to free her before the court-martial brought an unguessable new turn in his life. It no longer seemed possible to cut her off with a letter or with silence. He had to confront her, and take whatever pain and punishment she could inflict on him. It was a miserable errand on which he was embarked. He could hardly bear to think about it.

He tried to distract himself by talking to the bald fat literary agent beside him. His neighbor, however, was of the sleeping-pill school of air travel. For a while he cross-examined Willie to find out whether he had killed any

Japs personally or earned any medals or been wounded; but he had already lost interest, and was pulling papers out of his portfolio, when the plane began to jolt and flutter in the air over the Rockies. Thereupon he produced a bottle of yellow capsules, swallowed three, and slumped unconscious. Willie wished he had brought along his phenobarbital. In the end he drew the curtains, pushed back his chair, closed his eyes, and lost himself in sickly revolving thoughts of the *Caine*.

There were a few dreams of childhood which Willie could never forget, one in particular, in which he had seen God as an enormous jack-in-the-box popping up over the trees on the lawn of his home and leaning over to stare down at him. The scene in the anteroom of the Com Twelve legal office, in his memory, had the same quality of unreal and painful vividness. There, before his shut eyes, were the green close walls; the bookcase full of fat regular legal volumes bound in brown and red; the single fluorescent light overhead, throwing a bluish glare; the ashtray full of butts beside him on the desk, sending up a stale smell; the "board of investigation," a surly, thin little captain, his voice dry and sneering, his face the face of a nasty post-office clerk refusing a badly wrapped package.

How different it had all been from Willie's picturings, how unfair, how quickly over; above all, how small-scale and dreary! He had seen himself as an actor in a grand drama. In the privacy of his room, in his dark bunk, he had whispered to himself, "the *Caine* mutiny, the *Caine* mutiny," savoring the ring of the phrase, and imagining a long article in *Time* underneath that heading, greatly favorable to the heroic Maryk and Keith. He had even tried to envision Maryk's face on the cover of the news magazine. He had anticipated confronting an array of admirals across a green-covered table, justifying his act with quiet poise, with irrefutable facts. The memory of one daydream made him writhe. He had seen himself, the true key figure of the mutiny, summoned to Washington by President Roosevelt for a private chat in his office, convincing the President that the *Caine* affair was exceptional, that it was no indication of low morale in the Navy. He had even planned, in answer to Roosevelt's generous offer of restoration to any duty he chose, the simple reply, "Mr. President, I should like to return to my ship."

This tangle of technicolor folly had possessed his mind all during the Lingayen campaign and the return trip to Pearl Harbor. The suicide attack had happened so quickly, and caused so little damage (he had not even seen the Japanese plane before it struck) that it had merely served to enhance his picture of Maryk, and himself, and all the officers of the *Caine,* as cool-headed heroes.

The magic had begun to dim in Pearl Harbor with the arrival of Captain White, a good-looking, bright lieutenant of the regular Navy, obviously a trouble-shooter. Maryk had shrunk in a day to a subservient dull exec. The adventurous excitement in the wardroom had subsided. All the officers had begun walking humbly again, and guarding their words. White was arid, cool, and efficient. He acted as though the relief of Queeg had never occurred. He handled the ship as well as Maryk from the first, and he attracted the immediate loyalty of the crew. Willie's vision of the mutiny as a triumph of Reserve heroism over neurotic Academy stupidity languished; the Academy was back in charge, and master of the situation.

But Willie was still unprepared for the developments in San Francisco. He had never foreseen that the great *Caine* mutiny would be treated by the authorities as an irksome and not very pressing legal problem; that it would apparently mean little more to the legal office of Com Twelve than the pilfering of a truckload of lard. Days went by, while the ship rested in drydock, without any reaction to Captain White's report. And when the investigation at last began, there were no admirals, no green table, no summons from the President. There was only a cross-examination by a little man in a little office.

Was it this distortion in scale, Willie wondered, that had turned his irrefutable facts into slippery, badly described anecdotes which discredited himself, not Queeg, more and more as he told them? Was it the hostility of the investigating officer? Stories which he had counted on to damn Queeg seemed to tell themselves as descriptions of his own disloyalty or ineptness. Even the water famine, one of Queeg's grand crimes, sounded in his own ears like a prudent measure, and the crew's water-bootlegging in the engine room a rebellious act abetted by incompetent officers. What he could not convey to the investigator was the terrible distress everybody had undergone. The captain regarded him fishily when he spoke of the heat and the stack gas, and finally said, "I'm sure you suffered unendurable hardships, Mr. Keith. Why didn't you report the bootlegging to your commanding officer?" He knew he should have replied, "Because I considered him a coward and a lunatic——" but the answer that came out of his mouth was, "Well, er, nobody else did, so I didn't see why I should."

He remembered how he emerged from the interview with a terrible presentiment that he had hanged himself; a feeling which proved quite accurate. After the passing of five uneasy days he was summoned to the office of Captain Breakstone. The investigation report was placed in his hand. The cold blue-lined sheets felt horrible in his fingers before he began to read. He came to the words about himself with a sense of struggling in a nightmare; it was like reading a doctor's report that he was dying:

Recommendation (3)
That Lieutenant (junior grade) Willis Seward Keith USNR be brought to trial by a general court-martial on the charge of making a mutiny.

Willie accepted the brutal prospect of a court-martial with his mind, but his heart was that of a frightened rabbit, looking about for succor with wide shining eyes. He knew that he was still Willie Keith, just the innocent, good-humored Willie whom everybody liked, Willie, who could delight people by sitting at a piano and playing *If You Knew What the Gnu Knew*. Impaled by a terrible accident on the spike of military justice, his virtue seemed to be leaking from him like air from a punctured tire; he felt himself flattening slowly to his old self of Princeton and the Club Tahiti. A thought which had not passed through his mind for years was murmuring up from his subconscious: "Mother will get me out of it."

Supine in his tilted chair, his stomach straining against the tight safety belt each time the plane jounced, he spun a long morbid fantasy wherein his mother hired the country's greatest lawyers to defend him, and the long-faced officers of the court-martial were confounded by the brilliant legal minds arrayed at his table. He invented lengthy sequences of testimony, and saw Queeg wriggling under the lash of cross-examination by a defense counsel who resembled Thomas E. Dewey. The dismal dream became queerer and less coherent; May Wynn came into it somehow, looking old and hard, her skin hideously blotchy. Willie fell asleep.

But the plane flew over the spiky buildings of Manhattan in a violet-and-pearl dawn, and Willie woke and his heart revived as he peered through the round little window. New York was the most beautiful place on earth. It was more than that. It was the Garden of Eden, it was the lost island of sweet golden springtime, it was the place where he had loved May Wynn. The plane tilted, and glided downward. The gold-white sun appeared above the eastern clouds, brightening the air with slant rays. As the plane wheeled Willie saw Manhattan again, the Empire State Building, the Chrysler Building, Radio City, their lean shafts suddenly rosy above the purple haze which still veiled the city. There came into his mind's eye the beach of Kwajalein, the wide blue vacancy of the South Pacific, the orange puffs of shore batteries on the green hills of Saipan, and the pitching drenched wheelhouse of the *Caine* in the shrieking typhoon. In that instant, Willie understood the war.

"Half an hour late," grumbled the literary agent beside him, rasping shut the zipper of his portfolio.

When Willie stepped out of the plane to the gangway he was astounded by the feel of the frigid wind, cutting on his face, cutting in his lungs when he breathed it. He had forgotten what winter air was; and New York from the plane had looked deceptively springlike. He shivered inside his heavy bridge coat and pulled his white silk muffler closer around his throat. Coming down the steps, his breath smoking, he saw his mother waving gaily to him from behind a window of a waiting room. He ran across the strip of windy airfield. In a moment he was being violently kissed and hugged in the steam-heated room. "Willie, Willie, Willie! Oh, my dear, it's so good to feel you close again!"

Willie's first thought was, "How gray she is!" He was not sure whether it had happened in his absence, or imperceptibly before the war, and he was only now able to see it. Her red hair had dimmed to a nondescript grayish brown. "You look wonderful, Mother."

"Thank you, darling! Let me take a good look at you——" Holding his arms, she leaned back and scrutinized him, her face alight with joy. She was both disturbed and pleased at what she saw. Her son had suffered a sea change. This sunburned face, with its flat cheeks, prominent nose, and heavy jaw, was half alien. It was Willie of course, her Willie, and the boyish bow of the mouth she thought was the same; but—"You've become a man, Willie."

"Not quite, Mother," said her son with a weary smile.

"You look so trim! How long can you stay?"

"I'm flying back Sunday morning."

She hugged him again. "Five days! Never mind. I'll enjoy it more than any five years I've ever lived."

Willie told her very little during the drive homeward. He found himself minimizing the dangers of war and exaggerating the boredom, like all good tight-mouthed Americans in the movies. The more his mother pressed him for details the vaguer were his answers. He saw she wanted to be told that he had been snatched from the jaws of death innumerable times, and perversely he insisted that he had never been close to any real action. He was, in truth, a little disappointed at the absence of hair-raising escapes, or killings, or woundings, in his war record, now that he was back in the civilian world. It irritated him to be cross-examined. His natural impulse was to play up the true moments of danger, but an obscure shame prevented him from doing so. Taciturnity was a subtler and quite respectable form of boasting, and he made good use of it.

He had expected to enjoy real fireworks of nostalgia when he caught the first glimpse of his home; but the car turned into the driveway and rattled on the gravel up to the front door, and he merely stared stupidly at the brown lawn and bare trees. Inside the house was unchanged, but it seemed empty and still, and the pleasant aroma of frying bacon did not hide a pervading odor of camphor. The place smelled quite different than it had in the old days. He realized why almost immediately; there was no trace of cigar smoke. It had all aired out of the curtains and rugs and upholstery, long ago.

"I'll shower before we eat, Mother."

"Go ahead, Willie. I have plenty to do."

He picked up a newspaper in the hallway and glanced at the headlines as he trotted upstairs; *MacArthur Advances on Manila.* He came into his room, and tossed aside the newspaper. A gear seemed to shift in his mind, and his old identity began to operate smoothly. He felt no strangeness, no sense of contrast or of vanished time, no particular gladness at seeing his old books and phonograph. He undressed, hanging his uniform among his suits. Only the heavy gush of water from the shower head surprised him. He was used to the jagged sparse spray of the *Caine's* wardroom shower. The wonderful thick flow, the ease with which he could adjust the mixture hot and cold, seemed more luxurious to him than anything else in his home. On the *Caine* hot water was achieved by letting live steam into a half-clogged cold-water pipe. A small error in adjustment could boil one alive like seafood in a matter of seconds. More than once Willie had issued howling from a cloud of billowy steam.

On a whim, he took out his best tweeds, a beautiful soft tan suit which had cost two hundred dollars at Abercrombie and Fitch, and selected with fussy care a powder-blue wool tie, Argyle socks, and a white shirt with a buttoned-down collar. The trousers were too loose; the jacket struck him as overpadded and oversized. The tie seemed strangest of all when he knotted it, loud and effeminate, after two years of black ties. He looked at himself in the full-length mirror on the inside of his closet door. For an instant, his own face surprised him. He partly perceived the changes his mother had seen. He was concerned by a thinness of his hair at the forehead line. But the effect blurred even as he stared at himself; and it was just Willie again, looking tired and not very happy in loud clothes. He came downstairs, feeling clumsy and self-conscious, aware of the heavy pads on his shoulders.

He was hungry; and while his mother chattered happily about his handsome appearance he ate up a large platter of eggs and bacon, with several rolls. "You never drank coffee like this before," said Mrs. Keith, filling his cup for the fourth time, and watching him with mixed anxiety and respect.

"I'm a fiend now."

"You sailors are terrible."

"Let's go into the library, Mother," he said, draining his cup.

A ghost was in the brown book-lined room, but Willie fought down his feelings of awe and sadness. He dropped into his father's red leather armchair, selecting the sacred spot deliberately, disregarding his mother's wan sorrowful loving look. He told her the story of the mutiny. She fell silent after a few shocked exclamations, and allowed him to talk for a long time. The light in the room dimmed as heavy gray clouds rolled over the morning sky, blotting out the sunshine on the empty flower beds outside. When Willie finished and looked at her face she regarded him steadily and puffed a cigarette.

"Well, what do you think, Mother?"

Mrs. Keith hesitated, and said, "What does—have you told May about it?"

"May doesn't even know I'm in New York," he said irritably.

"Aren't you going to see her?"

"I guess I'll see her."

The mother sighed. "Well, all I can say is, Willie, this Old Yellowstain sounds like an abominable monster. You and the executive officer are perfectly innocent. You did the right thing."

"The doctors say different."

"You wait and see. The court will acquit your executive officer. They won't even try you."

His mother's blind optimism did not comfort Willie. On the contrary, it annoyed him exceedingly. "Well, Mother, not that I blame you, but you don't know much about the Navy, that's obvious."

"Maybe not. Have you decided anything about May, Willie?"

Willie didn't want to answer, but he was cross, and nervous; and telling the mutiny story had shaken his self-control. "Well, this will probably please you very much. I decided that it wouldn't work. I've given it up."

The mother nodded slightly, and looked down at her lap, appearing to suppress a smile. "In that case, Willie, why are you going to see her? Wouldn't it be kinder not to?"

"I can't just ignore her, Mother, like a whore I once spent a night with."

"You've picked up a little Navy language, Willie."

"You don't know Navy language."

"It's just that you'll be letting yourself in for a pointless, agonizing scene——"

"May's entitled to her scene."

"When are you going to see her?"

"Tonight, if I can. I thought I'd call her now——"

Mrs. Keith said, with doleful amusement, "You see, I'm not so dumb. I'm having the family over tomorrow night. I imagined tonight would be taken."

"It'll be the only night. You'll be all clear on the next four."

"Darling, if you think I'm happy about this you're mistaken. I share all your pain——"

"Okay, Mother——"

"Someday, Willie, I'll tell you all about a man I didn't marry, a very handsome and attractive and worthless man, who's still alive." And Mrs. Keith blushed a little, and looked out of the window.

Willie stood. "I'll make my call, I guess."

The mother came, put her arm around him, and leaned her head on his shoulder. Willie submitted. Outside a few thick flakes of snow drifted down through the black branches of the trees. "Darling, don't worry about your court-martial. I'll talk to Uncle Lloyd. He'll know what to do. Believe me, nobody's going to punish you for doing such a fine, daring thing."

Willie went to his mother's bedroom, took the extension telephone from the bedside table, and plugged it into the jackbox in his own room. He called the candy store in the Bronx. While he was waiting for an answer, he shoved the door shut with his foot. "May Wynn's not home," said a flat, vulgar voice, a woman with a foreign accent. "Try Circle 6-3475."

He called the other number. "Hotel Woodley, good morning," said the operator.

Willie knew the Woodley well: a shabby theatrical hotel on Forty-seventh Street. "May Wynn, please."

"Miss Wynn? One moment." There followed several repeated buzzes, and at last, "Hello?" But it was not May's voice. The voice was masculine.

"I'm trying to get Miss May Wynn's room," Willie said, with a horrid qualm.

"This is May's room. Who's calling?"

"My name is Willie Keith."

"Willie! Well, for Christ's sake! This is Marty Rubin, Willie, how the hell are you? Where are you?"

"I'm home."

"Home? Where? San Francisco?"

"I'm out on Long Island. Where's May?"

"She's here. This is terrific. Listen, Willie, did she know you were coming? She never said a word—— Just a second, I'll get her up——"

The pause was a long one. *"Hello! Willie!"*

"Hello, May. Sorry I woke you up——"

"Honey, don't be silly. I—I can't believe it! When did you get in?"

Willie had always disliked the threadbare "honey" of show-business chatter, and it grated on him especially when May used it, and more especially at this moment. Her voice was muffled and high, as it usually was when she had just awakened. "Flew in about an hour ago."

"Why didn't you let me know, honey? Gosh——"

"I thought I'd surprise you."

"I am surprised. I'm flabbergasted." There was a silence which was very dreadful to Willie. "Well, honey, when am I going to see you?" she said.

"Any time you want to."

"Oh, dear. Darling, you couldn't have picked a worse day. I have the grippe or some damn thing, and—we might have lunch—no, wait, there's something else—— Marty, when are we cutting that damned audition record? When can I get away? . . . Not till then? . . . Oh, Willie, it's such a mess! There's this radio show I have to cut a record for—it has to be today—I've been doping myself to try to get in some kind of shape—— Marty, honey can't we call it off? . . . Oh, Willie, you should have let me know——"

"Forget the whole thing. Don't get upset," Willie said, glaring at himself in the mirror of the closet door. "See you tomorrow, maybe."

"No, no! Honey, I'll be through around three—when, Marty?—three-thirty, Willie—meet me in the Brill Building, can you do that?"

"What and where is the Brill Building?"

"Oh, *Willie.* The Brill Building. Hell, I keep forgetting you're not a song plugger. Well, you know, across the street from the Rivoli—the big gray building—listen, it's the Sono-phono Studios, can you remember that? Sono-phono."

"Okay. Three-thirty. I'll be there. Don't you go to school any more?"

"Oh." May's voice became apologetic. "That. I'm afraid I've been playing hooky. I'll tell you all about it."

"See you later."

"Yes, honey."

Willie slammed the receiver so hard that the telephone went clattering off the table to the floor. He took off his civilian clothes, leaving them in a rumpled heap on a chair, and dressed in his uniform. He had two caps, a fairly new one, and the cap he always wore at sea, the gold trim of which was tarnished dull green. He selected the old cap and put a fresh cover on it, which set off more strikingly the tarnish of the ornaments.

The glory of Manhattan which Willie had seen from the airplane was nowhere visible at Broadway and Fiftieth Street when he came up out of the subway. It was the same old dirty crowded corner: here a cigar store, there an orange-drink stand, yonder a flickering movie marquee, everywhere people with ugly tired faces hurrying in a bitter wind that whirled flapping newspapers and little spirals of dry snow along the gutters. It was all as familiar to Willie as his hand.

The reception room of the Sono-phono Studios, some seven feet square, consisted of plasterboard walls, a plasterboard door in back, a green metal desk, and a very ugly receptionist with a plasterboard complexion, chewing a large wad of pink gum. "Yeah? What can I do for you?"

"I'm meeting May Wynn here."

"She ain't through. You can't go in, they're on mike."

Willie sat in the single yellow chair, opening his muffler and bridge coat. The receptionist glanced at his ribbons, counted the stars, and threw him an unsettling flirtatious leer. From behind the plasterboard he heard a man's voice, "Okay. Let's make this the master now." A small orchestra struck up, and then Willie heard her voice:

> *Don't throw*
> *Bo—kays at me——*

At once the heat and shabbiness of the *Caine* wardroom, and the hopeless hatred of Queeg, rushed into his mind, most incongruously mingled with sweet stirrings of his early love for May. An immense black sadness overcame him as the song went on. When it ended Marty Rubin opened the door and said, "Hi, Willie! Great to see you! Come on in!"

He was fatter than ever. His green suit was ill-chosen for his yellowish skin, and his tinted glasses were so thick that his eyes were distorted behind them to dots. He shook the lieutenant's hand. "You look marvelous, kid!"

May stood at the microphone, talking to two men in shirt sleeves. The musicians were packing their instruments. The studio was a bare room cluttered with cables and recording machines. Willie halted uncertainly inside the door. "He's here, May!" the agent called. She turned, ran to Willie, put an arm around his neck, and kissed him on the cheek.

"We'll get out of here in a few seconds, darling," she whispered. Willie stood with his back to the doorway, getting hotter in his heavy coat, while the girl talked for ten minutes with the agent and the men in shirt sleeves.

"I want a drink," May said, when they were alone at a table in the deserted upstairs room of Lindy's, "and then I want some breakfast."

"You're keeping queer hours—— What's that?" he said as May popped a white pill into her mouth.

"Aspirin. Feel my forehead." Her skin was hot. Willie looked at her with concern. She was haggard, her hair was carelessly pinned up on her head, and there were blue shadows under her eyes. She grinned sadly and a little defiantly. "I'm a mess, I know. You picked a great time to fall out of the sky, dear."

"You ought to be in bed, May."

"Bed is for those who can afford it—— Well, tell me about the war."

Instead Willie questioned her about herself. She was singing at a Fifty-second Street club, her first job in several weeks. Her father had been ill for half a year, and the fruit store, managed by her mother alone, was earning nothing. May was supporting the family. She had taken a room in a downtown hotel because she feared the long subway rides at night would give her pneumonia. "I'm kind of run down, Willie. School and night-club singing don't mix too well, after all. Sleep generally gets lost in the shuffle. I pass out on subways, in classes—it's awful."

"Are you giving up school?"

"No, no. I cut a lot of classes, that's all. I don't care. I don't want to be a Phi Bete. I just want to pick up some information. Let's talk French. I can talk French. *Avez-vous le crayon de ma tante?*"

She laughed. Her eyes seemed wild to Willie, and her expression was opaque. May drank off her coffee. "I've found out two things about my singing, Willie. First of all I haven't much talent—I really know that now—and secondly most of the other girl singers have even less. I can always scratch a living—until I become a hag, that is. Which, at the rate I'm going, will be next Tuesday. I'll tell you what. Let's go up to my room. I can lie down while we talk. I still have to sing tonight. Did I tell you that you are three times as good-looking as you used to be? You look more like a wolf than a bunny, now."

"You seemed to like the bunny——"

"Well, a wolf-like bunny is more nearly right. I think I'm a little loopy, dear. A martini before the first meal of the day is not a good idea. I must remember that. Let's go."

In the taxicab she suddenly kissed him on the mouth. He smelled the gin. "Do I utterly disgust you?" she said.

"What kind of question——"

"Sick, tacky—look at this dress, of all dresses I had to put on this thing—mixed up with crummy musicians in a crummy studio—we are star-crossed lovers, Willie. See, I told you I'd learn to read and write. Star-crossed lovers. Come, gentle night, give me my Willie. And when he shall die, take him and cut him out in lit-tle stars, and he will make the face of heaven so fine that all the world will be in love with night. Did you think I was living with Marty Rubin, dear, by any chance?"

Willie's face flushed. "All this on one martini?"

"And a temperature of, I would say, 101.8. We'll take it when we get home, just to check. Really, though, I don't call that very good luck. You telephone me after coming halfway round the world and a man answers. Star-crossed wires. If Shakespeare answers, hang up."

The taxi swerved sharply around a corner and she leaned against him. The smell of her hair was the same; sweet, exciting. His arm tightened around her. Her body was thinner than he remembered. She said, "Darling, tell all the little lieutenants on the *Caine* never to surprise their girls. Tell them to give their girls plenty, plenty of warning, so that they can get the men out of their apartments, and rest up for a week, and go to a beauty parlor, and work over all their little stupid bags of tricks. I am terribly impressed by your battle stars, Willie. You were never hurt, were you, sweet?"

"Not even close——"

"Do you know something? I have a slave. Real slave. Name of Marty Rubin. He has never heard of the Emancipation Proclamation. See the advantage of a college education! Promise me you won't tell him that Lincoln freed the slaves. Uncle Tom Rubin. I think I'd be dead if not for him, or have a couple of parents in the poorhouse, anyway. Wow! Home so soon?"

Her apartment was a wretched little room on a dark areaway. The bedcover, the rug, the chairs were worn to the gray threads, and paint hung in patches on the ceiling. She closed the door and kissed him passionately. "You're as big as a bear in that coat. Not bad for three dollars, this room, is it? Special favor to Marty that they let me have it. Sorry, there's no bathroom. Down the hall. Well, first of all, let's see about the good old temperature. Maybe I don't have to get into bed. Here, read my book of fame."

She watched him drolly, the thermometer pressed between her lips, while he turned over the leaves of the scrapbook. It was full of one-paragraph clippings. Featured on a page by itself, with an arc of gold stars pasted over it, was a long fulsome write-up, including a picture of May, from the New York *Daily News. May Wynn Latest Threat to Dinah Shore,* it was headed.

"I'd hate to tell you what I had to do to get that," May said through her teeth, biting the thermometer. She added,

"Not what you're thinking, however, from your expression." Willie hastily changed his expression with an effort of his face muscles. "Well, now, let's see." May held up the thermometer toward the window. "Why, not bad at all. Mere 101.2 Let's go horseback riding in Central Park."

"You get into bed. I'm going to call a doctor——"

"Now, dear, don't go rushing around making kettles of hot water and bathing your arms to the elbows. I've seen a doctor. I'm supposed to rest and take aspirin. The question is, what's the schedule? When do you have to go home to your mother?"

"The night is ours." Willie sounded insulted.

"Oh? That's wonderful." She came to him and put her arms around his neck. "Is it all right if I lie down, then? We can have a nice old chat—and I'll be all bright and beautiful for the evening."

"Of course."

"Well, then, you look out of the window for a minute. It's a gorgeous view." Willie obeyed. On the window sill across the air shaft, three feet away, were two bottles of milk, a tomato, and a package of butter, surrounded by little ridges of snow. The brick wall was black with grime. Behind him he heard quick feminine rustlings.

"All right, dear. Come and sit by me." May's dress and stockings were draped on a chair, and she was propped up on the bed, under the covers, in a gray rough bathrobe. She smiled wanly. "Hedy Lamarr, all set up for the seduction scene."

"Darling," Willie said, sitting and taking her cold hand, "I'm sorry I came at such a bad time—sorry I didn't let you know——"

"Willie, you're not half as sorry as I am. Only it's done, and there's no help for it." She clasped his hand between hers. "Dearest, I know you must have pictured me in a warm pink vacuum at home, writing you letters, and reading yours over a thousand times, and otherwise in a state of suspended animation. But that isn't what happens. Fathers get pleurisy, and stockings get holes in them, and I have to scratch for cash, and fellows make passes at me—which I can't even get too mad about because it proves I still have a stock in trade—but I've really been a pretty good girl." She looked up at him with shy weary eyes. "I even pulled a B-minus average on the mid-years. Got an A in Lit."

"Look, why don't you sleep? You knocked yourself out at that audition——"

"Which was a bust—I couldn't even see straight, waiting for you to show up——"

"Do you have to work tonight?"

"Yes, dear. Every night except Monday, the contract says—if Mama and Papa and May are going to eat—a lot of girls are just dying to substitute——"

"Why didn't you let me know you were in trouble? I have money——"

A look of fear came over May's face. She pressed his palm. "Willie, I'm no charity case—maybe I'm overplaying the scene, trying to cover up for looking so ratty. I'm in fine shape financially and every other way—I just have a lousy cold, see—haven't you ever had a cold?" She began to cry, pressing his hand against her eyes. Warm drops trickled down in his fingers. He held her close, and kissed her hair. "Maybe I'd better sleep. I am really shot," she said, in a low dry voice, her eyes hidden against his hand, "if I stoop to turning on the tears." She looked up at him and smiled. "What would you like to read? *Troilus and Cressida? The Crime of Sylvestre Bonnard* in French? Trevelyan's *History of England?* They're in that pile on the table——"

"I'll take care of myself. You turn in."

"Why don't you go out and catch a movie? Better than sitting around in this mousehole, listening to me snore——"

"I'll stay here." He kissed her.

She said, "This is wrong. You'll catch God knows what plagues."

"Go to sleep."

"Some home-coming. A weepy, drunken, jabbering sweetheart, passing out on you in a roach trap——" May slid down into the bed, and closed her eyes, murmuring,

"I have amazing powers of recuperation. Wake me at seven-thirty. You may have to dump over the bed, but get me up. I'll surprise you—just pretend we're meeting for the first time at seven-thirty——" She was asleep in a minute, her hair tumbled loosely, dark red on the white pillow. Willie looked for a long time at the pallid face smudged with lipstick. Then he took up *Troilus and Cressida,* opened it at random, and began to read. But as soon as he struck a speech about love, halfway down the page, his mind wandered off.

He was quite fixed now in his decision to break with May. Seeing her again had confirmed it. He was certain it was right. He estimated himself, as truthfully as he could and with no great pride in the result, as a rather mediocre middle-class intellectual. His ambition went no further than the life upholstered with the good things that money bought, and that meant his mother's or his wife's money, not university money. He wanted a wife, in the dim future, of his own kind, smooth, sweet, pretty, and educated, with all the small graces of good background and a moneyed family. May Wynn was bright, yes, unbearably attractive, maybe, though not at this moment. She was also vulgar, brassy, and overperfumed in the show-business way, and she had allowed him all sorts of liberties from the first, and had slept with him. She seemed a little soiled to him, a little cheap; and in every way jagged and wrong for his planned future. And she was a Catholic. May's disclaimer of any devotion to her faith had not convinced Willie. He was inclined to believed the general notion that Catholics never wholly abandon their religion and are capable of sudden great plunges back into it. He was very unwilling to complicate his life and the lives of his children with such a disturbing possibility.

Whether all this might have been swept away had he come back to a girl triumphant and gorgeous, the star of a hit musical comedy, it is impossible to say. He was at her bedside now in a shabby room in a dirty hotel, and she was sick and messy and broke. The schoolbooks made her seem more pathetic, not more desirable. She had made a bid to reform herself nearer to his tastes, and it had been a feeble failure. It was all finished.

She was sleeping with her mouth open, and her breath came quick, irregular, and noisy. The gray bathrobe had pulled open, uncovering her bosom. The sight made Willie uncomfortable. He pulled the blanket to her chin, and slumped in the armchair, and dozed.

"Am I seeing things?" said Willie, when the cab pulled up in front of the Grotto Club. "Where's the Tahiti? Where's the Yellow Door? Isn't this where——"

"This place used to be the Yellow Door," said May. "The Tahiti is gone. That Chinese restaurant used to be the Tahiti. Nothing lasts long on this godforsaken street."

"What happened to Mr. Dennis?"

"Died," May said, stepping out into the bitter dusty night wind.

She had been subdued and listless through dinner; and listlessly she waved at Willie as she vanished from his sight through the dressing-room curtain. He was amazed when she came out to sing half an hour later. She was fresh-faced and radiant. The customers, crowded in the smoky cellar between narrow walls of papier-mâché rocks interspersed with tanks of gloomy gray fish, listened in silence, and applauded loudly after each number. She acknowledged the applause with gleaming eyes and a genuine girlish smile, and sang on. She performed five numbers with undimming verve, gathered her full green skirt, and swept off the little stage as bouncily as a gymnast. "How does she do it?" he said to Rubin, who had arrived midway in the act, and was pressed beside him on the wall seat behind an infinitesimal table.

"Well, you ought to know, Willie, the show must go on. She's a pro. The customers aren't paying any less for their beer because May has a cold."

May came to their table with a yellow gauzy shawl around her throat and a black velvet jacket over her shoulders. Rubin rose and kissed her cheek. "Honey, maybe you ought to have colds more often. You're really putting out tonight."

"I feel fine—— Think I'm any better, Willie?"

"You're wonderful, May——"

"Don't lay it on, I'll know you're lying—— Where are you sneaking off to, Marty?"

"I have other clients. Get her to bed after the two o'clock show, Willie."

Willie sat on the little hard seat for five hours, talking to May or listening to her sing. Customers came and went, but it almost seemed that the departing ones handed their faces to the newcomers at the door to wear, so much alike did they all look. The air grew staler and the crowd noisier, and the fish in the tanks sank to the bottom and lay motionless, gaping and goggling in the slime. All charm had departed out of night-club surroundings for Willie. To earn a living amid such fusty make-believe struck him as a worse fate, even, than perpetual steaming on the *Caine*.

He told May nothing of the mutiny, though he took pleasure in making her laugh and gasp at stories of Queeg. She had recuperated startlingly. Her manner was bright and lively, and in the cellar gloom, with her make-up, she seemed rosily healthy. But Willie had been too scared in the afternoon by her appearance to feel free with her. The evening went by in restrained, good-humored, evasive chatter. May accepted his tone and followed it.

When they came into her squalid room back at the hotel, it was a quarter to three. Willie was suppressing yawns, and his eyes smarted. Without a word they took off their coats, lay on the bed, and kissed hungrily and wildly for a few minutes. Her forehead, her hands, felt hot to Willie's lips, but he went on kissing her anyway. At last with a common impulse, they slowed and stopped. She looked him full in the face, her eyes shining in the dim light of the floor lamp.

"Willie, we're all washed up, aren't we?"

It is the worst question in the world. Willie didn't have to answer. The answer was on his miserable face. May said, "Then why are we doing this?"

"You're right, as usual. I am a swine. Let's stop."

"No. I still love to kiss you, unfortunately." And she kissed him again, several times. But the spoken words had snapped the sweetness. They sat up, and Willie went to the armchair. "If only I hadn't had a cold," May said dolefully.

"May! May! This afternoon made no difference—it's just the kind of guy I am———"

"Darling, you don't know. It might have made all the difference in the world. Nobody loves a sick cat. However, it's all past history. It was an uphill struggle. Your letters were bad———"

"What can I say, May? You're the most wonderful girl I'll ever know———"

"Strangely enough, that's the truth. For you, I am. Only you're too young, or you love your mother too much, or something." She rose, and opened the zipper of her dress in an absent-minded way; went to her closet and changed into her bathrobe, not troubling to hide herself. The glimpse of her young body in the clinging slip was very painful to Willie. He wanted to gather her in his arms as he wanted to breathe, and he knew that it was absolutely impossible now. She faced him, her hands deep in the pockets of her robe. There was a tremor of uncertainty and pain about her eyes and mouth. "It's all quite definite, I suppose?"

"Yes, May."

"You don't love me?"

"It's all mixed up and lousy, May. Talking won't help it———"

"Maybe, but I'd like to tie up the bundle all neat and proper before I throw it into the cellar. If you don't love me, that does it, of course. You kiss as though you love me. Explain that."

Willie was unable to say that he loved May's mouth, but not enough to drag her through life with him—though that would have been putting it in the simplest terms. "I don't know what love is, May. It's a word. You'll always be the image of desire for me. That's a fact, but there's more to life than that. I don't think we'd be happy together. Not because of any lack in you. Call me a snobbish prig and let it go at that. Everything that's wrong between us is wrong with me———"

"Is it because I'm poor, or dumb, or Catholic, or what? Can't you put it in words, so I'll know?"

There is only one way to get off this particular kind of griddle. Willie looked at the floor and said nothing, while long seconds of silence ticked off. Every second brought another stab of hot shame and embarrassment, and his self-respect gushed out of the wounds. May managed to say at last, in an unembittered tone, though a shaky one, "Well, all right, Willie. It must be a load off your mind, anyway." She opened a drawer in a peeling, dirty bureau, and took out a bottle and a pillbox. "I'm going down the hall to doctor myself. I won't be long. Want to wait?"

"May——"

"Dear, don't look so tragic. It's not world-shaking. We're both going to live."

Willie, hardly aware of what he was doing, picked up *Troilus and Cressida* and read a couple of pages. He started guiltily when May came in, and put the book aside. Her eyes were red, and with her make-up removed, she was very pale. She smiled slightly. "Go right on reading, dear. Give me a cigarette though. I haven't dared to smoke all day, thought my throat would close up." She took an ashtray to the bed and lay back against the cushions with a sigh. "Ah, that tastes wonderful. Temperature, by the way, is down. Just a little over a hundred. Nothing like night-club air for what ails you. ♦ . . What are you going to do after the war, Willie? Going back to piano playing?"

"I don't think so."

"You shouldn't. I think you should teach."

" 'Those who can, do; those who can't, teach'—eh?"

"The world couldn't exist without teachers. It just seems right for you. I can see you in a university town, leading a nice quiet life, plugging Dickens faithfully as the years slip by——"

"Sounds heroic, doesn't it?"

"Willie dear, everyone does what he can do best. You talked me into wanting to read. It was quite an achievement."

"Well, I've thought of it, May. It would mean going back to school for a year——"

"Your mama will certainly see you through, won't she? . . . Especially *now*." May yawned like an animal. "Sorry, dear——"

Willie stood. "I don't blame you for being bored with me—and you must be dead——"

"Oh, sit down. I'm not bored with you, and I'm not angry at you." She yawned again, covered her mouth, and laughed. "Isn't it silly? I ought to be wailing and tearing my hair. My energy must be all out. Willie, I've gotten pretty used to this idea, really. I had a little hope at San Francisco—at Yosemite, I mean—but not after you talked to your mother and sent me home. However, it's done me no harm to have someone to be true to——"

"May—I knew what Yosemite meant to you—to me——"

"Now, dear, I didn't bring it up to torture your conscience. We both meant well. I was trying to trap you, I guess. I don't know. I'll have to take some psychology courses to figure myself out——"

"My mother doesn't hate you, May—it isn't her doing——"

"Willie sweetheart," said May, with a little tired sharpness. "I know exactly, but exactly, how your mother feels about me. Stay off that ground."

They talked some more, not much. She came to the door with him and kissed him affectionately. "You're very, very good-looking, all the same," she whispered.

"I'll call you tomorrow, May. Keep well." He rang for the elevator. She stood in the doorway, looking at him. When the elevator door was opened by a Negro in shirt sleeves, she suddenly said, "Will I see you any more?"

"Sure. I'll talk to you tomorrow. Good night."

"Good-by, Willie."

He did not call her the next day, nor the day after that, nor the day after that. He went to matinees with his mother, to dinner with his mother, to shows at night with his mother; he visited the family with his mother. When

Mrs. Keith urged him to go out by himself he glumly declined. One afternoon he went to Columbia and took a solitary walk through Furnald Hall. The incessant salutes of baby-faced midshipmen in khaki at first flattered, then depressed him. Nothing had changed in the lobby. Here was the leather couch on which he had told his father of his forty-eight demerits; there was the phone booth where he had talked to May a hundred times—and there was the knot of impatient midshipmen outside it as always, and inside was the youngster with a crew haircut crooning and giggling into the telephone. Dead lost time hung in the air. Willie hurried out of the building—it was midafternoon, gray and windy, and his mother would not be at the restaurant for a couple of hours—and so he went into a dim, shabby, empty bar on Broadway, and rapidly drank four scotch and sodas, which only seemed to make him a little dizzy.

His Uncle Lloyd joined them for dinner at Twenty-one. A banker in civilian life, he was now a colonel in Army public information, and he liked to talk about his experiences in the artillery in World War I. He was very grave about the mutiny. He told Willie long stories to prove how in the artillery he had had much worse commanding officers than Queeg, and had always conducted himself with true martial forebearance and loyalty. It was clear that he disapproved of Willie and thought he was in serious trouble. Mrs. Keith pressed him for a promise to help her son, but Uncle Lloyd only said he would talk to some of his Navy friends and see what the best procedure would be.

"Maybe they won't court-martial you after all, Willie," he said. "If this other fellow, this Maryk fellow, gets himself acquitted I guess that'll be the end of it. I hope you've learned your lesson by this time. War isn't a pink tea. Unless you can learn to take the rough with the smooth, why, you're just not worth a damn to your country in an emergency." So saying he departed for Washington, where he maintained a suite at the Shoreham.

Saturday night Willie was in his room, dressing to go to the opera. His eye fell on his wrist watch, and he

realized that in twelve hours he would be on an airplane,
returning to the *Caine* and the court-martial. His arm
reached around stiffly, like a lèver in an automatic
phonograph, and picked up the telephone. He called the
Woodley.

"May? How are you? It's Willie."

"Hello, dear! I'd given you up——"

"Is your cold better?"

"All gone. I'm in fine shape."

"I'm going back tomorrow morning. I'd like to talk to
you."

"I'm working tonight, Willie——"

"May I come to the club?"

"Sure."

"It'll be around midnight."

"All right."

It had never seemed possible to Willie that *Don Giovan-
ni* could be tedious. The opera had always been a wonder-
land of sound in which time stopped and the world dissolved in pure beauty. On this night he thought Leporello
was a coarse clown, the baritone a scratchy-throated old
man, Zerlina a screechy amateur, and the whole plot a
bore. He strained his eyes at his watch in the middle of
his favorite arias. At last it was done. "Mother," he said
as they came out of the lobby to the slushy street, "do
you mind if I go on the town by myself for a while? I'll
see you back home."

Her face showed how well she understood, and how
worried she was. "Willie—our last night?"

"I won't be late, Mother." He felt able to stuff her
bodily into a taxicab if she argued. She must have known,
because she signaled for a cab herself.

"Have a wonderful time, dear."

May was singing when he came into the crowded Grotto.
He stood at the bar, looking around at the admiring male
faces turned at the singer, his soul full of bitterness. There
was no place to sit when the show was over. She took
him by the hand and led him to her dressing room. The
glare of light in the hot, closetlike room made him blink.
He leaned against the make-up table. May sat in the chair

and looked up at him, glowing with an unfathomable sweet inner attraction, all different from her outside of rouge and white shoulders and round bosom half exposed by her tight singer's dress.

"I didn't tell you about something last time," Willie said. "I want to know what you think." He described the mutiny and the investigation to her in long detail. It felt like confessing; his spirit brightened as he talked. May listened calmly. "What do you want me to say, Willie?" she said when he was finished.

"I don't know, May. What do you think of it? What shall I do? What's going to happen?"

She heaved a long sigh. "Is that why you came tonight? To tell me about that?"

"I wanted you to know about it."

"Willie, I don't know much about the Navy. But it doesn't seem to me you have to do anything. The Navy is a pretty smart outfit. They won't condemn any of you for trying to save your ship. At worst, you made a well-meaning mistake of judgment. That isn't a crime——"

"It was mutiny, May——"

"Oh, hell. Who do you think you are, Fletcher Christian? Did you chain Queeg up and set him adrift in a boat? Did you pull knives and guns on him? *I* think he was crazy, whatever the doctors say—nutty as a fruitcake. Willie dear, *you* couldn't mutiny—not even against your mother, let alone a ship's captain——"

They both laughed a little. Though May's verdict was the same as his mother's, it filled Willie with hope and good cheer, whereas Mrs. Keith's opinion had seemed emotional and stupid. "Okay, May. I don't know why I had to load you down with my miseries—— Thanks."

"When are you leaving?"

"Seven o'clock in the morning."

May rose, and slipped the bolt on her door. "Noisiest musicians in the world work here." She came to Willie and put her arms around him. They exchanged a fearfully long, blind wild kiss. "That's all," May said, pushing herself out of his arms. "Remember it the rest of your life. You'll have to go. I find it hurts to have you around."

She opened the door; Willie walked out and threaded through the jostling dancers to the street.

He still had not the slightest understanding of why he had really come; he blamed himself for a late flare of desire crudely masked as a need for advice. He had no way of recognizing the very common impulse of a husband to talk things over with his wife.

Next day his plane left on schedule, in a sunny morning. His mother waved bravely from the sight-seer's boardwalk as the plane took to the air. Willie stared down at the buildings of Manhattan, trying to find the Hotel Woodley; but it was lost among the dingy piles of midtown.

33 · The Court-Martial—
First Day

Naval Courts and Boards opens with a melancholy section entitled "Charges and Specifications." It is only a hundred twenty-three pages long; not half as long as a twenty-five-cent mystery novel; and within that small compass the Navy has discussed all the worst errors, vice, follies, and crimes into which men may fall. It begins with Making a Mutiny and ends with Unlawful Use of a Distilling Apparatus. In between are such bloody offenses as Adultery, Murder, Rape, and Maiming, and also such nasty peccadilloes as Exhibiting an Obscene Photograph. These are sad, wearying, grisly pages, the more so for their matter-of-fact, systematic tone.

This shopper's list of crime, however, did not provide a charge or specification for the peculiar offense of Lieutenant Stephen Maryk. Captain Breakstone had quick-ly perceived that, though the affair was more like a mutiny than anything else, Maryk's invoking of Article 184 and his subsequent legalistic conduct made a conviction for mutiny unlikely. It was the queerest sort of twilight situation. In the end he fixed on the catch-all charge provided for rare or complicated offenses, "Conduct to the Prejudice of Good Order and Discipline," and with much care he drew up the following specification:

In that Lieutenant Stephen Maryk, USNR, on or about December 18, 1944, aboard the U.S.S. Caine, willfully, without proper authority, and without justifiable cause, did relieve from his duty as commanding officer Lieutenant Commander Philip Francis Queeg, USN, the duly assigned commanding officer of said ship, who was then and there in lawful exercise of his command, the United States then being in a state of war.

The judge advocate, Lieutenant Commander Challee, expected no difficulty at all in proving this specification. He was an earnest, bright young officer, holding his high rank on a temporary war promotion. A slight undercurrent of guilt was running through his days in San Francisco. He had requested the legal duty after several years at sea, because he wanted to spend time with his beautiful wife, a photographer's model; and he was a little ashamed of having had his request granted. He therefore pursued his duties with exceptional zeal, and he honestly regarded the conviction of Maryk, at the moment, as his personal war aim.

Challee estimated that the prosecution had a prima facie case. A charge of mutiny, he knew, would have been harder to prove. But Captain Breakstone's mild specification, in his view, was a plain description of the plain facts. The defense could not possibly deny that the event had occurred; Maryk had signed logs describing it. The key words were *without proper authority and without justifiable cause*. To establish their truth, Challee simply had to prove that Queeg was not and had never been a madman. He had the deposition of Captain Weyland in Ulithi, who had interviewed the captain of the *Caine* right after the mutiny. Three Navy psychiatrists of the San Francisco hospital, who had examined Queeg for weeks, were ready to testify in court that he was a sane, normal, intelligent man. At the investigation twenty chiefs and enlisted men of the *Caine* had averred that they had never seen Queeg do anything crazy or questionable. Not one officer or man, except the two parties to the mutiny, Keith and Stilwell, had spoken unfavorably of the captain. Challee had arranged for the appearance of several presentable sailors and chiefs to repeat their testimony.

Against this array there was only Maryk's so-called medical log. The board of investigation had dismissed it as "a whining collection of trivial gripes," commenting that all it proved was Maryk's latent and longstanding disloyalty. Challee was confident that the court would feel the same way. Every officer past the rank of junior-grade lieutenant had served, at one time or another, under an oppressive eccentric. It was simply a hazard of military life. Challee was fond of telling anecdotes which topped anything in Maryk's log.

The judge advocate knew that Greenwald had only one good point of attack: the question of criminal intent. He anticipated an eloquent harping on the fact that Maryk had acted for the good of the service, however mistaken his diagnosis of Queeg had been. Challee was fully prepared to demolish the specious sophistry which would follow, that Maryk was innocent of any offense.

He reasoned that Maryk, by willfully ignoring the whole weight of military tradition, and summoning up the mutinous effrontery to depose his commanding officer on the basis of such a wild error of judgment, had ipso facto convicted himself of "conduct to the prejudice of good order and discipline." If this were not true, if the precedent set by Maryk were to go unpunished, the entire Navy chain of command was in jeopardy! Any commanding officer who seemed queer to his exec was in danger of being summarily relieved. Challee was certain that a court of officers, especially a court headed by the austere martinet, Captain Blakely, would see that point. He counted, therefore, on a quick, satisfying victory over Barney Greenwald.

His estimate of the case was a good one. He erred only in his guess of Greenwald's probable strategy.

Willie Keith returned to the *Chrysanthemum* about eleven o'clock in the morning. He dropped his bags in his room and looked through the other rooms for *Caine* officers, but found only empty rumpled bunks. Then he heard faintly from the shower a bellowing of

> *Parlez-moi d'amour*
> *Rrrrrredites-moi des choses tendres . . .*

and he knew that Keefer was back. He found the novelist drying himself before a mirror, standing on wooden clogs. " '*Ja vous aim—uh*——' Willie, you old Dickens lover! How are you, my lad?"

They shook hands. Keefer's tanned body was scrawny, and his face was drawn as though he had not eaten in a week, but he was gay, and his large eyes gleamed oddly.

"Where's everybody, Tom?"

"Hither and yon. Ship's leaving drydock today so most of the boys are aboard. Steve's out with his defense counsel somewhere——"

"Whom did he get?"

"Some lieutenant off a carrier. Used to be a lawyer."

"Good?"

"Can't tell. Steve seems to like him. Mumbling, shambling kind of guy—— All kinds of hell breaking loose, Willie. Do you know about your pal Stilwell? He's gone crazy." Keefer flipped the towel around his shoulders and seesawed it briskly.

"What!"

"Diagnosis is acute melancholia. He's up at the base hospital. He was getting kind of funny there aboard ship, you know——"

Willie remembered very well Stilwell's brooding, sallow, pained face. Twice on the homeward voyage the sailor had asked to be relieved of the helm because of a blinding headache. "What happened, Tom?"

"Well, I wasn't here. The story is that he took to his

sack and just stayed there for three days, not answering musters, not going up for meals. Said he had a headache. Finally they had to carry him to the hospital. He was all limp and foul, Bellison says——" Willie wrinkled his face in horror. "Well, it was in the cards, Willie. One look at him and you know he's one of these tense burning-up-inside ones. And no education, and a year of riding by Queeg, and the mixed-up emotional background, and on top of it all a general court for mutiny hanging over him —it isn't mutiny, any more, by the way. That's another thing—— Got a cigarette? . . . Thanks."

Keefer wrapped the towel around his middle and clacked out to the saloon, exhaling a gray cloud. Willie followed, saying eagerly, "What's all this about the mutiny?"

"Steve's going to be tried on a charge of conduct to prejudice of good order and discipline. I told you that dried-up captain was out of his head, recommending trial for mutiny. I still don't think you guys have anything to worry about. The legal boys know they have a damn shaky case——"

"What about Stilwell? Is he going to appear, or what?"

"Willie, the guy's a vegetable. They're going to give him electric-shock therapy, I hear—— How'd you make out on leave? Did you marry the girl?"

"No."

"I had a pretty good leave," said the novelist, pulling on white drawers. "I think I've sold my novel."

"Hey, Tom! That's swell! What publisher?"

"Chapman House. Nothing signed yet, you know. But it looks okay——"

"Gosh, it wasn't finished yet, was it?"

"They read twenty chapters and an outline. First publishers I showed it to." The gunnery officer spoke casually, but powerful pride rayed out of his face. Willie regarded him with round eyes. The growing pile of yellow manuscript in Keefer's desk had been half a joke, after all. Novelists were mythical figures to Willie—dead giants like Thackeray, or impossibly remote, brilliant rich men like Sinclair Lewis and Thomas Mann.

"Will—will they give you a big advance, Tom?"

"Well, as I say, nothing's definite. If it all works out, five hundred or a thousand dollars." Willie whistled. "It's not much," Keefer said, "but for an incomplete first novel, well——"

"It's marvelous, Tom, marvelous! I hope it's a huge best seller! It will be, too. I told you long ago I wanted the millionth copy, autographed. That still goes."

Keefer's face relaxed in a foolish rosy smile. "Well, don't rush things, Willie—nothing's signed——"

Steve Maryk's spirit failed him in the very first moments of the court-martial, when the members of the court were sworn. Seven officers stood on a dais in a semicircle behind a polished red-brown bench, their right arms raised, staring with religious gravity at Challee as he intoned the oath from a battered copy of *Courts and Boards*. Behind them on the wall between the wide windows was a large American flag. Outside, green-gray tops of eucalyptus trees stirred in the morning sunlight, and beyond them the blue bay danced with light. It is a cruel unconscious trick of planning that has placed the court-martial room of Com Twelve on Yerba Buena Island, in such fair surroundings, with such a beckoning view. The square gray room seems all the more confining. The flag hangs between the eyes of the accused and the free sunlight and water, and its red and white bars are bars indeed.

Maryk's eyes were drawn to the face of the president of the court, Captain Blakely, who stood at the center of the bench, squarely in front of the flag. It was an alarming face; a sharp nose, a mouth like a black line, and small far-seeing eyes under heavy eyebrows, with a defiant, distrustful glare. Blakely was quite gray, and he had a sagging dry pouch under his jaw, bloodless lips, and shadowy wrinkles around the eyes. Maryk knew his reputation: a submariner, up from the ranks, beached by a heart condition, the toughest disciplinarian of Com Twelve. Maryk was shaking when he sat down after the oath, and it was the face of Blakely that had made him shake.

One regular lieutenant commander and five lieutenants made up the rest of the board. They had the look of any six naval officers passing at random in a BOQ lobby. Two of the lieutenants were reserve doctor; two of them were regulars of the line; one was a reserve of the line.

The large wall clock over Challee's desk ticked around from ten o'clock to quarter of eleven while various legal ceremonies, incomprehensible to Maryk, were performed. For his first witness, Challee called Lieutenant Commander Philip Francis Queeg.

The orderly went out. Everyone in the room watched the door. The ex-captain of the *Caine* entered, tanned, clear-eyed, in a new blue uniform, the sleeve stripes bright gold. Maryk had not seen him for almost two months. The change was startling. His last vivid recollection was of a little stooped potbellied figure in a gray life jacket and wet khakis, clinging to the engine telegraph, the bristly face green and twisted with fear. The man before him was erect, confident, and good-looking—and youthful, despite the few blond strands over a pink scalp. Maryk's nerves were jolted.

Queeg took his seat on a raised platform in the center of the room. His manner during the opening questions was courteous and firm. Never one did he glance in Maryk's direction, though the exec sat to the right of him, only a few feet away, behind the defense desk.

Challee went quickly to the morning of the typhoon, and asked the ex-captain to narrate the events in his own words. The reply of Queeg was a coherent, rapid sketch, in formal language, of the mutiny. Maryk admitted to himself that the facts were presented correctly; the external facts. Slight shadings of what had been said and done, and, of course, a complete omission of any details of how the captain had looked and behaved, sufficed to turn the whole picture inside out. As Queeg told the story, he had simply made every effort to hold fleet course and speed, and in face of worsening weather had managed to do so right up to the moment when his executive officer had un-expectedly run amuck and seized command. Thereafter, by staying on the bridge and judiciously suggesting necessary maneuvers to the frenzied exec, he had brought the ship safely through the storm.

The court members followed the account with sympathetic interest. Once Captain Blakely transferred a long ominous stare to the defendant. Before Queeg was finished Maryk had totally despaired. He looked to his counsel with frightened eyes. Greenwald doodled with a red crayon on a pad, drawing multitudes of little fat pink pigs.

"Commander," said Challee, "can you account in any way for your executive officer's act?"

"Well," said Queeg calmly, "it was a rather serious situation. The wind was force 10 to 12, the waves were mountainous, and the ship naturally was laboring very badly. Mr. Maryk had shown evidences of growing nervousness and instability all morning. I think when we took that last bad roll he simply went into panic and proceeded to act irrationally. He acted under the delusion that he and he alone could save the ship. His worst weakness was conceit about his seamanship."

"Was the *Caine* in grave danger at that moment?"

"I wouldn't say so, no sir. Of course a typhoon is an extreme hazard at all times, but the ship had ridden well up to that moment and continued to ride well afterward."

"Have you ever been mentally ill, sir?"

"No, sir."

"Were you ill in any way when Mr. Maryk relieved you?"

"I was not."

"Did you protest the relief?"

"As forcefully as I could."

"Did you attempt to resume command?"

"Repeatedly."

"Did you warn your executive officer of the consequences of his act?"

"I told him he was performing a mutinous act."

"What was his reply?"

"That he expected to be court-martialed, but was going to retain command anyway."

"What was the attitude of Lieutenant Junior Grade Keith, the officer of the deck?"

"He was in a state of panic as bad as Maryk's or worse. He consistently backed up Maryk."

"What was the attitude of the rest of the officers?"

"They were perplexed and submissive. Under the circumstances I don't suppose they had any alternative."

"What was the attitude of the helmsman?"

"Stilwell I considered the worst troublemaker on the ship. He was emotionally unbalanced, and for some reason was very devoted to Lieutenant Junior Grade Keith. He gladly participated in defying my orders."

"Where is Stilwell at present?"

"I understand he is in the psychiatric ward of the hospital here, with a diagnosis of acute melancholia."

Challee glanced at the court. "Is there anything else, Commander Queeg, that you care to state in connection with the events of 18 December aboard the *Caine?*"

"Well, I have thought a lot about it all, of course. It's the gravest occurrence in my career, and the only questionable one that I'm aware of. It was an unfortunate freak accident. If the OOD had been anyone but Keith, and the helmsman anyone but Stilwell, it would not have happened. Keefer or Harding or Paynter would have repudiated Maryk's orders and probably snapped him out of it in a hurry. A normal sailor at the helm would have disregarded both officers and obeyed me. It was just bad luck that those three men—Maryk, Keith, and Stilwell—were combined against me at a crucial time. Bad luck for me, and worse luck for them."

Maryk took the crayon from Greenwald's hand as Queeg spoke and scribbled on the pad, *I can prove I wasn't panicky*. The lawyer wrote underneath, *Okay. May not be necessary,* and around both statements he drew a large pig.

"The court would like to question the witness," said Blakely. "Commander Queeg, how long have you been in the naval service?"

"I am completing my fourteenth year, sir."

"In that time you have taken all the prescribed physical and mental examinations incident to entrance to the Academy, graduation, commissioning, promotion, and so forth?"

"Yes, sir."

"Does your medical record contain any entry reflecting in any way any history of illness, mental or physical?"

"It does not, sir. My tonsils were removed in the fall of 1938. That is the only entry that isn't routine."

"Have you ever had an unsatisfactory fitness report, or any letter of reprimand or admonishment, Commander Queeg?"

"Negative, sir. I have one letter of commendation in my jacket."

"Now Commander, the court would like you to account if you can for Lieutenant Maryk's opinion that you were mentally ill, in view of your background and service record." Challee looked quickly at Greenwald, expecting an objection to the question. The defense counsel sat head down, drawing on the pad. He was left-handed; his scarred wrist and hand curved around the moving crayon.

"Well, sir, I will have to point out that I assumed the command of an extremely disorganized and dirty ship. I saw I was in for a long tough grind. I was determined to bring that ship up to snuff, no matter how unpleasant the process might be. I took many stern measures. Lieutenant Maryk, I may say, from the first opposed my will in this regard. He didn't see eye to eye with me at all on this idea of bringing the ship up to snuff, and maybe he thought I was crazy to keep trying. His questionable loyalty and slackness forced me to bear down all the harder, of course, and—well, I guess that's the picture, sir. And as I say, I'll stand on the *Caine's* battle record under my command, despite all the trouble Maryk gave me."

There was an exchange of looks among the president, Challee, and Greenwald. The defense counsel rose for cross-examination. "Commander Queeg," he said respectfully, looking down at the crayon in his hand, "I should like to ask you whether you have ever heard the expression, 'Old Yellowstain.' "

"In what connection?" Queeg looked genuinely puzzled.

"In any connection."

"Old Yellowstone?"

"Old Yellowstain, sir."

"I have not."

"You aren't aware, then, that all the officers of the *Caine* habitually referred to you as Old Yellowstain?"

The judge advocate jumped to his feet. "I object to the question! It is impertinent badgering of the witness."

Blakely said frostily, "How does defense counsel justify this line of questioning?"

"If the court please, it is the assigned duty of defense counsel to disprove the words in the specification—I quote —*without authority, and without justifiable cause.* It will be the contention of the defense that the authority of Lieutenant Maryk was Articles 184, 185, and 186 of the *Navy Regulations,* and that his justifiable cause was the conduct, demeanor, and decisions of Commander Queeg during his command of the *Caine.* The sobriquet 'Old Yellowstain' used by the officers of the *Caine,* and the facts out of which that sobriquet arose, will be extremely relevant. I quote Article 185: *the conclusion to relieve his commanding officer must be one which a reasonable, prudent and experienced officer would regard as necessary from the facts thus determined to exist.*"

The president of the court worked his eyebrows while Greenwald spoke. "The court will be cleared," he said.

In the corridor, Greenwald lounged against the wall and remarked to Maryk, "Captain Blakely doesn't like Jews. Intonations on the name 'Greenwald.' I have absolute pitch for those harmonies."

"Jesus," said Maryk miserably.

"It won't make any difference. You're not supposed to love Jews necessarily, just to give them a fair shake. I've always had a fair shake in the Navy, and I'll get it from Blakely, too, despite the eyebrows."

"I don't think I have a chance at this point," mourned the exec.

"Queeg's doing nobly," said Greenwald. The orderly summoned them back to the courtroom.

"Before ruling, the court wishes to caution defense counsel," Blakely said, staring very hard at Greenwald. "This is a most unusual and delicate case. The honor and career of an officer with an unblemished military record of fourteen years' standing, including long combatant duty, is involved. The court recognizes that the defense is compelled to try to challenge the competence of that officer. Nevertheless, all requirements of legal ethics and military respect and subordination remain in force. The defense counsel will have to bear full responsibility for the conduct of his case, including indiscretions and abuses of his cross-examination privileges." The president halted, and intensified his stare at Greenwald, who stood behind his desk, looking down at his array of pigs. "Subject to the foregoing comment, the judge advocate's objection is overruled. Court stenographer will repeat the question."

The little yeoman in whites said tonelessly, "You aren't aware then that all the officers of the *Caine* habitually referred to you as Old Yellowstain?"

Queeg's head was down between his shoulders, and he squinted up at the air in front of him. He suddenly looked much more familiar to Maryk. "I am not aware of it."

"Commander," said Greenwald, "how many fitness reports did you write on Lieutenant Maryk, disregarding the one after he relieved you?"

"Two, I believe."

"One in January, and one in July?"

"That is correct."

"Do you remember their contents?"

"Well, they weren't bad fitness reports, as I recall."

"Did you give him the highest classification—Outstanding—in both of them?"

"Well, that was at the beginning. I may have."

"Photostats of the reports are available to refresh your memory, Commander."

"I can say definitely, yes, I was still classifying him as outstanding that early in the game."

"Isn't that inconsistent with your statement that from the first he opposed your wishes regarding the *Caine?*"

"No, there's no inconsistency, it's all how you interpret it. I don't use fitness reports to revenge myself on officers who disagree with me, and Maryk did know his job and— maybe I shouldn't have said from the first. In fact he started off at first like a house afire but he funked off very fast. That morning-glory type is quite common and I'm not the first captain who was fooled at first."

"Did you state in your report of 1 July that he was qualified for command?"

"Well, as I say, he started off like a house afire. If you want to know how he ended up why don't you bring up his last fitness report?"

"You wrote that report, Commander, did you not, after he relieved you on the grounds of mental illness?"

"That made no difference at all," exclaimed Queeg, with a touch of the old nasal voice. "The fitness report is not an instrument of retaliation or revenge—not in my hands, it isn't!"

"No further questions at this time," Greenwald turned to the court. "Commander Queeg will be called as a witness for the defense." The eyebrows of the president signaled astonishment followed by resignation. Queeg was excused. He walked out of the room hurriedly.

"Call Lieutenant Thomas Keefer," said Challee. The novelist came marching in, shoulders thrown back, head tilted a little to one side, his eyes looking blankly ahead. After being sworn he sat in the witness chair and crossed his gangling legs. His elbows lay on the arm rests and his fingers were laced across his stomach. His foot danced slightly all the time he testified.

Challee brushed through the opening questions in a monotone, then said, "Now, Lieutenant Keefer, coming to the morning of 18 December—where were you at the time Captain Queeg was relieved?"

"In the charthouse on the bridge."

"What were you doing?"

"Well, the weather was pretty terrible. Several of us were there, officers and men. We wanted to be on hand in case an emergency arose, but naturally we stayed out of the pilothouse, not wanting to clutter it up."

"Describe how you learned that the captain had been relieved."

"Mr. Maryk passed the word for all officers to lay up to the wheelhouse. When we got there he told us that the captain was sick and he had assumed command."

"Where was Commander Queeg at the time?"

"In the wheelhouse."

"Did he concur with Maryk's statement?"

"He did not. He continually protested and warned us that if we complied with Maryk's orders we'd be guilty of collusion in mutiny."

"Did Captain Queeg show any external signs of being sick?"

"Well——" Keefer shifted in his seat and for a moment encountered Maryk's painfully intense glance. Maryk looked away angrily. "Well, I have to say that at the height of a typhoon nobody aboard a four-piper looks very well. He was wet, and tired, and very tense-looking——"

"Was he raving, or foaming, or giving any other common indications of insanity?"

"No."

"Did he speak incoherently or gibberingly when he protested being relieved?"

"No, he spoke clearly."

"Did he look any worse than, say, Lieutenant Keith?"

"No, sir."

"Or Maryk?"

"I guess not. We were all tired, dripping, and knocked about."

"What was your response to Maryk's announcement?"

"Well, things were happening very fast and in a confused way. Captain Queeg was talking to us when the capsized *George Black* was sighted. Maryk began to maneuver to pick up survivors and for an hour that was all anyone thought about."

"Did you make any effort to persuade Maryk to restore Queeg to command?"

"I did not."

"Were you next senior officer to Maryk?"

"I was."

"Didn't you feel the seriousness of the situation?"

"I certainly did, sir."

"Didn't you realize that Captain Queeg's warning about collusion in mutiny was well founded?"

"I did."

"Why did you take no remedial action?"

"I wasn't present when the captain was relieved. I didn't know what he might have done in a critical moment to convince the executive officer that he was sick. And everyone was concentrating on saving first the *Black* survivors and then our own ship. There was no time for arguing. By the time the storm subsided the situation had crystallized. Maryk was in full command. The entire ship was obeying his orders. To oppose him at that point might have been a mutinous act on my part. I decided that for the safety of the ship my best course was to obey his orders until such time as higher authority endorsed or overruled his action. That was what I did."

"Lieutenant Keefer, were you aboard the *Caine* throughout the period when Captain Queeg was in command?"

"Yes."

"Did you ever observe evidences of insanity in him?"

Keefer hesitated, wetted his lips, and looked toward Maryk, who was gnawing a knuckle and staring out of the window at the sunlit trees. "I don't—I can't answer that question intelligently, not being a psychiatrist."

Challee said sternly, "Mr. Keefer, if you saw a man rolling on the deck and foaming at the mouth, or rushing up and down passageways screaming that a tiger was after him, would you venture to say that that man was temporarily deranged?"

"I would."

"Did Commander Queeg ever exhibit such behavior?"

"No. Nothing like that."

"Did you ever think he might be insane?"

"Objection," said Greenwald, rising. "Witness isn't an expert. Matters of opinion are not admissible evidence."

"Question is withdrawn," said Challee with a slight smile, and Blakely ordered it stricken from the record.

When Greenwald sat, Maryk slid the pad under his eyes, with a crimson scrawl all over the pigs: *Why, why, WHY??* Greenwald printed rapidly on a fresh sheet, *Implicating Keefer harms you. Two disgruntled bastards instead of one heroic exec. Take an even strain.*

"Mr. Keefer," said the judge advocate, "at any time

prior to 18 December were you informed that Maryk suspected Queeg of being mentally ill?"

"Yes."

"Describe how you learned this fact."

"At Ulithi, about two weeks before the typhoon, Maryk showed me a medical log he'd kept on Queeg's behavior. He asked me to come with him to the *New Jersey* to report the situation to Admiral Halsey."

"What was your reaction to the medical log?"

"I was dumfounded to learn that Maryk had kept it."

"Did you consent to go with him?"

"Yes."

"Why?"

"Well, I was stunned. And I—that is, he was my superior officer and also my close friend. I didn't consider refusing."

"Did you believe that the log justified the relief of Queeg?"

"No. When we arrived aboard the *New Jersey*, I told him as forcibly as I could that in my opinion the log would not justify the action, and that both of us would be liable to a charge of combining to make a mutiny."

"What was his response?"

"He followed my advice. We returned to the *Caine* and no further reference was made by either of us to the log or to Queeg's mental condition."

"Did you inform the captain of Maryk's log?"

"I did not."

"Why not?"

"It would have been disloyal and contrary to the best interests of the ship to stir up my captain against my executive officer. Maryk had evidently abandoned his intention to pursue the matter. I considered the matter closed."

"Were you surprised, two weeks later, when he relieved the captain?"

"I was flabbergasted."

"Were you pleased, Mr. Keefer?"

Keefer squirmed in his chair, peered at the fierce face of Blakely, and said, "I've said that Maryk was my close friend. I was badly disturbed. I ancipated that at best he would be involved in grave difficulties, and I thought all of us might also be. I thought it was a terrible situation. I was very far from pleased."

"No further questions." Challee nodded at Greenwald.

The defense counsel rose. "No questions." All seven members of the court turned to look at Greenwald. Blakely, his eyebrows at maximum altitude, said, "Does the defense intend to recall the witness at a later time?"

"No, sir."

"No cross-examination?"

"No, sir."

"Court stenographer will affirmatively note," said Blakely, "that the accused did not desire to cross-examine Lieutenant Keefer. The court will question the witness. . . . Mr. Keefer, the court desires that you describe any factual occurrences you observed which might have led a prudent and experienced officer to conclude that Captain Queeg might be mentally ill."

"Sir, as I've said, I'm not a psychiatrist." Keefer was now quite pale.

"Now as to this so-called medical log. You did read this log, Mr. Keefer. Were the facts contained in it known to you?"

"For the most part, yes, sir."

"But these same facts, which convinced Lieutenant Maryk that he ought to report the captain to Admiral Halsey, did not convince you, is that correct?"

"They did not, sir."

"Why not?"

Keefer paused, looked up at the clock, and back at Blakely. "Sir, it's not something a layman can intelligently discuss——"

"You have stated you were a close friend of Mr. Maryk. This court is trying to find out among other things any possible extenuating circumstances in his decision to relieve his captain. Did these facts contained in the log merely indicate to you, as a layman, that Captain Queeg was a highly normal and competent officer?"

There was an edge of irony in the tone. Keefer quickly

said, "Speaking from ignorance, sir, my understanding is that mental disability is a relative thing. Captain Queeg was a very strict disciplinarian, and extremely meticulous in hunting down the smallest matters, and quite insistent in having his own way in all things. He was not the easiest person in the world to reason with. It wasn't my place to question his judgments, but there were several occasions when I thought he bore down too hard and spent excessive time on small matters. Those are the things that were recorded in the medical log. They were very unpleasant. But to jump from them to a conclusion that the captain was a maniac—I was compelled in all honesty to warn Maryk against doing that."

Blakely beckoned to the judge advocate and whispered with him, then said, "No further questions. Witness excused." Keefer stepped down, turned, and walked out rapidly. Maryk looked after him with a small dismal smile.

In the afternoon session Challee began by calling Harding and Paynter. They were sullen witnesses. Once Paynter was admonished by the court for evasiveness. Challee pressed out of both of them a corroboration of Keefer's testimony: the captain had not seemed crazy after being relieved, and they did not know what had prompted the exec's decision. It became obvious in the questioning that they both disliked Queeg. But one after the other they were driven to admit that they had never observed him commit any acts of madness during his entire time of command.

In cross-examining Harding, Greenwald brought out that Stilwell had been restricted to the ship for half a year for reading on watch, and that the whole crew had been docked five days' leave in the States because some sailors had appeared at general quarters without life jackets. He drew from Paynter a description of Stilwell's court-martial.

Challee, in a belligerent re-examination, crowded the engineering officer hard. "Mr. Paynter, did Captain Queeg direct you to find Stilwell guilty?"

"He didn't order me to, no. The way he explained the law, though, he left no doubt what verdict he wanted."

"What verdict did you think he wanted?"

"Guilty, and a bad-conduct discharge."

"What verdict did the court hand down?"

"Guilty and deprived of six liberties."

"Did Captain Queeg attempt to have you change the sentence?"

"No."

"Did he give letters of admonition to the court?"

"No."

"Did he punish you in any way?"

"Well, yes. He said there would be no sleeping after 0800 in the wardroom. And he started keeping a black book on errors we made in writing logs."

"In other words, this cruel punishment consisted of orders to write accurate logs and not to sleep during ship's working hours, is that correct?"

"Well, at the time we were standing a one-in-three watch, and not to be able to sleep in——"

"Answer the question, please. Was that the extent of your so-called punishment?"

"Yes."

"No further questions."

Greenwald rose. "Mr. Paynter, what was the ship doing during that period?"

"Convoy duty in the forward area."

"Were you at sea much?"

"Practically constantly."

"Who were the OOD's?"

"Keefer, Keith, and Harding. I was mostly off the bill because of engine breakdowns."

"Were they all department heads?"

"Yes."

"And they were standing OOD watches, four hours on and twelve off, around the clock, week in and week out. How many hours of sleep could they average?"

"Well, see, two nights out of three you lose four hours— either the graveyard or the morning watch. And GQ at dawn—I guess about four or five hours—assuming no night GQ's."

"Were there many night GQ's?"

"Maybe a couple every week."

"Did Captain de Vriess ever restrict daytime sleeping of OOD's?"

"No. He used to urge us to grab sleep when we could. He said he didn't want any foggy zombies conning his ship."

The judge advocate re-examined briefly. "Mr. Paynter, did any of the OOD's die of overstrain?"

"No."

"Did they suffer nervous breakdowns?"

"No."

"As a result of this terrible persecution of not being allowed to sleep in working hours, were there any mishaps to the ship?"

"No."

The next witness was Urban. The little signalman's right hand trembled when he was sworn, and his voice quavered. The judge advocate led him to state that he had been the only person in the wheelhouse beside Queeg, Maryk, Keith, and Stilwell when the captain was relieved.

"What were your duties?"

"Kept the quartermaster's notebook, sir."

"Describe in your own words how it happened that Lieutenant Maryk relieved the captain."

"Well, he relieved him at five minutes to ten. I noted it in my book——"

"How did he relieve him?"

"He said, 'I relieve you, sir.' "

"Didn't he do anything else?"

"I don't remember for sure."

"Why did he relieve him? What was happening at the time?"

"The ship was rolling very bad."

Challee looked up at the court in exasperation. "Urban, describe everything that happened in the ten minutes before Captain Queeg was relieved."

"Well, like I say, we were rolling very bad."

Challee waited, his eyes intent on the sailor. After a long

silence he burst out, "That's all? Did the exec say anything? Did the captain say anything? Did the OOD say anything? Did the ship just roll in silence for ten minutes?"

"Well, sir, it was a typhoon. I don't remember too well."

Blakely leaned forward, scowling over his clasped fingers at the signalman. "Urban, you're under oath. Evasive answers in a court-martial constitute contempt of court, which is a very bad business. Now think over your answer."

Urban said desperately, "Well, I think the captain wanted to come left and the exec wanted to come right, or something like that."

"Why did the captain want to come left?"

"I don't know, sir."

"Why did the exec want to come right?"

"Sir, I'm a signalman. I was keeping the quartermaster's log. I kept a good log even though we were rolling so bad. I didn't know what it was all about and I still don't."

"Did the captain act crazy?"

"No, sir."

"Did the exec?"

"No, sir."

"Did the exec seem scared?"

"No, sir."

"Did the captain?"

"No, sir."

"Did anyone?"

"*I* was goddamn scared, sir. I beg your pardon, sir."

A member of the court, a reserve lieutenant with an Irish face and bright red curly hair, chuckled out loud. Blakely turned on him. The lieutenant began writing busily on a yellow pad. "Urban," said Challee, "you are the only witness to this whole affair who is not directly involved. Your testimony is of the utmost importance——"

"I wrote everything in the quartermaster's log, sir, just the way it happened."

"Logs are not supposed to contain conversations. I am trying to find out what was said."

"Well, sir, like I said, one wanted to come right and

one wanted to come left. Then Mr. Maryk relieved the captain."

"But the captain definitely did not act queer or crazy in any way at any time that morning—correct?"

"The captain was the same as always, sir."

Challee yelled, "Crazy, or sane, Urban?"

Urban shrank back in his chair, staring at Challee. "Of course he was sane, sir, so far as I knew."

"You don't remember anything that was said by anybody the whole morning?"

"I was busy keeping the log, sir. Except something about coming left or right, and about the storm being bad and all."

"What about ballasting?"

"Well, there was some talk about ballasting."

"To what effect?"

"Just talk about whether to ballast."

"Who wanted to ballast?"

"Well, the captain, or Mr. Maryk, I don't know which."

"It's of the greatest importance that you remember which, Urban."

"I don't know nothing about ballasting, sir. All I know is they talked about it."

"Was the ship ever ballasted that morning?"

"Yes, sir, because I remember I made a note in my log."

"Who gave the order to ballast?"

"I don't remember, sir."

"You don't remember much!"

"I kept a good log, sir. That was what I was there for."

Challee turned to Blakely, exclaiming, "I do not believe this witness is heeding the admonition of the court."

"Urban," said Blakely, "how old are you?"

"Twenty, sir."

"What schooling have you had?"

"One year in high school."

"Have you been telling the whole truth here, or haven't you?"

"Sir, the quartermaster isn't supposed to listen to arguments between the captain and the exec. He's supposed to keep his log. I don't know why Mr. Maryk relieved the captain."

"Did you ever see the captain do anything crazy?"

"No, sir."

"Did you like the captain?"

Urban said miserably, *"Sure* I liked him, sir."

"Continue your examination," said the court to Challee.

"No further questions."

Greenwald approached the witness platform, flipping the red crayon against his palm. "Urban, were you aboard when the *Caine* cut its own tow cable outside Pearl Harbor?"

"Yes, sir."

"What were you doing at the time that it happened?"

"I was—that is, the captain was eating me out—bawling me out—on the bridge."

"What for?"

"My shirttail was out."

"And while the captain was discussing your shirttail the ship steamed over its own towline?"

Challee had been regarding the defense counsel with wrinkled brows. He jumped up. "Object to this line of questioning and request the entire cross-examination so far be stricken from the record. Counsel has tricked the witness with leading questions into asserting as a fact that the *Caine* cut a towline, a material point that was not touched upon in direct examination."

Greenwald said, "The witness stated he had never seen the captain do anything crazy. I am attempting to refute this. *Courts and Boards* 282 says leading questions may be freely used on cross-examination."

The court was cleared. When all the parties returned Blakely said, "Defense counsel will have the opportunity to originate evidence later, and can recall the witness at that time. Objection sustained. Cross-examination thus far will be stricken from the record."

During the rest of the afternoon Challee called twelve chiefs and sailors of the *Caine,* all of whom testified briefly and glumly that Queeg had seemed much like any other captain, and had never to their knowledge done anything insane, either before the typhoon, during it, or afterward. The first of these was Bellison. Greenwald's cross-examination of him consisted of three questions and answers.

"Chief Bellison, what is a paranoid personality?"

"I don't know, sir."

"What is the difference between a psychoneurosis and a psychosis?"

"I don't know, sir." Bellison wrinkled up his face.

"Could you recognize a neurotic person as such if you encountered one?"

"No, sir."

To each of the twelve members of the crew, Greenwald put the same three questions and received the same answers. This litany, repeated twelve times, had a cumulating effect of irritation on Challee and on the court. They glared at Greenwald and fidgeted each time he went through the formula.

The court was adjourned after the testimony of the last sailor, Meatball. Maryk and his lawyer walked silently out of the court-martial building together. The last orange rays of a sinking sun were slanting across the bay, and the air was cool and sweet after the stale varnish-and-linoleum smell of the courtroom. They walked to Greenwald's gray Navy jeep. The gravel walk crunched loudly under their steps. "Have they got us on the run?" Maryk said quietly.

"Who knows?" Greenwald said. "We haven't gone to bat yet. You know this town. Where can we eat good?"

"I'll drive."

Greenwald drank a great many highballs during dinner. He evaded any talk about the court-martial, and filled the conversation with rambling dull information about Indians. He told Maryk that his real ambition had been to become an anthropologist, but he had gone into law out of crusading fervor, figuring that Indians needed to be defended more than to be studied. He said he had regretted the choice often.

He seemed queerer and queerer to Maryk. The exec abandoned hope—with his mind; he was convinced that Queeg, Keefer, and Urban had finished him off in the first day. But he clung to a shred of irrational faith in his strange defender. The prospect of being convicted was so awful that he had to believe in something. The maximum penalty was dismissal and fifteen years' imprisonment.

34 · The Court-Martial—
Second Day, Morning

"Okay, Lieutenant Keith," said an orderly, opening the door to the anteroom at two minutes past ten.

Willie followed him blindly. They passed through several doors, and suddenly they were in the courtroom, and Willie felt the shooting tingles in his arms and legs that he had felt when the *Caine* approached an invasion beach. The room was a frightening blur of solemn faces; the American flag seemed gigantic, and its red, white, and blue terribly vivid, like a flag in a color movie. He found himself on the witness platform, being sworn, and could not have told how he got there. Challee's face was gray and forbidding. "Mr. Keith, were you officer of the deck of the *Caine* during the forenoon watch on 18 December?"

"I was."

"Was the captain relieved of command by the executive officer during that watch?"

"Yes."

"Do you know why the executive officer took the action he did?"

"Yes. The captain had lost control of himself and the ship, and we were in imminent danger of foundering."

"How many years have you served at sea, Lieutenant?"

"One year and three months."

"Have you ever been in a ship that foundered?"

"No."

"Do you know how many years Commander Queeg has served at sea?"

"No."

"As a matter of fact, Commander Queeg has served over eight years. Which of you is better qualified to judge whether a ship is foundering or not?"

"Myself, sir, if I'm in possession of my faculties and Commander Queeg isn't."

"What makes you think he isn't in possession of his faculties?"

"He wasn't on the morning of December 18."

"Have you studied medicine or psychiatry?"

"No."

"What qualifies you to judge whether your commanding officer was in possession of his faculties on December 18?"

"I observed his behavior."

"Very well, Lieutenant. Describe to the court everything about your captain's behavior which indicated loss of his faculties."

"He froze to the engine-room telegraph. His face showed petrified terror. It was green. His orders were sluggish and vague, and not appropriate."

"Is it for the officer of the deck, Mr. Keith, a junior with one year at sea, to judge whether or not his captain's orders are appropriate?"

"Not ordinarily. But when the ship is in danger of going down and the captain's ship handling is increasing the danger instead of countering it, the OOD can't help observing it."

"Did Captain Queeg foam, or rave, or make nonsensical statements, or insane gestures?"

"No. He seemed to be paralyzed with terror."

"Paralyzed, yet he issued orders?"

"As I say, the orders were not helping matters, but making them worse."

"Be specific, Lieutenant. In what way were his orders making things worse?"

"Well, he kept insisting on going down-wind, when the

ship was yawing so badly it was broaching to. And he refused to ballast."

"Refused? Who asked him to ballast?"

"Mr. Maryk."

"Why did the captain refuse?"

"He said he didn't want to contaminate the tanks with salt water."

"After being relieved, did Captain Queeg go violently crazy?"

"No."

"Describe the captain's manner after being relieved of command."

"Well, actually, he seemed better afterward. I think he felt better as soon as he no longer had the responsibility——"

"No opinions, Mr. Keith. Tell the court not what you think, but what you observed, please. What did the captain do?"

"Well, he stayed in the wheelhouse. Several times he tried to resume command."

"In an orderly, sensible way, or in a wild, raving way?"

"The captain was never wild or raving, either before or after being relieved. There are other forms of mental illness."

"Tell us about some others, Mr. Keith." Challee's tone was coarsely sarcastic.

"Well, little as I know about psychiatry, I do know—well, for instance, extreme depression and vagueness, and divorcement from reality, and inaccessibility to reason—things like that——" Willie felt that he was stumbling badly. "Besides, I never said Captain Queeg issued rational orders that morning. They were rational only in so far as they were phrased in correct English. They showed no awareness of reality."

"In your expert opinion, as ship handler and psychiatrist, that is? Very well. Are you aware that Captain Queeg has been pronounced perfectly rational by professional psychiatrists?"

"Yes."

"Do you think these psychiatrists are also mentally ill, Lieutenant Keith?"

"They weren't on the bridge of the *Caine* during the typhoon."

"Were you a loyal officer?"

"I think I was."

"Were you wholeheartedly behind the captain, or antagonistic to him, at all times prior to 18 December?"

Willie knew Queeg had appeared on the first day, but he had no idea of what the testimony had been. He calculated his answer carefully. "I was antagonistic to Captain Queeg at certain isolated times. Otherwise I maintained a loyal and respectful attitude."

"At what isolated times were you antagonistic?"

"Well, it was usually the same basic trouble. When Captain Queeg oppressed or maltreated the men I opposed him. Not very successfully."

"When did the captain ever maltreat the men?"

"Well, I don't know where to begin. Well, first he systematically persecuted Gunner's Mate Second Class Stilwell."

"In what way?"

"First he restricted him to the ship for six months for reading on watch. He refused to grant him leave in the States when there was a grave crisis in Stilwell's family life. Maryk gave Stilwell a seventy-two-hour emergency leave and he returned a few hours over leave. And for all that the captain gave Stilwell a summary court."

"Wasn't Stilwell tried for sending a fraudulent telegram?"

"Yes, and acquitted."

"But the summary court was for fraud, not merely for being AOL?"

"Yes. I'm sorry, I spoke hastily."

"Take your time and be accurate. Do you think reading on watch in wartime is a negligible offense?"

"I don't think it warrants six months' restriction."

"Are you qualified to pass judgment on matters of naval discipline?"

"I'm a human being. In Stilwell's circumstances, the restriction was inhuman."

Challee paused for a moment. "You say Maryk gave Stilwell a pass. Did Maryk know that the captain had denied leave to Stilwell?"

"Yes."

"Are you testifying, Mr. Keith," the judge advocate said, with the air of having stumbled on something unexpected and good, "that Maryk, as far back as December '43, deliberately violated his captain's orders?"

Willie became rattled. It hadn't occurred to him that he would be disclosing this injurious fact for the first time. "Well, I mean it was my fault actually. I begged him to. I was morale officer, and I thought the man's morale—in fact, I think his present mental collapse is due to the captain's persecution——"

Challee turned to Blakely. "I ask the court to warn this witness against answering with immaterial opinions."

"Stick to facts, Mr. Keith," growled Blakely. Willie shifted in his chair, and felt his clothes all clammy inside. Challee said, "We now have your testimony, Mr. Keith, that you and Maryk and Stilwell connived to circumvent an express order of your commanding officer, a whole year before the typhoon of 18 December——"

"I would do it again, given the same circumstances."

"Do you believe loyalty consists in obeying only such orders as you approve of, or all orders?"

"All orders, except irrational persecution."

"Do you think there is no recourse in the Navy against what *you* think is irrational persecution, except disobedience of orders?"

"I know you can forward a letter to higher authority— via the captain."

"Why didn't you do that in this case?"

"I had to sail with Queeg for another year. The important thing was to get Stilwell home."

"It's an unlucky coincidence, isn't it, that the same insubordinate trio—Maryk, Stilwell, and yourself—combined in the deposing of your captain?"

"Stilwell and I just happened to be on duty when the captain went to pieces. Any other OOD and helmsman would have done the same."

"Maybe. Now, please tell the court any other instances of oppression and maltreatment that occur to you."

Willie hesitated for several seconds, feeling the weight of the court members' unfriendly looks like a pressure on his forehead. "Maybe you can make them all sound silly and trivial here, sir, but at the time they were serious. He cut off the movies for six months just because he wasn't invited to a showing by mistake—he cut off the water at the equator because he was annoyed by the detachment of an officer—he called midnight conferences on insignificant details with department heads who were standing a one-in-three deck watch. And he forbade sleeping by day so there was no chance to catch up on sleep——"

"We've had a lot of testimony on that sleep business. The officers of the *Caine* certainly wanted their sleep, war or no war, didn't they?"

"I said it's easy to poke fun at these things. But it isn't easy to conn a ship in formation in a rain squall when you've been up for seventy-two hours with maybe four hours' consecutive sleep."

"Mr. Keith, did Captain Queeg ever use physical torture on officers or men?"

"No."

"Did he starve them, beat them, or in any way cause anybody injury that will appear in the medical records of the *Caine?*"

"No."

"Did he ever issue punishment not allowed by regulations?"

"He never did anything not allowed by regulations, or if he did he backtracked immediately. He demonstrated how much can be done to oppress and maltreat within regulations."

"You didn't like Captain Queeg, did you, Lieutenant?"

"I did at first, very much. But I gradually realized that he was a petty tyrant and utterly incompetent."

"Did you think he was insane too?"

"Not until the day of the typhoon."

"Did Maryk ever show you his medical log on Queeg?"

"No."

"Did he ever discuss the captain's medical condition with you?"

"No. Mr. Maryk never permitted criticism of the captain in his presence."

"What! Despite the insubordination back in December '43?"

"He would walk out of the wardroom if anything derogatory was said of the captain."

"There were derogatory remarks about the captain in the wardroom? Who uttered them?"

"Every officer except Maryk."

"Would you say that Captain Queeg had a loyal wardroom of officers?"

"All his orders were carried out."

"Except those you thought ought to be circumvented. . . . Mr. Keith, you have stated you disliked the captain."

"That is the truth."

"Come to the morning of 18 December. Was your decision to obey Maryk based on your judgment that the captain had gone mad, or was it based on your dislike of Captain Queeg?"

Willie stared for long seconds at Challee's livid face. There were sharp steel teeth in the question. Willie knew what the true answer was; and he knew that it would probably destroy himself and Maryk. But he felt unable to carry off a lie. "I can't answer," he said at last, in a low voice.

"On what grounds, Lieutenant Keith?"

"Must I state grounds?"

"It is contempt of court to refuse to answer a question except on sufficient grounds, Lieutenant Keith."

Willie said thickly, "I'm not sure. I just don't remember my state of mind that long ago."

"No more questions," said Challee. He turned on his heel and sat down.

*   *   *

Willie was absolutely certain, in that instant, staring at the surgically cold faces of the court, that he had convicted Maryk and himself with his own mouth. He shook with boiling impotent rage at the flummery of court routine which prevented him from breaking out and shouting his self-justification; and at the same time he realized that he could never quite justify himself in the Navy's eyes. In plain truth, he had obeyed Maryk for two reasons, first, because he thought the exec was more likely to save the ship, and second, because he hated Queeg. It had never occurred to him, until Maryk took command, that Queeg might be really insane. And he knew, deep down, that he never had believed the captain was crazy. Stupid, mean, vicious, cowardly, incompetent, yes—but sane. The insanity of Queeg was Maryk's only possible plea (and Willie's too); and it was a false plea; and Challee knew it, and the court knew it; and now Willie knew it.

Greenwald rose to cross-examine. "Mr. Keith, you have stated you disliked Captain Queeg."

"I did dislike him."

"Did you state under direct examination all your reasons for disliking him?"

"Not at all. I wasn't given the chance to state half the reasons."

"Please state the rest of your reasons, now, if you will."

Words formed in Willie's mind which, he knew, would change the course of several lives and land him in trouble from which he might never extricate himself. He spoke; it was like punching his fist through a glass door. "My chief reason for disliking Captain Queeg was his cowardice in battle."

Challee started getting to his feet. Greenwald said quickly, "What cowardice?"

"He repeatedly ran from shore batteries——"

"Objection!" shouted the judge advocate. "Counsel is originating evidence beyond the scope of direct examination. He is leading the witness into irresponsible libels of an officer of the Navy. I request that the court admonish defense counsel and strike the cross-examination thus far from the record."

"Please the court," said Greenwald, facing into Blakely's glare, "the witness's dislike of Queeg was not only in the scope of the direct examination, it was the key fact brought out. The background of this dislike is of the utmost consequence. The witness has confessed ignorance of medicine and psychiatry. Things Queeg did, which caused the witness in his ignorance to dislike him, may in fact have been the helpless acts of a sick man. Defense will present material corroboration of all statements of the witness in this connection, and will in fact show that Queeg's acts stemmed from illness——"

Challee flared at Greenwald, "This is not the time for defense to present its case or make a closing argument——"

"The judge advocate has opened the question of Lieutenant Keith's admitted dislike of Captain Queeg," Greenwald shot back. "Evidence is tested as it arises——"

Blakely rapped his gavel. "Defense counsel and the judge advocate are admonished for unseemly personal exchanges. The court will be cleared."

When the parties of the trial came back into the room, Blakely had a copy of *Navy Regulations* open before him on the bench. He wore thick black-rimmed glasses which gave him an oddly peaceful professorial look. "For the benefit of all parties, court will read from Article 4, Sections 13 and 14 of the Articles for the Government of the Navy, before announcing its ruling.

"*The punishment of death, or such other punishment as a court-martial may adjudge, may be inflicted on any person in the naval service, who, in time of battle, displays cowardice, negligence, or disaffection, or withdraws from or keeps out of danger to which he should expose himself . . . or in time of battle, deserts his duty or station, or induces others to do so.*"

Blakely took off his glasses and closed the book. He went on in a grave, tired tone, "The court has said this is a delicate case. Defense counsel and the witness are warned that they are on the most dangerous possible ground. In charging an officer of the United States Navy with an offense punishable by death, and that the most odious offense in military life, equal to murder, they take on themselves the heaviest responsibility, and face consequences the seriousness of which cannot be overstated. The court now asks defense counsel in view of the foregoing whether he desires to withdraw his questions."

Greenwald said, "I do not so desire, sir."

"The court asks the witness to consider carefully the implications of his answers and state whether he desires to withdraw his answers."

Willie, his teeth chattering a little, said, "I do not so desire, sir."

"Subject to the foregoing," said Blakely, with an audible sigh, pushing aside the book, "the objection is overruled. Defense counsel will proceed with his cross-examination."

Willie told about Queeg's running from the Saipan shore battery which had fired on the *Stanfield*. He narrated in detail the episode at Kwajalein which had resulted in Queeg's being nicknamed "Old Yellowstain." He saw for the first time a change in the expressions of the court as he spoke. The frigid solemnity with which they had peered at him gave way slowly, and instead there were seven faces of men listening with interest to an amazing tale. Challee, frowning bitterly, scribbled pages of notes.

"Mr. Keith, who coined this name, 'Old Yellowstain'?" said Greenwald.

"I'm not sure, sir. It just sprang into existence."

"What did it imply?"

"Well, cowardice, of course. But it also referred to the yellow marker. It was one of those naturals. It stuck."

"Have you told all the incidents of cowardice that you recall?"

"Well, in any combat situation Captain Queeg inevitably would be found on the side of the bridge away from the firing. When we were patrolling near a beach, every time the ship reversed course the captain changed wings. Everyone noticed it. It was a common joke. All the bridge personnel will corroborate what I say, if they're not afraid to talk."

Greenwald said, "Besides these incidents of cowardice, what further reasons had you for disliking Queeg?"

"Well—I guess I've told the characteristic ones—well, for one thing, he extorted a hundred dollars from me———"

Challee stood wearily. "Objection. How long will these irrelevant unproven allegations be permitted by the court? The issue in this case is not whether Captain Queeg was a model officer, but whether he was insane on 18 December. Defense counsel has not even touched this issue. I suggest there is strong indication of collusion between defense counsel and witness to recklessly smear Commander Queeg and thus confuse the issue———"

Greenwald said, "The objection is identical with the last one court overruled. I repudiate the charge of collusion. Facts are facts, and need no collusion to be brought out. All these facts bear directly on the mental fitness of Captain Queeg to command a naval vessel, and as evidence they are nothing but clarification of Keith's dislike of his commanding officer, a fact established by the judge advocate at great pains in direct examination."

"The objection is identical," said Blakely, rubbing his eyes, "and it is overruled. Proceed with cross-examination."

"Describe this so-called extortion, Mr. Keith."

Willie told of the loss of the crate of liquor in San Francisco Bay. Captain Blakely began grimacing horribly. Greenwald said, "Did the captain order you to pay for the liquor?"

"Oh, no. He didn't order me. He made me admit that I was responsible for all acts of the working party because I was boat officer—although he had issued all the orders to the working party—and then he asked me to think over what I ought to do about it. That was all. But I was supposed to go on leave next day. My fiancée had flown out from New York to be with me. So I went to the captain. I apologized for my stupidity, and said I'd like to pay for the liquor. He took my money gladly, and signed my leave papers."

"No further questions," Greenwald said, and went to his seat. He felt a powerful grip on his knee under the table.

He quickly sketched a revolting cross-eyed pig in a steaming cauldron, labeled it "Queeg," showed it to Maryk, and shredded it into the wastebasket.

Challee re-examined Willie for twenty minutes, probing for contradictions and misstatements in his stories about Queeg; he got off a great deal of sarcasm at Willie's expense, but he did not manage to shake the testimony.

Willie looked at the clock as he left the stand. It was ten minutes of eleven. He was amazed, just as he had been on the morning of the typhoon, by the slow passage of time. He imagined he had been in the witness chair for four hours.

Challee called Captain Randolph P. Southard, a dapper, lean officer with a hard-bitten face and close-cropped head, whose ribbons and medals made three colorful rows over his breast pocket. The judge advocate quickly brought out that Southard was the commander of Destroyer Squadron Eight, and had commanded destroyers of several types, including World War I four-pipers, for ten years. He was Challee's expert witness on ship handling.

Southard testified that under typhoon conditions a destroyer rode just as well going down-wind as up-wind. In fact, he said, because of a destroyer's high freeboard forward it tended to back into the wind. Therefore, if anything, it was more manageable with the wind astern. He asserted that Queeg's efforts to stay on the fleet's southerly course had been the soundest possible procedure for getting out of the typhoon danger; and that Maryk's decision to turn north had been a dubious and dangerous one, because it had kept the ship in the direct path of the storm.

Greenwald opened his cross-examination by saying, "Captain Southard, have you ever conned a ship through the center of a typhoon?"

"Negative. Been on the fringes often but always managed to avoid the center."

"Have you ever commanded a destroyer-minesweeper, sir?"

"Negative."

"This case, sir, concerns a destroyer-minesweeper at the center of a typhoon——"

"I'm aware of that," Southard said frostily. "I've had DMS's under my command in screens, and I've read the book on 'em. They don't differ from destroyers except in details of topside weight characteristics."

"I ask these questions, Captain, because you are the only expert witness on ship handling and the extent of your expert knowledge should be clear to the court."

"That's all right. I've handled destroyer types in almost every conceivable situation for ten years. Haven't handled a DMS at the center of a typhoon, no, but I don't know who has besides the skipper of the *Caine*. It's a thousand-to-one shot."

"Will you state without reservation that the rules of destroyer handling would hold for a DMS in the center of a typhoon?"

"Well, at the center of a typhoon there are no hard-and-fast rules. That's one situation where it's all up to the commanding officer. Too many strange things happen too fast. But seamanship is seamanship."

"A hypothetical question. Assuming you are conning a destroyer in winds and seas worse than any you have ever experienced. You are wallowing broadside. You actually believe your ship is foundering. You are in the last extremity. Would you try to bring your ship head into wind, or stern to wind?"

"That's a mighty hypothetical question."

"Yes, sir. Don't you wish to answer it?"

"I'll answer it. In the last extremity I'd head into the wind if I could. *Only* in the last extremity."

"Why, sir?"

"Why, because your engines and rudder have the best purchase that way, that's all, and it's your last chance to keep control of your ship."

"But suppose heading into the wind would mean remaining in the path of a storm instead of escaping?"

"First things first. If you're on the verge of foundering you're as bad off as you can get. Mind you, you said the *last extremity*."

"Yes, sir. No further questions."

Challee stood at once. "Captain, in your opinion who

is the best judge as to whether a ship is in its last extremity?"

"There is only one judge. The commanding officer."

"Why?"

"The Navy has made him captain because his knowledge of the sea and of ships is better than anyone else's on the ship. It's very common for subordinate officers to think the ship is a goner when all they're going through is a little weather."

"Don't you think, though, sir, that when his subordinates all agree that the ship is going down the captain ought to listen to them?"

"Negative! Panic is a common hazard at sea. The highest function of command is to override it and to listen to nothing but the voice of his own judgment."

"Thank you, Captain."

35 · The Court-Martial—
Second Day, Afternoon

Dr. Forrest Lundeen was a stout, pink-faced commander with gold-rimmed glasses, and straight blond hair fading to gray. He was chief of psychiatry at the Navy hospital, and had headed the medical board which had examined Queeg. He sat comfortably in the witness chair, answering Challee's questions with good-humored alertness.

"How long did your examination last, Doctor?"

"We had the commander under constant observation and testing for three weeks."

"Who comprised the board?"

"Myself, Dr. Bird, and Dr. Manella."

"All three practicing psychiatrists?"

"Dr. Bird and Dr. Manella have been civilian psychiatrists. They are reserve officers. I have specialized in psychiatry in the Navy for fifteen years."

"What was the finding of the board?"

"Commander Queeg was discharged with a clean bill of health."

"No evidence of insanity was found?"

"None whatever."

"Does that mean that Commander Queeg is absolutely normal?"

"Well, normality, you know, is a fiction in psychiatry. It's all relative. No adult is without problems except a happy imbecile. Commander Queeg is a well-adjusted personality."

"Do you consider it possible that two weeks before you began your examination Commander Queeg was insane?"

"It is utterly impossible. The commander is sane now and has always been sane. A psychotic collapse leaves trauma that can always be detected."

"You found no such trauma in Commander Queeg?"

"None."

"Commander Queeg was summarily relieved of command of the U.S.S. Caine on December 18, 1944, by his executive officer, who stated that the captain was mentally ill. Do you consider it possible that on that date Commander Queeg was in such a state of psychotic collapse that the executive officer's act was justified?"

"Absolutely impossible."

"Is it possible for a sane man to perform offensive, disagreeable, foolish acts?"

"It happens every day."

"Assuming for a moment—this a hypothetical question —that the conduct of Commander Queeg throughout his command was harsh, ill-tempered, nasty, oppressive, and often showed bad judgment. Would that be inconsistent with your board's findings?"

"No. We did not find that he was a perfect officer. We found an absence of mental illness."

"From your knowledge of the commander, would you say he is capable of ill temper and harshness?"

"Yes. It's in the picture."

"Having discovered all that, you still say that the act of the executive officer in relieving him was unjustified?"

"From a psychiatric standpoint, completely unjustified. That was the unanimous conclusion of the board."

"Describe the background of your colleagues."

"Bird has special training in Freudian technique. He's a recent honor graduate of Harvard Medical School. Manella is one of the best-known psychosomatic men on the West Coast."

"State their present whereabouts."

"Bird is still on my staff. Manella was detached last week and is en route to the Philippines."

"We will place your report in evidence and hear Dr. Bird. Thank you, Doctor."

The judge advocate allowed himself a direct glance into Greenwald's eyes, and a thin cold grin. Greenwald came shuffling toward the witness platform, rubbing his nose with the back of his hand, looking down at his feet, and presenting a general picture of flustered embarrassment. "Dr. Lundeen, my background is legal, not medical. I hope you will bear with me if I try to clarify technical terms. I'll probably ask some elementary questions."

"Perfectly all right."

"You said Commander Queeg, like all adults, had problems, to which he was adjusted. Can you describe the problems?"

"Well, most of that information comes under the heading of clinical confidences."

"Yes, sir. Suppressing all confidential information, can you still describe in general the problems?"

Challee called out, "I object. Commander Queeg is not on trial. Lieutenant Maryk is. The question constitutes irrelevant probing of medical confidences."

Blakely looked to Greenwald. The pilot shrugged. "I rely on the judgment of the court. Evidence regarding disturbing factors in Commander Queeg's mental make-up is of the utmost importance to the issue, obviously."

With an annoyed glance at the judge advocate, Blakely ordered the court cleared. The parties were summoned back in less than a minute. Blakely said, "The question is material. Objection overruled. The doctor has the privilege of medical discretion in answering." Challee flushed, and slouched in his chair. The stenographer repeated the question.

"Well, you might say the over-all problem is one of inferiority feelings," said Lundeen, "generated by an unfavorable childhood and aggravated by some adult experiences."

"Unfavorable childhood in what way?"

"Disturbed background. Divorced parents, financial trouble, schooling problems."

"And the aggravating factors in adult life?"

"Well, I can't go into those too much. In general, the commander is rather troubled by his short stature, his low standing in his class, and such factors. Apparently the hazing at the Academy was a scarring experience." Lundeen paused. "That's about what I can say."

"How about his present family life?"

The doctor said reluctantly, "Well, you begin to tread on clinical ground there."

"But there are tensions, without describing them?"

"I won't answer further questions in that direction. As I say, the commander is well adjusted to all these things."

"Can you describe the nature of the adjustment?"

"Yes, I can. His identity as a naval officer is the essential balancing factor. It's the key to his personal security and therefore he's excessively zealous to protect his standing. That would account for the harshness and ill temper I spoke about before."

"Would he be disinclined to admit to mistakes?"

"Well, there's a tendency that way. The commander has a fixed anxiety about protecting his standing. Of course there's nothing unbalanced in that."

"Would he be a perfectionist?"

"Such a personality would be."

"Inclined to hound subordinates about small details?"

"He prides himself on meticulousness. Any mistake of a subordinate is intolerable because it might endanger him."

"Is such a personality, with such a zeal for perfection, likely to avoid all mistakes?"

"Well, we all know that reality is beyond the hundred-per-cent control of any human being——"

"Yet he will not admit mistakes when made. Is he lying?"

'Definitely not! He—you might say he revises reality in his own mind so that he comes out blameless. There's a tendency to blame others——"

"Doctor, isn't distorting reality a symptom of mental illness?"

"Certainly not, in itself. It's all a question of degree. None of us wholly faces reality."

"But doesn't the commander distort reality more than, say, you do, or any other person not under his tensions?"

"That's his weakness. Other people have other weaknesses. It's definitely not disabling."

"Would such a personality be inclined to feel that people were against him, hostile to him?"

"It's all part of it. Such a man by nature is constantly on the alert to defend his self-esteem."

"Would he be suspicious of subordinates, and inclined to question their loyalty and competence?"

"Maybe somewhat. It's all part of the anxiety for perfection."

"If criticized from above, would he be inclined to think he was being unjustly persecuted?"

"Well, as I say, it's all one pattern, all stemming from one basic premise, that he must try to be perfect."

"Would he be inclined to stubbornness?"

"Well, you'll have a certain rigidity of personality in such an individual. The inner insecurity checks him from admitting that those who differ with him may be right."

Greenwald suddenly switched from his fumbling manner to clicking preciseness. "Doctor, you've testified that the following symptoms exist in the commander's behavior: rigidity of personality, feelings of persecution, unreasonable suspicion, withdrawal from reality, perfectionist anxiety, an unreal basic premise, and an obsessive sense of self-righteousness."

Dr. Lundeen looked startled. "All mild, sir, all well compensated."

"Yes, Doctor. Is there an inclusive psychiatric term— one label—for this syndrome?"

"Syndrome? Who said anything about a syndrome? You're misusing a term. There's no syndrome, because there's no disease."

"Thank you for the correction, Doctor. I'll rephrase it. Do the symptoms fall into a single pattern of neurotic disturbance—a common psychiatric class?"

"I know what you're driving at, of course. It's a paranoid personality, of course, but that is not a disabling affliction."

"What kind of personality, Doctor?"

"Paranoid."

"Paranoid, Doctor?"

"Yes, paranoid."

Greenwald glanced at Challee, then looked around slowly, one by one, at the faces of the court. He started back to his desk. Challee rose. The pilot said, "I haven't finished cross-examination, I want to consult my notes." Challee sank into his seat. There was a minute of silence. Greenwald shuffled papers at his desk. The word "paranoid" hung in the air.

"Doctor, in a paranoid personality like Commander Queeg's, how do you distinguish between illness and adjustment?"

"As I've said repeatedly"—there was a tired, irritated note in Lundeen's voice—"it's a question of degree. Nobody's absolutely normal. Perhaps you're a mild manic-depressive. Perhaps I'm a mild schizoid. Millions of people live normal lives with these compensated conditions. Their physical analogues are a sway back, a heart murmur, something that is an individual weakness but not a disabling factor. You have to look for the disabling factor."

"Is this disabling factor an absolute or a relative thing, Doctor?"

"How do you mean that?"

"Well, could a man have a paranoid personality which

would not disable him for any subordinate duties, but would disable him for command?"

"Conceivably."

"Then as a communications officer he would not be mentally ill—but as captain of the ship he would be mentally ill, isn't that right?"

"You're jumbling up a lot of medical language which you use very loosely," Lundeen said huffily.

"I'm sorry, Doctor."

"In the case of Captain Queeg my board did *not* find him disabled for command."

"I remember that testimony, sir. Can you describe, Doctor, the point at which the paranoid personality becomes disabling?"

"When the man loses control of himself and of the reality around him."

"What are the symptoms of the disabled paranoid who finds reality too much for him?"

"Well, there can be various reactions. Withdrawal into torpor, or frenzy, or nervous collapse—it all depends on circumstances."

"Is the disabling factor likely to show up in personal interviews?"

"With a skilled psychiatrist, yes."

"You mean the patient would go into frenzy or torpor?"

"No. I mean the psychiatrist could detect the disabling mechanisms, the rigidity, persecution feelings, fixed ideas, and so forth."

"Why is a psychiatrist needed, Doctor? Can't an educated intelligent person, like myself, or the judge advocate, or the court, detect a paranoid?"

Dr. Lundeen said sarcastically, "You evidently are not too well acquainted with the pattern. The distinguishing mark of this neurosis is extreme plausibility and a most convincing normal manner on the surface. Particularly in self-justification."

Greenwald looked at the floor for half a minute. There was a rustle at the bench as all the court members, by a common impulse, shifted in their chairs. "A hypothetical question, Doctor, about a commanding officer with a paranoid personality . . . Assuming he does the following things: he becomes bewildered or frightened under fire, and runs away; he damages government property and denies it; he falsifies official records; he extorts money from his subordinates; he issues excessive punishments for small offenses. Is he disabled for command?"

After a long wait, with the court members staring hard at him, Lundeen said, "It's an incomplete question. Does he perform his duties satisfactorily otherwise?"

"Hypothetically, let us say so."

"Well, then, he—he is not necessarily disabled, no. He is obviously not very desirable. It's a question of your level of officer procurement. If you have other men as qualified as him for command, well, they would be preferable. If you're in a war and command personnel is stretched thin, well, you may have to use him. It's another war risk."

"Dr. Lundeen, would you, as an expert witness, say that Commander Queeg should be restored to command of a United States naval vessel?"

"Well, I—— The question's pointless. That's the province of the Bureau of Personnel. The man is not mentally ill. I've repeatedly stated that a paranoid disturbance, however mild, is a distorting condition and exceedingly unpleasant for associates. In war you make do with what you have. He isn't disabled."

"Would you care to have your son under Captain Queeg in battle?"

Lundeen glanced unhappily at the judge advocate, who jumped to his feet. "Objection. It is a personal emotion reaction that is being asked for, not an expert opinion."

"I withdraw the question," said Greenwald. "Thank you, Dr. Lundeen. Defense is finished."

Captain Blakely said, "The court wishes to clear up one point." The other court members looked tensely at the president. "Doctor, is such a thing possible—a temporary disability under stress, not amounting to a full collapse? Or—well, let me put it this way. Let's say a man with a mild condition is not disabled for all the usual stresses of command. Now let's say the stresses are multiplied manifold by a most extreme emergency. Would there be a loss in efficiency? A tendency to get confused and rattled, to make erroneous judgments?"

"Well, there might be. Extreme stress does that to almost anybody, sir."

"It's not supposed to do it to commanding officers."

"No, but practically speaking, sir, they're human, too."

"Very well, Doctor, thank you."

Challee resumed direct examination, and led Lundeen to assert several times, in different ways, that Queeg was not and had never been disabled. The doctor made these statements with aggrieved emphasis, occasionally looking sidewise at the defense lawyer.

"Dr. Bird will be my last witness, sir," Challee said to the court, as the orderly went out to call the second psychiatrist.

"Very well," said Blakely, glancing at the clock. It was five minutes past two. The lieutenant who came in was an extremely slender, youthful-looking man with dark hair, sallow skin, and sharp sensitive features. His eyes were brown, deep-set, large, and penetrating. There was something of the fanatic in his look. He was quite handsome.

Under Challee's questioning he confirmed everything that Dr. Lundeen had said about Queeg. In crisp, clear, yet gentle tones, he asserted that Queeg was fit for command now and had never been unfit. Challee said, "Did Dr. Manella concur with you and Dr. Lundeen in this opinion?"

"He did."

Challee paused, then said, "Did you find any indication that the commander had what is known as a paranoid personality?"

"Well, I would prefer to call it an obsessive personality with paranoid features."

"But this did not indicate mental unfitness?"

"No, it did not."

"Do the terms 'paranoid personality' or 'obsessive personality' occur in your board's report?"

"No."

"Why not, Doctor?"

"Well, terminology is far from exact in psychiatry. The

same terms may mean different things even to men of the same school. 'Paranoid personality' sounds disabling and really isn't, at least not for me or Dr. Lundeen or Dr. Manella."

"Then Commander Queeg was pronounced fit from three different psychiatric viewpoints?"

"Yes."

"You unanimously agreed, Doctor, that Commander Queeg is mentally fit now and must have been mentally fit on 18 December, when he was summarily relieved on the grounds of mental illness?"

"That was our unanimous conclusion."

"No further questions."

Greenwald approached the witness. "Doctor, in the Freudian analysis is there such a thing as mental illness?"

"Well, there are disturbed people and adjusted people."

"But *disturbed* and *adjusted* correspond roughly, don't they, to the terms *sick* and *well* as laymen use them?"

"Very roughly, yes."

"Would you say Commander Queeg suffers from inferiority feelings?"

"Yes."

"Based on what?"

"Very severe childhood trauma. But they are well compensated."

"Is there a difference between *compensated* and *adjusted?*"

"Most definitely."

"Can you explain it?"

"Well——" Bird smiled and settled back in his chair. "Let's say a man has some deep-seated psychological disturbance buried in his unconscious. It will drive him to do strange things and will keep him in a constant state of tension, but he'll never know why. He can *compensate* by finding outlets for his peculiar drives, by will power, by daydreams, by any one of a thousand conscious devices. He can never *adjust* without undergoing psychoanalysis and bringing the disturbance up from the unconscious to the light of day."

"Has Commander Queeg ever been psychoanalyzed?"

"No."

"He is, then, a disturbed person?"

"Yes, he is. Not disabled, however, by the disturbance."

"Dr. Lundeen testified that he was adjusted."

Bird smiled. "Well, you're in terminology again. Adjustment has a special meaning in Freudian technique. Dr. Lundeen used it roughly to mean that the patient has compensated for his disturbance."

"Can you describe the commander's disturbance?"

"Without an extensive analysis I could not describe it accurately."

"You have no idea of what it is?"

"Of course the surface picture is clear. Commander Queeg subconsciously feels that he is disliked because he is wicked, stupid, and personally insignificant. This guilt and hostility trace back to infancy."

"How has he compensated?"

"In two ways, mainly. The paranoid pattern, which is useless and not desirable, and his naval career, which is extremely useful and desirable."

"You say his military career is a result of his disturbance?"

"Most military careers are."

Greenwald glanced up surreptitiously at Blakely. "Would you explain that, Doctor?"

"I simply mean that it represents an escape, a chance to return to the womb and be reborn with a synthetic blameless self."

Challee stood. "How far is this totally irrelevant technical discussion going to be pushed?"

"Are you objecting to the question?" Blakely said, scowling.

"I am requesting the court to set limits to time-wasting by the defense in confusing irrelevancies."

"Request noted. Proceed with cross-examination."

Greenwald resumed, "Doctor, did you note any peculiar habit Commander Queeg had? Something he did with his hands?"

"Do you mean rolling the marbles?"

"Yes, did he do that in your presence?"

"Not for the first week or so. Then he told me about it and I recommended that he resume the habit if it made him more comfortable. And he did so."

"Describe the habit, please."

"Well, it's an incessant rolling or rattling of two marbles in his hand—either hand."

"Did he say why he did it?"

"His hands tremble. He does it to steady his hands and conceal the trembling."

"Why do his hands tremble?"

"The inner tension. It's one of the surface symptoms."

"Does the rolling of balls have significance in the Freudian analysis?"

Bird glanced at the court uneasily. "Well, you go into technical jargon there."

"Please make it as non-technical as possible."

"Well, without analysis of the person you can only guess at the symbolism. It might be suppressed masturbation. It might be fondling poisonous pellets of feces. It all depends on——"

"Feces?"

"In the infantile world excrement is a deadly poison and therefore an instrument of vengeance. It would then be an expression of rage and hostility against the world." The court members were exchanging half-amused, half-horrified side glances. Challee protested again about the waste of court time, and Blakely again overruled him. The president was squinting at the Freudian doctor as though he were some unbelievable freak.

"Doctor," Greenwald went on, "you have testified that the commander is a disturbed, not an adjusted, person."

"Yes."

"In laymen's terms, then, he's sick."

Bird smiled. "I remember agreeing to the rough resemblance of the terms *disturbed* and *sick*. But by those terms an awful lot of people are sick——"

"But this trial only has Commander Queeg's sickness at issue. If he's sick, how could your board have given him a clean bill of health?"

"You're playing on words, I'm afraid. We found no disability."

"Could his sickness, greatly intensified, disable him?"

"Very greatly intensified, yes."

Greenwald said with sudden sharpness, "Isn't there another possibility, Doctor?"

"What do you mean?"

"Suppose the requirements of command were many times as severe as you believe them to be—wouldn't even this mild sickness disable Queeg?"

"That's absurdly hypothetical, because——"

"Is it? Have you ever had sea duty, Doctor?"

"No."

"Have you ever *been* to sea?"

"No." Bird was losing his self-possessed look.

"How long have you been in the Navy?"

"Five months—no, six, I guess, now——"

"Have you had any dealings with ships' captains before this case?"

"No."

"On what do you base your estimate of the stress of command?"

"Well, my general knowledge——"

"Do you think command requires a highly gifted, exceptional person?"

"Well, no——"

"It doesn't?"

"Not highly gifted, no. Adequate responses, fairly good intelligence, and sufficient training and experience, but——"

"Is that enough equipment for, say, a skilled psychiatrist?"

"Well, not exactly—that is, it's a different field——"

"In other words, it takes more ability to be a psychiatrist than the captain of a naval vessel?" The lawyer looked toward Blakely.

"It takes—that is, different abilities are required. You're making the invidious comparison, not I."

"Doctor, you have admitted Commander Queeg is sick, which is more than Dr. Lundeen did. The only remaining question is, *how* sick. You don't think he's sick enough to be disabled for command. I suggest that since evidently you don't know much about the requirements of command you may be wrong in your conclusion."

"I repudiate your suggestion." Bird looked like an insulted boy. His voice quivered. "You've deliberately substituted the word *sick,* which is a loose, a polarized word, for the correct——"

"Pardon me, what kind of word?"

"Polarized—loaded, invidious—I never said sick. My grasp of the requirements of command is adequate or I would have disqualified myself from serving on the board——"

"Maybe you should have."

Challee shouted, "The witness is being badgered."

"I withdraw my last statement. No more questions." Greenwald strode to his seat.

For ten minutes Challee tried to get Bird to withdraw the word "sick." The young doctor was upset. He became querulous and dogmatic, and threw up clouds of terminology. He refused to abandon the word. Challee finally excused the balky, hostile psychiatrist. He introduced as evidence the medical board's report, the Ulithi doctor's report, several of Queeg's fitness reports, and sundry logs and records of the *Caine.* His presentation was finished.

"It's three o'clock," said Blakely. "Is the defense ready to present its case?"

"I only have two witnesses, sir," said the pilot. "The first is the accused."

"Does the accused request that he be permitted to testify?"

At a nod from his lawyer, Maryk stood. "I do so request, sir."

"Stenographer will affirmatively record that the statutory request was made. . . . Defense proceed to present its case."

Maryk told the story of the morning of December 18. It was a repetition of Willie Keith's version. Greenwald said, "Was the ship in the last extremity when you relieved the captain?"

"It was."

"On what facts do you base that judgment?"

Maryk ran his tongue over his lips. "Well, several things, like—well, we were unable to hold course. We broached to three times in an hour. We were rolling too steeply for the inclinometer to record. We were shipping solid water in the wheelhouse. The generators were cutting out. The lights and the gyro cut off and on. The ship wasn't answering to emergency rudder and engine settings. The radar was jammed out by sea return. We were lost and out of control."

"Did you point these things out to the captain?"

"Repeatedly for an hour. I begged him to ballast and head into the wind."

"What was his response?"

"Well, mostly a glazed look and no answer, or a repetition of his own desires."

"Which were what?"

"I guess to hold fleet course until we went down."

"When did you start keeping your medical log on the captain?"

"Shortly after the Kwajalein invasion."

"Why did you start it?"

"Well, I began to think the captain might be mentally ill."

"Why?"

"His dropping of the yellow dye marker off Kwajalein, and then cutting off the water, and Stilwell's court-martial."

"Describe these three events in detail."

Blakely interrupted the executive officer's account of the Kwajalein incident to question him closely about bearings and distances, and the gap between the *Caine* and the landing boats. He made notes of the answers. "After these three episodes," said Greenwald, "why didn't you go directly to higher authority?"

"I wasn't sure of my ground. That's why I started the log. I figured if I ever saw I was wrong I'd burn the log. If I was right it would be necessary information."

"When did you show it to Lieutenant Keefer?"

"After the strawberry business, months later."

"Describe the strawberry business."

Maryk told the story baldly.

"Now, Lieutenant. After the typhoon was over, did Captain Queeg make any effort to regain command?"

"Yes, on the morning of the nineteenth. We'd just sighted the fleet and were joining up to return to Ulithi."

"Describe what happened."

"Well, I was in the charthouse writing up a despatch to report the relief to the OTC. The captain came in and looked over my shoulder. He said, 'Do you mind coming to my cabin and having a talk before you send that?' I said I didn't mind. I went below and we talked. It was the same thing again at first, about how I'd be tried for mutiny. He said, 'You've applied for transfer to the regular Navy. You know this means the end of all that, don't you?' Then he went into a long thing about how he loved the Navy and had no other interest in life, and even if he was cleared this would ruin his record. I said I felt sorry for him, and I really did. And he pointed out that he was bound to get relieved in a few weeks anyway, so I wasn't accomplishing anything. Finally he came out with his proposal. He said he'd forget the whole thing and never report me. He would resume command, and the whole matter would be forgotten and written off—just an incident of bad nerves during the typhoon."

"What did you say to the proposal?"

"Well, I was amazed. I said, 'Captain, the whole ship knows about it. It's written up in the quartermaster's log and the OOD's log. I've already signed the OOD log as commanding officer.' Well, he hemmed and hawed, and finally said those were penciled rough logs and it all probably just amounted to a few lines, and it wouldn't be the first time rough logs had been corrected and fixed up after the fact."

"Did you remind him of the rule against erasures?"

"Yes, and he kind of laughed and said there were rules and rules, including the rule of self-preservation. He said it was either that or a court-martial for mutiny for me, and a black mark on his record which he didn't deserve, and he didn't see that a few scribbled pencil lines were worth all that."

"Did you persist in your refusal?"

"Yes."

"What followed?"

"He began to plead and beg. It went on for quite some time, and was very unpleasant."

"Did he act irrationally?"

"No. He—he cried at one point. But he was rational. But in the end he became terrifically angry and told me to go ahead and hang myself, and ordered me out of his cabin. So I sent the despatch."

"Why didn't you accept the captain's offer?"

"I didn't see how I could."

"But the danger from the typhoon was over. Didn't you think he could conn the ship back to Ulithi?"

"I'd already committed an official act and I didn't believe making erasures in the logs would change it. Also I still believed he was mentally ill."

"But you say he was rational."

"Captain Queeg was usually okay except under great pressure, when he tended to become mentally disabled."

"Then you had the chance, twenty-four hours later, of expunging the whole event from the official record with the captain's knowledge and approval?"

"Yes."

"Lieutenant Maryk, were you panicky at any time during the typhoon?"

"I was not."

"How can you substantiate your statement?"

"Well, I—well, by what happened. After relieving the captain I rescued five survivors from the *George Black* at the height of the typhoon. I don't think a panicky officer could have effected the rescue under those conditions."

"Did you relieve Captain Queeg willfully?"

"Yes, I knew what I was doing."

"Did you relieve without authority?"

"No. My authority was Articles 184, 185, 186."

"Did you relieve without justifiable cause?"

"No. My justifiable cause was the captain's mental breakdown at a time when the ship was in danger."

"No further questions."

Challee came toward Maryk, saying in a tone of open hostility, "Just to start with, Mr. Maryk, wasn't the captain on the bridge all the time you were *effecting* that rescue?"

"He was."

"Didn't he order you to come about and look for survivors?"

"After I'd already come about, he said he was ordering me to do it."

"Didn't he direct you in the whole rescue operation?"

"Well, he kept commenting on my orders."

"Could you possibly have effected that rescue without his orders, or comments, as you call them?"

"Well, I tried to be polite. He was still senior officer present. But I was too busy to pay attention to his comments and I don't remember them."

"Didn't he even have to remind you to do an elementary thing like putting the cargo net over the side?"

"I was holding off on the cargo net till the last minute. I didn't want it to be carried away by the seas. He reminded me, but he didn't have to."

"Mr. Maryk, what kind of rating would you give yourself for loyalty to your captain?"

"That's hard to answer."

"I'll bet it is. Four-oh? Two-five? Zero?"

"I think I was a loyal officer."

"Did you issue a seventy-two-hour pass to Stilwell in December '43 against the captain's express instructions?"

"I did."

"Do you call that a loyal act?"

"No. It was a disloyal act."

Challee was caught off balance. He stared at Maryk. "You admit to a disloyal act in your first days as executive officer?"

"Yes."

"Very interesting. Why did you commit a disloyal act?"

"I have no excuse. I didn't do that kind of thing again."

"But you admit starting your term as exec as you finished it, with disloyalty?"

"I don't admit to finishing disloyally."

"Did you hear sarcastic and insulting remarks passed by the other officers about your captain?"

"I did."

"How did you punish them?"

"I didn't punish them. I repeatedly warned them against the practice and I didn't allow it in my presence."

"But you didn't punish this outright insubordination? Why didn't you?"

"There are limits to what you can do in a situation."

Challee clawed over Maryk's story of the typhoon, catching him in minor inconsistencies and memory lapses. But the exec, with dull stolidness, admitted to mistakes and inconsistencies, and stuck to his story. Then the judge advocate switched to Maryk's background, and brought out that his grades had been lower than average in high school and college, and that he had had no training in psychiatry or any other science.

"Then where did you get all of these highfalutin ideas about paranoia?"

"Out of books."

"What books? Name the titles."

"Medical-type books about mental illness."

"Was that your intellectual hobby—reading about psychiatry?"

"No. I borrowed the books off of ships' doctors here and there, after I began to think the captain was sick."

"And you, with your background—did you imagine you understood these highly technical, abstruse scientific works?"

"Well, I got something out of them."

"Have you ever heard the expression, 'A little knowledge is a dangerous thing'?"

"Yes."

"You got a headful of terms you didn't understand, and on that basis you had the temerity to depose a commanding officer on the grounds of mental illness. Is that correct?"

"I didn't relieve him because of what the books said. The ship was in danger——"

"Never mind the ship. We're discussing your grasp of psychiatry, Lieutenant." Challee belabored him with dozens of psychiatric terms, asking him for definitions and explanations. He reduced the exec to glum monosyllables and frequent repetitions of "I don't know."

"In fact, you don't know what you're talking about when you discuss mental illness, is that right?"

"I didn't say I knew much about it."

"And yet you thought you knew enough to commit an act that might be outright mutiny, justifying yourself by your grasp of psychiatric diagnosis?"

"I wanted to save the ship."

"What right had you to usurp the captain's responsibility for the ship's safety—setting aside your psychiatric insight?"

"Well, I——" Maryk stared dumbly.

"Answer the question, please! Either your act was justified by your psychiatric diagnosis of Queeg—or else it was the most serious breach of naval discipline of which you were capable. Isn't that right?"

"If he wasn't sick it would have been a mutinous act. But he was sick."

"Have you heard the diagnosis of the qualified psychiatrists who have testified?"

"Yes."

"What was their diagnosis—was he sick or wasn't he on 18 December?"

"They say he wasn't."

"Lieutenant Maryk, did you think your ship-handling judgment was better than the captain's?"

"In normal circumstances the captain could handle the ship. Under pressure he became erratic."

"Isn't the reverse possible—that under pressure *you* became erratic, and couldn't understand the captain's sound decisions? Is that possible?"

"It's possible, but——"

"As between a captain and an executive officer, who is

presumed by the Navy to have the better judgment in ship handling?"

"The captain."

"Now, Lieutenant, your so-called justification consists in two assertions, doesn't it—one, that the captain was mentally ill, and two, that the ship was in a dangerous situation—correct?"

"Yes."

"The doctors have found that he wasn't mentally ill, haven't they?"

"That's their opinion, yes——"

"Then this court must presume that the captain's estimate of the ship's situation was right and yours was wrong, isn't that so?"

Maryk said, "Yes, except—just don't forget the doctors could be wrong. They weren't there."

"Then your entire defense, Lieutenant Maryk, boils down to this. Your on-the-spot snap psychiatric diagnosis —despite your confessed ignorance of psychiatry—is superior to the judgment of three psychiatrists after three weeks of exhaustive professional examination. That is your defense, isn't it?"

Maryk took a long pause, then said shakily, "All I can say is, they didn't see him when the ship was in trouble."

Challee turned and grinned openly at the court. He went on, "Who was the third ranking officer on your ship?"

"Lieutenant Keefer."

"Was he a good officer?"

"Yes."

"What's his civilian background?"

"He's an author."

"Do you consider his mind as good as yours? Or perhaps better?"

"Perhaps better."

"Did you show him this medical log of yours?"

"Yes."

"Was he convinced by it that the captain was mentally ill?"

"No."

"Did he dissuade you from trying to have the captain relieved, two weeks before the typhoon?"

"Yes."

"And yet two weeks later—despite the whole weight of naval discipline—despite the arguments of the next officer in rank to you, a superior intellect by your own admission, arguments that had previously convinced you your diagnosis was wrong—you went ahead and seized command of your ship?"

"I relieved him because he definitely seemed sick during the typhoon."

"Don't you think it's illogical, or fantastically conceited, to insist on your ignorant diagnosis now against the opinion of three psychiatrists?"

Maryk looked around unhappily at Greenwald, who was staring at the desk. The exec's forehead was covered with wrinkles. He swung his head back and forth, like an annoyed bull. "Well, maybe it sounds that way. I don't know."

"Very well. Now then. This amazing interview in which the captain offered to falsify official records. Were there any witnesses to it?"

"No, we were alone in the captain's cabin."

"Were any erasures made? Is there the slightest thread of tangible evidence to support your story?"

"The captain knows it happened."

"You rely for confirmation of this insulting libel upon the very officer you are libeling?"

"I don't know what he'll say."

"Are you predicting that Commander Queeg will perjure himself on the stand?"

"I'm not predicting anything."

"Is there a possibility that you imagined this story, which can't be confirmed or refuted except by the other interested party, to bolster your magnificent defense that you know more psychiatry than psychiatrists?"

"I didn't imagine it."

"But you *still* imagine your diagnosis of Captain Queeg is superior to the doctors'?"

"Only—only about Queeg on the morning of the typhoon," Maryk stammered. There was sweat on his brown forehead.

"No more questions," Challee said sarcastically.

Maryk looked to his counsel. Greenwald shook his head slightly, and said, "No re-examination." The exec came off the stand with a stunned expression. Blakely adjourned the court after Greenwald told him that the last defense witness, Captain Queeg, would appear in the morning.

36 · Queeg versus Greenwald

The defense counsel introduced as evidence photostatic copies of Maryk's fitness reports, and then called Queeg. The ex-captain of the *Caine*, taking the stand, was as debonair and assured as he had been on the first day. The exec marveled again at the change wrought by sunshine, and rest, and a new blue uniform. Queeg was like a poster picture of a commanding officer of the Navy.

Greenwald lost no time in getting to the attack. "Commander, on the morning of December 19, did you have an interview in your room with Lieutenant Maryk?"

"Let's see. That's the day after the typhoon. Yes, I did."

"Was it at your request?"

"Yes."

"What was the substance of that interview?"

"Well, as I say, I felt sorry for him. I hated to see him ruining his life with one panicky mistake. Particularly as I knew his ambition was to make the Navy his career. I tried as hard as I could to show him what a mistake he had made. I recommended that he relinquish command to me, and I offered to be as lenient as I could in reporting what had happened."

"What was his response?"

"Well, as you know, he persisted in the course that led to this court-martial."

"You say you felt sorry for him. Weren't you worried about the effect of the episode on your own career?"

"Well, after all, I knew the verdict of the doctors would turn out as it did. I can't say I was very worried."

"Did you offer not to report the incident at all?"

"Of course not. I offered to report the incident in the most extenuating way I could."

"How could you have extenuated it?"

"Well, I thought there were extenuating circumstances. A rough situation where a junior officer might well lose his head. And there was the rescue, which he brought off well under my direction. I was assuming mainly that by restoring command to me he'd acknowledge the error. It was the only course at that point that might have saved him."

"You never offered not to report the incident?"

"How could I? It was already recorded in the logs."

"Were the logs in pencil, or typed, or what?"

"That would make no difference."

"Were they in pencil, Commander?"

"Well, let's see. Probably they were—QM log and OOD rough log always are. I doubt the yeoman would have gotten around to typing smooth logs in all the excitement."

"Did you offer to erase the incident from the penciled logs and make no report at all?"

"I did not. Erasures aren't permitted in penciled logs."

"Lieutenant Maryk has testified under oath, Commander, that you made such an offer. Not only that, but you begged and pleaded and even wept to get him to agree to erase those few pencil lines, in return for which you promised to hush up the incident completely and make no report."

"That isn't true." Queeg spoke calmly and pleasantly.

"There isn't any truth in it at all?"

"Well, it's a distortion of what I told you. My version is the exact truth."

"You deny the proposal to erase the logs and hush up the story?"

"I deny it completely. That's the part he made up. And the weeping and the pleading. That's fantastic."

"You are accusing Mr. Maryk of perjury?"

"I'm not accusing him. He's accused of enough as it stands. You're likely to hear a lot of strange things from Mr. Maryk about me, that's all."

"Isn't one of you obviously not telling the truth about that interview?"

"It appears so."

"Can you prove it isn't you?"

"Only by citing a clean record of over eight years as a naval officer, against the word of a man on trial for a mutinous act."

"It's his word against yours, then, in this matter?"

"Unfortunately there wasn't anyone else in my cabin at the time."

"Commander, did you recommend to the commodore at Ulithi that Maryk be allowed to take the *Caine* to Linga-yen Gulf?"

"I thought that would come up. I did, yes."

"Despite the fact that, according to your story, you had seen him make a panicky mistake in a tight situation—a mistake of the most disastrous kind?"

"Well, I wasn't recommending him for command. The commodore put it to me that the Navy desperately needed minesweepers. He asked me to put aside personal considerations. I did put aside personal considerations. Maryk vindicated the training I had given him. And if as a result of that he gets acquitted and I carry a black mark for the rest of my naval career I'll still say I did the right thing."

"How could you be sure he wouldn't make another panicky mistake which would cost all the lives on the *Caine?*"

"Well, he didn't, did he? I took a calculated risk, and he didn't."

"Commander, the *Caine* took a Kamikaze hit at Lingayen, and yet Maryk brought the ship back safely. Was that likely in a man given to panicky mistakes?"

"Well, I understand it was a glancing hit, practically a miss. Anyway, for all I know, Keefer took charge in the pinch. Keefer is an outstanding officer, best on the ship. I relied more on him than on Maryk."

"Commander Queeg, did you ever receive a hundred ten dollars from Lieutenant Junior Grade Keith?"

"I may have. I don't recall offhand that I did."

"He testified that you did."

"I did? On what occasion?"

"On the occasion of a loss of a crate of yours in San Francisco Bay. He assumed responsibility and paid for the loss."

"Yes. I remember now. It was over a year ago. December or thereabouts. He was responsible for the loss, and insisted on paying, and so he did."

"What was in the crate that cost a hundred and ten dollars?"

"Personal belongings. I don't recall. Probably uniforms, books, navigating instruments—the usual."

"You remember the figure of a hundred and ten dollars?"

"Something like that, I don't recall exactly."

"How was Keith responsible for the loss?"

"Well, he was boat officer and in charge of the unloading. He issued foolish and contradictory orders. The men got rattled and the crate fell into the water and sank."

"A wooden crate full of clothes sank?"

"There were other things in it, I guess. I had some souvenir coral rocks."

"Commander, wasn't the crate entirely full of bottles of intoxicating liquor?"

After a barely perceptible pause—the skip of a heartbeat, no more—Queeg answered, "Certainly not."

"Keith has testified you charged him for thirty-one bottles of liquor."

"You'll hear plenty of strange distortions about me from Keith and Maryk. They're the two culprits here and they're apt to make all kinds of strange statements."

"Did you make this crate yourself?"

"No. My carpenter's mate did."

"What was his name?"

"I don't recall. It'll be on the personnel records. He's been gone from the ship a long time."

"Where is this carpenter's mate now, Commander?"

"I don't know. I transferred him to the beach at Funafuti at the request of the commodore for a carpenter. This was back in May."

"You don't recall his name?"

"No."

"Was it Carpenter's Mate Second Class Otis F. Langhorne?"

"Lang, Langhorne. Sounds right."

"Commander, there is a Carpenter's Mate First Class Otis F. Langhorne at present in damage-control school at Treasure Island, right here in the bay. Defense has arranged to subpoena him if necessary."

Queeg was obviously brought up short. His head sank between his shoulders. He shot a look at Challee. "You're sure it's the same one?"

"His service record shows twenty-one months aboard the U.S.S. *Caine*. Your signature is in it. Would it be useful to have him subpoenaed, sir?"

Challee said, "Objection to this entire interminable irrelevancy about the crate, and request it be stricken from the record."

Greenwald said, "The credibility of the witness is being established. I submit to the court that nothing could be more relevant to this trial."

Challee was overruled. The question was repeated. Queeg said, "Well, it's a question which crate Langhorne nailed up. I had two crates, as I recall now."

"Oh?" Greenwald paused for a long time. "Well! This is a new angle, not mentioned by Keith. Did Langhorne make both crates, sir?"

"Well, I don't recall whether I had both crates on that occasion or two crates on two different occasions. It's all very trivial and happened a long time ago and I've had a year of combat steaming in between and a typhoon and all this hospital business and I'm not too clear. As I recall now on two different occasions there were two crates."

"What was the other occasion?"

"I don't recall. It might even have been back in peacetime, for all I know."

"Did you lose both crates in San Francisco Bay?"

"As I say, I'm not clear on all this, I don't recall."

"Commander, there are many points in this trial which turn on the issue of credibility between yourself and other officers. If you wish I will request a five-minute recess while you clear your mind as well as you can on the matter of these crates."

"That won't be necessary. Just let me think for a moment, please." In the silence Blakely's pencil made a thin rattling noise as he rolled it under his palm on the bench. Queeg sat staring from under his eyebrows. "Kay. I have it straight now. I made a misstatement. I lost a crate in San Diego Harbor back in '38 or '39 I think it was, under similar circumstances. That was the one containing clothes. The crate Keith lost did contain liquor."

"Thirty-one bottles?"

"Something like that."

"How did you obtain thirty-one bottles of——"

Challee said, "May it please the court, *Courts and Boards* requires evidence to be developed briefly, materially, and relevantly. It is useless for me to stall this trial indefinitely with objections. I question defense's entire tactic of expanding on irrelevancies which confuse the issue."

Blakely said, "Court is aware of requirements of evidence and thanks the judge advocate for emphasizing them. Defense will proceed."

"How did you obtain thirty-one bottles of whisky, Commander, in wartime?" said Greenwald.

"Bought up the rations of my officers at the wine mess in Pearl."

"You transported this liquor from Pearl to the States in your ship? Do you know the regulations——"

Queeg broke in, "I'm aware of regulations. The crate was sealed prior to getting under way. I gave it the same locked stowage I gave the medicinal brandy. Liquor wasn't obtainable in the States, and was at Pearl. I'd had three years of steady combat duty. I gave myself this leeway as captain of the *Caine* and it was a common practice and I believe rank has its privileges, as they say. I had no intention of concealing it from the court and I'm not ashamed of it. I simply mixed up the two crates in my mind."

"Keith testified, Commander, that you gave all the orders to the boat crew which caused the loss of the crate."

"That's a lie."

"Also that you refused to sign his leave papers until he paid for the loss."

"That's another lie."

"It seems to be the issue of credibility again, sir—this time your word against Keith's. Correct?"

"You'll hear nothing but lies about me from Keith. He has an insane hatred for me."

"Do you know why, sir?"

"I can't say, unless it's his resentment against fancied injuries to his crony, this sailor Stilwell. Those two were mighty affectionate."

"Affectionate, sir?"

"Well, it seems to me every time Keith thought I looked cross-eyed at Stilwell there was all kinds of screeching and hollering from Keith as though I were picking on his wife or something. I don't know how else to explain the two of them ganging up so fast to back Maryk when he relieved me unless they were pretty sweet on each other and had a sort of understanding."

"Commander, are you suggesting there were abnormal relations between Lieutenant Keith and the sailor Stilwell?"

"I'm not suggesting a thing," Queeg said with a sly grin. "I'm stating plain facts that everybody knew who had eyes to see."

Greenwald looked around at Blakely. "Does the court desire to caution the witness about the gravity of this insinuated charge?"

"I'm not insinuating a thing, sir!" Queeg said nasally. "I don't know of anything improper between those two men and I deny insinuating anything. I said Keith was always taking Stilwell's part and it's the easiest thing in the world to prove and that's all I said or meant. I resent the twisting of my words."

Blakely, his face all wrinkled, said to Greenwald, "Are you going to pursue this topic?"

"No, sir."

"Very well. Go ahead."

"Commander Queeg, during the period when the *Caine* was towing targets at Pearl Harbor did you ever steam over your own towline and cut it?"

"Objection!" Challee was on his feet again. Blakely gave him a frankly irritated look and ordered the court cleared, motioning to the two lawyers to remain behind.

The skin of Challee's face was leaden gray. "I beg the court's indulgence. I must object. This towline business is the last straw. The tactics of the defense counsel are an outrage on the dignity of these proceedings. He's systematically turning this trial into a court-martial of Commander Queeg. He's not bringing out any evidence bearing on the issue. He's trying to smear and defame Queeg and nothing else."

Greenwald said, "Sir, the judge advocate has made it perfectly clear that he thinks he has a prima facie case in the report of the three psychiatrists. Maybe he wants the defense to switch to a guilty plea. But I say it's still up to the court, not to shore-bound doctors, however brilliant, to judge whether the captain of the *Caine* was mentally well enough to retain his self-control and his post during a typhoon. This is a direct argument to the issue. I have no way to conduct it except to review the witness's performance of duty in critical situations prior to the typhoon."

"Counsel will step outside," said Blakely.

"I must respectfully state," said the judge advocate, "that in my opinion, if my objection is overruled, and the reviewing authority disapproves the court's ruling, it will be a fatal error invalidating the entire proceedings, and a miscarriage of justice will result."

"Very well, clear the court."

There was a fifteen-minute wait. Blakely and the other court members looked grim when the parties returned.

"The objection is overruled. The witness will answer the question." Challee appeared stunned, sitting down slowly. The stenographer read the question about the towline from the record.

Queeg answered promptly, "Well, here's the story on that particular slander. I saw some AA bursts close aboard to starboard. I was gravely concerned that my ship might be within range of somebody's firing. We were in a gunnery area. I was watching the bursts. This same sailor Stilwell, a very dreamy and unreliable man, was at the helm. He failed to warn me that we were coming around the full 360 degrees. I saw what was happening, finally, and instantly reversed course, and I avoided passing over the towline, to my best knowledge. However, the line parted during the turn. There was a lot of vicious gossip, circulated mainly by Stilwell and Keith, to the effect that I'd cut the towline. I ascribed the mishap to a defective line in my written report to ComServPac. And he was cognizant of all this vicious gossip. And he knew all the circumstances. And he still accepted my report. It's on file. So I say it's conceivable that this vicious gossip was correct, but I consider it much more likely that the judgment of ComServPac in the matter can be relied on."

Greenwald nodded. "You were distracted, you say, by AA bursts. Did anything else distract you?"

"Not that I recall."

"Were you engaged in reprimanding a signalman named Urban at length for having his shirttail out, while your ship was turning 360 degrees?"

"Who says that—Keith again?"

"Will you answer the question, Commander?"

"It's a malicious lie, of course."

"Was Urban on the bridge at the time?"

"Yes."

"Was his shirttail out?"

"Yes, and I reprimanded him. That took me about two seconds. I'm not in the habit of dwelling on those things. Then there were these AA bursts, and that was what distracted me."

"Did you point out these AA bursts to the OOD or the exec?"

"I may have. I don't recall. I didn't run weeping to my OOD on every occasion. I may very well have kept my own counsel. And since this shirttail thing has been brought up—and it's a very typical Keith distortion, the whole business—I'd like to say that Ensign Keith as morale officer was in charge of enforcing uniform regulations and completely soldiered on the job. When I took over the ship it was like the Chinese Navy. And I bore down on Keith to watch those shirttails and he kept funking it and for all I know that's another reason he hated me and circulated all this about my cutting the towline."

"Ensign Keith did not testify on this point, Commander. Can you name any officer who will testify that he saw those AA bursts?"

"Maybe all of them did and then again maybe none of them did. It was fifteen months ago and we've been fighting a war and we've had much more on our mind than a few AA bursts off Pearl."

"Did you drop a yellow dye marker off Jacob Island on the first morning of the invasion of Kwajalein?"

"I may have. I don't recall."

"Did your orders include dropping the marker?"

"I don't recall. There have been several other invasions since."

"Do you recall what your first mission was during the invasion?"

"Yes. To lead a group of attack boats to the line of departure for Jacob Island."

"Did you fulfill that mission?"

"Yes."

"Why did you drop the dye marker?"

"I don't know for sure that I did drop one."

"Commander, the orders of the *Caine* on that morning are a matter of record, and there's no mention of dropping a dye marker. This court has heard repeated testimony to the effect that you did drop one. Do you deny that testimony?"

"Well, it sounds as though I may have dropped it to

mark the line of departure plainly, if I did it, but it's all dim in my mind."

"How far was the line of departure from the beach?"

"As I recall, a thousand yards."

"Did you stay close to the attack boats, leading them in?"

"Well, naturally, not wanting to swamp them with my bow wave, I was a bit ahead."

"How far ahead?"

"This all happened a year ago——"

"Fifty yards? Twenty thousand yards?"

"Well, I don't know. A couple of hundred yards, maybe."

"Commander, did you run a mile ahead of the attack boats, drop your marker, and retire at high speed, leaving the boats to grope to the line of departure as best they could?"

Challee leaped to his feet. "The question is abusive and flagrantly leading."

"I am willing to withdraw the question," said Greenwald wearily, "in view of the commander's dim memory, and proceed to more recent events."

"Court desires to question the witness," said Blakely. Greenwald retreated to his desk, watching the president's face. "Commander Queeg," Blakely said, "in view of the implications in this line of testimony, I urge you to search your memory for correct answers."

"I am certainly trying to do that, sir, but as I say these are very small points and I've been through several campaigns since Kwajalein and the typhoon and now all this business——"

"I appreciate that. If necessary the court can call a recess for several days to obtain depositions from officers and men of that attack group. It will facilitate justice if you can remember enough to give a few definite answers on points of fact. First of all, can you recall whether your orders contained instructions to drop a dye marker?"

"Well, to the best of my recollection they didn't. That can be checked against the record. But I believe I can say definitely that they didn't, as I recall now."

"Very well. Will you please repeat your explanation of why you dropped it?"

"Well, I guess to mark the line of departure plainly."

"Were those boats on the line of departure when you turned away from the beach?"

"As near as I could calculate, yes. This was all a matter of tangent bearings and radar ranges of course, but I brought them as close to the line as was humanly possible."

"In that case, Commander, if they were already on the line, what purpose did the dye marker serve?"

Queeg hesitated. "Well, you might say a safety factor. Just another added mark. Maybe I erred in being overcautious and making sure they knew where they were but then again I've always believed you can't err on the side of safety."

"From the time you made rendezvous with the boats, Commander, until the time you dropped the marker, what was the widest gap between you and the boats?"

"Well, distances are deceptive over water, particularly with those low-lying boats."

"Did you stay within hailing distance of them?" Blakely said with a slight acrid impatient note.

"Hailing distance? No. We communicated by semaphore. I might have swamped them if I'd stayed within hailing distance."

Blakely pointed at the redheaded officer at the far left of the bench. "Lieutenant Murphy informs the court that he was a boat officer in similar situations in three invasions. He says the common practice was to stay within hailing distance, never more than a hundred or a hundred fifty yards apart."

Queeg, slumped in his seat, looked out from under his eyebrows at the lieutenant. "Well, that may be. It was a windy day and the bow wave made a lot of wash. It was simpler to semaphore than to go screaming through megaphones."

"Did you have the conn?"

Queeg paused. "As I recall now Lieutenant Maryk did,

and I now recall I had to caution him for opening the gap too wide."

"How wide?"

"I can't say, but at one point there was definitely too much open water and I called him aside and admonished him not to run away from the boats."

"Why did your executive officer have the conn?"

"Well, he was navigator and for split-second precision instead of repeating a lot of orders back and forth——And it's all coming back to me now. As I recall I dropped the marker because Maryk had opened the gap so wide and I wanted to be sure the boats knew exactly where the line of departure was."

"Didn't you direct him to slow down when you saw the gap widening?"

"Well, but it was all happening very fast and I may have been watching the beach for a few seconds and then I saw we were running away. And so that's why I dropped the marker, to compensate for Maryk's running away from the boats."

"These are your factual recollections, Commander?" Blakely's face was grave.

"Those are the facts, sir."

Blakely said to Greenwald, "You may resume your examination."

The lawyer, leaning against his desk, said at once, "Commander Queeg, did you make it a practice, during invasions, to station yourself on the side of the bridge that was sheltered from the beach?"

Queeg said angrily, "That's an insulting question, and the answer is no, I had to be on all sides of the bridge at once, constantly running from one side to the other because Maryk was navigator and Keith was my OOD at general quarters and both of them were invariably scurrying to the safe side of the bridge so I was captain and navigator and OOD all rolled in one and that's why I had to move constantly from one side of the bridge to the other. And that's the truth, whatever lies may have been said about me in this court."

Greenwald, slack-mouthed, his face expressionless, kept

his eyes on the court members, who stirred in their chairs. "Commander," he said, as soon as Queeg subsided, "do you recall an incident during the Saipan invasion when the U.S.S. *Stanfield* was fired on by a shore battery?"

"I most certainly do." The ex-captain glowered at Greenwald, breathing heavily. "I don't know what lies have been sworn to in this court about that little matter, but I'll be glad to set the record straight on that, too. This same Mr. Keith we're talking about went hollering and screaming all over the bridge making a big grandstand play about wanting to fire on the shore battery when the *Stanfield* was in my line of fire and it was absolutely impossible to fire. And so I returned to my patrol station because that was my assigned duty, patrolling, not interdicting fire on shore batteries, and the plane was sunk without a trace and as for the *Stanfield* it was taking mighty good care of itself."

"What is the turning circle of the *Caine,* sir?"

"A thousand yards, but——"

"Sir, in swinging a thousand yards didn't the *Stanfield* move out of your line of fire to give you a clear shot at the shore battery?"

"For all I know the *Stanfield* paralleled my course. I never had a clear shot, that's all I know."

"Court desires to question the witness," said Blakely.

Challee stood. "Sir, the witness is obviously and understandably agitated by this ordeal, and I request a recess to give him a breathing space——"

"I am not in the least agitated," exclaimed Queeg, "and I'm glad to answer any and all questions here and in fact I demand a chance to set the record straight on anything derogatory to me in the testimony that's gone before. I did not make a single mistake in fifteen months aboard the *Caine* and I can prove it and my record has been spotless until now and I don't want it smirched by a whole lot of lies and distortions by disloyal officers."

"Commander, would you like a recess?" said Blakely.

"Definitely not, sir. I request there be no recess if it's up to me."

"Very well. Was the *Stanfield* hit during this incident?"

"No it was not, sir."

"Was it straddled?"

"It was straddled, yes, sir."

"And there was no way you could maneuver to lend it fire support? Did you try?"

"As I say, sir, it was in my line of fire and my estimate of the situation was that in the circumstances my duty was to get back on anti-sub station and not run around trying to make a grandstand play with pot shots at the beach and that was my command decision and I will stand on it as being in accordance with every existing doctrine, sir. It's a question of mission. My mission was patrol."

"Commander, wouldn't you consider returning enemy fire, directed at yourself or at a nearby unit, an overriding mission?"

"Definitely, sir, if the range was clear. The *Stanfield* was in my line of fire, however."

Blakely glanced at the other court members, his eyebrows puckered, and then nodded shortly to Greenwald. The lawyer said, "Commander, on the morning of 18 December, at the moment you were relieved, was the *Caine* in the last extremity?"

"It certainly was not!"

"Was it in grave danger at that moment?"

"Absolutely not. I had that ship under complete control."

"Did you tell the other officers that you had intended to come north, as Maryk did, at ten o'clock—that is, about fifteen minutes after the relief took place?"

Queeg plunged his hand into his coat pocket and brought out two glistening steel balls. "Yes, I did make that statement, and such had been my intention."

"Why did you intend to abandon fleet course, Commander, if the ship wasn't in danger?"

There was a long silence. Then Queeg said, "Well, I don't see any inconsistency there. I've repeatedly stated in my testimony that my rule is safety first. As I say the ship wasn't in danger but a typhoon is still a typhoon and I'd just about decided that we'd do as well riding it out head to sea. I might have executed my intention at ten o'clock and then again I might not have. I was still weighing all the factors but as I say I had that ship under control and even after Maryk relieved me I saw to it that it remained under control. I never abandoned my post."

"Then Maryk's decision to come north was not a panicky, irrational blunder?"

"His panicky blunder was relieving me. I kept him from making any disastrous mistakes thereafter. I didn't intend to vindicate myself at the cost of all the lives on the *Caine*."

"Commander Queeg, have you read Lieutenant Maryk's medical log?"

"I have read that interesting document, yes sir, I have. It is the biggest conglomeration of lies and distortions and half-truths I've ever seen and I'm extremely glad you asked me because I want to get my side of it all on the record."

"Please state your version, or any factual comments on the episodes in the log, sir."

"Well, now, starting right with that strawberry business the real truth is that I was betrayed and thrown and double-crossed by my executive officer and this precious gentleman Mr. Keith who between them corrupted my wardroom so that I was one man against a whole ship without any support from my officers—— Now, you take that strawberry business—why, if that wasn't a case of outright conspiracy to protect a malefactor from justice—— Maryk carefully leaves out the little fact that I had conclusively proved by a process of elimination that someone had a key to the icebox. He says it was the steward's mates who ate the strawberries but if I wanted to take the trouble I could prove to this court geometrically that they couldn't have. It's the water business all over again, like when the crew was taking baths seven times a day and our evaps were definitely on the fritz half the time and I was trying to inculcate the simplest principles of water conservation, but no, Mr. Maryk the hero of the crew wanted to go right on mollycoddling them and—or you take the coffee business —no, well, the strawberry thing first—it all hinged on a thorough search for the key and that was where Mr. Maryk as usual with the help of Mr. Keith fudged it. Just went through a lot of phony motions that proved nothing and—like thinking the incessant burning out of Silexes which were government property was a joke, which was the attitude of everybody from Maryk down, no sense of responsibility though I emphasized over and over that the war wouldn't last forever, that all these things would have to be accounted for. It was a constant battle, always the same thing, Maryk and Keith undermining my authority, always arguments, though I personally liked Keith and kept trying to train him up only to get stabbed in the back when—— I think I've covered the strawberry business and—oh, yes, Stilwell's court-martial. That was a disgraceful business, quite typical——"

Commander Queeg passed to a review of the court-martial, which was also, he said, a conspiracy of Keith and Maryk to discredit him. Then he discussed the failures of the laundry, the sloppiness of the mess statements and ship's service inventories, and went on from subject to subject in this way, cataloguing his grievances against his officers, mainly Maryk and Keith. He hardly paused for breath. He seemed unable to pause. His narrative became less distinct as he talked, his jumps in time and place more sudden and harder to follow. He talked on and on, rolling the balls, his face glowing with satisfaction as he scored all these successive points in his vindication. Greenwald strolled to his desk and leaned against it, listening respectfully. The court members stared at the witness. Challee slouched, biting his nails. The sentences became longer and more meandering. Blakely began to glance at the clock.

Queeg went on for eight or nine minutes in this way, and ended up, "Well, naturally, I can only cover these things roughly from memory but if I've left anything out why you just ask me specific questions and I'll tackle them one by one, but I believe I've hit the main points."

"It was a very thorough and complete answer, thank you," Greenwald said. He drew two glossy black photostats from a folder on his desk. "Commander, I show you authenticated copies of two fitness reports you wrote on Lieutenant Maryk. Do you recognize them as such?"

Queeg took the papers and said grumpily, glancing at them, "Yes, I do."

"Please read to the court your comment on Maryk of January 1944."

"I've already stated," Queeg said, "that at first he put on the act of a red-hot but cooled off in time——"

"We have that testimony, Commander. Please read the comment."

Queeg read in a choked voice a highly laudatory description of Maryk.

"Thank you, Commander. That was January. Now by July, six months later, had the *Caine* already been through the Kwajalein and Saipan invasions?"

"Yes."

"Had the following incidents already occurred: the water shortage, the coffee investigation, the Stilwell court-martial, and the suspension of movies, among others?"

Queeg hesitated. "Well, by then, yes, I think."

"Please read your comment of 1 July on Lieutenant Maryk."

Queeg stared at the photostat for a long time, hunched over, and began mumbling, " 'This officer has if anything improved in his performance of duty since the last fitness report. He is consistently loyal, unflagging, thorough, courageous, and efficient. He is considered at present fully qualified for command of a 1200-ton DMS. His professional zeal and integrity set him apart as an outstanding example for other officers, reserve and regular alike. He cannot be too highly commended. He is recommended for transfer to the regular Navy.' "

"Thank you, Commander. No further questions."

Greenwald walked to his desk and sat. The witness looked toward the judge advocate appealingly. Challee stood slowly, like an old man with rheumatism. He approached the witness stand, and seemed about to speak. Then he turned to Blakely. "No cross-examination."

"You are excused, Commander," Blakely said. Queeg went out of the courtroom in the same way that Maryk had seen him pass through the wheelhouse a thousand times—shoulders hunched, head down, feet scurrying, the balls rolling in his fingers.

Greenwald said, "Defense has finished its presentation."

"Recess until one o'clock," said Blakely.

37 · The Verdict

Challee had the face of a man sailing into a fist fight when he rose for his opening argument.

"If it please the court, I am almost at a loss to discuss the case the defense has presented. I have nothing to refute. It's no case at all. It has nothing to do with the charge or the specification. It has nothing whatever to do with the accused, or the acts for which he is undergoing a general court-martial.

"The defense counsel's very first question in this trial was, 'Commander, have you ever heard the expression "Old Yellowstain"?' I objected then, I object now to the entire strategy and tactics of the defense counsel before this court. His one idea has been to twist the proceedings around so that the accused would become not Maryk but Commander Queeg. To a certain extent he has succeeded. He has dragged out every possible vicious and malicious criticism of the commander from the other witnesses, and forced Queeg to defend himself against them in open court, on the spur of the moment, without preparation, without advice of counsel, without any of the normal privileges and safeguards of an accused man under naval law.

"All right. What has defense counsel proved in this orgy of mudslinging, insults, trick questions, and defamation? Let's assume that everything he tried to prove against Commander Queeg is true—which I don't for a moment concede—even so, what has he proved, I say, except that

Queeg was not a good officer? What has he tried to bring out except that the commander's term aboard the *Caine* was an unhappy mess of bad judgment and poor administration? Did that give Lieutenant Maryk the right of summary relief of command? Can this court possibly endorse the precedent that a captain who seems to be making mistakes can be deposed by underlings? And that his only recourse after that is to be placed on the witness stand at a general court-martial to answer every petty gripe and justify all his command decisions to a hostile lawyer taking the part of his insubordinate inferior? Such a precedent is nothing but a blank check for mutiny. It is the absolute destruction of the chain of command.

"The one issue in this trial was the insanity of Commander Queeg—the insanity, not the mistakes or misdeeds or poor judgment. The language of Articles 184, 185, and 186 excludes every possibility except the complete, utter, and unmistakable madness of the captain. The defense made no effort to establish such a justification for the simple reason that it never existed. Captain Queeg always was and still is as sane as any of us, whatever his errors may have been, and defense counsel knows it.

"Has any officer of this court ever sailed with a captain who committed no errors of judgment? Has any officer who has been in the Navy more than a few years failed to find himself under a captain with marked personal and emotional eccentricities? Naval command is the greatest strain that can be brought to bear on a person. The captain is a god—in theory. Some lapse more, some less, from that ideal. But the procurement policies of the Navy are rigid. That is why the presumption is always overwhelmingly on the side of the commanding officer in any dispute. He's a man who has been tried in the fire. Whatever his weaknesses—and they may even be grave weaknesses—he's a man who can command a combatant ship.

"In proof of this I need only cite the recorded fact that this case is the first in thirty years impugning the captain of a Navy ship under those articles. And even in this case the scientific findings of psychiatrists are forcibly and unanimously on the side of the Navy's system of command appointments. The doctors say that the Navy *did* know what it was doing in giving the *Caine* to Commander Queeg.

"With the leeway the court gave him, defense counsel brought out every single mistake, every single lapse of judgment that the captain of the *Caine* made or that some underling thought he made. The court knows that it all adds up to puling complaints against strictness and meticulousness—all but one point. That point is the imputation that this officer of the Navy was a coward under fire. I shall not discuss that point. I leave it to this court to determine whether a coward could rise to command of a combatant ship and remain undetected by his superiors through fifteen months of battle service. I count on the court to see the difference between bad judgment and poltroonery. I leave it to the court to reject this smear on the Navy.

"Let's look at the facts. Commander Queeg was given command of an obsolete, decaying, run-down ship. He brought it through fifteen months of combat unscathed, and carried out a multitude of assignments to the satisfaction of his superiors. There's no complaint against him on the record by his superiors—only by his underlings. He achieved this record of satisfactory battle service despite the hostility and disloyalty of his officers. He achieved it despite personal inner tensions, which the doctors have described—and which the defense viciously hammered at in a vain attempt to exaggerate them into insanity. Commander Queeg's achievement in the face of his own emotional difficulties and the disloyalty of his wardroom adds up, not to a bad record, but to a fine one, to an impressive one. He emerges as a loyal, hard-working, terribly conscientious officer who has been unjustly forced through a harrowing ordeal.

"The accused emerges without any justification. The defense counsel brought no psychiatrists to refute the findings of the medical board. He didn't because he couldn't have found any. Once the cloud of mudslinging settles down, the facts remain as they were at the outset. A commanding officer of a United States Navy ship was relieved of his command willfully and without authority. The claimed authority of Articles 184, 185, and 186 was voided by the medical board. No justifiable cause, either mental illness or any other, has been brought forward by the defense. It has been proved by expert testimony that Commander Queeg's ship-handling decisions in the typhoon up to the moment he was relieved were not only sensible and sound, but the best possible in the circumstances.

"The accused stands convicted by the facts. In his defense not one mitigating fact has been established. The court will reject, I am certain, the cynical, insulting attempt of the defense counsel to sway its emotions. The court will find the specification proved by the facts."

The contrast between Challee's manner and Greenwald's could not have been sharper. The pilot was soft, apologetic, hesitant after the judge advocate's passionate shouting. He kept looking from Blakely to Challee. He started by mentioning that he had undertaken Maryk's defense reluctantly at the judge advocate's request. "I was reluctant," he said, "because I knew that the only possible defense of the accused was to show in court the mental incompetence of an officer of the Navy. It has been the most unpleasant duty I've ever had to perform. Let me make one thing clear. It is not and never has been the contention of the defense that Commander Queeg is a coward. The entire case of the defense rests on the opposite assumption: that no man who rises to command of a United States naval ship can possibly be a coward. And that therefore if he commits questionable acts under fire the explanation must lie elsewhere."

Proceeding in the same calm, diffident tone, Greenwald reviewed all the damaging evidence against Queeg, laying especial stress on the points that had seemed to impress Blakely. He emphasized that both psychiatrists had admitted, in one form of words or another, that Queeg was sick. And he repeated over and over that it was up to the court, who knew the sea, to decide whether or not the sickness of Queeg was bad enough to incapacitate him. He referred briefly and apologetically to Queeg's behavior in court—his evasiveness, incoherence, changing stories, and inability to stop speaking—as further unfortunate evidence of his mental illness. He said very little about Maryk. It was all Queeg, Queeg, Queeg.

The court debated for an hour and ten minutes. Maryk was acquitted.

Maryk and Greenwald were surrounded on the sidewalk outside the court-martial building by a small jubilant knot of people. The exec's mother clung to him, weeping and laughing: a fat little woman in a green hat, with a round seamed face like a wrinkled photograph of her son's. Beside her stood the father, a heavy quiet shabby man, patting her shoulder. All the officers of the *Caine* were there. Willie Keith capered and shouted, slapping everyone on the back. All was noise and congratulation and joy. Greenwald was jostled by eager handshaking. "All right now listen, listen everybody," yelled Keefer. "Listen to me. We're going to celebrate!"

"Sure! Sure! Celebrate! Let's celebrate! Let's all get stiff! Fried! Boiled!"—a ribald chorus.

"No, will you listen? It's all arranged. Dinner at the Fairmont! I've hired a room. I'm paying. I'm rich!" shouted Keefer. "It's a double celebration! I got the contract on my novel in the mail this morning, and a check for a thousand bucks! It's all on Chapman House!"

Sailors a block away from the building turned to state in amazement at the frantic little group of officers yelping and dancing in the hot sunshine. "I will get monumentally drunk," cried Harding. "I will wake up in the alcoholic ward. And I'll love it." Jorgensen hugged and kissed the trunk of a eucalyptus tree in excess of joy. His glasses fell off and shattered. He peered around, giggling wildly. "Nothing but champagne will be served," yelled the novelist. "Champagne to toast the Fifth Freedom. Freedom from Old Yellowstain!"

Maryk blinked confusedly. "Greenwald's invited, isn't he?"

"Invited! Hell, he's the guest of honor," Keefer bawled. "A Daniel! A Daniel come to judgment! Momma and

Poppa, too! Wire your brothers! Tell 'em to fly down! Bring anyone you want!"

Greenwald said, "You guys have a fine time. Leave me out of it——"

The mother said through sobs, "You're a good boy, Steve. You never did anything wrong——"

"The hell with that," Maryk said to Greenwald, wriggling in his mother's embrace. "If you don't come I don't. It's all off."

"Man, don't ruin it," said Keefer, throwing his arm over Greenwald's shoulder. "What'll the party be like without the hero of the occasion?"

"You're the hero—a thousand bucks——" said the lawyer, disengaging himself.

Keefer cried, "I'll send a limousine and chauffeur for you——"

"That won't be necessary. Fairmont? Okay. I'll be there." Greenwald turned and started up the steps.

"Where you going, Barney?" Maryk said anxiously.

"Got to clean up the debris with Challee. You go along, Steve. See you tonight."

Keefer shouted after him, "Give Challee a crying towel, with the compliments of the *Caine!*" Howls of joyous laughter went up from the officers.

A huge green-iced cake baked in the shape of a book was the most prominent decoration of the table.

Multitudes, Multitudes
A NOVEL BY
Thomas Keefer

was written on it in flourishing letters of thick yellow sugar. It was surrounded by a bank of ferns and roses. The table was crowded with flowers, and candles, and silver, and bottles of champagne. Shreds of gold and silver foil from the wine bottles were scattered on the white cloth. It was seven o'clock, the chair at the head of the table was still vacant, and no food had yet been served. The officers were already boisterously drunk. Mr. and Mrs. Maryk smiled uncomfortably at the roistering jokes all around them, and laughed aloud whenever their son did. The exec sat at the right of Greenwald's empty chair, with his parents beside him. Opposite them were Keefer and Keith, side by side, sparking the merriment with a running fire of shouted jokes about Old Yellowstain. It was an inexhaustible topic. Jorgensen, at the foot of the table, was dissolved in howling giggles; tears ran down from his squinting bloodshot eyes. Several new officers who had reported aboard since the ship's return, and who had never seen Queeg, listened in wide-eyed wonder, and laughed uneasily at the jokes, and drank vast quantities of Keefer's champagne.

Willie was having a wonderful time. Though he suspected that Keefer had not been especially manly in the court-martial, he had no way of knowing the truth of the matter. Witnesses were not permitted to hear each other testify; and Maryk had never spoken a word against Keefer throughout the affair. All qualms had been forgotten in the grand wonder of the exec's acquittal, and Willie's release from fear. He drank as much of the novelist's champagne as anybody, excepting perhaps Harding. His old roommate of the clipping shack was in an alcoholic nirvana. From time to time Harding would get up and stagger to hug somebody, Keefer, or Maryk, or Paynter, it didn't matter who. He kissed Willie, maundering, "He gave me his hat to puke in. One of nature's noblemen, Willie Keith——"

Keefer said, "He'll probably have to do it again before the night's out." Willie thereupon seized a silver bowl of celery and held it under Harding's mouth, and Harding pretended to throw up, and it was a joke which made everybody roar except the two puzzled old folks. In this happy vein the party was proceeding when Keefer jumped up, yelling, "Here he comes! Fill your glasses! A toast to the conquering hero! Greenwald the Magnificent!"

The lawyer's blues were rumpled and baggy, and his walk was not of the steadiest, but nobody at the table was in a condition to notice. He came to the head of the table and stood stupidly, resting a hand on the empty chair, looking around slack-mouthed. "Party's pretty far along, hey?" he said, as wine splashed in a dozen glasses and all the officers shouted greetings. Keefer made his glass ring with a knife.

"All right, quiet, you drunken mutineers—— A toast, I say!" He lifted his glass high. "To Lieutenant Barney Greenwald—a Cicero with two stripes—a Darrow with wings—the terror of judge advocates—the rescuer of the oppressed and the downtrodden—the forensic St. George who slew with his redoubtable tongue that most horrible of dragons—Old Yellowstain!"

They all cheered; they all drank; they sang *For He's a Jolly Good Fellow* in bellowing discords. The lawyer stood, pallid and skinny, his mouth foolishly twitching in momentary grins. "Speech! Speech!" said Keefer, clapping his hands and dropping into his chair, and everybody took up the cry and the applause.

"No, no," Greenwald mumbled, but in a moment he was standing alone, and all the faces at the table were turned to him. The party settled into expectant quiet. "I'm drunker'n any of you," he said. "I've been out drinking with the judge advocate—trying to get him to take back some of the dirty names he called me—finally got him to shake hands on the ninth whisky sour—maybe the tenth——"

"That's good," Maryk said. "Challee's a decent guy——"

"Had to talk loud 'n' fast, Steve—I played pretty dirty pool, you know, in court—poor Jack, he made a wonderful argument—— *Multitudes, Multitudes,* hey?" He peered blearily at the cake. "Well, I guess I ought to return the celebrated author's toast, at that." He fumbled at a bottle and sloshed wine into a glass and all over his hands. "Biblical title of course. Can't do better for a war book. I assume you give the Navy a good pasting?"

"I don't think Public Relations would clear it, at any rate," the novelist said, grinning.

"Fine. Someone should show up these stodgy, stupid Prussians." Greenwald weaved and grabbed at the chair. "I told you I'm pretty far along—— I'll get to my speech yet, don't worry—— Wanna know about the book first. Who's the hero, you?"

"Well, any resemblance, you know, is purely accidental——"

"Course I'm warped," said Greenwald, "and I'm drunk, but it suddenly seems to me that if I wrote a war novel I'd try to make a hero out of Old Yellowstain." Jorgensen whooped loudly, but nobody else laughed, and the ensign subsided, goggling around. "No, I'm serious, I would. Tell you why. Tell you how I'm warped. I'm a Jew, guess most of you know that. Name's Greenwald, kind of look like one, and I sure am one, from way back. Jack Challee said I used smart Jew-lawyer tactics—course he took it back, apologized, after I told him a few things he didn't know—— Well, anyway . . . The reason I'd make Old Yellowstain a hero is on account of my mother, little gray-headed Jewish lady, fat, looks a lot like Mrs. Maryk here, meaning no offense."

He actually said "offensh." His speech was halting and blurry. He was gripping the spilling glass tightly. The scars on his hand made red rims around the bluish grafted skin.

"Well, sure, you guys all have mothers, but they wouldn't be in the same bad shape mine would if we'd of lost this war, which of course we aren't, we've won the damn thing by now. See, the Germans aren't kidding about the Jews. They're cooking us down to soap over there. They think we're vermin and should be 'sterminated and our corpses turned into something useful. Granting the premise—being warped, I don't, but granting the premise, soap is as good an idea as any. But I just can't cotton to the idea of my mom melted down into a bar of soap. I had an uncle and an aunt in Cracow, who are soap now, but that's different, I never saw my uncle and aunt, just saw letters in Jewish from them, ever since I was a kid, but never could read them. Jew, but I can't read Jewish."

The faces looking up at him were becoming sober and puzzled.

"I'm coming to Old Yellowstain. Coming to him. See, while I was studying law 'n' old Keefer here was writing his play for the Theatre Guild, and Willie here was on the

playing fields of Prinshton, all that time these birds we
call regulars—these stuffy, stupid Prussians, in the Navy
and the Army—were manning guns. Course they weren't
doing it to save my mom from Hitler, they were doing it
for dough, like everybody else does what they do. Question
is, in the last analysis—last analysis—*what* do you do for
dough? Old Yellowstain, for dough, was standing guard
on this fat dumb and happy country of ours. Meantime
me, I was advancing my little free non-Prussian life for
dough. Of course, we figured in those days, only fools go
into armed service. Bad pay, no millionaire future, and
you can't call your mind or body your own. Not for sensitive intellectuals. So when all hell broke loose and the
Germans started running out of soap and figured, well it's
time to come over and melt down old Mrs. Greenwald—
who's gonna stop them? Not her boy Barney. Can't stop a
Nazi with a lawbook. So I dropped the lawbooks and ran
to learn how to fly. Stout fellow. Meantime, and it took a
year and a half before I was any good, who was keeping
Mama out of the soap dish? Captain Queeg.

"Yes, even Queeg, poor sad guy, yes, and most of them
not sad at all, fellows, a lot of them sharper boys than any
of us, don't kid yourself, best men I've ever seen, you
can't be good in the Army or Navy unless you're goddamn
good. Though maybe not up on Proust 'n' *Finnegan's
Wake* and all."

Greenwald stopped, and looked from side to side. "Seem
to be losing the thread here. Supposed to be toasting the
Caine's favorite author. Well, here goes, I'll try not to
maunder too much. Somebody flap a napkin at me if I get
incoherent. Can't stay for dinner so I'm glad you called on
me to make a toast so I can get it over with. I can't stay
because I'm not hungry. Not for this dinner. It would in
fact undoubtedly disagree with me."

He turned to Maryk.

"Steve, the thing is, this dinner is a phony. You're guilty. I told you at the start that you were. Course you're only
half guilty. F' that matter, you've only been half acquitted.
You're a dead duck. You have no more chance now of
transferring to the regular Navy than of running for Presi-

dent. The reviewing authorities'll call it a miscarriage of justice, which it is, and a nice fat letter of reprimand will show up in your promotion jacket—and maybe in mine— and it's back to the fishing business for Steve Maryk. I got you off by phony legal tricks—by making clowns out of Queeg and a Freudian psychiatrist—which was like shooting two tuna fish in a barrel—and by 'pealing very unethically and irrelevantly to the pride of the Navy. Did everything but whistle *Anchors Aweigh*. Only time it looked tough was when the *Caine's* favorite author testified. Nearly sunk you, boy. I don't quite understand him, since of course he was the author of the *Caine* mutiny among his other works. Seems to me he'd of gotten up on the line with you and Willie, and said straight out that he always insisted Queeg was a dangerous paranoiac. See, it would only have made things worse to drag Keefer in— you know all about that, so as long as he wanted to run out on you all I could do was let him run——"

"Just a minute——" Keefer made a move to get up.

" 'Scuse me, I'm all finished, Mr. Keefer. I'm up to the toast. Here's to you. You bowled a perfect score. You went after Queeg and got him. You kept your own skirts all white and starchy. Steve is finished for good, but you'll be the next captain of the *Caine*. You'll retire old and full of fat fitness reports. You'll publish your novel proving that the Navy stinks, and you'll make a million dollars and marry Hedy Lamarr. No letter of reprimand for you, just royalties on your novel. So you won't mind a li'l verbal reprimand from me, what does it mean? I defended Steve because I found out the wrong guy was on trial. Only way I could defend him was to sink Queeg for you. I'm sore that I was pushed into that spot, and ashamed of what I did, and thass why I'm drunk. Queeg deserved better at my hands. I owed him a favor, don't you see? He stopped Hermann Goering from washing his fat behind with my mother.

"So I'm not going to eat your dinner, Mr. Keefer, or drink your wine, but simply make my toast and go. Here's to you, Mr. *Caine's* favorite author, and here's to your book."

He threw the yellow wine in Keefer's face.

A little splashed on Willie. It happened so fast that the officers at the other end of the table didn't know what he had done. Maryk started to get up. "For Christ's sake, Barney——"

The lawyer shoved him back into his chair with a shaking hand. Keefer automatically pulled out a handkerchief and dabbed at his face, staring dumfounded at Greenwald. Greenwald said, "If you want to do anything about it, Keefer, I'll wait in the lobby for you. We can go someplace quiet. We're both drunk, so it's a fair fight. You'll probably lick me. I'm a lousy fighter."

The other officers were beginning to mutter to each other agitatedly, glancing sidewise at Keefer. Greenwald strode out of the room, stumbling a little near the door. The novelist stood up. There was a thick, ugly silence, as though someone had just shouted a lot of dirty words. Keefer glanced around and uttered a laugh. No eye met his. He dropped back in his chair. "The hell with it. Poor guy is just crazy drunk. I'm hungry. He'll be around to apologize in the morning. Willie, tell them to bring on the chow."

"Okay, Tom."

The meal was eaten rapidly in a clinking quiet, broken by an infrequent low remark. When Keefer cut the cake there was a brief dismal scattering of handclaps. The party broke up immediately after the coffee. There were five unopened bottles of champagne still standing on the littered table.

Willie curiously scanned the lobby when he came out of the private dining room, but the pilot was gone.

VII

THE LAST CAPTAIN
OF THE *CAINE*

38 · The Kamikaze

Of all the people Willie encountered during the war Captain Queeg loomed largest in his memory, forever after. But there was another man who had an even greater influence on his life and character; a man whose face he never saw and whose name he never knew. The day after he encountered this man—it was late in June 1945—Willie Keith wrote an eight-page letter to May Wynn, begging her to marry him.

He was a Kamikaze pilot who destroyed himself in order to set the rusty old *Caine* ablaze at Okinawa.

Keefer was captain, and Willie was exec. The able trouble shooter, Captain White, had spent five months restoring order on the anarchical minesweeper and had passed on to his interrupted career in big ships. The four-pipers were falling into the hands of young reserves. Willie had become a senior-grade lieutenant on June 1; some of the old minesweepers even had jg's as execs.

The Bureau of Personnel had evidently decided that scattering the *Caine's* officers and crew was the best way to dissolve the bitterness of the Queeg days. Fully three quarters of the sailors were replacements. Farrington was the only other officer left from the mutiny time. Maryk had been detached from the ship a week after his acquittal, and sent to command an LCI, a humiliation which spelled the end of his naval hopes. Nobody knew what had become of Queeg.

Willie was running the ship. Keefer had retired into an isolation like Queeg's—except that he worked on his novel instead of solving jigsaw puzzles. Luckily for Willie, Captain White had taken a liking to him and had put him through intensive training, two months as engineering officer, two months as first lieutenant; he had been gunnery officer when the despatch came elevating him to the executive post. In all that time Keefer had been executive officer, a sullen, seldom-seen figure around the ship. He had never completely wiped from his face the yellow stain Barney Greenwald had thrown on it. The new officers and sailors all knew the story. The mutiny and court-martial were endless topics for gossip when Keefer and Willie weren't present. The general feeling on the *Caine* was that the novelist was untrustworthy and extremely queer. Willie was better liked, but for his part in the mutiny he was also regarded askance.

In the rare times when Keefer took the conn he was nervous, impatient, and harsh, and much given to pounding stanchions and yelling for instant execution of his orders. He wasn't a good ship handler; he had gouged the sides of oilers and tenders a dozen times. It was freely said that that was why he allowed Mr. Keith to do most of the conning.

Keefer had the conn, however, when the Kamikaze hit.

"There she comes!"

Urban's yell on the starboard wing was almost gay. But there was no mistaking the fright in Keefer's voice, the next second: *"Commence firing! All guns commence firing!"* At the same instant, not in response to the captain's order but spontaneously, came the popping of the 20-millimeters all over the ship.

Willie was in the charthouse, marking bearings along

the course line. The *Caine* was rounding the southern end of Okinawa en route to Nakagusuku Wan to pick up mail for the mine fleet. There had been no air-raid warning. It was ten o'clock in a gray cloudy morning. The sea was calm and lonely.

He dropped his pencil and parallel rulers and went scampering through the wheelhouse to the starboard wing. Pink curved dotted lines of tracer bullets pointed to the Kamikaze, about a thousand feet up, well forward of the bow, brown against the clouds. It was slanting straight for the *Caine,* wobbling clumsily as it came down. It was a small, flimsy, obsolete-looking machine. Its wings seemed to be stretching outward as it drew near, and the two red balls were plain to see. There were four streams of bullets converging on it; the plane was absorbing them all and floating down placidly. It was now quite big; a teetering, flapping old airplane.

"It's going to hit!" Keefer and Urban threw themselves to the deck. The plane, only a few feet away, tilted side-wise. Willie caught a glimpse of the goggled pilot through the yellow cockpit bubble. "The crazy fool," he thought, and then he was on his knees, his face to the deck plates. He thought the plane was coming right at him.

It seemed like a very long time before the Kamikaze hit, and Willie experienced a race of vivid clear thoughts as he crouched with his face to the cold blue-painted deck. The important point—the fact that changed his life—was that he felt an overpowering tearing regret at not having married May. Since jilting her he had been fairly success-ful in pushing thoughts of her out of his mind. When he was tired or upset they had come crowding back, but he had fought them off as products of weakness. This mighty feeling of longing for lost joy that possessed him now was different. It had the clang of truth. He thought he was done for, and above all his paralyzed terror towered the regret that he would never see May again.

The plane hit with the sound of cars colliding on a high-way, and a second later there was an explosion. Willie's teeth grated as though he had been punched in the face, and his ears rang. He staggered erect. He could see a puff of blue-gray smoke curling up from behind the galley deck-house, where the gun crew still sprawled in individual gray lumps.

"Captain, I'll call away GQ and then lay aft and see how it looks——"

"Okay Willie." Keefer rose, brushing himself with trembling hands, his unhelmeted hair hanging in his eyes. He had a dazed, vacant air. Willie ran into the wheelhouse and pressed the lever of the p.a. box. The helmsman and quartermaster watched him with frightened eyes. "Now hear this," he said loud and quick, "we have taken a Kamikaze hit amidships. Set condition Able throughout the ship. Away forward and after fire-fighting and damage-control parties——" Blue bitter smoke came wisping into the pilothouse. It stung his lungs like a dry cigarette. He coughed and went on, "Make your damage reports to the bridge. Turn on foam, sprinklers, and carbon dioxide as needed. Stand by magazine flood valves—ugh, ugh—but don't flood until ordered——"

He jerked the red GQ handle, and went out on the wing as the clanging began. He was amazed by the billow of smoke and blast of heat that struck his face. Tall orange flames were leaping as high as the mast behind the galley deckhouse and lapping forward toward the bridge—the wind was astern. Smoke in clouds boiled from the flames and rolled over the wing. "I thought you were going aft," Keefer shouted peevishly, his form dim in the smoke. He and the bridge gang were putting on life jackets.

"Aye aye, sir. Just going——"

Willie had to use elbows and shoulders to make his way down the well deck and the passageway through milling, yelling sailors dragging hoses, snatching life jackets, or just running. He broke through to the main deck. There was less smoke here than on the bridge; it was all blowing high and forward. Red flames, thick as oak trunks, were roaring out of an immense jagged hole in the deck over the after fireroom. Blackened sailors were stumbling out of the narrow hatch of the air lock. Pieces of the plane's wings were scattered on the deck. The gig was on fire. Hoses were tangled around on the deck and the fire-fighting parties, white-faced, helmeted, in life jackets, were fussing with fire-main connections or dragging red toylike handy-billies toward the hole. They uttered thin little shouts drowned by the banging of the GQ gong and the roaring from the exposed fireroom. The smell was of burning—burning oil, burning wood, burning rubber.

"What's the dope?" the exec yelled at a sailor staggering out of the air lock.

"Whole plane is down in there, sir! Whole goddamn place is on fire. Budge told us to get out. He's trying to shut off the main fuel valve—I don't know if he can get out any more—— I turned on the foam system before I came out——"

"How about the boiler?"

"I don't know, sir, the place is all steam and fire——"

"Do you know how to open the safety valves?" Willie screamed above the noise.

"Yes, sir——"

"Okay, blow 'em off——"

"Aye aye, sir——"

An explosion threw a round puff of white flame out of the fireroom. Willie staggered back. Fire was wriggling up the side of the galley deckhouse. Willie pushed through running sailors to Bellison, who was twisting a fire-main valve with a wrench. "Are you getting pressure on your main?"

"Yes, sir—looks like one hell of a fire, sir—are we going to abandon ship?"

"Hell, no. Put that fire out!" Willie yelled.

"Okay, sir. We'll try——" Willie slapped the chief's back and fought through the thronged passageway, stumbling over hoses. Coming to the bridge ladder, he was startled to see Keefer pop out of his cabin, carrying a lumpy gray canvas sack.

"What do you say, Willie? Have we got a chance?" Keefer said as Willie stepped aside to let him up the ladder first.

"I think so, sir. What's the sack?"

"Novel, just in case——" Keefer dropped the sack by the flagbag and squinted aft, coughing and clapping a handkerchief to his nose. The gun crews on the deckhouse were scrambling through smoke and fire, untangling hoses and swearing in screeches. The bridge sailors—radarmen, signalmen, soundmen—and three of the new officers pressed around Willie, their eyes wide open and staring.

"Captain, it doesn't look too bad yet—just one fire-room——" Willie began to describe the damage. But he had a strong feeling that Keefer wasn't listening to him. The captain was staring aft, his hands on his hips. Smoke streamed past his face. His eyeballs had an opaque yellow-ish look and were rimmed with red.

Clouds of screaming steam burst above the deckhouse. Keefer glared at Willie. "What went up then?"

"I told them to lift the safeties on number three, sir——"

On the galley deckhouse there was a sudden rattling explosion. A fireworks shower of flame—white, yellow, and streaking red—went shooting in all directions. Sailors tumbled down the ladders, yelling. Bullets whistled and pinged against the bridgehouse. "Oh, Jesus, there goes the AA," shouted Keefer, dodging for shelter. "This ship's going up, Willie. It'll be in the magazines in a min-ute——"

All three stacks boiled over with yellow dirty smoke like vomit. The vibrating of the main engines stopped. The ship glided, slowing, wallowing. The flames amidships cast an orange glow on the gray sea. "Water in the fuel lines." Keefer was gasping. "We've lost suction. Pass the word for all hands to——"

Three-inch shells began exploding in the ready box on the deckhouse with terrifying CRACKS! and sheets of white fire. Keefer screamed, staggered, and fell to the deck. Reeking waves of gunpowder smoke swathed the bridge. Willie crouched beside the captain, and saw several blue-dungareed legs climb up on the rail and leap over-board. Keefer said, "My arm, my arm," holding his shoul-der and kicking at the deck. Blood welled between his fingers and dripped.

"Captain, are you all right? The men are beginning to jump——"

Keefer sat up, his face twisted and sick. "Let's pass the word to abandon ship—— Christ, my arm feels like it's coming off—— I think I took a piece of a shell——"

"Sir, I swear I don't think we have to abandon yet——"

Keefer got up on one knee and staggered erect. He stumbled into the wheelhouse, and grabbed at the public-address lever with a bloody hand. "This is the captain speaking. All hands abandon ship——"

Willie, at the doorway, heard only the captain's weak voice in the wheelhouse, and no answering boom in the loudspeakers. "Sir," he shouted, "your p.a. is dead——"

The bridge sailors were huddled against the bulwark, like cattle seeking warmth from each other's bodies. "What do you say, Mr. Keith? Can we jump?" Urban cried.

"Stay where you are——"

Keefer came lurching out of the wheelhouse. A fresh explosion in the smoke on the deckhouse sent a rattle of metal against the bridge and a blast of heat. "This ship won't live another five minutes!" Keefer ran to the rail and peered aft. "Look, they're all jumping back there. The whole goddamn main deck must be going up." He dived through the bunch of sailors and clutched the canvas sack. "Let's go! All hands over the side——"

The sailors and officers began yammering, and jostled each other like subway riders in their eagerness to climb the rail. They bumped and pressed Willie, who was leaning out, trying to see aft through the stinging fumes. "Captain, nobody's jumping back aft—those guys in the water are all from the bridge!" One after another crewmen and officers were leaping off the wing into the water. Keefer had one leg over the bulwark. He clasped the canvas sack in his uninjured arm. He was climbing with methodical care, favoring his bloodstained arm. "Captain," Willie shouted at him, "they're not jumping back aft—they're not——"

Keefer paid no attention whatever. Willie seized him by the shoulder as he leaned out to jump. "Captain, I request permission to stay aboard with volunteers to try to get the fire under control!"

A flicker of understanding appeared in the novelist's glazed eyes. He looked vexed, as though Willie had said something particularly stupid. "Hell, Willie, if you want to commit suicide I can't stop you!" Keefer leaped out far, his skinny legs flailing the air. He fell into the water on his stomach and began pulling himself away from the ship. Heads bobbed all around him. Only Ensign Farrington remained on the bridge, leaning against the flagbag, wiping his eyes with his sleeve. Willie said harshly, "What's holding you back?"

"After you, sir." The ensign's collar-advertisement face was smeared with black, and he grinned half in fright and half in boyish enjoyment.

With the wheel untended, the *Caine* had meanwhile slewed around broadside to the wind, so that the bridge was rapidly clearing of smoke. The deckhouse fire had been blown apart by the explosion. There was only a dull yellow flickering here and there. The ammunition boxes were smoldering jagged ruins. Willie could see irregular flaring flames aft amid giant billows of white steam.

All at once his vision expanded. He saw the ocean and Okinawa again. There were the green quiet hills and the horizon. The ship was half turned around, so it took him a moment to get his bearings; then he realized that they had hardly moved since being hit. The peak of Yuza Dake still bore 320. The ship wobbled on a gently swelling sea. A trickle of yellow smoke dribbled from number-one stack. Scattered yells from amidships emphasized the calm silence. A couple of sailors in the water, drifted astern, were waving and shouting at the men on the ship. There weren't many who had jumped, so far as Willie could see, going from wing to wing: fifteen or twenty.

He felt an immense peace and personal power descend on him, wrapping his shoulders like a jacket. "I don't know but what we can save this bucket," he said to Farrington.

"Aye aye, sir. Can I help?"

"Can you start the Kohler—that putt-putt on the well deck?"

"Radio boys once showed me how, sir——"

"Light it off on the double. Cut in the p.a. switches. They're marked."

Farrington ran down the ladder. Willie scanned the men in the water through binoculars, and saw the captain about forty yards astern floating on his back, clutching the gray sack. The Kohler coughed, backfired, and began to chug like an old Ford. Willie went into the pilothouse. He was a little shocked at the sight of the wheel swinging back and forth, free. He got a power hum, pressing the p.a. lever. His voice blared over the decks:

"Now all hands, this is the executive officer. I ask you not to abandon ship. I've had no damage reports from any space but the after fireroom. The noise you heard was some ready ammunition popping on the galley deckhouse. Things looked pretty bad there for a minute. The captain gave permission to abandon but he also gave permission for volunteers to stay aboard and try to save the ship. Let's put out that fire and get some steam up to the main engines. Gunner's mates stand by to flood the magazines but don't do it unless I pass the word. Forward fireroom—if you can't get suction try shifting to the forward tanks. You probably have ruptured lines aft. Close off your stop valves so you don't get water backing up into the forward lines. Get the pumps going on this water we're throwing into the after fireroom. Keep calm. Just remember your drills and do what you're supposed to do. This ship can still steam into the harbor this morning under its own power. If we abandon it we'll all get dumped into the personnel pool on Okinawa. If we stick with it we'll probably pull an overhaul in the States. Stay with the ship."

Farrington came back to the bridge. Willie told him to take the wheel, and hurried aft. The passageway was empty. On the main deck sputtering red flames were poking up a little above the hole, all but smothered in fizzing gray clouds. Soapy foam and water ran in rivulets between the tangles of fire hose. Sailors and officers were jabbering by the life lines, well clear of the ragged crater. Some of them were smoking cigarettes. Fifteen or so clustered around the hole in the deck, pouring misty streams into the cavern of the fireroom. Some sailors were passing a hose down through the air lock, and from below there issued a stream of vile workmanlike cursing. The gig, charred but no longer afire, was being bailed out in methodical sloshes of greasy water by Meatball, sweating in his life jacket. Nobody was running any more.

On the deck outside the clip shack the pharmacist's mate was kneeling with two assistants, bandaging men lying on mattresses or in stretchers. Willie went to the injured men and talked with them. Some of them had been on watch in the fireroom. Their burns were swathed in thick yellow-stained bandages. There were men with gashes from the exploded ammunition, and one sailor with a crushed foot, swelled to twice its normal size and mottled green. Chief Budge was one of the burned ones.

"How goes it, Chief?"

"Okay, sir. Guess we got it licked. Lucky I got that main fuel shut off before I climbed out——"

"Did you take a muster? Did all your men get out?"

"I couldn't find Horrible, sir—he's the only one—I don't know, maybe he's around somewhere——" The chief tried to sit up. Willie pushed him back.

"Never mind. I'll find him——"

With a loud rumble number-one and -two stacks poured out a billow of inky smoke, and the ship vibrated. The executive officer and the chief looked at each other with grinning gladness. "Suction on one and two," said Budge. "We'll be okay——"

"Well, guess I'll get under way and pick up the swimming party. Take it easy, Chief——"

"Hope the captain enjoyed his dip," the chief said in a low voice. "He's got Queeg beat a mile for fast footwork——"

"Shut up, Budge!" Willie said sharply. He went forward. From the time the Kamikaze hit until suction was regained, seventeen minutes had elapsed.

During the rescue maneuverings in the next hour Willie retained the strangely clear vision and buoyant spirits and slowed calm time sense which he had acquired when

Keefer jumped overboard. Nothing seemed hard to do. He made dozens of quick decisions as damage reports poured into the wheelhouse and little emergencies sprang up in the wake of the conquered big one. He nosed the ship slowly among the swimmers, taking care to stop his screws whenever he came near them.

He turned over the conn to Farrington and went to the sea ladder when the captain was hauled aboard. Keefer was unable to climb; so a sailor dived into the water beside him and secured a line around his middle, and the novelist was fished out of the water doubled over, dripping, and clinging to the sopping gray sack. Willie caught him in his arms as he came up to deck level, and helped him to his feet. Keefer's lips were blue. His hair hung in strings over staring bloodshot eyes. "How the hell did you do it, Willie?" he gasped. "It was a miracle. I'll recommend you for the Navy Cross——"

"Will you take the conn now, Captain? Do you feel all right?"

"Hell, you're doing fine. Keep going. Pick 'em all up. I'll change my clothes—get pharmacist's mate to fix up this damn arm, it's killing me—— Did you take a muster?"

"Taking it now, sir——"

"Fine—keep going—give me a hand, Winston——" Keefer stumbled toward his cabin, leaning on the boatswain's mate's shoulder, leaving a trail of water on the deck. "I'll be up on the bridge in half an hour, Willie—take a muster——"

The list of missing men shrank as the ship picked up one swimmer after another. Finally there was only one name without a line through it on Willie's penciled sheet: Everett Harold Black, water tender third class—Horrible. A search party went wading through the gutted, flooded fireroom in hip boots. They found the missing sailor.

Keefer was on the bridge, his arm in a new white sling, when the report came up. The *Caine* was lying to in the waters where it had been hit. It was noon, and the sun was hot and dazzling overhead. A stale, sour smell of burning pervaded the sooty ship.

"Okay, that does it, Willie. Everybody's accounted for. . . . Poor Horrible—— What's the course to the channel entrance?"

"Zero eight one, sir."

"Very well, Helmsman, come to course 081. Quartermaster, make fifteen knots——"

Willie said, "Sir, I request permission to lay below and supervise removal of the body."

"Sure, Willie. Go ahead."

The deck sailors were rolling away the hoses, sweeping clanking debris off the deckhouse and main deck, and chattering happily about their own small heroisms. They greeted Willie with shouted jokes about a trip to the States. A cluster of them around the galley were munching crude thick sandwiches or snatching loaves from the cursing cooks, who were trying to light off the soup vats and get lunch ready. There was a line of sight-seers around the roped-off chasm in the deck. The voices of the search party echoed up from the dark watery fireroom as from a flooded tomb. A couple of the new ensigns who had jumped overboard stood at the rope in fresh khakis, peering down into the hole and laughing. They fell silent when they saw Willie.

He regarded them for a moment bleakly. They were buddies from a Western midshipmen school. They habitually whined and procrastinated about the officers' qualification course—didn't see any point to it. They grumbled about lack of sleep. Their carelessness in handling despatches and letters was unendurable. Moreover, they never ceased commiserating each other for the wretched fate of having been assigned to the *Caine*. He wanted to ask them sarcastically to write up a qualification assignment if they had nothing better to do than sight-see; but he turned away without a word and climbed down the air lock. He heard them tittering behind him.

The stink of burning and something worse than burning made him gag, as he backed down the narrow ladder of the shaft. He put a handkerchief over his nose and stepped into the fireroom. He slipped and stumbled on the wet, greasy catwalks. It was amazingly queer, it was like a nightmare, to see vertical white sunlight in the fireroom, and water sloshing in and out of the furnaces. The search party was far on the port side. Willie descended the last ladder; the water came up cold and slimy inside his trouser legs. He walked across the fireroom in water that fell to his ankles and then rose to his waist as the ship rolled. The sailors of the search party stepped aside and one of them directed a powerful electric lantern at the water.

"Wait till it rolls away, Mr. Keith. You'll see him pretty good."

Willie wasn't used to the sight of dead people. He had seen a few relatives laid out in plush-lined boxes in the amber gloom of funeral chapels, with an organ mourning sweetly through loudspeakers and a heavy smell of flowers filling the air. No undertaker had intervened, however, to prettify the death of Horrible. The water washed away for a few seconds, and the lantern beam showed the sailor clearly, pinned down and crushed by the battered engine of the Jap plane, his face and his dungarees black with grease. The sight reminded Willie of the mashed squirrels he had often seen lying on the roads of Manhasset on autumn mornings. It was shocking to soak in, all in an instant, the fact that people are as soft and destructible as squirrels. The dark waters sloshed back over the body. Willie fought down the tears and the nausea, and said, "This is a job for volunteers. Any one of you who can't stand it is excused——"

The search party were all of the black gang. He looked from face to face. They all had the expression that makes men equal, however briefly, before a dead body—a mixture of fright, bitterness, sorrow, and embarrassment. "Well, if you're all game, okay. The thing to do is rig a block and tackle on that crossbeam and get the wreckage off him. I'll get Winston down here with some canvas. Then you can lift him straight up through the hole in the deck with lines, instead of hauling him up ladders."

"Aye aye, sir," they said.

The man with the lantern said, "Want to see the Jap, sir? He's piled up on the port catwalk——"

"Is there much left of him?"

"Well, not a hell of a lot. It ain't too appetizing——"

"Sure, lead the way."

The remains of the Kamikaze pilot were frightful. Willie turned away after a glimpse of bones and charred purple meat, jammed grotesquely in a sitting position in the telescoped cockpit as though the dread thing were still flying; a double row of grinning yellow teeth burned all bare; and most appalling of all, undamaged goggles above the teeth sunk into the ruined face, giving it a live peering look. The smell was like a butcher shop.

"Well, sir, like the marines say, the only good one is a dead one," the sailor said.

"I—I guess I'll go and send Winston along——" Willie picked his way rapidly over the tangled rubbish of plane and deck plates and boiler fittings to the escape hatch and hurried up into the delicious streaming salt air.

Keefer slouched in the captain's chair on the bridge, pale and languid, and allowed Willie to bring the ship into the harbor. He took over the conn to anchor, giving orders in a flat, tired voice. Sailors on nearby ships stopped working to stare at the *Caine's* torn-up seared deckhouse and the huge black hole amidships.

Willie went below, discarded his wet, filthy clothes in a heap on the deck of his room, and took a steamy shower. He dressed in his freshest khakis, drew his curtain, and stretched out on the bunk, yawning. And then he began to tremble. It was just his hands at first, but it spread quickly to his whole body. The strange thing was that the sensation was not unpleasant. It sent a warm feeling and slight tingles all along under his skin. He buzzed with a shaking finger for a mess boy.

"Bring me a meat sandwich, Rasselas—anything, so long as it's meat—and hot coffee, *hot*—hot as live steam."

"Yassuh."

"I'm going to put my thumb in the coffee and if it don't blister you're on report."

"Hot coffee. Yassuh."

The trembling fit was dying down when the food came: two thick cold lamb sandwiches, and coffee hidden by its own vapors. Willie wolfed the sandwiches. He took from his desk drawer a cigar which he had received from Horrible, two days earlier; the sailor had passed a box around the wardroom upon being promoted to water tender third. He hesitated, feeling odd about smoking a dead man's cigar; and then he did smoke it, leaning back in his swivel chair, his feet on the desk. The usual after-pictures came into his mind. He saw the Kamikaze hitting the bridge instead of the main deck and mashing him. He saw himself ripped open by a flying fragment of the ready box; shot through the head by an AA bullet; burned to a grinning half skeleton like the Jap pilot by the explosion of a magazine. The thoughts were fearful and pleasing at once, like a good horror story; they whetted the extreme luxury of being alive and safe and past the hour of danger.

Then it occurred to him that Horrible's promotion had been his death sentence. Two days ago he had been transferred from the after engine room, which was now entirely undamaged, to the watch in the fireroom where he had died.

With the smoke of the dead sailor's cigar wreathing around him, Willie passed to thinking about death and life and luck and God. Philosophers are at home with such thoughts, perhaps, but for other people it is actual torture when these concepts—not the words, the realities —break through the crust of daily occurrences and grip the soul. A half hour of such racking meditation can change the ways of a lifetime. Willie Keith crushing the stub in the ashtray was not the Willie who had lit the cigar. That boy was gone for good.

He began writing in longhand the draft of a letter to Horrible's parents. The phone buzzer rang. It was Keefer, speaking in a quiet, decidedly cordial tone: "Willie, if you're all squared away would you mind coming up here for a moment?"

"Aye aye, Captain. Right now."

On the well deck many sailors were perched along the rails in the afternoon breeze, and there was a lively hum of chatter. Willie heard the words "Mr. Keith" repeated several times. The conversation died down when he stepped out of the hatchway. Some of the sailors jumped off the rail. They all regarded him with a look he had not seen on their faces before—directed at him. Long ago he had noticed them looking that way at Captain de Vriess after some neat ship handling. It was a wonderful look. "Hello, Mr. Keith," several of them said, quite pointlessly, since Willie went in and out of the hatchway twenty times every day without being greeted.

"Hi." Willie grinned at them, and went to Keefer's cabin. The novelist was on his bunk in a red bathrobe, resting against a pile of pillows. The sling hung empty around his neck, and the bandaged arm lay along the side of the bunk. He was drinking something dark brown in a water glass. He waved the glass at Willie, slopping the contents over the rim. "Medicinal brandy. Specific for loss of blood, prescribed by the pharmacist's mate—— Also I dare say for nerves tried by a day of heroism. Have some."

"I will, thanks, Captain. Where is it?"

"Locker under the bunk. Use the glass on the wash-bowl. Good stuff. Help yourself, and have a seat."

The brandy ran down Willie's throat like warm water, without the slightest sting. He rocked back in the swivel chair, enjoying the glow. Keefer said suddenly, "Ever read *Lord Jim?*"

"Yes, sir, I've read it."

"Good yarn."

"His best, I'd say."

"Curiously apropos to today's events." The novelist swung his head around heavily and stared at Willie, who kept his face politely blank. "Don't you think?"

"How, sir?"

"Well, guy jumps overboard when he shouldn't—commits this one act of impulsive cowardice—and it haunts his whole life——" Keefer drank off his glass. "Pass me the brandy. I just got this by visual. Read it."

He took the bottle and gave Willie a despatch. *CO Caine report Commodore Wharton aboard Pluto 1700."*

"Can you go, sir? Is your arm all right?"

"Hell, it's just stiff, Willie. A few muscles torn. Nothing.

No excuse whatever. I'm afraid I'll have to go. Will you come with me, please?"

"Certainly, Captain, if you think I'm needed——"

"Well, you know a little more about what went on than I do. Seeing as how I was safely in the drink all the time you were saving my ship——"

"Captain, your decision to abandon ship wasn't an act of cowardice, there's no point in your stewing over it. With the whole deckhouse blowing up and men jumping overboard and the flame and smoke and the general obscure picture, any prudent officer might have done the same——"

"You don't really think that," Keefer said, looking him straight in the face, and Willie took a swallow of brandy and didn't answer.

"Nevertheless," the captain said, "I'll be everlastingly grateful to you if you'll say as much to Commodore Wharton."

"I'll say it to the commodore."

After a silence Keefer said, "Why did you stay on board, Willie?"

"Well, Captain, don't forget, I'd seen the actual damage amidships and you hadn't. And you were wounded and shocked, and I wasn't—if things had been the other way around——"

"I would still have jumped." Keefer threw his head back on the pillows and stared upward. "See Willie, there is one lousy thing about having brains. Makes me worse off than Queeg. He could swallow all his own feeble self-protecting lies because he was a stupid man. But I can analyze. I'm imprisoned forever by the fact that I jumped. It has given me an identity. I can't forget that fact except by going paranoid like Queeg, and I'm pretty clearheaded. Not much guts, but a lot of brains. The combination is quite possible—in fact maybe there's a correlation, I don't know——"

"Captain, pardon me, you've been through a hell of a tough time and you've lost blood, and nothing you're saying about yourself makes any sense. You have all the guts anybody needs to——"

"Willie, it was you who left the steel balls on my pillow, wasn't it?"

Willie looked down at his glass. He had done that one morning after Keefer had rammed a tanker coming alongside and then screamed at the helmsman and put him on report. "I—yes, I did it. I'm sorry, Captain, it was a stupid thing——"

"I want to tell you something, Willie. I feel more sympathy for Queeg than you ever will, unless you get a command. You can't understand command till you've had it. It's the loneliest, most oppressive job in the whole world. It's a nightmare, unless you're an ox. You're forever teetering along a tiny path of correct decisions and good luck that meanders through an infinite gloom of possible mistakes. At any moment you can commit a hundred manslaughters. An ox like De Vriess doesn't see that or he doesn't have the imagination to be bothered by it— and more, he has a dumb oxlike sure-footedness for the right path. Queeg had no brains, but he had nerves and ambition, and it's no wonder he went ga-ga. I think I've managed to do pretty well—until today—haven't I?"

The tone of appeal made Willie hot with embarrassment. "Of course, Captain——"

"Well, it's been a struggle. Exec is nothing. It's command, command—I don't know, I might still have bulled through if not for that goddamn out-of-nowhere son of a bitch of a Kamikaze——"

Keefer's voice cracked, and tears spurted out of his eyes. Willie jumped up, averting his face. "Captain, I'll come back a little later, you're not well at all——"

"Oh, stick around, Willie. I'm okay. I just feel goddamn bad about being Lord Tom for life——"

Willie reluctantly leaned against the desk, still not looking at the captain. In a moment Keefer said dryly, "It's okay, I'm all right now. Have another brandy."

The tears were gone from his face. He held the bottle out to Willie. "Possibly the most humiliating aspect of the whole thing—I'm wondering whether after all my yapping, all these years, there isn't an occult wisdom in the Navy's mysterious ways. They put Roland on carriers, and sen-

tenced me to the *Caine*. And by some diabolical chance
we were both faced with the same test, a Kamikaze fire,
and Roland died saving his ship, and I jumped——"

"Captain, you're reading all kinds of meanings into a
random accident. Pull yourself together and forget it. If
you're going to see the commodore at 1700 you ought to
start getting ready—— Arm bother you?" Keefer was
grimacing as he sat up.

"Hurts like hell—that's another thing, I want to go to
the *Relief*—okay, Willie——" The captain swung his legs
out of the bunk, moving his arm carefully. "Have another
shot before we go?"

"No, thanks, sir——"

Keefer regarded him appraisingly, with a sullen smile.
"I wonder if you realize how much you've changed in two
years on the *Caine?*"

"I guess we all have, sir——"

"Not like you. Remember when you left that action despatch in your discarded pants for three days?" Willie
grinned. "I never told you, but De Vriess and I had quite
a talk about you that night. Curiously enough, it was I
who said you were a hopeless case. De Vriess said you
would be an outstanding officer eventually. I'll never know
how he could tell. You've got yourself a medal, Willie, if
my recommendation means anything—well. Thanks for
letting me weep into your brandy glass. I feel a lot better
for it." He reached for his trousers.

"Can I help you dress, Captain?"

"No, thanks, Willie—I'm not helpless—not physically.
What are they calling me in the wardroom, Old Swan-
dive?" His eyes glinted, and Willie couldn't help laughing
a little.

"Sir, everyone will have forgotten this thing in a week
—including yourself——"

"I'll remember it on my deathbed, if I die in a bed, or
wherever I die. Everybody's life pivots on one or maybe
two moments. I had my moment this morning. Well——
My mother didn't raise her boy to be a soldier. I'm still a
hell of a good writer, which is something. Whatever
Barney Greenwald thought. He probably would have

predicted I'd jump. Guess I jumped in the court-martial, too, though I still think I couldn't have helped Steve any by—— Well. Believe I'll have a last shot if you won't." He closed his belt dexterously with one hand, poured, and drank. "It is a very curious feeling for me," he said, "to be in a situation at last where words can change nothing. First time in my life, or I'm very much mistaken. Better shave, Willie."

"Aye aye, Captain."

"Hell, I guess you've earned the right to call me Tom again. Even Long Tom—I mean Lord Tom—I believe I am slightly fuzzy as of the moment. Nothing that a little fresh air in the gig won't fix. Or do we still have a gig? I forget."

"It looks pretty awful, Captain, but the motor still turns over——"

"Fine." As Willie put his hand on the doorknob Keefer said, "By the way——" He fumbled in the bookshelf over the desk and pulled out a fat black binder. "Here's the first twenty chapters of *Multitudes*. The rest of it is somewhat dampish. Like to look at it while you're relaxing tonight?"

Willie was astonished. "Why—thanks, sir—I'd love to. I was beginning to think I'd have to buy it to get a look at it——"

"Well, hang you, Willie, I still expect you to buy it, don't go gypping me on my royalties. Like to know what you think of it, though."

"I'm sure I'll like it very much, sir——"

"Well, bring that old comparative-lit mind to bear. And don't spare my feelings out of military deference."

"Aye aye, sir." Willie went out with the binder under his arm, feeling as though he had laid hands on a top-secret document.

Late that night he wrote to May.

39 · A Love Letter

It was long after midnight when Willie closed Keefer's
manuscript, put it aside, and went to the ship's office.
Snapping on the yellow desk lamp, he bolted the door
and uncovered the typewriter. There was dead silence in
the airless room except for the muffled creaking of fenders
between the hull and the side of the *Pluto*. (The *Caine* was
alongside the tender for repairs.) In the drawer for paper
he found some of the yeoman's tattered pornography,
and was amused by the fact that he didn't feel like
stopping to read it. He rolled paper into the machine and
wrote in a steady rattle, never pausing.

DEAREST MAY,

If there's one experience that's been typical of my
life on this ship, one memory I'll always retain, it's of
being shaken out of my sleep. I guess I've been
shaken out of my sleep a thousand times in the last
two years. Well, I've been shaken out of my sleep
regarding you, too, at last, and I only hope to God
it's not too late.

I know this letter is going to come as a bombshell
to you. Read it, darling, and then decide whether it's
worth answering. For all I know, I mean no more
to you now than any one of the dumb gawking
customers at the Grotto. But I must write it.

There's no point at this late date in apologizing for
not writing for five months. You know why I didn't
write. I came to what I then thought was the highly
noble conclusion that if I were going to break with
you I ought to break clean and not torture you with

any more double-talk correspondence. And since I had decided to duck out on you once for all because you weren't good enough for me—God help me—I didn't write.

I want you to be my wife. That's why I'm writing again. I know this beyond any question, it's the truth forever. I love you. I have never loved anyone, not even my parents, as I do you. I have loved you since the moment you took off your coat in Luigi's, if you remember, at which instant you were revealed as the most desirable woman—in my eyes, and that's all that counts for me—on the face of the earth. I subsequently found out that you were brighter than me and also had more character, but these were merely lucky accidents. I would have loved you I think if you had turned out to be a fool. So I guess physical attraction is at the bottom of it, and always will be. Maybe you don't like that, since you so easily attract droves of morons, but it's the truth.

The fact is, my sweet darling, that this sex attraction has almost ruined our lives because in my idiotic, immature, snobbish mind it came to seem a trap. After Yosemite my mother fairly talked me out of marrying you by hitting and hammering the idea that I was in the toils of sex. If you want to know what has changed I can't tell you. A lot of things have happened to me in the last five months, and the sum total of everything is that I have grown up five years in that time, and can now safely say that I am out of my adolescent fog, however far I am from being a man. I see this much clearly, that you and I are a once-in-a-lifetime miracle. I can't understand how or why you came to care for me, being stronger, wiser, prettier, possessed of more earning power, and in every way better than I am. Maybe my Princeton chatter helped, in which case thank God for Princeton. I know that the snob idea of marrying into a quote good family—large crimson unquote—can mean nothing to you. Whatever it is, your loving me is fantastic luck.

Sweetheart, this is like the breaking of a dam, I don't know what to write down first. The main thing is this, will you marry me the next time I come home? Whether the war is still on or whether it's over? I somehow think it will be over in a few months. If it is, here's what I want to do. I want to go back to school and get an M.A. and maybe a Ph.D. if the money holds out and then get a college instructor's job, I don't care where, but preferably in a small town. About money: it won't be my mother's money. Dad, God rest his soul, left me an insurance policy which can see me through two or three years of schooling; and maybe the government will help veterans the way they did in the last war. Anyway, that part can work out. By the way, my dad several times told me I ought to marry you, in an indirect way. He sensed that I'd found something wonderful.

I know I want to teach. As in everything else, you understood me perfectly in this regard. I've been exec now on the *Caine* for a couple of months (Christ, there's a lot of news I have to tell you—wait a while) and I've been running an education program with these Armed Forces Institute courses among the sailors. I can't describe to you the pleasure I get out of helping the men get started on subjects that interest them, and counseling them in their work, and watching them improve and learn. It *feels* like the work I'm cut out for. As for the piano playing, how far could I ever get? I have no talent. I can simply play the piano and invent slightly off-color rhymes, a nice parlor trick for Saturday nights. The whole night-club life, those damned customers with their dead floury faces and the stinking air and the same thing night after night after night—the whole stale gummy mess of pseudo-sex, pseudo-music, pseudo-wit—not for me. Not for you. You're like a diamond on a garbage pile, in those night clubs.

About religion. (First things first—there's so much to say!) I never have been religious, but I have seen too much of the stars and the sun and people's lives

working out, out here at sea, to go on ignoring God.
I attend services when I can. I'm a sort of pale Christ-
tian. Catholicism has always scared me, and I don't
understand it. We can talk about it. If you want to
bring up the children as Catholics, well, I guess a
Christian is a Christian. I would prefer not to be
married in a ritual I don't understand—I'm being as
frank with you as is necessary, because the chips are
down—but I will do that, too, if that's what you want.
All these things we can talk about, and they will
work out, if only you still love me as you did.

A fill-in on news (though I can't tell you where I
am or anything like that, of course). You can see
already that I'm not in the brig serving time for mutiny. Maryk was acquitted, mainly by legal trickery,
and so my case was dropped. That poor sailor
Stilwell went crazy—driven crazy, I guess, by Queeg,
whom I now feel as sorry for as I do for Stilwell,
they're both a couple of victims of war, no more and
no less. Last I heard Stilwell had pretty well gotten
over it after some shock therapy and was on the
beach doing some kind of limited duty. Queeg was
relieved by a marvelous Academy man who straightened out the ship in four months and then handed it
over to Keefer. So we have a novelist for a captain
now, quite a privilege.

I now see pretty clearly that the "mutiny" was
mostly Keefer's doing—though I have to take a lot
of the blame and so does Maryk—and I see that we
were in the wrong. We transferred to Queeg the
hatred we should have felt for Hitler and the Japs
who tore us off the beach and imprisoned us on a
wallowing old ship for years. Our disloyalty made
things twice as tough for Queeg and for ourselves;
drove him to his worst outrages and made him a complete psychological mess. And then Keefer put the
idea of Article 184 into Steve's head, and the rest
of the horror followed. Queeg conned the *Caine* for
fifteen months, which somebody had to do, and none
of us could have done. As to the typhoon, I don't

know whether it was best to go north or south, and never will know. But I don't think Maryk had to relieve the captain. Either Queeg would have come north by himself when things got bad enough, or strung along after some beefing and there would have been no damned court-martial. And the *Caine* would have stayed in action instead of holing up in San Francisco during the biggest actions of the war. The idea is, once you get an incompetent ass of a skipper —and it's a chance of war—there's nothing to do but serve him as though he were the wisest and the best, cover his mistakes, keep the ship going, and bear up. So I have gone all the way around Robin Hood's barn to arrive at the old platitudes, which I guess is the process of growing up. I don't think Keefer feels this way and I don't know if he ever will. He's too clever to be wise, if that makes any sense. Very little of what I'm saying is original, I got it from Maryk's defense counsel, an amazing Jew named Greenwald, a fighter pilot, probably the queerest duck I've ever known.

Keefer broke down and showed me some of his novel, finally. I guess you don't know that he sold the incomplete manuscript to Chapman House and they gave him a thousand dollars' advance. We had a dinner to celebrate, which turned into quite a horror for reasons which I'll tell you another time. Anyway, I read some chapters tonight, and I regret to say it looks awfully good to me. It doesn't seem very original in thought or style—sort of a jumble of Dos Passos and Joyce and Hemingway and Faulkner— but it's smooth, and some of the scenes are brilliant. It takes place on a carrier, but there are a lot of flashbacks to the beach, with some of the most hair-raising sex scenes I've ever read. It'll sell like hot-cakes, I'm sure. The name is *Multitudes, Multitudes*.

Though what you care about all this I'm sure I don't know. I just read back over what I've written and I guess it's the most idiotic and disjointed marriage proposal that's ever been composed. I guess

I'm writing a little faster than I can think, but what does that matter? The thinking's all over so far as my wanting to marry you goes. There's nothing left but the suspense, and it will be considerable suspense, of waiting to hear from you. Darling, don't think I'm drunk, or writing on a crazy impulse. This is it. If I live to be 107 years old, and whether you come back to me or not, I will never feel any differently about you. You are the wife that God sent me, and I was simply too fat-brained and childish to recognize you for three years. But I have I hope fifty years to make it up to you, and I just want the chance to do it. What more can I say? Maybe in love letters you're supposed to rave about the fair lady's eyes and lips and hair and swear eternal fealty and so forth. Darling, I love you, I love you, I love you, that's all. You're all I want, for the rest of my life.

It occurs to me, of course, that life as the wife of a drudge on a college faculty may not appeal to you. There's nothing I can say to that except that if you love me you'll come anyway and give it a try. I think you will like it. You don't know anything but New York and Broadway. There is another world of green grass and quiet and sunshine and pleasant, cultivated people, and I think after a while you will love it. Also you will be a spark of life in that environment—— It's somewhat soporific and unreal, that's its main drawback—and maybe you will spur me on to do some worth-while work instead of just droning the same drone from year to year. Anyway all this is around the edges. It all comes back to whether you still feel, as I now do, that we belong to each other.

For God's sake write as soon as you can. Forgive all my stupidity; *don't* revenge yourself by taking your time. Are you well? Still wowing the customers and causing pop eyes under all the crew haircuts lined up at the bar? The last time I was in the Grotto I wanted to fight ten guys for the way they were looking at you. Why I didn't recognize my feelings for what they were I will never know. As for Mother,

May, don't think about her, or if you do, don't be bitter. I suspect she'll come around. If she doesn't she will simply deprive herself of whatever pleasure she might have in seeing us happy together. Nothing she says or does will make any difference. Mother hasn't had much of a life, despite her money. At this point I'm sorry for her but not sorry enough to give up my wife for her. That's that.

Well, it's now a quarter past two in the morning, and I could easily write into the dawn and not be tired. I wish, my sweet, that I might have proposed to you in the most beautiful place in the world with music and perfume all around instead of pounding out an incoherent letter in a dismal ship's office, which you will receive all crumpled and dirty. But if this letter can make you half as happy as your answer saying yes would me, then no trappings could make it any better.

I love you, May. Write quickly, quickly.

WILLIE

He read this letter over perhaps twenty times, cutting a phrase here, inserting a sentence there. He finally became numb to its meaning. Then he copied it all over on the typewriter, dropped the papers in his room, and made himself a cup of coffee. It was four o'clock when he picked up the smooth draft and read it for the last time. He got a very clear picture of how it would strike May: astounding, somewhat groveling, wild, and babbling —but still, the truth. There were a dozen more places where he wanted to correct it, but he decided to let it go. It was impossible to make it a good, dignified letter; he was in a bad, undignified position. He was crawling back to a girl he had jilted. No words could change that. If she still loved him—and he was fairly sure she did, judging by their last kiss—then she would swallow his foolishness and her pride and accept him. That was all he wanted, and this proposal sufficed for it, if any would. He sealed the letter up, dropped it in the ship's mailbox, and went to sleep, feeling that life from now on, failing another

Kamikaze, would be an empty wait while his letter went halfway around the world and the answer returned the same long way.

Not only Willie was becalmed; the *Caine* was, too. The resourceful repair men of the *Pluto* quickly patched up the damage on the deckhouse; but they grubbed around in the smashed fireroom for two weeks, and concluded that mending the boiler was not a job for them. It could be done, they said, only by diverting an excessive amount of the tender's time and resources. There were more useful Kamikaze victims to be mended—new destroyers and destroyer escorts. So the hole in the deck was plated over, and the *Caine* was ordered away from the tender's side to an anchor berth far up the harbor. There it sat, while the Okinawa campaign ended and the operations officer of ComMinePac tried to make up his mind, among a thousand other preoccupations, what to do with it.

The ship still had two boilers in the undamaged fireroom with which it could make twenty knots or so. Early in July the operations officer, Captain Ramsbeck, came aboard and they went out to sea for a run, stirring up the barnacles for the first time in weeks. Ramsbeck explained to Keefer and Willie that MinePac was reluctant to send the old ship back home for overhaul while there was any life in it. Once out of the forward area it would probably not return in time to be of any help in the massive sweeping duty which lay ahead. The *Caine* steamed smoothly on the trial run, and Keefer said he was willing and anxious to take part in the next operation. Willie pointed out that some four-pipers which had been converted to seaplane tenders ran perfectly well on two boilers. Ramsbeck seemed favorably impressed, as much by the attitudes of the captain and exec as by the *Caine's* performance. Next day he sent them the operation order for a sweep in the China Sea, with the *Caine* penciled in.

One morning a couple of days before the sortie for the sweep, Willie was in his room writing the war diary for June, and taking long pauses to wonder why he hadn't yet heard from May. The gangway messenger knocked at the open doorway and said, "Pardon me, sir. The *Moulton* is coming alongside." Willie ran up to the main deck. The bow of the other DMS was swinging in beside the forecastle, and he could see his old friend Keggs on the bridge, sunburned and salty-looking, leaning over the bulwark and shouting orders. Willie jumped across the gap as soon as the lines were secured and met Keggs coming down the bridge ladder.

"Captain Keggs, I presume?"

"Damn right!" Keggs threw a long arm around his neck. "Am I addressing Captain Keith?"

"Exec Keith. Congratulations, Ed."

When they were settled in the captain's cabin of the *Moulton,* drinking coffee, Keggs said, "Well, it figures, Willie. I've been at sea six months longer than you. You'll have the *Caine* by December." The horse face had acquired authority and poise; it was almost a stallion's face now. Keggs looked younger, Willie thought, than he had at midshipmen school three years ago, desperately poring over ordnance textbooks in the dawn. They spoke mournfully about Roland Keefer for a while. Then Keggs said, looking at Willie sidewise, "I see you're not talking about the *Caine* mutiny——"

"You know about it?"

"Willie, it was all over the DMS outfit. All we heard was scuttlebutt, though—nobody ever got the straight dope —is it still restricted or something?"

"Of course not." Willie told him the story. The captain of the *Moulton* kept shaking his head incredulously, and a couple of times he whistled.

"Maryk's the luckiest guy in the Navy, Willie. I don't know how he ever got off——"

"Well, as I say, this lawyer was sensational——"

"He must have been—— Want me to tell you something? One night down in Noumea I got drunk with the exec—under the Iron Duke, this was—and he quoted Article 184 to me by heart. And he said he was just waiting for the Duke to do one really impossible thing, and he'd nail him. But he never mentioned it to me again.

You should have seen the way Sammis made him crawl, too——"

"They never do that one thing, Ed. That's the catch."

Seventeen days before the end of the war, the mine-sweeper *Caine* finally swept a mine.

They were out in the China Sea, in a double line of minesweepers that stretched five miles across the water. The sun was low in the east, dazzling white. Sweeping had begun at sunrise, and the ragged line of ships was advancing cautiously over the shallow green sea into the mine field. The mine popped up suddenly in the *Caine's* wake and wallowed low in the water, a big rusty ball knobbed with little horns. Keefer, squeaking with excitement, ordered a dye marker dropped. The signalmen ran up the warning flag hoist. Behind them a subchaser headed for the mine and began shooting at it with machine guns. It went up with a terrific roar and whoosh, in a tower of pink-and-white spray a hundred feet high. All along the sweep formation mines began to bob up. The water was spotted everywhere with yellow-green markers. The *Caine* was in the second line, so the sailors began to watch the water ahead anxiously.

In less than a minute they saw a mine dead ahead in a mantle of yellow water. Keefer danced three times completely around the bridge, yelling contradictory maneuvering orders, as the *Caine* bore down on the mine and the guns hammered away at it. They were within a hundred feet of it when it vanished, with a hellish howl and a tremendous cataract climbing to the sky. Then the lookouts spotted another mine ahead on the port side, and almost at the same moment the *Caine* cut loose two more mines. There was pure bedlam on the bridge for five minutes.

But every novelty, even a deadly novelty like mine-sweeping, gets its bloom rubbed off quickly and settles into a routine. By the time the *Caine* had swept seven mines and exploded half a dozen, it became clear even to the nervous captain that the process wasn't a hard one, nor, with luck, mortally dangerous. So he went to the other extreme, and became very debonair in his conning, and nuzzled up so close to a couple of mines in order to shoot at them that he scared Willie badly.

There was an other-worldly strangeness about that morning for Willie. He had long ago become convinced that it was part of the fate of the *Caine* never to sweep a mine. The irony had seemed a fitting crown for the ship's freakish career. He had studied up his minesweeping, all the same, but he had really thought the manual was just another useless book in the safe, like the Dutch and French codes. He had even begun, quite irrationally, to disbelieve in the existence of mines. All the mess of gear on the fantail, then, really served a purpose! The paravanes did dive below the level of anchored mines and kite there on an even keel; the cutting cables actually did cut the mine moorings; and the mines really were iron balls that could blow up a ship. It was one more proof—Willie was getting used to them by now, but he still felt uneasy shame when another cropped up—that the Navy more or less knew what it was doing.

The minesweeping career of the *Caine* was destined to be brief—to that extent his instinct had been right. Willie was just beginning to enjoy the perilous game when the fuel pumps of number-one boiler collapsed, and the ship was slowed to twelve knots. This reduced the maneuverability of the long vessel below the safety point in an area of drifting mines. The OTC ordered the *Caine* to drop out of line and return to Okinawa. It was just before noon. An auxiliary minesweeper, one of the clean-up ships in the rear, steamed forward to close the gap, and the *Caine* faltered and turned away. Keggs, on the bridge of the *Moulton* next in line, waved good-by to Willie and sent him a blinker message: *Lucky. Maybe I'll try throwing a wrench in my pumps, too. See you later.*

On the way back they had the melancholy pleasure of setting off one more mine floating miles behind the sweepers. Willie was the one who spotted the grim brown ball. He watched the mine through the glasses, feeling a sort of proprietary affection for it as it resisted the hail of machine-gun bullets splattering it. Then suddenly it wasn't there, replaced in an eye blink by a column of boiling pink water; and World War II was over for the U.S.S. *Caine*.

Nobody knew that at the time, of course. The ship limped into Buckner Bay (as Nakagusuku Wan had been renamed), and Keefer sent a despatch to the *Pluto* requesting a period alongside. Next day he received an acid official letter from the tender. Owing to a rush of more urgent work, the *Caine* could not be accommodated alongside until late in August. Keefer was ordered to make every effort to do his own repairing, using material the tender would be glad to furnish.

So again the old minesweeper swung at anchor in the bay, accumulating rust and barnacles. Willie had plenty of time to worry about May, and he began to be very nervous. Six weeks had passed since he had sent off the proposal. In the interim he had written several times to his mother, and she had answered the letters. He comforted himself with the usual reasonings of men overseas. His letter or May's had gone astray in a Navy foul-up. A typhoon had damaged the ship carrying the mail. May wasn't in New York. Wartime postal service was erratic at best—and so forth and so forth. None of these thoughts cheered him much because he knew how fast and reliable the armed forces mail really was. Two weeks to twenty days sufficed in Okinawa for a letter and a reply. The men were writing hundreds of letters, having nothing better to do, and Willie was very familiar with the mechanics of delivery. He grew gloomier with every day that passed. Three times he wrote passionate pleading letters and then tore them up because he felt like a fool when he read them over.

One afternoon he came into his room and saw on his desk a fat envelope addressed in a feminine handwriting —not his mother's rounded slope, May's spiky vertical hand, he thought in an electrifying instant, and fell on the letter. He tore it open frantically. It was from Lieutenant (jg) Ducely. A large folded newspaper page fell out of the envelope to the floor.

DEAR WILLIE,

I thought you and whoever's left on the old hell ship would get a bang out of the enclosed. I'm back in Public Relations—90 Church, thank God just a stone's throw from my favorite bars—and this thing passed across my desk yesterday afternoon. I'm supposed to file it but I wrote for another copy, and am sending this on. I guess Old Yellowstain has been put out to pasture for good, which ought to please you. Stuber Forks, Iowa! I die laughing just saying that over and over to myself. Well, he can't run a supply depot up on a reef, anyway.

We have heard all kinds of vague stories about the great *"Caine* mutiny" back here. It's become a kind of legend, though nobody knows what really happened except that Maryk got acquitted. Well, wouldn't you know, with my two battle stars and actually having been on the fabulous *Caine* and all I am the grizzled sea warrior around here, and of course it just murders me, but naturally I play it big. I could have a harem of Waves, if I cared for big behinds and hairy legs, but I guess I am a little fussy. Especially as I am practically engaged. This will probably kill you. When I got back—you remember all those letters I wrote home about that girl in the *New Yorker* ad— well, a pal of mine in Batten, Barton, Durstine and Osborne actually tracked her down for me, and she is probably the most beautiful girl in New York, Crystal Gayes (her real name is a Polish jawbreaker) a very well-known model, and a really sweet kid. I have had a lot of Stork Club duty in the past six months, and my boy, believe it or not, it beats the dear old *Caine*. By the way I saw your inamorata May Wynn singing at some club and she looked mighty fetching but I didn't get a chance to talk to her.

Well, Willie, I hope you've forgiven me for all the times I threw you. I am not made of your stern stuff. I never told you how terrifically I admired you for standing up under Old Yellowstain's persecution, though I know most of it was my fault. I am just a grasshopper, I guess, but you, my boy, are a cross between John Paul Jones and a Christian martyr.

Well, if you ever get home, look me up in the phone book. My mother is Agnes B. Ducely. Best regards to the boys, and stay away from those Kamikazes.

Sincerely,
ALFRED

P. S. Note that O.Y. is still lieutenant commander. His AlNav came out in March, so I guess he was passed over, and that is curtains, of course. Hooray.

Willie picked up the newspaper sheet. It was the front page of the Stuber Forks, Iowa, *Journal*. A feature story at the bottom was ringed with red crayon. There was a two-column picture of Queeg, sitting at a desk, pretending to be writing with a pencil, and looking into the camera with a sly half-smile. Willie felt a qualm of shock and disgust, seeing the face.

BATTLE-SCARRED PACIFIC VETERAN
NEW EXEC OF LOCAL NAVY DEPOT

The story, written in the stiff wordy prose of a high-school theme, made much of Queeg's exploits on the *Caine*. There was no mention of the mutiny or the court-martial. Willie stared at Queeg's face for a long time, then crumpled the sheet, went into the wardroom, and tossed it through the scuttle into the sea. At once he regretted it; he knew he should have shown it to Keefer. He was upset by the reminder of old horrors, and by the brief mention of May, and most of all by bitter envy of Ducely. He knew that this was a foolish feeling. He wouldn't have traded places with Ducely; but he had the feeling anyway, nasty and strong.

When the news of the atom bomb came through, and then hard upon it the announcement that Russia had declared war on Japan, a complete change took place in the officers and the men of the *Caine*. There were holiday faces on the decks and in the passageways. The talk was of peacetime plans, of marrying, of going to school, of setting up in business. There were die-hards in the crew who maintained that it was all propaganda, but they were cried down. Every day the admirals sent out stern warnings that the war was still on; they made no impression.

Like the others, Willie began to calculate his chances for getting out of the Navy; but about the decks he kept a stiff face, and pushed the ship's routine along against the current of merry relaxation among the crew. It annoyed and amused him at once to see the new officers clustering like bugs around the wardroom radio, exclaiming impatiently at the delay in announcing Japan's surrender. The more recently aboard, it seemed, the louder they complained. The ship's doctor in particular (the *Caine* had a doctor at last, a June arrival) announced at frequent intervals his entire disgust with the government and the Navy, and expressed his belief that Japan had surrendered a week ago, and the whole thing was being kept secret while laws were hastily drawn up to keep the reserves in service for another couple of years.

On the evening of August 10, a more than ordinarily silly movie was being shown on the forecastle. Willie sat through a reel of it, and then went below. He was on his bunk in his room, reading *Bleak House,* when he heard the jazz music on the radio break off sharply. "We interrupt this program to bring you an important news bulletin——" He leaped to the deck and scampered to the wardroom. It was the surrender announcement: just a couple of sentences, and then the music resumed.

"Thank Christ," Willie thought, in tremendous exaltation, "I made it. I came out alive."

There was no noise topside. He wondered whether anybody else on the ship had heard it. He went to the scuttle and peered out at the moonlit harbor and the dark bluish mass of Okinawa. Then he thought, "Keefer will take her to the boneyard. I will never be the captain of a United States warship. I missed."

A military band blared from the radio, *When Johnny*

Comes Marching Home. A single green star shell suddenly burst over Okinawa and floated slowly down near the moon. Then, all at once, an unbelievably brilliant cascade of lights and fireworks began rising from the island: a million crimson streams of tracers, countless blue and white searchlights fanning frantically back and forth, red flares, green flares, white flares, star shells, a Fourth of July display many miles long of ammunition suddenly sprayed to the starry black heavens in a thank-prayer for peace. And a masculine chorus boomed from the radio,

> *When Johnny comes marching home again,*
> *Hurrah, hurrah,*
> *We'll give him a hearty welcome then,*
> *Hurrah, hurrah——*

Now the deck overhead began to thunder with the dancing and jumping of the sailors. And still the bursts of color rose from Okinawa in million-dollar streams, a glory of triumphant waste, and the rattle and roar of the guns came rolling over the water, and the ships in the harbor began firing, too, and then Willie heard the *Caine's* 20-millimeters rattling as they had rattled at the Kamikaze, making the bulkheads shudder.

> *And we'll all be gay*
> *When Johnny comes marching home.*
> *Oh, when Johnny comes marching home again,*
> *Hurrah, hurrah——*

For an instant Willie was marching up Fifth Avenue in the sunshine in an immense parade of the Navy, and crowds on the sidewalk were screaming cheers, and ticker tape was falling across his face as he marched. He saw the towers of Radio City, and the spire of Saint Patrick's. His hair prickled on his skull, and he thanked God for having sent him to the *Caine* to fight in the war.

> *And we'll all be gay,*
> *When Johnny comes marching home.*

The vision vanished, and he was staring at the battered radio on the green bulkhead. He said aloud, "Who told those sons of bitches they could fire the 20's?" He ran topside.

The Navy's first AlNav announcing a point system for discharge was on the Fox skeds within a week. It caused howls and curses and screams of pain throughout the minesweeper, as though the ship had been hit by a torpedo. Willie scribbled a rapid sum of his points and saw that he would be discharged, according to the AlNav, in February 1949. The point system was weighted so as to get rid of married men and old men. There was no credit for overseas service or for combat.

He was not disturbed. The AlNav was monstrous, of course, but he was certain that it would be suspended in a couple of weeks, as soon as the wave of anguished screeching had traveled back up the chain of command and splashed over into the press. He could picture clearly what had happened. This point system had been drawn up in wartime and filed away for a remote future; and all at once it had been snatched out of the files and placed on the skeds before anyone troubled to realize its implications. Meantime the world had gone from night to day, from war to peace. Wartime thinking had become instantaneously obsolete, and the Navy was lagging a bit.

Meantime, there was the decrepit *Caine* to worry about. The repair program at Okinawa had halted in chaos. Multimillion-dollar refittings, night-and-day labor without regard to expense, were now things of the past, a past as remote as Gettysburg though only a week away in calendar time. The repair officer of the *Pluto,* a harassed little commander behind a desk piled a foot high with documents, his wrinkled face as gray as mimeographed paper, snarled at Willie, "How the hell do I know what to tell you, Keith?" (It was Willie's fourth visit in a week; he had been turned away by the yeoman the first three times.) "Everything is snafued from here to Washington and back. *I* don't know whether the Bureau will authorize spending another forty cents on a four-piper at this point.

Maybe the survey board will just decide to let the ship rot here." He pointed at a wire basket overflowing with yellow flimsies. "See that? Every one is a ship with troubles. Want to get on the list? You can be 107, maybe."

"Sorry to have troubled you, sir," Willie said. "I realize how snowed under you are——"

The perspiring commander responded at once to the friendly tone. "You don't know the half of it. Like to help you, Keith. We all want to go home. Look, I'll send you a couple of chief shipfitters for seventy-two hours. If between them and your crew you can fix those bloody fuel pumps you'll have a ship to ride home in. That's all you want, isn't it?"

When Willie got back to the ship he called the black gang together on the forecastle. "It's up to you," he said. "If they decide to survey this bucket we'll sit on the beach with the dogfaces for a year waiting our chance for a ride back. Fix the pumps and you've got your private limousine to take you home, maybe in a week. How about another look at the pumps?"

The pumps were repaired in two days.

An order went out to all the destroyer-minesweepers in the harbor to prepare to go to Tokyo to sweep the harbor in advance of the victorious fleet. The *Caine* wasn't included. Keefer went with Willie to the MinePac office on the *Terror*. They tried to convince Captain Ramsbeck that they were ready for sea, but the operations officer reluctantly shook his head. "I appreciate your spirit," he said, "but I'm afraid the *Caine* is washed up. Suppose you had another breakdown en route? This is the typhoon season. Would you like to ride out a typhoon with twelve knots of power?" Willie and Keefer looked at each other with rueful grins of defeat. Standing side by side on the flying bridge that afternoon, they watched the minesweepers stream out of Buckner Bay.

"Well, I would have liked to see Tokyo," Keefer said. "I think they will write on my tombstone, *Almost, but not quite*. What movie have we got for tonight?"

"Roy Rogers, Captain."

"Why does God go to so much trouble just to make me

feel lousy? I think I'll fast for a month and try to get the answer in a vision."

So the *Caine* swung to its rusted, mossy anchor in an almost empty harbor, and the officers and crew listened to the surrender ceremonies over the radio.

The new point system came out almost exactly when Willie had anticipated it would, early in September. It was a workable, fair plan. It released half the crew of the *Caine,* and also the captain. Willie's exit date was the first of November. When Keefer saw the AlNav he became tremendously excited. He summoned the executive officer to his cabin. "Ready to take over the ship, Willie?"

"Why—why sure, sir, but who'll give it to me? I've barely got two years at sea——"

"Hell, Willie, you're more qualified than De Vriess was when he got the *Caine.* Two years of war cruising is like fifteen years of peacetime duty. *I* say you're qualified. I said so in the June roster of officers. It's a cinch. We'll get MinePac to send a despatch to BuPers—if you're willing. If I wait for the Bureau mill to grind out a relief for me I'll still be in Okinawa when the war with Russia starts."

"I—well, sure, I'd *like* to take over, sir——"

The officer personnel section aboard the *Terror* was filled with a milling mob of captains and execs on errands similar to Keefer's. The language of the AlNav was plain. It was an explosively sensitive reaction of the Navy to a squall of public opinion. Release was mandatory except in cases which endangered the security of the United States. Every exception had to be reported to the Secretary of the Navy in writing, signed by the admiral heading the fleet or force involved.

When the turn of Keefer and Willie came, the personnel officer hastily leafed through the papers and snapped at Willie, "Two years of sea duty and you think you can handle a DMS?"

Keefer interposed, "It's been pretty intensive duty, sir."

"Well, all right, that's not the point. I'm in one hell of a squeeze play, *that's* the point. *I* have to recommend these reliefs, and *I* take the rap if some silly young red-hot runs his ship up on a rock. And the admiral says don't recommend anyone who isn't qualified, or else, and the department says don't hold back anyone who's got enough points for release, or else." He mopped his brow with a handkerchief and glanced at the growling line of officers behind Keefer. "I've been getting this double talk all day. Naturally you say he's qualified, Keefer, you're all on fire to go home. I'm staying in this outfit. I'll have to answer for it——"

Keefer said, "He's up for a Navy Cross, if that's any help." He told how Willie had saved the ship in the Kamikaze disaster.

"Well, he sounds like he might be able to handle it at that. I'll send the despatch. The rest is up to the bureau."

Three days later the morning Fox sked produced an action message for the *Caine*. Willie had been haunting the radio shack. He carried the sheet to the wardroom and broke the code hastily.

He was captain.

Keefer was all ready to leave; he had been packing since the day the AlNav arrived. Ten minutes after the despatch came the crew was at quarters for the ceremony of transfer of command. Ten minutes after that Willie and Keefer were at the gangway with the ex-captain's bags. The gig was away exchanging movies. Keefer stared out over the harbor, drumming his fingers on the life line.

"Tom, I sure thought you'd want to take her into the boneyard," Willie said. "A ride through the Panama Canal and all—you could have stayed on—it would just have been another couple of months, after all——"

"You talk that way because your escape date is November 1. You've forgotten what freedom smells like in the nostrils, Willie. It's like the smell of all the beautiful women and all the good liquor in the world distilled into one essence. It makes you crazy for it. These minutes waiting for the gig seem longer to me than a month under Queeg, which was longer than ten years of normal living. You'll know what I mean on the last night of October."

Willie said, "No sentimental ties to the good old *Caine?*"

The novelist's face wrinkled. He looked around at the

rusty deck, at the peeling stacks. The smell of stack gas was strong. Two half-naked sailors were skinning potatoes by the clip shack, cursing each other with monotonous obscenities.

"I've hated this ship for thirty-five months, and I feel now as though I'm just beginning to hate it. If I were to stay aboard, it would only be to see how much deeper hate could get for an inanimate object. Not that I really think the *Caine* is inanimate. It's an iron poltergeist sent into the world by God to ruin my life. And it hasn't done a bad job. You can lay my ghost, Willie. I'm tired of it—— Thank Christ, there's the gig."

"Well, Tom, this is it." They shook hands, and watched silently as the boat drew near. The OOD and the new exec, a lieutenant junior grade who had previously commanded a yard minesweeper, stood at a respectful distance from the two commanding officers.

Willie said, "I guess this is a real parting of the ways. You're going on to a brilliant career, I know you are. You're a fine novelist, Tom. I'm going to bury myself at some poky college and that'll be the end of me. I'm not good for much else."

Keefer bent to pick up his handbag, then looked Willie straight in the eyes. His face was distorted as though by a spasm of pain. "Don't envy me my happiness too much, Willie," he said. "Don't forget one thing. I jumped."

The bell clanged. Keefer saluted, and went down the ladder.

40 · The Last Captain of the *Caine*

Willie moved his belongings into Queeg's room (he could think of it by no other name) and lay down on the bunk. It was an immensely queer sensation. Once, when he was sixteen, his mother had taken him to Europe; during a guided tour of the palace at Versailles, he had lingered behind the crowd of tourists in the imperial bedroom, and had leaped over the velvet rope and lain on Napoleon's bed. He was reminded of that now as he stretched out on the bunk of Captain Queeg. He smiled at the association, but he understood it. Queeg was once for all the grand historical figure in his life. Not Hitler, not Tojo, but Queeg.

His mind was painfully divided between the thrill of command and the misery of May's lengthening silence. He wanted so much to share this great news with her! He well knew that the *Caine* was a dirty old broken-down hulk—and that only because it was such a pitiful caricature of a ship had he been entrusted with it—and yet his blood ran quick with pride. He had risen from his fumbling, incompetent beginnings as Midshipman Keith to the command of a United States warship. Nothing could erase that fact. Luck and merit were mingled in the event, but the event stood. It would be on the records of the Navy so long as the Navy existed.

After a while he went to the desk and wrote this note to May:

My DARLING:
    Three months ago I wrote you a very long letter, and I have received no answer. I feel impossibly

616

sheepish about repeating what I said, because I can hardly believe you didn't receive it. If by some wild chance you didn't *please* let me know quickly—you can send a wire to me now, I think—and I will write it again with extra flourishes. But if you got it—and I must believe you probably did—then your silence says everything that has to be said. I will still look for you when I come home. I want to see you face to face.

I am at Okinawa. Today I relieved Keefer as captain. I came through the war unscratched, and, I'm sure, a little better for having been somewhat useful for the first time in my life.

I love you——

WILLIE

Then he wrote to his mother.

Even at anchor, on an idle, forgotten old ship, Willie experienced the strange sensations of the first days of a new captain: a shrinking of his personal identity, and a stretching out of his nerve ends to all the spaces and machinery of his ship. He was less free than before. He developed the apprehensive listening ears of a young mother; the ears listened on in his sleep; he never quite slept, not the way he had before. He had the sense of having been reduced from an individual to a sort of brain of a composite animal, the crew and ship combined. The reward for these disturbing sensations came when he walked the decks. Power seemed to flow out of the plates into his body. The respectful demeanor of the officers and crew thrust him into a loneliness he had never known, but it wasn't a frigid loneliness. Through the transparent barrier of manners came the warming unspoken word that his men liked him and believed in him.

He gave them fresh reason to do so in his first week as captain. A typhoon brushed past Okinawa one night, and Willie was on the bridge continuously for thirty hours, maneuvering finely with his engines and rudder to keep the anchor from dragging. It was a horrible night. The newcomers aboard did a lot of worrying and praying; the crewmen who had lived through December 18 were less terrified. When gray dawn broke over the heaving, white-capped harbor, it revealed a dozen ships stranded on beaches and reefs all around the bay, some high and dry, some lying on their sides in shallow water. One of the wrecks was a DMS. Of course the sight of these unhappy ships made everyone on the *Caine* feel especially snug and smug and comfortable; and Captain Keith was established as a hero.

New storm warnings kept coming in all day. More typhoons were loose in the South Pacific, and the paths of two of them indicated that they might hit Okinawa. When the waves in the harbor subsided Willie rode over to the *Moulton* in his gig. The DMS squadron, back from the Tokyo sweep, were ranged in the south anchorage. He burst in on Keggs in his cabin.

"Ed, are you ready for sea?"

"Hi, Willie! Sure—— Need fuel and chow and such, but——"

"I want to get the hell out of here. MinePac doesn't know what to do with me. He's afraid to send me to sea because I might have another breakdown. Come on over to the *Terror*. Maybe we can talk him into letting both of us go. You can escort me."

Keggs looked scared and perplexed. "Willie, we don't originate sailing orders in this outfit."

"Listen, boy, everything's broken wide open. None of the big brass knows what to do from day to day. The war's over. It's all different——"

"Well, sure, but we still aren't——"

"Ed, what can we lose? Wouldn't you *like* to be under way for home at 0900 tomorrow?"

"Would I? Jesus——"

"Then come along."

They tracked down the operations officer in the ward-room of the *Terror*, drinking coffee alone at the end of a long table. He greeted Willie with a friendly smile. "How'd you keep that old wreck of yours afloat in the blow, Keith? Well done. Have some coffee. You, too, Keggs."

The two captains sat on either side of the operations officer. Willie said at once, "Sir, I want to take the *Caine* back to the States. Now. Today. I don't want to ride out any more typhoons with the engine plant I've got."

"Wait a minute, Lieutenant. Nobody asked you for suggestions about sailing orders——"

"I'm acting for the safety of my ship——"

"You're not seaworthy——"

"I am as of the moment. My crew fixed the pumps. Sitting here through the next two typhoons isn't going to make me any more seaworthy——"

"Well, you can always be surveyed here, you know—there's a board on the way——"

"But I can still get her home. She has scrap value you'll lose if you scuttle her here——"

"Well, I don't blame you for wanting to get home. We all do. But I'm afraid——"

"Sir, how does the admiral feel about the *Giles,* laying up there on Tsuken Shima on her side? It's not going to be any credit to MinePac to have another major vessel wrecked. The *Caine* is in no shape to stay. The safe course is to send us out of this typhoon area. I have a crew to think about."

"And suppose you break down in mid-ocean?"

"Send Keggs along, sir. We're all up for decommissioning. The high-speed sweeps are finished. Anyway, I won't break down. My crew will hold her together with chewing gum and baling wire, I swear, so long as the bow is pointing to the States."

Ramsbeck stirred his coffee, and regarded Willie with wry appreciation. "I'm hanged if you don't make out a case. We're up to our ears here, we can't think of everything—— I'll talk to the admiral."

Two days later, to the tremendous rejoicing of both crews, the *Caine* and the *Moulton* received orders to proceed to the Naval Supply Depot in Bayonne, New Jersey, via Pearl Harbor and the Panama Canal, for decommissioning.

* * *

It cost Willie Keith an unexpected pang to steam away from Okinawa. He stood on the bridge looking back at the massive island until the last green hump sank into the sea. At that moment he really sensed the end of the war. He had left his home three years ago and come half around the globe; he had pushed as far as this strange, unknown place; and now he was going back.

He couldn't get used to steaming at night with lights showing. Every time he glanced at the *Moulton* and saw the yellow flare from the portholes, the red and green running lights, and the blazing white masthead light, he was startled. Instinctively he still observed all the black-out regulations; crushed his cigarette before emerging from his cabin, slid through the curtains of the charthouse so as not to leak any rays, and held his finger over the lens of his flashlight. It was uncanny, too, to be on the bridge at night and not hear the gurgling pings of the sound search. The sight of all his guns untended, trained in, and covered with canvas made him uneasy. For him the sea and the Japanese had been one enemy. He had to keep reminding himself that the vast ocean did not spawn submarines of itself as it did flying fish.

He spent long night hours on the bridge when there was no need of it. The stars and the sea and the ship were slipping from his life. In a couple of years he would no longer be able to tell time to the quarter hour by the angle of the Big Dipper in the heavens. He would forget the exact number of degrees of offset that held the *Caine* on course in a cross sea. All the patterns fixed in his muscles, like the ability to find the speed indicator buttons in utter blackness, would fade. This very wheelhouse itself, familiar to him as his own body, would soon cease to exist. It was a little death toward which he was steaming.

When they tied up in Pearl Harbor, the first thing Willie did was to go to the Navy Yard's telephone exchange and put a call through to the candy store in the Bronx. He waited for two hours, slouching on a battered couch and leafing through several tattered picture magazines (one of them had a detailed forecast of how Japan would be invaded, and predicted that the war would end in the spring of 1948). The operator beckoned him to her desk at last and told him that May Wynn was no longer at that number; and the man on the other end didn't know where she could be reached.

"I'll talk to him."

The candy-store proprietor was spluttering. "You really calling from Pearl Harbor? Pearl Harbor? It isn't a joke?"

"Look, Mr. Fine, I'm May's old friend Willie Keith who used to call her all the time. Where is she? Where's her family?"

"Moved away. Moved away, Mr. Keith. Don't know where. Five-six months ago. Long time—— Shaddup, you kids, I'm talking to Pearl Harbor——"

"Didn't she leave a number?"

"No number. Nothing, Mr. Keith. Moved away."

"Thanks. Good-by." Willie hung up, and paid the operator eleven dollars.

Back at the ship his desk was piled with mail that had accumulated at Pearl Harbor, most of it official. He turned the envelopes over eagerly one by one, but there was nothing from May. An odd-sized bulky brown envelope from the Bureau of Personnel caught his eye and he opened it. In it was a letter and a little flat maroon box. The box contained a ribbon and a medal—the Bronze Star. The letter was a citation signed by the Secretary of the Navy, praising him for putting out the fire after the suicide attack, and concluding with the formula, *Lieutenant Keith's heroism over and above the call of duty was in the highest traditions of the Naval Service.*

He sat and stared at the medal numbly for many minutes. He began to open the official mail. It was the usual mimeographed or printed matter for a while; then he came on a letter which was typed.

From: The Chief of Naval Personnel.
To: Lieutenant Willis Seward Keith, USNR.

Subject: Improper Performance of Duty—
Reprimand for.
Reference: (a) Court-martial Order #7–1945.

Enclosure: (A) Copy of Reference (a).

1. In accordance with reference (a) enclosed, the Bureau finds that your conduct in the matter of the irregular relief of Lieutenant Commander Philip F. Queeg USN of command of the U.S.S. CAINE on 18 December 1944 constituted improper performance of duty.

2. Your attention is directed to the comments of the convening authority, the Bureau, the Judge Advocate General, and the Secretary of the Navy. In accordance with those comments, you are reprimanded.

3. A copy of this letter will be placed in your promotion jacket.

"Well," thought Willie in a whirl, "a medal and a reprimand. Nice morning's haul."

He scanned the close small type of the court-martial order. There was a page and a half of comment by Com Twelve, the convening authority. He judged that it must have been written by Breakstone and signed by the admiral. The acquittal was disapproved. Willie knew this created no danger for Maryk, because he couldn't be tried again; but it unquestionably meant the end of his naval career.

. . . The medical board recommended that Lieutenant Commander Queeg be restored to duty. No evidence was found of any mental ailment. It must be concluded that the actions of the accused showed gross ignorance of medical facts, and extreme want of judgment in placing reliance on his uninformed opinions in order to commit an act with the most serious and far-reaching possibilities. . . . These comments extend with pertinence if lesser force to the actions of the witness Lieutenant Keith, the officer of the deck. The testimony of Lieutenant Keith leaves no doubt that he did not comply reluctantly, but rather sided wholeheartedly with the accused in his actions.

The convening authority believes the specification proved beyond a reasonable doubt . . .

. . . There is in this case a miscarriage of justice whereby an officer escapes punishment for a serious offense and a dangerous precedent has been established. The fact that the ship was in hazard does not mitigate, but rather intensifies the responsibility of the accused. It is at times of hazard most of all that the line of naval discipline should be held rigidly, especially by senior officers on a ship. . . . A ship can have only one commanding officer, appointed by the government, and to remove him in an irregular manner without referring the matter to the highest available authority is an act exceeding the powers of a second-in-command. This doctrine is emphasized, not weakened, by the description in Articles 184, 185, and 186 of the exceedingly rare circumstances in which exception may be made, and the intentions of the Navy Department to this effect are therein expressed with the utmost clarity and vigor.

In the endorsements that followed, the higher authorities all concurred emphatically with Com Twelve's comments.

"Well, I concur too," Willie thought. "That makes it unanimous, so far as the case of Lieutenant Keith goes. . . . Poor Steve."

He brought out of a drawer the red cardboard clip folder in which he kept the documents of his naval career. There one on top of the other were his orders to Furnald Hall and to the *Caine,* his commission, his promotions, and his applications for transfer to submarines, ammunition ships, underwater demolition squads, mine-disposal units, secret extra-hazardous duties, and Russian language school, all of which he had submitted in moments of despair during the Queeg year, and all of which Queeg had disapproved. He carefully inserted the citation and the letter of reprimand side by side, and sealed them in, thinking as he did so that his great-grandchildren could puzzle out the inconsistency at their leisure.

* * *

Three weeks later, on the morning of the twenty-seventh of October, Willie sat in the cabin, muffled up in his bridge coat, reading Pascal's *Pensées,* a book he had pulled out at random from one of the suitcases piled at his feet. His breath smoked. The air streaming through the open porthole was raw and dank. Outside were the shabby sheds of the supply depot, and beyond them the gray muddy flats of Bayonne knobbed with oil tanks. The *Caine* had been tied up for three days alongside a dock, stripped of its guns, empty of ammunition and fuel. All the paper work was done. It was the end of the trail. The decommissioning ceremony was half an hour off.

He fumbled inside his clothes, drew out a pen, and underlined in ink the words of the book, "Life is a dream, a little more coherent than most." In the weeks since leaving Pearl Harbor he had felt more and more that he was living in a dream. It didn't seem possible that he had himself conned a ship through the great locks and steamy green ditches of the Panama Canal; that he had sailed past the coast of Florida and picked out with binoculars the pink stucco home on the shore of Palm Beach where he had spent seven childhood winters; that he had brought a United States ship of war through the Narrows into the harbor of New York, threading among hooting ferryboats and liners, and had seen the spiky skyline and the Statue of Liberty from the bridge of his own ship, he, Captain Keith of the *Caine.*

His rise to command had seemed queer enough at Okinawa, but there, at least, his Navy identity had still possessed him. Coming to the East Coast, nearing his home, seeing the landmarks of his old life rising up real and unchanged, he had felt his military personality dissolving, drifting away into the sea air like vapor, leaving a residue which was only Willie Keith. It was this transition that made the days and nights dreamlike. He was no longer a naval officer—but he was no longer Willie Keith, either. The old personality didn't fit; it seemed as odd as an outdated fashion.

There was a rap at the door. "Come in!"

His exec stood at the threshold and saluted. "Ship's company is at quarters, Captain."

He laid aside the book and went out on the forecastle. He returned the crew's mass salute and stood facing them, on the rusty empty circle where the number-one gun of the *Caine* had been fastened for thirty years. A stiff wind blew a swampy oily smell over the deck, and flapped the crew's pea jackets. The sun shone feebly yellow through the gray smoke and mist over the harbor. He had prepared a long, sentimental speech. But he looked around at the faces and his heart became cold. He had nothing to say to these strange ensigns and jg's. Where were Keefer, Maryk, Harding, Jorgensen, Rabbitt? Where was Ducely? Where was Queeg? The skimpy crew appeared as alien as the officers. All the men released on points were gone. He saw a few familiar faces: Budge, fat and stolid, had ridden all the way; so had Urban and Winston. Most of the others were sullen draftees, married men with children who had been dragged from their homes in the last months of the war.

Willie pulled the decommissioning order out of his pocket and read it aloud in a high, strained voice over the wind. He folded it away and looked around at the ragged thin ranks of the crew. A forlorn end, he thought. A truck rattled past on the dock, and a crane was snorting at a nearby pier. The cold wind stung his eyes. He felt he had to say something.

"Well, most of you are pretty new to the *Caine*. It's a broken-down obsolete ship. It steamed through four years of war. It has no unit citation and it achieved nothing spectacular. It was supposed to be a minesweeper, but in the whole war it swept six mines. It did every kind of menial fleet duty, mostly several hundred thousand miles of dull escorting. Now it's a damaged hulk and will probably be broken up. Every hour spent on the *Caine* was a great hour in all our lives—if you don't think so now you will later on, more and more. We were all doing part of what had to be done to keep our country existing, not any better than before, just the same old country that we love.

We're all landlubbers who pitted our lives and brains against the sea and the enemy, and did what we were told to do. The hours we spent on the *Caine* were hours of glory. They are all over. We'll scatter into the trains and busses now and most of us will go home. But we will remember the *Caine*, the old ship in which we helped to win the war. *Caine* duty is the kind of duty that counts. The high-powered stuff just sets the date and place of the victory won by the *Caines*.

"Lower the flag."

The exec brought him the ragged remnant of the commission pennant. Willie rolled up the narrow bunting and stuffed it in his pocket. He said, "I want the jack, too. Have it wrapped for mailing and bring it to my cabin."

"Aye aye, Captain."

"Dismiss the men from quarters."

The chief of the decommissioning detail was waiting at his cabin door. While Willie was handing over the keys and records the yeoman brought him the last logs to sign. Steward's mates came in and out, taking his bags to the dock. A sailor entered with the wrapped union jack. Willie addressed it to Horrible's parents, and told the sailor to mail it. At length his chores were done. He went down the abandoned gangplank, not saluting. There were no colors to salute and no officer of the deck. The *Caine* was junk.

A yard jeep drove him to the gate, where his mother was waiting in a new tan Cadillac. Mrs. Keith had been driving to Bayonne every day since the arrival of the *Caine*. It was natural and inevitable now that she take him home. But Willie didn't like it. "She drove me to the Navy's gates," he thought. "Now she's driving me back home. The little boy is through with the sailor game."

He had been utterly unsuccessful in his efforts to track down May. She seemed to have vanished from the world. He had called Marty Rubin's office a dozen times, but the agent was out of town. His mother had uttered not a word about May, and that irritated him, too; he interpreted it as a bland assumption that she had won the fight once for all.

He was quite wrong. Mrs. Keith was avoiding the subject out of fear. Her son made her uneasy. Even since his visit in February he appeared to have aged; the change was in his eyes, his gestures, his bearing, and the very timbre of his voice. From the ruddy careless boy of three years ago he had evolved into a peculiarly gray-toned, nondescript adult. All she wanted was that he come back to live with her in the big empty house. Once he came home, she thought, he might thaw and become more himself again. She was terribly afraid of saying anything that would give him the cue to declare his independence.

"It must be sad to leave your old ship after all these years," she greeted him.

"Happiest moment of my life," he growled, aware that he was echoing words of De Vriess spoken two years ago. He slumped glumly beside her, and they drove in silence almost an hour. When they were crossing the Triborough Bridge Willie suddenly said, "I've been trying to locate May. She seems to have disappeared. You haven't heard from her by any chance, have you?"

"No, Willie. I haven't."

"I wrote to her in June, asking her to marry me. She never answered."

"Oh?" Mrs. Keith kept her eyes on the road.

"Does that surprise you?"

"Not very much. You spent your last night with her, you know, in February."

"It surprised me. I did break with her. I didn't write for five months after that. Then one day I wrote." He watched his mother's face. "Are you very upset?"

"There's nothing to be upset about, from what you tell me."

"Will you be upset if I marry her? If she'll have me, I will. That's definite."

Mrs. Keith glanced at him for an instant. She was a timorous gray-headed old woman in that look, and Willie suddenly felt warmly sorry for her. Then she turned to the road again, and her determined strong profile was the same as ever. She waited a long time before answering.

"You've grown up. You know everything I can tell you. If you're still seeking out May, she must have qualities I've never had a chance to observe. I hope she doesn't hate me."

"Of course not, Mother——"

"I wouldn't want to be shut out of your life, whatever you do. I'm rather short on sons."

He leaned over and kissed her cheek. She said in an agitated voice, "Why now? You haven't kissed me since you've been back."

"I've been in a fog, Mother. When I find May I'll be normal again, maybe——"

"Bring her home and let me get to know her. Were you fair to me? Didn't you hide her away like a cheap liaison? I took her at the value you set on her, Willie. That's the truth."

It was a good shot—only partly true, he thought, because his mother's possessiveness had a violent life of its own—but a fair criticism of himself. He was relieved by his mother's apparent surrender. "I'll bring her home, Mother, as soon as I find her."

He called Rubin's office as soon as he brought the bags from the car. This time the agent answered. "Willie! It's about time. I've been waiting for a couple of months for you to show up——"

"Where's May, Marty?"

"What are you doing now? Where are you?"

"Home in Manhasset. Why?"

"Can you come into town? I'd like to talk to you."

"Where's *May*? Is she all right? What are you being so mysterious about? Is she married or something?"

"No, she isn't married. Look, can't you come in? It's kind of important——"

"Of course I can. I'll be there in an hour. What's it all about?"

"Come on in. Come to my office. The Brill Building. I'll wait here for you."

Rubin's "office" was a desk in a cluttered room that had four other desks occupied by four other agents. Rubin stood as soon as Willie came in the door, and picked up a loud plaid overcoat draped on the back of his chair. "Hi, Lieutenant. Let's go where we can talk."

He said nothing about May as he led Willie along Forty-seventh Street and turned up Seventh Avenue. He asked eager questions about the Kamikazes and minesweeping. Willie interrupted at last. "Look, Marty, I want to know——"

"I know what you want to know. Here we are." They went through a revolving door into the crowded ornate lobby of a popular tourist hotel. Willie knew it well. He immediately recognized, even after three years, the de-odorant perfume that characterized the place; every hotel in New York has its own unchanging smell. Marty led him to a large glass-covered signboard in mid-lobby, and pointed. "There's your girl. She's stopping here."

NOW NIGHTLY IN THE GORGEOUS AZTEC LOUNGE
THE SHIMMERING MUSIC OF

Walter Feather

AND HIS SAXOPHONE
WITH THE ORCHESTRA
"Heaven in a Horn"
AND SONGS BY

Marie Minotti

"Broadway's Beloved Bombshell"

There was a picture of a saxophonist and May together at a microphone. "Now you know," Rubin said.

"What do I know? Why did she change her name?"

"Said the other one didn't bring her any luck. She's been with Feather since about two weeks after you left, Willie. She's—she's mixed up with him."

The words and the tone made Willie very sick. He stared at the saxophonist's picture. He had rimless glasses, a flat thin stage smile, and a long nose. "He doesn't look like much——"

"He's a prime no-good. Married and divorced twice—I've been fighting it, but—she just gets sore at me——"

"Christ, May has more sense than that——"

"He caught her on the bounce, Willie. You threw her down pretty hard. He's a fine musician, he has a lot of moola, and he's as smart as Einstein about women. He's a little god in his own crowd. May—well, she's pretty innocent, Willie, for all her wise-guy line——"

"What's the story? Are they engaged, or what?"

"The story—the story he tells her—is that his last divorce isn't final yet. Maybe he really wants to marry her—I don't know—we're hardly talking any more——"

"It's that bad?"

"Oh, she still pays me the ten per cent. She doesn't have to, we never had anything on paper. I know for a fact Feather advised her to stop paying. But she pays. Not that I ask her. We had a hell of a fight over your letter—sorry I got my nose in your affairs, Willie—but I said something about Feather being a draft dodger, and she wasn't buying any cracks about Walter at that point——"

"I've got to talk to her, Marty."

"Well, let's take a look. They might be rehearsing."

They walked to the Aztec Lounge and heard music through the closed doors painted with green-and-yellow feathered serpents. The band was playing *Anchors Aweigh*. "See, a special welcome for you," Rubin said. "Come on in." They slipped through the doors. The big garish room had a wide polished dance floor and a multitude of empty tables. Green paper palms screened the doorway. Through them Willie saw May on the orchestra platform, singing. He was terrifically startled. Her hair was bright blond.

"Let's wait here awhile," Rubin said. He leaned against the wall with his hands in his coat pockets, peering at the stage through his thick greenish glasses. "How do you think she looks?"

"Fierce."

"Feather likes his vocalists blond."

The music slowed and died in the middle of the number. The leader was rapping with his stick. "Honey, what's so tough about that phrase?" he shouted. "Let's take it again from C——"

With an impatient sweep of her head May said, "Walter, I hate this damned song. Why do we have to do it? Such corn——"

"Look, baby, when that parade breaks the place will be jumping with Navy. We'll be doing it all night——"

"Well, you do the vocal. I can't stand it——"

"What parade?" Willie whispered.

The agent grinned. "How unconscious can you get? Don't you know today's Navy Day?"

The band struck up again. May sang a few bars and stopped, looking at Feather obstinately. He shrugged and waved the band silent. "Like some coffee, Marie?"

"Anything."

"Break for a half hour," Feather said to the musicians. They scraped their chairs and walked off the platform, chattering. May threw a camel's-hair coat around her shoulders. She and Feather came toward the door, walking side by side in an automatic closeness that jarred Willie's nerves. He stepped out from behind the palms, acutely conscious of his gold-buttoned bridge coat and white scarf and tarnished hat.

"Hello, May."

The girl staggered back a step, putting her hand on Feather's arm. Her mouth fell open. She stammered, "Good God, Willie. Did you want me to drop dead? How —how long have you been here?"

"Just came. Didn't want to interrupt——"

"I—Walter, this is Willie Keith—Captain Keith, or Lieutenant Keith—I don't know, which is it? Are you still captain of that minesweeper?"

"I decommissioned her this morning——"

Feather held out his hand. "Glad to meet you, Willie. Marie's told me about you——" They shook hands. Feather was not bad-looking; the lobby picture was unfortunate. He had a pleasant, keen expression. The eyes were wrinkled and shadowed, and the plentiful brown hair had streaks of gray. His grip was firm and his voice strong, good-natured, and attractive.

"Hello, Marty," May said coldly.

"Well, how about you two guys joining us?" the band leader said. "We're just going to grab a bite——"

"I'd like to talk to you, May," Willie said.

"Well, fine, let's all drop into the grill," Feather said.

"I'd like to talk to you, May," Willie repeated dully.

The girl glanced timidly at Feather. She had a trapped look.

"Whatever you want, Marie," the musician said carelessly. "There isn't a hell of a lot of time——"

She caressed the bandleader's hand. "I won't be long, Walter. You go ahead."

Feather raised one eyebrow. He nodded, and smiled at Willie. "All dressed up for the parade, Lieutenant?"

"I'm not parading."

"Oh. Too bad. Well, come around tonight. Bring a friend. As my guests."

"Thank you."

"Come on, Marty," said the bandleader. "Have coffee with me."

May and Willie were alone in the vast dance room painted with Aztec designs. The rows of empty tables and chairs were bleak and mournful. Willie said, "Why the hell did you dye your hair?" His voice made a thin, hollow echo in the room.

"Don't you like it?" They were confronting each other not two feet apart, like prize fighters.

"No. I think it's cheap and hard."

"Thank you, honey. Every night-club columnist in town has complimented me on the improvement."

"Night-club columnists are maggots."

"You've come back in a sweet mood."

"Do you want something to eat?"

"It doesn't matter. You said you want to talk to me. This is as good a place as any if you want privacy."

They went to the nearest table and sat. Willie threw open his coat and pulled his scarf off. May clutched her coat around her. He thought she was shivering. She said, "You look all different."

"Why didn't you answer my letter?"

"What did Marty tell you?"

"Never mind Marty."

"You always hated him. You never believed what a friend he was to you. God knows why he likes you——"

"Didn't you think I was entitled to an answer? Just one line saying no thanks, I've got me a bandleader and I'm a blonde?"

"I don't have to listen to you get nasty. Just remember, my friend, you kicked me into the gutter. If somebody picked me up what do you care?"

"May, everything I said in the letter still goes." He wanted to add "I love you," but he couldn't. There were too many grinning Aztec masks all around.

The girl's look softened. "It was a wonderful letter, Willie. I cried over it. I still have it. But you wrote it four months too late."

"Why? Are you engaged, or married? What's happened?"

May looked away.

A twist of pain crossed Willie's face. He said flatly, "Are you his mistress?"

"That's a corny word. Mistresses went out with Dickens, dear."

"Are you, May?"

She faced him. Her face was so white that her make-up looked garish. "Well, what the devil do you think? What do grown people do when they're together night and day like me and Walter—play marbles? Everybody knows about us. You and your goddamn stuffy, stupid questions." Tears stood in her eyes.

Willie could hardly talk. His throat was closed up. "I— all right, all right, May."

"So I guess that takes care of everything, doesn't it?"

"Not necessarily—I just——" He leaned his head on a fist. "Give me ten seconds to get used to it——"

"Is that all it'll take?" she said bitterly. "You're broad-minded."

Willie looked at her and nodded. "Okay, it's absorbed. Will you marry me?"

"Now you're being noble. Nobility is your long suit. You'll think better of it in the morning and back out gracefully——"

"May listen, I love you, and I always will. Every name you call me I deserve. Everything that's happened is my fault. We might have had a perfect love, the springtime thing that's in all the books. I wrecked that. But you and I belong to each other, I know that." He took her hand. "If you love me, May, marry me."

May didn't take her hand away. He thought he felt a little pressure. The blond hair troubled him very much. He tried not to see it. "What changed you, Willie? You're different, really you are."

"I almost died, and I realized that all I regretted was you." He knew it was a good speech, but to himself he was wondering whether he really wanted her after all. But the momentum of his emotions was impossible to arrest. May was inside this creature somewhere and he was going to have May.

She said wearily, "Willie, what do you want me to do? Come to a college with you on the GI bill and make chops on an electric grill for you and wash diapers and talk about books? I'm making two-fifty a week steady."

He leaned to her and kissed her. Her lips smiled under the kiss. He jumped to his feet, pulled her up, and kissed her passionately, and this time she responded in the old way. She leaned back in his arms, and said huskily, "Amazing. That still works."

"Then that's all——"

"Not by a long shot. Sit down, beautiful sailor." She pushed him into his chair and sat, and put her hand over her eyes. "However, it makes for confusion, a little bit, I'll say that. Surprises me——"

"Do you love this Feather?"

"If you call love what we had, those things don't happen again. And thank God for that, I say."

"He's old."

"You're young. In many ways that's worse."

"You can't kiss two people the way you just kissed me. You're not in love with him."

"Sex takes up a very small part of the day, anyway."

"It makes the rest of the day worth living."

"You could always talk fast. Be honest, Willie, what's the point of coming back out of nowhere like this? It's all dirty and broken and finished. It was wonderful but you ruined it."

"It isn't all sex. Our minds run the same way. We're talking just as we always did. Even these painful things we're saying are alive and worth hearing and exciting, because we're saying them to each other——"

"I've gotten so I like money."

"Then I'll give you money."

"Your mother's."

"No, I'll go into business if you really want it. I can make a go of whatever I put my hand to——"

"I thought you wanted to teach."

"I do, and I think you're talking through your hat about money. You're stalling."

May looked bewildered and desperate. "Don't you know what a horrible beating I took from you? I thought our love was good and dead. I was glad of it——"

"It's not dead. It's our life, still——"

She scrutinized his face coldly. "Okay, since you're being so noble I feel like telling you something. I don't care if you believe it and I don't intend it to change anything. Just so's you know there are two noble people in this deal. I haven't slept with Walter. So there's no question of rescuing the poor lost waif." She grinned sarcastically at his stunned look. "Too much for you to swallow, no doubt. I told you, I don't care——"

"Christ, May, of course I believe you——"

"Not that he didn't try, God knows, or doesn't keep trying in his nice way. But there's a catch. He really wants to marry me. And he's not a grabbing college boy. Seems he isn't divorced yet. And I have this coarse Catholic prejudice against getting into bed with a married man. Nobody else would believe this, no reason why you should——"

"May, can I see you tonight after the show?"

"No, Walter's having a party———"

"Tomorrow morning?"

"Good God, *morning!*"

"Afternoon?"

"You're still thinking in Navy terms. What can civilized people do in the afternoon?"

"Make love."

She suddenly laughed aloud, richly and deeply. "You fool. I said civilized people, not Frenchmen." She looked at him with a flash of the gaiety that had been their way together. "You know, you're still Willie, after all. You looked so damn forbidding there for a while———"

"It was the hair, May. It threw me completely. You had the most beautiful hair in the world———"

"I know you liked it. It was Walter's idea. He's cold-blooded about it. He's taken surveys and everything. The dopes like their singers blond, that's all." She put her hands to her hair. "Is it really so awful? Do I look like a tramp or something?"

"Sweetheart, my love, stay blond the rest of your life. I don't even know what you look like. I love you."

"Willie, how did you almost get killed? What happened?"

He told her the story of the Kamikaze, watching her eyes. The look in them was familiar. He thought May was glancing out through the windows of the singer. She was still there.

"And—and then you wrote that letter?"

"Same night."

"Didn't you want to take it all back in the morning?"

"Here I am, May. I even tried to phone you from Pearl Harbor———"

"It feels funny to hear you call me May. I'm getting used to Marie."

"I got this for my colossal heroism." He pulled the Bronze Star out of his pocket, opened the box, and showed it to her. May's eyes gleamed in admiration. "Here, take it."

"Who, me? Don't be crazy."

"I want you to have it. That's the only good I'll ever get out of it——"

"No, Willie, no——"

"Please——"

"Not now. Put it away. I don't know, maybe another time—it's—— Thanks, but put it in your pocket."

He did, and they looked at each other. She said after a while, "You don't know what I'm thinking."

"I hope for the best."

"We might try another kiss. As long as you're a hero." She stood, pushed aside his coat, and clung to him, kissing hard. With her face against his shoulder she said faintly, "I always did think I would like to have your kids—before. I—I don't feel that way about Walter, it's different—— Willie, this thing would need an iron lung and—and then I don't know—you'd never forget Walter—neither would I —honestly, you're being hard on me. I was all back in one piece until an hour ago——"

"Were you happy?"

"Happy? Happy is when you don't have a broken leg, so far as I know." She began to cry.

"I swear you're wrong, May——"

She pushed herself away from him suddenly and pulled a mirror out of her coat pocket. "God, if Walter sees me in this condition, things will really start popping." She began to work hurriedly at her make-up. "Willie, you devil, you've never been anything but trouble for me, you're my haunt." Powder flew in little clouds from the puff. "Imagine you wanting to raise the kids Catholic! That's the point in the letter where I started to cry—it was so absurd, talking about the kids. *What* kids? . . . Look at those eyes. Burnt holes——" Some musicians came strolling through the curtains on the stage. May glanced at them over her shoulder. Her smile faded and her face set in a businesslike look. She put her make-up away. Willie said quickly, "I'll see you tomorrow?"

"Oh, sure, why not? I'll have lunch with you. But I have to make records at three-thirty."

"And tomorrow night?"

"Willie, don't start pressing me. And don't start build-

ing things in your head. This talking has gone all wrong—
I feel drunk—it proves nothing—— Look, do me a favor
and wipe off that lipstick——" She looked uneasily at the
musicians again.

He stepped to her side and said in a low voice, "I love
you. We'll be happy. Not comfortable. Happy. Not two-
fifty a week. Happy. Happy in love."

"So you say. I'll see you tomorrow."

Willie said, "I also like your eyes and your face and
your voice and your mouth. I don't want to leave you.
Make it breakfast instead of lunch, breakfast at seven
o'clock. I'll check into this hotel so I can be within a few
floors of you——"

"No, no, not breakfast. Don't check in. Don't be crazy.
The war's over, there's time, all kinds of time. Willie, get
that look off your face, and go away, for God's sake, I still
have to work——" She turned away abruptly, trembling,
and walked toward the stage, hugging her coat about her.

The door opened and Walter Feather came in. "Hi,
Lieutenant. If you want to see the Navy parade, it's coming down Fifth Avenue now. You can hear the drums in
the street."

They faced each other for a moment, and there was
something in the bandleader's face that unaccountably reminded Willie of Tom Keefer—the mocking condescension
perhaps, or perhaps a softness under the brightness. He
felt encouraged. He had matched Keefer.

"Thanks, Feather. I guess I'll go have a look at it." He
glanced at the stage. May was watching them, holding a
sheet of music. He gestured good-by to her, and she barely
nodded. He went out into the street.

Brass-band music was echoing down the side streets. He
hurried to Fifth Avenue, worked to the front of the crowd,
and watched the Navy's blue ranks marching by. The
music made him straighten up in his heavy bridge coat. But
he felt no regret at being on the sidelines. His mind was
full of the fight that lay ahead. He was going to make May
his wife. He did not know what manner of life they could
find together, he did not even know whether they would

be happy, and he did not care now. He was going to make May his wife.

Torn paper was flying in the air over the victorious marchers; and now and then a scrap drifted down and brushed the face of the last captain of the *Caine*.